Every Second Counts

Emma Berry

Every Second Counts

Spiderwize
Remus House
Coltsfoot Drive
Woodston
Peterborough
PE2 9BF

www.spiderwize.com

A CIP catalogue record for this book is available from the British Library.

ISBN: 978-1-911596-75-2

EVERY SECOND COUNTS

By
Emma Berry

Other books in the Massenden Chronicles include

Series One
Ribbons and Rings
-
The Interlopers
-
Riding High
-
Perfect Partners
-
Time Will Tell
-
Twists and Turns

Series Two
Full Circle
-
A Family Affair
-
Every Second Counts

Principal Families in the

Massenden Chronicles

The West Family

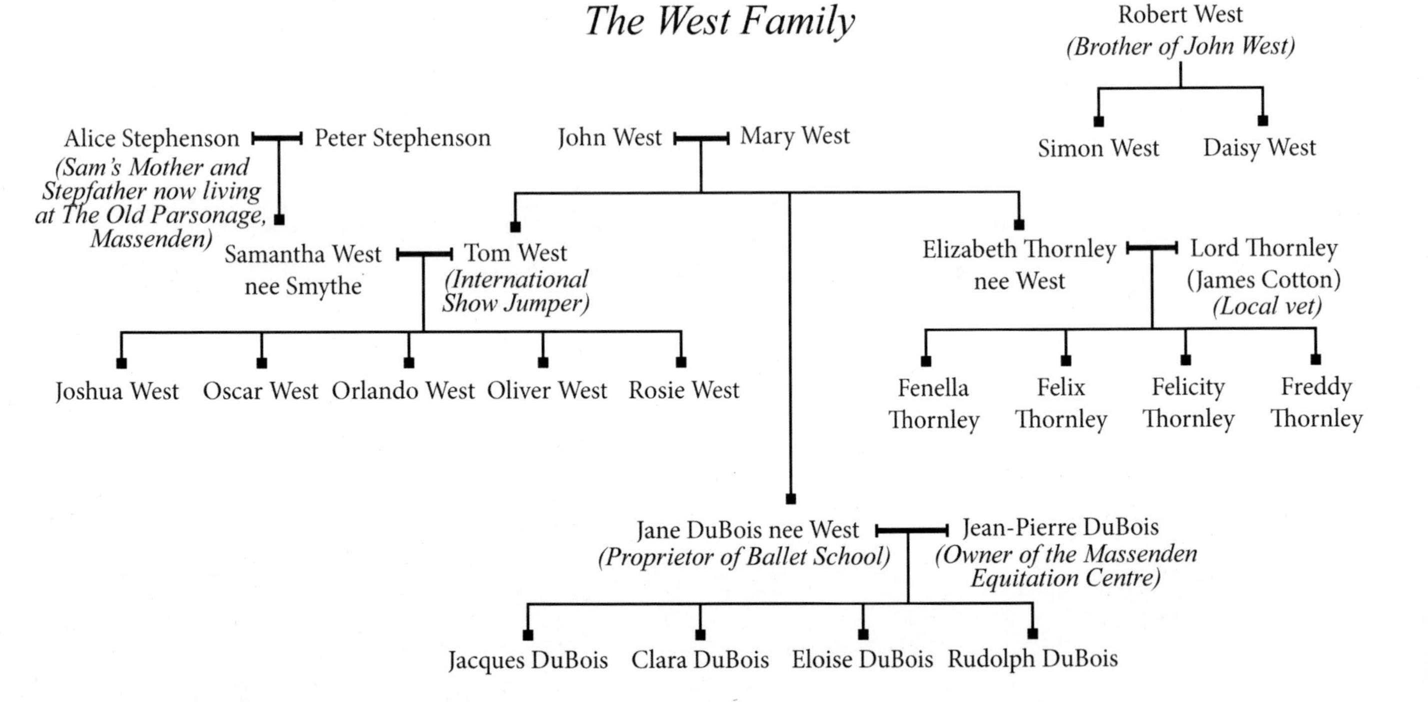

The Wright-Smith Family

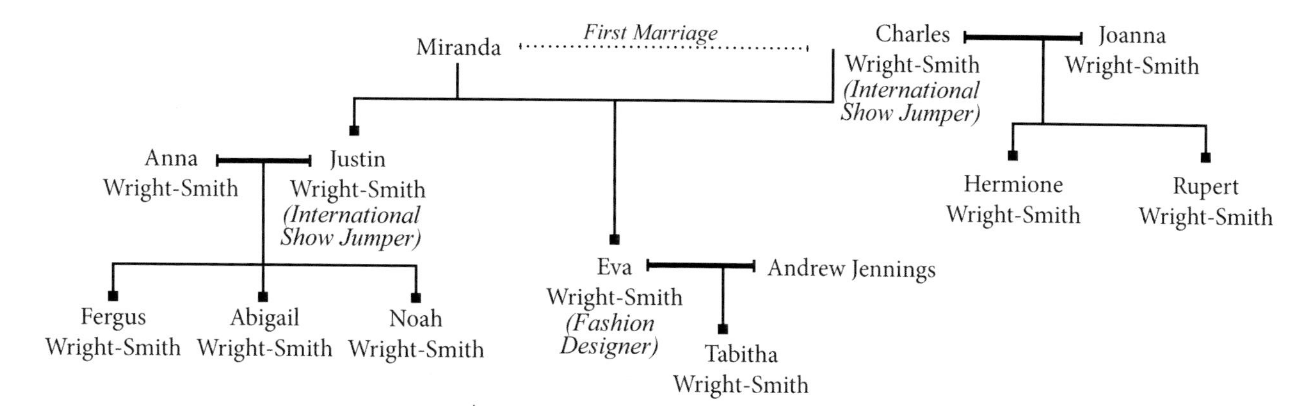

The Silvestre Family

Dominic Silvestre
(Manager of Lake House Stables)

Genevieve Silvestre

Anne-Marie Silvestre
(Adopted)

The Carstairs Family

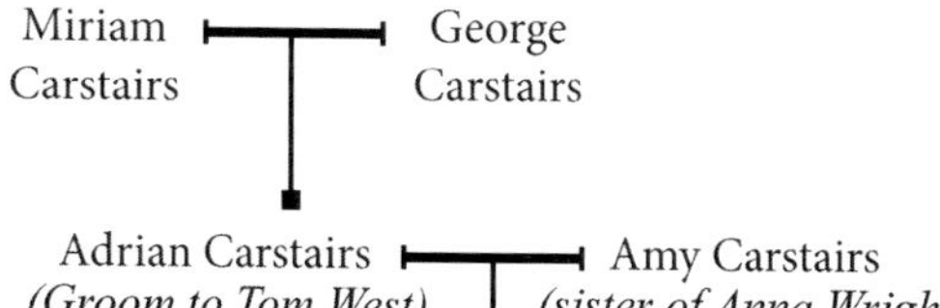

For those who prefer cms.

12.2h.h. = 128cms.

13.2h.h. = 138cms.

14.2h.h. = 148cms.

EVERY SECOND COUNTS

CHAPTER 1

It was twelfth night and Lake House had taken on a truly magical aura. Different coloured lanterns were strung all the way down the drive, passing Lake House until they reached the huge marquee, which had been erected on the grass beside the lake.

It was a clear, frosty evening, the full moon shining on the huge lake, and there were a myriad of bright stars in the cloudless sky. Floodlights were illuminating the lake and the whole atmosphere was enchanting and slightly surreal.

A smaller marquee was in situ on the lawn in front of the house where an aroma of beef burgers and onions was already in evidence. A disco was playing and *The Gang* and many of their school friends were already gathering in various large and small groups. John-Pierre's grooms, the brother and sister Trish and Tony, and Tony's wife Lilia, who was Jane's assistant in her ballet studio, had the dubious pleasure of keeping an eye on the proceedings inside the smaller marquee, but the youngsters were enjoying themselves, letting off steam in the way only young people can.

Tom and Sam West had walked up to Lake House from their home, Woodcutters, which was situated at the far end of the lake, with their five children. Their youngest child, Rosie, was wearing her smartest jeans with a fleecy lined sweatshirt and the triplets, Oscar, Orlando and Oliver, were similarly attired. Their oldest son, Joshua, was wearing his new dark, green cords, which his Aunt Lizzie had given him for Christmas, and a thick yellow polo neck jumper. He would soon be twelve and was suddenly developing an interest in the latest style of clothing. He was a striking young lad, with dark curly hair like his mother, and piercing blue eyes inherited from his father, of which young Georgia Norton was already very aware.

Georgia's father was Giles Norton – probably better known as Patsy Sanders – the extremely popular author of a number of crime fiction novels. His latest, *'A Woman Scorned,'* was currently flying off the bookshelves. Before he had discovered his talent for writing, Giles had been a captain in the army. He had been posted to Afghanistan when Georgia had been a small baby, only to lose a leg within six months of arriving there. His wife, Clarissa, had not been able to come to terms with his disability and had made an abrupt exit from their home with his next door neighbour and one time best friend, leaving Giles grieving with not only a missing leg but also minus his wife and his child. Now he was renting Two Theobald's Row, one of the four Georgian cottages Tom and Sam had bought eighteen months ago. Ten-year-old Georgia was living with him and now in her final year at the Primary School. Giles had been persuaded to come to the ball by his neighbours, Esther and David Collins, whose daughter, Charlotte was Orlando West's particular friend.

Giles was well aware his dancing days were certainly behind him but he was a gregarious character and he knew there would be several fellows happy to chat with him.

Oscar West was on cloud nine. Genevieve and Dom Silvestre, Charles right hand man, were walking by the lake with the West family, accompanied by their daughter Anne-Marie. She had collected her Christmas present from the opticians that morning. Her spectacles were now a thing of the past and the new contact lenses were securely in place.

Anne-Marie and Oscar West, Tom and Sam's most boisterous triplet, had been inseparable since the day they had met in the play area at a huge horse show in Aachen in Germany. They had been toddlers at the time but their chance meeting had turned into a long, lasting friendship.

Young romances certainly ran in the West family. Tom's parents John and Mary had fallen in love when they had been at their playschool after a fight over a pot of paint, and Tom and Sam had followed in their footsteps when Tom's little black pony, Twinkletoes, had introduced them when Tom had been nine years old and Sam about to have her eighth birthday. Now several of their children seemed to be following the trend of the West family – not least Oscar and Anne-Marie.

Oscar couldn't take his eyes of Anne-Marie. After she had collected her lenses, Genevieve had taken her to the hairdressers in Ashford and her hair had been beautifully styled. 'Cor, Annie,' Oscar had said when he had set eyes on her. 'Cor Annie. You look – you look ---' he saw his father giving him a warning glance. Oscar's language could be questionable. 'Nice,' he ended rather tamely. 'Really nice.'

Rosie West was running on ahead. She could see Gus Wright-Smith waiting for her by the entrance to the marquee. Like Joshua – he was wearing cord trousers. His were dark grey and he too was wearing a polo neck jumper. Rosie had soon joined him and they had disappeared into the marquee where they joined Gus' sister Abby and his father's young half brother and sister, Rupert and Mimi. Soon, *the gang* was all together ready to enjoy their evening.

Beside the lake, the larger marquee was already buzzing with chatter and laughter as everyone was greeting each other and finding their tables. This was the final fundraising event for the rebuilding of Marigold Bloomfield's animal sanctuary in Ribbenden, which was a mere two miles from the larger, neighbouring village of Massenden. A horrendous fire had devastated the sanctuary the previous summer, resulting in the loss of the huge barn and also the row of old, wooden stables. The number of small animals which had perished in the fire didn't bear thinking about, but thanks to the valiant effort of the fire brigade and many local residents, including

Justin Wright-Smith and Tom West who had risked their own lives, the small ponies which had been in the stables had been saved, and Tom had staggered out of the burning inferno with the huge Great Dane x Irish Wolfhound puppy, Boswell. Now firmly ensconced at Woodcutters, guarding Sam and the children with his life whilst Tom was away jumping on the continent, as he so often was.

The tiny Shetland pony, Amelia, was safely at Lake House Stables, being ridden by Justin's youngest son, Noah. The little boy was only twenty months old, but could often already be seen in his little basket saddle beside his father on one of his big show jumpers.

Justin's father, Charles, and James Cotton, alias Lord Thornley, both multimillionaires, were funding the ball and the children's disco, and now sixty five thousand pounds had been amassed over the last six months. Marigold Bloomfield was the guest of honour, sitting between James and Charles. She was aware the village had been raising money for her sanctuary, but she was in total ignorance of the massive amount she was about to receive when the clock on the stables at Lake House would strike midnight.

Rosie's little Sparkler, on whom she had won so many trophies had been rescued from the sanctuary the previous year, along with several other ponies, not least Orlando and Joshua Wests' Torchlight and Doppelgânger. Perhaps the most significant of all was Tom's beautiful bay mare, Clementine.

At midnight the miniscule little Amelia would be led into the marquee with the cheque attached to a huge velvet bow round her neck, and the fundraising would finally reach its conclusion.

James' parents, had joined Charles and his second wife Joanna, and soon Sam's mother and stepfather, Alice and Peter Stephenson and John and Mary West, were chatting and laughing together, as Charles glanced towards the entrance to the marquee. He could scarcely believe his eyes; he blinked once and then twice as his estranged daughter, Eva, was walking towards him accompanied by her partner Andrew Jenkins, clutching a bundle that looked unmistakably like a baby.

Eva had refused to acknowledge her father since the day he had announced he had fallen in love with Joanna and would be divorcing his wife of twenty-two years. She had just been coming to terms with the divorce when her mother, Miranda, had been tragically killed in a plane crash. Eva could blame no one but her father. She had refused to speak to him at her mother's funeral and in spite of repeated phone messages and letters had totally ignored his request to meet her, refusing to acknowledge the fact that for the last fifteen years of their marriage her parents had endured a miserable life.

For Justin, it had been a different matter. He had sensed the unhappy atmosphere that had surrounded Lake House and he realised the difference Joanna had made to his father's life, but now he too was watching in amazement as his sister was slowly approaching their father.

She stopped in front of him, saying in her abrupt way. 'I thought you might like to meet Tabitha – your youngest grand daughter,' and thrust the baby into Charles arms. The baby seemed to smile at him. He held her little hand as her fingers curled round his, and looked at Eva.

'She's beautiful, Eva, just perfect,' and to Eva's discomfort, she detected tears in her father's eyes.

'I thought it was high time she met her Grandpa and I would rather like to meet my nephews and niece and my young half brother and sister. Tabitha is staying with Jane's baby sitter this evening and Andrew and I are sleeping at Jane and Jean-Pierre's for what will be left of the night. You can meet Tabitha again in the morning. I'll take her to Bramble Cottage now and come back as soon as she has settled.'

Eva hadn't yet addressed Joanna, but she hadn't failed to notice the way she had been looking at her father, touching his shoulder as he had gazed at the baby.

Maybe Justin was right. Perhaps her mother and father should never have married. Justin had once told her his father's first love had been killed when they had been riding his motorbike. He had married Miranda on the rebound and according to Justin the marriage had been doomed from the outset. Eva half smiled at Joanna and left with Andrew and the baby, as Charles tried to recover his composure.

Justin had been as stunned as his father when he had met Eva in the entrance to the marquee. Eva had told her brother several times that she would never forgive their father and that in her opinion he had as good as killed her mother. Now Justin prayed the tide was turning. He was certain his father would grasp the olive branch Eva was offering with both hands.

He met Eva as she was making her way to her car, about to take Tabitha to Jane's cottage. 'Well, Eva, that wasn't so bad, was it?'

Eva looked at Justin. 'Actually, it was a bit of a shock. Dad looks older.'

'Of course he does, you idiot.' Justin told his sister. 'You've ignored him for the past twelve years, what do you expect? He was forty-two when Mum was killed – he's fifty-four now, but he's happy, Eva. You may find it difficult to forgive Joanna, but she truly loves him, and there is absolutely no doubt for the last twelve years she has made him really happy. Surely you wouldn't wish for anything else? Anyone of us can make a mistake and unfortunately that was the case with Mum and Dad. I'll see you later and introduce you to Gus and Abby. You'll have to wait until the morning to see Noah. Hopefully he is fast asleep. There's a lot of noise coming from the youngster's marquee - they're all going to crash out on the floor at Lake House later on.'

The ball was in full swing by the time Eva and Andrew returned, this time accompanied by Jane and Jean-Pierre who had been delayed by their little son, Rudi, who had been particularly fractious, but was now sleeping peacefully under the watchful eye of the kindly home help, Dorcas who had the dubious pleasure of looking after the youngsters for the evening.

They joined Sam and Tom, and Justin and Anna, and Jane

introduced them to David and Esther, who had just arrived with Giles. They were a large party and soon realised they were short of one chair. 'I'll go and find another,' Jean-Pierre offered.

'Don't worry, Pierre,' Sam told him, 'I'll sit on Tom's knee. He won't mind.'

Tom was well aware Sam had been flirting with him from the moment their children had disappeared into the disco. He was also under no illusion that she knew his stomach was turning cartwheels. She was wearing the beautiful bronze evening dress she had worn the night they had gone to Gervaise Castle. She had been seventeen and he had been eighteen. It was the evening he had given her her precious ring. The different stones spelt dearest, and she never took it off her finger. Thirteen years ago, she had been an extremely pretty girl, now she was an elegant, beautiful woman, but to Tom she was still his precious little Sammy, who he had loved since he was nine years old. She slid onto his lap and put her arms round his neck, letting her fingers tangle in his blond curls. He gently kissed the top of her hair and then said rather gruffly; trying to hide the emotion he was feeling. 'Let's dance. Sammy.'

He took her into a corner of the marquee and slid his hand down her back, letting it rest on her shapely bottom, as the other one pulled her close. 'Sammy, darling, have you got butterflies in your stomach and is your heart crashing?' he asked, as he kissed her neck. She gazed into his eyes. She didn't have to answer.

'Sammy?'

' Ummm.'

'Do you wish we were at Woodcutters?'

'Ummm.'

'So do I.'

She laughed. 'You're still a randy old devil, Thomas West.' She guided him into the corner of the marquee where the light was dim and pulled his head down until she could reach his lips.

'Ad infinitum, my Thomas.'

‘Oh, God, Sammy – yes please – ad infinitum – for sure.’

Eva was gazing across the marquee. ‘Are those two for real?’ she asked Jane.

Before Jane could answer, Elizabeth, who had just joined the group, broke in.

‘Tom and Sam are impossible, they still behave like love sick teenagers and they even kiss in front of their children. No wonder Ozzie and Rosie have these fixations with Anne-Marie and Gus.’

Jane was shocked. ‘Lizzie, just because you hide your emotions, there’s no need to criticize Tom and Sam or Rosie and Oscar. They are the dearest children and if Oscar didn’t have Anne-Marie’s innocent friendship he would probably be a complete disaster. Tom and Sam’s love has always been special, Lizzie. We’ve always known that. If Sophie had killed Sam when she stabbed her last year, Tom’s life would have been over too. Thank God Charles found her in time.’

Elizabeth gave her sister a half smile. ‘Oh, well, I suppose we are all different, and I adore my rock,’ and she smiled at James, ‘ and I suppose you and Jean-Pierre enjoy your little tiffs, as you choose to call them.’

Jane took Jean-Pierre’s hand and kissed it. ‘We haven’t had one for some time, have we Pierre?’

‘Non, ma Cherie, and I don’t particularly want one either. You know what always ‘appens, Janie.’

‘Well, Pierre, I think little Rudi was a very good result – but now I think no more tiffs and no more babies either. Come on, Pierre, let’s see how your feet are behaving today,’ and she whirled him away to join Tom and Sam.

‘Shall we, my shrimp?’ James smiled at Elizabeth and then waltzed her steadily round the edge of the marquee, holding her as though she was a piece of exquisite, breakable porcelain.

Giles was happily chatting to David and Esther as Eva looked at Andrew.

'Come on, Andrew, there's something I want to ask you.' And she almost tugged him onto the dance floor.

'It's leap year,' she informed him, without any preamble.

'So, what is remarkable about that?' he asked her.

'It means the woman can propose to the man.'

'So?'

'Andrew, we have rubbed along together for over ten years, we now have our precious little Tabitha. How about getting married?'

'Good God, Eva, I suppose we could'

'So what is your answer then, Andrew?'

'It seems it could be one of your better ideas.'

There was a pause in the music as everyone returned to the table. Eva was holding Andrew's hand and looking at Justin who was sipping his glass of white wine.

'Andrew and I have just decided to get married,' she announced in her abrupt way. 'I've just proposed to him – after all it is leap year, and he appears to have said yes.'

Justin lost no time. He picked up a serving spoon and banged it on the table. There was an immediate hush around the marquee. 'Important announcement,' he yelled to the now silent gathering. 'Eva and Andrew have just decided to get married, so raise your glasses everyone.'

There was a scraping of seats as everybody raised their glasses. John was the first to recover his surprise. 'To Eva and Andrew and their dear little Tabitha,' and he clinked his glass with Mary's as everyone reiterated. 'To Eva and Andrew,' although some of the newcomers to the village had no idea who they were toasting.

Charles and Joanna walked over to Eva and Andrew. Eva put her arms round her father, kissing him for the first time in over twelve years. 'I'm sorry, Dad. I should have understood, but it's not too late, is it? You can watch Tabitha grow up. I think she will love her grandpa,' and then to Charles delight, she turned to Joanna, saying, 'and her granny,' and gave Joanna a hug. 'Now I will have a dance with my dad, whilst Andrew gets acquainted with Joanna.'

Charles felt a ton weight had been removed from his heart, as he smiled through his tears at Eva. 'Eva, you have to know the truth. I am really, really happy with Joanna. I didn't want to hurt your mother, but when the heart is involved somethings become unavoidable. That may sound a very weak and feeble excuse but I am afraid it is true. Tomorrow you must meet your brother and sister – Rupert and Mimi, and Justin's three lovely children, Tabitha must get to know her cousins. When are you and Andrew thinking of getting married?'

'I'm not sure. He only just knows he IS getting married!! I would love to have the reception here, at Lake House. Perhaps just a lunch in the dining room. I think it will just be my family and my friends here. Andrew's father is teaching in Botswana. He went out there just before Christmas with his latest lady friend. It would be nice here.'

'It would be perfect, Eva, and this is the best start to the New Year I could possibly wish for. Now, I should return to my special guest, Marigold, but come here for lunch tomorrow and really get to know your extended family.'

Eva smiled. 'We will look forwards to that and you and Joanna can get to know Tabitha.'

The dancing continued until ten o'clock, when the buffet was served and at midnight, Justin hurried to the nearest stable where Amelia had been hidden. He led her to the marquee with the cheque tied onto the velvet bow, which hung round her neck.

John had been unanimously voted to be the person to present Marigold with the cheque. He had known her since he had been a small boy.

When Marigold saw the size of the cheque, she was totally overcome. 'You are the dearest, kindest people on this earth. I know you have all joined in raising this money for my sanctuary. So many of you have been involved and this has been the most wonderful evening for the culmination of all your efforts. I thank you all from the bottom of my heart and I hope many of you will come to the opening of the new accommodation at the sanctuary later in the year.'

Everyone broke into song, giving a rousing rendition of *'For she's a jolly good fellow,'* before a cab arrived to take the almost overwhelmed Marigold home – whilst the dancing continued until the early hours of the morning, long after all the youngsters were lying fast asleep in their sleeping bags wherever they could find a space on the various floors of Lake House.

It had been an evening to remember – an evening when Massenden had been a true village, as everyone had reveled in the charm and romance of the beautiful old Queen Anne House, with its shimmering lake, by which a group of people were wending their way home on the crisp winter's night.

Tom and Sam were holding hands as they walked with Dom and Genevieve. Slightly behind them, Esther, David and Giles were chatting to Peter and Alice and John and Mary.

'I wonder who has bought the tea rooms,' Alice said to no one in particular. 'I see it's under offer.' No one had any idea, but all would soon be revealed and someone was going to receive an almighty shock.

CHAPTER 2

When John and Mary walked into the kitchen they noticed a light was flashing on their answer phone. John was tempted to ignore it until the morning, but then decided he was still wide-awake so he might as well answer it. He was completely taken aback when he heard his young brother Rob's voice. '*Hi, John, Just to let you know I am coming back to work in London on the first of March. Can you find a house to rent somewhere near you for the kids and myself. Will call you again tomorrow, Love to Mary. Rob.*'

Robert was eleven years younger than John, who had just been starting his first year at the Grammar School when Robert had been born. It was many years later that John learned his mother had suffered several miscarriages between the births of her two sons.

Robert had worked for an engineering company in London after graduating at Leeds University – Old Tiles and the sheep had never captured his interest and soon after his twenty-fifth birthday his firm had transferred him to their offices in Sydney where he had very soon become acquainted with the budding young Australian actress, Lois Carmelo.

Robert had an obsession for fast cars and before long he had joined a racing team, Force Carmelo, which was sponsored by his firm. The owner of the team happened to be his boss, Wayne Carmelo, and before long Lois and Robert had entered into a steamy relationship, which six months later had culminated in a glamorous wedding at the local yacht club in Sydney, of which Lois' father was also a patron.

Robert had never met Lois' mother who was American and had left her wealthy husband for an even wealthier rock star soon after Lois' first birthday. Her father had never sought to marry again, spending his spare time with his racing team or on his opulent

One day perhaps Tabitha will stay here. And all your old toys will be waiting for her.'

Eva sat down beside him and put her arms round him. 'So, you never really hated me then, Dad? Mum always told me Justin was your favourite.'

Charles was astounded. 'Eva, I know we should never speak ill of the dead, but that is the most wicked thing she could ever have told you. There was never any difference, just as I love Mimi and Rupert in exactly the same way. I cannot believe she could have said such a thing. That's something I can never forgive.'

'I shouldn't have believed her, Dad, I'm as much to blame as she is, but at least we have the chance to put things right, and I've missed you, Dad, and you are lucky to have found Joanna. I can see she loves you for yourself, not for your money or who you are. You deserve her, Dad. Now I am going to leave Tabitha with you and Joanna for an hour whilst Justin drags me off to see this mansion he has bought, and I want to meet Gus and Abby and Noah, too. I am sure you and Joanna will be fine with Tabitha, but Andrew is doing a sketch of Amelia in her stable if you should need him.' She kissed her baby and laid her on Charles' knee. 'I will see you both in time for lunch,' and she ran to meet Justin at the front door.

Justin was pleased, mainly because the work on the house was progressing far more quickly than he had imagined it would and also because Eva was obviously impressed.

'Wow, Justin, I thought the view from our garden in Winchelsea was amazing but this is superb. What a gorgeous garden. This place must have cost you an absolute bomb.'

Justin looked serious. 'For once money didn't matter to me, Eva. I hadn't spent any of the fortune Mum left me. I went to see my bank manager and he advised me to invest in property. The next day Tom and I were riding round Back Lane when we met the gardener who Tom knew. He showed us the house and the stables and that was it. He told us it was going on the market the following week, by the end of that afternoon it was mine, and now all we want to do is to move in. It's amazing to think the motorway and the channel tunnel are a mere five miles away and we can't hear any traffic at all. It's a perfect situation. The horses are always travelling to and from the continent and next year Gus will be getting the bus at the end of Back Lane to the Grammar School, and the Primary is only five minutes walk for Abby and Noah when he starts there.'

'Noah is gorgeous, but he's really tiny, Justin.'

'He's great, Eva. He nearly didn't make it, he was very premature, but then so was Gus, and look at him now. He's got the heart and courage of a lion.'

Eva laughed. 'Which he already appears to have given to little Rosie West.'

'They're like Tom and Sam, Eva. *Ad infinitum*!'

'Well let's hope they will be as happy as they are, Justin. Tom and Sam haven't changed one iota. I was watching them last night. They really are unique, but Sam is still just as beautiful as ever – fancy – five children and still possessing a figure like a model. It's no wonder Tom can't take his eyes off her.'

'Do you remember Sophie Stevens, Eva?'

'Good God, yes. Always trying to seduce poor old Thomas!!'

'Well she overdid it last year in Brussels,' and Justin told her of Sophie's wicked plan to compromise Tom and then stabbing Sam. 'Dad found her just in time, Eva. Another five minutes and he would have been too late.'

'God, what happened to Sophie? Wherever is she now?'

'Nowhere, Eva – probably in hell. She took an overdose and polished herself off.'

'Crumbs! Talk about a woman scorned, Justin.'

Justin looked startled. '*Crikey*!' He thought, '*crafty old Giles. That's what he's called his latest novel. I saw Sam reading it the other day. I don't think she can have realized it's based on that morning,*' but happily for everyone, especially Giles, Justin decided to keep his thoughts to himself. As far as he was concerned that dreadful incident was definitely best forgotten.

CHAPTER 3

Alice had been keeping her eye on the Massenden Tea Shop, which was almost next-door to Peter and her home, The Old Parsonage, on the village green. She had seen the present owner, Martha, at the W.I. meeting the previous week and asked her who had bought it but she had been annoyingly vague.

'It's under offer,' she had told Alice, 'but there are lots of planning issues and licenses to obtain before any sale can go through. It's all very much in the balance at the moment.'

Alice hadn't noticed any new faces in the vicinity of the tearooms or even around the green and for the moment Martha was still serving her famous cream teas and morning coffees.

One day shortly afterwards, when Georgia Norton got home from school, she saw two letters on the dining room table addressed to herself. One was from Eleanor, her best friend at her old school, St. Swithins, and the other was from her mother. She immediately recognized the handwriting and the French stamp.

She opened Eleanor's letter first. It was full of life at St. Swithins. Apparently Eleanor was now in the junior hockey team. There had been a brilliant surprise at the start of the term when they had discovered their *Bête Noir*, Miss Carnoustie had left the school and returned to teach in Scotland. She had been in charge of Eleanor and Georgia's dormitory the previous year and both girls had been totally in awe of her. According to Eleanor, the new French teacher was now in charge of the six girls in Dorm 1V and was an absolute singe, often letting the lights stay on until ten o'clock instead of the obligatory nine thirty. She ended by telling Georgia about two fab new boys who had arrived at the neighbouring boy's school, St. Crispin's, – and who she had met at church and already inveigled into her particular group. Georgia smiled to herself. Eleanor was a wolf where the boys were concerned and she had never mentioned Joshua West to her friend. He was her secret. She sighed as she admitted to herself he never singled her out for attention, but he rarely seemed to talk to anyone except his cousins Jacques, Eloise and Clara. She had long ago decided she wasn't going to give up hope and she looked at the photograph she had persuaded Charlotte to take secretly at a big horse show the previous year. Unbeknown to Joshua, Charlotte had surreptitiously caught an excellent image of her patting Ganger and smiling up at her hero. It sat in pride of place on her bedside table.

Georgia folded her friend's letter and turned to the envelope with the French stamp. She opened the thin paper slowly and started to read. *'Darling Georgia, I hope school is going well and that you are still happy at the Primary. Granny says she saw you last week and that your eleven plus exams start very soon. I do hope you will get to the Grammar School with Charlotte, and Granny says Gus and the triplets are all hoping to join Joshua at the boy's Grammar, too.*

I have some rather important news I think you should know. Paul and I have decided to go our separate ways. He is determined to buy a chain of beach bars in Portugal and that is not a route I have any desire to follow. I am very fond of Paul, but not enough to give up my life doing something that is not what I would be happy with. Maybe it is because there is someone else always lurking somewhere in the back of my heart. Luigi and Maria are also unhappy at the thought of working in beach bars and they have agreed to come with me wherever I should end up, hopefully running an Italian style bistro. They have been with Paul and myself since we started our restaurant here in France, which incidentally we have already sold. Paul and I have agreed to share the proceeds and the business will finish on the 3ist March.

I have already seen a property that has taken my fancy, but there is a lot of water to flow under the bridge before any deal can become a fait accompli, for which reason I cannot tell you any more details but I should know the outcome of the planning decisions before the end of February. It is a huge step for me to take and I need to be sure I am doing the right thing. I will of course let you know as soon as I have any news'. She then went on to ask Georgia about Fire Cracker and *The Gang,* and finished by saying she hoped Giles was well and that she had heard his latest book was a best seller.

Georgia showed the letter to Giles. His vulnerable heart missed a beat when he read that she was splitting up with Paul and then dropped abruptly as he read there was someone else in a corner of her heart. He wished that it could be himself and then he immediately chastised himself for being stupid. There was always something that would stand in their way like a solid brick wall, and he kicked his prosthetic leg hard with his good one, immediately wishing he hadn't as he felt a pain shoot up to his thigh. He wondered where Clarissa was anticipating her new business would be and hoped it wouldn't be too far for Georgia's visits. He didn't know or had never met Luigi and Maria, but Georgia had told her Luigi was a brilliant chef and Maria was excellent in front of house.

When Georgia had gone to bed Giles shivered and decided to light the fire. Within five minutes the coals were blazing in the duck's nest grate and the flames were casting shadows against the walls in the dimly lit room. For once Giles' lively imagination was quiet, and Herbert Holmer, the highly efficient detective and hero of his books, was not discovering obscure clues or about to unearth an unsolved murder. Giles' thoughts were travelling back over the years. He could barely recall a time when he hadn't known Clarissa. They had started at Primary School together in Chilham, the pretty village near Canterbury, with its castle dominating the background of the village street, with its antique shops and heavily beamed tearooms. He and Clarissa had both passed their eleven-plus and progressed to their Grammar Schools in Canterbury, which is where he had met Tom West. Giles had eventually gone to Sandhurst Military Academy, and Clarissa to Pru Leith's famous Cookery School. He remembered meeting her in London and going back to the flat she shared with three other girls, and vividly recalled the first time they had made love on the very cramped back seat of his elderly mini and then a year or two later sampling the delights of the slightly more roomy jeep.

He recalled the pride on his parent's faces when he had received his first pip, and then his second when he had reached the lofty heights of lieutenant. Soon he had proposed to Clarissa, vowing that nothing could ever tear them apart.

He closed his eyes, enjoying the warmth of the fire. He gazed into the flames and could see Clarissa in her white wedding dress, he remembered their idyllic life together in their army quarters in Aldershot – then the day he had received his three pips as he reached the rank of captain, which was the same day Clarissa held him close and told him he was to become a father.

He got up and walked over to the old oak bureau, carefully opened an envelope and pulled out a photograph of himself with his arm round Clarissa as they both gazed down at their beautiful baby girl, little Georgia. The photo had been taken the day before he had received confirmation of his posting to Afghanistan. They had held each other close as Clarissa promised faithfully she would send him a picture of Georgia every single week. Ten days later, after a night of heartbroken passion, his pal, Eddie had wrenched him away from his sobbing wife and manhandled him into the vehicle, which was taking them to the aeroplane that was waiting to fly them to Afghanistan. Little did he dream as he left England that morning that he might never again make love to Clarissa.

He clenched his hands as he stared at the photograph, then carefully replaced it in its envelope and went back to his chair by the fire. His mind took him back to one afternoon six months after he had arrived in Afghanistan. He could still feel the pain that had racked his body as he and several of his confederates trod on the mines after they had left their stricken Land Rover. He could still see his shattered left leg and hear the screams of the other injured men. Some were more fortunate than himself, but some much less so as they lay dead beside him. He recalled the helicopter taking him to hospital and eventually being flown home to England where he had spent months in rehab before having his prosthetic leg fitted, finally coming back to his parent's home in Kent where Clarissa and Georgia were waiting for him.

His parents had tactfully gone away for the weekend, leaving the house free for his reunion with his little family and then Giles shuddered as he relived the next few minutes. He could hear Clarissa screaming. 'No I can't Giles – I'm sorry it's your leg – I can't let it touch me, -- I'm truly sorry,' and picking up Georgia had fled to the spare bedroom and locked the door. Two days later there was no sign of her or the baby. She had gone and so had his neighbour and childhood friend, Paul. The divorce had been rapid. His own parents had been wonderful and so too had Clarissa's. They were ashamed of their daughter and most of his friends had shared their opinion. *'Surely,'* they had thought, *'if you truly loved someone the fact that their body was not perfect was no reason to turn away from them?'*

Giles had one thing that had saved his sanity. When he had been in the rehab he had been laying in his bed one evening and the image of a good looking young man in a dark suit and a brown trilby hat had crept into his mind. With every passing minute he had become more and more of a reality, as Herbert Holmer - private detective - was born, and so too was Patsy Sanders. - Herbert Holmer had many, many passionate affairs, but for Captain Giles Norton, highly decorated military officer, there had been none. Clarissa's behaviour had shaken him to the core and he never wished to be humiliated again, but in spite of everything that had happened and whatever his own parents and Clarissa's parents and all his friends thought of his ex-wife, he still loved her with every inch of his heart and he longed for her every single night, as his fictional detective Herbert Holmer indulged in an extremely fulfilled life.

Giles sighed, pulling himself out of his reverie. He switched on the reading lamp and opened his computer. He typed in his new title, *'Stranger Things May Happen,'* and started to write. Hebert

Holmer was off to Las Vegas on his next investigation, which involved an extremely glamorous young lady and her devious, scheming mother who was out to seduce the cunning detective.

When Georgia came down in the morning, the first chapter was written and Giles Norton alias Patsy Sanders was asleep with his head on the still open computer.

CHAPTER 4

The impending arrival of Rob West and his family meant urgent changes had to be made. John and Mary realised it was not going to be possible for them to move into Old Tiles Oast. When they looked at their diaries they discovered it was let almost solidly through to the autumn, with the first couple arriving on the twelfth of March. Most were return visitors who had fallen in love with the oast on their visits the previous year.

Tom's grooms, Adrian and Amy unwittingly solved the problem when they told Tom they would like to change cottages with Amy's parents, Miriam and George, rather than move to the little oast house Tom had just converted near the woods which led to Woodcutters. They liked being next door to one another and Adrian's parents assured Tom that they were more than happy to move to the smaller Crofter's Cottage, whilst Amy and Adrian wanted nothing more than to be next door to them in the larger Shepherd's Cottage. Amy loved the motherly Miriam, who was soon to become her mother-in-law, and Miriam had already offered to look after the baby for a few hours a week when Amy felt ready to return to her duties as part time groom for Tom and Sam at Woodcutters.

Dom was obliging as always and agreed to move into Tom's Little Oast for a few weeks until Theobald's Place was ready for Justin, upon which Dom and Genevieve would move up to South Lodge. Everyone seemed happy with the arrangements and Tom was sure he would not encounter any problems letting the Little Oast once Dom was ensconced at South Lodge.

Charles wanted to pay for Dom's move but the Frenchman waved aside the offer. Charles' grooms, Sheila and the mightily strong Erica had already offered to help move the furniture in one of the horseboxes and John had felt the least he could do was to help as well, considering it was his own brother who was causing the upheaval.

George and Adrian had completed their very simple moves in less than a morning. A good deal of Miriam and George's furniture had stayed in Shepherd's Cottage. They just took their bedroom suite and the furniture that was in the sitting room. The rest they left for Adrian and Amy who were extremely grateful. Each of the cottages had an identical semi detached garage in the lane behind the gardens, so they kept their cars and all their outdoor paraphernalia where they already were.

Miriam was quite happy. She made the tiny bedroom, where Gus had once slept, into her sewing room and as long as George had his large television in the sitting room to watch his football and cricket, he was more than satisfied.

The following day, Genevieve, Dom and Anne-Marie were firmly ensconced in The Little Oast. Genevieve had watched it being transformed over the past few months and had peeped inside several times. She thought it was unique, filled with character and charm and she knew if it had just been the three of them and Tin Tin, their dog, she would have asked Dom if they could have stayed there, but her mother needed her own space and at South Lodge she would have a large bedroom with its own en-suite and the playroom would become her private sitting room. Also, Genevieve would still have a fourth bedroom for her paying guests, which had been such a financial help the previous year, and now even though Dom was a partner in the Lake House complex and receiving a generous salary Genevieve enjoyed having her guests, especially as often they were old friends and acquaintances from Toulouse, where Dom had worked for so long.

Anne-Marie loved living in the oast. She had the little bedroom in the roundel and she had soon discovered she could see Woodcutter's Cottage and Oscar's bedroom. At nine o'clock every evening she and Oscar both flashed a torch through their windows three times, to say goodnight to each other. She could watch Tom and Rosie and the boys schooling their horses and ponies in the jumping paddock just in front of the cottage, and a few days before Christmas Tilly had loaned her Tom Thumb. He was just under thirteen hands but Anne-Marie was a slim girl and he was all she could ask for. Now Tilly was at the Grammar School with Mimi, time was short and she found Bits n Pieces took up most of her time and she was pleased to see Anne-Marie and her little Tom Thumb joining the gang at Lake House.

Tom had explained to Anne-Marie that Twinkletoes was thirty years old and his days of teaching young people to ride had sadly but realistically drawn to a close. He was to spend the rest of his days under the watchful eyes of John and Mary in the paddock at Old Tiles with his old donkey friends, Cobweb and Moth. He had been the perfect schoolmaster to countless children, not least having been the instigator of Tom's illustrious career and Tom always reckoned he owed everything to his little, black pony.

Anne-Marie understood and now she was happy with Tom Thumb, who was grazing in one of Tom's paddocks near The Little Oast with Sam's Welsh Mountain Pony, Snow Queen, who had recently returned to Woodcutters after completing her duties at The Old Manor House now Fenella had acquired Poupėe.

Elizabeth's young twins, Felix and Flicka, were both young tearaways – completely different characters to the rather delicate, reserved Fenella and they were already riding Sam's little Dartmoor ponies, Hunca Munca and Timmy Tiptoes.

Sam had decided to put Snow Queen, who was a registered section A mare, to a well known Riding Pony stallion. He belonged to the owner of Ladybird, a beautiful pony Sam had shown for his owner for many years when she had been a teenager. Ladybird's owner specialized in breeding children's show ponies and she had suggested Sam should bring Snow Queen to her beautiful grey stallion, Showman of Thelmington. Sam had been thrilled and she and Susan were going to take Snow Queen to Oxfordshire to the Thelmington Stud in April in the trailer Tom had given her for

Christmas. It was a beautiful trailer, matching the silver blue tone of her People Carrier, which now had a strong tow-bar attached to its rear.

Sam had no idea Tom had bought it for her and when she had seen it outside the stables on Christmas morning she had hugged him until he could scarcely breathe. Now she could take any of the children if they needed to go to a separate venue and she could also take her horse, Chim Chim to the various dressage events she was hoping to enter with the riding club this coming year.

There were just two weeks before Rob's arrival but before that there was a big weekend of jumping to look forwards to at the Massenden Centre. It was going to be a huge event for two members of *The Gang*. Rosie was to make her debut in the thirteen two competition with Le Duc de Toulouse who she had taken over from Oliver. Tom was his usual phlegmatic self – trusting in both his young daughter and the talented Duc.

At the Massenden Centre, things were not quite so calm as Jacques prepared to ride the new Junior Foxhunter pony his parents had given him for Christmas. Jean-Pierre had asked Jock, the trusted Scottish dealer and long standing friend and team mate of Charles to look for a young pony with an outstanding jump for thirteen year old Jacques. As he usually did, Jock had come up trumps, this time with a beautiful chestnut gelding a friend of his had discovered in Galway, at a dealer's yard that Charles' late godmother, Lady Hermione Macdonald, had often visited and bought from with great success.

The Flying Fox was a full fourteen two pony, just six years old. He had entered four Junior Foxhunter competitions in Ireland the previous autumn, being placed in the first three and triumphing in the fourth. Jock himself had witnessed the win and had been more than mildly taken with the impressive, chestnut pony. He had phoned Jean-Pierre from the showground and a deal had been struck there and then. Jock had taken The Flying Fox, or Foxy, as he was better known back to Scotland with him and a week before Christmas, Ernst had driven up to Jock's yard and the pony had been carefully concealed at Woodcutters until late on Christmas Eve, when armed with a bright torch, Tom had manfully walked up to the Centre where Ernst had put the beautiful pony in a freshly prepared stable. At eight thirty on Christmas morning, when Jacques went to feed his pony Beau Geste, he noticed the chestnut Flying Fox with tinsel plaited into his mane and a big card round his neck. Jacques could barely read what it said as tears misted his sight, but he could just make out. *'To dearest Jacques with all our love from Mum and Papa. Bonne Chance with The Flying Fox. Xx'*

Now the big day had arrived and Jacques was walking the Junior Foxhunter course with his father and Tom. 'There's absolutely nothing for you to fear, Jacques. Just stay calm and do your best. You have got a super pony.' Tom told his nephew.

Even Clara had come to watch her brother and all the family had gathered in the box in the grandstand with the Wests and the Wright-Smiths.

Jacques felt butterflies in his stomach. He was well aware his dad would have paid a high price for this superb animal and he didn't want to let him down. He shortened his reins, trying to remember everything he had learned from Charles and Tom. He pushed with his heels and felt Foxy change gear and as they cantered through the start the butterflies flew away and the adrenalin flowed as the beautiful pony was flying, clearing every fence with inches to spare. It was the best feeling in the world, and all too soon it was over and he was trotting back into the collecting ring where his father and Tom were waiting for him. He was smiling; he knew this was going to be the first of many ponies and horses he would jump with the Massenden prefix.

For once, Tom let his emotion show. 'Brilliant round, Jacques. You've got a truly superb pony. He's a real star. You're a lucky, lucky young man and you have a very generous dad. Now go and walk Foxy round the edge of the practice area. There don't seem to be too many clears – just keep him settled.'

There was never any doubt about the eventual winner. Jean-Pierre was both ecstatic and relieved. He hadn't even told Jane how much he had paid for the pony. Tom knew, but he had told no one except Sam. He had seen a tiny snippet in the corner of a horsey magazine. *'Exceptional price paid for the highly talented Novice Jumping Pony, The Flying Fox. An undisclosed buyer has paid nine thousand pounds and The Flying Fox is now believed to be jumping in the South of England with his lucky new owner. We wish them well.'*

Sam had been shocked. 'Is Pierre crazy, Tom?' she asked her husband.

Tom smiled. 'Not crazy but ambitious. We all do things in a different way. I baulked at paying seven thousand for Fizzy for Ollie, but obviously Pierre can afford it and he will probably get his money back if Foxy goes on to win H.O.Y.S. but as you well know that's not the easiest thing to do, even on the most talented pony. I think our boys will probably have something to say about that too, not to mention Rupert, Mimi and Gus, but game on – we shall just have to wait and see.'

The twelve two class was next and as Tom more than half expected, Rosie and Sparkler were the easy winners with her cousin, Eloise and Pierrot a long way behind her in second place and Abby and the ever reliable Fuzz Buzz in third. Elizabeth was beside herself with joy as Fenella and Poupée took fifth place. It was Fenella's first competition and Poupée had jumped steadily and carefully as James had hopped from one leg to the other in the collecting ring.

Sam was sitting with Joanna, Genevieve and Anna in the box whilst the men walked the thirteen two class with Rosie and the boys.

'We're not going to let you win, Rosie.' Oscar told her. 'Lando and I are both going to do our damndest to beat you.'

'Nice one, Oscar,' Tom told his son sarcastically. 'Rosie doesn't need any favours from you or Orlando, and I sincerely hope Gus won't give her any either. She's perfectly capable of jumping round here in a good time – all I want her to do this year are nice, sensible clear rounds. She and the Duc have all the time in the world. Now go and check the distance in that double again, please, boys.'

Oscar grinned at his father. 'Aye, aye, Sir. At your command,' and he saluted his father cheekily and sauntered back to the aforesaid double, carefully checking the distance between each jump.

Justin was walking behind them with Gus, who ran up to Rosie. 'Take care, Rosie. These jumps are higher than you are used to.'

She pinched his arm. 'Worry pot, Gussie. Course I'll be careful but if Dad thinks I'm going to crawl round here, he's got another think coming,' and she tossed her pretty, little face in the direction of her father.

Gus looked unconvinced. 'Dad says I mustn't go slowly on purpose. He says it's not fair to Hamlet – but Rosie please be careful.'

She laughed at him, teasing him. 'Well, at least you can't run and hide your face Gussie, you're jumping directly after me.'

Gus had gone red. 'How do you know, Rosie?' he asked. 'Who told you?'

'Oh, Gussie, all *the gang* know but I don't mind. I think you're ---I think you're –O.K.' And with that she hurried out of the school with her father, who lifted her onto the Duc.

Gus felt sick. - So all *The Gang* knew he was a coward and all because he didn't want to see Rosie get hurt.

He looked at his father. 'I don't want to jump, Dad. I don't feel well,' and he ran into the stand and up the stairs. He burst into the box where Sam, Josh and Oliver were sitting with Anna and Abby, and Joanna was eating a sandwich with Charles and Mimi.

'I'm not bloody jumping – I'm not a bloody coward – I'll bloody well watch Rosie from up here. I'll show you all I'm not a bloody wimp.' And with that tirade over, Gus Wright-Smith burst into tears.

Everyone listened in shocked horror. This wasn't Oscar West, this was dear little Fergus Wright-Smith. Even Mimi was stunned into silence.

'I don't want to be a coward,' Gus was now sobbing. 'I just don't want Rosie to get hurt.'

Anna took his hand. 'Come on, Gus. Rosie will be worried if she sees you're not in the collecting ring. Let's find Daddy and Hamlet. I can't always watch Daddy, and I know Sam sometimes hides her eyes when Tom is jumping Opal or The Wizard and I'm sure Joanna sometimes doesn't watch Grandpa. We're all cowards when we're frightened for someone we're really fond of. Tom wouldn't let Rosie ride The Duc if he didn't think she was capable of doing it, so come on, let's go and find Hamlet.' And she led Gus out of the box and found Justin who was looking anxiously for Gus, as he held on to Hamlet in the collecting ring.

'He's better, Justin,' Anna told her husband. 'He'd better get Hamlet warmed up quickly.'

Justin was well aware Gus had been crying, but he chose to ignore the fact. 'Come on, Gussie, let's pop Hamlet over the practice jump.'

Gus looked at his father. 'Dad, why am I afraid when Rosie jumps? I didn't think I was a coward.'

' If someone is a special friend you are not a coward if you care about them.'

'*The Gang* all knows, Dad.'

'Knows what, Gussie?'

'That I hide my eyes when Rosie is in the arena. The worst thing is, Rosie knows too.'

'*The Gang* are your friends, Gus, but when jumping is our sport we just have to be brave, not only for ourselves but for the ones that are closest to us.'

'So why am I frightened for Rosie then, Dad?'

'One day, when you are several years older, you will realise why.

But for now, just have fun with her and all your friends, because once you grow up nothing is ever quite the same again. Now come on, off you go on Hamlet and let Tom worry about Rosie.'

Anna arrived back in the box just in time to see Oscar and Humbug shooting into the school. 'Is Gus O.K. Anna?' Sam asked her friend. 'Poor little chap. Growing up can be hell.'

'He's all right, Sam. He's just gutted Rosie will think he's a coward. He's upset she knows he can't watch her.'

'Rosie won't hold it against him, Anna. She's far too fond of him and Oscar won't dare open his mouth. He's frightened when Anne-Marie just canters.'

Sam sighed. 'Oh, dear, Humbug looks his usual effervescent self. Tom says Oscar makes him excited on purpose and he's almost as bad with Whisky. Oh, glory, now it's my turn to hide my eyes, here come Rosie and The Duc.'

All eyes were now firmly on Rosie. She wouldn't be nine for another three months and she was a slight little girl, but Tom had assured Sam that the Duc was a much easier ride than Sparkler.

Charles was watching with interest. In his opinion little Rosie West was the best eight-year-old rider in the country. All of Tom's children could see exactly when to tell their ponies to take off. It was a gift their father had obviously passed on to them, and as he watched the new partnership he was shaking his head in disbelief. Rosie had the beautiful quiet style of Tom, the only difference was the fact that she was extremely vocal and her voice could be heard urging The Duc de Toulouse at every jump.

She passed Gus in the entrance and shouted. 'Good Luck, Gussie,' and he solemnly raised his hand in acknowledgement. He breathed a sigh of relief – she was O.K. - and his young heart lifted as he and Hamlet started their round.

Rosie rode up to Tom. 'Well done, sweetheart. Really, well ridden. Walk the Duc round with Gus and Hamlet when they come out of the school. Keep away from Oscar and Humbug. That pony is completely bonkers today. I'm just going to help 'Lando at the practice jump.'

Gus was coming through the exit. Hamlet's round had been impeccable. Rosie called to him. 'Gussie, come and walk round the edge with me and the Duc.'

They walked quietly round together until finally Gus asked, 'Rosie, are you ashamed of me?'

He received her beautiful smile. 'Of course not, Gussie, but really you have no need to worry about me, you know.'

'I can't help it, Rosie. You're my special friend, you see.'

Rosie smiled again and said in an offhand voice. 'Oh, I've always known that.'

Gus looked both shocked and embarrassed. 'Rosie, I have never, never told you that.'

Rosie laughed. 'No, not yet, Gussie, but you will one day. Probably when I'm riding Bamboozle.'

'Who on earth is Bamboozle?'

'Lily's last foal. He's going to be my Foxhunter pony when I'm older. When I am eleven, he will be six. Dad says that's perfect. You'll be thirteen then, Gussie. I wonder if you will still hide your eyes when I jump.'

It was Gus' turn to smile. 'I don't wonder, Rosie. I know I will. Always.'

Rosie looked and saw Tom beckoning her to the practice jump. 'Good luck in the jump off, Gussie. Dad is calling me. I'll see you later.'

'Good luck, Rosie, and please take care.' But she was cantering across the sand school towards Tom without a care in the world.

There were only six in the jump off and they were all part of *The Gang.* Rupert and The March Hare had joined Gus, Rosie, Orlando, Oscar and Georgia.

Oscar was the first to jump. Humbug was almost pulling his arms out of their sockets but the game boy somehow steered the hot little piebald pony round the course, but Oscar knew he had gone very wide to the final jump – it had been almost impossible to turn Humbug and Tom was fast coming to the conclusion that maybe he would try Humbug with a Pelham bit. He was reluctant, but he knew it could be the solution that would stop Humbug pulling.

Tom shot inside the school to watch Rosie. He soon realized that she was ignoring his instructions, as she and The Duc were flying. She was two seconds faster than Oscar. Tom knew her time was going to be a force to be reckoned with but he was pretty certain it could be beaten, but none of the ensuing ponies could afford to make any mistakes. He wasn't wrong, as Gus and Hamlet were faster and clear.

Rosie rode over to him. 'You were supercalifragilisticexpialaidocious, Gussie.' She called out happily.

Orlando and Jet Stream were fractionally slower than Rosie, but the March Hare and Rupert were benefitting from all the coaching Charles was giving his young son and they now had an awesome understanding with each other and they were faster than anyone. Georgia was the last to jump. She was thrilled even to be in the jump off at all and was probably more delighted than any one with her sixth place.

Oscar put Humbug back in the horsebox – he was determined to do better in the next class with Whisky, but he loved Humbug and he kissed the pony's nose and gave him a handful of nuts. He had been totally unaware of his father watching him but Tom was pleased. Oscar had the right attitude. Tom knew his young son would be disappointed to have come fifth in the previous jump off, but his love for his feisty little pony was obvious. Oscar was a good sport, and in Tom's eyes that showed an excellent character.

He checked Whisky's girth and gave Oscar a leg up onto his second mount. 'Try to keep Whisky calm Ozzie, walk round the practice area until I get there. Don't attempt the practice jump and put yourself to jump as near the beginning of the class as you can.

I will be with you as soon as I have helped Ollie and 'Lando. Josh has already gone down on Lily. Go and walk round with him.'

As soon as Oscar had disappeared, Tom turned his attention to Orlando and Torchlight and then Oliver and Buck's Fizz. He put the saddle onto Ganger, ran the stirrups up and led him down to the practice area – ready for Josh to jump onto once he had competed with Tiger Lily.

He could see Justin putting the jump to the right height for Gus and his skewbald, Pie in the Sky – Mimi was cantering round on Lord of the Rings, whilst Charles held her second ride, the lovely grey mare Babushka. The last of *The Gang* to arrive in the collecting ring was Jacques and Beau Geste.

There were twenty-four entries altogether, including Karl and Helga's daughter Heidi. Their son, Nicholas, was in his first senior year and he would be entering the Young Rider's the next day. To Mimi's delight, Nicholas had fallen out with Kristina, his girlfriend of the previous year, and Mimi had decided she would wear her favourite jeans and sweatshirt and her cherry red anorak, and if her mother wasn't looking, pinch some of her lipstick in an effort to attract the attention of the almost silver haired German boy. Mimi was twelve – going on sixteen – and Joanna had already realized her young daughter was a handful. Charles laughed and called Mimi his little minx, but Joanna's outlook was not so open-minded and she had already decided their daughter needed a reasonably firm hand. Not enough to alienate her but sufficient to keep her under control.

Joanna need not have worried as far as the blond Nicholas was concerned. He had already turned his attention to the Dutchman, Pieter's, eighteen-year-old daughter, who was visiting The Massenden Centre with her father for the first time. Nicholas was having a wonderful time in the caravan with Margareta, whilst her unsuspecting father was enjoying a cultural visit to Canterbury and enjoying the architecture of the majestic old Cathedral with two of his Dutch teammates.

The fourteen two class was well under way. Rosie was in the box, watching her brothers with Sam. She clapped, as first Whisky and Oscar and then Lily and Josh jumped clear. Two girls she didn't know had four and eight faults and then Rosie stood up as Gus and Pie in the Sky trotted through the big doors at the end of the school. Sam smiled as she saw Rosie cross her fingers. She didn't move as Gus jumped his round, but as he left the school she turned to Sam. 'Mummy, Gussie looked just like a prince. A real fairy tale prince.'

Sam smiled. She wouldn't really describe Gus as a prince – just a nice looking young boy, with big grey eyes and a rather charming smile, and then she remembered when she had been younger than Rosie and a prince with a mop of blond curls and piercing blue eyes had ridden up her drive on a little black pony. She remembered pulling herself out of her wheel chair and staggering towards him. He had caught her as she had started to fall and as she had looked up and smiled at him, she had thought – *' my prince – he must have come from his castle. ---- And he's still my prince*,' she thought to herself. To everyone else he had been Tom West, the farmer's son, but to her, he was her very own prince. '*Maybe we all have one prince in our lives if we're lucky,'* she thought, '*and perhaps that's who Gus is. Rosie's own Prince Charming.'*

She smiled at Rosie. 'Perhaps he is, Rosie, and maybe you are his princess.'

'Is Dads your prince, Mummy?'

'Always, Rosie, always.'

Rosie had turned her attention back to the competition. 'Here's 'Lando and Torchlight, Mummy,' and she watched her brother as Torchlight cleared every jump.

By the end of the competition there were ten clear rounds. 'I'm going to find Dads in the collecting ring, Mummy.' 'Alright, but be careful and stay with Daddy.'

'I might talk to Gussie or the trips,' and she had run down the steps.

The jump off had started and Whisky and Oscar had jumped a fast clear, as Josh and Lily followed them into the school.

Gus was waiting by the entrance. He heard Rosie's voice. 'Good luck, Prince Charming, cos that's what you look like on The Pie.'

The doors opened as Josh came out with an unlucky four faults. Lily had just caught the gate with her back leg.

Gus gave Rosie one last smile. He felt he could do anything – she had told him he was a prince. He felt almost like a king as he patted The Pie, and together they jumped the round of the afternoon. No one could catch them. Not even Mimi or Josh and Ganger.

Justin lifted Rosie in front of Gus on The Pie, as they rode back to the horsebox. 'I said you were a prince, Gussie.'

'Maybe you are a princess, then Rosie.'

CHAPTER 5

Mary was waiting at Honeysuckle Cottage for Dom and Adrian to arrive with the horsebox and an assortment of furniture she had bought at the auction in Canterbury the previous day.

She and John had suddenly realised Honeysuckle Cottage was devoid of any creature comforts. She had sent a text to Rob who had asked her to buy the bare necessities, which would tide him over until the freight arrived from Sydney a few weeks later.

Fortunately the kitchen was well fitted with all the electrical goods and a modern gas cooker, and Joanna had scoured the attic at Lake House and discovered various utensils and cutlery, along with a kitchen table and four chairs, which had been sitting there since she herself had left Honeysuckle Cottage over twelve years ago.

She also found a pile of bed linen and Nicholas and Emily's old duvets – all neatly tied up in black plastic bags, and Mary unearthed a spare duvet at Old Tiles for Rob.

She had bought an almost new double bed at the auction and a pair of brand new bunk beds, which John would dismantle and put in each of the youngster's bedrooms.

She had purchased an old but comfortable settee and two chairs and a glass coffee table, as well as three capacious chests of drawers. The whole lot had cost less than two hundred pounds and she felt Rob could afford to have a massive bonfire when his smart, Australian furniture arrived in a few weeks time.

There were fitted carpets in all the bedrooms and Amtico flooring downstairs and by the time the furniture was unloaded and in situ, Mary decided that although far from luxurious, at least the cottage looked reasonably welcoming.

The following morning, John left for Heathrow. The plane was due to land at nine thirty, but Rob had warned his brother that getting through customs could be a lengthy business owing to Daisy's Silky Terrier, which would be travelling in the hold.

Rob certainly hadn't been mistaken and it was already well into the afternoon before they were leaving the airport, joining the queue of traffic on the M.25 as everyone was trying to get home to the South East. John turned the radio on as he realised all his passengers were fast asleep. He stopped at a filling station where he noticed a large bowl of water. He lifted the little terrier, Peanuts, ignoring her growls, snapping teeth and smelly breath and took her to the bowl. She refused point blank to have anything to do with the water and John shut her firmly in the back of the Range Rover with the luggage, as she gave him one final growl.

At seven thirty, exhausted after the long, slow drive, John was finally pulling up in front of the farmhouse. A succulent smell of roast lamb greeted him as Mary opened the back door before all hell was let loose as Peanuts leaped out of Daisy's arms, rushing up to John's dachshunds, Mac and Mabel, who were none too happy to see an intruder entering their domain. There were squeals and growls, followed by a gnashing of teeth. Five minutes later, Mary was driving John to the A. and E. with a gash across his hand requiring at least four stitches and Peanuts was firmly locked in the kennels behind the Victorian stables.

Rob didn't bother to apologise.

'God, what little monsters you've got,' was all he said, totally ignoring the fact that Peanuts had been the instigator of the fight.

John was trying to stem the flow of blood as Mary told Rob. 'Help yourselves, Rob. Everything is ready,' only to be told.

'Oh, we don't eat meat, we'll just eat the veg,' with which Mary pulled John into the car, slamming the door and driving twice as fast as she usually did, on her way to the hospital.

'Damn and blast, Mary. What a ghastly little dog. They can get it to Honeysuckle a.s.a.p. and it's not welcome at Old Tiles again. I'm not having Mac and Mabel's noses put out of joint. It had better not go near Boz – he would eat it in one mouthful. At least the journey from Heathrow was quiet, they were all three asleep after the first five minutes.'

When John and Mary arrived back at the farm a full two hours later, after John had had four stitches and a tetanus booster, Rob was lolling on the settee in the lounge watching a documentary, ironically about Sydney harbour. There was no sign of Simon or Daisy.

The supper dishes were sitting on the table, and the leg of lamb congealing in its own fat in the oven.

'Where are your youngsters, Rob?' John asked his brother.

'Oh they wandered upstairs to watch a television in one of the bedrooms. What's happened to dad's sheep, John?'

'MY sheep went a while ago, Rob. Two hundred sheep with no help wasn't too clever. I've let the land to the local Equitation Centre of which I am now a sleeping partner. It's going well and Mary runs the B. and B. in the farmhouse.'

Rob gave John an odd look. 'Can't think that Dad would have approved of that, John.'

John was ready with his answer. 'Well, I do remember he did have two sons, Rob. I don't remember you ever taking any interest in the farm. At least I gave up thirty years of my life to those sheep.'

'Well, what about your son? I gather he ponces about with his horses.'

'Tom works all hours God gives him and so do his wife and his five kids.'

Even Rob could feel things weren't going too well and he gathered Simon and Daisy. 'I think we'll make a move across the road to this cottage, Mary. Just point us in the right direction.'

Mary walked to the farm gate and pointed to Honeysuckle Cottage, handing him the key. 'I've left bread and milk and some tea and coffee. There is a selection of cereals and some honey and marmalade, but I think you have forgotten something - Peanuts. I don't think we really want her here,' and Daisy ran to the kennels to retrieve her bad tempered pet.

Mary sighed as she walked back to the farmhouse. 'Not a good start, Johnny. Oh dear, not a good start at all,' she said, as she looked at John's very sore hand.

The next morning Rob disappeared to London to introduce himself to the staff at Carmelo Enterprises U.K. leaving the two youngsters to entertain themselves. By mid morning they were bored with their own company and after shutting Peanuts in the kitchen, decided to explore Old Tiles farm.

The schools were on half term holiday and they wouldn't be making their presence felt there until the following week.

'Come on, Daise,' Simon was yelling in his Australian drawl, 'let's see what this paltry little English farm has to offer. I can tell you, Daise, as soon as I hit eighteen I'll be back on that plane to Oz. This place stinks already. I'm going to get Dad to fix up Skype so I can chat with Marlene, and he can jolly well pay for her and her mum to come over here in the summer holidays.'

Marlene had been Simon's girlfriend for the past six months. She was the daughter of one of Rob's many lady friends, who had latterly started to get too possessive for Rob's liking and was one of the reasons he had been pleased to accept the move to London.

Daisy was more open-minded. 'I'll reserve judgment, Si. Last night Mary mentioned a gang. They might be O.K. She said one of them might ask us to join.'

'That's O.K. for you Daise,' her brother drawled, 'you're only eleven. I want my own sheila not a gaggle of immature brats.'

He slammed the farm gate shut and then spied Thunder and Twinkletoes grazing with the donkeys in the small paddock. Daisy, who was by far the more timid of the two stroked Twink but Simon had noticed a head collar slung over the stable door. He ran across and put it on Thunder, attaching the rope to either side of the headpieces. Before Daisy could say a word, he had plucked a large thorny stick from the hedge and leaped onto Thunderbird, shouting to his sister to close the gate behind him.

'I don't think you should be doing this, Si,' Daisy was yelling, but he was already almost out of sight, thrashing Thunder with the stick and kicking the old pony's sides.

He soon noticed the cross-country course and turned the sweating pony towards it, just as Tom, Sam and the family were on their way to pay a visit to Mary and John and to introduce themselves to the new arrivals. The first thing Tom saw was his beloved Thunder flying over a huge brush fence – catching his back leg on the top and turning a somersault as his rider flew through the air, getting dazedly to his feet and trying to pull Thunder up at the same time.

Even Oscar had never heard the expletive Tom used, as he threw Madame's reins to Sam and tore to the stricken pony. Joshua was even quicker than his father and reached Simon seconds before Tom, whilst Sam was trying to stem Rosie's screams, as the triplets stood like shocked statues beside her. She had already guessed who the lad was and she soon feared for his life as Tom raced towards him but Josh was already there and Sam saw Joshua's fist flash and the boy struggling on the ground as Josh hit him again and again.

By now Orlando and Oliver were crying as well as Rosie, and Oscar was running to join in the fight with Josh, as Simon was now standing up and a real fight had broken out.

Tom was past caring about the boys. He was phoning the vet. He had helped Thunder to his feet with the help of John, who had heard the commotion from the lambing shed where he had just helped one of the Jacob sheep give birth to triplet lambs. He had grabbed the quad bike and was soon gasping at the scene in front of him.

His first job was to separate the two boys, which was no mean feat. Blood was pouring down their faces. Simon had a badly cut eye and Josh's jaw was feeling very odd. Fortunately, Oscar's wounds were superficial. John called Mary on his mobile. '*Mary – emergency, sweetheart. Bust up on the cross-country course. That bloody boy has had an accident with Thunder. Can you bring the*

Range Rover as quickly as possible, there's blood everywhere? I've no idea where Daisy is.'

Mary glanced through the kitchen window. '*I can see her sitting on the fence talking to Twink and the donkeys. She seems to be behaving herself. What's happened to Thunder?'*

'Not good, Mary. Tom's sent for the vet but Josh and the boy had a full on fight. They've hurt each other pretty badly, I am afraid you and Sam will have to take them to the A. and E. The trips and Rosie can stay with me. Lollipop has just had triplets. They can watch over those. I think another Jacob is about to give birth. Daisy had better stay here too. Can you be as quick as you can and bring her with you?'

Mary pulled everything off the hob and out of the oven and ran to the Range Rover. She called to Daisy and told her to get in the car and they were soon racing towards the cross-country course. She gasped when she saw Tom with Rob's son and Josh with blood pouring down both their faces, and then burst into tears when she saw the stricken Thunder, whose front leg was dangling a foot above the ground.

Tom was as white as a sheet – partly with anger and partly with distress as he looked at his beloved old pony.

'Get that boy out of my sight before I kill him, Mum and put him in the front of the car beside you, Sam can sit in the back with Josh. Trips, you and Rosie go with Grandpa John. Put the ponies with Twink and do you think you can manage to lead Madame to the Victorian stables, Oz? Ollie you lead Humbug and Fizz, Rosie you take Sparkler and if this girl is any more sensible than her brother, she can lead Ganger. Dad will take Chim Chim for you, Sam. Get going as quickly as you can, Mum. I've rung James. He's on his way.'

Thunder was looking towards the paddock where Tom could hear Twinkletoes neighing and Cobweb and Moth both giving, mournful brays.

As Mary and Sam disappeared with the boys, they passed James bumping across the paddock with his Land Rover towing the horse ambulance and a young trainee vet sitting beside him.

James was visibly upset. His mind shot back over sixteen years when he and Tom had first seen Thunder in Shady Sid's filthy yard. He had been a special pony from that moment – not only to Tom – but also to everyone who knew him.

He took one look. 'Let's see if we can get him into the ambulance, Tom. Poor old chap. We must get him X Rayed. It's just possible he's torn a tendon. Let's hope nothing is broken.'

With a lot of help from John, James and the young vet, Tom managed to lead Thunder into the ambulance and with Tom and Marcus, the young trainee vet on either side of him, James drove slowly back to the surgery.

In the lambing shed, one of the Jacob sheep was about to produce twins. The trips, Rosie and Daisy were all sitting on straw bales. The first little lamb arrived but it needed help, however, before John could help it, the second lamb was struggling to be born. To John's amazement, Daisy picked up the first lamb, cleared its nose of the membrane and swung it round and round by its feet. Before long it was breathing happily and tottering towards his mother and sister.

'Well done. Daisy,' John smiled at the young girl.

'I often helped Donovan. He had the farm near us in Sydney. He taught me about lambing. I think he's O.K. now, Uncle John.'

The triplets were impressed. Rosie looked at Daisy properly for the first time. 'Do you want to come and say hello to my pony, Sparkler?' she asked.

'O.K.' Daisy drawled and John breathed a sigh of relief as he heard her telling Rosie and the triplets that her pony Popcorn and her brother's stock horse, Melchior, would be arriving in two days time.

Fortunately for everyone, after a quick phone call to Jean-Pierre telling him of the traumatic morning, he had agreed to take the two newcomers at livery. In the interest of all, John decided the further apart Josh and Simon were kept, the better it would be for everyone.

Meanwhile Sam and Mary were sitting in the A. and E. with a boy either side of them. Josh's jaw was feeling very strange and Simon's right eye was almost closed.

Eventually they were shepherded into the doctor's surgery. 'Well, well, what have we here? Bit of a fisticuffs I imagine.'

He dealt with Josh's jaw, putting three stitches in his chin and telling him to eat very soft food for the next few days. He then cleaned up Simon's eye, stitching his cheek, and with a warning that he didn't wish to see either of them ever again, ushered them out of the room, but not before Sam heard Josh muttering out of the corner of his mouth. 'If anything happens to Thunder of if you ever touch one of our ponies again, you're a dead man.'

Simon glowered at Josh. 'When my stock horse, Melchior arrives on Thursday I wouldn't even want to go within a mile of your potty, old has been.'

Sam caught hold of Joshua and pushed him into the car as she saw the look on his face. 'Don't listen to him Josh. He's just an ignorant kid.'

'Kid.' Simon glowered at Sam. 'I'll show you what a kid I am when my sheila comes over here in the summer.'

Sam chose to ignore him. She hadn't yet met Tom's Uncle Rob, but she sincerely hoped he was a damn sight better than his obnoxious son.

James was shaking his head. 'I'm sorry, Tom, there's a small bone that's broken in the leg. I can operate – he will have to be in a plaster cast for about six weeks but he won't be in any pain. At the worst he could end up slightly lame. It will be expensive but I imagine where Thunder is concerned money won't be an issue.'

'Can you absolutely guarantee he won't be in pain, James?'

'Yes, but I doubt if he can ever be ridden again, but you had retired him anyway.'

'There's nothing to think about, then James. Do the op as soon as you can.'

'I'll do it this afternoon, Tom. He will have to stay here for a few days and then he can just amble about as he pleases. He will have to wear the cast for about six weeks, and Tom, I won't charge my time – I couldn't – not for Thunder.'

'God, you're a good mate, James but I shall be taking Twinkletoes back to Woodcutters and Thunder can join him there. Honeysuckle Cottage is too near Old Tiles for my liking and that young lad will definitely not be welcome at my home, whatever relation he is. Josh and he half killed each other this morning. I wonder whether Sam and Mary are still at the A. and E. God, what a start. I haven't met the girl properly yet, but as far as I am concerned, Uncle Rob can definitely pay your vet bill. I just hope those two boys don't kill each other on the school bus next week. Oh, God, poor Thunder. Call me as soon as he's had his op, James. Now do you want me to get him into a stable?'

'Thanks, Tom, then I'll run you back to Old Tiles.'

'It's O.K. James. I'll walk – it's not far and it might cool my temper before I meet that young thug again.'

In fact Tom didn't meet Simon again as the young man informed Mary he wanted to go straight home. Mary was only too pleased, and when she arrived at Old Tiles she was more than a little relieved to see Rosie and Daisy talking to Sparkler. There was no sign of the triplets but Sam was not surprised when she discovered them with John, stolidly munching their way through a lemon drizzle cake.

Sam had already received a call from Tom and she ran to meet him as she saw him walking towards the farmhouse.

She put her arm round him and as he noticed the tears in her eyes, his own emotions overcame him – they turned into the Victorian stables and both wept into Madame's soft neck.

'Poor, darling Thunder,' Sam sobbed. 'No wonder Josh tried to beat him up.'

'I'm mighty glad he did, Sammy. It certainly saved me a job and he wouldn't have got off so lightly if I had had anything to do with it. Maybe the girl isn't as bad as her brother. At least Rosie seems to be getting on with her, but one thing is for certain, none of my kids will invite that lad to join *The Gang.'*

'No, Tom, but the rules are that only one member has to invite him and he'll be in.'

'Well Gussie and Abby won't I'm sure, nor Jacques.'

'Maybe not, Tom but who is a little minx as far as boys are concerned?'

'No, Sammy, surely not!!'

'Well don't hold your breath, my Thomas.'

Rosie had asked Sam if Daisy could come back to Woodcutters and Sam had taken pity on the young girl. It wasn't her fault that she was encumbered with an obnoxious, older brother and with Tom's rather reluctant agreement, Sam put a saddle and bridle on Twinkletoes and with the command that no one would do more than walk, a very subdued cavalcade made its way back to Woodcutters.

Rosie had obviously taken a liking to Daisy and they spent the rest of the afternoon playing with Holly and Boz after Rosie had introduced her to all the horses and ponies.

'Is your brother always stupid?' Rosie asked in her usual direct way.

'He's often in trouble. He tried drugs once at school and he was often caught smoking. Then he met Marlene and became a bit more sensible.'

'Who is Marlene?'

'Marlene Longfellow. One of Dad's floozie's daughters.'

'What's a floozie?' Rosie wanted to know.

'Sort of like a dolly bird.'

'Oh, Dad had one of those.'

Unfortunately for Rosie, Tom was just walking across the lawn to go into the kitchen and make himself a cup of tea. He had been schooling Opal and was waiting nervously for James' phone call to tell him Thunder had come out of the anesthetic. He overheard Rosie's cheerful remark and thundered. 'Rosie. How many times do I have to tell you I have never had a dolly bird? That was Oscar's stupid idea. You know that perfectly well.'

Daisy smiled at him. 'Oh, my dad had several, all at the same time, that's quite normal.'

'Maybe it is in your father's eyes, Daisy, but certainly not in mine. What time do you expect your Dad home this evening?'

'He said he would be back by six thirty and then he would take Si and me to a MacDonald's in Ashford. He says they do Veggie Burgers.'

'Fine, I'll walk back with you, I need to break the news to my Uncle Rob that he will be receiving a considerable vet's bill. Where is your brother now?'

'He told me he was going to explore the village.'

Simon had indeed wandered down to the village green where he had come across a group of boys about his age playing cricket.

He sat on a seat, ready to make fun of them, until he realized they were better than average players.

After a while, a huge hit from the batsman sent the ball flying in his direction. He caught it adeptly and threw it back to the bowler.

'Thanks, mate. Do you want to join us? We haven't seen you before. Are you new to this joint?'

Simon decided to be affable, 'Yea. My dad and my sister and I arrived yesterday,' he replied in his distinctive drawl.

'Where are you from mate?' The lad who was fielding nearest to him asked.

'Sydney.'

'What are you doing here? Are you on holiday?'

'No. My dad's firm have moved him to London.'

'London! What you doing in Massenden, then?'

'My uncle lives here. At the farm down the lane.'

'Are you a West?'

'Yea, Simon West. My dad is Rob West. John West's brother.'

'So you know old Josh?'

'Too well,' Simon growled, and for the first time the lad noticed Simon's swollen cheek.

He laughed. 'Don't say old Josh has been swinging his left hook. It's the most lethal in the school. What have you done to upset his lordship? It takes a lot to rattle Josh; he's usually pretty solid. It's his young brother, Oscar, that's the feisty one.'

'I rode one of their bloody ponies. It was a stupid old thing – tipped me up on one of the cross-country fences. His dad wasn't best pleased.'

'I bet he wasn't. The whole of that family live for their horses and ponies but Josh is a good guy. He only started at the Grammar last term. He doesn't play cricket or footie, he rides his ponies all over the country but he really likes his boxing. He's the best under fifteen in the school.'

One of the boys who had been batting sauntered up to Simon. 'D'you want to play? The girls usually congregate here about five o'clock. If you're interested.'

Simon didn't hesitate. 'Sure thing I am. Bring on the sheilas.'

When a group of about fifteen girls arrived a couple of hours later, Simon decided maybe Massenden had more to offer than he had first imagined.

When Rob arrived home an hour later, he discovered his son ensconced on the settee with his arm round a young girl in a skimpy black skirt, a figure hugging sweater and half a chemist's shop plastered on her face. Marlene already appeared completely forgotten. At the same time, his nephew was standing scowling on the doorstep with a piece of paper in one hand and Daisy standing beside him.

It was not the best reunion with Tom, whom he hadn't set eyes on for over twenty years.

'Uncle Rob, I presume,' Tom stated with no preliminary niceties. 'I'm Tom and I am afraid I have bad news for you. Your son saw fit to try to ride my old pony over the cross-country course at the farm this morning. Thunder is now in residence at the local vets with a broken bone in his leg. Here is the bill. You're lucky it's not larger. Fortunately for you the vet also happens to be my brother-in-law and one of my very good friends and has elected not to charge for his time. He was with me the day I rescued Thunder almost twenty years ago. I think you will find your son has temporarily lost some of his looks. My son, Josh saw to that, although by the look of things he still appeals to the village girls. On the other hand your daughter and my girl, Rosie, have had a really good time together – she is welcome at Woodcutters anytime.'

Rob was completely taken aback. Tom had been a tiny lad when he had last seen him with two baby sisters toddling behind him. Now he was staring at a strapping man, with an athletic body and extremely good looks.

'Come in, Tom, I'm sorry. Si is missing Oz. at the moment. He'll soon settle down. I didn't realize your dad had made so many changes to our farm.' He emphasized the word, *our*, which did nothing to improve Tom's mood. The farm had been left to his father, of that he was under no illusion. Rob had never shown the remotest interest in it and when Tom's grandfather had died, the extremely pleasant, modern bungalow in which he had been living at the time had been left to Rob, and Tom assumed he still owned it. It looked over the sea at Greatstone and as far as Tom knew it was let to an elderly couple and their daughter.

'There have been changes at *Dad's* farm, yes,' and he emphasized the word Dad, 'but all for the better. The farm and Dad were struggling. The sheep weren't really paying their way. Now the Equitation Centre rents the land and Dad is a sleeping partner, he and Mum have more time to enjoy life together.'

'Oh, your dad was always too soft with Mary.'

'Yes, and you will soon discover I have exactly the same attitude towards my wife, Samantha, and now I will leave this with you and I would be grateful if you would pay it pronto, Uncle Bob. Vets don't appreciate being kept waiting. If your young daughter wants to spend the day with Rosie tomorrow she's welcome. Sam is taking Rosie into Canterbury, maybe Daisy would like to go with them – obviously Simon has already discovered his own entertainment,' and Tom nodded pointedly at the boy and girl sprawled on the elderly settee.

'He's met up with a group of young lads who play cricket on the green. He's meeting them tomorrow, apparently some of them go to the Grammar School.'

Rob turned to Daisy. 'Would you like to go with Rosie and her Mum to Canterbury tomorrow, Daise?' he asked the girl in the Australian drawl he appeared to have acquired.

Daisy nodded and Tom told her Sam would pick her up at ten thirty.

Rob opened the envelope and looked at the vet's bill. 'Christ, they know how to charge.'

'Well, unfortunately, thanks to your son, Thunder has a pretty badly damaged leg. He hasn't just got a scratch on the knee you know.'

'Oh well,' Rob sighed. 'I'll send them a cheque tomorrow, Tom. Sorry about the pony – but boys will be boys. Si will have his own nag to ride on Friday. It's obviously got a bit more stamina than your old fellow.'

Tom chose to ignore this remark. It wasn't worth the effort of retaliating. 'I wouldn't think he'd be riding for a day or so. His horse will be pretty stiff after being freighted up in the plane; Jean-Pierre will insist they are rested until after the weekend.'

'That won't please Si. How about this gang? How do they join?'

'They don't actually join – they have to wait to be invited and I'm afraid I'm pretty sure that won't be by one of my lads. Fortunately it's all up to the kids. I have nothing whatsoever to do with it, but it doesn't look as if he's going to be too lonely,' and Tom glanced at the settee again before he walked through the door and back to Woodcutters.

It had been an inauspicious beginning and sadly for Thunder the consequences had been dire.

The next morning, as soon as Tom had given Adrian instructions, he rushed to the Veterinary Surgery where he found Thunder standing in his stable pulling at a haynet. His leg was in a plaster cast and Tom noticed the pony was obviously trying not to put any wait on the damaged limb.

James came out to greet him and they looked at Thunder together. 'He's sore, Tom but I am afraid that is inevitable, but he's interested in his food, which is a good sign and his temperature is normal. It's just a matter of time and rest. He should stay here for a couple more days and then we'll get him back to Woodcutters. What's that bloody boy doing with himself today, Tom?'

'He seems to have met up with some lads who he found playing cricket on the green. Actually, they're not a bad crowd. He seems to have got entangled with a girl already, so hopefully he will be kept well entertained and out of my sight. Sam and Rosie are taking Daisy to Canterbury. Thank goodness she appears a quiet little kid. It's a strange life for them really, with a mother that's all over the world making films. Daisy told Rosie she hasn't seen her for over two years, and I can't see her bothering to come over here unless her film world brings her. I've given Uncle Rob your bill. He said he would send a cheque today. Let me know if there's a problem but I don't think he's short of a bob or two.'

Tom put his arms round Thunder's neck and kissed his nose. 'I'll come and see you again this evening, old boy. Thanks again, James, I'll see you tomorrow evening. I promised Sammy I would come and have a drink at the club. I think Jean-Pierre is sorting out the dressage team for their first competition in a couple of week's time.' With a last pat on Thunder's neck, he drove back to Woodcutters and a morning schooling his horses.

Sam was in a shoe shop with Rosie and Daisy. When Sam had called at Honeysuckle Cottage to collect Daisy the girl was clutching an envelope which contained five twenty pound notes.

'Dad says can you take me to the shoe shop and buy me some shoes for school and a grey skirt and blue jumper?' Sam wasn't thrilled. The shoes were no problem but the uniform for the Grammar School could only be obtained from one particular shop in Ashford. She sighed, knowing that Daisy would hate to start at the school without the correct uniform and resigned herself to the fact that she would have to make a detour via Ashford on the way home.

She took Rosie to the hairdressers and after looking at Daisy's unkempt mop, asked the stylist if she could cut the girl's hair into a well-shaped bob. Daisy wasn't too keen, but Sam ignored her protests and was soon in a large shoe shop trying to persuade Daisy into a sensible pair of school shoes. At last this was accomplished and they were meeting Anna and her three children for lunch in Marks and Spencer. To Rosie's delight, Anna suggested she should come home with her for the afternoon whilst Sam had the unenviable task of parking in Ashford and getting Daisy kitted out for the following week.

That evening all the family went to see Thunder. He whinnied when he saw them and hobbled to the front of his stable but Tom was pleased to see his ears were pricked and his eyes bright, and he was even more pleased when the most senior vet, Mathew Parker, told him he could take Thunder home the following afternoon.

Tom decided to put him with Twinkletoes, who would keep him company and his heart felt lighter as the crisis seemed to be over its worst.

The following afternoon, at the same time as Thunder was arriving back at Woodcutters, a huge horsebox was pulling into the yard at the Massenden Equitation Centre. Daisy was impatiently waiting with Sam and Rosie as Simon tore into the yard on a bicycle he had borrowed from one of his newfound cricketing pals.

The driver was opening the ramp and Sam caught her breath as a beautiful Australian bred pony tiptoed into the yard. He was exactly fourteen hands high and had a handsome, intelligent head, with large brown eyes, set perfectly on his arched neck.

'Have you shown him, Daisy?' Sam asked.

'Noow.' Daisy drawled. 'I've just hacked him around the ranch where we kept him with Melchior. I'd like to do dressage, though. I've watched it on the telly.'

'Well, you have come to the right place. I can help you if you like, Daisy. I used to show my horse Chim Chim, and now I am going to do dressage with him with the Massenden Riding Club.'

'Fair dinkum. You bet I would.'

'Well, give him the weekend to settle and we'll see how we get on in Jean-Pierre's sand school.'

'Wow. Thanks Aunty Sam.'

In contrast to Popcorn, Melchior was a stockily built, dark bay horse, just under fifteen hands. Simon seemed underwhelmed by the sight of his horse, patting him quickly and then heading straight back to his new pals and the thought of Coleen, who had promised she would come with her group of girlfriends to the village green at five o'clock.

He wished he hadn't insisted Melchior had accompanied Popcorn to England. The two-legged fillies he had just met would, he was certain, prove far more entertaining and for Melchior the future looked extremely unpromising.

Tom, Adrian and Josh had taken Sam's new trailer to the vets and collected Thunder. Adrian drove the Range Rover, whilst Tom and Joshua steadied the pony.

Thunder's ears were pricked as Tom led him carefully down the ramp. He could hear Twinkletoes whinnying as the little black pony noticed his friend emerging from the trailer. Joshua ran and caught Twink and soon he and Thunder were stabled next to each other. The following morning they would graze together in the smallest paddock near the cottage.

Josh and Simon had not encountered each other again and Sam was praying no incidents would occur on the bus when school resumed after the weekend. Fortunately for everyone, several of the girls he had just met would also be there and Simon's attention would most probably not be on Joshua. At least, that was Sam's fervent hope.

CHAPTER 6

On Wednesday evening the bar at the Massenden Equitation Centre was rapidly filling. Twelve members had been short listed for the dressage team. The club was hoping to be able to enter an A. and a B. team with two reserve riders for each team.

The many members who were not interested in taking part in the dressage competition were going to be involved in a highly competitive General Knowledge quiz, which Susan and James had devised.

With the wine and beer being consumed in more than average quantities, the competition was getting slightly raucous as the members of the various teams argued mildly over the correct answers.

Tom was sitting at a table with his parents who had stoically invited his Uncle Rob to join them. Elizabeth was with them as well, doing her best to be polite to the uncle she hadn't seen since she had been three years old and of whom she had no recollection at all.

She had heard all about the incident with Thunder from James, and had just endured a tirade from her uncle about the money-grabbing vets in England. According to him, the bill for Thunder's operation would have been at least half the price had the accident occurred in Australia. She immediately decided to tell James never to give a discount for anything that might befall Melchior or Popcorn and certainly not the bad tempered Silky Terrier, Peanuts, as she looked at the stitches across the top of her father's hand.

Only half of Tom's attention was focusing on the quiz – the other half was admiring Sam and Chim Chim. She stood out from the rest of the riders, partly because of her stunning figure and partly because she and Chim were in total accord with one another.

He suddenly heard Rob asking his father. 'Who is that stunning chick on the big black horse, the one with the fab figure? Has she got any strings attached to her, John, or is she up for grabs?'

The next thing Rob knew, he was lying prone on the thick green carpet, which covered the floor of the bar.

Sam had glanced up at the same moment as Tom's fist was flashing. She had thrown Chim's reins to Jean-Pierre and flown up the stairs, which led from the school to the gallery and bar.

The first thing she noticed was a man, almost the image of her father-in-law and extremely like her husband, lying still on the floor, and John holding on to a seething, white faced Tom, as every contestant in James now forgotten quiz looked on in amazement and not a small amount of horror.

'Tommy! What on earth have you done?' Sam gasped as she gazed at the stricken man who was by this time trying his best to sit up. Tom was still glaring at him.

'Meet my wife, Samantha, Uncle Rob, and for your information she does not only have strings attached - she has bloody chains too, and let me tell you, those are firmly fixed to me.'

Rob had by now managed to get himself onto rather unsteady feet. 'Bloody hell, Tom. It was only a bit of lighthearted banter. Nothing for you to get fired up about.'

'I don't think so, Uncle Rob. You can bloody well look elsewhere for your sheilas as you like to call your women.' With which he turned and stalked out of the bar, walking briskly to Lake House where Justin and Adrian were instructing *the gang*.

Sam was left looking bewildered. 'What on earth is up with Tom, John?'

'A mixture of my crassly stupid brother and my insanely jealous son, I am afraid, Sam.'

'Oh dear,' and she looked straight at Rob. 'What on earth did you say to him?'

'I only asked John who the glamorous chick on the black horse was and whether she was a free agent. The next thing I knew that young thug had floored me.'

Sam laughed. 'You don't know your nephew very well yet, *Uncle* Rob,' and she stressed the word *uncle,* 'but let me put you straight. No. I am not a free agent. Crazy as my husband may be, I am very firmly shackled to him and I can assure you those chains will never be broken. I just want to make myself clear. Now I must relieve Jean-Pierre of my horse and re-join the rest of my group.'

Tom's temper was still blazing. He fervently wished his Uncle Rob and his blasted kids were still ten and a half thousand miles away in Sydney, let alone ensconcing themselves in Massenden. Tom was always fair. *'No,'* he thought, '*that's not quite right. Little Daisy seems a nice enough kid.'*

He had been more than a little upset by Thunder's accident. He was well aware that before too many more winters had passed he would have to come to terms with losing the ponies he had had for so long, but he wanted to be in control of when they died. He didn't want some freak accident taking them away. He would know when their lives were no longer of an acceptable standard and then he would not hesitate to say goodbye to them but at the moment, Thunder and Twinkletoes were in the rudest of health, or they had been before Simon's callous act. The donkeys would be his father's decision, which he would respect, but they too spent their days lazing happily under the old oak tree in front of the kitchen window at Old Tiles.

Just before Christmas he had asked James to come and put Rascal down in his stable at Woodcutters. His rasping cough had worsened and Tom immediately knew what the kindest thing was to do. It had been a bad day for the whole family, but Tom had instilled into his children that sometimes there was only one way to be kind.

As he neared the indoor school at Lake House, Tom's heart lurched as he realized with a shock that Black Satin was now twenty-four and his faithful labradoodle, Bertie, was already fourteen. He wished animals could live as long as human beings, but they didn't, and sadly that was a fact of life.

By the time he was entering the school his temper had evaporated and he stood by the door watching his five children, and what seemed like an ever-expanding *gang,* trotting through a grid of poles and jumping a cavaletti at the end. He noticed Daisy had been invited into the close-knit *gang*. Justin had obviously loaned her Guy Fawkes, who was still waiting in the wings for Abby to grow into.

Tom acknowledged Daisy seemed a competent rider and from the expression on her face, was obviously enjoying herself.

Justin, who hated quizzes of any description, was starting to build a small jumping course for the younger children and Tom instinctively walked over to help his friend.

Justin looked surprised. 'Tom, what the hell are you doing here? Don't say your quiz team have kicked you out.'

Tom smiled ruefully, 'I think I kicked myself out actually, Just. I flattened my Uncle Rob.'

'You what?'

'Gave Uncle Rob a quick upper cut.'

'God, Tom, You are a complete and utter liability. What the hell had he done?'

'Asked my Dad whether Sammy was up for grabs.'

'Tom, you're crazy, or that bloody left hand of yours is. What on earth were you thinking of?'

Tom shook his head. 'I don't know. I just lost my rag I suppose.'

'So where is Sam now?'

'Still at the Centre with Chim. Sorting out their dressage teams. I expect she's hating me at this minute,' he added gloomily.

'So, you love her so much, you've left her to ride home alone?'

'God, Just. I didn't think of that.'

'As far as Sam is concerned, Tom, you don't think, you just act.'

‘ I had better go back and find her.’

‘She will ride back as far as here with Jo and Anna. Dad’s baby-sitting Noah this evening, Anna said she would text me when they are leaving the Centre. Charlotte’s Dad is walking up here to collect her and Georgia, and I think they’re taking Daisy home too. I said they could borrow Guy for the evening and turn him out with Charlotte’s pony. It’ll be so much easier when the evenings are lighter and they can all ride back through the woods together.’

The older children were just completing their jumping course when Justin received the text he was expecting from Anna.

‘They’re on their way, Tom, they’ll be here in five minutes.’

Tom wasn’t certain what sort of reception he was about to receive from his wife and he waited by the stables in some trepidation.

Sam was feeling pleased. She, Joanna, Jean-Pierre and Tony had all been selected for the A. Team and Trish, Anna, and two men who lived in Ribbenden called Guy and Patrick would make up the B. Team. The competition was to be held the following Saturday at a Riding Club between Ashford and Dover. She was chatting and laughing with Anna and Joanna, at the same time wondering what her erstwhile husband was up to and she wasn’t altogether surprised to see him waiting by Topsy Turvy’s stable.

Tom looked at Sam rather hesitantly. ‘The kids have gone on ahead. I told them to put the ponies in their paddock and then have a shower.’

He took Chim’s bridle and led him to the mounting block, leapt up behind Sam and turned the horse towards the lake and the path, which led to Woodcutters.

Sam had had every intention of being cross. She had worked out in her mind exactly what she was gong to tell him, but as she felt his arms round her waist and his hands creeping under her jacket, she sighed. ‘Oh, Thomas West, what a weakling I am. I so wanted to be cross with you, but I can’t. I just want you to chain me right by your side forever, my idiotic, insanely jealous husband. Never undo those shackles, Tommy. Never.'

She heard Tom groan. 'Sammy, for God's sake make this bloody horse trot.'

'Why, Tommy?'

He laughed, 'I want to get home, my Sammy,' and then he groaned again. 'Sammy, I don't want to think about next week. Friday – three weeks in the States – God it's heaven and hell loving you and leaving you. Hell when we're apart and heaven when we're together. Thank God when I am too old to go off on these tours.'

'But Tom, by then we might be too old to reach heaven.'

Tom jumped off Chim and gently lifted Sam out of the saddle – holding her close. 'Never, my darling, I promise you. Heaven will always be there. You know what I am always telling you, we are *ad infinitum*, and I shall definitely put padlocks on them.'

'On what, my Thomas?'

'On those damn shackles, of course.'

Sam laughed. 'Tom, I wonder what colour your uncle's eye is right now?'

Tom growled. 'Jet black I hope. Sodding man. It's the very least he deserves as far as I am concerned.'

Sam had watched Daisy riding her grey pony, Popcorn, in the dressage arena at the Equitation Centre. Daisy's riding was slightly rough but Sam could see possibilities in both the girl and the pony and had told Daisy she would help her over the coming weeks. She also suggested she should join the Pony Club with *the Gang*, where she would have the chance to compete in their annual dressage tests.

Daisy immediately showed interest and Sam promised her Rosie and the boys would take her with them to the meeting in the first week of the Easter holidays.

Simon had ridden Melchior precisely once, galloping him flat out round Jean-Pierre's biggest paddock, riding Western style, wearing chaps and a stetson. Jean-Pierre was not amused.

'You can leave that 'at at 'ome in future, young man. 'Ard 'ats only 'ere.' And I suggest you walk your 'orse for at least twenty minutes before you turn 'im out in 'is paddock. You need to 'ave more consideration for your 'orse. 'E is not a machine.'

Simon pulled a rude face at Jean-Pierre's back, muttering under his breath about ignorant 'frogs', ignoring his instructions and turning the sweating Melchior straight out in the paddock with Popcorn. Unfortunately for him, he was about to catch the extremely sharp side of Jean-Pierre's tongue, who had not trusted the young lad and had turned back to the paddock, only to see Simon walking nonchalantly through the gate, swinging Melchior's head collar.

Jean-Pierre marched straight up to Simon and grabbed the head collar. 'Put this straight back on your 'orse and now I demand you will walk 'im for 'alf an hour or your 'orse will leave my yard toute suite. You comprehend what I am saying?'

Simon did at least understand authority. He had witnessed it several times at his boarding school in Australia and he couldn't fail to recognise it now. He sulkily replaced the head collar onto Melchior and began his thirty-minute walk hating every thing about Jean-Pierre, England and the rain, which was now starting to fall heavily onto his Stetson. When he had finished, he walked back through the grounds of Lake House. He didn't care whether or not he was trespassing. He had realized it was a short cut back to Honeysuckle Cottage.

As he passed South Lodge, he noticed the quad bike parked by the gate. Justin had nipped home from the stables to collect Noah, intending to give him a ride on Amelia. Unfortunately, he had left the key in the ignition. Simon had seen the bike at Old Tiles, the day he had ridden Thunder. Without any delay or second thought, he switched on the ignition and the next minute was tearing through the stable yard, then past the lake and through the woods to Old Tiles – finally leaving the quad by the entrance to the lane opposite

Honeysuckle Cottage. He ran down to the village green where Coleen was waiting, whilst Justin who was totally mystified was phoning his father.

'Have you pinched the quad bike, Dad? I left it by the gate at South Lodge whilst I ran in to pick up Noah. When I came back it had gone.'

Charles was equally nonplussed. *'Of course I haven't, Justin. You know I've got my own bike. It's by my back door. Why would I want the other bike? Who the hell can have taken it? Have you asked Dom or Tom?'*

'Tom has gone for a hack with his kids – it can't possibly be him. I saw Dom half an hour ago. He said he was just about to ride Organza and take Anne-Marie and Tom Thumb with him.'

'Oh, God.' Justin sighed, *'I suppose I shall have to call the police. I'll call Tom on his mobile just to double check he doesn't know anything about it.'*

A short while after, Tom's mobile was ringing in his pocket. He pulled it out with some difficulty and noticed it was his dad. *'Tom, I've just driven home and noticed a quad bike at the farm gate. I've taken the keys out of the ignition. Have you any idea what it's doing there?'*

'I've a damn good idea, Dad. Where's that little rat, Simon West? It's just been nicked from South Lodge. Justin has just called me. He had dashed indoors to get Noah to take him to the stables to ride Amelia, when he got back to the gate the bike had vanished. That bloody boy is a complete liability. Can you take the bike to the farmhouse? One of us will collect it in the morning.'

'Will do, Tom, and later on this evening I will have words with that boy. Thank goodness the schools start again soon. Let's hope he won't cause chaos there.'

'I've warned Josh not to go near him. Unfortunately Justin and I are flying out to Canada and then the States for three weeks. Miami and Mexico.'

'Yea, Dad, it may sound exciting but do you really think we enjoy leaving Sammy and Anna, not to mention our kids. Look after Sammy for me, Dad. I know she hates it when I'm away. She's got her dressage competition on Saturday and I think she's going to help Daisy with her pony, and Dad, make sure my uncle keeps his filthy hands off her.'

'Tom, I think your Uncle Rob does actually know where to draw the line, he had no idea Sam was your wife the other evening. Anyway I'm sure Mary will have a day in Canterbury with her and perhaps Anna will go too. She must miss Justin.'

'Anna has got quite a busy time at the moment. Old Griggs has nearly finished Theobald's Place. She and Justin are hoping to get all the carpets fitted as soon as we get back from this tour and then they are booked to move in on the first of April.'

When Tom had finished speaking to his father, he called Justin. *'It's O.K. Just. I've located the quad. That young bugger, Simon, must have taken it. Dad just called me. He discovered it by the entrance to the farm.'*

'Bloody boy. What time will you be picking me up tomorrow morning, Tom?'

'We need to be at Heathrow by eleven thirty, so half past eight should be about right.'

'O.K. I'll be ready. I've just had a call from Sheila. She and Erica are fine and the horses are settled in their stables in Ottawa and apparently there is an enormous six-berth caravan awaiting us. Might have been useful in the past but not much cop for two staid married men. Actually, Anna is a bit down.'

'So is Sammy. Perhaps they can have a few days out together. Anna could take Topsy and Sam could take Star to Camber if the weather is nice now Sam's got her trailer. Adrian would hitch it up for her. I'll suggest it to her. We shall be back for the Easter Show but then we've got Paris. I'm determined to take Sammy to that. Alice has said she will have Rosie and Josh and I'm sure Mum and Dad would have the trips. I would quite like to take Josh with us,

I'm a bit worried about leaving him anywhere near that wretched Simon. Anyhow, we've got ten days to decide about that once we get back from the States.'

That night Tom held Sam extra close. 'Keep those shackles padlocked whilst I am away, Sammy.'

'Tommy, I hate this. It never gets any better.'

He pulled her so close she could scarcely breathe. She could feel the strong beat of his heart against her bare breast and his lips crushing hers. At last they fell asleep – Tom's arms still holding her tightly. She woke in the middle of the night and glanced at the clock on the bedside table. Three forty five. In just over four hours he would be gone. She tightened her hold, he didn't wake but she heard him sigh in his sleep and whisper her name. '*She wouldn't cry when they said goodbye*,' she told herself firmly, she was determined not to upset him. That luxury could come later when he had gone and when the children were at school. She knew he hated these partings as much as she did.

Rosie was tearful – Josh and Ozzie were quiet – and Orlando and Oliver had left all their cereal, whilst both Sam and Tom were toying with their toast.

Dom hooted in the drive. He was collecting the triplets and Rosie and taking them to school. Tom kissed Rosie and hugged all his boys. Rosie was sobbing, Orlando was crying and Oliver was silent. Only Oscar appeared his usual self as he greeted Anne-Marie. Tom waved as the Range Rover disappeared, then loaded his luggage and gave Sam one final kiss.

He watched in the mirror as she turned and hurried indoors. He had just reached the end of the drive when he realized he had left his passport on his desk in his study.

He quickly reversed down the drive and hurried through the kitchen into his study. There was no sign of Sam. He picked up his passport and then stopped abruptly – he opened the playroom door and his heart broke. Sam hadn't heard him. She was lying on the settee, her head buried in a cushion. Boswell had a paw on her knee and Holly was desperately trying to lick her face. Her body was heaving as she sobbed.

Tom ran across the room and picked her up. 'Sammy, my precious, precious one.' He held her in his arms, stroking her hair. 'My Sammy, I came back for my passport. Darling, I have to go. It's breaking my heart too, but I must go and pick up Justin. Look after my family for me whilst I am away. I love you all so much.' He gave her one last passionate kiss and then tore himself away. He got into the Range Rover and quickly phoned his mother. *'Mum, I'm worried about Sam. She's really upset. I have to get Justin or we shall miss the plane. I'm late already. We need to get to Heathrow.'*

He heard his mother's voice. *'Don't worry, Tom, I will take her to Rye later to see Eva and Tabitha and I will make a big casserole for everyone this evening. Dad and I will look after her, Tom. You go and get Justin, and take care in the States.'*

Tom knew he had the best Mum in this world. He knew she was busy with the B. and B. but she was always there and he knew she would never let him down.

He put the car into drive and drove to South Lodge where he found Justin trying to extricate himself from Noah, who was hanging on to his legs, and Anna who was clutching his waist, weeping into his chest.

Ten minutes later, as they finally left Massenden, the two men looked at each other. 'God!' they both said at the same time, 'this is pure hell. Why don't we both just stack shelves in the super market or dig up the roads?'

Tom sighed. 'Could you live without your horses, Justin?'

Justin's answer was prompt. 'Never. Could you?'

'Not a hope in hell.'

As they drew near Heathrow, Tom's mobile was ringing. He

pulled onto the hard shoulder and answered. He heard Sam's voice. *'Tommy, my darling. I'm sorry. I let you down. I upset you.'*

'Sammy, sweetheart, you could never, never let me down. I hate leaving you, but look on the bright side – I am already over an hour nearer to seeing you again, but take care and always remember you and I are ad infinitum.'

'For ever, my Tommy. A million kisses.'

'Two million my darling, and I will call you as soon as we get to our first destination.' He turned off his mobile as Justin's was ringing. *'I love you Anna,'* he was saying.

The girls had no idea, but Mary and John were at that very moment hatching a plan. Joanna, Alice and they themselves would have all the children and they had already booked flights for Anna, Sam and little Noah to fly to Miami for the men's second venue. They would leave the following Wednesday and return the next Monday.

Tom had been absolutely correct. He had the best parents in this world.

When Mary called Sam and told her what they had done, she was over the moon.

'The children will be absolutely fine, Sam. Your Mum has said she will have Rosie and Josh and we will have the trips. No problem, darling. We thought Anna wouldn't want to leave Noah, but Joanna and Charles are more than happy to have Abby and Gus.'

'Mary, how can I thank you. But I insist we pay for our tickets. No way will we let you do that. We won't tell the men we're coming. We'll give them a surprise. I'll ring Anna straight away. She will be thrilled.'

Anna was equally excited and agreed not to let Justin know they were coming. *'I'm glad we're taking Noah, Justin will be really pleased to have his baby with him.'*

Two evenings that week Sam rode Chim to the Centre to practice the dressage test with Jean-Pierre, Tony and Joanna. She went an hour early, put Chim into a stable and walked to the indoor school where she was very soon joined by Daisy and her very attractive pony, Popcorn.

Sam immediately became immersed in helping Daisy. Her riding lacked finesse but Sam knew it would only be a matter of a short time before that would come. The pony was compliant and by the end of forty-five minutes, Sam was more than satisfied. 'Good girl, Daisy. I'm coming here again on Thursday for another practice with Chim, so if you can manage, meet me here at the same time and we will have another session.'

'Thanks, Aunty Sam, that was really great.'

'You've got a lovely pony, Daisy. We'll look for some show classes in a month or two and start working on the Pony Club dressage test. By the way, where's that brother of yours? Melchior needs riding. How often did he ride him in Australia?'

'Quite often, his girl friend kept her horse on the same ranch. They both rode Western style together. I don't think Coleen is interested in riding.'

'And what about Simon?' Sam asked. 'Is he interested in his horse?'

'He used to be Aunty Sam, but now there is only one thing he seems to be interested in.'

'Oh and I can guess what that is.'

To Sam's surprise Daisy's answer was not quite what she was expecting.

'He's obsessed with learning to speak different languages. He speaks fluent Italian – German and Spanish and before we left Australia he had started to learn Mandarin.'

'Goodness, Daisy, not what I expected at all.'

'He wants to be an interpreter. I know he can be wild and difficult but he is actually very clever.' Daisy thought for a moment and then added. ‘Oh, but Aunty Sam – he does like his Sheila’s too. But I’m not very keen on his latest one, all she thinks about are soaps and chat shows.’

CHAPTER 7

That evening John met his brother for a pint of beer in the Bear. 'Look, Rob,' he told his brother. 'I appreciate your kids are probably not finding the transition to a new country easy, but there are some things that go beyond the limit and one is taking other people's property. Like pinching the quad bike from Justin's gate and tearing over my land on it.'

Rob tried to bluster. 'That's only the sort of thing most boys of his age might do, John. I think he was fed up with that frog, Jean-Pierre. He'd had words with him about Melchior. Apparently he wasn't happy about him riding Western style without a hard hat.'

'Jean-Pierre has to adhere to strict rules, Rob. He runs his establishment to a very high standard. That's why he has so many international riders attending his shows and his courses. As you are well aware he is our son-in-law, and Mary and I are not only extremely fond of him, we are also proud of both him and the Centre. If Simon insists on riding Western style I am sure the livery stables at Stanhurst wouldn't object. It's every man for himself there, but Simon would have to get a bicycle and get himself there. It's about five miles or so towards Canterbury.'

'Oh I doubt if he could be bothered to do that. I probably should have sold Melchior before we left Australia. Simon spends more than half his time listening to C.D.s'

'Oh god, Rob. Heavy metal? Rap?'

'No, no, John. Languages. He's obsessed with them. He's learning as many as he can. I'm certainly not discouraging him. He's into Mandarin at the moment.'

'Good heavens, Rob, you do surprise me. I thought all Aussie boys were into was sport.'

'Oh, he's into that as well. He wants to join the tennis club. He could probably give you a run for your money, John. I don't stand a chance when I play against him.'

'Well, if he behaves himself, Justin Wright-Smith would probably give him a good game, he's a cracking all round sportsman. He used to play cricket too, but now of course he doesn't have the time at the weekends. Charles has a fantastic hard tennis court at Lake House and a superb gym as well as an indoor and an outdoor swimming pool. Charles doesn't suffer fools lightly though. Simon needs to improve his behavior before he gets invited there, but I will take him to the tennis club with me at the weekend if you like.'

'Thanks, John. Anything to get him out of the clutches of that dreadful, empty headed Coleen. Thank God she doesn't go to the Grammar School, at least she won't be on the school bus every day. Daisy seems to have settled down far more easily. Your hot headed son's wife seems to have taken her under her wing.'

John laughed. 'You are safe for a bit, Rob. Tom is in the States for a few weeks with his horses. Justin has gone with him. We're having the kids between us and Sam and Anna are flying out to meet up with them in Miami for five days.'

'So does Tom make a good living jumping his horses, John?'

John laughed again. 'He's a millionaire twice over, Rob. He works bloody hard though. All hours God sends him and he has to make huge personal sacrifices. He hates being away from Sam. Especially since last year.'

'Why? Did she have a fling with someone whilst he was out of sight?'

'Certainly not, Rob. Sammy adores Tom. No, it was terrible; a maniac of a woman who wanted to steal Tom attacked her. He had rejected her since they were kids. She suddenly flipped and attacked Sam whilst Tom was in Belgium. Thank God Charles found her with minutes to spare, but it rocked the whole village.'

'Christ! What happened to this woman?'

'She went home and took a lethal overdose. The police broke

into her house and discovered her body that afternoon. Strange thing, that house seems to provoke unhappiness. The couple that bought it was only there a short while before there was a massive scandal and now there is a divorce going through. You will probably meet Caroline Mawgan-Whitely. Nice woman with three young children. The girls are at St. Swithins but they keep their ponies at Lake House. Daisy will certainly meet them in the holidays. I know they are both members of *the gang*. The husband had an affair with his next door but one neighbour, Tamara Adams. I expect you remember Richard Adams; we used to buy our feed from his dad. If I remember correctly you and he fell out when you had that steamy affair with his sister when you were both in the sixth form.'

'Do I not. Richard knocked me clean out as Moira and I were creeping up to her bedroom. Mortifying. He was several years younger than I was, if I remember rightly he was your Tom's sparring partner when they first started at the Grammar. I remember the Mawgan-Whitely family too. Didn't they live in that lovely old house on the green, almost opposite the old Primary School? There were two boys, quite a bit younger than me. They had ghastly parents – really fancied themselves.'

'Yes, they went to live in France, and Sam's mother, Alice and her husband Peter, bought the Old Parsonage from them, and they still live there. You will meet them soon, I am sure. They're a super couple.'

John stood up having finished his beer. 'Must get back, Mary's got a Spanish couple staying at the farm. I said I'd help her get the room ready.'

'I'll have a word with Simon about Melchior, John, and tell him you'll take him to the tennis club on Saturday afternoon. That may inspire him not to go flying over our land on quad bikes which don't belong to him!!'

Rob's words, *our land,* didn't go unnoticed by John. 'Your land, I think you meant to say, Rob. I'm sorry if you feel hard done by, but that was Dad's wish. You can read Dad's will if you like, Rob. I kept a copy in the safe. You could always sell the bungalow on the coast, Rob; it should be worth a pretty penny now. It's in a superb position with that glorious sea view.'

'No, John, I'm financially O.K. at the moment. Luckily my job pays me well. I must admit I still feel a bit miffed about the farm, but I suppose you always were Dad's favourite.' And with that final remark, ignoring the fact that John had run the farm single-handed for the past thirty years, he sauntered out of the pub back to Honeysuckle Cottage to confront his young son.

CHAPTER 8

Sam pulled back the curtains and peered out of her bedroom window, enjoying as she always did, the magnificent views over the lake towards the old Queen Anne House.

It was seven o'clock on Saturday morning and daylight was just breaking. As far as she could make out she could see the sky was clear, and she felt the first tinge of excitement as she thought of the Massenden Riding Club's debut dressage competition now almost upon them.

The children were all still fast asleep. Sam pulled on her working jeans and a thick jumper and after a quick cup of tea, went into the tack room and gathered her grooming kit.

She brushed Chim until his black coat was gleaming and then found her scissors and black thread. Half an hour later, he was sporting an extremely neat row of plaits. His tail had been immaculately pulled the previous afternoon.

Sam stood back and admired her stunning horse and her recent hard work before putting on his red stable rug. She put the grooming kit and a tin of hoof oil beside his stable and went back indoors to cook herself a hearty, warm breakfast. There was already a message on her mobile. '*Good luck today, my darling, and to the rest of the team. I'm missing you like mad, loads and loads of love, Tom xx.*'

At eight thirty, Adrian's mum and Dad, Miriam and George arrived at the cottage. George would muck out the stables with the boys whilst Miriam and Rosie were going to make a big casserole and a rhubarb crumble for their meal when Sam got home that evening.

Sam kissed Rosie, hugged the boys and begged them all to behave themselves. She went to the stable and carefully put Chim's travel bandages on his legs and tail and soon heard Jean-Pierre's large, green horsebox pulling up at the gate. Tony ran into the yard and as

Sam led Chim, he carried her saddle and bridle into the horsebox and put the grooming kit and the hoof oil into a corner of the luton. He jumped back into the horsebox as Sam climbed into Joanna's Range Rover, where Anna and Trish were already ensconced. Guy and Patrick, the two men from Ribbenden, would make their own way in Guy's Land Rover and trailer to the equitation centre where the competition was to be held.

Most of the teams had met many times before and they were looking with interest at the debutants from Massenden. The home riders of Heron's Court were also fielding two teams and it wasn't long before they let it be known to the newcomers that their A. Team had been unbeaten for the last three years and they were obviously confident this would continue. Jean-Pierre kept extremely quiet. He had tremendous faith in his A. Team. Tony and Sam were well above average and although he was a modest man, he knew his own dressage was one of the best when he competed with the French team. Joanna was the least experienced, but even she was calm and reliable.

Sam was to start for their team, followed by Tony, then Joanna and finally Jean-Pierre.

Jean-Pierre didn't think the B. Team stood much chance of a place but they were all determined to enjoy themselves and with Trish leading them, Anna and Guy in the middle and Patrick as the anchorman, he hoped they would do well enough to be encouraged to do more competitions in the future. On occasions he had been asked to judge at various venues and he watched the riders from the first four teams with interest, acknowledging that without a doubt, the rider from the home team had a very well schooled horse and was a very experienced rider. As he had expected, by the end of her routine she was well in the lead.

He held his breath as Sam and Chim trotted up the centre line, stopping squarely and still in the middle. Chim looked magnificent and as always, Sam herself was immaculately turned out. She was so used to showing Chim, often under pressure, especially at H.O.Y.S., that performing a dressage test held no fears for her. Jean-Pierre watched appreciatively as she made the transition from one movement to the next, executing a perfect pirouette at the end of the arena in front of the judges and doing a wonderful extended trot down the side, ending with a passage down the centre line, before standing squarely to a halt as she made her salute, finally making a calm exit out of the arena.

Jean-Pierre waited for her marks with bated breath. He noted the shocked horror on the faces of the Heron's Court team as Sam's score was announced. They were far better than that of their first rider. Sam took Chim back to the horsebox and put him in his stall with a large hay net and then sat with Jean-Pierre. It would be at least another two hours before he would have to fetch his horse.

It wasn't long before her mobile was bleeping. Her heart leapt, hoping it was Tom and then she realized it would not yet be 7a.m. in Ottawa. Soon she could hear Rosie. *'Mummy, have you done your test yet? Was Chim a good boy?'*

'Yes, darling, we've just finished and Chim was extremely good but so far only the first rider from each team has gone, at the moment Massenden are leading, but it's very early days.'

'Oh, Mums, so Chim must have got a really good score.'

'Yes he did, Rosie, but as I told you there is a long way to go. What are you up to?'

'Making a yummy chocolate cake with Miriam. Can I call Dads?'

'Yes, but not for another hour, it's only quarter to seven in Ottawa at the moment. He's probably still fast asleep.'

'O.K. Mums. Shall I tell him you're missing him?'

'Yes, but don't make him sad.'

'Charles is going to take us all for a lesson this afternoon. Can I take The Duc?'

'Be very careful, Rosie. Stay with Joshua on your way up to the school.'

'O.K. Daisy's coming too, she's going to ride Guy Fawkes cos

Popcorn doesn't like jumping and Anne-Marie is bringing Tom Thumb. Oz is going to meet her at Old Tiles, opposite Back Lane. Georgia and Charlotte are coming too.'

'All right. Just be really careful.'

'Course, Mums. Love you.'

'Love you too, Rosie.'

Sam smiled at Jean-Pierre. 'It sounds as though Charles has got an exhausting afternoon ahead of him. All *the gang* is descending on Lake House for a lesson.'

'I expect Dom and Adrian will be there to lend a hand. When is Anna's baby due, Sam? It must be really imminent now.'

'Next Thursday officially, but babies aren't always too reliable, as you know only too well, Pierre.'

By the end of the second round the Massenden team was still just in first place but their lead had been cut to a slender four points and after the third rider from each team had completed their test they had dropped a place and the Heron's Court team were smiling smugly once more. Joanna was blaming herself. 'Don't be silly, Joanna,' the rest of the team were reassuring her. 'Hercules is the least experienced of all the horses in our team. He certainly did his best. Our B. Team is doing well. They're currently in fifth place. Trish and Guy were brilliant.'

Tom had called Sam during the morning. *'Sammy, how is it going?'*

'Good, as the scores stand at the moment, we are lying in second place but we've still got our trump card to play. Pierre is our anchorman. He's just gone to get Rigoletto.'

'I gather from Rosie Chim was a good boy.'

'Um – actually we're still in pole position for individual first place but I expect most of the teams are saving their best until last, like we are. The B. team is doing well. Trish was super and so was Guy, one of the chaps from Ribbenden. They're in fifth place but all the scores are really close. What are you doing?'

'Missing you like hell, but Justin and I are having a good meeting here. We both won a big class yesterday. Madame is really on song. It's the big Grand Prix tonight. I think it's probably being televised but don't forget the time difference.'

'I can't wait to see you, Tommy. We all miss you so much.'

'It's hell, Sammy. God. Two and a half more weeks! It feels like a lifetime. Good luck for the rest of the day. A million kisses, my darling. Ad infinitum.'

'Oh, Tommy, forever, darling,' and she slowly turned off her mobile but she was hugging her secret to herself. It wouldn't be two and a half weeks – just a mere five days and they would be together. She shivered with delight as she turned to greet Anna.

'Justin has just called me,' Anna informed Sam. 'Apparently they are missing us like mad. I kept our secret though; I can't wait until we surprise them on Wednesday. Our teams seem to be doing quite well, Sammy. You and Chim were brill. Your team is just five points behind Heron's Court A. team now. It's all up to Pierre.'

As Jean-Pierre made his entrance he needed to score ninety-five points to overtake the leading team. Rigoletto was not Jean-Pierre's top ride but the Frenchman made all his horses look brilliant and without a doubt he was showing his International class. They finished their test with an amazing score of ninety eight points, which had catapulted them back into the lead and that was how they were destined to stay. The B. team had finished in a creditable fourth place. Jean-Pierre had won the individual first prize with Sam in second place. The Heron's Court team was in shock. They had forgotten what it was like to be beaten but they acknowledged they had more than met their match that day and took their defeat in good spirit. There would always be another day, but they feared the Massenden team was there to stay.

CHAPTER 9

Sam was kissing Rosie and hugging the boys. 'Now please be very good with Granny Mary and Grandpa John,' Sam was begging the triplets, 'and Genevieve will take you straight to ballet with Anne-Marie after school, Rosie. She has got your leotard and your ballet shoes and after the class she will take you to Granny Alice's. Tomorrow, Dom will gather you all together and you will go to Lake House for a lesson with Charles, and on Saturday Dom will take you to the show in Sussex. Auntie Elizabeth and Uncle James will be there and so will Charles. Take great care and do exactly what you are told. I shall be home on Monday, possibly in time to meet you from school but if not Miriam will be there and she will stay with you all at Woodcutters until I get back.'

Anna had arrived with Gus and Abby and to Sam's relief Rosie ran into the school with them. The triplets had already disappeared and Sam called to Anna. 'I will pick you up in half an hour,' and she sped home to gather all her things into the car.

Three hours later the plane was rising high above the clouds on its way to Miami – the sunshine and the blue sea waiting invitingly ahead of them. As they landed, they realized the time in London was five hours ahead of that in Florida and after the nine and a half hour flight it was still only mid - day in Miami. The day already seemed upside down to both of them as Anna was wondering how little Noah would adapt to the time change. At the moment he was full of life as Anna strapped him into the cab as they set off for the showground.

When they got out of the cab they could see the deep blue sea sparkling and lapping almost against the side of the arena.

Sam had been with Tom before the children had been born, but for Anna it was the first time and she stood for a moment, completely entranced by the whole magical scene which lay in front of them.

'We had better see if we can locate Tom and Justin's caravan. If we can't find it we'll look for their stables. They won't be far from their horses and certainly Erica and Sheila will be in the vicinity.'

In the end it was little Noah who spotted Justin who was emerging from a huge caravan. 'Dadda, dadda,' he was shouting, trying to escape from his buggy.

Anna quickly unstrapped him and the little boy ran towards Justin shouting, 'Dadda, wait for Noah.'

Justin turned round with a start – a look of amazement covering his face when he noticed his young son running as fast as his little legs would take him. He picked Noah up in his arms. 'Noah, what are you doing here?' And then he saw Anna pushing the buggy, waving to him, and Sam bringing up the rear with their two suitcases.

Less than half a minute later, Anna was in his arms and Sam was glancing round for Tom.

'Anna, darling. God this is amazing but where are Gus and Abby?'

'With Joanna and Charles. They have been brilliant and so have Tom and Sam's parents. We're here to support you until Monday when you move on to Mexico.'

'Where's Tom?' Sam asked Justin.

'He's just gone to check the horses. Madame is getting a bit stressed. She is in season and one of the stallions belonging to a Spanish rider is right opposite her. Pedro is a nice chap. He's moving his stallion further away and putting one of his teammate's geldings opposite her. It's not doing Madame or the stallion any favours as things stand. Wait in the caravan for him, Sam, He won't be long. I'll take Noah and Anna for a nice cool drink in the bar and then show Noah the sea.'

He helped Sam lift the suitcases into the caravan and then disappeared with his arm round Anna, at the same time as he pushed Noah in his buggy.

Sam looked round the caravan, which was enormous. There

was a bedroom either end with the living room and kitchen in the middle. She noticed an excellent cooker and a more than adequate refrigerator.

She unpacked her clothes and hung them beside Tom's in the wardrobe. There was a slight aroma of the aftershave that Rosie had given him for Christmas and Sam pressed her cheek against his shirt, longing for his return.

The unpacking finished, she sat on the bed and picked up her latest Patsy Sanders thriller, anxious to find out whether Herbert Holmer had uncovered any more clues about the mysterious woman who had suddenly disappeared, when she became aware of Tom's voice. She heard him sit down at the table in the living area and realized he was talking to someone on his mobile and two seconds later she realized he was talking to herself or rather to her voice mail.

'Sammy, darling,' she heard him say. *'Where on earth are you? I've already left three messages on your answer phone. Please, darling, call me as soon as you pick up this message. I'm missing you like hell.'*

Sam crept out of the bedroom and into the living area where Tom was sitting with his back to her. She tiptoed up behind him and kissed the gold curls at the back of his neck.

He jumped violently. 'What the hell?' and he swung round furiously and then his expression changed. 'Sammy, Sammy, my sweetheart, convince me I'm not hallucinating. Last night I dreamt you were in an aeroplane with Satin. He was the pilot and he was looping the loop. He was up to his old tricks again. I told him to bugger off. Oh Sammy, but where are the kids?'

Sam couldn't answer at first because at that moment her lips were otherwise engaged but finally she managed to tell him. 'Rosie and Josh are with Mummy and Peter and the trips are at Old Tiles. It was your Mum and Dad's idea. They were truly amazing and now we are here until Monday when you and Justin fly on to Mexico.'

'We?'

'Of course. Anna is here too, with little Noah. They have taken Noah to have a cold drink and then they are taking him to the beach.'

Tom sighed. 'God, this is amazing. We were missing you both like hell. We only arrived here early this morning and I've spent most of that time trying to calm Madame, but now Pedro has moved his stallion away from her I think she is behaving herself. Kaspar did really well in Ottawa. He won two huge classes. They've all got a day off today. Our first competition isn't until tomorrow evening. I'll take you to one of the bars by the beach tonight. We'll see if we can find the one we went to before the kids had arrived in this world. Re-kindle old memories.' He told her with a wicked smile.

Sam laughed. 'I don't remember much about the bar, all I can recall is what happened after we had visited it, Tommy.'

He kissed her and grinned. 'As I said, my Sammy. Re-kindle old memories.'

'Randy old devil, my Tom. But for now, let's go and see if we can find Justin and Anna and see what little Noah thinks of the beach."

On Saturday afternoon Tom and Justin's mobiles bleeped at almost the same moment. Tom heard Joshua's voice sounding very excited. *'Dad, we've had an amazing day in Sussex. Charles is really chuffed. First of all Rosie and Sparkler were brilliant in the twelve two class, then she and the Duc beat everyone and to crown it all, Ganger and I won the fourteen two class. Gussie and The Pie were second and Lando was third with Torchlight. Mimi is in a real strop. Babushka and Lordie both had four faults, so did Ollie and Jacques but he won the Foxhunter Class again with his new pony.'*

Tom realized there was no mention of Oscar. *'What happened to Oz today?'* he asked Joshua.

'He didn't come. He fell off Humbug in the school last night and hurt his wrist. Gramps took him to the A. and E. It's not broken, just badly sprained. He can't ride for at least a week. Granny Mary

took him and Anne-Marie to the circus in Canterbury. He said it was great.'

'Where is Rosie now?'

'She's having supper with Gus and Abby at Lake House.'

'Say really well done to her when she gets back, Josh, and congrats to you and Ganger.'

'He was fantastic, Dad, but you should have seen Rosie. I don't think Charles could believe his eyes. She's really got the hang of The Duc. Charles turned down a huge offer from some American millionaire on your behalf. He knew you wouldn't want to sell him. He says you are the worst dealer in Europe, Dad.'

Tom laughed. *'Do you want a quick word with Mum, Josh?'*

'I would, but Granny Alice and Peter are taking me and Georgia to the Italian restaurant in Ashford to celebrate my win and Georgia's dad is just ringing the door bell. Must go. Good luck tonight, Dad.' And he had gone.

Justin was also putting his mobile back into his pocket. 'That was Gus. Apparently Rosie and The Duc were amazing. Dad turned down an offer of seven thousand pounds on your behalf, Tom. Some American computer buff wanted him for his daughter. Dad knew it wasn't even worth calling you. Gus was second but he said he and Hamlet couldn't get near Rosie's time.'

'I know, I've just been speaking with Josh. I'm surprised little Madam hasn't called me herself but I gather from Josh she is otherwise engaged. Apparently she's having supper with Gus and Abby at your Dad's. I wish I had been there to watch her round. According to Josh it was amazing and he did O.K. too. Not sure what's up with him. Apparently he's dining Italian with Georgia this evening. Alice and Peter are treating them. Josh is quite a dark horse, Justin. Poor old Oz is out of action. He had a fall off Humbug in the school yesterday and apparently he can't ride for a week. Mum took him to the circus with Anne-Marie. God, I hope that was a wise move. Knowing Oz, he's more than likely to emulate some of the stunts. He's probably concocting a high wire across one of Dad's barns as we speak.'

Justin laughed. 'Luckily he's got Anne-Marie to keep him under control, Tom. Those two are the most unlikely pairing on this earth, but my goodness what a difference those contact lenses have made. Just a brace on her teeth for a year or two and Ozzie won't know what has hit him!'

Justin grinned at Tom. 'Come on, let's see if we can do as well as our kids – can't let them push their old dads into the shade,' and he and Tom changed into their riding gear and sauntered off to the stables to find Erica and Sheila and their immaculately groomed Kaspar and Lightening Strikes.

The girls had settled themselves in the grandstand with Noah almost asleep on Anna's lap, healthily drunk by all the sea air and sunshine he had absorbed that afternoon. He was pulling his hair and rubbing his ear, which Anna knew was a sign that within a few minutes he would be fast asleep. She wasn't wrong, his eyes were tightly closed as the first rider, who was the Dutchman Pieter and Charles' former ride Lady Madonna, entered the floodlit arena with the almost midnight blue sea in the background and several yachts or mini cruisers as Sam thought of them, moored in the distance. Pieter and Madonna were clear until the middle element of the extremely, tricky treble, and left the arena with four faults and Pieter visibly disappointed.

This round set the trend for many that followed, and only Hans and his bay mare Gretchen and the Spanish rider Pedro with his grey stallion that had a Spanish name which was every commentators worst nightmare, but which Pedro and most of the riders referred to as Romeo, were clear until Justin and Lightening joined them.

Tom was the penultimate rider. Kaspar was full of life, appearing to be taking the floodlights and the atmosphere around the arena in his stride. He was eager and strong as he approached the first jump – his ears were pricked and he was pulling hard but although Tom could feel his arms aching, he felt he was in control until he was approaching the ominous treble. He knew his stride was wrong. Kaspar was taking off too far away from the first element but the horse decided to take matters into his own head and flew, landing too close to the second part. Tom was waiting for the horse to stop, instead of which, Kaspar seemed to rise like a helicopter, clearing the huge upright and before Tom could gather his reins or his thoughts Kaspar was flying over the final spread as Tom somehow regained the stirrup he had lost, and shortening his reins was back in control to finish the course with what he considered had been the luckiest and most hair raising clear round since The Likely Lad had bolted with him in a thunderstorm in Germany when he had been a sixteen year old lad.

Justin had been watching from the side of the practice area. 'God, Tom, I thought you were a goner. I don't know whether Kasper is the cleverest or the maddest horse I have ever encountered.'

Tom was patting Kaspar. 'I think even Satin in his heyday would have stopped in the middle of that treble – we were so wrong. I don't think he's clever or mad. I think he's the bravest horse I've ever ridden.'

'Are you going to withdraw from the jump off and take fourth place? There are only four clear rounds. You will still win a tidy sum.'

'Withdraw!!! Are you raving mad, Justin?'

Justin shook his head. 'No, Tom, but I fear you are.'

In the stand, Sam had finally stopped shaking and Anna was calmly telling her. 'Don't worry, Sam. He'll never risk jumping that treble again. He's sure to be happy with fourth place,' but Sam shook her head.

'Anna, there is only one person who really knows my husband, and unfortunately I can guarantee we shall have to endure it all over again.'

The jump off was soon underway and so far only Justin was clear. Hans and Pedro were second and third with four faults and fast times, when Kaspar cantered into the arena. The crowd was silent; most had not expected to see the pair again. This time Tom had the eager Kaspar under strict control. He stopped and reined back four paces before letting Kaspar break into a canter and pass through the start. This time there were no histrionics as the horse and rider flew in total accord, cutting Justin's time by over three seconds.

The spectators rose to their feet, everyone appreciating the brilliance of both the horse and his rider. Kaspar was bucking as he left the arena and Tom was laughing, blowing a kiss into the stand where he knew Sam was sitting, except that like everyone else with the exception of Anna, who had little Noah fast asleep on her lap, she was standing applauding the only man she had ever loved in her life. He was crazy – he was brave – above all he was her Tom.

Anna was smiling at her friend. 'Does he ever think about anything other than his horses, Sammy?'

Sam laughed. 'Oh yes, Anna. I can assure you in two hour's time his horses won't even enter his head. He won't be Tom West, brilliant rider and horse whisperer - he will just be my Tom. Ad infinitum, Anna.'

'What does that mean?' Anna asked.

'Forever and ever.' Sam told her with a happy sigh as she watched Tom receiving a gold watch, an enormous trophy and a very handsome cheque.

'Forever and always since I was eight years old.' And she stood up and blew Tom a kiss as he and Kaspar cantered round the arena in front of Justin, Hans and Pieter and as the latter three exited through the double doors, he let Kaspar fly round the wonderful arena under the starlit sky, and the blue sea in the background sparkled along with Kaspar and his super talented rider.

The next afternoon it was Justin and Pickwick's turn to shine after Madame and Tom had exited with an unfortunate four faults. Noah was awake, calling, 'Dadda, Dadda,' as Justin and Pickwick did their lap of honour, and much to the amusement of the spectators around them he called. 'Noah here, Dadda. Noah see'd you Dadda.'

It was still early. The watch Tom had won the previous day was telling him it was just four thirty. Erica and Sheila took care of the horses as Tom and Justin changed into shorts and T. shirts, before they strapped Noah into his buggy and with the girls in the briefest of sundresses, made their way to the wonderful beach.

It had been an amazing few days but they were all only too aware that first thing in the morning the men would be on their way to Mexico and their wives and Noah would be winging their way back to Heathrow.

That night, Tom held Sam close. 'It's been an amazing few days, my Sammy, and this time next week Justin and I will be on our way home. Only six days and we will be together again and then after that, Paris. We'll take Josh and Rosie with us. Justin is going to bring Noah and Gus. Apparently, Lizzie has asked Abby to stay at The Old Manor House with Fenella and Mum says she loves having the trips.'

He kissed Sam again. 'Sleep tightly my darling and always remember, if my body isn't with you, my thoughts most definitely are. Ad infinitum, my Sammy. Forever and always,' and he fell asleep at the end of a perfect few days.

CHAPTER 10

Sam had just walked down to the village shop. She had decided to make a chocolate and Guinness cake, which John had been raving about. Mary had given her the recipe; apparently one of the W.I. ladies had brought one to the meeting the previous week and after sampling it, the members had clamoured for the recipe. It was now high on John's wish list and Sam was aiming to make one and put it in the freezer for Tom when he arrived home late on Sunday evening.

It was a lovely morning and all the dogs had followed Sam through the woods and over the fields to Old Tiles. She had left them in the kitchen with Mac and Mabel and Spick and Span whilst she had hurried on to the shop. Once she had completed her purchases she decided to call at The Old Parsonage to collect Rosie's leotard, which she had forgotten to put in her case. As she passed the tearooms she saw a notice in the window. She peered at it and read. *'Thank you to everyone who has supported my tearooms over the past thirty years. I shall miss you all, but the time has now come for me to move on and The Massenden Tearooms will be open for the last time on Saturday the 30th of March when any resident of the village will be treated to a cream tea. Martha.'*

As Sam was reading the notice a white van pulled up beside her and a young man with extremely long hair and faded, torn jeans leapt out and changed the sign, which currently read *UNDER OFFER* - to - *SOLD.*

Sam hurried the few yards and turned into the drive, which lead to The Old Parsonage, where she found her mother with a pair of secateurs, snipping the faded heads off the last season's hydrangeas.

'I've just popped in to collect Rosie's leotard,' she told Alice. 'She says she left it in the chest of drawers in the small bedroom.

I'll just run upstairs and get it. She will need it after school for her ballet class.'

Sam found the leotard and ran back downstairs, telling Alice. 'I see the tearooms are definitely sold. A young man has just changed the sign. Martha is leaving at the end of March. She is inviting the villagers to a free cream tea. Perhaps we can go together with Mary and Joanna. Genevieve would probably like to come too and Anna if she's not in the middle of moving house. Do you know who has bought it?'

Alice was intrigued. 'No, when I asked Martha, nothing was definite. I'll ask her again if I see her at the W.I. meeting next week. Peter read something in the local paper under the Planning Notices. He thought they wanted to extend the opening hours and to sell alcohol. It could be exciting but I shall miss Martha's coffee. The W.I. ladies often meet there for a chat on a Wednesday morning. I do hope if it's going to be serving food in the evenings it won't take customers away from The Bear. Roy relies on his regulars who go there to eat, although sometimes it would be nice if he varied the menu. It's very predictable. We shall just have to wait and see, but I shall do my best to find out and I will let you know if I happen to see anything of the new owners. I'll let you know what changes are on their way.'

As Sam crossed the green and walked home up Back Lane she noticed the postman on his daily round. He was delivering a very significant letter. It was addressed to Miss Georgia Norton and the postmark on the envelope was French. He called out to Sam asking her. 'How's that young rascal? Not driving any more Range Rovers I hope?'

Sam laughed, 'No, thank goodness. I think he learned his lesson that day.'

The postman had been the first person on the scene the morning Oscar had stolen his father's Range Rover and crashed into the utility room, severely damaging not only the Range Rover but himself as well.

Wednesday was ballet day and it was Sam's week to do the *'ballet run.'* Anna took the triplets back to South Lodge with Gus, and Sam took a carload of girls to Jane's ballet class. To Jane's surprise, Mimi was still coming regularly, wobbling her way through pirouettes and battement tendus. She got off the school bus at the entrance to the Equitation Centre with several other girls from the grammar school, including Clara and Tilly, and ran down the drive to Jane's studio beside the Indoor School just in time for the four thirty class.

It was almost five thirty before Sam had deposited all her passengers and Georgia and Charlotte ran into their neighbouring cottages calling, 'Goodnight. See you in the morning.'

Georgia put the key in the front door and ran into the dining room where she discovered her father lost in some far eastern country with Herbert Holmer, a tantalizing woman and a seedy hotel.

When he heard his daughter, Giles pulled himself back to the reality of Theobald's Row as Georgia threw her arms round him, giving him a bearlike hug and kissing his cheek. 'Hi, Dad! Anything to eat?' This was her standard greeting, every evening without fail.

'Cut yourself a piece of cake. There's one I bought from the farmer's market yesterday morning and I'll put a couple of shepherd's pies in the oven in half an hour. The trip's gran had a load of her homemade pies at the market. I've stocked up for the next few days. By the way, there's a letter for you on the kitchen table. It looks as though it's from your mum.'

Georgia picked up the letter and recognized her mother's handwriting. She went out into the paddock to talk to Fire Cracker and leaned against his stable door with one hand stroking his soft neck whilst she tore the envelope open with her teeth - shook the letter out and started to read, *'Dearest Georgia. Thank you for your letter. I am glad you didn't find your exams too difficult and so pleased you are having fun with the gang and your pony. I can now tell you my news. For a little while I shall be living with Granny and Grandpa in Tunbridge Wells. Paul and I close the restaurant here at the end of the month and he will be going straight off to Portugal. We have been together for almost ten years and of course it is a huge step to be taking. I shall miss him terribly but in my heart I know it is the right time to make this break.*

I told you a few weeks ago I had found premises, which I really liked. It has been run as a tea room for many years and I had to get the relevant planning permission to turn it into a licensed bistro and I also need to do quite a few alterations to the living accommodation upstairs. Luigi and Maria are going to run the bistro with me and they also have a twelve year old daughter who will obviously be coming with them, so we need to turn the accommodation into two separate flats. One will be for me and there will be a larger one for Luigi and his family.

Now is the real news. I hope you will be pleased. I am buying the tearooms on the green in Massenden. The bistro will be called La Casa sul Verde. (The House on The Green). I hope you will be happy to think that I will be living so near you.

It is best that you stay with your dad. My hours will be long, as of course the majority of our business will be done in the evenings. My apartment will be small and you have your pony with you – also I know Daddy is very happy to have you living with him.

I haven't yet told him that I have bought the tearooms. I hope he won't mind that I shall be living so near but I am sure he understands that our lives moved on a long time ago and I am certain that both he and I are mature enough to cope with the inevitable occasional meeting. Please, Georgia, do not think that I am coming to Massenden for any reason other than that I believe I have discovered the perfect premises, in a charming spot, with of course the huge added attraction that you can pop in and see me after school and in the holidays.

Maybe you will want to tell Daddy and tell him I enjoyed his latest book. Look after yourself and I will meet you as soon as I am back in England. We could enjoy a little shopping therapy in Tunbridge Wells. My very fondest love, Mummy.'

Georgia was almost eleven years old but she was mature enough to realize that this was not going to be easy and her first thoughts flew to her father. She was well aware that although he had enjoyed the company and the occasional dinner out with several different women – mostly through the publishing world – she was certain there had been no special woman in his life since her mother had left with Paul, ten years ago. She was also only too aware of the photograph standing on the chest of drawers, of her mother and himself, which his father had taken on the day of their engagement. It stood beside a very recent one of her jumping Fire Cracker, which he had taken himself at the Massenden Show.

In two weeks time it would be Joshua's twelfth birthday and Georgia's eleventh and they had already decided they were going to ask Adrian and Dom to take the big horseboxes to Camber Sands and all *the gang* would ride in the sea. Sam and Mary had already offered to make a massive picnic and they would join the youngsters at lunchtime, bringing Anna and Noah with them in Sam's large People Carrier.

Everything had been perfect in Georgia's young world until she had opened this innocuous looking letter.

Her first feeling was of pleasure. It would be nice to see her mother without having to be put on euro star and worrying whether she would be able to find her when she got to Calais, and then being left to her own devices when she had reached her mother's bistro. After re-reading the letter, she suddenly had the feeling of being abandoned. It was obvious her mother didn't want her to stay with her, let alone live with her, although the girl admitted to herself she would never agree to leave her father. She knew he was often not on the same planet as she was – travelling the world with Herbert Holmer, but he was always there for her – generous and kind – making certain she was happy, and chatting to her about her day as they ate their evening meal, which he laughingly called *'Dad's Hour.'*

Georgia's mind swept half a mile up the lane to Woodcutters.

She thought of Josh and his brothers and Rosie. When his dad was at home he was always laughing – calling Sam darling – sometimes teasing her, but there was always a feeling of love and she realized all too well, that for her own father, a very important part of his life was missing.

Suddenly, she was frightened. How was her father going to react to this news? Maybe he wouldn't wish to stay in Massenden. She buried her head in Fire Cracker's neck. She was sure he would live somewhere where she could take her pony, but she wanted to stay here, in Massenden and go to the Grammar School with Charlotte and Mimi. She loved *the gang* and her lessons with Charles or Justin and Adrian. She wanted to beg her father to stay, but how could she if his life was to become unbearable?

Suddenly, everything was too much and she wanted to talk to someone. Not her father, but someone who would understand her fears. She didn't know exactly why her mother had left her father for Paul, but she had often noticed him throw his prosthetic leg across the room in frustration and she had a feeling the leg may have played a significant part in the break up of his marriage.

It had started to rain heavily but Georgia needed a friendly face and she immediately knew whose that was. She folded the letter and pushed it into the pocket at the side of her school skirt. She put the bridle on to Fire Cracker – clambered on his bare back, not stopping to go indoors to fetch her hard hat, and with the rain pouring down on her dark hair and seeping through her school shirt, trotted across the lane, through the gate into Old Tiles Farm and galloped beside the cross country course, through the woods and into the stable yard at Woodcutters, where Rosie and Josh, who were on stable duty that evening, were checking the ponies. They were covered from head to foot in bright yellow oilskins and sou wester hats. The only part of them that was visible was a pair of bright blue and a pair of dark brown eyes.

Joshua caught hold of Georgia as she slithered off the back of the saturated pony, which he led into the only empty stable as Georgia was crying, 'I want to see your Mum.'

'Georgia,' Josh told her. 'Go with Rosie. Mum is baking in the kitchen. I'll rub Fire Cracker down with some towels and try to get him dry. Rosie, tell Mum I will be back in about half an hour.'

As he started to dry the pony, Rosie anxiously took hold of Georgia's hand and led the dripping wet girl into the kitchen.

Sam was just taking the Guinness chocolate cake out of the oven. It both smelt and looked good and she was just sampling a small piece, which had stuck in the bottom of the tin, thinking *'Umm, Tom will love this.'*

She gasped in horror when she saw a soaking wet girl standing in her kitchen dripping over the floor, not recognizing her for a moment.

'Georgia's here, Mummy. She's just ridden Fire Cracker up through the woods.'

Sam could now see who was beneath the dark hair, now plastered to her face, with large drops of rain dripping from the shirt, which was clinging forlornly to Georgia's slender body.

'Georgia, darling,' and she clutched the girl as she threw herself sobbing into Sam's arms.

'Georgia, whatever has happened?' Sam was immediately imagining some accident had befallen Giles. Maybe he had fallen down the stairs or tripped in the garden.

'Dad's fine, but I don't know whether he will be once I have shown him this.' And she handed the now very wet letter to Sam.

Before she opened it, Sam turned to Rosie. 'Rosie, run a really hot bath – take a handful of my bath salts and find a big towel in the airing cupboard – then ask one of the trips for a pair of jeans and one of their thickest sweaters. They should fit Georgia. Go as quickly as you can, that should stop her shivering. Meanwhile I will make a really hot cup of chocolate.'

As Rosie and Georgia disappeared, Sam sat down and peeled

open the now very wet envelope. A few of the words had run into each other but most of it was still legible.

After she had read it, the first thing she did was to call Giles. His phone rang for a long time, for the simple reason he was searching the paddock with Charlotte's father, David for any sign of the missing pony or his daughter.

As they heard the phone ringing in the distance, David patted Giles arm. 'I'll go, old pal. I can probably catch it before it rings off.' He tore through the paddock and into Giles' dining room where his mobile was lying beside the computer. He grabbed the phone, to hear Sam's voice, to his relief saying, *'Is that you, Giles? I've got a very wet Georgia here.'*

'No, it's David. Giles and I were in the paddock looking for Georgia and her pony. We heard the phone ringing and I knew I stood more chance of reaching it before it rang off. Here comes Giles now. I'll hand him over to you.'

He turned to Giles. 'It's Sam, Giles. Georgia is at Woodcutters.'

Giles grasped the phone. *'Sam, thank God.'*

'I am afraid she is soaked through, Giles. She is with Rosie who has run her a hot bath. You stay there. I'll give her a hot drink and some casserole with my lot and then she can stay the night with Rosie. There is something I need to tell you, Giles. Don't worry; it's nothing terrible, just something that has upset Georgia. Could you pop up here in a couple of hours when the youngsters have gone to bed? There is something I think you should see. I've put Georgia's clothes in the drier, they will soon be dry again and I will take her to school in the morning with Rosie and the trips.'

'Has it got anything to do with that letter from Clarissa?'

'Yes, it has, Giles. Please don't worry, but I think you should know the contents.'

'God, Sam. She's not taking Georgia to some God forsaken place. She's really happy in Massenden with your five and the rest of the kids.'

'That's certainly not what is in her mind I can assure you, Giles. I'll see you around eight thirty.'

To Sam's relief the hot bath had done it's trick and Georgia was now enjoying a casserole with the triplets and Rosie. Josh was almost as wet as Georgia had been and was indulging in a hot shower. Fire Cracker had taken exception to the yellow oilskins Josh had been wearing and he had abandoned them, getting soaked as the saturated pony shook his body violently several times, showering Josh with cold rain water.

An hour later, Sam had settled all the youngsters, although she thought she could detect muffled voices coming from a certain young man's bedroom. She was pretty certain Oscar was watching East Enders on his television. She trudged back upstairs and followed the voices to Oscar's bedroom door. She went in to the room to be greeted by the sight of her son completely dead to the world, his T.V. remote lying on top of his duvet having slipped out of his lifeless fingers. On the screen were a semi naked man and woman indulging in a steamy kiss, as the well-known signature tune started its drumbeat to denote the end of the episode. She shook her head in the direction of her sleeping son – the look of innocence on his countenance completely belying his wayward character. She turned off the television, placing the remote well out of his reach, dropped a light kiss on the scar on his cheek and firmly closed the bedroom door.

Oliver and Orlando were fast asleep only Joshua was still wide-awake.

'What's the matter with Georgia?' he asked Sam in a whisper.

'She had a letter from her Mum telling her she's buying the tearooms near Granny Alice. She's afraid her Dad will be upset, but I'm sure it will all work out in the end, Josh. Things usually do.'

'So is Georgia's mum going to make cakes and scones like Martha does?'

'No, she's going to have an Italian bistro.'

'Wow. I love Italian food, Mum.'

Sam smiled, 'So do I, Josh. Now go to sleep or you won't be awake in time for your bus in the morning.'

'Night, Mum.' And the ever-compliant Joshua turned out his bedside light.

Half an hour later, Giles was knocking on the front door. He was still extremely disturbed. Most people came to the kitchen door and Sam was struggling with the heavy bolts and the chain, which secured the old, oak door.

'Sorry, Sam. Have I come to the wrong door?'

'It's O.K. Giles. Most people come through the kitchen,' she told him. 'After Sophie broke in I had these huge bolts put on the door. They're not used very often and they get a bit stiff. I must ask Tom to oil them when I remember. Come into the sitting room. Would you like a glass of rosé? I'm going to indulge.'

Giles decided he might well need one. 'Yes please. That sounds great.'

'Read this whilst I go and get a couple of glasses,' and Sam handed Giles the letter, which she had dried on the top of the range.

She poured two glasses of wine and then as an afterthought cut two slices of the cake she had just made for Tom. When she returned to the sitting room, the letter was lying on Giles' knee and he appeared to be staring into space and to Sam's horror she could detect a tear in his eye. She was used to the children crying but not grown men. On the very rare occasions Tom was reduced to tears, she would hug him and kiss him but she could hardly do that with Giles, so she told him. 'Giles, she won't take Georgia from you It's obvious she is a business woman. She's not cut out to be a mum.'

Giles looked sadly at Sam. 'Nor a wife I'm afraid, Sam. How can I bear to live so near and yet so far from her? Sam, she wasn't always so hard and distant. For the first year of Georgia's life we were a perfect little family. Thank God we are unable to see into the future. I would never have believed how my life could change so quickly.'

'Giles, I don't know what happened, but I imagine Clarissa fell in love with Paul whilst you were in Afghanistan.'

'It wasn't like that, Sam. It was this that finished our marriage,' and he slapped his prosthetic leg in anger.

'Your leg? But why?'

'It repulsed her, Sam. She wouldn't come near me. Two days after I came back to my parent's home from rehab she had disappeared with Paul and Georgia. Paul had always fancied her, I was well aware of that. We had all grown up together. She liked him, yes, but nothing more until he became the better option. She asked me for a divorce but she never married Paul. When Georgia was seven she wrote to me telling me she had arranged for her to be a boarder at St. Swithin's. Georgia had stayed with me three or four times a year at my parent's house. I loved her so much. When I heard of Clarissa's plans for her I was shocked. I went to see Clarissa and insisted Georgia came to me every weekend. God, Sam, she was just a little girl, only seven years old, almost being abandoned by her mother.

Clarissa was only too glad that I was willing to take over the responsibility of Georgia – just asking that she should spend the larger portion of the school holidays with her. Lately she seemed to want her less and less and after I moved to your cottage it was obvious Georgia's life was beginning to revolve round the friends she was making here in Massenden. She begged me to let her leave St. Swithins. That was the last time I met Clarissa. We had a meal in Folkestone and discussed Georgia's future. She agreed Georgia could live with me and go to the Primary School, then hopefully on to the Grammar with Charlotte.'

Sam had listened to every word Giles had told her. 'I don't think you will have any problems, Giles. It doesn't sound as though she will want to take over Georgia's life. If you want my opinion, she appears to be an extremely selfish person, but maybe I shouldn't pass judgment. All I ever wanted was to marry Tom, live with him in Woodcutters and love my family. I am lucky. I have achieved all that and as a bonus have enjoyed my garden design business but I have never let that supersede my wish to be the best mum I could possibly be, and Giles, I can honestly say, with my hand on my heart, I have never, never glanced at any one but Tom and if ever, God forbid, some tragedy might have befallen his body, I would still have wanted him. The thought of leaving him would never have entered my head. You must know all women aren't like Clarissa. Ten years is a long time to be alone. Giles. You must have had a few flings over the years.'

'Never, Sam. There's no way I am going to be rejected again. *Ever*. Besides Sam, whatever Clarissa has done, I want her every single night. I lie awake thinking about her. There has never been anyone else. Georgia has no idea. God, I must be a weak man but I can't help my feelings. Our love was perfect, it could never be the same with anyone else but I know no one else could possibly understand how I feel.'

'I can, Giles. Of course I've kissed Pierre and James and Justin when they have given me a present or when I have been saying goodbye to them but I have never experienced a passionate kiss or made love to anyone but Tom,' she laughed. 'Giles, I am one hundred per cent certain it's been the same for Tom. Maybe we're lucky but it has always been the same for us, so perhaps we would be the only people who understand exactly how you feel towards Clarissa.'

'Clarissa obviously thinks we have both moved on. Maybe she has and it won't be difficult for her, but I can guarantee, Sam, for me it will be pure hell, knowing she is barely five hundred yards from my bed, probably with some fellow, whilst I am aching for her in every part on my body, except in this bloody leg which is impervious to all feeling,' and he hit it again with the full force of the palm of his hand. 'For Georgia's sake I will stay here. She has to have some stability in her life. I'm afraid she worships your eldest son, Sam, but she has lots of good friends, especially Charlotte, and I am not prepared to disrupt her life. I shall just have more and more adventures with Herbert Holmer.'

'Will Herbert ever get married do you think, Giles?'

Giles response was immediate as he almost spat the words. 'Never, never. He has more sense; he will never put himself in the position where he can be humiliated. No woman in any of my books is ever going to have that pleasure.'

In that moment, as Sam saw Giles out of the back door, reassuring him she would take Georgia to school in the morning, the fictitious Herbert Holmer became a real person, for as Giles walked into the rain and hurried down the garden path Sam watched as he pulled an old, brown, trilby hat from his pocket and placed it at an angle on his head. Herbert Holmer was none other than Giles Norton. Herbert Holmer's steamy affairs were Giles way of coping with his life, sadly devoid of the woman he longed for, Georgia's mother, Clarissa.

Giles made his way home, asking himself many questions as he reflected on the letter which had shaken him to the very core of his heart, as Sam poured herself another glass of wine, turned on Classic F.M. and found herself listening to the moving slow movement of Bruch's violin concerto. She closed her eyes between sipping the wine and turned her mind to the as yet unknown Clarissa Norton. Although she knew Giles and Clarissa had been divorced for ten years, according to Giles she had never seen fit to marry the man she had run away with. She tried to put herself in Clarissa's position but she found it impossible. She couldn't help thinking that the vast majority of army wives in her position would certainly be devastated, but at the same time tragic as the injuries might be, still had their husbands to love, when some of their friends only had the shattered remains of the man they had married and the father of their children flown home in a soulless aeroplane. She thought of her own mother. She knew there had been very little of her father to be buried but Alice had had to cope. Sam was sure she would have very little sympathy for Clarissa, who was very soon to be her next-door neighbour.

She finished her wine and poured herself another glass. It was very rare for her to drink on her own but tonight with the haunting music in the background she felt she needed it. She walked to the bureau and for once it wasn't Tom's photograph her hands went to - but to a tall, smiling young man with dark, brown hair curling under his peaked cap – a wide smile on his face as he gazed down at Alice who was sitting on a garden chair, holding a little girl who looked exactly like Rosie. It had been the very last picture that had ever been taken of Captain Joshua Smythe and his wife Alice and their young, daughter Samantha.

Sam placed the photograph carefully back in its place and picked up one of Tom and herself holding hands as they came out of Massenden Church on their wedding day, almost twelve years ago. She ran her finger down his face and then kissed the photo through the glass as the phone rang.

'Tommy, Tommy. Are you alright?'

'I'm very all right, my Sammy, apart from being thousands of miles away from you. Kaspar has excelled himself. He won the big class tonight and now we're in pole position for the Grand Prix on Sunday afternoon. I am catching the plane at six o'clock, that's eleven o'clock in Massenden. I'll be home early on Monday morning. I can't wait, my darling. Justin is over the moon, too. Pickwick came third, just Mikel and Grey Knight in between us. Madame is in the big class tomorrow, but what have you been up to, my little one?'

'Working on a design for Caroline Mawgan-Whitely. She wants her garden simplified. Reggie had all those weird pergolas put everywhere breaking up the views, but it's not difficult, I should have finished it by the weekend. Actually I was just kissing you when the phone rang.'

Tom laughed. *'I wish, my Sammy.'*

'I was feeling nostalgic and I was looking at the photo of my dad – my real dad. The one on the bureau and then I looked at our wedding photo and kissed you.'

'Oh, darling. But why were you feeling nostalgic?'

'I've had a strange evening, Tommy,' and she revealed the happenings of the past few hours.

'It's sad, Sammy and difficult to understand what Clarissa did, but perhaps it would be fairer to wait until you meet her before pre-judging her. We all seem to suffer from a fear of something. - I hate bats. - you are terrified of the channel tunnel and being shut in a lift. Maybe she suffers from a fear of false limbs or coming to terms with imperfections, but I do agree it was a desperately callous thing to do to poor old Giles. He's going to find it bloody hard to avoid her in a small place like Massenden.'

'Tom, I think Giles has become Herbert Holmer.'

'Who the hell is Herbert Holmer?'

Sam had forgotten Tom didn't share her enthusiasm for crime busters.

'Herbert Holmer is the hero in all Giles' books. He has a different steamy affair in each book but Giles told me Herbert would never get married. He said he wouldn't risk putting him through the hell and heartbreak of a divorce.'

'Good God, Sam. Thank heavens I don't have to make love to a book, however good the storyline might be and however seductive the heroine.'

'Tom, I only meant Giles' writing comes through his own broken heart.'

'Well I'm still truly thankful I've got the real thing who I shall see on Monday morning. Good night, my darling. Sweet dreams and no more wine this evening!!'

'Tom. How do you know?'

'Your voice is just the teeniest, weeniest slurred, my Sammy' and he laughed as he switched off his mobile.

Sam put the empty bottle in the re-cycling box, went upstairs and ran a hot shower. She slipped between the crisp, clean sheets she had put on the bed that morning, picked up her favourite photo of her smiling husband, laid it on the pillow and shut her eyes, all thoughts of Giles and Clarissa banished as her mind wandered happily to Monday morning. She decided she would cancel the two clients who were due to visit her office to discuss their front gardens. Monday morning would be exclusively Tom time – and she shivered in happy anticipation as her eyelids gently closed.

At Two Theobald's Row, Giles was not indulging in wine. He decided he needed something stronger to blot out the evening of reality and to re-enter the fictitious world of Herbert Holmer, and a large tumbler of neat whisky was standing beside his computer.

After an hour he decided maybe the whisky might not have been such a good idea. Tonight Herbert Holmer seemed extremely elusive. He was having difficulty finding the detective that night. He pulled on the brown trilby, ignoring the fact that it was still soaking wet after his excursion through the woods on his way home from Woodcutters. He reached for a case from which he extracted a thin cigar. This was a rarity indeed. Smoking was something Giles did only in extreme circumstances, unlike Herbert Holmer who was rarely to be seen without a cigarette or cigar in his mouth.

At last Giles discovered Herbert in an exotic bedroom with a dark haired Eastern woman with an abundance of sensual beauty and wearing very scant clothing. But as Giles took another large slurp of whisky and a puff on the cigar, the face of the woman was changing. It was slowly becoming a face he recognized only too well and a body he had loved so often, and as Herbert Holmer leapt into bed with the only girl Giles had ever loved, huge sobs racked the author's body and for the first time in his life he hated the detective who had made him a multi millionaire.

Giles slammed the computer shut, with Herbert Holmer firmly inside and refilling his glass, staggered up the stairs, as the image of Clarissa, naked in a bed in Beijing with Herbert Holmer stubbornly refused to leave his tormented mind.

CHAPTER 11

Sam was busy slicing another chocolate Guinness cake. The first two had completely disappeared, along with a multitude of sandwiches, quiches and many other delicacies eaten amongst the sand dunes at Camber, whilst the ponies pulled at their hay nets as they dried off in the sun after an invigorating hour cantering and trotting through the waves. The weather had played its part well and that day Joshua and Georgia had become twelve and eleven years old.

Georgia was thrilled. She now had a beautiful new saddle with a deep seat and knee rolls – it was the same make as the majority of *the gang* already had. Charles, who was an extremely good customer of the local saddler had, on the instruction of Giles, borrowed three saddles and chosen the one he thought most suitable for Fire Cracker, who was now fully equipped with his new saddle and a smart new bridle with a red velvet brow band. Clarissa had played her part, and the previous day a large parcel had been delivered to 2. Theobald's Row. It contained an extremely well fitting chestnut brown riding jacket and a pair of cream jodhpurs.

Sam as always had been practical and after the debacle of a few evenings ago, had driven to Rye to the sailing shop, and now thanks to all the West family, Georgia was well equipped for the heaviest of downpours, and a pair of leather riding gloves bought with Joshua's pocket money completed her outfit.

Joshua was feeling extremely grown up. He had received an envelope containing a chequebook and a bankcard. Tom and Sam had opened an account for him. Tom remembered how useful his Post Office account had been when he had needed the money to buy Thunderbird and Truly from the unsavoury Shady Sid nearly twenty years ago. Joshua's account already showed a very healthy balance of five hundred pounds, thanks to the generosity of not only Tom and Sam but also of his grandparents and his Aunts

Lizzie and Jane. He had already decided he would put any money he should win with Ganger or Lily into the account. His father had told him the story of Thunder and Truly and he wondered whether one day his own bank account might come to the rescue of some forlorn creature.

Georgia had given him a blue baseball cap with the motif of a horse jumping a large brick wall above the peak. He was wearing it at a jaunty angle as he sat between Georgia and Mimi.

Mimi was not at all happy. She had given Josh a very smart biro and pencil with his name on the side, beautifully presented in a green leather case. He had smiled and thanked her, but she was well aware he preferred Georgia's baseball cap. He was laughing with Georgia as they shared a huge piece of the chocolate cake with Charlotte and Orlando. She looked towards Jacques but to add to her chagrin he was deep in conversation with Tilly.

Mimi stood up and went to join her brother as he played a game of pocket chess with Eloise. Gus and Rosie were searching in the rock pools with Abby holding onto little Noah and Anne-Marie and Oscar were devouring the last of the egg sandwiches. Mimi felt alone. Everyone seemed to have paired up with someone else. Eventually she went to talk to Daisy who was listening to Oliver, who had brought his guitar and was playing folk music a little distance away from the main group. Clara had joined them and they were joining in the songs, singing the ones they knew the words to.

'Where's your brother today, Daisy?' Mimi asked the girl. 'Did he feel a party on the sands was beneath his dignity?'

'Nooow, Mimi,' Daisy drawled. 'He's searching for a new sheila. He's fed up with Coleen already, thank goodness. He says he's looking for something a bit more classy.'

'What's a sheila, Daisy?' Mimi asked.

'It means a girl friend in Australia, Mimi.' Daisy explained.

Mimi immediately wondered how classy she would be in Simon's estimation. He had not gone unnoticed by her on the school bus. She imagined the triplets would look very like him in three year's time.

'Why doesn't he bring Melchior and join *the gang*?' she asked Daisy.

'He hasn't been invited,' Daisy told her. 'None of our cousins will ask him.'

Mimi smiled artfully at Daisy, knowing full well she was putting the cat amongst the pigeons. 'Well, I'm asking him now. You can relay my invitation to him, Daisy. The rules state that only one member has to issue an invitation and that's just what I have done,' and Mimi stuck her tongue out at Joshua and Jacques' back sides before going to sit beside Josh.

'Well, Joshua West,' she smiled evilly at him. 'We've got a new member for *the gang.*'

Josh looked round the group. 'I thought Daisy was already a member. I thought Rosie had invited her. That's fine. She's a nice kid.'

Mimi gave him an even more ingratiating smile. 'Oh, it's not Daisy but I've just asked her to tell Simon I've invited him to join us and the rules say there is nothing you or anyone else can do to stop me asking whosoever I wish.'

Josh was not unlike his father. Tom was easy going for the majority of the time, but occasionally, as Sam had learned at a very tender age, his temper would ignite and flare like a beacon, only to be extinguished a very short while later. It was very rarely directed at her, but when they had been teenagers she remembered one morning when she and Justin had slipped on the ice outside the stables at Lake House. They had fallen in a heap together on the frozen concrete and she recalled the expression on Tom's face as he had appeared round the corner of the stables as she lay laughing with Justin, his hands on her bum as he tried to help her to her feet. Tom had stormed off on Satin, shouting a tirade of abuse at the laughing pair, only to feel remorse racking his body less than an hour later, as he had tied Satin to a post outside the village shop and bought the biggest box of chocolates he could find.

She was clearly reminded of this moment as Josh turned on Mimi, throwing the case with the pen and pencil into her lap. 'You bloody, stupid, little cow. You're a bloody thoughtless idiot. Have you already forgotten what that ------- moron did to Thunder?'

Sam was startled into action. As far as she was concerned, Josh had just used a totally forbidden word, which to the best of her knowledge she had only heard Tom use once, the morning a few weeks ago when he had seen his beloved Thunderbird lying on the ground.

'Josh. You should be ashamed. I'm absolutely mortified you could even think of using that word.'

'Why? Dad used it the other day when he saw Thunder.'

'Those were extreme circumstances. Josh, and you will apologize to Mimi at once.'

'No way, Mum. Mimi is just a stupid, insensitive, little girl. I used to think she was my friend. Christ, how mistaken I was. Enjoy yourself with Simon, Mimi. He's probably all you deserve.' He stood up, pulling a rather shaken Georgia with him, and pushing his baseball cap at an even more jaunty angle, kept hold of her hand as he walked to the rock pools to join Rosie and Gus.

Mimi went to sit beside Joanna who was trying to brush aside Sam's apologies. Mimi was visibly upset and there were tears in her eyes as she looked at the biro with Josh's name on the side. She picked up Rudi's spade, which was lying abandoned by the picnic basket whilst he indulged in a nap, and dug a deep hole in the sand, which interspersed the grassy dunes. She put the pen back in the box beside the pencil and laid it in the bottom of the hole, covering it with the golden sand. She looked sadly at Sam. 'It's disappeared for ever, Sam, like my friendship with Josh. He hates me.'

'Hate is a very strong word, Mimi. What you have done is not the most sensible thing you will ever do. Josh and Simon may be cousins but I am afraid they will probably never be friends, but one day, Mimi, Josh will forgive you. Satin has often told me you and Josh will always be friends and he is usually right – so cheer up, Mimi.'

'But Josh likes Georgia.'

'Of course he does, Mimi, and he likes Abby and Charlotte and all his cousins. You and Josh are just twelve years old. You both have a lot of living and growing up to do and many competitions lie ahead for you all with your ponies.'

'But Gus and Rosie and Ozzie and Anne-Marie?'

'They all have to grow up too, Mimi. I know Tom and I loved each other when we were very young, but it is very rare that young love lasts, and even we hit a huge bump on the way, namely Black Satin. Life has a strange way of sorting itself out, just let it take its own course, Mimi, and now you have invited Simon to join the gang your task is to keep him well away from Joshua. I've had one visit to the A. and E. on their behalf and I have no desire to have another.'

It was Sunday evening and at last all the family was quiet. Fortunately there was no Eastenders to lure Oscar into bad ways and there wasn't a sound even from his bedroom. He was sitting by the window looking across to the Little Oast waiting for Anne-Marie's goodnight signal. He had put the piece of seaweed she had found for him over the mirror on his chest of drawers. He glanced in the mirror and ran his finger over his scar. The tan he had caught from the sun that afternoon was almost concealing the line which ran down the side of his face. He went back to the window as the first red light flashed across the paddock. He flashed his own torch three times in reply. It had been a good day, but all days were good when Annie was with him, added to which it was not he who was in trouble with his mother. For once it was his older brother. It was unheard of, but it had made Oscar the happiest youngster in

Massenden. He flashed his torch one last time, took the piece of seaweed off the mirror and jumped into bed.

When Sam opened his bedroom door to kiss him goodnight he was fast asleep. The damp seaweed was adorning his neck. Sam smiled – all was obviously well in Oscar's little world.

Orlando and Oliver were both fast asleep but Rosie was sitting up in bed drawing a card. It was of a pony and its rider was wearing a large, golden crown.

'Rosie, it's late. What are you doing, sweetheart?'

'Drawing a picture to give Gussie in the morning. Just to remind him he's a prince.' And Rosie sighed. Her eyes were closing but suddenly she opened them again. 'Mummy, what did that word mean that Josh said to Mimi?'

'Something very unpleasant, which I hope I never hear anyone in this family utter again.'

'Oh, but I heard Dads say it to Justin when Kaspar trod on his reins and broke them.'

'Well, Rosie, Daddy is in for a serious telling off.'

Rosie laughed. 'I think Dads might enjoy that, Mummy.'

'You know far too much for your age, young lady. Now go to sleep and sweet dreams.'

'Oh they will be, Mummy. I shall dream of my prince and his castle.'

Sam smiled and shut Rosie's bedroom door. Rosie might possibly dream of her prince but she knew she was definitely going to see hers tomorrow morning and she ran downstairs to attend to the chocolate Guinness cake for her erstwhile husband, who she had decided she was going to deal with the moment he set foot in the house.

'*Roll on tomorrow morning.*' She thought, hugging herself in eager anticipation.

CHAPTER 12

Boswell and Bertie were sitting firmly by the door and Holly was staring longingly at her lead. Sam laughed, putting her car keys back on their hook on the dresser. 'Come on, you lot,' she called to Rosie and the triplets. 'I'm going to take pity on the dogs, we will all walk to school this morning, it's a beautiful day.'

Unfortunately, she had only glanced in one direction failing to see an ominous black cloud which was appearing over the trees from the west and a quarter of an hour later, as Rosie skipped up the school drive in pursuit of Gus and Abby, followed by her slightly less enthusiastic brothers, the heavens opened and Sam and the dogs rushed to take shelter under the nearest large tree, but not before they were all four soaked through as Sam's thin cardigan and her light weight jeans clung to her body. After ten minutes, she decided it was not to be just a passing shower and hastened as fast as she could back to Woodcutters, where she threw her saturated clothes straight into the washing machine and rushed upstairs to take a hot shower.

She relaxed as the shower wash and the hot water warmed her body and she was singing happily, wondering whether Tom's plane had landed yet and if so, how near home he was, when she saw a shadow stretching across the shower room floor and the wickedly smiling face of the object of her thoughts.

'Wow, Sammy,' he was laughing. 'I was hoping for a warm welcome home but I didn't expect to be set on fire,' and he was hurling his clothes on the floor, oblivious of everything except the vision of his wife, with shower gel frothing over her delectable body. As his arms crept round her, he laughed again. 'God, Sammy, talk about an unconventional welcome home!!'

She was stroking his curls, which were now in tight ringlets, sticking to his scalp.

'This is actually not what I had in mind, Thomas West. You were supposed to have both a slice of a 'come and try me' chocky cake made with Guinness, which is now your Dad's firm favourite, and also a slice of my tongue giving you a stern telling off.'

'Me!! A telling off.'

'Yes, my Thomas.'

'I don't like the sound of that at all, Samantha West.'

'No and I don't like the sound of the word Rosie heard you using when Kaspar broke his reins.'

'God, did I say something bad?'

'Yes, and so did your son when he was yelling at Mimi yesterday.'

'Oscar!! Yelling at Mimi!!'

'No, Thomas, not Oscar - Joshua.'

'Josh. God, did it begin with a B?'

'Sadly no, Thomas, go a little further down the alphabet and you will hit the right letter.'

To Sam's annoyance, Tom only laughed. 'Sorry, Sam, but they were brand new reins. I hadn't even paid the saddler for them, but I had no idea Rosie was around. Still, I'm sure she's heard Gussie saying it.'

'Gus!!!'

'Oh, yes, I only have to read his lips. He often says it when Hamlet or The Pie have a pole down – after all, he's only saying what he hears his dad say.'

'Tom! Do you say it too?'

'Of course, it's only a way of letting off steam.'

'And 'Lando and Ollie? I needn't even mention Ozzie I suppose, and surely not Rosie?'

'No, not Rosie. The boys are only growing up, Sammy, but I can't believe Josh would say that to Mimi. Whatever had she been up to?'

'Asking your cousin, Simon to be a member of *the gang.*'

'----.' Tom swore.

'Tom, how can I try to make the boys into little gentlemen when their own father leads them astray?'

'Sammy, be honest. Do you really want a family of Little Lord Fauntleroys? Because if you do then I fear you are fighting a lost cause – and surely darling, you quite fancy me, even though I might sometimes indulge in making my feelings felt. Now, come back where I know you are dying to be and stop worrying about the inevitable - our boys are fine. They just want to be men before they are even teenagers,' and he opened his arms again and turned the shower on full blast as she screamed, before he kissed her soundly.

An hour later, Tom had devoured almost half the cake. 'Gosh, this is good, Sammy – no wonder it's Dad's favourite. The horses should be arriving this evening. It's been quite a trip for them. Madame and Kaspar can have a month off, I'll concentrate on Opal and Clementine.' Tom broke off as his mobile suddenly rang. *'Adrian,'* Sam heard him say. *'Are you O.K. You're where? At the hospital – Amy's had a little girl – congratulations – Molly. That's lovely. Take the rest of today and tomorrow off and I will see you on Wednesday. Dom will help me with the horses and the kids can do their own ponies after school. Sam will help them. She's mouthing congratulations. Love to Amy. See you on Wednesday.'*

He turned to Sam. 'Amy's baby girl is called Molly Anna. She's just over eight pounds and everything is fine. She will be home tomorrow and Miriam is ready to help. They're getting married next week. Best rags out, Sammy. Reception at some hotel just outside Maidstone.'

'That should be the last wedding for ages, Tom. There's only Giles and Caroline Mawgan-Whitely who are single. Oh and Richard Adams, now he's divorced Tamara.'

'There's Trish, too, don't forget, Sam. I hope one day she will find someone else to love. She obviously adored her late husband. I like Trish, she deserves to find someone who will make her happy, but at least she seems to have settled into Theobald's Row and Jean-Pierre says she and her brother have made a terrific difference to his own work load at the Centre. Apparently he's been picked for the French European Event Team again. Pity he's a frog. I think our own event team could do with a boost. Let's hope we show jumpers can keep the Union Jack flying, and now I think I am going to catch up on my jet lag. A couple of hours sleep should put my clock back in order. Don't worry about any lunch for me, that cake will last me until supper time, but give me a shout at half past two, I'll come and collect the kids from school with you. Let's walk. The dogs would enjoy that. We could call into Old Tiles and say hello to Mum and Dad. The kids would like to see them. I'm going to crash out, don't go without me, I can't wait to see Rosie and the boys.'

'Have a good sleep. I'll take Chim round the lake for an hour.'

'There is an alternative, Sammy. You could join me in our bed.'

'Darling, I thought it was sleep you were requiring!!'

Tom laughed. 'You're right sweetheart. Actually I am almost dead on my feet, your time is probably better spent with Chim at the moment,' and he staggered up the stairs and threw himself fully clothed onto the soft mattress. Two minutes later, whilst Sam was saddling Chim, he was dead to the world.

As Sam rode round the lake she could see Topsy Turvy coming towards her. Little Noah was on the leading rein, Amelia trotting serenely beside Anna and Topsy.

'Anna how is Justin? Tom's dead to the world.'

Anna smiled. 'He just sat down on the settee, took Noah on his knee and was snoring his head off within five minutes. They're exhausted, Sam. I think some people imagine they live the life of playboys. If only they knew. I am going to be really firm and insist Justin takes time off to help me move into Theobald's Place. Mr. Griggs has finished the house; he's just started converting the coach house. We won't move the horses and ponies from Lake House until it's finished and we've found a good groom, but tomorrow Just and I are going to choose our curtains and carpets.'

'Would you like me to have Noah for the day, Anna.'

'Sam, that would be really great, but surely you will want to be doing something with Tom.'

'Anna, I am sure you know Tom well enough after all these years to know exactly what he will be doing. If you let me have Noah's buggy, I'll push him up to the stables and lead him round the lake on Amelia. The dogs would appreciate the walk I'm certain.'

Anna still looked dubious. 'If you're sure, Sam that would be fantastic, we would be able to give all our attention to what we really need for the house. Actually the old floorboards in the sitting room and the dining room look superb now they have been sanded and polished. I think we are abandoning the idea of fitted carpets and getting some Chinese rugs. I'm really excited. How long is Tom likely to be asleep for?'

'At least three hours. Probably until I wake him to fetch the children from school.'

'Come and see the house. Mr. Griggs has got the key. We can put the horses and Amelia in the stables.'

Sam needed no second bidding and turned Chim around, retracing her steps, then trotting slowly past Woodcutters and through the wood towards Back Lane with Noah squealing in delight as he bounced up and down rather erratically in the little basket saddle.

Sam had seen Theobald's Place shortly after Justin had bought it in the autumn, but now after several months in the capable and artisan hands of Mr. Griggs and his men a complete transformation had taken place, although the original Georgian features had been sympathetically retained apart from the kitchen, which made Sam catch her breath. A brand new grey A.G.A. had been installed in the old inglenook fireplace. It was fired by gas but unlike the A.G.A at Old Tiles it could be turned off and re-ignited whenever it was needed, which meant the kitchen didn't get unbearably hot in the warmer weather, which was something Mary often complained of and had persuaded John to buy an electric cooker for the summer months.

A reclaimed double butler's sink sat under the window set into black marble worktops, which emphasised the elegant eau de-nil cupboards, which covered the vast walls.

There was an archway through to what had once been the old scullery and was soon to be the dining end of the kitchen and the old pantry had been divided into an extremely useful utility room with a large American style fridge freezer and a family sized washer – drier. The shower room boasted the Victorian Royal Doulton white toilet pan embellished with Wedgwood blue flowers. It had been removed from the bathroom upstairs together with the old cistern, now renovated and fitted high up the wall with a long chain, at the end of which was a round brass knob, which at that moment was taking every bit of Noah's attention.

The bedrooms on the first floor all had their own en-suite wet rooms and a range of wardrobes down one side of each room. Every bedroom had an amazing view of the grounds and two of the rooms looked across the huge pond to the old stables. The top floor, however, was in Sam's estimation the piéce de resistance of the wonderful old house. The bedroom was massive, with the most amazing vista across to Lake House on one side and Old Tiles Farm on the other. A door led to a large dressing room with antique style oak wardrobes on either side. Obviously one had been built to house Justin's clothes, the other for Anna's. A further door opened into a palatial bathroom with a huge bath on it's four stubby cabriole legs standing in the middle of the room on a very impressive grey marble plinth. There was a double shower, two identical Victorian style basins and a loo with an oak seat, with another cistern high above on the wall. The pull at the end of the chain was in the form of a brass horse's head. Anna had discovered it in a brocanté shop in Paris. With it she had unearthed a matching light pull and had given them to Justin for part of his Christmas present. He had laughed and teased her, but she knew he liked them when she heard him asking Mr. Griggs to take great care when he fitted them to the chains.

Sam wandered back to the bedroom and looked out of the huge Georgian window, where in the distance she could see Woodcutters. She could also make out a blond figure, which was Tom, talking to a black horse, which she recognized was Satin.

'So much for him sleeping, Anna. There's Tom talking to Satin and Thunder. He just can't keep away from his horses. I love, love your home Anna, but I think I had better get back. Tom and I are going to walk to school and then call in at Old Tiles. Would you like me to collect Abby and Gus?'

'It's kind, Sam, but I think Justin wants to be at the school gate. He's been missing them dreadfully. Three weeks is a long time.'

'That's fine. – Drop Noah off whatever time you like in the morning and whatever you do, don't hurry back. We'll have a lovely day and if the weather is like this, we'll have a picnic in the garden.'

Sam got back to Woodcutters to find Tom munching an enormous cheese and tomato sandwich.

'I suddenly felt ravishing. You've had a long ride?'

'I met Anna and Noah and we went to see the finished Theobald's Place. It took rather a long time to get there with Amelia's little legs.'

'And? Your verdict?'

'Gorgeous. Mr. Griggs has excelled himself. I can't believe Justin - who not many years ago wouldn't contemplate a home of any description, now has a mansion which almost resembles a palace. It's truly beautiful, extremely tasteful and with a kitchen to die for.'

'Sam, you're not envious are you? You don't crave for a mansion, do you?'

'Tommy, I wouldn't swap Woodcutters even for Buckingham Palace! There is nowhere on this earth that would tempt me to contemplate leaving here. I fell in love with it the very first time you showed it to me even though it was full of cobwebs and spiders and now it may still be a cottage, albeit quite a large one, it is our own palace, my darling, and my own handsome prince just happens to live there.'

Tom pulled her to him and kissed her until eventually she laughed. 'Darling, I'm sorry to interrupt but if we don't go this very minute, the children will be abandoned at the school gate. You've got something to look forward to later, though.'

Tom kissed her again. 'I think I might have a very good idea what you have in mind,' he laughed.

'Yes, toad in the hole.'

'Whaat! Never mind, that always puts me in the right mood.'

It was Sam's turn to laugh. 'Dearest Tom, if my memory serves me correctly you are always in the right mood!!'

'Well,' Tom replied, pulling the curl on her forehead. 'Aren't you the lucky one then?'

'Tom, I think we are both lucky,' and she caught his hand and picked up the dog's leads before they set off through the woods, making their way to the Primary school.

The children were just leaving their classrooms and soon the triplets were tearing towards the gate – followed by Rosie and Gus and not far behind Charlotte and Georgia.

Just as Tom and Sam were about to leave, Lizzie made her late arrival, screeching to a standstill outside the gates. Mrs. Abrahams did not appreciate the late and unseemly arrival of Fenella's mother but as she also happened to be Lady Thornley, not a word of reproach was ever uttered. Fenella never worried if her mother was late, she always had Eloise to keep her company, as Jane was almost as erratic as her sister. In September, Felix and Flicka would have left the nursery and moved into the reception class. Elizabeth was well aware she was nearly always the last parent both in the morning and the afternoon. James had often reproached her mildly, saying. 'Shrimpkin, don't you think you could manage to leave the house just five minutes earlier?' and she would reply. 'Oh, Jamie, I think our clocks are always five minutes slow.'

James would smile indulgently, saying. 'Oh, well, I suppose someone has to be last, but drive carefully, my shrimp,' and he would kiss her goodbye, always arriving in his surgery at precisely ten minutes to nine. Never one minute before neither one minute after.

Tom was gathering Rosie in a bear-like hug, as Sam's mobile rang. '*Sam, it's Giles. Is there any chance you could take Georgia home with you? I've been in London at the hospital since ten o'clock this morning having a fitting for the latest model in prosthetic legs!! They're running terribly late with the appointments. I've called Esther but she's taking Charlotte straight to her grandmother's. She and David have some important business dinner this evening. I don't really like leaving Georgia alone. I know it's a big ask with Tom only just getting home --- but?'*

Sam cut him short. *'Of course that's O.K., Giles. Tom will be tied up with the horses this evening anyway, they're arriving back from the airport around five thirty. We're just collecting the children from school now and Georgia is actually standing right in front of me. Tom and I walked down and we're calling at Old Tiles on our way home. Don't worry – Georgia can do her homework with the trips. I know they've got an exam tomorrow, so there's no riding for them this evening, much to their disgust. Just collect her whenever you are back.'*

'Thanks a million, Sam. I hope this bloody new leg is going to be all it's cracked out to be! The surgeon assures me I shall feel like a new man. Oh, gosh, sorry Sam, they're calling my number. Thanks again – must go. See you later.'

Sam turned to Georgia. 'Georgia, darling, your dad has just phoned. His hospital appointment is running very late. I've told him you can come back to Woodcutters and have supper and tea and do your homework with the trips.'

Georgia's expressive face lit up. 'Cool, Sam. Will Joshua be there?'

'Yes, he gets off the five fifteen bus. He will be home in time for supper.'

'Cool,' Georgia repeated with an even brighter smile.

'We're going to Old Tiles to see Granny and Grandpa on the way home,' Sam told the children. 'Grandpa John has two sets of twins he thinks you would like to see. Two of the Jacob ewes obliged this morning, and Granny Mary has finished the jumper she has been knitting for you, Rosie. The one with the horse's head on the front.'

'Smashing.'

'You can wear it to the Pony Club party next week, Rosie.'

'I'm not going.'

'Not going. Of course you are, Rosie. Fenella and Abby would be really upset if you didn't go with them.'

Rosie looked even more mutinous. 'I am *not*, *not* going, Mummy. All the gang except Abby and Fen are going to the eleven and over party in the evening. I refuse to go to the baby one in the afternoon. I'm not going without Gussie and he says he won't go to the evening one either. If I am old enough to be chosen by the Pony Club to represent them at the horse show in London, then I'm old enough to go with the trips and Josh to the evening party. Fen will be O.K. She can go with Abby.'

'We will discuss this later, Rosie.' Sam knew Lizzie would have plenty to say if Rosie didn't attend the party, but she did have a sneaky sympathy for her young daughter. What Rosie had said was true. The Pony Club had chosen her to represent them in London before Christmas and she had won the event for them, but facts were facts and it would be another two years before she would be eligible to join the rest of the gang at the evening party. Sam never asked Tom to pull rank on behalf of any of his children. Rosie just had to learn the hard way. Rules were rules and they were something that were never broken by the Massenden Pony Club however talented a young rider might be, or even if her father was the number one rider in the world.

Rosie didn't argue with her mother, but hugged her secret to herself. Gus and she had hatched a plan and it definitely did not include the Massenden Pony Club.

As Sam and Tom made their way across the Village Green in the direction of Old Tiles Farm, Georgia suddenly spotted a very familiar figure. She left the triplets and tore across the immaculately mown cricket pitch, shouting. 'Mummy, Mummy.'

Sam looked towards the tearooms where she could see a dark haired woman about her own age, shaking hands with Martha.

Georgia had flung her arms round the very attractive woman who was currently kissing her daughter, asking Georgia. 'Georgia, what are you doing?' and then she noticed Sam and Tom and their family. 'Goodness, these must be the triplets I've heard so much about.'

Georgia smiled at her mother. 'This is Orlando, this is Oliver and this is Oscar,' she said, pointing at each one in turn, 'but you'll never remember which is which, Mummy. And these are their sister, Rosie, and their Mum and Dad.'

Martha had disappeared into the tearooms and closed the door as Clarissa told Tom and Sam. 'I'm Clarissa Norton, I expect you know Giles, my ex. I am the new owner of the '*about to be*' Italian Bistro, La Casa sul Verde. I've just been chatting to my builder,' she explained.

Tom smiled. 'Wow, sounds very posh. Sam and I love Italian – so do the kids. I've known Giles for years. I knocked him out in the sparring ring the first week we started at Grammar School together. In spite of that we remained good friends!! He rents one of our family cottages in Back Lane,' and he pointed, 'just over there. We live the other side of the Green, past Old Tiles Farm and through the woods. My parents live in the farm, which is where we are making our way. Sam's mother and stepfather will be your neighbours, they live just there in the Old Parsonage. When do you hope to open?'

'If everything goes to plan on the first of June, I have to make quite a lot of alterations to the living accommodation. I have an Italian couple that is going to have a flat on the first floor and I am going to have the attic converted into my own little space. Luigi will be my chef and will cook all the main courses. My own forté will be the sweets. Luigi's wife Maria will be in front of house. Luckily they both speak excellent English and so does their daughter, Luca. She is hoping to go to the Grammar School with you in September, Georgia.'

Georgia, who was looking rather dubious asked. 'So will I have a bedroom in your apartment then, Mummy?'

Clarissa shook her head. 'No, I'm afraid it is a tiny space, darling, but Daddy's cottage is really only a very short distance away. We shall be able to see each other very often.'

'At Daddy's?' Georgia asked, and Sam didn't miss the look of wistfulness in the girl's eyes when her mother answered. 'No, Georgia, you will have to come here,' she decided it was time to make a move towards Old Tiles, hoping the little lambs would bring a smile back to Georgia's sad face.

'Well, all the very best of luck with your new venture,' she told Clarissa. 'I'm sure we shall be sampling your food before long.'

Oscar grinned at Clarissa. 'Yes, Mum and Dad are always going into Ashford. There's a fab Italian place there. They think it's the tops, but I think I might bring Annie here and see if your food is any good.'

Sam was immediately covered in embarrassment, although Tom had turned away to hide his amusement. Oscar was just being Oscar, saying exactly what he was thinking, and was now giving Clarissa his most charming smile but not missing her discomfort when she noticed the long scar running down his face, partly hidden by the navy blue baseball cap, which he was, as usual, wearing at a jaunty angle.

Clarissa was feeling sick. She knew it was wicked, but she just couldn't help it. She couldn't fight the phobia she had about scars and imperfections to the human body, which had ruined both her marriage and her life. She tried to smile at Oscar as he told her. 'Annie is my girlfriend. She's French and she's very beautiful.' He was very astute and was well aware she was finding his scar offensive and continued firmly. 'She doesn't mind my scar. She says I'm still exactly the same Oz I was before I drove into the utility room in Dad's Range Rover.'

Tom felt an even more urgent need to prise Oscar away from this conservation, which was rapidly becoming very personal.

'Come on, all of you, we must press on. Georgia is coming home with us whilst Giles is at the hospital.' He explained to Clarissa.

Neither Sam nor Tom failed to note the look, quickly hidden, but a definite flash of anxiety that had shot across Clarissa's extremely attractive countenance.

'What's wrong with Daddy, Georgia? Is he ill?'

'No, he's having a new leg. Apparently it will be brilliant. The specialist says he will feel like a new man,' she sighed. 'Daddy is spending most of his time in Beijing at the moment.'

'In Beijing?'

Georgia smiled. 'He's having an affair with a really sexy woman.'

Clarissa had grown suddenly pale. 'Daddy is?'

'No, Mummy. Herbert Holmer of course, but you know how Daddy gets lost in his story lines.'

'No, I don't really, Georgia. Daddy was in the army when we were married and when you were born. He didn't have Herbert Holmer for company then.' *'Nor a horrible prosthetic leg,'* she thought to herself.

'Anyway, I'll call you on your mobile, Georgia. I'm staying with Granny and Grandpa in Tunbridge Wells. Next time I'm here we will go out to lunch at the pub and I will show you inside La Casa sul Verde.'

'Can Daddy come too?'

‘He wouldn’t be interested, darling,’ and she kissed Georgia before getting into her car and driving away.

Georgia turned to Sam. ‘I think perhaps Daddy would be interested, Sam.’

‘Maybe, one day he will, Georgia, but for now, let’s go and see these baby lambs and then we must get back to Woodcutters before Josh’s bus gets there.’

CHAPTER 13

The visit to Paris was looming on the near horizon and Sam was already sorting out clothes for Rosie and Josh to take to France and a mountain of gear for the triplets to take to Old Tiles. Mimi and Rupert were staying at Lake House under the supervision of Joanna's mother, Brenda, who was hoping she wasn't going to have any problems with Mimi. Fortunately Mimi had a most uncharacteristic and unexpected love for babies and Eva had promised she would bring Tabitha to Lake House for lunch on the Sunday and Amy had said she would love it if Mimi came to help her bath Molly in the mornings. It was the rest of the day that was worrying her grandmother but Charles had assured her the gang would be meeting every afternoon under the supervision of Adrian, and Brenda was determined not to let Joanna be aware that looking after her granddaughter was not the idyllic pleasure it once had been.

Rupert would be no trouble she was certain. He had recently rescued two bicycles from a skip outside one of the cottages in the village and was patiently taking them apart, endeavouring to end up with one useable mode of transport. Charles thought it highly unlikely the end product would ever transpire but if it did nothing else, it was occupying every one of his young son's spare hours.

When Oscar suddenly discovered Dom was taking Anne-Marie and Genevieve to Paris all hell let loose. In the end for the sake of a peaceful life for everyone else, and to Mary's secret relief, Tom and Sam agreed he could go to Paris with them and she was currently squeezing another pair of jeans into his bag.

Two days before they were due to leave for Paris there was the small matter of the Pony Club parties. To Sam's relief Rosie had ceased complaining and at three o'clock Tom watched her run through the door of the Village Hall before continuing his journey to Ashford to have his hair, which was almost curling onto his shoulders, severely cut after Sam, both his sisters and his mother had told him he looked like a tramp. He had glanced in the mirror and could see their point and had agreed to drop Rosie at the hall on his reluctant way to what he maintained was one of the biggest wastes of time life could throw at him.

Mary always laughed. She had had problems with Tom and the barber from the age of two and a half when he had wriggled and screamed as the poor man had struggled to cut the gold curls that were almost half way down his back. Now, thirty years later, he was still the worst fidget Mr. Timms had ever encountered. He decided to cut Tom's hair extremely short. *'I shan't see him again for another six months,'* he told himself, *'and his triplets are almost as bad.'*

Whilst Tom was watching in horror, as his gold locks descended onto the floor and a short back and sides was rapidly taking shape, Abby and Fenella were wondering why Rosie wasn't at the party playing charades and pass the parcel.

At six o'clock Sam was still getting over the shock of the strange looking man in her kitchen, who swore he was still her husband however unrecognizable he might appear.

'Darling, whatever has Mr. Timms done to you?'

'Bloody man, it was all over the floor before I could stop him. Still the plus point is I shan't have to endure him or waste any more money for at least another six months,' he scowled.

Sam laughed, 'I don't think Mr. Timms looks forwards to your visits any more than you enjoy going there, Tom. Whenever I take the trips or Josh he always asks, *'and will I have the pleasure of cutting your husband's hair soon, Mrs. West?'* When I say, *'I doubt it,'* he breathes a huge sigh of relief and says. *'Thank goodness, he's such a fidget, but he always has been. I'm quite surprised I haven't cut one of his ears of before now.'*

Tom scowled again. 'Well it's your fault if you don't fancy me any more, Sam. You made me have it cut.'

'And your mum and your sisters, and even your daughter. It's O.K. darling. You look quite er – er – manly!!'

'Manly – what the hell did I look before, then?'

Sam laughed and thought. ' Still manly!'

'So that's how I always look then?'

'It would appear so, my handsome hulk, and now I must go and fetch Rosie from the party. It will be finishing in five minutes. Mimi, Rupert, Gus and Annie are calling for the trips and Josh at seven o'clock. They can walk down to the hall together and I'll pick them up at ten thirty.'

Sam picked up her car keys and three minutes later was sitting in the Village Hall car park waiting for Rosie. She waited patiently as the children emerged in small groups, all running to their waiting parents. After what seemed an eternity, Lizzie emerged with Abby and Fenella. She saw Sam and came across to the car greeting her, looking rather surprised to see her sister-in-law. 'Whom are you waiting for, Sam?' she asked.

'Don't be silly, Lizzie, Rosie of course. What on earth is she doing?'

'But, Sam, it's you who are being silly, Rosie wasn't at the party.'

'Of course she was. Tom dropped her off at three o'clock on his way to the barbers.'

'Oh, so we managed to convince him he looked like a highly undesirable vagrant.'

'Yes, yes, Lizzie. But where is Rosie?'

'I've no idea, Sam. She certainly wasn't at the party. I've been helping all the afternoon. I never even caught a glimpse of her.'

Sam started her car and shot out of the car park. Lizzie shuddered as she watched a Range Rover slam on its brakes, miraculously missing the silver people carrier by less than a foot, the irate and shaken driver raising his fist and shouting obscenities at Sam who was totally oblivious of the carnage she had almost caused. Shaking from head to foot she tore down the road turning into Woodcutters and pulling up by the front door with a screech of brakes. She tore into the paddock where Tom was leading Opal across the yard towards his stable. Sam's screams terrified the horse who reared up, tearing the rope out of Tom's hand, flying through the gate, which Sam had left open and galloping and bucking round the lawn, quickly decimating Tom's much cherished grass.

Tom was about to swear until he saw Sam's waxen face and heard her frantic screams.

'She's gone, Tom. She's not there.'

'Sammy, darling, what on earth is the matter?'

'Oh, Tom. Oh, Tom. Rosie's gone. Someone's taken her. Ring the police quickly.'

Fortunately, Opal had realized he was alone in the garden and he flew over Sam's sculptured privet hedge, landing safely back in the stable yard where he came to an abrupt halt in front of Madame's stable.

Adrian was in the yard feeding the ponies. He shot Opal into his stable as he watched Sam and Tom tearing back towards the cottage.

Two minutes later, Tom was talking to the police and ten minutes later they were in the drive at Woodcutters, parked alongside Sam's people carrier.

The police were baffled. Tom was adamant he had seen Rosie go through the Village Hall doors.

As the police were asking what to Sam seemed totally useless questions, Tom's mobile rang. He grabbed it and answered *'Tom West.'*

'Tom, it's Justin. Is Gus with you? We haven't seen him since mid afternoon. Apparently, according to Dom, he didn't turn up for a session with the gang. I thought he had gone to Theobald's Place with Anna and Noah, and Anna thought he had taken Hamlet for a jumping lesson with Dom. No one has seen him. We're worried sick. Anna wants me to call the police.'

'The police are actually here in our kitchen, Justin. Rosie didn't

go to the Pony Club party this afternoon, although I actually watched her go into the Village Hall. We've been frantic but now it doesn't take a genius to believe they are together somewhere. Little devils! Earlier in the week Rosie was being really bolshie about having to go to the junior Pony Club party. She said Gus wasn't going to the evening one either. She went without a murmur this afternoon, though. Where the hell can they be? I'll ring you back, Just. I must tell the police the latest development.'

'O.K. Tom. I'm just rushing down to Theobald's Place to make certain they're not having a picnic there. It's unlikely; Anna and Noah were there until half past four. At least Rosie will be safe with Gus, Tom.'

'Small comfort to me I'm afraid, Justin. Fond as I am of your young son, he is only just eleven years old. I would like to know exactly where they are.'

'I'll call his mobile, Tom and let you know as soon as I get a reply.'

Sam was still clutching Tom as he turned to the policemen. 'I am assuming she is with Fergus Wright-Smith from Lake House. He has also not been seen since mid afternoon. They are the most unlikely pair of youngsters to get into trouble but I wish to God I knew where they were.'

'How old is this lad?' the sergeant asked Tom.

'Just eleven and Rosie is nine.'

'We'll call head quarters and get our squad cars to look out for them. Would they be likely to have much cash on them?' the sergeant asked Tom.

Tom thought. 'How much money do you think Rosie has, Sammy?'

'Probably between fifteen and twenty pounds, I don't know about Gus. He's probably got more. He's just had his birthday. Try Rosie's mobile again, Tom.'

Tom waited but there was no reply from the little girl so he left a message. *'Rosie, Mummy and I are really worried. Where are you?*

I presume you are with Gus. The police are at Woodcutters. Call me immediately you get this message.'

Rosie looked at Gus. 'Dad has just left me a message, Gussie. I think I had better let him know I am O.K. I shan't tell them where we are. I'll just tell them we'll be home about half past nine.'

'Hells bells, Rosie, here's a message from Dad, I'll say the same as you. Then they needn't worry.' And the two youngsters sent their texts.

At Woodcutters, Sam was still clutching Tom. The boys had already left for the senior Pony Club party. They hadn't wanted to go. Orlando was tearful and the other boys, including Oscar were extremely quiet. Tom had promised he would call Joshua as soon as he had any news. Suddenly a text came through on his mobile. He read it and looked at both Sam and the two police officers. 'As we thought, she is with Gus. Little Madam doesn't say where they are but informs me they will be back here at nine thirty.'

John and Mary were busy entertaining a family of four who were having a holiday at Old Tiles on the recommendation of their cousins, Karl and Helga Becker. John was just carving a succulent leg of lamb when the phone in the kitchen rang. He answered it and took a minute or two before he realized to whom he was talking.

'Filippo Greco?' he repeated.

'Yes, Mr. West. I own the Italian restaurant in Ashford. I really need to speak to your son, Tom or to his wife, but it would appear they are ex-directory. We are rather concerned. We had a table for two booked under the name of West. We were expecting your son and his delightful wife, but two youngsters turned up. My wife and I are worried; they seem very young to be out alone in the evening. We wonder if their parents know they are here. I don't recognise the boy but the little girl certainly belongs to your son.'

John was alarmed. *'Has the boy got dark, wavy hair?'*

'Yes, yes, he has.'

'I'm pretty certain I know who he is. He's Tom's partner's son. No worries there. He's a nice kid but he's only eleven and Rosie is only just nine. Can you make certain they don't leave your restaurant? They are far too young to be in Ashford alone in the evening. I'll call Tom at once and ask him to get in touch with you straight away and thank you and your wife for being so vigilant.'

'Mary, that was Filippo from Italiano's in Ashford. Rosie and Gus are eating there alone.'

Mary did not appear concerned. 'Tom must have taken them to Ashford by car, I expect he's picking them up later but you had better ring him and check, just to make sure it's all legit.'

One minute later, John was talking to Tom.

'Tom, I've just had Filippo on the line.'

'Filippo?'

'From Italiano's in Ashford. It would appear Rosie and Gus are dining there alone. I imagine you took them there but I thought I had better check with you, Filippo is a bit concerned.'

'God, Dad. Sam and I are nearly out of our minds. We've even had the police here. Rosie played truant from the Pony Club party this afternoon. She was furious she couldn't go to the evening do with Gus. They must have decided to do their own thing. Why does this weird young love run through our family? Sam and I were once at loggerheads with the vicar but at least I was sixteen. Rosie and Gus are carrying this to extremities. I must call Justin at once. He and Anna are worried sick too. One of us will go and get them. There is no way they are wandering about in Ashford on their own.'

'Don't worry, Tom.' His father told him, *'I've asked Filippo not to let them out of his sight until someone comes to fetch them.'*

Tom called Justin. *'Little blighters, Justin. Dad's had a tip off. They're living it up at Italiano's in Ashford.'*

To Tom's annoyance, Justin laughed. '*I told you Rosie would be perfectly safe with my son, Tom.*'

'Justin, maybe in a few year's time I will trust your son. At the moment he is not the issue – it's the thought of two youngsters, vulnerable to any unsavoury people who could be walking the streets. I'm on my way to get them straight away.'

'I'd better go, Tom. You sound a bit overwrought.'

'I am not overwrought, Justin. I am a perfectly normal dad who does not appreciate his young daughter going behind his back, for which I can assure you she will receive due punishment, but yes, perhaps you had better get them and insist Rosie sits in the back of the car on her own and can you tell Filippo I really appreciate his help?'

'O.K. Tom. I can assure you Gus isn't going to get out of this lightly. Why the hell didn't they just ask one of us to take them to Italiano's?'

'Because, Justin, they bloody well knew what the answer would be. They would have been at the village hall whether they liked the idea or not. You had better get going before those devious little devils escape from under Filippo's nose.'

Filippo was keeping an eagle eye on the young boy and girl who were pulling some notes out of the back pockets of their jeans. He nudged his wife who hurried to the table, saying.

'I've a little treat for you before you leave,' and then putting a large glass bowl of ice cream in front of the two youngsters.

'Wow, thanks,' Gus grinned at the kindly, plump, Italian woman.

Rosie wasn't really hungry. She was actually beginning to feel a little bit sick – not because she had eaten too much but because now the main part of her adventure with Gus was over, she was looking through the window, realizing it was already getting very dark and there were several groups of noisy teenagers standing in the doorways of the shops. She was sure Gus would look after her, but a big part of her was wishing her dad was with them too.

Filippo's wife, Gina was getting anxious. Justin had been held up by a minor accident on one of the roundabouts approaching Ashford but at last the Italian woman breathed more easily as she noticed a Range Rover pulling up on the double yellow lines outside the restaurant.

Rosie had gone to the ladies' room and Gus was carefully counting their money and looking at his watch. There was only one bus every hour to Massenden and it would definitely not be a good thing to miss the one that left at nine o'clock. He failed to notice his father coming through the door, until a shadow was cast over the table and a hand came down firmly removing the notes from his clasp. He gasped and looked up. 'Dad. What are you doing here?'

'What do you think I am doing here, Gus? Where is Rosie?'

'She's in the loo. We need to catch the nine o'clock bus.'

'Gus. You and Rosie are most definitely not catching any bus. The reason I am here is to take you home. What ever were you thinking of, Gus. Sam thought Rosie had been abducted when she discovered she hadn't been to the party this afternoon. They called the police, who are definitely not amused.'

'The – the – the ppppolice, Dad?'

'The police, Gus.'

Rosie appeared from the loo, her eyes almost popping out of her head when she noticed Justin.

'Gus, why is your dad here?' but as she noticed the ever increasing groups of youngsters, although she would never let Gus know, part of her was really pleased Justin was there.

Justin had gathered Gus and Rosie's money and was paying Filippo, at the same time giving him a large tip for keeping a fatherly eye on the delinquents.

As Justin ushered them into the car, a noisy group of about ten boys and girls brushed past them. They were shouting and laughing, drinking beer out of cans.

Rosie noticed a boy with a blond head with a mass of curls. The boy looked very like her own father, or rather how she imagined he had looked a long time ago. The boy had his arm round a slim, dark haired girl. Rosie stared at the low cut dress and short skirt, the black mascara and the ruby red lipstick and pulled Justin's arm. 'Justin, there's Simon – my cousin. He looks as though he has had too much to drink already.'

'How old is he, Rosie?'

'Fourteen.'

'Right. Get in the front of the car, Gus and you in the back, Rosie,' and Justin locked the door and ran after the group of youngsters. He caught hold of the blond boy's arm and found himself looking at the image of Tom when he had been riding The Likely Lad.

'Simon West?'

Simon was frightened He had no idea who Justin was, but imagined he was a plain-clothes policeman.

'Come with me,' Justin ordered and pulled the boy in the direction of his Range Rover. 'Get in. I'm taking you home.'

He pushed Simon onto the back seat where Rosie was sitting. 'What the hell is she doing here?' he asked Justin. 'She's my cousin.'

'I'm well aware of that, Simon. I am taking her home too.'

'Are you a plain-clothes cop, because if you are, I haven't done anything wrong? I was just out with a group of my mates.'

'Simon, my name is Justin Wright-Smith. I am a business partner of your cousin Tom. I also have a bone to pick with you. You stole my quad bike.'

'I borrowed it. I didn't steal it. I left it at the farm.'

'In my eyes you stole it, but the reason I am taking you home is that you are too young to be roaming the streets with that gang of lads. Fortunately for you I am not the police, but next time it could well be them and you would be in serious trouble, not least with your father,' and Justin put the car into drive and shot forwards.

Halfway home and having negotiated several roundabouts Justin felt a hand shaking his shoulder. 'Could you stop mister, I'm about to throw up?'

Rosie looked at her cousin in disgust. 'Well, don't do it over me, Simon,' and as Justin slowed to a stop she pushed him onto the grass verge.

Almost an hour later, after two more stops and Simon complaining British beer must be naff, Justin stopped in front of Honeysuckle Cottage and marched Simon up the path to the front door, only to discover Robert firmly ensconced on the sofa with a familiar face. He was hastily adjusting his trousers, as Tamara Adams pulled on her shirt.

'What the hell are you doing barging in here?' he asked Justin rudely.

'I suggest you ask your son the answer to that question, Robert. – Good evening, Tamara. Shame Robert hasn't got a Roller but I gather Reggie Mawgan-Whitely hasn't got his any more either. Sorry to have interrupted your – er – evening, Robert. Just watch your young son – but I should think he's already thrown up all the beer he'd been drinking by now,' and Justin hurried back down the path to tell Gus exactly what he thought of young lads of eleven who saw fit to take his friend's even younger daughter on a bus to Ashford instead of attending the Pony Club party with the rest of *the gang*.

It was not a comfortable evening for Gus and certainly no better for Rosie who would very shortly be confronting Tom who was far from happy.

The next day, they learned that their entries for an important two-day show in Sussex had been cancelled, and they would not even sit on their ponies for two weeks once they had returned from Paris. Simon however had got off extremely lightly. 'Just go to your room,' Rob had ordered his son, turning his attention back to the far more entertaining Tamara Adams, slowly undoing the buttons on the front of her blouse, as Simon disappeared to his room completely unconcerned. He found a totally unsavoury film on his skybox and wondered whom the blond chick was who sat behind the cousin he despised on the school bus each morning.

CHAPTER 14

To Rosie's disappointment when they arrived in Paris Gus was nowhere to be seen. She noticed Abby pushing Noah to the huge ice cream stall in his buggy. 'Where's Gussie?' she asked her friend.

'He's not been allowed to come to Paris. Mummy was furious with him about the Pony Club Party. He's staying with Rupert and Mimi. He's mad. He's not speaking to Mummy at the moment. Daddy was going to let him come but Mummy put her foot down. He's not allowed to ride either. He's helping Rupert with some old bicycles.'

Rosie was livid. She was also upset, realizing that it was mainly on her behalf that Gus had not gone with the rest of the gang to the party. She turned away from the ice cream kiosk and found a stall selling cards. She searched the stands and eventually found one depicting a boy and a dog, which faintly resembled Gus and Santa. She went back to the caravan, slamming the door, not helping her current rocky relationship with her own mother when the small table Josh had put his lemonade on toppled over and sticky liquid wended its way over the floor and onto Boz's extra large paws.

Sam frowned at Rosie. 'For goodness sake, Rosie, look what you have done. Not only is the floor in a mess but Boz is too.'

'It stinks, Mum.'

'Right, Madam. I imagine this involves a certain young man.'

Suddenly it was all too much for Rosie. She put her arms round Sam's waist and sobbed. 'It's my fault Gus is in trouble.'

'No, Rosie. You are both equally to blame. You both have to realize you can't always do or have exactly what you want. Life isn't that simple I'm afraid. What you did was extremely irresponsible and very thoughtless. I see you have bought a card. I sincerely hope it's for Auntie Lizzie apologizing for not going to the party, which she spent a long time organizing, making sure you would all have a lovely tea.'

'It's for Gussie,' Rosie hiccupped.

'Well in that case, you had better go back to the stall and choose a really nice card for Auntie Lizzie, and whilst you are about it you had better buy two stamps.'

Rosie was still feeling belligerent. 'I can't speak French.'

'I can assure you, Rosie, if you point to the place where the stamps should be the lady will understand exactly what you want.'

Rosie left the caravan in the same black mood in which she had entered it and Sam shuddered again as the door slammed and she just managed to catch the bottle of lemonade before the rest of it spilled over Boz, who was frantically licking his paws.

There was no sign of Oscar. He and Anne-Marie were in Paris with Genevieve sampling a creperie near the Eiffel Tower, and Joshua was proudly riding Madame Bovary round the practice area beside his father and Kaspar. Madame was now ten years old and as Tom looked at his eldest son he thought that possibly in five years time he would ask Charles if he could hand the mare to Joshua. At fifteen she would be past her prime but would most likely still be the perfect schoolmistress for a young lad to start on his senior career in the Young Rider's Classes.

As they returned to the stables, they passed the various trade stands where Josh noticed his young sister sitting alone at a table. She was laboriously writing her 'apology' card to her Auntie Lizzie – her tongue sticking out and a frown on her forehead as she deliberated what she should say. In the end her message was extremely short. *'Dear Auntie Lizzie. Sorry I didn't come to the party the other day but actually I don't want to belong to the Pony Club any more if I can't come with Gus and the Gang. I don't think Gussie wants to come any more either. Now I am in Paris and Gus hasn't been allowed to come. It's all the Pony Club's fault. I shall have a really boring week. Love Rosie'.*

She picked up the card with the boy and the dog, '*Dear Gussie. Paris stinks. I'm sorry it's my fault you're not here. Josh is in a good mood because Dad's letting him ride Madame and Oz is happy because Genevieve has taken him into Paris with Anne-Marie. It's only me that's miserable because you're not here.'*

A shadow fell across the table as Tom sat down on the empty chair opposite her, holding two ice creams. He handed her one and winced at the withering look he was receiving. It wasn't nice he decided, to be at odds with your young daughter, who was telling him in no uncertain terms. 'If you think an ice cream is going to make me happy then you couldn't be more wrong. Nothing will make up for Gussie not being here,' and her huge, brown eyes, so like Sam's gazed mournfully at him.

'Rosie, I know Gus is your special friend but you have got Ozzie and Anne-Marie here and Josh and Abby as well. You've got plenty of friends around you.'

'But Daddy, they're not the same. You're always telling me you did everything with Mummy when you were young.'

'I certainly did a lot with her, Rosie, but I was often with Justin or James and all my Prince Philip team mates. It's good to have lots of friends when you're young and it still applies when you get older. The Pony Club helps you to make friends with other boys and girls who have the same interests as you do.'

'I've just told Auntie Lizzie I'm not going anymore.'

'I think you are, Madam. The Pony Club teaches you to be a good sport. That life isn't always about winning trophies and money, and I want all my family to understand that.' He put his hand in his pocket. 'Go and buy another card, Rosie.'

'But Dad, it took me ages to write this one' ---

'Too bad, I'm afraid sweetheart,' but he watched as she walked back to the stand and bought an identical card. Her message this time was extremely short. *'Sorry Auntie Lizzie but I won't be at the party next year either. Not until I can come with Gus and the rest of the gang. I hope you and Uncle James are well, love Rosie.'*

She stuck the stamps on the cards and as Tom watched her drop them into the letterbox he fervently hoped this would be the end of this unfortunate storm in a teacup and would very soon be forgotten.

At Two Theobald's Row Giles was sitting in front of his computer. Georgia and Charlotte were at Lake House with the members of *the gang* who had not gone to Paris with the exception of Gus, who was scrubbing his hands and finger nails, trying to remove the grease, which had accumulated during the course of the morning as he had helped Rupert dismantle the frame of one of the bicycles. Having accomplished this to the best of his ability and having used almost half a tin of Swarfega, he took his mobile into the garden and sent Rosie a long text message. '*Wish I was with you in Paris, or that you were here. Not even allowed to go near the stables. I thought about creeping out of bed at night and having a ride round the lake but not worth risking getting caught. Might be in even more trouble. Another ten days to go. Life stinks at the moment in more ways than one. My hands got all oily and I've had to use masses of Swarfega to get the black grease off. Don't know whether Rupert really knows what he is doing. Apparently Veronica and Vanessa Mawgan-Whitely are home and are at Lake House with the gang. Daisy seems to be jumping Guy Fawkes cos Popcorn doesn't like jumping. According to Rupert she's quite good. Eloise says her dad is fed up with Simon. He hardly ever rides Melchior and Trish has had to exercise him. Mimi has asked Simon to join the gang, so suppose he will be there this afternoon. Poor old Adrian. Give my love to Abby and a big kiss to Noah, missing you, Gus.*'

Giles was scratching his hair as he wrestled with the idea of emulating Herbert Holmer who had just acquired a bulldog puppy. He found his finger pressing Safari and then typing in

English bulldog He now had his new prosthetic leg. He had been to London that morning and so far what the specialist had told him was proving to be true. He had walked from the hospital to Charing Cross Station and not felt a single twinge and had felt he was walking on air. He had silently thanked all the researchers who through their hard work and dedication were making his life more and more tolerable.

As he had turned into Back Lane he had involuntarily glanced towards the top of the green to the soon to be opened Casa sul Verde. He had cursed his ridiculous heart as it leapt when he had glimpsed a slim young woman with dark curly hair, almost reaching her shoulders, stepping into a navy blue Volvo. He had a strict conversation with himself.

'Forget the woman, Giles, for God's sake.'

'But how can I?' His wayward side answered.

The sensible side replied. *'Just because you've got a new leg it will always be the same.'*

'But it's pretty good,' romantic heart answered.

'Yes, but it will never be made of your own flesh and bone – forget her you idiot'.

'I can't. I can't – God help me.'

He had drawn up in front of Two Theobald's and rushed to his computer in search of solace from Herbert Holmer who had no inhibitions about arms, legs, or in fact any other part of his body. He had discovered his alto ego lying on a rug, playing with a young woman very much resembling Clarissa and an enchanting round, fat ball, which turned out to be a young bulldog puppy with the name of Boris.

Now, an hour and a half later and two chapters further into the intriguing life of Herbert Holmer, Giles was staring at a photograph of four bulldog puppies. Apparently they were just ten weeks old and ready to leave their mother. Giles decided if Herbert Holmer could cope with a roly-poly puppy then so could he, but in his heart he knew the puppy would need exercise, and where better to take him for his daily constitutional than round the green past the Casa sul Verde. He was well aware he was submitting himself to daily torture but he didn't care. All he required was just a glimpse of Clarissa to lighten his day.

He heard Georgia calling goodnight to Charlotte and called to her. 'Come and look at my computer.'

She ran into the dining room expecting to read about one of Herbert Holmer's latest escapades, instead of which she found herself gazing at four rotund bulldog puppies.

'Dad, why are you looking at puppies?' she asked her father.

'Herbert has got one now, Georgia and I think I should follow his lead. How would you like a drive to Eastbourne tomorrow and help me choose one?'

'Choose one – for us, Dad? Our own puppy. Gosh! Can Charlotte come with us?'

'You can certainly ask her if she would like to.'

The words were barely out of his mouth before Georgia was crashing on the front door of Number One Theobald's Row.

Esther opened the door as Georgia was gabbling. 'Please can Charlotte come with Dad and me to Eastbourne tomorrow? We're going to choose a puppy. Dad has suddenly decided he wants to exercise his new leg every day. He's going to buy a bulldog puppy and he's already found a litter on the Internet. He says we will leave here at ten o'clock.'

Esther smiled at the excited girl and told her. 'Charlotte is just seeing to Bouncer and Catherine Wheel. You'll find her in the paddock. As far as I am concerned she can certainly go with you and your father.'

With that Georgia ran through the kitchen door to find her friend filling two hay nets. It was soon agreed that Charlotte would join Georgia and Giles at ten o'clock the next morning.

In the end, Giles had one more passenger than he had bargained for when Georgia received a phone call from Orlando.

'Charlotte has told me she is going to see a puppy tomorrow morning with you and your dad. Is there room in the car for me as well? Ollie's got a rehearsal tomorrow morning for a concert he's doing with his guitar next week, I've asked Gran and she says I can come with you if your dad says it's O.K.'

Giles didn't mind. He was just relieved it wasn't Oscar who wanted to come. He told Georgia to tell Orlando he would pick him up at the farm gate at ten o'clock.

In Paris, Sam's mobile was ringing. *'Mum, it's 'Lando. Georgia's dad is taking Charlotte, Georgia and me to see some bulldog puppies somewhere near Eastbourne tomorrow morning. Gran says I can go. Ollie's got a rehearsal in Ashford. Grandpa John is taking him to the music school. I was going to help Rupert with his old bicycles but Gus text me and said it's not much fun. He spent most of the afternoon cleaning the oil off his hands. Giles says he'll buy us some lunch in a village he knows on the way home.'*

'That's fine 'Lando, but why does Giles want a bulldog? It seems rather a strange breed.'

'Cos Georgia says a man called Herbert someone or other has got one.'

Sam laughed. *'That's the detective he writes about'* Lando. *At least it won't need much exercising.'*

'According to Georgia, he wants to walk round the green everyday to exercise the new leg he got in London today.'

Sam had a good idea why Giles wanted to walk round the green and she didn't think the only reason was his new leg. *'Don't hurt yourself, Giles'*, she thought. *'She's caused you more than enough pain already'* – and her mind turned to the attractive brunette, Clarissa, whose acquaintance Tom and she had recently made outside her new venture, La Casa sul Verde.

CHAPTER 15

Orlando was sitting on the farm gate eagerly awaiting Giles. As he heard the church clock striking ten, as if on cue, the silver Volvo came into sight. Giles indicated to the vacant front seat and Orlando clambered in, carefully placing his grandmother's camera in the front pocket of the car. He wanted to take a picture of Giles' puppy with its brothers and sisters before it left the litter.

Georgia and Charlotte were sitting in the back with an elderly blanket folded between them, ready for the puppy to sit on whilst making the journey back to Massenden. Giles didn't want any mishaps on the back seat.

'Do you want a boy or a girl?' Orlando asked him.

'I'm not sure yet, Orlando but Herbert has got a boy called Boris, so I shall probably have the same.'

Orlando wondered who Herbert was and fleetingly wondered whether Giles was gay until he vaguely remembered his mother mentioning a detective called Herbert Holmer when she had been reading one of Giles' books. He had also heard her saying to his father, *'I do hope Giles isn't in for more heartbreak. I think it's rather insensitive of Clarissa to set up her new business in our village.'*

At half past eleven, mainly due to Giles excellent sat nav they were crawling down a very narrow lane in the extremely attractive village of East Dean – about four miles from Eastbourne. As the lane twisted and turned they finally pulled into the drive of a charming, red brick cottage where they could see a large penned area enclosing several bulldog puppies. A rotund bitch and an equally rounded, middle-aged woman were advancing towards them, a broad smile lighting up the latter's pleasant countenance. She shook hands with Giles and then greeted the three children warmly, immediately offering Giles a cup of coffee and as if by magic producing squash and biscuits for the youngsters.

She informed Giles she had already sold the largest bitch, but the other four puppies were all still available and having introduced them to Denzel, who was the father of the puppies and snoring very loudly, they proceeded excitedly into the enclosure in the garden.

It was extremely well constructed with a large kennel in one corner. The puppies were playing together, whilst their mother looked on placidly, occasionally giving the odd growl when the over exuberant puppies attempted to get her to join in their game. The bitch was considerably smaller than her brothers, but Giles had no hesitation in choosing his puppy. He had fallen for the smallest of the three boys. He liked the cream coat and the even brown markings round its eyes and the brown saddle across its back.

The children loved them all but Orlando thought of Bertie and Boz and the effervescent Holly and couldn't help wondering why Giles had chosen this particular breed with its plump body, supported by extremely short cabriole legs and its strangely pushed-in nose and he could still hear the older dog, Denzel snoring loudly enough to waken the dead. Then he remembered Giles' limp and he realized this was probably the perfect breed for him, for surely the boy thought, these weird stubby legs would not need much exercise.

He took a photograph of the mother and her pups before Giles carried the puppy back to the house to collect his pedigree and a bag of food to which he was already accustomed.

As Giles was writing a hefty cheque, Georgia noticed a copy of *To A Woman Scorned* lying on the coffee table. 'Oh,' she said involuntarily, 'you're reading my Dad's latest book.'

Mrs. O'Hara, the breeder, laughed. 'Oh no, dear. That's by my favourite author, she's called Patsy Sanders.'

It was Georgia's turn to laugh as her father was handing her a cheque signed Giles Norton. 'Patsy Sanders is my dad. Everyone thinks she's a woman – Dad and I are always laughing about that.'

Mrs. O'Hara looked at Giles. 'Herbert Holmer. He has a bulldog.'

'He most certainly has. Why else would I have one?' But the

lady was grabbing her book, handing it to Giles. 'Please could you sign it, Mr. Norton? I've got everyone of your books.' And with that she rushed upstairs to appear two minutes later with all eight of Giles notorious books, which he carefully signed on the flyleaf of each one, telling her. 'I'll send you a copy of the next one. I'm half way through at the moment, but I think it may be some while before I finish it. I think little Herbert here is going to take up a lot of my time from now on. I shall walk him round the village green at least twice a day. '*And we shall sit on the seat opposite La Casa Sul Verde',* he added silently to himself. '*Just one glimpse - one short glimpse. That's all I'm asking for.*'

Fortunately Georgia was completely unaware of her father's ulterior motive for obtaining the now snoring Herbert who was lying rather ungainly on the rug in between Charlotte and herself.

Giles drove to a nearby village where Mrs. O'Hara had told him of a teagarden where the puppy would be welcome and excellent sandwiches could be purchased.

They drove alongside the South Downs to the small village of Jevington where they soon turned into the car park, which led to the tea garden.

Giles had placed the rug on the grass and Herbert immediately closed his eyes and fell asleep as Georgia sat beside him making certain he didn't stray off the rug. He had already had his first injections but he needed to see James the following week for his final pricks.

They were all enjoying a huge plate of sandwiches when the garden gate opened and a man appeared with a rucksack on his back, leading a large black horse. He sat on a bench just inside the gate as the horse stood quietly beside him looking round at the other occupants in the garden.

Orlando leapt up, grabbing his gran's camera and walked up to the man, smiling and asking him. 'Wow, can I take a photo of you and your horse? I've never seen one in a tearoom before, well a garden at a tearoom. What's his name?'

'He's called Lani,' the man told Oscar with a smile.

'How old is he?'

'He's nineteen but he still loves his hacks over Beachy Head.'

Orlando patted Lani. 'My dad's horse Black Satin is twenty-four now, but he still hacks him out with us. He doesn't jump anymore though.'

The man, whose name it appeared was Glyn, looked at the young boy with his gold curls and piercing blue eyes. He reminded him of someone he'd often seen and admired on the television. 'What's you name, young man?' he asked Orlando.

'Orlando. Orlando West.'

'I think your dad is my idol. Is his name Tom?'

'Yea. Tom West. I'm staying with my gran at the moment cos dad and mum are in Paris. Two of my brothers and my sister are there with them but I said I would stay with Ollie cos he's in a concert next week. He's rehearsing. He sings and plays the guitar when he's not riding his pony Buck's Fizz. Is Lani a Welsh Cob?'

Glyn was impressed by the young boy's knowledge.

'Yes, he's a registered section D. Welsh Cob, I've had him over fifteen years.'

Orlando held Lani whilst Glyn mounted, and then pulled three pony nuts out of his pocket, which he gave to Lani before opening the gate for him as he and Glyn made their way back to Eastbourne across the South Downs. Orlando went back to the girls who were lying on the rug with Herbert, who was by now wide-awake and trying to chew the buttons off Georgia's jacket.

Giles bought them all an ice cream before Herbert was lifted back into the car and was making his way to his new home in Massenden.

That night his whimpers and wails could be heard all over the cottage and he spent the entire night snoring loudly on Giles' duvet.

Whilst Giles had been choosing his new sleeping companion, the men had been working hard in Paris and they had all qualified for the Grand Prix on the Sunday afternoon. Tom had chosen to ride Kaspar and he had not been disappointed when he had finished in an excellent third place behind Charles and the German Hans Weiss, with Justin and Jock in fourth and fifth places. Kaspar would rest the next day, whilst Madame would enter the speed class after which, after much debating between Tom and Sam, Clementine was to make her debut in the Puissance.

It would be the first Puissance Tom would have attempted since his success with Satin at the tender age of seventeen, when he hadn't a care in the world and danger was not a word he was associated with. Now he was a father of five children and he had promised Sam the minute he felt Clementine starting to falter he would pull out. Tom knew she was capable of jumping well over seven feet as unbeknown even to Sam, she had proved to him several times in the school at Lake House.

Sam wasn't exactly happy, but she realized Tom wasn't quite the headstrong teenager he had once been now over fourteen years ago and also that Clementine wasn't a highly charged character like Black Satin, but even so, as she acknowledged to Anna and Joanna, she would be more than happy when the ordeal was over, but Oscar and Joshua could barely wait until the following evening. Oscar insisted that one day he would jump the big wall at Olympia and he was determined to do it at an even younger age than his father had done.

Earlier that evening, Madame had jumped cleanly into fifth place in the class Justin had won on his old friend, Mr. Pickwick.

At eight thirty all the Lake House supporters were ensconced in a box at the side of the arena in full sight of the big, red wall.

Rosie was holding Sam's hand and Oscar was sitting between Anne-Marie and Joshua, barely blinking and not taking his eyes of the huge jump his father and Clem were about to attempt.

Clementine was not one of the fastest horses on the current

circuit and Charles was awaiting her appearance in the Puissance with interest. Speed was not a factor in this class and he was certain this could be her forté.

He sat on one side of Sam, remembering her fainting at his feet as Satin had pranced into the arena fourteen years ago to clear the wall and take the trophy and the enormous cheque that went with it.

The class was small with only ten entries. They did however include Hans Weiss and his latest Puissance horse, Scarlet Ribbons. By the end of the third round only four of the original ten starters were left in the competition, and of those one was Han Weiss and another was Tom West, and after the fourth round there were only two left to fight it out.

Hans Scarlet Ribbons was getting more and more excited and white foam was appearing over her neck and chest. Meanwhile, Clementine remained herself, calm and unflustered.

As the red wall reached seven feet two inches, the judges asked both Hans and Tom. 'Do you wish to continue?'

Tom's answer was spontaneous. 'Of course, Clem is enjoying herself,' but to his amazement Hans declined. 'Scarlet has had enough; she's getting too excited. I'll call it a day.'

Tom was disappointed. Clem had felt as if she could go on forever – but in the box, apart from Oscar, everyone was relieved when the announcement came over the public address system that Han Weiss was withdrawing his mare, Scarlet Ribbons, therefore Tom West and Lake House Clementine were the automatic winners.

'Cor, what a swizz, Clem was going brilliantly. Dad must be sick.' Oscar complained.

At that moment Sam didn't care how her husband was feeling. She was just happy it was all over before she had fainted at Charles' feet.

Oscar followed Tom back to the stables, stroking Clementine. 'Cor, Dad. That was – that was whatever that funny long word Rosie's always saying, and bloody exciting. Cor. Five more years and you can let me ride Clem in the Puissance at H.O.Y.S. You were seventeen – I'll bloody do it at sixteen.'

Tom shook his head at his son in despair. 'Oscar, please for the last time of asking will you refrain from using that word. You know it upsets your Mum and probably Clem isn't too pleased to hear it either.'

Oscar's high spirits could not be dampened. 'O.K. Dad,' and then, completely oblivious of Hans, who was following just a few feet behind them added in his loudest voice. 'I thought Hans was like you, Dad – but God what a pathetic wimp, but it was obvious Clem was going to beat him. He's a bloody coward.'

Hans had had his horse's interests at heart and his temper had reached boiling point, when he heard Tom's quiet voice remonstrating once again with his son. 'Oscar, will you stop using that word and Hans is definitely neither a wimp nor a coward. One day, hopefully, when you are a lot more mature, you will learn when your horse or pony has had enough. If you are as good a horseman as Hans is then you will understand when it is the right time to stop before your horse injures itself.'

'Oh. Like when Humbug starts pulling my arms out. But that's fun Dad.'

'You are an over enthusiastic young boy, Oscar who has not had to endure three broken legs like Hans has.'

'Wow *three* broken legs. Does he screw them back on like Georgia's Dad?'

'No, Oscar, usually when you break your leg it's put into plaster and after several weeks the bones have joined together again. Giles accident was quite different. His legs were blown to pieces by a mine. It was impossible to mend it.'

Oscar was finally silenced until he turned round and noticed Hans behind him. He gave the German a sympathetic look. 'Actually, I don't think you are too much of a coward Mr. Weiss and I'm so glad you don't have to screw your legs back on like Georgia's father. I'm going to jump Clem in the Puissance when I'm sixteen and I've already talked to Satin about it. He says Clem and I are definitely going to win. I shall be even younger than my dad was and I'm certain my girlfriend won't be feeble like Mum was. Annie won't faint at anyone's feet.'

Hans laughed at Tom's fury as he told his son. 'Mum is not feeble, Oscar. How can she possibly be when she has to put up with your nonsense all and every day and anyway by the time you are sixteen you and Annie may not even be talking too each other?'

Oscar shook his head at his father in disbelief. 'Dad, if there is one thing I am even more certain about than winning the Puissance it's that Annie will be watching me with every one of her fingers and her toes crossed. We are like you and Mum. Ad infinitum.'

Tom was silenced by those earnest words. He had simply no more to say. He just hoped his young son's heart would never be broken, but five years when you are a young teenager is a very long time, so much could lie ahead and happily for everyone concerned, he could not know that the monumental mountain Oscar and Anne-Marie would one day have to climb would be even larger than the enormous red brick wall at H.O.Y.S.

Giles was exhausted. He felt that matchsticks were holding his eyes open. He was on the phone speaking to James.

'James, I'm really sorry to bother you, but can you suggest anything I can do to keep a puppy quiet at night? I bought a bulldog pup three days ago and I haven't slept since. The only place he will lie is on my pillow and either snores in my ear or licks my face all night.'

James laughed. *'You must be firm from the beginning,'* he told Giles – steadfastly ignoring the fact that eight years after acquiring The Pooch, the little dog still slept at the end of their bed. *'Put him firmly in his basket in the kitchen – leave the radio on, preferably with voices talking and put a reasonably loud ticking clock in his bed. I can guarantee it will work.'* And a vision of The Pooch floated in front of him once more. *'Anyway it's definitely worth a try. When does he have his final injections?'*

'At the end of next week.'

'Well, I suggest once he's had those, take him round the green just before you go to bed, a walk sometimes helps to settle a puppy. I wish you luck, Giles, but I'm afraid I am a mere vet, not an animal behaviourist.'

'I'll try anything James.' And having put the phone down, he went into the dining room and wound up the antique mantle clock, which had been his grandmother's pride and joy - wrapped it up in a tea towel and placed it in Herbie's basket. He then borrowed an old radio from Esther and turned to Radio Two.

That night there was a slight improvement and by the time Herbie's injections were due Giles was once more enjoying unbroken nights.

'Thanks, James,' he said, as James deftly administered Herbie's final jabs and put the kennel cough drops up the snorting little nose. 'Your advice was first class. Not a sound for the last six nights. I shall certainly recommend you to every new puppy owner I come across,' and the happy author strode out of the surgery with the portly little bulldog rolling after him on its short stubby legs, whilst a perplexed vet was shaking his head. *'Where on earth had Elizabeth and he gone wrong with The Pooch,'* he was asking himself.

CHAPTER 16

Finally, after what seemed for ever, Rosie and Gus's suspensions were over and at half past eight that same morning there was a frantic knock on the kitchen door at Woodcutters and Rosie rushed to it, tugging it open and clasping Gus round his waist, telling Sam. 'We're going for a ride, Mum.'

Sam looked at her young daughter. 'Hold on a minute, young lady. Just where are you off to?'

'Round the lake to the stables, Daisy is meeting us there with Popcorn, then we're going to meet Oscar and Anne-Marie at Old Tiles and then ride back to the school where Charles is going to give *the gang* a lesson. Joanna is making a picnic for us all after we've had a swim and a work out in the gym. After lunch Gus, Abby, Daisy and I are going to play tennis at Lake House.'

'Well your day seems well planned, Rosie. Miriam will be here all day. Be sure to be home by six o'clock all of you and she will give you your supper. I told you last evening, I am going to take Snow Queen to Gloucestershire with Susan. She is going to share the driving with me. Daddy is jumping in Antwerp at three o'clock our time this afternoon – you can call him just before you have your supper and see how Opal got on in the Nation's Cup. Give him my love and tell him I will speak to him after the evening competition he's doing with The Wizard.'

'O.K. Mums, we'll be good,' and Sam crossed her fingers hoping they all meant what they were saying as she loaded Snow Queen into her silver trailer, happily totally oblivious that today would be the last time she would enjoy the luxury of Tom's generous Christmas present.

Sam and Susan both fell in love with the beautiful show pony stallion and having said goodbye to Snow Queen for the next few months and enjoyed a delicious lunch with Anna, the owner of the stud and given a hug to the now long retired Ladybird, set off with Susan behind the wheel, arriving back at Woodcutters at six forty five to discover her offspring devouring a chicken casserole with Miriam. According to her there had been no unforeseen problems during the course of the day and to Sam's total surprise Rosie was now begging for a tennis racquet for her forthcoming birthday. Tennis was a sport quite alien to Tom and herself but apparently Rosie had really enjoyed her afternoon and now tennis was high on her agenda. John was an excellent player and when later that evening Sam told him how much Rosie had enjoyed her first attempt at the game, he immediately told her he and Mary would give her a racquet for her birthday. Apparently they could buy it through the Massenden tennis club who had a discount arrangement with the local sports shop.

The following morning, Sam glanced at the calendar, which hung above Tom's desk in his study. *The first of April. April fools day.* It was a day she had hated since she had been fourteen years old and she and Tom had ridden to the old quarry in Ribbenden. There was an old millpond at the bottom and they had tied The Likely Lad and Moonstone to a strong branch of a large oak tree. They had sat down by the pond and Tom had handed her a plastic box of sandwiches he had made. When she had opened the lid she had found she was staring at an enormous black spider. Her screams had rung out across the quarry as she had thrown both the container and the sandwiches far into the middle of the pond. Tom had rolled on the grass laughing, his unkempt blond curls falling wildly onto his neck and his blue eyes sparking with fun, *April fool*, he had yelled, *fooled you Sammy.* He was still laughing until he realized Sam was almost hysterical. The expression on his laughing face had changed and he had held her close. Soon the fear of the spider had disappeared but she was now afraid of the feeling that was overpowering her body. She had pulled away from him, running to Moonstone, leaving him to clear up the picnic - by the time he had done that she was galloping, flying back up the hill towards

Massenden and Honeysuckle Cottage where she had slammed the door and run to her bedroom, leaving Moonstone loose to eat the grass in the garden. Five minutes later she had received a text. *'Sammy, I'm truly sorry - I never meant to frighten you. It was only a silly piece of black plastic.'*

She had sent him a text back. *'It's not the spider Tom. It's myself I'm afraid of. I want us to go back to being children again. I don't want to grow up.'*

Tom's reply had been immediate. *'We have to, my Sammy, there is no going back but I promise I will always look after you. Always.'*

Sam had hated that date ever since and now here it was once again. She brought herself back to the present. One day all her boys and Rosie would have to grow up – but not just yet she told herself. Let them enjoy being children for as long as possible, but she sighed as she watched Gus as he helped Rosie into his grandfather's Range Rover, his young hands firmly propelling her small bum into the rear seat and then sitting down beside her.

The more advanced show jumping members of *the gang* were off to a large affiliated show in West Sussex. Charles huge horsebox was loaded with Pie in The Sky, Hamlet, Lord of the Rings and Babushka in the front and Rupert's Alfie and The March Hare behind them with Rosie's Sparkler and The Duc at the very back in the last two places. Dom was driving and Charles bundled Rupert and Mimi into the Range Rover to join Rosie and Gus.

Tony was driving the The Equitation Centre's large green and white box with Beau Geste and The Flying Fox, Eloise's little Pierrot, Tilly's Bits n Pieces and Joshua's Ganger and Lily. They set off behind Charles with Jean – Pierre following in his Range Rover with Josh and Tilly as well as his own youngsters.

Elizabeth was late as usual, partly because the twins were in a particularly fractious mood with each other and partly because she was never on time. At last, Poupée was established in the front stall, with Torchlight beside her and when at last Jet Steam and Buck's Fizz were installed, Elizabeth's groom Maurice leapt into the driving seat and started the engine, as Fenella sat beside her mother in the Thornley's B.M.W. with Orlando and Oliver separating the still squabbling twins.

Only Sam's trailer, now attached to Tom's Range Rover was left in the yard at Woodcutters. Sam helped Oscar load Humbug and Whisky, and then kissed both him and Anne-Marie before they climbed into the back of the Range Rover. Sam patted Humbug and Whisky and waved goodbye to Adrian and the two children. As they disappeared out of the drive, she shut the yard gate and went to talk to Satin, who was crashing on his stable door. She offered him a handful of pony nuts, but he refused to take them, blowing in her face and throwing his head up and down, almost hitting it on the lintel over the stable door. He was obviously upset about something and Sam wished Tom were there to ask him what was the matter.

She couldn't stay all day talking to Satin; she was going straight to South Lodge to collect Noah who she was looking after for the day. She could already see two enormous removal vans outside South Lodge and four men going in and out carrying boxes and crates and various pieces of furniture. Justin and Anna's big day had finally arrived and when Gus and Abby arrived back from the show they would be taken straight to Theobald's Place.

It was with a great deal of relief that Anna handed Noah to Sam. He was clutching his riding hat in one hand and Justin's old, threadbare teddy, from which he refused to be parted, in the other.

It was a gloriously warm, sunny morning and Sam drove straight to the stables, put the basket saddle on to Amelia, pushed Noah's hat firmly on his head, squashing Ted Bear in the basket beside the toddler.

Ten minutes later, as Noah was chuckling and Sam's legs were beginning to tire from obeying the little boy's constant urge to trot faster, she heard her mobile ringing. She pulled it out of her pocket; at the same time keeping a firm hold of Amelia. She looked at the incoming number and certainly didn't recognize the caller.

'Hello,' she answered, still out of breath from her exertion with Noah and Amelia.

'Is that Mrs. Samantha West?' an unfamiliar voice asked her.

'Yes, yes. Who is that?'

'You won't know me. My name is Lance Cole. I am a solicitor from Ashford. I'm afraid I have some bad news.'

Sam's legs shook, her thoughts immediately rushing to Tom who was in Antwerp with James.

'Bbbad news?' she managed to whisper to this unfamiliar voice.

'I am afraid there has been an accident about four miles from Massenden at Three Lanes Cross. Now first of all, the children are not seriously hurt. They are however, trapped in the back of the vehicle. A boy and a girl about eleven or twelve years old, they have been cut and are bruised, but fortunately the boy managed to throw his jacket over the girl's face saving her from the worst of the glass. She was sitting on the side of the car that was hit. I was following the trailer and was the first on the scene. I've sent for the emergency services and they are on their way but I've talked through the broken window to the young lad and he says he wants his mum and dad. He gave me your number.'

Sam was shaking from head to foot, trying to think quickly whom she could ask to look after Noah.

'Oh, my God. My God. I'll get there as soon as I possibly can. I'm a little way from my car at the moment. I'm looking after a friend's small boy but I will be with you shortly. What about the driver, our groom, Adrian, and the ponies?'

'The whole lot is on its side at the moment. The driver looks bad I am afraid. He's not moving and certainly not conscious. The trailer is badly damaged, I can hear some movement but I can't do any more until the fire brigade arrives with their cutting tools. I've also called the local vets. I think they will be needed. There is a huge tail back of traffic in each direction; the lorry that hit your family is right across the road. It is foreign. It appears to be from

Poland. Oh, thank God, I can hear sirens. I had better ring off.' As he did so Sam tore back to her car, after calling Old Tiles.

John immediately promised to come to Lake House with Mary who would take Noah back to the farm for the day and he would take Sam to Three Lanes Cross.

The rest of *the gang* had no idea any problems had occurred and were proceeding happily to the borders of West Sussex. Elizabeth was completely oblivious of the near miss she had had. Her sat nav had taken her down an extremely narrow lane and to her relief she was just re-joining the main road, bypassing the accident of which she was totally unaware. She noticed a long backlog of traffic in the opposite direction and vaguely wondered what had caused it, but fortunately had no idea of the carnage that lay behind her. If she had ignored her sat nav, which she often did it would most likely have been her B.M.W. the lorry would have hit.

Fortunately, John knew all the neighbouring farmers and he immediately got permission to drive through their fields, thus avoiding the seemingly unending line of traffic. He pulled up at the gate nearest to Three Lanes Cross and ran, his heart thumping as he saw the scene in front of him. As he arrived he saw his young grandson and the little French girl being carefully lifted out of the rear of the Range Rover, realising a car any less solid and the fate of the two youngsters would have been a completely different story. They were both covered in fragments of glass, which was embedded in their hair and their clothes and Anne-Marie had a long, deep gash on the side of her right leg.

Sam had finally reached Oscar and Anne-Marie and was clutching them to her at the same time looking with horror at Adrian, who was still entangled in the twisted metal.

She was being ushered into a waiting ambulance with the two children almost before she knew where she was, and was on her way to Maidstone.

The air ambulance had arrived. It had been established that Adrian had severe head injuries and it was waiting to fly him to London as soon as it was possible to extract him from the tangled mess.

Another fire engine had now arrived and had cut the trailer free and a hoist was endeavouring to right Sam's once beautiful trailer. At last it was possible to cut open the groom's door. As John looked inside he turned away and was violently sick in the hedge. He was a farmer who had experienced many tragedies and difficult situations over the years, but this was the most heartbreaking he had ever encountered. The partition was smashed to pieces and Whisky had definitely come off the worst.

Mathew Parker, the chief vet from the Massenden practice ended his suffering in less than a minute. Humbug had fallen on top of the partition and was struggling to get back on his feet as large pieces of jagged wood were puncturing his neck, his body and his legs, but at least he was alive.

With John's help and also that of two local farmers, once the side of the trailer had been cut away it was possible to remove Humbug and get him into the horse ambulance. With the young assistant vet driving and Mathew and the two farmers supporting Humbug, at the same time trying to stem the flow of blood from the worst of the wounds, they were travelling as fast as was feasibly possible to the horse surgery in Massenden at the rear of the veterinary practice.

John turned his attention back to Adrian who was by now almost free of the twisted metal. He was breathing but unconscious. Once he was in the air ambulance John got back into his Range Rover and drove back to Massenden drawing up at Shepherd's Cottage where he could see Amy sitting on a garden bench, happily nursing her two-week-old baby. Miriam's husband George was mowing the lawn next door.

John walked slowly up to the older man who looked more than a little surprised to see John who was deathly white, telling him. 'George, I am afraid I have some terrible news. A Polish lorry has smashed into Tom's Range Rover, which Adrian was driving with the trailer to Sussex. Anne-Marie and Oscar were in the back.

Fortunately they are not badly hurt but I'm afraid your son is in a bad way. He is being air lifted to hospital in London with head injuries.'

George was staggering in front of John who put out a hand to steady him. 'God, John. Poor, poor Amy. We must tell her at once and get her to London.'

As George broke the news to Amy, John caught the distraught girl as she fell into his arms.

'We'll find out which hospital he's being taken to, Amy and I will drive you and Molly there. Get some nappies and a warm shawl and I'll ring the police and find out where they are taking him.'

At that moment John's phone rang. It was the police. *'Right, I will bring his wife and their tiny baby straight away. It will probably take us a couple of hours. It all depends on the traffic.'*

He turned to Amy. 'They have taken him to Moorfields in London. I'll set the sat-nav. Bring all you need for Molly and we'll get going.' In less than five minutes, with Molly's buggy in the back of the Range Rover, John was tearing out of Massenden choosing the route Elizabeth had taken earlier, avoiding the scene of the accident. It was the last thing John wanted Amy to see.

In Maidstone hospital, Sam's mobile was ringing. It was Tom. *'Darling, what the hell has happened?'*

'Tom, I've been trying to get you, you weren't picking up your phone.'

'Sorry but James and I were exercising the horses. We'd turned our mobiles off but Mathew Parker has just got hold of James.'

'Tom, what did he tell James? I'm in Maidstone hospital in the A. and E. with Ozzie and Anne-Marie. They have been so lucky. They've got lots of minor cuts and bruises and Anne-Marie has one nasty gash on her leg but they will be allowed home either this evening or tomorrow morning but I left with them before they had got the trailer open or freed Adrian. What did Mathew tell James?'

'Sammy, I am afraid it is really bad news. Ozzie is going to be devastated. Whisky is dead and Humbug really badly injured. I have told Mathew to do everything possible to save him. I am getting the one o'clock flight back to Gatwick. I'll get a cab straight to Maidstone hospital and we'll tell him together. Dad has taken Amy and Molly to Moorfields Hospital in London. Adrian has severe head and eye injuries It's not good, Sammy. I've called Justin – he's left for Sussex. He'll give Dom his Range Rover and drive the horsebox home. Dom and Genny will want to be with Anne-Marie.'

Sam couldn't answer. *'Sammy, are you still there?'*

Sam sobbed. *'Yes, yes, Tommy. Satin was upset when the trailer left this morning. He was trying to tell me something. I wish you had been there, you would have understood what he was saying. He knew something bad was going to happen. What about the lorry that hit Adrian?'*

'Barely a scratch on the driver. Sod's law, but I shall sue him for every penny I can get. Apparently there are several reliable witnesses who saw him coming straight across the road without even slowing down. God, poor little Amy - poor, poor girl. James is flying home too. Neither of us feels like jumping at the moment. We both just want to get home. Sally will drive the horses to Massenden this evening. God, I can't bear the thought of seeing Ozzie's little face. Poor kid, he dotes on Humbug and Whisky. Poor, little sod.'

By the time Rosie's class was over, the whole of the Lake House group was getting more and more anxious.

Where on earth could Adrian and Oscar and Anne-Marie be?

By the end of the next class Dom and Genevieve were sick with worry. They had tried calling Anne-Marie's mobile but were not receiving a reply and when they tried to call Oscar it was also to no avail. Just as Mimi was about to mount Babushka, Charles couldn't believe his eyes when he saw Justin running across the showground towards the collecting ring.

'Dad,' he gasped, completely out of breath. 'There has been a really bad accident. A Polish lorry has crashed into Tom's Range Rover and trailer. As you know Adrian was driving. He has been airlifted to Moorfields Hospital in London. Oz and Anne-Marie are in Maidstone A. and E. Sam is with them. They're shaken and cut and bruised but nothing too terrible. They were extremely lucky. Sadly it's not the same happy scenario for the ponies. The trailer was a complete write off. Whisky is dead and Humbug has terrible injuries. Ozzie doesn't know yet. Tom and James are flying home as we speak, and he and Sam will tell him together. Dom must take my Range Rover to Maidstone to Anne-Marie and I will drive the horsebox home.'

'Where is Anna?' Charles asked his son.

'Jean-Pierre has sent Tony and Trish to Theobald's Place to help her with the move. I had to get here A.S.A.P.'

Dom and Genevieve were racing across the practice area towards Justin and Charles. 'What's happened? What's happened?' Dom was asking Justin.

'Dom, there has been an accident. I promise you Anne-Marie is not badly hurt. She and Oz are with Sam at the A. and E. at Maidstone Hospital. A foreign lorry hit the Range Rover and trailer. Unfortunately Adrian has come off the worst. He has severe head injuries, but Oz was very quick to react and threw his jacket over your little one's face. They have got cuts and bruises and Anne-Marie has a large gash on her leg but the main problem is shock, so it's possible the hospital might want to keep them there overnight, but they have been extremely lucky. Unfortunately, Whisky and Humbug are a different story. Oz doesn't know yet, but Whisky is dead and it's highly likely Humbug may never compete again. It's too early for Mathew Parker, the chief vet to know. He is pulling out all the stops but Humbug is currently having a blood transfusion, he has so many deep puncture wounds. Tom and James are flying home this afternoon. Sam is not telling Oscar anything until Tom is with him too. Poor lad, his heart is going to break. Anyhow, now you must take my Range Rover and get to Anne-Marie. Take care and I promise you she is not in any danger at all. Sam says they have both been given something to make them sleep for a few hours. I will drive the horsebox back to Massenden.'

Dom looked gratefully at Justin. 'Justin, but your move?'

'That's O.K, Dom. That's a minor detail in the circumstances. Jane has sent Tony and Trish to help Anna and Mary is looking after Noah at the farm. Poor Amy. They have only been married a week and little Molly – just two weeks old. Let us pray Adrian comes out of this coma soon. Now give me the keys of the horsebox and here are the ones for the Range Rover.' The two men exchanged keys before Dom and Genevieve ran to the Range Rover and started their journey to Maidstone.

Mimi rode up to Justin and her father. 'Justin, why are you here? I thought you and Anna were moving today.'

'We are, Mimi, but there has been an accident.'

Mimi looked at Justin. 'Something has happened to Ozzie and Anne-Marie, hasn't it?' she almost whispered.

'Yes, Mimi, I am afraid it has. We all need to get back home. Ozzie and Anne-Marie are in Maidstone Hospital. They have lots of cuts and bruises but fortunately neither of them is seriously hurt, but sadly, Adrian has had to be flown to a hospital in London. He has bad head injuries. John has taken Anna and Molly to be with him.'

Fortunately, Mimi was so upset for Anna and Molly she forgot to ask any questions about the two ponies.

'I will go and cancel the rest of out entries Dad, whilst you gather all the kids together,' and Justin hurried in the direction of the secretary's tent, where he met Lionel, who looked more than a little surprised to see him.

'Justin, I thought you were moving house today. I thought that's why you were unable to be in my Nation's Cup team in Antwerp yesterday?'

‘It was, Lionel. I’m only here because there has been a terrible accident near Massenden this morning. Both Oscar’s pones were involved. Whisky is dead and it’s touch and go with Humbug. It will be months before he can jump again, if indeed he is ever able to. Oz is in hospital with Anne-Marie. They were in the back of the Range Rover. Sam is waiting for Tom to get home before they break the news to him about the ponies. Poor kid. I know he is a young rascal but he loves those ponies so much. We shall have to find him something else to ride as soon as possible or he is going to be totally lost. The worst of all though is Tom’s groom, Adrian. He’s been flown to London with really bad head and eye injuries.’

Lionel had an immediate image of Oscar’s cheeky face. He had a soft spot for the little boy who had jumped fearlessly on the strong Whisky and the hotheaded Humbug. He suddenly recalled a very special pony, which was wasting its life either standing in its stable or wandering aimlessly around its paddock. Lady Lavinia Causton-James, otherwise the Countess of Markeley and owner of Goldfinger had often discussed her granddaughters and their shameful neglect of the brilliant pony. He decided to phone her that evening when he got home.

The children were all standing in a circle, some like Mimi, Josh and Jacques holding their ponies who had been due to jump early in the next class.

‘I’m sorry kids, but we have to get home straight away. There has been an accident. Now, I promise you ‘Lando and Ollie, although Oz is in hospital, he is not badly hurt. Just cuts, bruises and shock and it is the same for Anne-Marie, but I am afraid Adrian has been badly hurt. A lorry hit them at Three Lanes Cross as they were leaving Massenden this morning.’

In spite of Charles’ reassuring words, Orlando and Oliver were sobbing and Rosie was screaming as she turned and hid her face in Gus’s chest. It was Josh who asked Charles, ‘The ponies, Charles? What about the ponies?’

Charles had no intention of telling them the bad news here at the show. That could wait until they were home and Tom and Sam were with them. He just told Joshua. 'They are quite badly hurt, Joshua, but for now we all need to get the ponies loaded and make our way home. All of you travel back in the same vehicle as you came in this morning. Justin will be driving the Lake House horsebox instead of Dom who has gone to Maidstone to be with Anne-Marie.'

Whilst the sad cavalcade was making its way back to Massenden, Tom had arrived at the hospital. Oscar and Anne-Marie had both woken from a two-hour sleep and were half-heartedly eating a fish pie and some frozen peas.

Shortly after Tom's arrival, Dom and Genevieve had rushed into the ward, relieved to see their young daughter sitting up and at least making an effort to eat her supper. The doctor had spoken with Sam and suggested it would be best if both Oscar and Anne-Marie stayed overnight in the children's ward and would go home after he had seen them again the following morning. To Genevieve's relief she had been told she and Dom could stay at the hospital with the children who had been put together in a small side ward.

Sam and Tom knew they needed to get home to the rest of their children. They had to tell them the devastating news. Tom had called James who had gone straight to the surgery to see Humbug. Apparently he was heavily sedated and still having a blood transfusion although he did appear to be holding his own. Sadly he had lost his left eye, in spite of Mathew's desperate attempt to save it, but the task had proved impossible.

Tom asked James to make sure that Whisky's ashes were put in a casket and they would bury him under the acer tree next to Rascal.

Tom sat on the edge of Oscar's bed as Dom took Anne-Marie's hand.

'Oscar, there is something you have to know.'

Oscar saw the look on his father's face. 'Dad, are the ponies O.K.? Whisky and Humbug?'

'Oz, there is no easy way to tell you this. You have to be extremely brave. I'm sorry, so sorry but Whisky is dead and Humbug is very badly injured. Darling Ozzie, just hold me and cry as much as you want to.'

At last Oscar asked Tom. 'Where is Humbug?'

'He's with Uncle James at the surgery. He's having a blood transfusion like Mummy had last year.'

'How long will it be before he can jump again?'

'Ozzie we don't know yet. It's too early even for the vets to know, but he might find it difficult. He has lost his left eye you see.' At which Oscar sobbed and sobbed until at last, completely exhausted, he fell asleep in Tom's arms.

Tom's mobile bleeped. It was James. *'Tom, I'm back home and I've got all your family here. Lizzie suggests they stay here tonight. We've turned the ponies out in one of our paddocks, then you and Sam can stay at the hospital with Ozzie, I imagine he is pretty cut up.'*

'Yes. Not good, James. He's distraught. He has cried himself to sleep.'

'Look, Tom. I'm fairly used to dealing with having to give my clients bad news, would you like me to tell the rest of your family? I'll take great care of Rosie. Gus and Abby are here too. Theobald's Place is in chaos at the moment. Mary is hanging on to Noah for the night so that Anna and Justin only have to get one bed sorted. Of course Anna is desperately concerned about Amy. It could be a good thing for Rosie to have Gus with her. They can all have a sleep over in the old nursery, we've got masses of sleeping bags.'

'Thanks a ton, James, you're a friend in a thousand.'

James sat all the children round the kitchen table, at the same time siting Rosie on his knee. 'First of all, the good news. Oscar and Anne-Marie will be home tomorrow morning. They have both got lots of cuts and bruises and they have had a really bad shock, but Oscar is very, very unhappy and your Mum and Dad are going to stay at the hospital with him tonight.'

James noticed Oliver and Orlando were both sucking their thumbs and Rosie was clutching his hand tightly. Joshua was staring at him with wide eyes as he continued, 'I know you are all going to be really sad too, but unfortunately the lorry didn't just hit the Range Rover, it hit the trailer as well. Humbug is at the surgery. He has lost a lot of blood and he has had a blood transfusion. He has lots and lots of cuts and bruises but worst of all he has lost one of his eyes. He will be able to see perfectly out of his right eye but we shan't know for many weeks or even months whether he will ever have the confidence to jump again.'

'So is Whisky at home, Uncle James?' Orlando asked.

James tightened his grip on Rosie. 'I'm really sorry *gang* there is no easy way to tell you – I am afraid Whisky is dead. You must all help Ozzie, it is a huge shock for all of you, but for Oz, for the moment it is the end of his world.'

Without any hesitation, Orlando, Josh and Rosie spoke together. 'He can borrow Lily,' this was from Josh. 'I will ask Charles if he can ride Jet,' from Orlando and finally from Rosie, 'or the Duc,' but everyone was crying, including Elizabeth. It was a truly dreadful evening.

The following morning Anne-Marie and Oscar were safely back in their homes, scarred and bruised but thankfully with no serious injuries apart from Oscar's broken heart. Anne-Marie was helping Genevieve gather all her clothes and special books and toys, putting them into suitcases and boxes ready for the move to South Lodge in two day's time.

Now, once more bereft of his Range Rover, Tom had borrowed Sam's car and driven to London to see Adrian, who had regained consciousness for a few minutes, but had now drifted back into oblivion. The triplets all wanted to see Humbug. They insisted they were going to sit by his stable at the surgery all day.

Sam didn't argue with them. She made them a packet of sandwiches, took a bottle of lemonade out of the fridge and rang the surgery to ask Mathew Parker if he had any objections. When he said he hadn't, she sent them on their way.

Joshua was helping George with the mucking out – without both Adrian and Amy, Tom was extremely short staffed. Joshua was aware George's thoughts were not in Massenden but miles away in London thinking about his son and worrying about Amy and little Molly. Suddenly he heard footsteps and looked up to see his grandfather and heard him saying. 'Thought you could probably do with some help here, George,' and picking up a hayfork, immediately plunging into action.

'I know Tom is on his way to London. We are all praying for your son, George. There is going to be a massive enquiry into this accident. We have some excellent witnesses, including one lady who says she drives that route every day and just missed being hit by the same lorry last week in exactly the same place. Tom and Charles won't rest until they get more than adequate compensation. Luckily everything at Lake House Stables is well insured but that is no compensation for you and your family at the moment and for what your poor son is suffering.'

'It's not good news. John. Adrian had a severe hemorrhage behind his eyes. He is in the best hospital he can possibly be but even they fear for his long-term eyesight. Poor, little Amy. Married for just one week and with tiny little Molly. Poor kids. Life is just not fair. How are Oscar and the little girl?'

'I gather Oscar is devastated about Whisky. Sam says he is sitting in the recovery stable at the vet's surgery where Humbug is. Poor pony has lost an eye. God, what a terrible, terrible day.'

Sam watched as just after three thirty she saw Tom walking up the path. Her heart sank as she saw the look of total exhaustion in the demeanor of his body language and the greyness, which seemed to be covering his face.

He walked past her without even acknowledging she was there – went into the sitting room, opened a cupboard and poured himself a glass of neat whisky, then sat on the settee with his head in his hands. She left him alone for a few minutes and then made herself a cup of tea and sat beside him on the settee. To her dismay, she realized Tom was crying. She put her arms round him asking him. 'Darling, please tell me? Surely Adrian is still with us?'

'God, Sammy, this is a true, true nightmare, Yes, the surgeons are pretty sure he will pull through but unfortunately the front of the lorry came right through the side of the Range Rover. That crazy idiot must have been going at some pace. It hit the back of Adrian's head, causing a bad hemorrhage behind his eyes. He regained consciousness about an hour before I left. He was distraught. He couldn't see anything and he had no idea who any of us were or even his name. Amy is beside herself. He had no idea who was talking to him and certainly no inkling that Molly was his daughter. I spoke to the surgeon. He said it was too soon to know what recovery he will make. They are going to do lots more tests once he is in a fit state to have them.'

Sam slipped her hands under Tom's shirt, undoing the buttons and laying her head on his chest. 'Oh, Tom, whatever have Adrian and Amy done to deserve such a terrible tragedy. It's not fair. If you can manage without the car tomorrow, I will take Anna and Miriam to the hospital. I know they are desperate to see Amy. Jane says Noah can go and play with Rudi. It's really sad for Justin and Anna too. They had been looking forwards to moving to their lovely new home and now they can't think of anything except Adrian and his lovely little family.'

'Apparently the police have got several excellent witnesses, especially the solicitor who spoke to you on his mobile. He saw everything. I suspect it may well be *'the clink'* for that Polish maniac. By the way, where are the trips?'

‘They’ve been sitting with Humbug in his stable at the surgery all day. James says Humbug has been lying down sedated most of the day. Apparently Oz has been lying beside him with his arms round him.’

‘Poor kid. It’s getting late; I’ll go down to the surgery and walk home with them. Where are Rosie and Josh?’

‘Josh has been mucking out the stables here with your dad. George had to go home – he wasn’t feeling too good. I think he had a bit of delayed shock but Miriam is with him. Now Josh and Rosie have gone for a ride to Theobald’s Place. They’re going to ride round the paddocks there with Gus and Abby. I told them to be back here by seven o’clock. I’ll walk down to the surgery with you. I would like to see Humbug too.’

Sam kissed Tom’s chest gently and did up the buttons on his shirt, then gently pulled him to his feet, slipping on her cardigan and walking with him to find the triplets.

As they reached the stable at the back of the surgery they could hear Oliver and Orlando trying to persuade Oscar to come back with them to Woodcutters and eat some supper. ‘I can’t leave Humbug,’ they could hear Oscar sobbing. ‘I want to make sure he doesn’t die like Whisky.’

Oliver was trying to placate his brother. ‘He isn’t going to die, Oz. You heard what James told us. He said Humbug must be a very strong pony because he is so much better today.’

‘I just want to see Whisky again,’ Oscar wept. ‘He’s probably gone to heaven and I don’t expect I will be allowed there when I die cos of the bad words I’ve said and cos I stole Dad’s Range Rover that time.’

Tom and Sam had heard every word. Sam pulled Oscar to her, overcome with emotion for her most vulnerable son. ‘Ozzie, darling, when you are an old, old man I am sure you and ‘Lando and Ollie will all go to heaven but not for a very, very long time.’

‘And will Whisky still be waiting there for me?’

Sam had to tell him the truth. 'No one knows where any of our dogs or ponies or any of our pets go to when they die, Ozzie but I am sure, wherever he is, Whisky will be watching over you and he will be happy when he sees you doing well, whoever you are riding.'

'So he won't be upset if I ride another pony?'

'No, Ozzie, he won't mind at all. Now say goodnight to Humbug. It's time he went to sleep and we will all come and see him first thing in the morning.'

To Sam's relief Oscar kissed Humbug's neck and walked back to Woodcutters, where an hour later she could hear the very distinctive signature tune of a certain programme. She sighed, but decided to turn a blind eye for that evening and even Tom agreed with her.

An hour later, Sam crept upstairs. Rosie, Oliver and Orlando were fast asleep and Joshua was looking at his iPod but Oscar was holding a photo of Whisky. He was asleep, but Sam could see traces of recent tears, which had dried on his cheeks. He suddenly opened his eyes as if sensing she was there and he looked at her sadly. 'I loved Whisky so much, Mum. Why do bad things have to happen?'

'Sadly,' Sam told Ozzie, 'although lots of good things happen in our lives unfortunately one or two bad things come along too.'

'Has anything bad ever happened to you, Mum?'

'A long, long time ago when my Daddy was killed by a mine, and then I had my accident, and last year too, when Sophie Stevens hurt me.'

'But you're happy now?'

'Of course, Ozzie, gradually the bad things fade and more good things happen.'

'Like being with Dad.'

'Yes, that's a wonderful thing.'

'Annie won't ever leave me will she Mum?'

'I hope not, Ozzie.'

'I'll always look after her, Mum. I'm glad I managed to put my jacket over her face. I would hate her to have a scar like mine.'

'Ozzie, we never even think about your scar. It's fading every year. Soon it will be a thing of the past too, and you were a brave boy to look after Annie.'

'But I love her you see, Mum. I think we're like you and dad. *Ad infinitum.'*

Sam kissed him and closed the bedroom door quietly. *'Darling Ozzie, I hope so,'* she thought. *'Oh, Ozzie I hope so.'*

CHAPTER 17

Three days later there was some good news and some that was not so good.

Humbug was making extremely good progress and Mathew Parker had promised Oscar that if the pony had no setbacks in the next few days he would most likely be able to go back to Woodcutters the following week once his wounds had healed and there was no risk of him picking up an infection. Oscar was happier and although he had been inconsolable when the family had gathered round the Acer Tree in the garden and buried the casket containing Whisky's ashes beside those of Rascal's, he now appeared to be over the worst of his grieving and was counting the hours until Humbug would be allowed home and turned out in the paddock nearest the cottage with his old friend Black Satin.

However, for Adrian, the outlook was not so bright. Although his life was no longer in danger, he was still suffering from severe amnesia, not remembering anything of his life before the accident and with just a very limited amount of vision from his left eye and nothing at all from the right one.

Lake House Stables was paying for Amy and little Molly to stay in a small hotel near the hospital until more tests had been completed and Adrian's future would be more easily assessed.

Tom realized he was in dire need of a groom. He prayed with all his heart that one day Adrian would return to the stables and decided to contact an agency to see if any temporary grooms were available. If so, they could live in The Little Oast, which Dom and Genevieve were moving out of that day.

Anne-Marie and Oscar were sad that they would no longer be able to flash their torches through their windows at nine o'clock each evening until Joshua suggested they sent each other a very simple text. Just - *'goodnight.'* Oscar wished he had thought of it himself but was gracious enough to say. 'Wow thanks, Josh – great idea,' as they walked together to the surgery to see Humbug.

Tom was in luck. The agency had just received an application from a Canadian brother and sister who were travelling round Europe wanting to stay for six months in as many different countries as they could over the next five years. Not surprisingly, being interested in horses, especially show jumping, they were well aware of the name Tom West and that afternoon they were having a cup of tea and sampling a piece of Sam's Guinness cake in the garden at Woodcutters. They had arrived in an elderly camper van, sensibly attired in their riding gear and carrying their hard hats.

Tom's first impression was good and soon he was saddling Madame and Clementine for the brother and sister and Kaspar for himself and they were all three riding round the lake and through the woods as Tom wanted to show them The Little Oast.

They were more than a little taken aback when they realized they were not expected to live in their extremely basic camper van and less than half an hour later, Jules and Hannah were shaking hands with Tom and Sam after a phone call to the agency. They would be starting work at Woodcutters the following Monday.

Tom and Sam were then thrown into an immediate quandary wondering where they could obtain the bare necessities to furnish the cottage. There was not a stick of furniture in The Little Oast and certainly Jules and Hannah's sole possession was their camper van. Once again it was John who was their saviour. Tom had mentioned their predicament to him when he had once again come to Woodcutters to help Tom with the stables. Later that evening Tom had two phone calls. The first was his dad. *'Tom, I've got you some furniture, have you got a spare hour to help Rob and me get it into your horse box?'*

'Uncle Rob, Dad?'

'Yes, I just got here in time – he was about to have a massive bonfire. His freight arrived from Australia yesterday. He and Simon

had dragged all the old furniture into the garden. I arrived just in time to stop an almighty inferno.'

'Your are amazing, Dad. Sam has just made our supper, and then I'll be on my way to Honeysuckle with the horsebox. We'd better shift it tonight in case it rains.'

Two hours later, with rather begrudging help from Rob and Simon, the four men had moved all the furniture into The Little Oast, and when Sam peeped in the next day, she was sure Jules and Hannah would think they had died and gone to heaven, after the sparse comfort of the camper van.

After the exertion of moving all the furniture and negotiating the narrow stairs in the Little Oast, Tom was exhausted. Sam made two cups of her special mixture of hot chocolate and Horlicks. It was only ten o'clock but after the trauma of the past few days they were promising themselves an early night, when the phone rang. It was unusual for the landline to ring so late and Tom ran into the kitchen, his heart beating fast, as he prayed neither Adrian nor Humbug had suffered a relapse. It was somewhat to his relief when he heard Lionel's voice saying, *'I'm sorry it's so late, Tom. I hope I haven't disturbed you or Sam but I wanted to be certain your youngsters were out of earshot. I wondered whether you had any idea who Oscar might be riding in the immediate future? I know from what Justin told me, Humbug would be out of action for a long time. I know the boy must be devastated. Is your groom making any progress?'*

'He's not too good, Lionel. He suffered a severe blow on the back of his head. At the moment he is in Moorfields, he has very restricted vision in one eye and nothing in the other but worse still he has no recollection of who he is or who any of us are – not even his young wife, Amy or his two week old daughter. It's devastating. We're all totally gutted. My dad is helping in the stables here, but fortunately I've managed to get temporary grooms for six months, a brother and sister from Canada. They're starting on Monday. I didn't want anyone permanent. Sammy and I are praying Adrian will recover.

He's worked for me since he was a schoolboy of fourteen. If you are calling about the Nation's Cup in Dublin, Lionel, I will make it with Kaspar. I'll share Justin's caravan. We'll travel together with Charles."

Lionel breathed a sigh of relief. *'Good. Jock will make up the team. We are in dire need of some points.'*

Tom laughed. *'We'll do our best Lionel. How's Cavalier? Has your wife done any more long distance rides on him recently?'*

Tom learned that apparently she had ridden fifty miles and raised a thousand pounds for Cancer Research.

'Actually, Tom,' Lionel was saying – *'I was ringing you about a rather super pony that is wasting the best years of its life. Do you remember the Countess who Oscar thought was the Queen?'*

Tom laughed again. *'Poor lady, God knows what rubbish Oscar said to her.'*

'Well it couldn't have been all bad, Tom. She wondered whether he would like to ride her rather super J.A. Palomino pony, Goldfinger. She bred him herself and her eldest granddaughter brought him on through Foxhunters and qualified him for H.O.Y.S. She's seventeen now, but unfortunately her younger sister has lost all interest in riding – she spends all her time rowing on the Thames. The pony hasn't competed for the last year. He's only ten, apparently lively but very well schooled with a lovely temperament. She has asked if you would like to bring Oscar to try him. She was really upset when I told her about Whisky.'

'Does she want to keep the pony at her place or would he live here?' Tom asked.

'You would need him at Woodcutters, Tom. There is no one to exercise him here, but I know him well and I can guarantee he is a super pony.'

'I'll talk to Sam and then to Ozzie and ring you back after breakfast tomorrow morning.'

'Fine, maybe you could come to lunch on Friday and bring your trailer.'

'Um, Can't do that I'm afraid, Lionel. My Range Rover and Sam's trailer are both in police custody at the moment, or rather what is left of them are. They will be vital evidence at the trial, but Sam's people carrier has a tow bar, I'll ask Jean-Pierre if we can borrow the Equestrian Centre's trailer. I'll call you in the morning and thanks a ton. It's more than kind and I am pretty sure Ozzie will jump at the opportunity.'

There was no sign of Sam in the sitting room. Tom picked up the two empty mugs and rinsed them under the tap before saying goodnight to Bertie and Holly, giving them a small dog biscuit and taking one upstairs for Boswell, who he was almost certain would be lying on the landing outside their bedroom door guarding Sam as he did night after night even if Tom was at home.

As Tom went up the stairs he could hear Sam's voice. He realized she was in Oscar's bedroom and he could hear her telling him. 'Darling Oz, I'm sure it's not Mathew or James or any of the other vets. Humbug was much better today and soon he will be home in the paddock with Satin.'

'But something might suddenly have happened to him, Mum. I don't want him to die. I don't want him to die.'

Sam was relieved when she heard Tom coming up the stairs. He was running. He had heard enough and his heart broke for Oscar, who had the reputation of being a tough little imp but underneath his strong language and his wild ideas, Tom knew was the most vulnerable of all his children.

He sat beside Sam on Oscar's bed and gently removed the picture of Whisky that his young son was clutching. He stood it on the table beside Oscar's bed. Oscar was looking at him with fear in his eyes. 'Dad?' he asked. 'That phone call. It was to say Humbug is dead wasn't it?'

'Ozzie, it most certainly wasn't. I am sure Humbug is fast asleep.

It's very late. That was Lionel on the phone. Do you remember the Countess who gave you your rosettes at H.O.Y.S?'

Oscar nodded. 'She was nice. She said she would see me next year, but now she won't – I haven't got a pony now, unless Humbug can jump with one eye.'

'Ozzie, I am not promising he will, but there are one or two horses currently jumping the big courses who for one reason or another have had the misfortune to lose an eye. We shall have to be patient and wait and see and you will have to do all you can to help him – but Ozzie, the Countess has a pony which her granddaughter rode for her. Now she is out of juniors and her young sister is involved with a different sport. The pony hasn't competed for over a year. The Countess would like you to come to her house and try him. Would you like to do that?'

'Would Whisky have minded if I did, Dad?'

'No. I know he wouldn't Ozzie. He would have said go on Oz, have a shot at it.'

'What do you think, Mum?'

'I agree with your Dad. Whisky would be pleased for you.'

'I like the Countess. She's almost a queen. What's the pony called?'

'Goldfinger. He's a palomino.'

'I shall never love him like Whisky but I would like to go and see him. I must jump – it's all I want to do in this world.'

'All right then Oz. I'll call Lionel in the morning and we'll go and see him as soon as it's convenient for Lady Lavinia.'

'Who is Lady Lavinia?'

'That's the Countess' name.'

'That's really nice. It suits her cos she's really nice too. Can we go tomorrow?'

'I don't think quite so soon, but I'll fix something with Lionel in the morning,' and he watched with relief as Oscar's eyes started to close as he clutched Tom's old, much loved Jacko monkey. He waited until he was certain Oscar was asleep and then put his arm round Sam and crept up the stairs to the top of the house where Boz was lying by their bedroom door, eagerly awaiting the biscuit which he knew Tom would give him. After munching the prized titbit, the huge dog laid down again with one ear listening – guarding Sam as he did every night.

Tom walked to the window and looked towards the stables and the paddock nearest the cottage. The moon was shining over the lake and suddenly he could see Black Satin swimming across the water, leading Humbug, with a beautiful palomino pony following them, its pure white mane and tail shimmering as it floated in the water. Then suddenly in the bright moonlight, Tom was aware of another pony swimming a little way behind. It looked rather like Pierrot but it was bigger and its mane had been hogged, there was a boy looking remarkably like one of the triplets sitting on it's back. Tom turned to tell Sam to come and have a look, but she was already fast asleep and when he turned back to the lake, the moon was still shining, but Black Satin and the three ponies had all disappeared, then when he looked at the stables he could clearly see Satin's head looking over the door towards the cottage before moving away to the back of his stable.

Tom climbed into the old feather bed still wondering about the identity of the unknown pony, he pulled Sam towards him and fell asleep, to dream of Oscar winning H.O.Y.S. and Lady Lavinia, Countess of Markeley presenting the cup, but Oscar wasn't riding the palomino, Goldfinger, he was sitting on a bouncing bay pony with a thick black forelock and a bristly hogged mane. Tom had no idea who it was or where it had come from.

After a further phone call to Lionel and quick arrangements for the rest of the family, it was agreed that Tom and Sam would take Oscar to meet Goldfinger the next day. Charles and Dom gallantly offered to have the whole of *the gang* at Lake House. They would start with a session in the gym, before Charles would give them a lesson in the school, after which they would all eat their picnic lunches before Sally would take them for a hack round the lake and through the woods to Old Tiles where Alice and Mary would provide cakes and squash. The day would end with a swim at Lake House in the indoor training pool. John would stay at Woodcutters until Sam and Tom got back from Lady Lavinia's home, which was in a village near Oxford.

After some begging and cajoling, Tom had given in to Oscar's pleas that Anne-Marie should accompany them. 'She must meet the Lady Countess, Dad. I told her I had a French girl friend called Annie.'

Tom felt he was being weak as he gave in to Oscar's incessant demand that she came and he rang Lionel again.

Lionel laughed when Tom apologized. *'Don't worry, Tom. He obviously takes after his dad in more ways than one. I know Lavinia is laying on a picnic in the garden, one more little girl won't make any difference I'm sure.'*

Dom was rather reluctant when Tom asked if Anne-Marie could come with them. 'I am afraid for her after the accident, Tom.'

'I understand, Dom, but life should go on as normal for Anne-Marie. You know Sam and I will be ultra careful,' and finally Dom agreed she could go with them.

That evening, Sam made a mound of various sandwiches, wrapped them in foil and put them in the refrigerator with Josh's name on one of the packets. He was like his father and loved marmite, which the triplets and Rosie couldn't abide.

By the time the four siblings had finally left for Lake House the next morning, Anne-Marie had arrived at Woodcutters and Oscar was impatiently hopping from one foot to the other whilst Tom talked to his father who had once again come to help George in the yard.

Tom was asking George for the latest news of Adrian. Apparently his eyesight had improved very slightly and he now had very blurred vision in both of his eyes, but he still didn't know who he was or recognize Amy or Molly, but he was now able to walk to the shower room and the day room and was sitting in a chair most of the time listening to the radio. The present was perfectly lucid but his life before the accident appeared to have been buried. He talked to Miriam and Amy, but he was like a stranger and spoke only about his life in the hospital. He held little Molly but only because Amy placed the baby in his arms. He had no idea she was his daughter. Amy stayed stoically strong in front of him, but when she and Molly got back to the small hotel where they were staying, she sobbed uncontrollably. She was frightened of what lay ahead and for the inevitable day when Adrian would leave the hospital and she would not only have Molly to look after but also a husband who had no idea who she was and worse still neither who he himself was. The future was not bright and she hugged the tiny baby to her in the rather claustrophobic hotel room where her meal was brought to her every evening. It was easier than taking Molly to the crowded dining room.

With a final request to Joshua to look after Rosie, Oscar and Anne-Marie climbed into the back of the People Carrier and with Jean-Pierre's large trailer firmly attached to the tow bar, Sam drove carefully through the village, first stopping at the vets where Oscar was thrilled to find Humbug grazing in a small paddock adjacent to his stable. James was talking to him and smiled when he saw Tom and Oscar.

'He's doing really well, Oscar. Just the deepest wound needs to grow a scab and then you can take him home. We shall keep his eye socket covered for a while though. It will have to be checked at least twice a week until we are certain no infection can get inside.'

Oscar was smiling. 'That's alright, Uncle James. Ollie or 'Lando will bring Fizz or Torchlight and walk on the outside of Buggy. I can easily lead him down to the surgery.'

'We'll see when the time comes,' James told the enthusiastic boy. 'I can probably drop into Woodcutters on my way home from the surgery. Now have a super day and I hope all works out well with this pony you are going to see,' and with a final pat on Humbug's neck, Oscar ran back to the car and leapt in beside Anne-Marie who was telling Sam how her grand-mère might not be living with them for much longer as she had met a gentleman on the cruise who lived in Canterbury and had asked her to live there with him. Sam chuckled. Obviously even at seventy-five one was not too old for a romance and good luck to her, she thought.

Sam was driving extra carefully. She could see in the mirror that every time she approached a road junction Anne-Marie was clutching Oscar's arm and once when a large white van pulled out of a side turning in front of them causing Sam to stop abruptly, she noticed her hide her face in Oscar's jacket. She made a mental note to warn Genevieve that her daughter had been more affected by last week's trauma than perhaps they had realized.

Tom appeared to have no such qualms. Sam glanced at him thinking he was very quiet and noticed he had fallen asleep. *'Darling Tom,'* she thought. *'He works so hard and I know he has taken Adrian's accident really badly. Anyone who isn't au fait with the life of a show jumper has no idea what an exacting life it is, even if you are at the top and have grooms to help you. At the end of the day, the horses are Tom's responsibility. They have to be schooled on the flat, hacked out and jumped in the sand school. They aren't like a tennis racquet or a bag of golf clubs that can be put away in a cupboard and forgotten about – they are living creatures that rely on him to make certain they are fit, happy and healthy and Tom is still only thirty-two years old. God willing, he has at least another twenty-five or maybe even thirty years ahead of him in this competitive and often dangerous sport.'* She sighed and put her hand briefly on his knee. He immediately opened his eyes and smiled at her. 'Shall we have a quick break and a coffee, Sammy? I need something with some caffeine to wake me up. I think there's a motorway stop a few miles further on. We're making really good time. We don't want to be early.'

He turned to tell Oscar they would soon be stopping but to his surprise both he and Anne-Marie were fast asleep. The previous week had certainly taken its toll on everyone.

Sam had set her sat nav and at ten minutes to one she found herself driving down an extremely narrow lane, lined on each side by a long row of lime trees. 'Tommy, I hope I don't meet another car or worse still a lorry,' but apart from several groups of young rabbits playing on the verges, the lane was deserted. Her sat nav was soon telling her to turn left. As she did so, she found herself driving down a long tarmacked drive – on one side was a huge lake with large clusters of pink and yellow water lilies, floating like islands across the water. Swallows and swifts were dipping their wings as they flew from one side of the lake to the other, grabbing whatever small insects happened to cross their flight paths.

On the other side of the drive, bluebells and anemones were stretching like a carpet under a variety of shady trees. At the end of the drive Sam could see a beautiful Queen Anne House, very similar to Lake House. She parked carefully in a corner of the sweeping drive. Oscar picked up his bag, which contained all his riding gear and Sam gathered the bunch of Samantha roses she had picked that morning.

Lady Lavinia was looking out for them and she greeted them in the drive, surrounded by six miniature, longhaired dachshunds, almost identical to John's Mac and Mabel. Anne-Marie was enchanted. 'Oh, they are beautiful,' she cried.

The Countess smiled at her. 'Come to the conservatory.' She told the girl and led them through the sitting room to a huge glass conservatory where there was a large playpen in which four dachshund puppies were chewing an old slipper.

‘Cor, Lady Countess,’ Oscar told her. ‘My Grandpa John would love these. They are the same colour as Mac and Mabel. Grandpa rescued them after a big fire at the animal sanctuary. They live with his sheepdogs Spic and Span at Old Tiles Farm.’

Eventually, Oscar and Anne-Marie were prised away from the puppies and they followed the Countess into the garden where a picnic had been laid in a large summerhouse, which overlooked the far end of the lake. It was almost entirely covered in clematis Tetra Rosa and an early climbing rose. The garden was full of rhododendrons and azaleas and to Sam’s delight, many different varieties of her favourite Japanese Acers. She noticed the back of the Queen Anne house was covered from end to end with a pale blue wisteria.

Sam’s eyes were riveted to every aspect of the garden, as she told Lady Lavinia. ‘Your garden is just perfect. Could I walk round it after we’ve eaten our lunch? The azaleas are simply sensational and the scent from the yellow species is quite amazing.’

Lady Lavinia had been stunned by Sam’s beauty. She had understood from Lionel that Tom West had a beautiful wife and Lionel had also mentioned their charming garden, which he had already taken his wife Miriam to see. ‘Of course you can, and you must tell me the name of these beautiful roses you have brought me.’

Sam laughed. ‘They are called Samantha rose. Tom planted them in our garden before the cottage was officially ours. Actually, planning gardens is my job. Although I have to restrict how many projects I take on these days. Five children and one big boy require quite a lot of attention, especially in the kitchen department. I try not to work too much in the school holidays. I like to ride out with them all and go to as many shows as I can, but at the moment I am redesigning the flowerbeds for Justin Wright-Smith. He’s just moved to a lovely old Georgian house with a beautiful walled garden, but Anna wants to bring more soft colours into the borders.’

To Sam and Tom’s surprise, a middle-aged gentleman with old denim shorts emphasizing his very nobly knees, greeted them as they entered the summerhouse. They had thought Lady Lavinia to be a widow but were now being introduced to the very much alive Lord Aristotle, Count of Markeley, or Totty as his wife referred to him. He immediately offered to take Sam on a tour of the garden, as after they had finished the picnic, Lady Lavinia, Tom, Anne-Marie and Oscar made their way to the stables.

Tom wasn't too sure about leaving Sam with the rather lecherous gentleman who had a definite glint in his eye as he perused Sam in her very becoming summer dress, but Oscar was pulling him towards the Countess' old Land Rover in which she was going to drive them to the stables. With one final warning glance at Sam, he rather reluctantly sat down on a very torn front seat beside Lady Lavinia and settled two of the dachshunds on his knee, before they bumped at breakneck speed across the uneven grass towards the stables, where he could see a palomino head sporting a pure white mane watching them as they approached.

Oscar had changed into his riding clothes in the downstairs loo. It was very similar to the one Gus had shown him in Theobald's Place except the flowers on this loo were painted a musty pink and there was just a piece of thick string attached to the high cistern. There were pictures of horses all around the wall and several of a lady jumping them – Oscar thought it was probably his Countess. It was obviously a long time ago. She was wearing extremely thick, baggy jodhpurs and a bowler hat and some of the horses had docked tails.

As they got out of the Range Rover, a youngish man who was obviously a groom came up to Lady Lavinia, addressing her courteously, 'Good afternoon, My Lady.'

She smiled at him 'Good afternoon, Lawrence. This is young Oscar West. He is going to see how he gets on with Goldie. Could you saddle him up, please?'

Lawrence almost bowed. 'Very good, My Lady,' and he hastened to Goldfinger's stable.

Oscar and Anne-Marie had walked over to a small paddock where two Shetlands and a larger, very light bay pony were grazing. The bay was probably a little over fourteen hands and had a hogged mane and a dark black, bushy forelock and tail.

He walked straight up to Oscar, blowing in his face. Oscar felt something special as he stroked the pony's neck. 'You're super,' he told the pony. 'Why are you with these Shetlands and why haven't you got any shoes on?'

The pony blew in Oscar's face again. Oscar turned to Lady Lavinia. 'What's his name?' he asked her.

'Hanky Panky.'

Oscar smiled. 'I like that. He's lovely and he can talk.'

'What do you mean – he can talk?' the Countess asked Oscar.

'I just felt something strange. As if he was trying to tell me something. Doesn't anyone ride him, cos he hasn't got any shoes on?'

Lady Lavinia shook her head. 'Not now, dear. He's twelve. My grandson used to ride him, but he hasn't been ridden since he was eight when Christian was out of juniors. My granddaughters couldn't manage him, the grooms lunge him two or three times a week but there is no one here that is capable of riding him. He's very strong and quite a handful.'

Oscar was no shrinking violet – he always asked a direct question expecting an answer in a similar vein. 'Could I try him, Madam Countess? I think he would like me to ride him.'

Tom looked embarrassed, 'Oz, the Countess is very kindly letting you try Goldfinger.'

'I know Dad, but Hanky Panky can talk to me.'

Tom looked at Lady Lavinia. 'You may not be aware,' he explained. 'But I can talk to most horses. My boys seem to have inherited my idiosyncrasy. Black Satin tells me lots of things and most of them come true. I was about nine when I discovered I could talk to my little pony Twinkletoes. It's the reason I can usually ride all the difficult horses like Satin and Opal and my beautiful Misty'

Lady Lavinia looked at the young boy. She noticed Hanky Panky's eyes were following him and decided before she made any decision she would see how he fared with Goldfinger, who was a true gentleman – the complete opposite of Panky, who was hot, strong and a handful.

The groom was soon leading the palomino up to Oscar and Tom was giving him a leg up. There was a large sand school on the far side with a selection of ramshackle jumps, which had definitely seen better days. With the help of the groom, Tom did his best to build a reasonably stable course. Oscar trotted Goldfinger into the school. Lady Lavinia turned to Tom. 'Do whatever you want Tom; you know what your son is capable of. Goldie is a good pony but he's not very fit at the moment.'

It was obvious Goldfinger was a steady, reliable pony and Oscar was at ease straight away, although he was trying not to think of the effervescent Whisky or his bouncing Humbug as the superbly mannered Goldfinger cantered evenly on both legs and then cleared the jumps without so much as a single tug on the reins. Tom raised the jumps once as he realized not only was the pony extremely eye catching, he was also very talented. It was also soon obvious it was Lady Lavinia's wish that Oscar should become Goldfinger's new jockey.

'Would you like to ride Goldie for me?' she asked him.

'Yes please, he's a lovely pony, but I would love it if you would let me try Hanky Panky, Madam Countess. I love your Goldie, but I'm used to quite naughty ponies, like Whisky and Humbug.'

To Lady Lavinia's consternation, she suddenly noticed Oscar's eyes fill with tears and she noticed Anne-Marie put her hand on his knee. She suddenly remembered H.O.Y.S. and Oscar saying. *'I'll give this rosette to Annie – she's my girlfriend - she loves pink and green,'* and she thought of the prancing, little piebald pony he had been riding – she called to Lawrence. 'Can you saddle Hanky Panky, please?'

'Hanky Panky, Madam, are you sure?'

'Yes please. Lawrence,' and five minutes later Oscar was sitting on a bouncing ball of fire just as Sam and Totty, alias Lord Markeley arrived in the paddock in a golf buggy.

'What on earth is that lad doing on Panky, Lavinia? Have you taken leave of your senses?'

'That remains to be seen, Totty, but somehow I don't think so.'

Oscar and Panky were fast approaching the sand school and were still in one piece as Anne-Marie slipped her hand into Sam's. 'Ozzie says Hanky Panky asked him to ride him, Sam. I hope he was listening properly.'

Sam held her breath but so far Oscar seemed to be in control. In fact Oscar was happy for the first time since Whisky had died and Lady Lavinia was happy for the first time since her grandson Christian had gone to university. Ten minutes later, as she watched the young lad and the pony flying over the jumps, her mind was made up. As Oscar bounced up to her she had tears in her eyes. Oscar was beaming. 'He's fantastic Madam Countess – he's supersonic.'

'Would you like to jump both the ponies for me, Oscar, until you are out of juniors. How far ahead is that? How old are you now?'

'Just eleven. I've got five more years in juniors and yes please, if Dad says I can then that would be great. Would you like the prize money and the trophies if I win any but could I give the rosettes to Annie cos she never gets lovely big ones at the Pony Club Show. She's only just learned to ride, you see.'

'I don't want anything, Oscar. Just the pleasure of seeing the ponies I have bred jumping at all the big shows. Would you like to meet Goldie's mother?'

'Cor – you bet,' and Lawrence was asked to fetch the mare from a nearby paddock whilst Oscar was begging his father to let him ride Hanky Panky.

Completely unbeknown to his son, Tom realized he had seen Hanky Panky before, just the previous evening. He was the pony who had been swimming with Satin in the lake behind Humbug and Goldfinger. Oscar had been riding him and obviously Satin was certain success would come their way. *How did the old black horse see into the future?* Tom shivered. It was uncanny but as he looked at Sam, he remembered Charles' words the day Sophie Stevens had stabbed her. *'If it hadn't been for Black Satin, Tom, I would have been too late.'* He would never know, but all he knew was that he would be eternally grateful and he was certain it wouldn't be Goldfinger that Oscar would have the big successes on, for Satin had told him last night that Oscar and Hanky Panky were going to be almost invincible. A new partnership was about to be born.

He too had seen something special, not least the sparkle that had miraculously returned to his son's eyes. 'O.K. Ozzie,' he told the boy, 'but you will be very busy. Don't forget Humbug will need a lot of your time. He will need to be lunged at the very least and you will certainly probably be able to hack round the lake on him, more than that, we don't yet know.'

Oscar silenced his father, 'Dad, I'll just get up two hours earlier. I'll work like mad. Panky is special, I know he is and Goldie's super too,' he added almost as an afterthought.

Sam and Anne-Marie were admiring Goldie's palomino mother, Golden Rain who was heavily in foal. Goldie had been her first foal and now he was ten, she was still only fifteen and according to Lady Lavinia was in foal to a sixteen hand-jumping stallion. She smiled at Oscar. 'Just right for you when you leave juniors, Oscar.' And she wasn't speaking in jest. She was going to keep a very close eye on young Oscar West. *'One day,'* she was thinking to herself, *'this young man could be jumping Golden Rain's as yet unborn foal, of that there can be no doubt.'*

After Oscar had thanked Lady Lavinia many, many times, the two ponies walked calmly into the trailer this time with Tom driving,

Hanky Panky and Goldfinger and the fearless Oscar West, the carbon copy of his famous father were soon to become a force to be reckoned with at every show they entered and back at Woodcutters,

Black Satin was nodding his head. He was always right and he nodded it again, just for good measure.

CHAPTER 18

April had launched into May and Oscar had certainly not been idle. The day after Hanky Panky and Goldfinger had arrived at Woodcutters, he had asked Sam. 'Can Annie and I get the bus to Ashford this morning?'

'To Ashford, Oz, why do you need to go to Ashford?'

'I need a really good alarm clock, Mum. I must get up at half past five every morning. Annie has asked Genevieve and she has said she can come with me. She wants to buy some water paints in Smiths. I've got the money for a clock and enough to buy us one course in Fillipo's. We'll get the two o'clock bus home and when Dad gets back from London he said he would give me a school on Panky, but before that I shall ride Goldfinger up to Lake House.'

Tom and Charles had already left for London where they were visiting Adrian whose eyesight was improving slowly each day but who still couldn't recall any of his life before the accident, nor did he recognize any one, talking only of things that had occurred in the hospital.

Sam was just about to tell Oscar if he looked after Anne-Marie with the utmost care he could go on his quest for an alarm clock when Orlando suddenly decided he and Charlotte would like to go with them. She suddenly felt a lot happier at the thought of the steady, reliable Orlando being with them and gave the boys twenty pounds so that they could all enjoy one of Gina's delicious sweets and with one final warning to Orlando and Oscar to look after the girls – she waved them goodbye.

Oliver and Joshua were on stable duties, helping George in the yard and Rosie and Gus were playing tennis with Justin at Lake House. It appeared to be their latest craze.

Sam looked at the blue sky and the sun, which was casting

dappled shadows through the Acer trees across the lawn, and pushed aside the plans for the reconstructed borders she was working on at Theobald's Place that were lying on her desk in the chalet, instead she shrugged her shoulders, picked up her latest Patsy Sanders' book and walked across the grass to her lounger, which she pulled into the sun. Before she settled down she went into the kitchen and brought out a glass and a jug of lemon squash, picked up her mobile and settled down to an extremely rare morning, with no one but the dogs to interrupt her total absorption in the exploits of Herbert Holmer and his as yet unsolved mystery.

An hour and a half later, her phone rang. It was Tom. Apparently Charles and he had arrived at the hospital to find Amy in a very distressed state. She had taken Molly to see Adrian as she had done every day. Usually he just stared at them, answering her questions politely, but never once recognizing her. Today, however, it had been different.

'Why do you keep coming to see me and bringing this baby with you?' he had asked her.

'Because I am your wife, Adrian and this is your little daughter, Molly.'

'It's kind of you to visit a total stranger, but it's really not necessary. I'm sure you have more interesting things to do, and why do you call me Adrian?'

'Because that's who you are, Adrian Carstairs and we are Amy and Molly Carstairs.'

'Never heard of them – but Adrian is an O.K. name. I suppose it is as good as any other. Perhaps you could just read me the supper menu before you go.'

'Of course, Adrian, but Molly and I are not going anywhere.'

'Well, that's up to you I suppose, Amy, but I think I'll listen to some music on my headphones.'

A short time later, the specialist came in to see Adrian. He smiled at Amy.

'I would like a word with you, Mrs. Carstairs. Come into the side ward. I think we need to talk in private.'

Amy picked up Molly and followed the professor into a small room. He took Amy's hand and smiled kindly as he asked. 'May I call you Amy?'

Amy nodded, too miserable to utter a word.

'I am afraid you are going to have to be very patient, Amy,' the professor told her. 'We have to hope that something will suddenly jog your husband's memory back into place but I have to warn you this could take a very long time and at the very worst, but I pray this will not be the case, he might never remember his past. His eyesight is improving which is a positive you must hold on to. I understand it is extremely hard and upsetting for you but it is important you are with your husband. Some very small thing you may say could suddenly penetrate his subconscious mind. It is an intolerable situation for you but when he is stronger, a visit to his home could help jog his memory but do remember however much it upsets you, he is not meaning to hurt you. What are his interests?'

Amy looked at the professor through her tears. 'His horses, his job as a groom, giving lessons to the youngsters. His bosses, Charles Wright-Smith and Tom West are coming to see him this morning but the last time Tom came Adrian had no idea who he was.'

'It may be a good idea to take Adrian to the stables in a week or so. If Mr. West could persuade him to ride one of his quietest horses that could help the situation. It's worth trying anything. Hopefully his eyesight will have improved significantly by that time.'

As Amy was leaving with the professor they met Tom and Charles, who had just arrived in the ward. Tom was holding a large photograph album containing many pictures of Satin, Misty and one or two of Adrian himself riding Midnight Fantasy and of him as a boy jumping Thunderbird.

The professor quickly told Tom and Charles of his plan to get Adrian to Lake House to see the horses and even to ride with Tom in the school.

Tom immediately agreed and as soon as Adrian was able, the hospital car would drive him to Massenden.

It was obvious Adrian still had no idea who Tom and Charles were. He glanced at the album, but it was extremely difficult for him to see it and he certainly didn't recognise himself. 'Who is that boy?' he asked Tom as he looked at himself and Thunder at H.O.Y.S.

'That's you winning the junior show jumper of the year.' Tom told him, but Adrian just stared at him with a vacant expression.

When Adrian's lunch arrived, Charles looked at Amy. 'Come on, little one. Tom and I will take you out to lunch. You need to get out of this place for an hour or two – you can feed Molly in the ladies.' He didn't give Amy any time to argue as he took her arm and led her firmly out of the hospital and into the warm sunshine.

Sam put the phone down beside her book and went indoors with a heavy heart after her conversation with Tom, hoping the lunch he and Charles were going to give Amy would at least give the girl a small boost. She ate her sandwich and then lay back on the lounger and closed her eyes, only to open them ten minutes later when her phone rang again, this time it was James. *'Is Tom there?'* he asked Sam.

'No, James, he's in London with Charles. They are visiting Adrian but Tom has just rung and told me he still has no idea who they are. Apparently Amy is at breaking point and he and Charles are taking her out to lunch. They felt she needed to get away from the hospital for an hour or two. Is everything O.K. with Humbug?'

'It most certainly is. He's ready to come home. I've got the trailer hitched up. I was going to bring him back to Woodcutters on my way home to lunch.'

'That would be wonderful, James. Oscar and Anne-Marie have gone on the bus to Ashford but he would be thrilled to find Humbug here when he gets back. I'll make certain a stable is ready for him.

I know Josh and Oliver mucked them all out with George before they hacked up to Lake House.'

Half an hour later, James drove into the yard. Sam ran to meet him as he was lowering the ramp of the trailer. Satin had trotted up to the five bar gate and was shaking his head and whinnying as Humbug walked slowly into the yard. James led him to the stable where Sam had already filled the manger with hay and placed a large bucket of cool water in one corner. Humbug took a long drink and then, with his ears pricked, called back to Satin over his stable door.

'Let's bring Satin into the stable next to Humbug's good eye so he can see him and give him a day to settle down next to his old friend and then tomorrow they can go out together in the small paddock.'

Sam was thanking James. 'Oz will be over the moon; he's been to Ashford to buy an alarm clock. He says he is going to get up at five thirty every morning and walk Humbug round the lake before he has a work out in the gym with Rosie and his brothers and the Wright-Smith family.'

'He's a good kid, Sam. If he goes on like this I can guarantee he has a great future ahead of him, and talk of the devil – here he is.'

Oscar had seen the trailer in the yard. 'Why is Uncle James here, Mum?'

James covered Oscar's face with his hands and walked him towards the stables. He stopped in front of Humbug and removed his hands from Oscar's eyes. 'Open them Oscar.'

Oscar let out a yell, which even frightened Satin. 'Buggy –oh Buggy,' and tears of sheer joy were pouring down his face as he hugged his little piebald pony. He opened the bag he was carrying and first of all handed Sam a very squishy, white, paper bag.

'We bought one of Gina's special Tiramisu's for you,' he told her. It was almost unrecognizable, as Oscar had sat with it on his lap in the sun on the top of the bus, but Sam kissed him.

'Ozzie, how lovely, you kind boy. I'll just run and put it in the fridge for a little while. Maybe I'll share it with Dad for our supper.'

'O.K. Mum, and look – if this doesn't wake me up, then nothing will,' and he proudly showed her the enormous, red alarm clock, which was destined to awaken him at precisely five thirty every morning.

He put his hand into the pocket of his jeans and pulled out twelve pony nuts. He gave three to Humbug and then three each to Hanky Panky and Goldfinger before patting Black Satin who greedily snatched the remaining three.

'Where are the others, Ozzie?'

'Annie is getting Tom Thumb ready, she's going to meet me at the stables. Orlando is helping Charlotte with Catherine Wheel – they're going to ride tandem back here, then 'Lando is going to grab Torchlight and I'm taking Goldie. Dad says he will come with me to our paddock this evening and see how I get on with Panky. He's going to bring Madame. He says she could be a good influence on Panky.' And with that he saddled Goldfinger just as Charlotte and Orlando trotted into the yard on Catherine Wheel.

As the weather developed it's pattern of warm spring evenings and the mornings grew lighter with each day, Oscar was quickly establishing a strong rapport with both Goldfinger and Hanky Panky and on the last Saturday of the month he was entering the big Junior Open Class at the Massenden Show with both of the ponies.

Oscar was full of optimism but Tom was realistic. Not only would there be stiff opposition from many of the Lake House Gang, there were several other extremely capable riders from many parts of the country who frequented the ever increasingly popular show.

Oscar had put hours and hours of hard work into schooling both the ponies and now both they and Oscar were extremely fit. If there was any justice in this world, both Charles and Tom felt the young lad certainly deserved his fair share of it.

Lionel had not told anyone that he was bringing Lady Lavinia and her husband Totty to see how Oscar was progressing with her ponies, whilst he was going to make his first notes with Tim Gregson for the Junior Championships, which were to be held the following year.

The morning of the Show dawned bright and warm and by ten o'clock the Junior Foxhunter Class was well under way and the horsebox park was rapidly filling with a long stream of boxes turning through the gates of the Centre. As the jump off finally began and was eventually won by Jacques and his Flying Fox, Tom took Rosie and Sparkler to the practice area where they met Eloise and Jean-Pierre, the latter more than a little on edge.

'What's up, Pierre?' Tom asked his brother-in-law.

'I 'ave an important person to look after.' he told Tom. 'She is going to present the cup to the winner of the fourteen-two class later on this afternoon.'

'Leave Eloise with Rosie, Pierre, I'll look after her.' And it was with much relief that Jean-Pierre made his way back to the box, where unbeknown to any of *the gang,* Lionel, Lady Lavinia and Totty were waiting for the smallest ponies to commence their class, which began with the entrance of Virginia Mawgan-Whitely and Pixie Love. She and her sister, Veronica were still having lessons with Charles or Dom, and Charles watched with pleasure as his pupil jumped a pleasing clear round. Her mother, Caroline was standing with Charles - she was obviously delighted, giving Charles a hug. 'You've done wonders with her,' she told him. 'Veronica is really looking forwards to jumping Groucho later on.'

Charles was more than pleased as he envisaged several more hundred pounds winging their way out of Caroline's silver purse straight into his golden one!! He turned his attention to Abby and Fuzz Buzz who as always jumped a slow but immaculate clear round, which was soon followed by a significantly faster one by the ever willing Sparkler, aided in no mean way by an extremely vociferous Rosie.

Totty looked at Lady Lavinia. 'That child is going to be a beautiful woman one day, my dear. She has all the attributes and charm God saw fit to give her mother.'

Lionel was smiling. 'Sam has retired her beautiful stallion, Chim Chim,' he told Totty, 'but they were a real force to be reckoned with and she looked amazing in her sidesaddle habit, but she is also a very talented garden designer. You should visit Woodcutters one day. It's a lovely old cottage and the garden has a very Japanese influence. Sam loves her Acers although that young rascal Oscar demolished her pièce de résistance when he drove Tom's Range Rover through the middle of it. Tom's yard is immaculate, as you would expect. He has got a Canadian brother and sister working for him for six months whilst that poor lad, Adrian languishes in hospital. I gather he still has no idea who he is – so dreadful for his young wife. Tom was telling me the hospital is going to send him to Lake House in a car next week and Tom is going to lead him round the school on Madame. The specialist hopes it could help him. The only good news is that Humbug has made huge strides. Apparently Oscar rode him round the lake with Tom and Satin last week. According to Tom he was his usual bouncing self. Thank God for that.'

'Well, Lionel, I am really looking forwards to seeing how Oscar is getting on with Goldie and Panky. I'm not expecting miracles, just a nice steady round. Not that that's easy as far as Panky is concerned. I called Tom last week and he said he was cautiously optimistic.'

Lionel laughed. 'That translates to - they are getting on like a house on fire, Lavinia.'

By now, the jump off was under way and the six young girls who had jumped clear were waiting their turns.

'Where the hell have all the young lads got to?' Charles grumbled.

Tom smiled. 'We shall have to wait for Rudi and Noah to grow a bit, Charles. Meanwhile, bring on the girls.'

All the other parents and their young offspring rather unsportingly hoped that Rosie and Sparkler would have a fence down and to his shame, the thought had even crossed James' mind – but as they flew round the course, cutting every corner, he could only feel admiration for his young niece. He watched Abby and Fuzz Buzz as the little dun pony refused to be hustled out of his normal, careful rhythm, finally finishing a full ten seconds behind Rosie. After Pixie Love and Virginia had jumped into second place, Eloise smiled at Tom. 'I'm going for it, Uncle Tom. I don't think Pierrot can catch Sparkler but I'm going to try my hardest to beat Virginia's time,' which she did – going into second place behind Rosie.

The girls stayed in that order, as eventually to James' delight, Fenella and Poupée finished just half a second behind Pixie Love. Abby was fifth and a little girl unknown to *the gang* came sixth with an exceedingly fast four faults.

Sam had come into the collecting ring ready to go back to the horsebox with Sparkler and get Rosie mounted on Le Duc. She was standing with Tom as they watched their daughter receive the small cup – a large, red rosette and an envelope with fifteen pounds inside it.

As Rosie exited the arena, Tom was aware of a bay pony ridden by a familiar young lad racing towards him. He leapt to one side pulling Sam with him, as Justin, who had also arrived in the collecting ring was marching up to his young son, who having seen Rosie coming out of the arena, had leapt off Hamlet, throwing his arms round Sparkler's neck, smiling engagingly at Rosie.

'That was brilliant, Rosie, absolutely brilliant. Supercali and all the rest of it,' but his smile faded quickly as Justin took hold of his arm.

'Gus. Your behavior is disgraceful. You very nearly knocked Sam over. You know very well that no one ever, ever races through the collecting ring like that. Go at once and apologise to Sam and then hand me Hamlet whilst you walk the course with your Grandpa.'

Sam took Rosie to get Le Duc whilst Tom waited with Orlando. It felt strange to have only one of the triplets in this class, but although Tom was keeping his thoughts to himself, not wishing to raise Oscar's hopes before he himself was certain, he was fully expecting Humbug to be competing again before too long. Although Oscar hadn't jumped him yet, Humbug was totally relaxed when hacking, and the previous evening Tom had taken Oscar into the indoor school and schooled him on the flat. Humbug seemed to be coping admirably with just the one eye and next week he would let Oscar jump him over the cavaletti.

Rosie was walking towards him with Sam beside her. Sam held Le Duc and Jet Stream whilst Tom walked the course with her and Orlando. It was very similar but a little higher than the one she had just jumped with Sparkler.

As Lady Lavinia watched Rosie and Le Duc, she turned to Totty and Lionel. 'I really think I can relax. I truly believe Goldie has a home for life. That little girl is outstanding. When Oscar is out of juniors, she can jump him for me. Perfect,' and she smiled again when three quarters of an hour later, Rosie was once again receiving a cup. Rupert and The March Hare were two seconds behind her and Gus was another second slower than Rupert, with Orlando and Jet Stream and Veronica Mawgan-Whitely and Groucho in fourth and fifth places.

Even Tom was surprised. Le Duc had been good when Oliver had ridden him, but now with Rosie he was in a class of his own, but all he said was 'Good girl, Rosie – well ridden.' He wanted to keep her feet firmly on the ground and both Justin and Charles both fully understood how he felt and kept their congratulations very low key.

The course was soon being altered for the Fourteen-two Class, whilst the participants gathered in the collecting ring, amongst who was an extremely excited and determined Oscar. He was jumping

Goldfinger near the beginning and Hanky Panky close to the end. He knew Annie was sitting in the stand with Georgia, Charlotte and Rosie. As he walked the course and glanced at the stand, he suddenly glimpsed another familiar figure sitting in the director's box with Jean-Pierre and Jane. He pulled Tom's sleeve. 'Dad, dad – there's my Countess.'

Tom's heart sank. He too had seen the good lady, he didn't want Oscar to be nervous or feel any pressure but Oscar's next words put his mind at rest. 'Wonderful, Dad. She can see how fit Goldie and Panky are and I'm going to do my damnedest to get a clear round on one of them.'

It was at that moment that Tom realized that maybe what Sam and many other people were always telling him was true and perhaps Oscar did take after him, for whatever the circumstances when he himself was jumping, whether it be here in his home village of Massenden or at one of the most important events in the world, nothing ever fazed him. It was one of the reasons he was very rarely out of the top five-ranked show jumpers in the world and it looked very much as though Oscar was blessed with the same laid back attitude.

Oscar followed his brother, Joshua into the arena. Josh and Lily had jumped an immaculate clear round, as had Mimi and Babushka before them. Oscar cantered calmly in front of the stands, waving his hand nonchalantly to Lady Lavinia as he passed her box.

'Oh dear, Lionel, he's noticed I'm here.'

'Well it doesn't seem to have had an adverse effect, Lavinia,' and they held their breath as the beautiful golden pony lived up to his name.

Lady Lavinia clapped her hands. 'Wonderful. They have got an amazing partnership already. Quite remarkable.'

As the class continued, so the clear rounds were mounting and by the time Oscar and Hanky Panky pranced into the arena there were already sixteen pairs through to the jump off, many of those being current members of *the gang*. Oscar didn't wave to Lady Lavinia this time. He needed both his hands to keep a firm hold on the extremely lively pony, but he was used to riding the effervescent Humbug and the ill-fated Whisky, who had been almost as strong.

Sam was holding Tom's hand tightly as they watched together from the edge of the entrance of the arena, but from the moment Oscar and the cocky bay pony, with his hogged mane and jet black forelock shot through the start and over the first three jumps, Tom was aware he was watching a very special partnership, and as Panky flew over the last jump, he held Sam close and for once he was showing more than a little emotion.

'Oh, darling, I am so, so pleased for him. He has come through the most heartbreaking experience. He knew the moment he set eyes on Panky he had met a very special partner. He's a brilliant pony and although I should never say it because he is my son, I must – he has a very, very special jockey. Whatever he does in the jump off, I am really proud of him – and of my other boys too. They are all through to the next round.'

'You must be proud of Rosie too, Tom.'

'Darling one, of course I am, but she is well aware of that. She's not exactly a shrinking violet, is she?'

Sam laughed. 'Well I certainly agree with you there, my Thomas. Now here come Mimi and Babushka. Mimi had four faults, but Gus and Pie in the Sky set a fast clear round and as the ensuing competitors tried to beat him the faults started to come thick and fast. Oscar was sensible, he followed his father's advice and didn't try to beat Gus' fast time and he and Goldfinger went into third place behind Josh and Tiger Lily, but Oscar was saving the best until last - he had a tough task ahead as Joshua and Ganger had now jumped into the lead.

Oscar was totally focused. He forgot about Annie, his father, his brothers and even his Countess. All he could see was the green grass and the brightly painted jumps. He spoke briefly to his pony. 'Come on, Panky, let's show everybody what we are made of.'

The pony appeared to nod its head as it sped through the start

– the atmosphere was electric. Many of the spectators and almost all the other competitors knew of the devastating loss Oscar had so recently had to endure. Everyone recognized his love for his ponies. He was giving away nothing, as he turned Hanky Panky in the air, cutting every corner on the course, finally taking out a stride before flying over the final oxer. There was no contest; he had beaten his older brother's time by over three seconds. The crowd were on their feet, even though many of them, including his aunts Lizzie and Jane abhorred his sometimes over exuberant manner and the appalling words he used far too often, but there were many who were taken aback by the obvious tears which were flowing down his young, scarred face, as he threw himself into his mother's arms crying. 'I did it for Whisky, Mum. I had to. I hope he was watching wherever he is.'

Sam was hugging him. 'Ozzie, I hope so too. I'm sure he most probably was, and Lady Lavinia most certainly was. She will be thrilled.'

Oscar scrubbed away his tears with the back of his hand, sniffed hard and remounted Hanky Panky to lead the winners into the arena.

To his delight, he saw his Countess coming towards him with a silver cup, slightly larger than the ones Rosie had won earlier that day. Trish was walking beside her, holding a large tray of various two coloured, velvet rosettes. They were almost as grand as the ones he had received at H.O.Y.S.

Lady Lavinia was smiling at him saying. 'Well done, Oscar.'

'Oh, Madam Countess, Panky was fab – I knew you were watching and Mum says she thinks Whisky might have been too, but actually I 'm not too sure cos what's left of him is buried in a metal box under the Acer tree in the garden. I think I will go and ask the vicar if it's possible that a little bit of him might be in heaven. She's sure to know.'

He looked carefully at the rosettes. 'Could I have the red and black one, please. I usually give my rosettes to Annie, but I think I will keep this one. It's rather special and I am sure that's what

Panky is going to be – but I'll give Goldie's to Annie. Do you think you could try and save the pink and green one? That's her favourite colour.'

Lady Lavinia (his very own Countess) smiled. 'I think you had better choose Goldfinger's now, Oscar. It will save me coming back down the line.'

'Cor, thanks a million, Madam Countess. That's bloody kind of you, and now I shall definitely see you at H.O.Y.S. with Panky. Bloody great,' and he gave her his most disarming smile as Joshua glared at him as he heard his words, but he had to admit, his brother was bloody good. Lady Lavinia merely smiled. She couldn't have been more pleased with her day.

CHAPTER 19

Anne-Marie was painstakingly painting a small, square, white card with a pony's head in one corner. She was using her gold paint to colour it, leaving a white star in the middle of its forehead. She finished the picture by painting a white main and then after she had written in black biro, '*Oz and Goldfinger's first rosette, Massenden Show, fifth place.*' She then pinned it on her bedroom wall with the green and pink rosette immediately below it. It now took pride of place beside the rosettes Oscar had given her that he had won the previous October with Whisky and Humbug.

She wiped away a tear as she thought of Whisky. Oscar and she had cried together several times but today he was happy and although she knew no pony would ever take Whisky's place it was obvious Oscar already loved the aptly named Hanky Panky. Tomorrow evening she was going to ride Tom Thumb with Oscar and Humbug to Lake House where he was going to jump the pony over Charles' cavaletti. It had been a good week. She had heard that she had got her place at the grammar school with Georgia, Charlotte and Eloise and all the triplets, Gus and Rupert would be joining Joshua and the obnoxious Simon West at the boy's grammar school in September.

It had been a particularly good week for Oliver – he had passed his grade four guitar exam and his grade three piano exam with honours.

Anne-Marie noticed the light outside the window was fading. She glanced at her watch - she was three minutes late – she picked up her mobile. *'Good night, Oz. I've just hung the gorgeous rosette on my wall – you were brill. See you tomorrow evening – sleep well – Annie X'*

There was already a text on her phone from Oscar. *'Have just had a quick buzz on Buggy. Dad came with me on Satin – we cantered round the lake – Buggy on fine form. Mum says I can go to church in the morning – want to ask the vicar if she thinks Whisky can see me jumping. 'Lando and Ollie are coming with me. I know you can't come too because you're one of those Roman somethings, but never mind, I'll see you in the evening. Good night – Oz x.'*

The next morning, the triplets put on their cleanest jeans and a blue check shirt and walked through the woods and across the fields past Old Tiles Farm to the village green. The church clock was already telling them it was two minutes to ten but the bells were still ringing and they ran through the door and flung themselves down at the back of the church.

Orlando could see Georgia and her father. He was holding something on his lap and Orlando was pretty certain it was Herbie. Further up the church he could see Veronica and Virginia Mawgan-Whitely and their mother and in the very front pew Susan and Bill Cotton.

They enjoyed singing the hymns except that they missed the first two verses of every one whilst they struggled to find the right number in the hymn book, but the lady vicar, who was known for her long sermons seemed to be talking for a very long time and Oscar's mind wandered to the Massenden Horse Show and whether his father had jumped yet.

He pulled his mobile from his jacket pocket. *'Dad, Oz here. How is the show? Have you jumped yet? We're going to walk straight to the Centre after we've left here. The hymns are O.K. but the vicar is talking for an awfully long time. Hope she finishes soon cos Ollie wants the loo. Think he had better call at Granny Alice's before we walk to the Centre. Don't think he would make it. See you soon, Oz.'*

As Oscar put his mobile down on the front of the pew, he noticed a discreet arrow on the wall, pointing to the vestry. He read – TOILET- He nudged Oliver who crept out of the pew in relief. He heard a bleep. The lady in front of him turned round with a frown, which Oscar ignored as he picked up his mobile and read his father's reply. *'Tell Ollie Mum thinks they have recently built a loo at the back of the church. No, I haven't jumped yet. Be very careful when you cross the main road to the Centre. Be sure to use the crossing. Dad.'*

Oscar replied. *'It's O.K. Dad. Ollie's found it. All well. Thank goodness, I think the vicar has finished talking. Oz.'*

At last the final hymn was being sung and the boys were putting their two-pound coins into the collection purse, which Bill Cotton was bringing to each pew. Ten minutes later they were filing out of the church in a slow moving queue as everyone shook hands with Marcia Thomas, the lady vicar.

When the triplets eventually reached her, she smiled kindly at them. She knew exactly who they were. The Primary School children traipsed solemnly into the Church every Friday afternoon during the term time and she had known every child since she had come to the parish when she had replaced the Rev Brownlee, Tom and Sam's bête noir, who had left the village a few years ago.

'Hello boys,' she greeted them, admirably hiding her surprise at seeing them gracing her service. 'How nice to see you in church. Is Mummy with you?'

'No, I came cos I wanted to ask you something very important,' Oscar told her.

'Well, I hope I am able to help you. Which of the triplets are you?'

'Oscar.'

'Well, Oscar, what is worrying you?'

'There was an accident, Mrs. Vicar.'

The accident had been well documented in the local newspaper with a picture taken the previous year of Oscar on Whisky at the Massenden show.

'I know dear, and I was very, very sorry. I know you lost your pony.'

'That's what I want to ask you. Mum and Dad aren't sure but you must know cos you are a friend of God's. After Whisky died he was,' Oscar searched for the right word, 'creamed – and James brought him back in a box, which my dad buried under one of the trees in our garden - but I want to know whether a tiny bit of him could be in heaven. I want to know if he can watch me jumping.'

The vicar was nonplussed – in all honesty she thought it unlikely but she could also see the look of hope in the young boy's eyes. 'I can't be certain, Oscar, but perhaps his soul is there and then maybe he could see you, and he was cremated, dear, not creamed.'

'Oh, and what exactly is a soul?'

'It's a spirit.'

'Wow, like a ghost. Thanks Mrs. Vicar. Ghosts sometimes creep around the house at night. I might see him then. Wow that would be great.'

The vicar was looking rather uneasily at Susan and Bill who were standing directly behind the triplets, when to her relief she heard Oscar saying to his brothers. 'Come on Ollie and 'Lando, let's go and tell Dad. The Vicar says Whisky can see us. He's probably sharing a stable in heaven with Rascal. Bye, Mrs. Vicar,' and the three boys ran off across the green.

Marcia Thomas was shaking her head. 'Oh, Mrs. Cotton, may God forgive me. I think I have just told a lie, but at least the little lad's mind is at rest. Surely I've only committed a very small sin.'

Susan patted her arm. 'I think you have just made a young boy very happy and I'm certain that is no sin, Marcia, and what's more, I am certain Tom and Sam will be eternally grateful! Poor Oscar, he adored that pony.'

Orlando was running ahead of his brothers, trying to catch up with Georgia and her father. Herbie was waddling along behind them – he had sat on Giles' knee during the service, not uttering a single bark or a whimper. 'Georgia,' Orlando was gasping for breath as he reached her. 'Ollie. Oscar and I are going to the Centre to watch my dad and Justin and Charles. Can you come with us? Mum's taken a picnic. There will be masses of food she always makes far too many sandwiches. Rosie and Josh are already there with Gus and Abby.'

Giles had no objections, he had an appointment with Herbert Holmer and would be working on his computer all the afternoon and as Georgia ran off with the triplets, he sat on the seat opposite La Casa sul Verde with Herbie on the seat beside him, hoping for just one brief glimpse of a woman who prayed on his mind every moment of his waking hours, and who was having an on-going affair with his alter ego, the dapper detective Herbert Holmer.

CHAPTER 20

The following Wednesday afternoon, Tom was sitting on the seat near the stables, which overlooked the lake, holding Midnight Fantasy's bridle, waiting for the hospital car, which was bringing Adrian for a re-union with his little horse. The specialist at the hospital thought by going back to Massenden, maybe something, however small, would jog Adrian's memory and bring him back from the dark abyss he was currently lost in.

Amy and Miriam were at Shepherd's Cottage where Tom was going to lead Adrian. He would have tea there, before Tom would take him back to the stables and the car, which would then drive him back to the hospital.

Amy had had a long discussion with Adrian's specialist, an extremely well esteemed professor called Patrick Masters. He had told Amy that now Adrian's eyes had recovered seventy per cent of their sight and were still improving almost daily, he would soon be ready to leave the hospital and move to a rehabilitation clinic for a month, after which, he told Amy, he would come home and it would be Amy's responsibility to look after the husband who had no idea who he was.

She was still visiting him every day and they had developed a friendly relationship, which was something Patrick Masters told her he hoped could induce a resurgence of his love for her. Fortunately for Amy she had the devotion of Adrian's parents, Miriam and George, but they too were experiencing the same heartbreak as she was. At the moment, their son had no idea who they were.

Amy had shown him the pictures of their wedding. He had acknowledged the fellow looked remarkably like him but he had handed them back to her saying. 'I'm sorry, he certainly does resemble me but I am afraid it means nothing. The last thing I can remember is waking up here, my life before that has gone, but I do look forwards to your visits, you've become a really good friend.'

Patrick Masters had assured Amy she must take the positives from this. Adrian was certainly not rejecting her or little Molly, who he always welcomed with a smile. One thing was certain; Amy was determined to get her husband back, however long it might take.

Tom could see the large black car coming down the drive to the stables. He stood up and led Fantasy towards it, greeting Adrian as he stepped out of the large limousine accompanied by a man a little older than himself who was one of the special carers whose job it was to accompany patients such as Adrian on one of these missions.

He shook hands with Tom and stroked Midnight Fantasy. Tom was smiling at Adrian, who was trying to remember where he had seen Tom.

'I'm Tom. I came to see you in hospital with Charles, the other day. This is your horse, Midnight Fantasy. I thought you might like to see him and I will lead you down to the cottage where Amy is waiting with some tea for us. Then I'll bring you back here and maybe if there is time you can give Fantasy a good brush.'

Adrian looked uncertain. 'Amy? Is that the girl with the baby who comes to see me in hospital? She's nice. I thought she lived in London near the hospital.' He was stroking Fantasy. 'I like her. Is she a single mum? She never brings a fellow with her, just a rather cute baby.'

Tom was nonplussed – never one to be lost for words, for once he was struggling. 'She appears to be single at the moment, Adrian, but hopefully her chap will soon rediscover her.' It was the best reply he could think of and he changed the subject asking Adrian, 'Would you like a leg up?'

'A leg up? What's that?'

'I'll help you on to Fantasy.'

'I think I can manage,' and to Tom's complete surprise, put his foot in the left stirrup and landed gently into the saddle, picking up the reins with a natural ease. Sally appeared leading Madame.

'Hello Adrian, I'm Sally, one of the grooms here,' but all she received in return was an empty smile. She held Fantasy's reins whilst Tom leapt into the saddle saying. 'Thanks Sally. Come on, Adrian, let's go.'

They walked round the lake, chatting companionably about Fantasy. It was only too obvious that the stables, the lake and not least Tom himself meant nothing to Adrian as he chatted about his boys and Rosie before deliberately riding up to Woodcutters. He had called Sam on his mobile when he had seen Adrian arriving at Lake House asking her to be at the cottage gate – he was leaving no stone unturned as he strove to find something that would stir Adrian's lost memory.

He led Adrian to the gate, where Sam was waving. 'Hi, Adrian,' she called.

Adrian looked uncertain. 'Hello,' he replied, but there was no recognition whatsoever.

'This is my wife, Sam, Adrian and this is our home, Woodcutters.'

Adrian was looking at the cottage, when suddenly, Boswell came racing out of the front door, which Sam had left open and ran straight up to Fantasy, where he started clawing at Adrian's leg.

He laughed. 'How odd. Your dog seems to know me.' The dog was staring unflinchingly at Adrian's vacant face. He gave a small wine and pawed the young man's leg again.

'He's nice. What's his name?'

'Boswell, but we call him Boz. He's Sammy's guard dog.'

'He's smashing. It's strange, I think I've seen him somewhere before. Did you bring him with you when you visited me in hospital?'

Tom was almost holding his breath. 'I don't think Boz would have been appreciated there, Adrian.'

'Well, I'm certain I have seen him somewhere before.'

Patrick Masters had emphasized that Adrian should not be taxed in any way and Tom said no more as they said goodbye to Sam and the dog and continued on their way to Shepherd's Cottage and Amy. 'Shall we trot?' he asked Adrian.

'Trot?'

'Yes. Go a bit faster. Are you up for that?'

'Sure. I think I must have done this before. It feels familiar and comfortable.'

Tom pressed Madame's sides gently and still holding the leading rein, he and Adrian trotted together through the woods. To Tom's delight and he was not altogether surprised, he noticed Adrian rising in complete harmony with Fantasy. He was obviously enjoying himself. 'Smashing,' he said as he smiled at Tom, who noticed that for the moment the vacant expression had left Adrian's face.

They trotted up to the stables in the corner of the small paddock opposite Shepherd's Cottage and although Adrian appeared completely oblivious of his whereabouts, Tom's eager eyes noticed him running up his stirrups, before undoing the girth, laying it carefully across the seat of the saddle, then looping the reins over one arm and easily removing the bridle before patting Fantasy, carefully closing the stable door and then following Tom across the paddock and up the front path to the cottage.

Inside the cottage Miriam was doing her best to stem Amy's anxious nerves. 'Don't expect too much, dear,' she was telling her daughter-in-law. 'Remember Mr. Masters told us we mustn't do or say anything which might upset Adrian. We must let things happen in their own time. It will be very hard, but we must both be strong,' and the brave woman gathered herself together as she saw her son making his way up the path to the front door chatting to Tom. She kissed both the men on their cheeks, glancing hopefully at Adrian's face, but it was only too obvious he had no recognition of his own mother. She swallowed her disappointment and walked back into the cottage where Anna was sitting on the settee feeding Molly.

Tom, who had watched Sam feeding his own children many,

many times was not the least bit embarrassed but Adrian was looking distinctly uneasy and the huge lump in Amy's throat was hurting as she recalled his arms round her on this same settee, and how they had laughed at their greedy little girl, the very evening before the accident.

Adrian turned away and found his eyes looking at a photograph of Amy in a pale, blue dress, standing beside a young man who looked very familiar and he questioned what he was doing beside this beautiful girl and also why Tom was standing beside them in a dark grey suit.

He was puzzled but said nothing and to his relief Amy had fastened her dress and was placing the baby back in its buggy.

He liked Amy. She looked pretty in her simple cotton, flowered dress, which showed off her figure, which was still a little fuller than usual after the recent birth of Molly. He felt an emotion he was unable to define, but which vaguely stirred his mind, creeping over his body but one thing he was sure of, was that he didn't want to go back to the hospital, he would far rather stay here with this pretty girl and the little baby which seemed to be always smiling at him, but all too soon, Tom was glancing at his watch. 'We had better saddle up the horses, Adrian. Your car will be waiting.'

'I wish I didn't have to go back, Tom. I wish I could stay here, I feel safe here.'

'Maybe you can, Adrian. Anyway we will see if the hospital will let you come back here soon,' and he vowed he would make certain they would, because another small incident had occurred. 'I'll just pop up to the loo if that's O.K.' Adrian had said to Amy, and before she had time to reply he had disappeared up the stairs, through the bedroom to the bathroom. He seemed to know exactly where it was. Even Amy was heartened and when he had left with Tom, she hugged Miriam.

'Did you notice? He remembered where the bathroom is, that's the first encouraging sign.' But it wasn't - it was the second and the moment the car had driven away from Lake House, Tom was on the telephone to Patrick Masters.

'Adrian seemed to vaguely recognise my dog, Mr. Masters, and I noticed he knew exactly where the bathroom was situated in the cottage. You have to go through the bedroom to find it. He remembered that. Also he rode as if he had never been out of the saddle. The visit was definitely beneficial. If he can come here again before long one of us will ride with him and I know Amy would welcome him at the cottage again.'

'It's Wednesday today, Mr. West. How about next Monday at the same time?'

'Fine, I'm competing at the weekend but I'll make certain I'm here on Monday afternoon and I'll bring our dog with me.'

Amy was feeding Molly when the front door opened and she heard Anna calling. 'Co-ee, Amy, can I come in?'

'Anna, of course, I'm just feeding Molly.'

Anna was carrying a basket containing a small cottage pie and a punnet of raspberries. 'I've brought you a little treat for your supper, Amy and I wanted to know how Adrian coped with his visit this afternoon.'

Amy sighed. 'Anna, it's so hard to tell what he is thinking. He has no recollection of his life before the accident at all; his earliest memory is waking up in the hospital and not being able to see anything. Although he noticed our wedding photograph and I saw him looking at it, it seemed to mean nothing at all to him. I think he likes me – he's friendly and he seems to have a bond with Molly, although he has no idea she is his daughter. Tom phoned me a little while ago and he is convinced Adrian recognized Boswell and he also said he seemed totally relaxed riding Fantasy although he obviously didn't realize he was riding his own horse. He told Tom he wished he could stay here. He didn't want to go back to the hospital. The really odd thing was, he knew exactly where the loo was. He went straight up to the bedroom and into the en-suite – not to the main bathroom. Anna, I am so frightened. I just don't know what lies ahead for Molly and myself - the only thing I know for certain is that I still love him to bits and I shall do everything in my power to get my old Adrian back,' and by now the tears were running down Amy's expressive face.

'Amy, don't go rushing to London tomorrow,' Anna begged her sister. 'Dom and Genevieve have said they will go to the hospital in the morning after Anne-Marie has gone to school. Now Tom has the Canadian grooms the stables can manage without Dom for a day. Bring Molly to Theobald's Place and we will spend the day together in the garden. You've not seen the house since we have got ourselves straight. We will just have a really quiet day, it will help to recharge your batteries.'

Anna could see Amy was dithering. 'Adrian will be fine, Amy, and a day in the fresh air would do Molly a power of good. She needs to get some colour into her little cheeks.'

To Anna's relief, Amy agreed she would push Molly to Theobald's Place in time for lunch and spend the afternoon in the garden.

Whilst Anna was at Shepherd's Cottage, Adrian was in the hospital car talking enthusiastically about his afternoon and the excitement of riding a horse called Fantasy. He suddenly said to Jack, his carer. 'Tom introduced me to his wife. She was beautiful and they had a super dog called Boswell. Strange – I'm sure I had seen him before. I asked Tom if he had brought him to the hospital, but he laughed and said *'I'm sure Boz wouldn't be welcome there.'* Odd, I'm certain I had met him before. He wasn't the type of dog you would forget. He was enormous and strangely enough he seemed to know me. He rushed straight up to me and pawed my leg.

We had tea in a pretty garden with Amy – you know – the girl who visits me at the hospital with the baby. I really like her – she's friendly and little Molly is cute. There was a photograph of Amy with a chap – he looked a bit like me, perhaps I've got a brother or a cousin. I wish I could remember. It bothers me. It was odd though. I needed the loo before I left and I seemed to know exactly where it was. I felt as if I'd been in the cottage before, can you ask Professor Masters if I can go there again and I would like to ride Fantasy again too.'

As soon as they had arrived back at the hospital Jack went straight to the professor's office and told him. 'I've had a really interesting conversation with Adrian on the way back here, sir. He is positive he knew Tom's dog and according to him he felt he had ridden before, everything came completely naturally to him, but perhaps the most significant thing of all, he knew exactly where the loo and the en-suite were in the cottage. He told me he likes Amy and wants to go there again – he also said he would like to ride again.'

Patrick Masters nodded. 'I've already had an encouraging phone call from Tom West, Jack. I've arranged for you to take him to Massenden again on Monday afternoon. Tom says he will make certain he is available and he will bring the dog with him. Although I believe this will be slow progress, Jack, the signs are most definitely encouraging.'

That same evening, the future was also looking even more promising for Oscar and Humbug. Tom had decided to give his son half an hour's schooling on both Humbug and Hanky Panky and he was riding the bigger pony beside Oscar, past the lake to the indoor school where Dom had built a small jumping course for Humbug, who was now bouncing beside Hanky Panky, who in turn was giving Tom the most uncomfortable ride he had endured for a very long time. The pony's feet never seemed to be on the ground, he was as strong as Kaspar and Tom was marveling that his young son could control this ball of fire, let alone jump clear round a jump off course and when Oscar said. 'He's super isn't he. Dad?' Tom replied sardonically. 'Well he's certainly unorthodox, Oz.'

'What does that mean, Dad?'

'Mad. Oz. Plain mad.'

'Yea, but bloody good fun, dad.' Tom found he couldn't disagree. He and Oscar obviously had the same taste.

When they reached the school, Justin was opening the large sliding door. Tom and Oscar both shot through it into the school where Justin had just finished schooling Pickwick, who was leaving for Paris at the end of the following week for a big three day show in which Tom and Charles would also be participating. It was going to be a busy weekend as on the Saturday, the boys were all going to a large show near Dorking, but to the girl's annoyance they would all be going to Jane's studio where they would be taking their ballet exams. They had been both disappointed and furious when they had realized these coincided with one of their favourite shows and it wasn't until Tom had negotiated with Sally and Erica to drive the big horseboxes to Camber Sands on the Sunday that they had gradually stopped grumbling, especially when they were told they could spend the day round the pool at Lake House once the exams had been accomplished. Joanna and Genevieve were going to have the dubious pleasure of accompanying the girls to the ballet studio, whilst Anna, Elizabeth and Sam were going to oversee the boys where Sam was going to lead Noah and Amelia in their first leading rein class.

Noah had recently discarded the basket saddle and was already rising to the trot on Gus' very first German saddle that Justin had given him when he had still been riding Mr. Magic. Anna had bought Noah his first tiny pair of brown leather jodhpur boots, a pair of cream jods and a brown tweed jacket. She would pick a tiny white rose bud from the garden, and she knew that whatever the outcome, she was going to be bursting with pride when Sam led little Noah into the arena for the first time and she wished Justin could be there to enjoy the experience too. Noah would be a miniature of his father as he sat on the miniscule Amelia.

Humbug was flying and Oscar was smiling. In the school at Lake House his beloved Buggy was listening to his every aid – it was impossible to believe that it was less than two months since the ill fated accident and how amazingly well Humbug had learned to cope with just one eye. Charles had crept into the corner of the school – even he was astounded – he and Tom raised the jumps and once again, Humbug flew. Tom pulled a handful of nuts from his pocket and fed them to the eager pony. Oscar had jumped to the ground and buried his face in Humbug's mane. Tom could see his young son's shoulders were heaving. He was only too aware of how badly Whisky's death had affected Oscar, added to which, the trauma of Humbug losing his eye had only added to his misery. Now the exhilaration and delight of discovering Humbug was showing no signs of distress had overcome the boy, whom it was hard to believe was only just eleven years old.

At last he looked at Tom. 'Dad Buggy is going to win at H.O.Y.S. He can. I know he can. He was brilliant.'

'We'll take it slowly, Oz, and you could well be right. I m going to Paris next weekend but when I get back there's a mid-week show in Essex. It's your half term that week, so you and I and Humbug and perhaps Goldfinger will have a special day out together and we will see what we can do without your brothers and sister on your back side.'

'You won't tell 'Lando and Ollie I cried, will you, Dad?'

'Of course not, Ozzie. Now let's see what mood Panky is in tonight.'

Charles watched almost in awe, as having held Humbug whilst Tom raised the jumps for the bigger pony, he then saw Oscar at his very best. He obviously had a very special relationship with this unorthodox pony but they were foot perfect and he was applauding this plucky boy seemingly without one ounce of fear in his body, with genuine admiration. Apart from possibly Joshua, Charles could think of no other junior who could have controlled this prancing ball of fire.

Tom encouraged and praised his children when he felt it was deserved but he never got carried away by any of their performances.

As Oscar walked Hanky Panky round the school to cool him down, Charles smiled at Tom. 'You must be so proud of him.'

Tom's answer was immediate. 'I'm proud of all my kids, Charles, whenever they try their best, whether it's their riding, Rosie's ballet or Oliver's music but what I am proud of is the tremendous fortitude Oscar has shown recently. He is still heartbroken about Whisky's death but he is getting on with his life, learning how to deal with adversity and with that Sam and I will give him every scrap of help we possibly can.'

Tom and Oscar walked back to Woodcutters and as they reached the cottage, Oscar asked his father once more. 'You promise, you won't tell, but Buggy was brilliant, wasn't he Dad?'

'He always was a feisty little bugger, Ozzie, a bit like his rider and he obviously still is. I'm proud of you both. You are a lucky boy; you've got three superb ponies. I know you will never forget Whisky and no one would expect you to, but it's time to move on and tonight I will send the entries to the show in Essex. During this week, school the ponies as often as you can on the flat but don't attempt to jump Hanky Panky or Humbug until I am back from Paris when we will have another session together before the show.'

'Thanks. You're a great Dad.'

'And I have four sons and a great daughter too,' Tom thought.

Sam glanced at Oscar as he ran into the kitchen ahead of Tom. He was smiling, but she was his mother, and she was well aware he had been crying. She was also sensitive enough not to ask any questions. She was well aware that Oscar was still traumatized by the accident; however, he was smiling at her as he took his place at the supper table beside Orlando and Oliver, telling her. 'Buggy was brilliant, Mum. He didn't knock a single fence down and he was bouncing like a trampoline!!'

Sam laughed at his words. 'That's wonderful Ozzie.'

'Yea, and Dad's taking me to a show in Essex when he gets back from Paris.'

Rosie was highly put out. 'And what about me?' she asked Tom.

'You can come too Rosie but you will only bring Sparkler. I want to pay extra attention to Humbug in the thirteen two class. 'Lando and Josh, you are going to a show in Berkshire that day with Justin and Gus and Abby, and Charles is taking Mimi and Rupert to Hampshire. There are a lot of shows in the South of England that week, probably because it is half term. You've got your music school next week, haven't you Ollie?'

'Yea, we're staying in a boarding school in Buckinghamshire. It should be great. There's going to be a jazz section. Don't forget to come to the concert on the Sunday evening before I come home."

'Rosie and I are coming with your Grannies and Grandpas, Ollie, and Jane and Clara are coming too. Dad and the boys are jumping in Sussex.'

Rosie wasn't too pleased about this arrangement, she would far rather have been going to the show with Gus and her brothers, but for once Sam had been adamant – she was to have a day out with her grandparents. When Sam had a certain expression on her face, then Rosie knew there was simply no point at all in arguing.

Later that evening, when the boys and Rosie had gone to bed, Sam asked Tom. 'Why had Ozzie been crying?'

'He asked me not to mention it to the other boys, Sam. He's still really cut up over Whisky. It's going to take a long time for him to forget that morning. It will probably never vanish completely but hopefully as he has success with Goldfinger and Hanky Panky it will fade. He was overcome when Humbug jumped so well. He's an amazing little pony and Ozzie is desperate to get him to H.O.Y.S. He deserves to be helped. That's why I'm taking him to Essex without the others. We'll see what he can do.'

'Tom. The boys are so lucky. You're not just the best husband in the world, you are the most fantastic Dad.'

'But I love you all, Sammy. It's as simple as that.' And he kissed her as he picked her up and carried her up the stairs.

Adrian's second visit to Massenden the following Monday was interesting. It was pouring with rain and Tom decided the only place they could ride was in the school. He wanted to see how Adrian would cope without being led and he decided to ride Oscar's Goldfinger to Lake House. He was a sensible, calm pony, quite capable of carrying a lightweight adult, which Adrian most certainly was.

When Adrian saw Goldfinger he made no comment – just stroking his neck whilst Boz, who had followed Tom to the school was leaping all over him. He laughed. 'I love your dog, Tom. I'm really sure he knows me – I wish I could remember where I have seen him before. I think he was with another big dog.'

This was extremely interesting. Tom was sure Adrian was referring to Bertie. He waited to see if he was going to say any more, wondering if he would mention Holly, but instead he turned to Goldfinger saying. 'What a super pony, Tom.'

'Yes, Oscar rides him,' but Tom noticed there was no flicker of recognition at the mention of his son. He sat Boz in the corner of the school, telling him to stay. The big dog immediately obeyed Tom's command, curling into a huge ball and closing his eyes.

Tom held Goldfinger whilst Adrian mounted and then watched as the younger man gathered the reins. 'Walk round the school Adrian whilst you get to know Goldie. He's extremely well schooled. He won't suddenly do anything untoward. When you feel ready trot on and then canter if you want to.'

Before long Adrian was smiling broadly as he cantered round and round the school on both reins.

Tom called him into the middle of the school. 'How good is your eyesight now, Adrian?' he asked.

'Eighty per cent perfect, or so they tell me,' he told Tom.

'So can you see the jumps clearly?'

'Yes. It's only when I read I need glasses.'

'O.K. then Adrian, I've built you a little course. Have a walk round first whilst I hold Goldie and then see how you get on.'

Tom watched with interest. Adrian had certainly lost none of his skill and he and Goldfinger were jumping in perfect harmony.

'Wow, he's super, Tom. I think I've done this before – but I don't think it was on this lovely pony.'

Tom raised the jumps once and then put Goldfinger in one of the empty stables and asked Adrian's driver to take them to Shepherd's Cottage. Boswell sat in the back with Tom. When they reached the cottage he made sure he was well away from Amy's feisty little dog, Scruffy, who was curled up in the corner of the settee. He wagged his tail as Adrian came into the room, but unlike with Boswell, Adrian showed no sign of recognizing him.

He was obviously pleased to see Amy and kissed her cheek as she came to greet him with Molly in her arms. He kissed Molly's forehead and stroked her face, smiling at Amy. 'I'm sure she has grown since I was here the other day, Amy,' and he produced a small teddy bear which he had bought in one of the small towns on his way to Massenden. It was obvious he liked Amy and as they ate the ham and egg sandwiches and the Victoria Sponge she had made, he was telling her about Goldfinger and the jumping course Tom had built for them. 'I'm sure I had jumped before Amy, but the reins felt different. I kept feeling for another one.'

Amy glanced at Tom – he nodded at her – Fantasy had a Pelham bit with two reins attached to it, Goldie had a simple snaffle with just the one rein – it was another very small step in the right direction.

There was another three quarters of an hour before the car would take Adrian back to the hospital, Tom stood up. 'I must get back to the horses, Amy. It seems to have left off raining and the sun is trying to come out, why don't you and Adrian push Molly down to Old Tiles. Mum would love to see her?'

'Would you like that?' she asked Adrian.

Adrian was happy just to be with Amy. He liked her – he felt safe with her and he had fallen in love with Molly. 'I don't know where Old Tiles is, but yes, if we've time that would be great.'

As they walked past the cross-country course, he asked Amy. 'What are those huge jumps?'

'They belong to the Massenden Equitation Centre. Tom's brother-in-law, Jean-Pierre and his partner James Cotton own it. They sometimes have competitions here.'

Amy wasn't sure if he had understood but soon they had reached Old Tiles where they found Mary picking gooseberries. She rushed to the buggy to look at Molly and then smiled at Adrian, who obviously had no idea who she was. 'Hello, Adrian, I'm Mary, Tom's mother. You've been here lots of times.'

Adrian stared at her blankly. 'Have I?' was all he replied.

Mary gave Amy a large bag of gooseberries.

'I'm sorry we can't stay, Mary but Adrian's car is waiting to take him back to London but I wanted Molly to get some fresh air before it rains again and I shall top and tail these gooseberries whilst I watch T.V. this evening.'

As they walked back and drew near Shepherd's Cottage she felt Adrian take her hand. 'Amy, I like coming to see you and Molly. I already feel I know you well.'

Amy turned and kissed him very gently on his lips. 'Me too, Adrian, I feel I know you very, very well and you can come here as often as you like. Molly likes seeing you too. I'll bring her to the hospital when I come on Thursday. Perhaps you could ask your professor if I could take you out to lunch,' and with that promise she kissed him again gently as he clambered into the car, waving as they drove away. Amy felt happier than she had done for several weeks. She felt a small stride had definitely been made.

CHAPTER 21

Sam was leading Noah round the large arena with about twenty other small children and their hopeful parents, whilst Anna was taking a multitude of photographs on Justin's second best camera. She had firmly refused when he had offered her his Leica, which after his horses and now probably Theobald's Place was his most treasured possession. The camera she was using was considerably less valuable and also very much easier to manipulate.

At the same time, Dom was taking a video on his iPod.

Sam was very experienced in the show ring and she was making certain the larger Welsh Mountain and Dartmoor ponies were not overshadowing tiny little Amelia. The previous afternoon, she had helped Anna bath the little skewbald mare. They had dried her with Anna's hair dryer before plaiting her bushy mane into neat little balls.

Amelia's temperament was superb as was Noah's and together, as Sam was well aware, they made a really appealing pair.

It was unusual for a toddler of Noah's tender age to have his natural seat and to be able to rise to the trot, which he did admirably, never missing a single stride. Sam had four godchildren of which Noah and Rudi were the youngest. She loved them all but Noah was special. He was the baby who had battled against all odds to survive and now he was giving her his cheeky grin, looking so like his father and his grandfather too, as she led him into the front line which the judges were starting to assemble.

Noah was the third little rider to do the individual show after which the judge walked up to Sam, who she had recognized. 'How old is he?' she asked. 'I thought Rosie was your youngest.'

Sam laughed. 'Sadly he's not mine. He's my little godson and he is two but he's very small for his age. He was a very prem baby.'

The judge smiled at Noah and then asked the next child to do her individual show.

The class took a very long time and Sam could see Noah was becoming bored. She had not had five children of her own without becoming extremely resourceful and soon Noah was listening entranced to a story she was quickly making up about a naughty cat who had chased a bird up a tree and was now waiting for the fire engine with a big ladder to come and rescue him. Noah's eyes were huge, when Sam suddenly realized they and four mothers were being asked to trot round again. 'Best bumps, Noah,' she told the little boy.

Amelia trotted steadily and Noah was smiling at the judge – a little girl on a beautiful Welsh Section A, pony, not unlike Snow Queen, was called in first and then to Sam's joy, the steward was beckoning to Noah.

Soon Sam was fastening a big blue velvet rosette onto Amelia's bridle. Noah, however, was asking. 'Auntie Sammy, Did it reach?'

'Did what reach, darling?' Sam asked him.

'The ladder, Auntie Sammy, did they rescue the naughty cat?'

'Yes, Noah, and he was so afraid he never chased another bird again.'

'That's good but I very hot. Where's my Mummy? Do you think she will let me have an ice-cream?'

Sam looked at Noah in his tweed jacket. The sun was blazing down – she undid the buttons and folded the little coat over her arm as she led him back to Anna, who was soon hugging both her and Noah at the same time.

'Brilliant, Noah,' the boys were all shouting and with Gus holding one of his hands and Joshua the other, he toddled beside them to the ice-cream kiosk.

The judge was watching – he had looked small on the pony – but she hadn't realized he was barely more than a baby. She walked across to Anna. 'Anna,' she said recognising her, 'Justin's wife.

I thought that child was special and I thought I recognized that wicked smile.' The judge had once had a brief fling with Charles many moons ago. 'He's got the Wright-Smith style and what a smashing little pony.'

'She's our rescue pony,' and Anna told her about the fire at the sanctuary. 'Her two year old son is growing up on my friend's farm. He looks exactly like her, he's gorgeous.'

Ten minutes later, Amelia was dozing in her stall in the horsebox whilst Noah was fast asleep in his buggy under a large tree by the side of the arena where the junior jumping was about to commence.

Whilst Sam was triumphing with little Noah, Joanna, Elizabeth and Genevieve were arriving at Jane's ballet studio, with six young girls who appeared to be taking everything in their stride, plus Mimi whose nerves, at the very thought of a ballet exam, were as usual struggling to get the better of her.

Somehow she had passed her first three exams and now in her burgundy leotard was about to embark on her Grade 1V with some of her school friends and the very talented Clara Dubois.

Joanna was surprised that Mimi had persisted – but she had – and now she was facing the extremely po-faced examiner, Françoise Corvière, who had her own exclusive ballet school on the outskirts of London. Jane's heart had sunk when she had received confirmation of who her examiner was going to be and she had asked the bar staff at the Equitation Centre to produce the best lunch they possibly could in an attempt to thaw the ice cold Madame Corvière, who was now in her mid-sixties and who, in the past had examined Jane herself several times before she had gone to the ballet school in London.

When the three mothers crept into the waiting room, which had a large notice blue tacked to the door saying 'QUIET PLEASE. EXAMS IN PROGRESS.' they found Jane waiting for the bell to ring, which would be the summons to let her know the examiner was ready for Lilia to lead in her ten little primary pupils. This first exam was in the form of a class rather than a strict exam and

Lilia was allowed to officiate. The following exams were without any guidance or sign of a teacher and Jane had to wait with the anxious mothers, listening through the wall trying to ascertain what was going on.

During the Grade1 exam to Jane's consternation, on several occasions she heard the music pause and then start again. *'Oh dear, she thought, someone has gone wrong.'* With most examiners she wouldn't have worried, but when that person was Françoise Corvière she was well aware from past experience this was not a good sign.

Fenella, Abby and four of their friends from the Primary School were soon disappearing through the door into the studio. Jane had made sure their hair was immaculate and the seams of their tights ran in a straight line down the back of their legs and when she knew there was nothing more she could do, would sit them on a chair giving them a selection of books to read.

Madame Corvière suddenly sat up a little straighter as the exam got under way and the Hon. Fenella Thornley executed her echapée sautés. With her pink and white complexion and her pale gold hair in a neat bun, Fenella resembled a delicate piece of porcelain and it was with an effort that the harsh examiner managed to turn her attention to the other little girls.

Rosie and Eloise were looking at a book together. Jane had put almost an entire can of hair lacquer on Rosie's mop of thick curly hair – but she was finally satisfied as she slipped a green, velvet scrunchy around her dark bun. With their gold skin, brown eyes and almost black hair, Rosie and Eloise could have been taken for sisters rather than cousins. Usually, Rosie's curls would cascade in a wayward fashion onto her shoulders, whereas Eloise's hair was long and straight, usually either tied neatly in a ponytail or sometimes plaited, but today with their neat buns, they looked more like siblings.

Madame Corvière glanced at the list that Jane had left on the table. She soon realized Eloise Dubois was Jane's daughter. She recalled Jane as a little girl taking this very exam – after all, she asked herself, who could possibly forget her? It was she who had first suggested to Jane's teacher in Canterbury that the child should try for a scholarship to the renowned ballet school. She looked at the list again. Rosie West – West – that name rang a bell, surely that had been Jane's surname

'Are you Madame Dubois' niece?' she asked Rosie.

Rosie had never heard of the word shy. 'I sure am and Tom West is my Dads and I am going to be his big horse, Kaspar when I do my interruption bit in the middle of the exam,' and she smiled her mother's smile which was impossible to ignore – even if you were a hardened examiner.

'I think you mean interpretation, Rosie.'

Rosie smiled again. 'Oh well, I'll still be my Dad's horse whatever the word is,' and this time it was the two cousins that François Corbière found it hard to wrest her eyes from.

Just as Rosie and Eloise were coming back into the waiting room, Joanna's mobile was bleeping and there was a message. *'Hi, Mum, It's Rupert – just to let you know Alfie and I won the twelve two class without Rosie there to thwart us, so I shall be at H.O.Y.S. with him. Little Noah came second in the leading rein class and he's been asleep ever since. We're just going to have lunch, then it's the thirteen two class. Had a call from Dad – he won the accumulator in Paris this morning. Good luck to Mimi. Rupert xx'.*

As Genevieve and Joanna took the children to the bar in the Equitation Centre, and Jane carried a tray with a lace cloth and a delicious chicken salad – followed by strawberries and cream into the studio for Madame François Corvière to partake of, Sam and Anna were sitting on some hay bales that had been placed around the arena, plying the boys with sandwiches and bowls of strawberries which Sam had picked in the garden half an hour before they had left. Noah was still asking Sam questions, wanting to know what colour the cat had been and whether he had been chasing a robin, which was the only bird he could recognize.

Dom and Josh went to the horse box to get the thirteen two ponies ready for the younger boys whilst Sam and Anna watched Noah grinning in his buggy as the strawberry ice-cream Anna had bought him dribbled down his chin.

The thirteen two class turned out to be a fiercely fought battle between Gus, Rupert and Orlando who were the only clear rounds, with Rupert and The March Hare beating Gus and Hamlet by half a second and Orlando less than a tenth of a second behind Gus.

Oscar turned to Anna. 'Dad's taking Humbug and me to a show in Essex next week. I'm probably going to take Goldie too. I think Rosie and Sparkler are coming and 'Lando and Josh are going with Justin and Gussie to another big show somewhere else. Ollie's going to a music week for half term, so he won't be jumping.' He hurried with his brothers to get ready for the next class in which the Lake House stables were going to participate in full force.

Sam was proud of her boys as she watched them with Dom in the practice area. He had his hands full in more than one way as he manfully held Lily and manipulated the practice jump at the same time and he was heartily glad he hadn't got Hanky Panky to contend with as well. He had caught a glimpse of him in the school at Lake House the other evening and had marveled at Oscar's ability to stay in the saddle and Tom's unconcerned attitude as his son just about kept control of the super charged pony.

He looked at the beautiful, calm Goldfinger and found it hard to comprehend why Oscar preferred the tempestuous and aptly named Hanky Panky. Anne-Marie had told him. 'Ozzie says Goldie is a bit boring, Papa – he says it's exciting to ride Panky - he says he's much more like Whisky.'

'I don't think Whisky was quite as much of a handful, Cherie - but I think Oscar takes after his father - he can talk to these difficult animals and they respect him.'

Dom brought his mind back to the present and put the poles to the correct height and then satisfied all the boys had jumped them three times, told them to walk quietly to the collecting ring. He was holding Lily for Joshua who was jumping her near the end of the class. The boys walked the course together. Fortunately they were well trained in this task and Joshua was making sure they all counted the strides between the double of jumps at least twice.

The triplets always caused a ripple of interest whenever they walked the course together. It was impossible to tell Orlando and Oliver apart and Oscar was only distinguishable by the baseball cap he always pulled low over his face, as he tried to hide the scar he detested so much.

Josh and Ganger opened the class – jumping an impeccable round – followed by an equally impressive one by Gus and his Pie in the Sky. There were several girls and two boys who were unknown to *the gang*, only one of whom succeeded to jump a clear round and then Josh started as he noticed a girl with bright chestnut hair riding a dapple grey pony. He recognized her immediately and as he glanced at his mother he saw she was clutching Anna's arm. She too had seen Florence Faulkes-Williams. He called to Rupert. 'Come and hold Ganger for me – I must speak to Mum.' He ran to his mother asking her. 'Mum, are you O.K.?'

He noticed his mother was extremely pale but she told him. 'I'm perfectly alright, Josh. It's just Florence is the image of her mother when I first met her. It's – it's – uncanny, but don't worry, I'm fine," and together they watched the red headed girl exit the arena with an excellent clear round under her belt, as Oliver who was completely unconcerned passed her in the entrance with Buck's Fizz. Unlike his brothers, Oliver was not yet interested in girls. He didn't seem to have inherited the family tendency for young love and he had no idea who Florence was, his mind was totally engrossed with the task ahead and he reaped his reward and would be joining his brothers in the jump off.

Oscar was only interested in his Annie and he hadn't even noticed Florence in spite of her flaming red hair and her eye-catching pony. He felt he was riding in his Granny Mary's rocking chair as Goldie almost took himself round the course. He knew he was very lucky to have been asked to ride this beautiful gelding but as he cantered out of the ring he couldn't see where he was going – the tears were falling fast as he longed for his beloved Whisky.

Dom was quick to notice - he gave Ganger to Rupert again and followed Oscar who was riding towards the horsebox. He saw him tie Goldie to the horsebox and climb in through the groom's door and after a moment he followed him inside.

Amelia was lying in the straw in her rater large stall and Dom swallowed a lump in his throat when he noticed Oscar lying with his arms round her sobbing into the tiny pony's neck.

He went and sat beside the distraught boy, putting his hand gently on his shoulder. 'Hey, lad. You've just jumped a fantastic round.'

Oscar sobbed even more. 'But it wasn't on Whisky – it wasn't on Whisky.'

'No, it wasn't Oscar, but Goldie was doing 'is best for you. 'e's a beautiful pony and although 'e will never take Whisky's place 'e wouldn't want to, and you owe it to 'im to do your very best Oscar and to make Anne-Marie proud of you.'

'ANNIE – Dom you won't tell Annie I cried will you. She'd think I was a wimp. I'm not really, Dom. It's just I still miss Whisky so much. I like ponies that are hot and fizzy like Humbug and Panky. When Rosie's a bit older I shall ask my countess if she can ride Goldie for her. She would love him, but she's only just big enough for The Duc – so I'll ride him until she's - um – um – say eleven.'

Dom pulled Oscar up and brushed the straw off his clothes. 'I promise I won't say a word to Anne-Marie and now we 'ad better go and look at the jump off course with your brothers.'

Sam was wondering where Oscar had disappeared to and was relieved when she saw Dom showing him the jump off course. She had been watching Orlando and Torchlight and had not realized he and Dom had vanished.

By the end of the class there were ten clear rounds. The jumps were raised and the clock was now going to play its part and before long, Joshua and Ganger were cantering through the start.

The jump off was fast and furious and when Oscar and Goldfinger entered the arena Gus and Pie in the Sky were in the lead.

Dom had walked to the entrance beside Goldfinger. ''e 'as got a 'uge stride Ozzie – 'e covers the ground faster than you think because 'e is such a smooth ride and because 'e does not not mess around you can turn 'im on a sixpence. Go for it lad, Make Whisky proud of you.'

Which is exactly what Oscar did and for the first time he realised that it wasn't always the hottest, most effervescent pony that was the fastest. Goldie was well in the lead and it stayed that way until the last pony had jumped.

Suddenly an announcement was being given over the public address system. *'Sir Michael Faulkes-Williams who has kindly sponsored the class will present the prizes.'*

Oscar was looking with interest at the tall man who was handing him the cup and a very large red, velvet rosette. 'Is your wife a countess, sir?' he asked.

Michael Faulkes-Williams was a little taken aback, especially when Oscar added. 'My dad's only a mister but he's always telling my mum she's a princess.'

He smiled. 'I'm sure she is Oscar and a very pretty one too.'

'Oh, yes, she's dad's Dolly Bird, as well.'

Michael Faulkes-Williams smiled faintly and moved to the next boy who was Gus and who to his relief just said. 'Thank you, sir, I shall give this to Rosie cos she couldn't come today,' and he moved down the line until he came to his own daughter, Florence. 'Well done, darling, Mummy would have been really proud of you and Caprice was superb,' and with the final rosette distributed, he turned and left the arena as quickly as he could. He had noticed Sam and the horror of his late wife's horrendous final act swept over him as it so often did. He turned to the pretty woman beside him who was the second Lady Faulkes-Williams. 'I'll just make sure Caprice is safely in the trailer and then we'll get home. I feel as if I have had enough of horse shows for a while.'

At Massenden, to Jane's relief, the ballet exams were over and even Mimi seemed to have survived the ordeal.

Madame Corvière had said farewell, telling Jane. 'I have seen some really promising dancers today, Jane, and it was very refreshing to find such beautifully turned out children – not a single hair out of place. I'll send you the reports in the next few days but I can tell you there are no disasters.'

'None?'

'No. One of the older girls was a little wobbly on her arabesque but she was extremely sensible and asked if I would let her do it again. I really don't mind that. It showed enterprise I thought.'

'Was that Hermione Wright-Smith?'

'Yes, what a nice girl. Not the best arms, I have to say, rather stiff but I could see she was doing her utmost to please me. Most commendable.' And with that she had snapped her brief case shut and stepped elegantly into her small B.M.W. as Jane turned to Lilia and her pianist, handing them both a large bouquet of roses and lilies.

'Thank you both for all your help today, there is no way I could possibly have managed without either of you.'

'It was a pleasure, Jane,' the pianist told her, 'and by the way I noticed the examiner appeared to be taking a great deal of interest in Clara.'

Jane smiled. 'Oh well, I shall know the worst and the best by the end of the week but obviously there weren't any disasters,' and she locked the studio door behind her and went in search of Jean-Pierre and a stiff brandy in the bar.

CHAPTER 22

Josh was only twelve but he was an extremely perceptive, intelligent boy and he realized his mother had been far more shaken by the sight of Florence Faulkes-Williams than she was willing to admit. He remembered the girl at the Massenden Show with her mother a few months before Sophie's wicked attack and he realised how much Florence resembled her late mother with their bright chestnut hair and their loud voices. It was four o'clock in Sussex and Josh knew that in Paris it would be one hour later. He thought his Dad would most likely be having a sandwich and maybe a cup of tea before getting ready for the evening competition and he decided to call him. Fortunately his surmise had been correct and Tom was currently munching his way through a ham sandwich with Justin and Charles, when he was aware that his mobile was ringing.

'Dad, it's Josh.'

'Josh. How has your day been?'

'Fine. Ozzie and Goldfinger won the Junior Open – Gus and Pie were second and Ganger and I were third and fifth with Lily, but something rather odd happened today and I think Mum is a bit disturbed.'

'Mum. What was wrong, Josh?'

'Florence Faulkes-Williams was jumping. She's grown a lot since we last saw her and now she looks exactly like her mum. I saw Mum clutching Anna and she has been quiet ever since. I just thought maybe you should call her.'

'Thanks, Josh – will do and well done all of you. I will be home tomorrow evening – look after Mum.'

'Of course, Dad. Good luck tonight,' and Joshua switched off his phone.

Tom turned to Justin and Charles. 'Damn and blast – as you

probably gathered that was Josh. Apparently Florence Faulkes-Williams was at the show and according to Josh now she's older is the spitting image of Sophie. Josh is concerned. He said Sammy was clutching Anna – damn –damn- damn – it's the last thing Sammy needed, or though I suppose if Florence is on the circuit the kid's paths are bound to cross fairly frequently. I'll give Sam a call and make sure she's O.K.' and he left Justin and Charles and made his way back to the caravan.

He dialed her mobile and she answered almost immediately. *'Sammy, darling, it's Tom.'*

'Tommy, aren't you supposed to be jumping?'

'Not until seven thirty – but remember we are an hour ahead of British time. I gather all the kids jumped well and little Noah surpassed himself.'

'How do you know?'

'Josh has just called me. Darling, are you O.K.?'

'Did he tell you about Florence?'

'He did. Would you like me to come home?'

'Darling Tom, of course not. I was really startled for a few minutes, she is the image of Sophie when we first knew her, but she is just a harmless young girl – it was a bit odd seeing Sir Michael presenting the prizes to our boys, but I promise you darling I am absolutely fine, just win the big class this evening and don't worry one tiny bit about me. I've got my four boys to look after me – and not least my faithful Boz.'

'Sammy, you don't know how I hate being away from you.'

'Dearest Tom, after all these years I promise I do know because it is the same for me but you will be home tomorrow evening and I will have your favourite toad in the hole waiting for you. Now promise you won't worry about me. Don't forget tomorrow I'm going to Camber with all the gang.'

'Enjoy it, my darling. I'll call you again after the Grand Prix has finished. Ad infinitum.'

'For ever and always, my Tom.'

The Grand Prix was an overwhelming success with Kaspar in first place, Justin and Mr. Pickwick second and Charles and Dr. Faustus fractionally behind them in third place.

Charles, who was the senior partner at Lake House, looked at Tom and Justin as they were making their way back to the stables. 'How about cutting out the speed class tomorrow, chaps. I know of a much better way to spend the day – let's get the first shuttle back to Dover tomorrow morning and drive straight to Camber. The horses have all excelled themselves today – I don't mind driving the horsebox. We'll hitch the caravan up to the Range Rover and Erica can drive it back to Massenden. Let's give the girls a surprise and ourselves a day off. Who says aye?'

Tom was delighted – he was worrying about Sam and her unfortunate meeting with Florence, and Justin had already made the decision to withdraw Pickwick from the speed class. 'Aye – Aye, Dad,' he said and Tom nodded his head enthusiastically.

'Not a word to the girls either of you, we'll get to Camber, wait until we see them and then meet up with them in the sea. Early start though. I'll set the alarm for five o'clock.'

Justin groaned but Tom was happy – early mornings had never been a problem for him. Charles laughed at the expression on his son's face. 'You can sleep in the horsebox, Justin. Tom and I will share the driving.'

'O.K. Dad, but just make certain I move myself from the caravan into the cab before you drive away.'

Tom phoned Sam as he had promised but didn't mention a word about their changed schedule, just telling her. *'Kaspar was ace, Sammy, and Pickwick and Faustus were pretty good too. Sleep well and I'll see you tomorrow.'*

'So Kaspar won then, Tommy? I'm in bed already. I've made a massive picnic. I'm sure there is enough to feed an army but the

weather forecast for tomorrow is brilliant and it's going to be a really hot day. I just wish you were going to be with us.'

Tom felt a tiny white lie was necessary as he replied. *'So do I, my darling – take great care – now a million kisses. Night, night'* and he watched as Charles carefully set the alarm clock for five o'clock.

The sun had already risen as Charles drove the horsebox around Paris, getting onto the Auto Route leading to Calais. The traffic was extremely light at that hour on a Sunday morning and they had soon left the suburbs of Paris many kilometers behind them, making good progress towards the port. There was no problem getting a place on the shuttle and in less than an hour, with Tom now driving, it was barely nine o'clock on a glorious English, Sunday morning and having missed out on breakfast in France, they pulled into a large roadside café which had a bright yellow and blue sign outside advertising all day breakfast. Having woken Justin who had still been sleeping and ordering the most unhealthy breakfast consisting of an enormous plate of fried food, they were trying not to think how horrified their wives would be if they were aware of the huge amount of cholesterol their men were consuming.

By the time they had eaten a leisurely breakfast, brought Justin to life with four cups of strong coffee, and then driven along the coast from Dover to Camber Sands it was almost eleven o'clock before they had they parked the horsebox in the shadiest spot they could find. They noticed four horseboxes already in the park and as they glanced across the grassy dunes and the golden sand they could see a large string of horses and ponies making their way towards the sea, which was shimmering under the heat of the sun.

Charles looked in astonishment. 'My God, more than half of Massenden must be down there. I can even see Rudi perched up in front of Jean-Pierre on The Whistler and your little Noah and Amelia, Justin, with Anna leading him from Topsy. Crikey, Tom, I can see your sister, Jane on a little horse.'

Jean-Pierre had persuaded Jane to join them with the little horse,

Cassandra, that she sometimes rode in the evenings in the school or hacked round the extensive boundaries of the equitation centre whenever she and Jean-Pierre could find a spare hour together in their busy lives.

Charles and Tom let down the ramp ready to unload their horses whilst Justin went in search of the nearest loo. 'Bloody hell, why on earth did you two persuade me to drink half a gallon of coffee, Dad?'

'Well, something needed to wake you up, you lazy old sod.'

Charles held Pickwick and Faustus whilst Tom led Kaspar into the sunlight and as Justin rejoined them, his mission accomplished, he and Tom fastened the ramp and securely locked the cab. As they mounted the horses they looked over the dunes and could see Genevieve sitting with Giles and the now rotund little bulldog, Bertie, and Charlotte's parents, David and Esther.

They walked the horses carefully across the sand and Tom and Justin waited whilst Charles attracted David's attention, who after the initial shock of seeing the three huge horses standing on the sand, walked over and relieved Charles of their wallets and the keys to the horsebox.

It was low tide and the sand seemed to stretch forever. Soon they had picked their way through the sand castles and the picnicking families and broken into a trot as they had drawn nearer to the sea. They were all three riding bareback – their saddles were too precious to risk a soaking of seawater and Charles and Tom were both hoping the unpredictable Faustus and Kaspar would not put in too many unexpected pranks. Justin was unconcerned – he didn't recall Pickwick ever throwing even the minutest buck and as he reached the edge of the sea he cantered through the waves as Faustus reared high and Kaspar gave three enormous bucks as the two men clutched their horse's manes, somehow staying on their slippery backs and Justin and Pickwick flew through the waves, soon catching up with Susan on Daddy's Girl who was walking beside Mary and Chance. Just ahead of them, Anna was leading

Noah sitting in his basket saddle. Anna didn't want any mishaps in the sea and much to Noah's annoyance he was firmly strapped in the basket.

Justin pulled Pickwick to a walk and rode abreast of the tiny skewbald mare. Noah squealed when he looked up and saw his father towering over him. 'Dadda, Dadda,' he called, startling Anna.

'Justin, whatever are you doing here? You should be doing the speed class in Paris.'

'Well you might sound more pleased to see me, Anna. The truth is we all did well yesterday in the Grand Prix and we decided we would give the horses and ourselves a day off.'

Noah was holding his arms out to Justin. 'I can't take you, Noah. I've got to hold on to Pickwick. You hold on to Amelia's reins and we'll have a little trot.' He turned to Anna, 'Well at least my son is pleased to see me.'

Anna blew him a kiss across Amelia's skewbald head. 'Of course I'm over the moon, Justin – it was just a shock when you suddenly appeared. Where are Tom and your dad?'

'Hopefully not drowning in the sea. The last time I glanced at them, Faustus was on two legs and Dad was hanging on to his neck. Kaspar was leaping around like a frog about ten feet above the waves with Tom clutching his mane. Not too funny when you are riding bareback I must admit. So how is my Anna?'

'Happy now you are here, Just.'

'That sounds highly satisfactory then, my darling. Is there a beach shop here do you think?'

'There is – well I don't think it's exactly a departmental store but I'm sure it sells most things you might require on the sands. What is it you need?'

Justin laughed. 'Well, I don't think it would be too appropriate to go skinny dipping here in the middle of the day, and the sea does look very enticing.'

'Oh, your swimming trunks are in the car, Justin. You obviously left them there after you had swum at Lake House the other day. Abby found them on the floor, they are probably still a bit damp, but they would soon get wet anyway.'

Justin was pleased. Although he was now an extremely wealthy man he still objected to spending one single penny on trivialities unless it was totally necessary. 'Brill. Have you remembered to bring Noah's armbands?'

'I most certainly have, and Jane has got Rudi's. We've told them they must have a rest for an hour after the picnic and then we will take them into the sea.'

'Smashing, hold tight little man and we'll have a short canter,' and as he held Pickwick in an extremely collected canter, Amelia's little legs flew like small rockets as Noah shrieked with delight as he bounced up and down in his basket.

Meanwhile, Tom and Charles were now in control of their mounts and trotting to catch up with the group who were fast approaching the entrance to Rye Harbour where there were never many people and it was usually possible to canter across the soft sand.

Sam and Joanna were riding together. Sam had brought Lily and Joanna was riding Babushka. They both jumped, as two shadows appeared beside them on the sundrenched beach and Sam felt a hand stroking her arm. She turned with a start and found herself looking into Tom's laughing face.

'Darling, oh darling – wicked – but why didn't you tell us you were coming?'

'Well, first of all we weren't certain we would be able to get on an early shuttle, but fortunately for us most frogs don't seem to move very early in the morning and secondly, we wanted to surprise you. The horses were superb yesterday,' and Tom laughed, 'and so were we three musketeers, so we thought we all deserved a day off.'

'It's wonderful,' and Sam's face was gazing at her husband, 'but what a shame you haven't got your swimming trunks.'

'We have though, Sammy. Charles and I always keep a pair in the horsebox – there's often a pool near the showground or sometimes even on the complex itself. Something to look forwards too later, I think, I trust your bikini is safely under those jeans?' and his eyes were glinting as brightly as the sun on the waves.

Charles was still slightly preoccupied trying to quieten the still plunging Faustus as Babushka tried to bite his grey neck, but Joanna put her hand on his thigh simply saying, 'It's so good to see you, so good, my darling.'

Justin and Anna were the first to walk back to the horsebox. Justin changed into his trunks, which smelt faintly of the chlorine from Charles indoor pool and carried Noah back to the rugs, which the girls had laid out on the sand. He lay down in the sun with Anna and Noah who was already falling asleep between them and when Abby and Gus threw themselves on the sand beside them he felt his life was totally complete. He held Anna's hand a shade more tightly as Gus stood up and ran to meet Rosie whose face was already tanned from the sun and the sea and sighed in contentment, not giving a single thought to the thirty riders and horses negotiating the speed class in Paris at that very moment – his life was perfect here on the crowded sands. He covered Noah's head with a tea towel as the sun blazed down and watched Abby and Gus build a massive sand castle with the rest of *the gang*. He smiled at Anna who was pouring him a glass of Chablis from a bottle she had taken from the icebox. She had changed into her very fetching swimsuit – he sipped the wine. 'Very cool, Anna,' he told her and it didn't take a brainbox to know that he wasn't referring to the wine.

Tom had put Kaspar back into the shade of the horsebox with a hay net and a rubber bucket of water that was fixed to a hook on the side of his stall so that he couldn't kick it over. He gave him a small handful of nuts, which he always kept in his pocket and then jumped into the groom's compartment where he discarded his jeans and pulled on his swimming trunks before rejoining Sam who was waiting in the shade with Lily.

There was not one ounce of fat on Tom's muscular body. Sam

remembered when she and Tom had been children his grandfather had found an old D.V.D. of a Tarzan film. Tom had been a stocky little boy. At the end of the film he had turned to Sam and said. 'I'm going to ask Mum if I can go to the gym in Ashford,' which he did. – When, at the age of twelve he had met Charles Wright-Smith with his fabulous gym in the cellars at Lake House, he had spent three quarters of an hour there every day, then swimming in the indoor pool, making full use of both facilities, which Charles himself would use whenever he could find the time. By his fourteenth birthday Tom's puppy fat had completely disappeared as his muscles developed and he grew taller, and now Sam shivered as she looked at the hunk of a man who was walking towards her in the briefest of swimming trunks, his gold curls, which had grown considerably since his last visit to Mr. Timms, glowing beneath the sun, and his blue eyes blazing, with Sam wasn't certain, but thought could be a mixture of both love and desire.

He put Lily in the box whilst she changed into her dark blue bikini – throwing a paler blue sarong around her shoulders.

Tom had never hidden his emotions – he loved Sam and he didn't care who knew. He took one look at her and pulled her into the nearest sand dune saying nothing but kissing her until she could scarcely breathe. Suddenly she could hear Oscar's voice telling Orlando. 'Buggy really enjoyed that 'Lando but next time we come here I'm going to ask Dads if I can bring Panky. I wonder where Mum is.'

Mum was at that very moment making a supreme effort to cool her own emotions and not least those of her husband. She managed to pull her lips away from his muttering. 'The boys – they're coming back to the horsebox. I think you had better go and help them and then later, my darling, I'll race you out to the old raft.'

Tom gave her one last kiss. 'God, Sam, how can I stay so cool with my horses and yet one touch from you and I'm totally lost,' but before she could reply he had pulled her up and out of the sand dune, startling the boys.

'Dad, how on earth did you and Mum fall into a sand dune? You should be more careful. You should look after Mum - that's why I'm holding on to Annie and Tom Thumb – girls need looking after.'

Tom was still struggling with his emotions but he managed to smile at Oscar. 'Ozzie, if you can look after Anne-Marie half as well as I look after your Mum, then she will be a very lucky girl believe you me.'

The electricity was still sparking through the air between Tom and Sam as Charles and Joanna joined then on the rug. Charles suddenly looked up and gave a whoop of joy. 'Eva, what are you doing here?' and he was holding out his arms to Tabitha who was dressed in a pink candy striped sundress with a matching hat covering her sparse head of hair. Andrew was carrying her buggy over the sand as she smiled at Charles.

'Joanna phoned me and told me *the gang* was coming here today and we wanted to join everyone.' And as Charles settled back on the rug cuddling his smallest grand daughter, his cup of happiness was full. All his family was around him; it was an afternoon to savour and he was going to enjoy every minute of it. *Sod the speed class in Paris* he was thinking.

CHAPTER 23

On Monday morning Oliver was feeling slightly apprehensive as he kissed Sam goodbye before joining his friend. Eddie lived in Ribbenden, next door to Marigold Bloomfield's sanctuary and his mother, Marcia, knowing Sam had four other children, had offered to take Oliver with her own son to the boarding school where the music school was being held.

With promises that she and Rosie would come with his grandparents to the concert the next Sunday afternoon, Oliver hugged his mother one final time and as they turned out of the gate of Woodcutters, finally started to look forwards to the week ahead. It was the first time he had been parted from his family. He clutched his guitar more tightly and half wished he would be competing against his brothers with Buck's Fizz instead of worrying about scales and arpeggios and whether the music was to be played in D Sharp or E Minor or some other key.

Rosie and the other boys had ridden through Old Tiles across the farm to a gate, which led into Back lane. They were going to Theobald's Place to meet Gus and Abby and then they would ride through the large paddock at the bottom of which, Jean-Pierre had agreed that Justin could put a gate that would lead into the far corner of his cross country course. The children could ride beside the jumps and then across the yard to the indoor school. It was a huge help for all *the gang* who lived in Back Lane and for the West children too and now the main road was no longer the threat it had always posed.

Usually *the gang* had their lessons in the school or the jumping paddock at Lake House, but today Jean-Pierre had suggested they should come to the Centre and as it was a warm, sunny day Dom and Justin had decided to school them in the outdoor arena which was already set out with its beautiful, solid show jumps over which Jean-Pierre had been schooling The Whistler and Flêche d'Or.

Sam was in the kitchen at Woodcutters making a mid-morning cup of coffee for Tom, at the same time appreciating the succulent aroma of the large joint of lamb she was roasting. Adrian was coming to lunch at Woodcutters, where Amy and Molly would join them.

She could hear Tom whistling as he walked across the garden. He had ridden round the lake with his two Canadian grooms, Jules and Hannah. The lake had been abundant with wildlife – not least a swan with six baby cygnets and a multitude of moorhens and shell ducks with their babies, then the icing on the cake had been the kingfisher which had flown across the lake in front of them, its jewel like feathers flashing in the morning sun.

Tom felt he needed something calming and relaxing after his emotions had been highly charged the previous day at Camber with Sam upsetting his equilibrium in her provocative swimsuit. He smiled at her as she carried the tray with two cups and a jug of coffee across the lawn to the seat under the rose arbour with its abundance of climbing roses and honeysuckle, the scent of which was permeating the air.

'How are you getting on with Jules and Hannah, Tom?' she asked.

'Well, they're both really nice. Good riders and hard workers. Apparently, they were telling me they have both joined the tennis club as visitors for the summer. They seem to have settled really well and are ready to make their own amusement. I gather they have already met Mum and Dad at the club and Uncle Rob and the obnoxious Simon, who according to them is a really crack player. I only wish he would take a bit more interest in Melchior. Jean-Pierre is really anxious – he says he is a good little horse. He's had words with Simon but apart from tearing round the fields a couple of times a week, that's all Simon does with him. Pierre's not happy at all. He wants to speak with Uncle Rob about the situation. You can't have a horse standing doing nothing in a field for days on end and then gallop it flat out for an hour. His wind will go and the poor horse won't be fit for anything. Anyhow, Adrian should be here in an hour. I've just time to take Kaspar round the lake before he gets here. I'll see you at twelve. Have you got one more kiss left, Sammy? Or did I have them all last night?'

Sam giggled. 'Thomas West, you are quite insatiable, but maybe you left just one tiny one behind,' and she kissed him gently at the same time pushing him off the seat. 'No Tommy – I said one little one – how would you like burnt lamb and charred potatoes for your lunch?'

Tom laughed. 'I'd prefer another kiss, but I'll be good. Jules was getting Kaspar ready – he'll be waiting,' and he walked reluctantly to the stables.

Disappointingly, there was very little progress that day as far as Adrian was concerned, although Boswell sat beside him, gazing into his face, occasionally thumping his tail. 'I'm sure I've met him before,' Adrian repeated what he had said on his previous visit.

'You have seen him here with Sam and myself, Adrian. You've met him lots of times and Bertie and Holly too.'

Adrian shook his head in frustration. 'It's driving me crazy. I can remember everything that has happened since I woke up in hospital but before that, my world is empty; I wouldn't even know whether I am really Adrian Carstairs. Amy says she is my wife – but how can I be certain? I only know I like her and I love little Molly.'

They had finished their lunch, Amy was feeding Molly and Sam was stacking the plates in the dishwasher. Tom took two cups of coffee into the garden.

'Adrian, it must be extremely disconcerting for you, but all I want is to help you. I have known you since you were a schoolboy of fourteen – you had a horse called Hercules and you needed money to keep him at livery. You came to work for me every morning before school and again every evening and then when you left school you came here as my groom and to jump some of the young horses. A few years ago, I gave you Midnight Fantasy – he's your own horse, Adrian and when we've finished our coffee you can ride him round the lake. Sam will look after Molly and Amy can join us. She can ride Goldie. Adrian, Amy is your wife – I promise you. Shepherd's Cottage is your home. You share it with Amy and your little daughter, Molly. Please believe me Adrian. Soon you will be leaving the hospital and Amy will be there to look after you.'

Adrian had tears in his eyes. 'All you are telling me means nothing, Tom. The more I try to remember, the emptier my head seems to be. I want to believe you and I think I must have ridden before because it all seems so natural. Amy seems to want me at her cottage – she has said she will look after me. I'd like that – but would it be right? Would it be fair to her?'

'It's what she wants to do more than anything, Adrian. Now let's go for this ride. Here comes Amy and Sam is going to sit in the garden with Molly.'

Tom felt depressed. He didn't really think he had made any progress but his mood lifted as they rode around the lake and Amy and Adrian were exclaiming over the little cygnets and when the kingfisher flashed over the water as it had done earlier that morning, Tom felt maybe that was a good omen.

That evening, Tom and Oscar rode up to the indoor school at Lake House, Tom once again riding the irrepressible Hanky Panky and Oscar bouncing beside him on Humbug. The schooling session was a success and as Oscar gazed at the cygnets as they walked quietly back by the lake he smiled at his father. 'Buggy says he's going to win on Wednesday, Dad and Panky says he's going to try his damnedest.' Then he sighed. 'I wonder what Ollie is doing right now, Dad. 'Lando and I have been thinking about him all day and we think we will miss the show on Sunday, Dad. Josh will go with you. 'Lando and I would like to be with Ollie at his concert.'

Tom realized, not for the first time, how his triplets depended on each other – they had their own personalities but the bond between the three boys was like an iron chain.

Wednesday finally arrived. Oscar had barely slept for the past two nights and he was too excited to eat any breakfast.

Orlando and Joshua had already left for Lake House. Joshua was riding Lily with Orlando beside him on Torchlight and Hannah following them on Ganger, leading Jet Stream. She was going to travel in the horsebox with Sally who would be driving, whilst Anna and Justin would follow in Anna's people carrier with their three children plus Joshua and Orlando. Justin and Anna had already admitted to each other that it was with a great deal of relief they would not be responsible for the over zealous Oscar that day.

Oscar was in fact leading Humbug into Tom's largest horsebox as Rosie stood at the bottom of the ramp waiting to lead Sparkler into his stall, whilst Jules hung onto Hanky Panky who was plunging from side to side impatient to follow Humbug into the horsebox.

Charles had just acquired a Foxhunter gelding from Jock who had received a call from one of the late Lady Hermione's faithful dealers in Holland telling him he had just got hold of four excellent six year old horses with great potential. Jock had duly gone over to Holland, and had been highly impressed by the stallion, two geldings and a beautiful chestnut mare. He had called Charles who had agreed to buy two of the horses whilst Jock's middle daughter would bring on the stallion and one of the geldings. Charles was happy to take the mare and the other gelding, which Dom was supposed to be jumping, but when Charles knew Justin and Tom were going to different shows and had a space in their boxes, suddenly Tom found he was entered in the Foxhunter Class with Swallow Tail, who was about to follow Hanky Panky up the ramp, with Clementine filling the final stall.

After a good deal of grumbling, Justin had finally given in to his father's wishes and the chestnut mare, Conchita was standing in her stall looking disdainfully at Amelia who was going to do the leading rein class with little Noah.

The previous afternoon, Tom and Justin had schooled the two horses over the fences at Lake House and they had to agree with Jock that both the mare and the gelding appeared to have an enormous amount of raw talent.

Sam had decided to stay at Woodcutters with the dogs. She and Sarah had a huge project designing the garden around a new care home for the elderly that had just been constructed. It was a lucrative contract and they were keen to get the plans finished as soon as possible and with no distractions other than the dogs Sam decided it should be possible to make a good deal of progress, especially as Sarah's mother had offered to have her nine month old granddaughter Chloe for the whole day and as Tom drove out of the yard, Sarah swept into the drive and work would commence.

Tom had decided to travel without a groom. Rosie was quite capable of looking after Sparkler and without his brothers to distract him, Oscar would cope with Humbug – Tom wasn't quite so sure about Panky, but the two horses could stay in their stalls whilst Tom helped Oscar with the challenging pony.

The show was being held at a new venue this year and the organizers had certainly pulled out all the stops to make it as attractive as possible, with three large rings – a more than adequate parking area for the horseboxes with excellent facilities and a variety of trade stands and eating bars.

They had made excellent time and Tom suggested before they even opened the ramp they should buy themselves a drink and something tasty to eat.

Oscar had been wishing he had eaten some breakfast almost the minute after they had left Woodcutters and he followed Tom enthusiastically to an excellent refreshment tent where he and Rosie had a lemon milkshake, whilst Tom enjoyed a steaming hot cup of strong coffee. They spotted a plate of Danish pastries and each munched their way through two of the mouthwatering offerings.

They looked at the junior jumping arena, which was already set out for the 12.2h.h. ponies and Tom walked the course with Rosie twice. He couldn't see any particularly problematical fences and half an hour later, Rosie and Sparkler were making their way to the collecting ring.

When Rosie jumped at the Massenden Centre or at the big show in Sussex she recognized most of her rivals but all the competitors here were strange faces. She had no idea how fierce the opposition was going to be.

'Just do your best, Rosie, sweetheart, that's all I shall ever ask of you,' Tom reassured her, and as she cantered into the arena six riders had gone before her and there was still no sign of a clear round.

Sparkler was on form and Rosie was smiling as she rode through the exit as Tom was trying to ward off a large, red-faced man who was offering him a ridiculous amount of money for Sparkler.

'I'm just not interested in selling my daughter's pony,' he told the man – as he had told many people before.

'Three thousand, five hundred,' the persistent man almost shouted at Tom.

Tom decided to be sarcastic. 'Oh, I'm sorry, I didn't realize you were deaf,' and he turned to the back page of the schedule, pulling out his biro and writing in large letters –NO – and then catching hold of Sparkler's bridle led Rosie away from the collecting ring.

Oscar's eyes were wide open. 'Bloody hell, Dad – that was a massive amount of money.'

'Money isn't the most important thing in life, Oscar, as I hope you will come to appreciate and I wouldn't have sold a venomous snake to that odious man. Come on, Rosie, we'll look at the jump off course whilst Ozzie holds onto Sparkler and don't sell Rosie's pony if that creep comes back whilst we're gone. Don't even answer him, Oz – we won't be long. Now let's see what turns you can make Rosie, but I don't think there are too many clear rounds anyway.'

Rosie took Tom's hand. 'Dads, I don't like that man, he keeps staring at Sparkie. I'm going to stay on him whilst Ozzie rides Humbug and Pankie. He might steal him from the horsebox.'

'Darling Rosie, I'm quite sure he wouldn't do that but you can ride him if you want to.' Rosie was beginning to cast doubts in his mind and he decided whilst he jumped his horses in the afternoon he would make certain the horsebox was well and truly locked.

There were only three clear rounds, one of which was an over fat boy on a stocky pony with a hogged mane. It didn't take a detective to realise he was the red faced man's son. The boy rode with spurs and a stick, which he held pointing towards heaven and hands that made Tom sweat. He was following Rosie's immaculate round on Sparkler. She had listened to Tom and had cut every corner he had pointed out. The boy was undoubtedly strong but he was also exceedingly rough – his legs crashing against the pony's sides. He was much wider than Rosie at every corner and as he flew through the finish with his legs flailing like windmills he was three seconds slower and two seconds behind the girl who jumped into second place.

Rosie and Sparkler were well on their way to H.O.Y.S. as she cantered out of the arena clutching a large cup, an envelope and a rosette, which was almost as stunning as the ones Oscar's countess had presented him with the previous autumn.

Rosie was already pulling her mobile out of her pocket. 'Are you ringing Mummy, Rosie?' Tom asked her.

'Mummy – of course not, Dads, I'm calling Gussie. Whatever made you think I was phoning Mum?'

Five minutes later she was smiling. 'Gus is really proud. Noah and Amelia won the leading rein class – apparently Justin is over the moon. He took him into the ring. Gus hasn't jumped yet, neither have 'Lando or Josh, but Abby rode Guy Fawkes for the first time and they were second. She said Guy was really fast after Fuzz Buzz.'

The course was being raised for the next class. 'We'll wait until it's finished, Oz and then we will walk it together before we get

Humbug out of the box. If we put you down near the end then you will have plenty of time to warm him up. There are quite a few numbers already on the board, go and put yourself down as near twentieth as possible, that should give us at least half an hour, possibly a bit more.'

Oscar picked up the chalk and put his number on the board. 'I'm number twenty one, Dad.'

'Fine, Oz. They seem to have finished the course, don't go far away, Rosie whilst Oz and I walk it.'

Rosie could see the red-faced man with a plump girl who was obviously the sister of the lad who had been in the previous class. She could also see the girl who had come second sitting on her pony watching her father who was walking the course with a slightly older girl. She rode up to the girl she had just beaten and smiled, asking her. 'What's your pony's name?'

'Sailor Boy,' the girl smiled. 'What's your pony called?'

'Sparkler. Is that your dad and your sister?'

'Yes, who are you with?'

'My brother and my dad. Ozzie's pony had a bad accident – it's the first time he's jumped since he lost his eye.'

'Lost his eye?'

'Yes, a lorry hit the trailer he was in. Oz's other pony Whisky was killed, now a lady has asked Oscar to jump her pony for her. He's really bouncy and strong. Oz is jumping him in the next class. He's called Hanky Panky – but Oz likes strong ponies.'

'Well I hope he beats that horrible Bill Strawbridge.'

'Who is Bill Strawbridge?'

'He's the brother of the younger boy in our class and the sister who is in this one. Dad calls him Bully Bill. He says one day he will report him for excessive use of the whip.'

'Do you always come to this show?' Rosie asked her. 'I've

never been before, my other brothers have gone to a different show in Sussex.'

Cassie was curious. 'How many brothers have you got?'

'Four, but Ozzie 'Lando and Ollie are triplets and Josh is a year older.'

Cassie was taken aback. 'Gosh, and have you any sisters?'

Rosie laughed. 'No I'm the only girl, thank goodness. Do you live in Essex?'

'No, quite a distance away, we live in a village near Lincoln. This show used to be a little further away in the next village but now it's moved here it's much nicer.'

'And where do the Strawbridge's live?'

'Unfortunately in the same village as we do. Jake Strawbridge has got a scrap metal yard. Dad says it's an eyesore. I don't like him – he wants to buy every pony that beats his horrible children and then when the latest pony doesn't win, he sends it to the local horse sale.'

Rosie shuddered. 'He wanted to buy Sparkler this morning. My dad wouldn't listen – Dad's still got his first pony, Twinkletoes, he's thirty now.'

'Does your dad still ride?'

'Yes, yes, he's' – and Rosie bit her tongue. 'He's riding in the Foxhunter class this afternoon,' and she left it at that. Rosie was finally learning a little bit of tact and diplomacy, and when Cassie Lewis asked her. 'What does your dad do?' she replied. 'Oh, he works with horses.'

Tom and Oscar had finished walking the course and came up to Rosie. 'We're going to get Humbug, Rosie.'

'Can I stay here with Cassie, Dads?'

Cassie's mother was sitting on a rug with a small toddler, she smiled at Tom, thinking she had seen him somewhere before. 'I'm not moving from here,' she told him. 'The girls can watch the show classes in the next ring. I'll keep an eye on your daughter and Cassie will introduce her to some of her friends. I'm Suzie Lewis and my husband who is with our older daughter, Clare, is Mike. He's enjoying a day off on terra firma – he's usually way up in the sky at the weekends. He's a pilot, so his weekends are usually pretty full.'

Tom smiled. 'I'm Tom and this is my son, Oscar. If you're sure, I know Rosie would love to meet some of the other kids, we're a bit out of our usual territory here, we have come up from the bowels of Kent. I won't be long. Thanks a million.' And he and Oscar hurried away to get Humbug from the horsebox whilst Suzie struggled to remember where she had seen him before.

Tom was finding it impossible to believe Humbug had lost an eye as he stood in the warm up area before prancing up to the practice fence, as full of life and enthusiasm as he had ever been.

Tom was sharing the practice fence with Clare's father, Mike, who was grinning at him. 'I love these weekends when I can get to the shows with Suzie and the kids – it always makes me feel nostalgic – there's a very distinctive smell of horse droppings, wet turf and quite often damp leather. I had my own horse until I went off to train to be a pilot. Now I don't get too many Saturdays off. How about you or are you a white collar worker in the city?'

Tom laughed. 'No, definitely not. Like you, I'm nearly always working on a Saturday but at least I still get the chance to ride.'

'You mean to say you've still got your own horse?'

'Well, yes, yes, I have.'

'Have you brought it today?'

'Yes, I'm doing the Foxhunter and the Open.'

Mike looked taken aback. 'The Open! I think you said you hadn't been to this show before, – it used to be held just down the road in the next village – I don't want to scare you, but THE OPEN!! Wow – it's huge.'

'Gosh, well I shall just have to hang on and hope then.'

‘But will your horse jump them?’

‘Oh, yes, Clementine will jump anything.’

‘And you?’

‘I shall certainly do my best.’

‘We shall look out for you. We always stay until the end of the show. Cassie and Clare won’t entertain leaving until the final whistle has blown. What’s your Foxhunter horse called?’ Mike asked Tom.

Tom’s mind went blank – he had barely made the acquaintance of the horse. He glanced in the schedule, and then grinned at Mike. ‘I couldn’t remember. I’ve only ridden it once. Ah, here we are, Swallow Tail – it belongs to a friend.’ He missed the odd smile that passed over Mike’s face as he turned to Oscar and asked him. ‘All set, Oz?’

‘Sure thing, dad, and Buggy says he can see just as well with only one eye.’

Mike started, then looked at the pony more closely – sure enough there was a large cavity where Humbug’s eye should have been.

Tom noticed him looking. ‘This is Buggy’s first outing since his accident – he seems to be coping well but we won’t know for certain until he has been in the arena. Just walk him round quietly now, Oz until it’s your turn. I’ll be watching with Rosie. Good luck.’

‘I’ll bloody well do my damnedest, Dad.’

Tom sighed. ‘I know you will, Oz.’ He turned to Mike. ‘Apologies for his language, Mike, but actually Oz has been through a lot recently, his other pony was killed. A lorry hit our trailer.’

‘Poor kid. Is that how he came by the scar on his face?’

‘No, I’m afraid that happened a year or so ago – little bugger stole the keys to my Range Rover. He didn’t get very far. Just demolished half the garden and most of the utility room.’

‘Christ! Is he your only son?’

Tom laughed again. ‘No, Sammy and I have two more exactly

like him. Oscar is one of triplets and then there's our older son Joshua. He's dark, like Rosie and their Mum. They're at another show today. They've gone with some friends from our village.'

Tom wished Clare good luck and went to find Rosie who was now surrounded by a group of girls and boys who were obviously regulars at this show and all seemed to know Cassie. Rosie was obviously blissfully happy, but she cantered over to him as Humbug bounced into the arena with all of his old panache and aplomb.

Mike was standing by Tom waiting for his daughter to take her turn directly after Humbug who was currently bouncing round the arena in his old flamboyant way as he almost tore Oscar's arms from their sockets but at the same time, clearing the jumps with inches to spare.

Mike turned to congratulate Tom and was taken aback when he saw him wiping a tear from his eye. 'I'm sorry, Mike. You will think what a wimp of a chap but Humbug is so special. We've had him since he was a yearling and Whisky was his brother who we bred ourselves. It's been a truly torrid time recently. Oz is going to be over the moon, but as Oscar rode up to Tom he jumped off the pony, and buried his head in Humbug's striped mane.

'Why is your brother crying?' Cassie asked Rosie.

'Because he's happy.'

'If that is the case, why is he crying?'

'Cos we didn't know whether Buggy would ever be able to jump again.'

Oscar was now smiling at Tom through his tears. 'Dad, he's still my old Humbug. He's the bravest and the most super pony on this earth.'

'He is Ozzie and you are a mighty brave boy too. It could all have gone horribly wrong, but you were there to make certain it didn't. Now come on, let's look at the jump of course and see what he can do.'

They walked with Mike and Clare and studied the jump off course together. Mike was intrigued – Tom obviously had experience of jump off courses as he heard him pointing out several short cuts to his son.

There were more clear rounds in this class including Jake Strawbridge's daughter. She rode in exactly the same style as her younger brother and as Tom watched her in the jump off his mind was made up. After the class was over he would have a word with the judges. He had noticed blood on the pony's flanks - it was unacceptable and should not be tolerated at any show, least of all one that was affiliated to the British Show Jumping Association.

Tom watched Oscar and Humbug flying, twisting over the jumps in a class of their own. Mike's elder daughter jumped an extremely competent round and Tom decided she obviously had an extremely good instructor.

'Who looks after your daughters, Mike- they're both very stylish riders?'

'We're lucky. When possible we take her to a chap called David Mason but he's often on the continent in the Nation's Cup teams – then his father coaches the girls. It's not cheap but in my opinion money well spent. The girls are at the village Primary School and hope to go on to the Grammar School in Lincoln. Suzie and I prefer to give them free education and a few out of school extras.'

The class had now ended and the results were being given out. *'In first place, Oscar West, riding Lake House Stables, Humbug. Second, Clare Lewis on Mike and Suzie Lewis' Flying High and so on until in sixth place Carla Strawbridge on Jake Strawbridge's Million Pound Girl'.*

As Oscar came out of the arena as Rosie had done in the class before, he was holding a substantial silver cup – an envelope containing a cheque and a red velvet rosette, which he was going to give to Anne-Marie.

'Wait there for five minutes, Oz. I'll not be longer than that.' Tom could hear Carla Strawbridge shouting abuse at her father and could see the blood where Carla's spurs had thudded into her pony's sides. Half a minute later he was knocking on the front of the judge's wooden stand where they sat to peruse the horses and ponies.

Tom knew almost every judge in the country and they recognized him immediately. 'Tom, good to see you here.'

'It's a super venue, Patrick and I'm sorry to spoil your day but that girl who came sixth – her pony is bleeding. I'm sorry but that sort of callous riding makes me see red.'

The judges shook their head. 'Don't worry, Tom, it hasn't gone unnoticed – we've asked her to bring the pony to us and our duty vet is going to look at it. The brother is almost as bad and the worst is yet to come in the next class I'm afraid, but thanks for your vigilance, Tom and your kids are amazing. That little grey is a dream pony – but then it's got an amazing little girl in the saddle. I've seen the piebald at H.O.Y.S. a year or so ago with your older son.'

'Humbug is Oscar's ride now? Oz is a bit overwhelmed at the moment. Buggy was involved in an accident two months ago – I'm sure you were too far away to see but he lost an eye. This was his first outing and Ozzie is thrilled to bits.'

'He's a great kid but where are the rest of your boys?'

'Justin Wright-Smith has taken them to Sussex. I wanted a quiet day with Ozzie. The boys can get very competitive when they are jumping against each other and I wasn't sure how Humbug would react to the arena, but he was great.'

'We shall see you in the arena later on, I believe, Tom.'

'You certainly will but you will see Oscar again first. He's jumping a very tricky pony that belongs to the Countess of Markeley but Oz likes a challenge and Hanky Panky is certainly that.'

As Tom left the judge's box he noticed Jake Strawbridge and his daughter. He was berating the vet, his face an even deeper shade of red, as the young man examined the pony's flanks. When Tom and Oscar went to the horsebox later to fetch Hanky Panky, the cattle truck next to him was preparing to leave the showground with three yelling children and their father shouting abuse at every official manning the lorry park, vowing never to return to this venue.

Oscar breathed a sigh of relief. 'Cor, Dad, now I can safely leave Panky in the horsebox when I've jumped him, I hated that man and that ghastly girl told me Buggy should have been put down. I've never seen them before and I hope I never set eyes on that podgy girl again.' He led Humbug into his stall, tying a small bucket of pony nuts on the hook before unloading Hanky Panky.

Suzie and Mike looked at each other as an announcement was coming over the public address. *'Now we have Oscar West and the Countess of Markeley's Hanky Panky.'* They watched in awe as the highly charged pony and the young lad who was the image of his father literally pranced their way effortlessly over the now substantially higher jumps. They were in a class of their own and a buzz was going around the spectators. Who was this boy who they had never seen in this area before?

This time there were no tears as Oscar trotted up to Tom holding yet another cup and another buff envelope. 'Wow, Dad, he was damn good. Crumbs, I felt I was bouncing up to the clouds. If you give me the keys, I'll put him back in the box.'

'Oscar, you know I don't trust you with keys if they have any connection with four wheels. We'll tell Rosie to bring Sparkler and then we'll eat Mum's picnic.'

Rosie was still with Cassie and her group of friends. 'Dads, please, please can Sparkie and I do the races this afternoon. Cassie and her sister are training for the Prince Philip team and they're going to do them. Please, Dad, I promise I will look after Sparkie?'

Tom wanted his children to have fun – not always to be counting strides and remembering twisting jump off courses and he told her. 'O.K. Rosie, we'll put Sparkler in the box whilst we have lunch. Give him to me and you go and enter him over there at the

Secretary's Tent.' As he handed Rosie a twenty-pound note Oscar looked at him. 'Cor can Buggy do some of the races too, Dad?'

'It might be difficult for him, Oz, but you can try if you promise not to be disappointed if he can't twist through the poles.'

'Cor, Dad. Thanks, he'll be O.K. I'll help him.' And Tom was pretty certain he would.

Having loaded Hanky Panky and tied Sparkler and Humbug to the horsebox, Tom retrieved Sam's picnic hamper from the cab and laid out the rug she had carefully folded. He opened the basket and smiled – on top was a card – *'Enjoy, my darlings.'* And as he looked at the sumptuous feast inside he knew there was no doubt that they would.

Rosie couldn't wait to get back to her newfound friends and with a stern warning to both Rosie and Oscar to take care, Tom put the now empty hamper back in the cab and led the almost unknown Swallow Tail down the ramp. He was not Tom's usual type of ride but occasionally it was relaxing not to be sitting on a ball of fire like Opal and Kaspar and by the time he had completed his round Tom liked him even more. He had tremendous scope and ability – he had plenty of blue blood in his veins and he certainly wasn't lacking in speed as he demonstrated in the jump off, with the best jockey in the world showing him the way.

Soon, Tom was locking a fourth trophy in the refrigerator and securing the horsebox. Swallow Tail was on his way and Charles was delighted when he received a text from Tom who soon had a reply. *'Get him up to Grade A a.s.a.p. Then we'll flog him for a small fortune – fifty-fifty as usual Tom.'*

Tom shook his head. Charles was almost impossible but he knew he wouldn't let him rest until he had agreed. He didn't really need the added pressure of jumping Foxhunter courses – that was supposed to be Dom's domain but the horse was an easy ride and he was sure either Jules of Hannah could exercise him every day and as he crossed every finger he possessed, maybe in the not too distant future Adrian too would be hacking him round the lake.

Tom wandered back to see how his children were faring and as he half expected, Humbug and Sparkler were already festooned with rosettes in various colours but mainly blue and red.

Rosie was in the ten and under section with Cassie and Oscar in the fourteen and under with Clare. The competition was strong but Humbug appeared to have lost none of his skills or his joie de vivre and Oscar was happy even though his arms were aching from his shoulders to his wrists.

He had walked across to the main arena to watch the Foxhunter jump off. Clare laughed and told Oscar, *'Swallow Tail!'* That's the name of my Dad's Hawk.'

'Hawk,' Oscar asked.

Clare laughed. 'Airplane, Oscar.'

Oscar stared in disbelief. 'You are kidding! Your Dad flies a Swallow Tail!' and never one to be shy, he turned to Mike.

'Your plane's a Swallow Tail. Wow – Wow – Wow. If I wasn't going to be a show jumper, that's what I would like to do. Dad and Mum took us to Margate last summer to see the display over the sea. Wow – Wow – it was AMAZING. Wow!!'

Mike laughed at the enthusiastic boy. 'We'll ask your dad if he can bring your brothers and Rosie and you to the open day and the museum and you can see my plane on the ground.'

'Wow!!' was all Oscar could say.

Mike wandered over to the refreshment marquee to get a coffee for Suzie and himself. As he waited in the queue he stood behind three teenage girls who were talking excitedly. 'I can't wait to see Tom West in the Open with his gorgeous Clementine. I've seen them on the telly lots of times. Fancy the World No. 1 being here of all places. He's a fab rider and a gorgeous hunk of a man. Unfortunately he's got a really stunning wife and five children. That boy jumping the piebald and the bay pony is one of his sons and his little girl won the 12.2.h.h. Class earlier, apparently she looks just like her Mum.'

Mike who adored his wife Suzie but was extremely like Charles Wright-Smith had once been, had the reputation of being an outrageous flirt and thought. *'Hmm, maybe she would like to see my Swallow Tail too!'*

When he arrived back with the cups of coffee, he gazed in amazement at the enormous bay mare towering over Sparkler as they watched Oscar doing the apple bobbing race, immersing his head into the bucket of icy cold water, knowing full well the trick of pressing the apple against the side of the bucket whilst grabbing it with his teeth. This accomplished in two seconds, he jammed on his hat, vaulted lightly onto Humbug's back and flew to the finish as the water cascaded from his golden curls onto his white shirt.

'Bloody hell that water was cold, Dad. We've just got the musical sacks, then that's that. There's twenty-five quid for the pony and rider with the most points and I think Buggy and I are in the running for that. Cor! What a smashing day,' and he galloped into the arena to stand beside a sack. As the music blared out, Tom's memory went back to his very first Pony Club show over twenty years ago. Twink had been festooned in rosettes as Sparkler and Humbug were now and as Tom watched his son's technique of going slowly as he drew close to a sack and then galloping onto the next one, he laughed at the intent expression on his face. Suddenly, he heard his name being called over the tannoy and he tore himself away from the shrieking children and cantered Clem calmly across the showground.

A few minutes later a voice echoing across the huge arena was stating how lucky they were to have the privilege of Tom West and his mare, Lake House Clementine supporting their first show at this new venue.

At the side of the arena Rosie and Oscar were standing with Cassie and Clare as they watched their famous father jumping one of his classically superb clear rounds. Oscar was clutching an envelope and a little statue of a galloping horse, which he had been told he could keep and he was going to give it to Anne-Marie. Humbug had won the Gymkhana Championship.

When Tom had finished his round and was walking Clem round – keeping her muscles supple before the jump off, Oscar told Rosie. 'Stay here, Rosie, I will be back in a few minutes,' and he cantered across to the trade stands where he had seen a stall advertising a local horse and pony rescue centre, with photographs of several horses which had arrived at the centre in appalling condition and then six months later, going off to their new homes almost unrecognizable. There was a tiny Shetland pony about the size of Amelia in a trailer by the side of the stand, who like Humbug, had lost an eye. He dismounted and led Humbug up to a lady who was wearing a green overall with Fairfields Horse and Pony Rescue Centre written across the front.

Humbug was not too happy about the side of the marquee, which was flapping in the wind, but Oscar gamely hung on to him, handing the envelope with the twenty-five pounds inside it to the lady. 'I'd like you to have this for your rescue centre please. You see Humbug lost his eye in an accident recently. He and I would like to help another pony who has been unlucky.'

The lady smiled at Oscar, patting Humbug at the same time. 'Is your Mummy happy about you giving away your prize money, dear?' she asked Oscar, who told her, 'Mum's not here, I'm with my Dad. He's in the arena now – look' - and he pointed at Tom and Clementine.

'Your Dad is Tom West?'

'Yea and he rescued Clem from our local sanctuary. He wouldn't mind and I really want to help,' with which he turned Humbug away from the marquee and watched his father and Clem collecting a similar buff envelope and a superb silver trophy.

After Tom had signed as many autographs as he possible could, he dismounted and led Clementine up to another marquee. It was for the Riding for the Disabled and as he handed his not inconsiderable cheque to the nonplussed gentleman all he could see in his mind was a beautiful little girl with long, curly, black hair and a smile which had stolen his heart.

'I want you to have it,' he smiled at the gentleman, 'yours is a charity very close to my heart and it always will be,' and with one final handshake he led Clementine back to the horsebox and then re-joined Oscar and Rosie.

Mike and Suzie were about to leave – their young son asleep in his buggy.

Oscar was tugging Tom's sleeve. 'Cassie and Clare's Dad's plane is called Swallow Tail too – you know, you took us to Margate to see their display last year. He says if you take us to their open day on the airfield he'll show us his Swallow Tail. Please, Dad, please.'

Tom laughed. 'So, Mike, you won't be flying me to Rome or Paris in a Boeing 737?'

Mike grinned. 'No, and you won't be lunging young kids round a muddy field.'

'Well, I often do that. The kids in our village have formed their own gang – my partners give them lessons every week and when I have a spare day I have been known to lunge a fair few of them, but give David Mason my regards if you see him before he goes off to Spruce Meadows for a few weeks and tell him we'll meet up when he gets back. He's a first class chap. Your girls are lucky. How about Clare and Cassie coming to stay with us and joining *the gang* for a week in the summer holidays if they can put up with my four boys?'

Cassie and Clare were jumping up and down. 'Please, please, please.' they were imploring their mother and Tom and Mike were exchanging phone numbers and arranging that Sam and Suzie would sort out a suitable week in the forthcoming holidays.

The traffic was heavy and Rosie had fallen asleep long before they had reached the Dartford Tunnel but Oscar was still bubbling with Humbug and Panky's successful day. He had already called

Anne-Marie and told her he had lots of rosettes to give her and a little horse to put on the table by her bed and that Rosie and he had spent the day with two really nice girls who were going to come and stay at Woodcutters in the holidays. There was silence for a while and then Tom heard Oscar telling her. 'They were O.K. Annie but not French or beautiful like you.'

Tom smiled to himself. In his opinion they had both been extremely pretty girls and once again he wondered at his son's overwhelming attraction for the strange, little Anne-Marie Silvestre.

Rosie's mobile was bleeping and Oscar plucked it off her lap. *'Rosie, it's Gus.'*

'Rosie's asleep, Gussie. We've had a really smashing day though. Dad let us do the gymkhana with Buggy and Sparkler. How about you?'

'Jet won the thirteen two class and Hamlet was second, then Josh and Ganger won the fourteen two and 'Lando and I tied with exactly the same time for second place with Torchlight and The Pie. Lily was fifth. Then that new mare Dad is riding won the Foxhunters. She's a super mare. Dad says he wants to buy her before Gramps gets a fantastic offer for her. Tell Rosie to call me when she wakes up.'

'O.K. Gus – but – Gus – we met two girls and guess what – their Dad flies a Swallow Tail – he's asked us to the airfield to see the plane. Dad says he'll take us in the autumn when the planes aren't doing so many displays.'

'Wow – Oz. Can I come too?'

'Sure thing, Gus, see you tomorrow. Rosie and I will ride over to your house – cheers.'

That evening Tom had his arm round Sam as they enjoyed a glass of red wine in the sitting room.

'Sammy, thank you for that fantastic hamper, I'm afraid we ate every single bit of it and the kids had a super day. We met up with a really nice family,' and he told her about Mike and Suzie and their girls, at the end of which a slightly bemused Sam was agreeing the girls could come and stay and join *the gang* for a week and she made sure their phone number was safely in the phone book in her mobile before snuggling into Tom's ever ready arms.

'So, do I see a load more silverware on the dresser which will all need cleaning, my darling? Did Clem win a large cheque?'

Tom's hand had slipped under her shirt and she snuggled even closer. 'She did, my Sammy but actually I didn't bring it home.'

'Oh, Tommy, did you loose it?'

'No, my darling – the Riding for the Disabled had a stand at the show. I made it over to them. I think you know why.'

Sam undid his shirt and laid her head on his bare chest. 'How much, Tommy?'

'Two and a half thousand pounds.'

Sam's arms tightened round him. 'My Tom, is it any wonder I love you so much?'

'All I could see was a beautiful little girl in a wheelchair – smiling at me – stealing my heart for ever and there was never any question, I knew what I wanted to do and maybe, just maybe it will help another little boy or girl realize their dream to walk and run again. By the way, I wonder where Ozzie put his money. He won twenty five pounds with Humbug for winning the most points in the gymkhana races.'

He heard Oscar talking to Josh and Orlando as they went up the stairs to bed. 'Hey Ozzie,' he called out, 'you haven't lost that twenty five pounds have you?'

'I haven't got it Dad, I gave it to the Horse and Pony Rescue stand because I was so pleased Buggy was his old self. I knew you wouldn't mind.'

'I'm proud of you Oz and I am perfectly certain Buggy is too.' He turned back to Sam.

'I have five wonderful kids who are so lucky because they

happen to have the most beautiful mum in this whole world, who I am now going to kiss extremely thoroughly. My precious little Samantha West.'

CHAPTER 24

The following afternoon, a flier came through most of the letterboxes in the more affluent part of Massenden. Clarissa had paid three boys who practiced their cricket on the green, one of whom was Simon West, to deliver them. He hadn't particularly wanted to, but he had seen a sweatshirt he liked in the shop at the tennis club – he had pointed it out to Rob who at the time had his eyes firmly fixed on Tamara Adam's extremely short tennis skirt and had barely listened to his son, just saying. 'Well you will have to buy it out of your allowance then, Si,' as he followed Tamara onto the tennis court hoping he could be her partner, which would give him every advantage of catching more than one glimpse of her delectable bum with which he was already very well acquainted.

Simon had subsequently scrutinized his money box and had discovered he was ten pounds short of the money he required – so rather begrudgingly he had taken the bundle of leaflets and was currently walking the length of Back Lane, which to his annoyance included the long drive to Theobald's Place - it also included No.2 Theobald's Row, where Giles was currently in Istanbul with Herbert Holmer.

Herbie barked and got up in his usual languid manner – he didn't rush to the door - that was not in the little dog's nature but he waddled over to the mat and started to chew the piece of paper.

Giles stood up, walked over to the little dog and pulled the paper from his mouth. There was to be a local election the following week and he thought it was most probably from the Lib Dems or the Conservative party – the local Labour candidates never bothered to canvas in Back Lane, they concentrated their efforts on the Council Estate at the far end of the village. He was just going to screw it into a ball and see how good his aim was as he eyed up the waste paper basket, when he spied the word Casa. He quickly smoothed out the now very crumpled flier and a minute later was burying his head in Herbie's plump little body, whilst the puppy licked the tears from his face.

'Christ, why am I so feeble?' Giles was asking himself. *'I was yelled at by the Sergeant Major when I was at Sandhurst – asked to do near impossible feats by my Commanding Officer – I never wavered. Why then, why do I only have to think of Clarissa and I want to blub like a small kid. God help me – because I certainly can't help myself,'* and he read the flier again.

La Casa sul Verde is delighted to announce it will be opening for business on Saturday 10th of June at 7.30p.m.

A glass of champagne will greet you from 7.p.m. onwards courtesy of Clarissa, Luigi and Maria who will be proud to introduce you to their varied menu of delicious Italian food.

Booking essential. Please phone the following number 303030 or e-mail casasulverde@overthemoon.com.

Giles was just making himself a cup of tea when Georgia burst through the door, flinging her arms round his neck, asking her usual question. 'Anything to eat, Dad?'

He pointed to the cake tin. 'Help yourself, sweetheart. I had a shop up at the farmer's market. Mary had a stall – I bought one of her smashing chocolate guiness cakes and a lemon drizzle too.'

As Georgia noticed the flier on the table, she looked at her father. 'Mum sent me a text, Dad. She asked whether I would like to help pass the champagne and then have a meal with Luigi's daughter, Luca and she says I can invite a friend. I thought I would invite Josh. Would you mind, but you will be coming anyway won't you, Dad? You wouldn't miss Mum's big day.'

Giles swallowed hard. *He wouldn't cry in front of Georgia, he just wouldn't.* He made a play of going back into the kitchen to refill his teacup, at the same time saying. 'Mum wouldn't want me there, Georgia,' and then before he could help himself, added. 'She's no time for imperfections.'

Georgia gave the last piece of her cake to the drooling Herbie and ran into the kitchen, throwing her arms round his neck. 'You are the most perfect Dad in this world. It's not you who is the loser – it's most definitely Mum, and now I am going to ride up to Woodcutters with Charlotte and ask Josh if he will come to La Casa on Saturday. You're sure you don't mind, Dad?'

'You must support your mum, sweetheart and on Sunday you can tell me all about it.' Georgia hugged him again and five minutes later he watched her going through the gate into Old Tiles and cantering towards Woodcutters with Charlotte beside her.

He gave a deep sigh. He could never leave here – it would break Georgia's heart and as far as he was concerned one broken heart in a family was more than enough. He turned back to his computer as he searched the colourful streets in Istanbul for the elusive Herbert Holmer.

He had finally discovered his alter ego following a swarthy man through a seamy Market place, when he was brought back to reality by a knock on the kitchen door and his neighbour's voice calling. 'Giles, are you busy, old man, or can I come in?'

'Enter, David. What brings you here?'

'This,' and David pushed the flier in front of Giles' eyes.

'I've already had a chat with Georgia. Clarissa has asked her to help at the champagne reception and then to invite one of her friends to have dinner. She's just rushed off to Woodcutters with your daughter to see if she can persuade Joshua to escort her!!'

'Esther and I are going to make up a party, Giles. All Theobald's Row is coming except for Betsy who prefers to stay with her guinea pigs. She says she will have Bertie.'

'But why would she want Bertie?'

'So you don't leave him here alone. There is no way you're not coming with us. You like Trish and Tony and Lilia, and Joyce is good fun too.'

'I – I – I can't David. You don't understand. Clarissa would be embarrassed. It would ruin her evening if I was there.'

'Don't be daft, Giles. She chose to open a bistro in this village where she knew damned well you were already living. She can't pick and chose who her patrons are. Anyhow, Esther has already booked the table and you are coming even if we have to manhandle you to get you there. Understood?'

'God, David. I want to – you will never, never know how much I want to be there – but' –

'No buts. You are coming, and you can look after Trish. Apparently she hasn't been out to dinner since her husband died last year. At least you can make sure she has an enjoyable evening and you never know, you might even sew seeds of doubt into Clarissa's concrete heart. We'll leave here at ten to seven and walk across the green, before which you can take Herbie to Betsy's. Best suit, old man. I'll see you on Saturday; I've got a business meeting in Amsterdam until the weekend. Could you just keep an eye on the cottage? Esther is coming with me and Charlotte is staying with Rosie and the boys for a couple of nights – she's taking her pony with her.'

'Fine, no trouble at all, David – but about Saturday evening.' –

'Absolutely no buts, Giles. Lock Herbert Holmer in some seamy nightclub for the evening and come and enjoy the real world and what I hope will be some extremely good Italian delicacies. We'll look after you. A few glasses of Chianti and you won't know where you are.'

Giles groaned. 'I shall know where I won't be though, David.'

'Where is that?'

'In bed with Clarissa.'

'Oh, Giles – get that wretched woman out of your mind for God's sake, man.'

'Do you think I don't want to, David. Do you really think I enjoy tormenting myself day after day?'

'Come on, Giles, it's a lovely evening and I've got a bottle of Chablis in the fridge – the girls won't be back for a while – let's grab Esther, go and sit in the garden and indulge ourselves. You can bring Bulldog Drummond if he can manage to waddle that far,' David added as he glanced at the rotund little canine.

'Oh, he can walk round the green, David. We do that every evening – we stop on the seat half way.'

'I know you do, you besotted idiot, Giles.' David thought to himself as the two men walked up the path and sat in the garden, whilst Esther brought out the Chablis and a bowl of crisps. After his third glass, Giles discovered he was even looking forwards to his visit to La Casa sul Verde!!

Fortunately, the Lake House Stables were having a weekend at home before leaving for Aachen and the big Grand prix the following Wednesday and the stables would be attending the opening in full force. After much persuasion from Anna, Amy had agreed to leave baby Molly in the capable hands of Miriam and George and join the large group.

Mary and John were coming with Susan and Bill Cotton and Elizabeth, James, Jane and Jean-Pierre.

Hannah had agreed to stay at Theobald's Place, glad that her brother had drawn the short straw and had the unenviable task of overseeing the triplets, not least Oscar, who had already informed Jules he was allowed to watch anything he liked on the television in his bedroom until half past ten. Jules thought this was highly unlikely, but decided if it ensured a peaceful evening, then who was he to interfere.

Charles and Joanna were fortunate – they had a resident baby sister in the form of Joanna's mother and for the moment, Anne-Marie's Grandmere was still at South Lodge. However, there was soon to be a wedding and Madame Louise Lacoste would soon become Mrs. Frank Holywell, living in the nearby village of Tollshurst. The cruise she had saved so diligently for had reaped its reward and a ceremony was going to take place at a well-known hotel near Ashford.

Charlotte wasn't certain about her evening. It was to be spent helping Betsy clean out the guinea pig cages and get some of them ready for a show the next day to which Betsy had insisted Charlotte should accompany her. Charlotte didn't know which would be worse. The smell of the diesel from the exhaust or the stink of the guinea pigs in their travelling boxes in the boot of the Volvo!!

By the time six thirty on Saturday evening arrived and Georgia had disappeared in the only skirt she possessed other than her grey school uniform, and a silk shirt her mother had sent her on her birthday, Giles was fluctuating from heady anticipation to sick despair as his hand hovered over the telephone. He was on the point of calling David to say he had suddenly developed a stomach bug. His neighbour, however, was an astute man and before Giles could dial the number, there was a knock on the front door and David was telling him. 'Come and have an aperitif in our garden first – Joyce and the trio from number four are already there.' And Giles had no alternative other than to hand Herbie to Betsy and follow David meekly into his garden.

By the time they were making their way across the village green, Giles was wondering whether his supposedly amazing prosthetic leg was not living up to its reputation when he realized he had just downed two enormous glasses of sparkling wine on a totally empty stomach. He had completely forgotten his mid-morning snack as his mind had been engaged with Herbert Holmer who was having a highly adventurous afternoon in a brothel in Istanbul in his search for an extremely elusive middle eastern princess who had mysteriously disappeared on a visit to the city of Ankara and had reportedly been seen two days ago in Istanbul with a gentleman of infamous notoriety.

As they arrived at La Casa sul Verdi, Georgia was the first person to spot him. 'Dad,' she shrieked, as he stood in the doorway looking extremely handsome in his dark grey suit, white shirt and the tie of his old army regiment, which was the only one he possessed. To his delight as Georgia screamed his name, he noticed the wine spilling over the glasses on the tray Clarissa was holding. 'Gilie,' she squealed, which tortured his stupid heart. How many times in the past had she whispered, 'I love you Gilie,' but to his pride, he kept his composure and when she told him, 'I didn't expect to see you here,' he replied nonchalantly. 'Didn't you, but of course I wanted to wish your new venture every success?' and he handed her a small posy of pink and white roses with one tiny red rose bud in the centre. It was identical to the one she had held on their wedding day. She half smiled and then checked her next words as Giles pushed Trish to the fore. 'I don't think you know Trish Snowfield, Clarissa, like you, she is a newcomer to the village,' with which he took hold of Trish's arm firmly, leading her to the table where Tony and Lilia were sitting with Joyce, but not before he noticed Clarissa had spilled a good deal more of the wine. However, as David glanced at the menu Giles was holding, he noticed it was shaking like the proverbial leaf.

Once the champagne had been disposed of Clarissa disappeared into the kitchen where she donned a large white apron as she took charge of the enticing sweets, which would later be appearing on a trolley, which Maria would take round to each table.

The wine was flowing and after two more glasses, Giles was searching for the loo. Mission accomplished, he was making his slightly unsteady way back to his table when he came face to face with Clarissa as she came out of the kitchen. She caught hold of his arm. 'It's really good to see you here this evening, Gilie.'

Giles felt a lump forming in his throat but he managed to answer gruffly. 'Don't call me that Clarissa. I'll never be your Gilie again – just Giles with a bloody false leg,' and he almost pushed her out of the way as he rejoined his table.

Clarissa turned and hurried back into the kitchen. Luigi gave her a long stare. He had known her over ten years. 'Why the tears, Clarissa?'

'It's your wretched onions, Luigi – why should they be tears?'

Luigi wasn't fooled – there wasn't an onion in sight!!

The bistro was buzzing – every table full of laughter and bonhomie. Sam and Tom were smiling at each other as they watched Georgia doing her utmost to get Joshua to respond to her innocent, flirtatious eyes, but sadly for Georgia they were well aware that at that moment the only girl their son had eyes for was his piebald mare, Tiger Lily, about whom he was enthusing to the Italian girl, Luca.

Rob West and Tamara Adams were sitting at a table for two in a secluded alcove but for once Rob's eyes weren't focusing on her bum or her boobs, the latter of which were revealed in abundance beneath a seductively plunging neckline. He had his eyes firmly fixed on the owner of La Casa sul Verde – wondering how he could convene a private meeting with the dark haired beauty.

Giles was well aware of the direction in which Rob's eyes were roaming and his mood was darkening by the minute. Unfortunately for Rob, the sweets were about to be served and Clarissa's attention was focused only on those.

The evening had without doubt been an unequivocal success. Two well-known local food critics had been enjoying the meal and Clarissa and her team were obviously going to receive many complimentary reports.

It was almost half past eleven when the diners finally drank the last dregs of their coffee and gathered their jackets – the majority preparing to walk to their homes.

Clarissa and Luigi were standing either side of the doorway receiving assurances from every single diner that they would be back many times in the near future.

'Let me know if you have a particular day when you are not too busy at lunch time, Clarissa,' Sam asked. 'Rosie and the boys can come for a treat with some of their friends. Oscar in particular loves Italian food.'

Clarissa tried to suppress a shudder as she recalled the cheeky, young lad with in her opinion, a disfiguring scar running down the side of his face, but she promised Sam that she would let her know the best day for them all to come once the summer holidays had started.

The last to leave were the group from Theobald's Row – mainly because they were waiting for Georgia to collect her coat and say goodbye to Luca and Josh. David and Tony shook hands with Luigi and then kissed Clarissa. Giles was mildly and pleasantly drunk. He wasn't sure if his lips slipped or whether it had been intentional but whereas David and Tony had merely brushed Clarissa's cheek, somehow his own lips had briefly discovered her mouth. The kiss had lasted less than two seconds, but as Giles walked home, his entire body was on fire as the stupid tears he couldn't control were running down his cheeks.

Georgia had gone back to La Casa to pick up the menu, which she wanted to keep. She was startled when she noticed her mother's eyes glistening with tears and even more so when she ran across the green catching up with her father. 'Dad what's the matter with you and Mum? Why are you both crying? I thought the evening was wonderful.'

'So did I, Georgia – every single bit of it.' But he was thinking only of that very last moment. He glanced across the green to Tony who was holding both Lilia and Trish's hands. He had enjoyed the evening, Trish had been great company and they had laughed a lot but with one huge feeling of anguish, his heart was confirming what he had known for the last ten years, there was only one girl that would ever catch it and once, many years ago, when they were still at school, he had caught hers but in spite of having a leg that was the best money could buy, it would never be good enough for the girl he would love all the time he was walking on this earth. All he wanted at that precise moment was to go back to the Bistro and feel her lips again – she was like a drug – an addiction – but one that he was certain he would never be able to overcome.

Clarissa was finally in her own tiny apartment. Reliving the evening. It had undoubtedly been a huge success. She was absolutely sure of that. The food had been enjoyed, nothing had gone wrong, except, at the very end when she had felt the lips that had once kissed her so passionately when they were young, before Georgia was born and for the first few years before his army career had taken him away from her. She picked up the posy of roses he had given her earlier and put it in a small glass vase which she place on her dressing table, after carefully taking the bright red rose bud from the centre and putting it inside the heaviest book she possessed then placing several more large volumes on top. She wanted to keep it forever in the drawer by her bed beside a faded red rose that had once adorned the centre of her wedding bouquet.

Clarissa knew the reason she had never been able to accept Paul's marriage proposals which he had made at regular intervals – what she felt for him had not been enough – each time he asked her to marry him or have a child with him there had been a familiar face staring at her over Paul's shoulder.

Clarissa buried her face in her pillow. *'Oh Gilie, Oh Gilie –Why, why am I such a coward? I love you so much but I cannot overcome this terror I have. Why, I even freaked out because a poor little kid with a scar running down his face wants to come to my restaurant. Giles, why did you kiss me? I thought my life was under control – now it's in turmoil,'* and Clarissa tossed and turned until the small hours of the morning, until as she heard the church clock striking four o'clock, she fell into an exhausted sleep, as at two Theobald's

Row, Giles finally slept, with Herbert Holmer still in his brothel in Istanbul, no nearer solving the mystery of the missing princess than he himself was to controlling the erratic beating of his heart.

The reviews in the local papers were all raving about the food and the ambiance their critics had experienced during their evening at La Casa sul Verdi on the tranquil village green in the heart of the Wealden countryside, after which the telephone was ringing continually with customers anxious to try this exciting new venue for themselves. Clarissa wondered who a Mr. Robert West was. He had booked a table for himself and his son and daughter for three evenings in the forthcoming week. Clarissa had not gone unnoticed by the ever-roaming eyes of Rob West who was beginning to grow anxious of Tamara Adam's subtle suggestions that maybe it was time she moved into Honeysuckle Cottage. This was the last thing Rob wanted – he wished to be free and the shapely Clarissa had definitely caught his eye.

Clarissa was totally unaware of Robert's plan to set out to beguile her as she sat in Dr. Taylor's waiting room, trying not to look at Jules who had just cut his hand and was currently dripping blood over the pristine floor.

'You had better see Dr. Taylor before me,' she told him and he thankfully shot into the surgery, emerging some minutes later with his hand neatly bandaged but on his way to the A. and E. at the nearest hospital where he had been told he would have at least four stitches. Clarissa watched through the window as he clambered into an extremely old campervan, which he drove noisily out of the car park, backfiring as it made its way to Ashford.

Dr. Taylor's face appeared round the door. 'Next,' she smiled and Clarissa made her way into the surgery.

'I don't think we have met before,' the doctor smiled at Clarissa. 'I hope all went well for you on Saturday evening. Unfortunately I left it too late to book a table but we're coming *en famille* next

Saturday. We're really looking forwards to it, but how can I help you this morning?'

Clarissa sighed. 'I don't know whether anyone can ever help me, Dr. Taylor. I have a terrible phobia, which is ruining my life. I would give anything to overcome this fear and I am afraid you will think I am a very weak and cruel person.'

'I think that is for me to decide, don't you, Clarissa? Is it all right if I call you that?'

'Of course, Doctor.'

'Would this phobia include you ex-husband or your young daughter, Georgia?'

'You know Giles, Doctor?'

'Yes, when Georgia was given the pony he made sure her tetanus jabs were up to date. A very commendable precaution and I suggested he should update his own too. I have to say I found him a charming man and an extremely conscientious father. He has obviously fought through several years of pain but now, with all the new technology he has made an amazing recovery.'

'But – but it's still there, Doctor. That's the trouble. His body will never be perfect.'

'But Clarissa many, many people have a deformity or disfiguration of some type. I have one patient who has lost both an arm and a leg. Now, six years later, he is working in a bank and just last month his wife produced the most beautiful baby girl. They are so happy – they already had a young son when he had his accident – now they have their perfect little family.'

'I can't help myself Dr. Taylor – that's the trouble – I have this terrible fear. I can't look at or be near anyone who has even quite a small imperfection. I couldn't even look Tom West's young son Oscar in the eye. He knew – I could see the scorn on his face. When Giles first came home from the rehabilitation centre I couldn't bear him near me. I fled from our bed and took Georgia next door where an old friend of Giles and mine lived. I ran away to France with

Paul and Georgia. Giles was shattered but I begged him to divorce me and he reluctantly agreed. I stayed with Paul for ten years but although I was really fond of him I would never consider marrying him of having his children. There was always someone in the way. Someone I had loved since I was a schoolgirl. Fortunately, Giles had discovered his talent for writing and I think he lives his life through his fictitious characters.'

The doctor looked straight at Clarissa. 'Why did you choose to come to Massenden where you knew full well Giles had been living for the last two years?'

'It wasn't easy to find the right premises which had the potential to be turned into a bistro. I thought I was mature enough and sufficient time had passed that I would be able to cope and I thought Georgia would be able to see both her parents.'

'And you obviously have discovered you still have feelings for your ex-husband?'

'More than just feelings. After the meal on Saturday most of the men gave me a kiss on the cheek – they had all enjoyed their meal and their wine – the ladies were kissing Luigi, my chef and business partner. I think Giles had consumed rather more wine than he should have done – somehow he kissed me on the lips – it was very brief –but Dr. Taylor, I thought my life was in order but it's not – oh it's *so* not – I love him so much, but you see it's hopeless because there's one part of him I could never have near me. I'm sure I don't have to tell you what that is. Doctor is there anyone or anything that could help me?' with which Clarissa burst into tears.

The doctor handed her a tissue as she asked. 'And Mr. Norton – Giles – has he a girlfriend or a partner that you are aware of?'

Clarissa tried to smile. 'According to Georgia, he spends all his time with Herbert Holmer getting involved in the most outrageous crimes. Oh, and then of course there's Herbie – the bulldog pup he has just acquired. He walks it round the green at precisely nine thirty every evening- I often notice him sitting on the seat opposite La Casa. My parents are very fond of Giles – he often takes them out for a meal. They told me he once said he would never put himself in the position where a woman could ever reject him again. I wish we could at least be friends. Occasionally we meet to discuss anything that affects Georgia. Even when I was with Paul, Giles always treated me with respect - he never appeared bitter or unkind but then that's typical of him, he always had a very strong character. It's difficult to decipher his true feelings. I am desperate to overcome this obsession doctor, above all for Giles but also for innocent little boys like young Oscar West.'

'Were you aware of this phobia when you were a child, Clarissa?'

'No, but when I was about fourteen I was cycling with a school friend when she hit a huge pot hole and crashed off her bicycle. We were in a lane at the back of the village where we lived. Claudia was screaming. It was a hot day and we were wearing shorts I looked at her leg – it was facing the wrong way – her kneecap was at the back of her leg. Instead of helping her, I fainted. Fortunately a lady who was walking her dog phoned for an ambulance, but I had let Claudia down. She made a full recovery but she never spoke to me again. She told all our friends I was a coward. It was shortly after that I started going out with Giles – he used to laugh at me because I couldn't watch him play rugby, or dive off the high board but he never called me a coward – not once. It was after Claudia's accident that my phobia started but I was a teenager never for one moment imagining how this irrational fear would ruin three lives – Giles', Georgia's and my own.'

'Giles is obviously aware of your phobia? The reason you rejected him?'

'Oh, yes. - I screamed –I told him, don't let it touch me. I can't be near it.'

'And how did Giles react?'

'Giles was still recovering from months in hospital and rehab – still feeling weak. He cried, but I gathered Georgia and ran next door to Paul who I knew had been in love with me since we had all been at school.'

'But you had visited Giles many times when he was in hospital?'

'Yes, yes, but at first he was always in bed and then later in a chair or walking with a stick in the grounds at the re-hab. He was always dressed - it was the first night when he came home to his parent's house. They went away for the weekend so that Giles and I could be together with Georgia. That evening when we went to bed, I watched in horror as Giles took off his leg and I saw – I saw,' – but Clarissa couldn't continue.

'You saw what was left of his leg.'

'Yes, oh yes, that's when I screamed. He pulled me closer – he was crying – and then oh, Dr. Taylor – I hit him – he let me go and I ran, God forgive me, even if Giles can't.'

'You were a young wife, Clarissa, all you could see was this broken man, his army career finished and his life drastically changed for ever. He had to come to terms with this – there was nothing he could do about it but, sadly for him, you had an alternative, which you chose to take. Many wives would have coped but for you, the phobia you unfortunately have made this impossible. You knew what you were doing was hurting a very troubled man but your panic was beyond your control. Fortunately for Giles, he has discovered a way to obliterate the real world and lose himself in the life of his alter ego, Herbert Holmer.'

The doctor paused and smiled at Clarissa. 'Oh yes, like many people, I am addicted to his books, but Herbert is merely Giles himself in disguise. Now I am only a G.P. but I think you should see a counselor who is qualified to help people in situations like yourself. You are obviously at least on amicable terms with Giles, and that is a good start. Maybe the counselor will suggest you try to arrange a day out together with Georgia – perhaps to the theatre or a trip to the Tower of London or somewhere like that, she might even suggest hypnotherapy could help you, but are you willing for me to arrange for you to see someone?'

Clarissa thought for a moment and then made a huge effort to smile. 'Yes, please, because whatever Giles might think of me. I can't go through the rest of my life like this. I'm not really the hard, unfeeling person I must appear to everybody.'

'Not everyone, Clarissa, I for one am certain you are not. I'll call you as soon as I have fixed an appointment with the most suitable counselor I can find to help you in your situation, but before then I shall look forwards to visiting La Casa sul Verde on Saturday evening,' and as she gave her one more smile, Clarissa left the surgery with just the suspicion of a spring in her step.

CHAPTER 25

Orlando and Oscar were tying balloons on the entrance to Marigold's sanctuary and Josh, Mimi and Jacques were all standing on steps nailing bunting across the new building, which was able to house more than fifty small mammals. Dom was hammering horseshoes that Rosie had diligently painted in a variety of colours over the doors of the six new stables, which now graced the yard opposite Marigold's beautiful old Elizabethan house, which had miraculously escaped the ferocious fire that had blazed almost exactly a year ago.

The committees from both the Ribbenden and the Massenden W.I.s were laying out a buffet lunch, with elder flower and lemonade cordial for the youngsters and on a nearby round table several bottles of champagne in cool ice buckets were waiting to bubble into the glass flutes at precisely mid-day when John West was to cut the gold ribbon in front of the main gates to the sanctuary.

Betsy would then put the first in-mates into their cages. They were the two rabbits and two guinea pigs that Sam had rescued on the day of the fire. Betsy had looked after them for almost a year but now they were to be the first little creatures to be re-homed.

Marigold already had a long list of guinea pigs, rabbits, hamsters and gerbils and even a large rat who would be arriving later that day and only that morning she had received a phone call about three puppies that had been discovered in a ditch, hidden in a thick cardboard box. She knew that before long the new building would be abounding with animals of all shapes, temperaments and sizes.

Marigold was almost overcome as she made a short speech thanking everyone who had worked so hard raising the money to make this morning possible and as the visitors started to leave, Rosie and Anne-Marie were begging to be allowed to stay behind and help Marigold settle the new animals as and when they arrived. Dom finally gave in to their pleas arranging to return for them at five o'clock, by which time both girls were clutching a small carrying box with holes in either side.

'What are you doing with those?' he asked.

'Marigold has given them to us – they're gorgeous.' Rosie told him and as she opened the lid a small way, to Dom's dismay he could see what was undoubtedly an extremely young golden hamster.

'And I presume you 'ave one too?' he asked Anne-Marie. She smiled disarmingly at her father.

'Oui, papa, but mine is pure white and I shall call him Tiddly Winks and he can sit in the corner of my bedroom.'

'Et Tin-Tin?'

'Papa, you know Maman doesn't allow Tin-Tin upstairs. You and Maman won't have to do a thing – you won't even know he is in the house.'

Dom sighed and gave in but Rosie met with much stiffer opposition. Sam was adamant. 'It will live in the tack room, Rosie. You know Boswell and Holly are always going in and out of your bedroom. It's either that or it goes straight back to Marigold's.' Sam was not the mother of five children for nothing – she had learned to be firm a long time ago and after borrowing a very small cage from Betsy, the hamster was installed on the shelf in the tack room. The matter was not open for even the smallest discussion.

Later that evening, there was great excitement at Woodcutters as two of the four imminent foals arrived within one hour of each other. Star produced yet another piebald colt. He had almost identical markings to those of Humbug but he was obviously going to be much larger and as Tom looked at him he thought he would be about the same size as Tiger Lily. 'Take care of him Rosie,' Tom told the excited little girl. 'In four years time you will be nearly fourteen – just the right age when we come to back him – you can choose his name.'

Rosie thought for a long time, watching the foal as he began to suckle his mother - he suddenly looked up at her and tossed his head in the air as if to say *'just look at me.'*

Sam laughed. 'Cheeky boy – Mr. High and Mighty.'

Rosie hugged her mother. 'Mum that's a super name.'

'What, Cheeky Boy?'

'No silly, High and Mighty. Cos one day he and I are going to jump mighty high together. I'll call him Mighty for short.'

Tom smiled at her. 'That's great, Rosie and don't forget, before that you've got Bamboozle to think about.' And then he let out a yell. 'Wow, look at this,' and Grace was just expelling the most exquisite light chestnut filly foal with a pure white mane and tail and a gleaming white star on her forehead. Josh had just arrived in the yard and was gazing at the beautiful foal – the filly wobbled as she took her first step and then everyone caught their breath as she tipped her head on one side and looked at them – she was simply perfect. Josh looked at Tom and Sam. 'Gosh. I'm just spellbound.'

Tom grinned. 'You've hit the nail on the head, Josh. That's what we all are at this moment, *'spellbound,'* and that's what we'll call her. Lake House Spellbound and you can back her in four years time, she may well be your first Foxhunter horse, we'll have to be patient and wait and see. Two down, two to go. I think we've got another couple of weeks to wait for Misty and Chintz's big days, their foals will probably be bigger than this one but I guarantee they can't possibly be any more beautiful. I'll ask Anna if she would like to push Molly here and keep and eye on them with Hannah whilst we're in Aachen. It would give her something to look forwards to and if there is anything they are worried about with either the foals or their mums, they can call James straight away and they can keep an eye on Misty and Chintz at the same time.'

'How long will you be away for, Dad?' Josh asked Tom.

'The horses are leaving the day after tomorrow and Mum and I are flying out to Germany with Charles and Joanna on Tuesday. We'll be back here on Sunday evening but I will call you every morning and evening. Justin's not coming this year – he's going to Rotterdam the following week with Jason and a couple of younger riders. He'll be looking after *the gang* this week. Dorcas will be arriving tomorrow evening. Just make sure you all tell her when you are going up to Lake House so that she knows where you are. I shall speak to Ozzie and 'Lando later. Where are they by the way?'

'They've gone to Lake House to help Rupert with his bicycles. He's taken them apart, now he's trying to make one good one out of all the bits.'

Tom sighed. 'Get the Swarfega ready, Sammy darling, I rather think they will need it.' And he sighed with pure joy as he looked at the latest arrivals, Lake House High and Mighty and Lake House Spellbound, wondering what lay in store for them.

The following afternoon, Sam left with Rosie and the two remaining triplets, calling for Mary and Susan as they made their way to Buckinghamshire to be reunited with Oliver and to listen to the concert the eighty boys and girls from various youth orchestras from the south of England would perform in the historic old school hall. They were filled with pride as they listened to Oliver's renditions of two of Scot Joplin's most famous pieces, The Maple Leaf Rag and the Entertainer on the piano and his school's group of various Chris Barber and Humphrey Lyttelton's iconic pieces when Oliver performed with his electric guitar with six other boys on various instruments.

Not for the first time, Sam wondered in which direction Oliver's life would take him. Her other three boys and even Rosie's futures were plain to see but at the moment, Oliver could go in one of two directions and as far as she and Tom were concerned they would not influence him in either way. Only time would eventually tell, but she was even more uncertain when having heard about the foals from Orlando and Oscar, he tore into the paddock and having duly admired the new arrivals, called his brothers and Rosie, and as Sam looked out of the window all she could see were the triplets and their sister cantering along the path beside the lake.

Two minutes later, Tom and Josh arrived back in the yard with The Wizard and the Foxhunter horse, Swallow Tail and Joshua's Lilly and Ganger. They had obviously had an excellent day as they staggered into the cottage under the weight of three more trophies. Swallow Tail was proving to be a star and had beaten Justin and his mare Conchita by a mere two hundreds of a second and The Wizard had excelled himself in the Open. The afternoon had ended in style for Joshua as Ganger had prevailed in the Junior Open and with the triplets and Rosie not there to thwart him, Gus had won the thirteen two class with Hamlet.

Jean-Pierre was becoming increasingly worried about Simon's horse, Melchior who spent most of his time standing by the gate watching the other horses as they went about their daily exercise. Daisy was worried too, even more so when Jean-Pierre asked her. 'What time does your father get 'ome from London, Daisy? I want to 'ave a word with 'im about Simon's 'orse. "E 'asn't been ridden for more than a week. 'E is 'ere on full livery, if 'e was 'alf livery I could use 'im in the school for lessons. 'E is a good 'orse and this life 'e is leading at the moment is not benefitting 'im at all. "Ow old is 'e Daisy?'

'He's eight – he's a year older than Popcorn.'

'Right, so what time is your dad 'ome this evening?'

'He gets off the train in Ashford at twenty past six and he's usually in the house about a quarter to seven but he often stops at the pub for a drink on the way home.'

'Well, I shall be at your 'ouse at a quarter past seven. I wait for 'im if 'e is not there. This situation with Melchior cannot go on. Where are you going with Popcorn?'

'I'm taking him to your dressage area. Auntie Sam is helping me with the test for the Pony Club Day. Lots of the gang are going to try the test too, even Mimi with Babushka and Anne-Marie is going to have a go with Tom Thumb. Auntie Sam is going to

Germany tomorrow but she says she will give us all another lesson next week.'

Jean-Pierre was well aware of the Pony Club Dressage test, which was fast approaching. He had been helping Eloise and Pierrot for the past few weeks. He smiled at Daisy. – 'If you get everyone here by five thirty tomorrow evening I will give you another run through with Eloise.'

Daisy was thrilled. She had noticed Jean-Pierre on his beautiful horse Flèche d'Or executing what appeared to be a very complicated movement in this very school.

'Thank you, Jean-Pierre, I'll tell *the gang* at school tomorrow and Rosie can tell the younger girls who are still at the Primary School. I think there are eight of us altogether including Fenella Thornley who is the youngest. We're in two groups. Ten and under and fourteen and under.'

Jean-Pierre smiled at Daisy's enthusiasm. 'That's fine – I will be 'ere at five thirty sharp. I'm not teaching until seven thirty, which will give us plenty of time. If it's wet, we'll go into the school but somehow I doubt it will be, the weather forecast for the next few days appears to be excellent.'

Daisy trotted Popcorn round the edge of the school whilst she waited for Sam and Rosie, who she could soon see as they appeared in the distance, trotting down the drive towards her.

Whilst Daisy was enjoying a happy hour with Sam who was both patient and encouraging, the same could certainly not be said of her brother.

His *'chick'* as he described his latest fancy piece had not appeared at their appointed meeting place earlier that afternoon. He had waited for three quarters of an hour before he received a text message. *'Hi, Si. Won't be able to meet u. Have gone 2 Canterbury 2 the cinema with Peter Giles. Hope u've not been waiting. Carla.'*

Simon had never before encountered the experience of being stood up and to say the very least, he was not at all pleased and his mood did not improve when a couple of hours later there was an imperious knock on the front door, which he opened to find himself confronting the *odious frog* who he despised.

'What do you want?' he asked Jean-Pierre rudely.

'I wish to 'ave a word with your father about Melchior.'

'What's wrong with the brute?'

'There is nothing wrong with 'im at the moment but there very soon will be if you don't give 'im regular exercise.'

'I've got better things to do with my time than ride round your crumby fields on my own. There aren't even any decent chicks to have a bit of fun with.'

'If that's 'ow you feel about my establishment then I shall 'ave no option other than to ask your father to make other arrangements for Melchior. Maybe if you 'ave developed other interests in your life it would be best for you and your 'orse if you let me use Melchior in my school.'

Simon was just about to tell Jean-Pierre he couldn't care less how many old cronies rode his horse when he saw his father's figure striding up the cottage path to the front door.

Rob hadn't much time for the handsome Frenchman, who in his ignorant opinion spent most of his life showing off on his horses – on the other hand he appreciated that Daisy was probably happier when she was with his bloody nephew's wife, Sam, and *the gang* with whom she seemed to spend almost every spare moment, than she had been at any time in her short life. He was the first to acknowledge that his children had experienced a most unorthodox childhood. – They very rarely, if ever, mentioned their mother from whom about twice a year they would each receive a parcel containing the most inappropriate clothing, which in less than no time he would have taken to the nearest charity shop. Daisy talked incessantly about her Aunties Mary and Sam and her Uncle John and in his heart, Rob knew it was very much thanks to his brother and his family that his young daughter had settled into Massenden so quickly.

It had been an entirely different story for Simon. It had all started the very first morning with the highly irresponsible act he had committed with Thunderbird, which he knew neither Tom nor Joshua were ever likely to forget. Fortunately Simon and Joshua's lives didn't cross paths too often. The only time they met was on the school bus where Joshua always sat with his cousin Jacques, ignoring Simon and fortunately for all concerned was completely unaware of the lecherous looks Simon was giving Mimi Wright-Smith as he watched fascinated as her long blond hair swung across her shoulders as she talked animatedly to her friend, Clara Dubois.

For the time being, Simon was happy spending his time with the gang of boys and girls who he met on the village green – but he was biding his time - waiting for Mimi to grow older, when he would make his move, blissfully unaware that she and Josh had been friends for as long as anyone could remember and Joshua's lethal left hook would never hesitate to flash if circumstances suggested it needed to be used and that would apply not only to his family but extended to any member of *the gang* and as everyone knew the outcome was not pleasant and should be avoided at all costs.

Rob made a quick decision, swallowing his irritation at the sight of Jean-Pierre in his sitting room. 'To what do I owe this pleasure – fancy a glass of vino, old chap?'

Jean-Pierre had no desire to be anything but pleasant, after all this bumptious man was his wife's uncle, all he wanted was the best outcome for the unfortunate Melchior, so he replied affably. 'That sounds great, Rob.'

Rob went to an opulent drinks cabinet in the corner of the sitting room and asked Jean-Pierre. 'What's your tipple? Red or white?'

'Whichever you prefer to open, Rob. I'm teaching again in an 'our's time so I must limit myself to one glass. So it's up to you – it will be you who 'as to finish the bottle.'

'I'll open the white then. Tamara Adams is coming round later. She'll help me finish it. She wants to move in with me but I need to break it to her that's not on my agenda. I'm sure I'm not the perfect dad, but at the end of the day Si and Daize have to rely on me, they've had a tough time recently having to acclimatize themselves to a completely new lifestyle. For Daize it's been relatively straightforward, mainly thanks to my hotheaded nephew's beautiful wife, Sam. God knows how she's ever stuck with that arrogant chap for so long, but she's been brilliant helping Daize with Popcorn. She seems to be wrapped up in some competition at the moment but it's not been so easy for Si, his tastes are a bit more sophisticated than Daize's *gang* and Massenden doesn't seem to have much to offer him.'

Jean-Pierre was still reeling from the remarks about his brother-in-law, who also happened to be one of his best friends but he decided that in the interests of Melchior, he would ignore the unkind words and reveal his reason for being at Honeysuckle Cottage.

'Actually, it's Simon I need to discuss with you, or more accurately 'is 'orse, Melchior. The 'orse is sad. It is not getting enough attention or exercise. Your son rides 'im once a week if the 'orse is lucky. You are paying me a lot of money every month, which from your point of view is good money thrown away. I feel we must reach a compromise. I am willing to take the 'orse on 'alf livery, which means I 'ave the use of Melchior for my clients three evenings a week – the rest of the time 'e is there for Simon to ride whenever 'e wishes. At least the 'orse will be fitter and 'ave something to look forwards to.'

Rob looked at Simon. 'How does that idea appeal to you, Simon?'

The lad looked at Jean-Pierre boldly. 'Well, I'm sure your old cronies wouldn't tire him out and if that means I haven't got to waste my time at your yard, then so much the better as far as I am concerned.'

Jean-Pierre ignored Simon's appalling manners and turned back to Rob. 'My suggestion would be that we try this arrangement for the next six months. 'Alf livery is exactly as it sounds – you give me 'alf the amount you are paying me now and Melchior will be well looked after. If Simon's riding days are over then we could talk again at the end of the six months. I am sure I could buy 'im from you for the school or often some of my students ask me to look out for a sensible 'orse for them but one thing I 'ave to tell you and that is I cannot 'ave that 'orse in my stables wasting 'is life. If you and Simon don't agree to my suggestion, I'm afraid your only other option is to find another livery yard for 'im where the main idea is to take your money and not concern themselves with the welfare of your 'orse. Take a few days to chat with Simon and let me know your decision,' and Jean-Pierre drained the last few drops of the Australian white wine, but as he stood up to leave Simon suddenly spoke. 'Let the old dears ride him, Dad, I might go and give him a good old blow out once in a while when I've nothing better to do. Thank goodness I don't take after my cousins who don't even know one end of a cricket bat or a tennis racquet from the other, but if they want to spend their time poncing around with a bunch of pony mad girls that's up to them.'

Jean-Pierre shook his head. 'I will pretend I didn't 'ear that remark, Simon, but I suggest you watch your cousin Tom on the television. I think you will be surprised when you see the ratio of men to women riding in the Nation's Cup Teams and in the big Grand Prix. It is at least eight to one in favour of the men and I don't think those men are poncing around as you just suggested.'

'Huh. I'm certainly not going to waste my time looking at my cousin on television when I spend half my time avoiding him in the flesh, and his creepy son is one worse.'

Jean-Pierre was completely shocked. 'You will take back those remarks, Simon West and I think it is best if you find other accommodation for Melchior straight away, Rob.'

Simon turned on his father. 'Sell the bloody animal to this frog, Dad – I'm through with horses,' with which he turned and slammed out of the house.

‘It would probably be the best thing in the interest of everyone, not least the poor innocent ‘orse.’

‘How much would you give me?’

‘One thousand five hundred pounds. I can assure you that is a very fair price and I am certainly not interested in ‘is tack. I am afraid we don’t ride Western style at my Centre.’

‘I wouldn’t have a clue about the price, Jean-Pierre but as your wife is my niece I suppose I just have to trust you. All I know is, I paid four thousand Australian dollars for Melchior and Daisy’s Popcorn.’

‘Well you’ve done O.K. then and I can guarantee by the time Sam has given Daisy a few more lessons, Popcorn will be worth a good deal more than you paid for ‘im. I will put the cheque through your letter box tomorrow then and I’m pretty sure your son will never come to regret his decision,’ and with that the two men shook hands, and the next minute, Jean-Pierre was passing Tamara Adams on the garden path.

CHAPTER 26

The next morning, having sent Josh on his way to the school bus, Tom and Sam were hugging the triplets and a slightly tearful Rosie at the Primary School gate. Just as Sam's conscience was beginning to smite her she saw Gus and Abby running down the drive with Anna holding Noah who was waving to them from Amelia's back. They each grabbed hold of one of Rosie's hands and to Sam's relief she was laughing as she ran up the drive with them in pursuit of her brothers.

Tom took Sam's hand. 'She'll be fine, darling. One look from Fergus Wright-Smith and she has forgotten all about us!!'

'I know, Tom. I'm just a hopeless case. I want to be with you in Germany more than anything in this world but at the same time I hate leaving the family.'

'That's because you are a Super-Mum, my darling and not a bad wife either,' he teased.

'Just not bad, my Thomas?' After which remark Tom gave all the mothers and the few fathers gathered round the gate an impromptu demonstration of an extremely mouth watering kiss!!

Elizabeth, who had just arrived at the gate with Fenella and the twins turned to her sister in disgust. 'Poor Sam, I really don't know how she puts up with him, he's almost obscene!!'

Jane laughed at her.

'Puts up with him, Lizzie!! She encourages him all the time. You can bet your life they will be snogging in that plane all the way to Aachen!! If Sam hadn't had her womb removed when Rosie was born I swear they would have at least a dozen children by now!!'

To Jane's consternation Elizabeth wasn't laughing, in fact there was more than a suspicion of tears in her eyes as she asked Jane. 'Have you time for a coffee? I need someone to talk to.'

'Lizzie, what's wrong with talking to James? You and James? There's nothing wrong between you is there? Your solid rock isn't crumbling, surely?'

'Of course not, Jane – please can I come to the cottage and talk to you?'

'What. Now?'

'Please, if you've time. I'm really frightened.'

'Darling Lizzie, what's wrong? Have you spoken to *The General*?'

'No, no. I don't want to tell her until I have spoken with you.'

'Follow me straight to Bramble Cottage and we will sit in the garden with a coffee. Pierre has gone for a hack with Tony and Trish so we can talk in peace.'

Jane was worried. Whatever could have happened to upset her sister's well-ordered life? She pulled into the drive of Bramble Cottage with Lizzie close behind her and soon she was carrying two cups of coffee into the garden. Two minutes later she was shaken to the core when Lizzie burst into tears, burying her face in her hands.

'Darling Lizzie, tell me quickly. What ever is wrong? Where is James?'

'He's at work, Jane, he doesn't know there is anything wrong.'

'Then you haven't had a mighty fall out with him?'

'Of course not, Jane, how could I ever fall out with my wonderful rock?'

'If he is such a rock Lizzie, then why are you with me? Why aren't you with him, telling him what's worrying you?'

'I can't Jane. I need you to come to Doctor Taylor's with me. I've managed to get an appointment this morning. I think I'm really ill, Jane. I've found a huge lump.'

Jane felt the world dropping from under her feet. 'A lump, Lizzie?' she managed to whisper. 'Where? In your breast?'

'No – no – in my stomach.'

'When did you discover it?'

‘A few days ago. I haven’t felt very well for several weeks now. I’m not hungry and I want to sleep all the time. My periods are all over the place, too. Please help me, Jane. I’m so frightened.’

Jane put her arms round Elizabeth. ‘What time is your appointment?’ she asked.

‘Ten fifteen this morning.’

‘Right – in the car. With any luck Doctor Taylor might see us a bit early.’

Unfortunately the waiting room was full and Jane tried to calm her sister as it gradually drew near to their appointed time. Finally, one hour later, at a quarter past eleven, Jane was propelling a shaking Elizabeth into the surgery.

The doctor smiled and then looked worried as she noticed the evidence of very recent tears. She had known Elizabeth since she had come home from the hospital with Mary – a tiny premature baby who had fought for her life.

‘My dear, Elizabeth, whatever is wrong?’

‘I’ve found a huge lump, Doctor. I haven’t felt myself for the past three or four months and my periods seem to be almost non existent.’

‘Lie on the couch and let me have a feel.’

To Elizabeth and Jane’s surprise, the doctor was smiling. ‘You are in for a shock I think Elizabeth, but unless I am an extremely bad doctor, you are about four and a half months pregnant. Does James know you haven’t been feeling too well recently?’ ‘No, no. I was so afraid. I wanted to see you before I worried him. How can it be when I had to have all that I.V.F. treatment to enable me to have the twins?’

‘I imagine because of your past history you have not done anything to prevent a pregnancy occurring?’

‘Well no. No, we haven’t. Even James didn’t think we would ever have any more babies.’

‘Well, just to be certain, I am ringing the hospital – we

will get an emergency scan done this afternoon, just to set your mind completely at rest. Can you manage that?' Jane smiled. 'I'll take her Dr. Taylor. I'll ask Lilia to take my ballet classes this afternoon. Lizzie has already told me James won't be home for his lunch today – he's the other side of Canterbury checking Jim Crane's cattle for T.B. We'll get some lunch after Lizzie has had her scan.'

The doctor made a swift phone call. 'They can fit you in at one thirty, Elizabeth. Give me a call as soon as you get home.'

'But why have I had these odd little periods?'

'That's not too unusual. Your body is warning you to take life quietly. Definitely no more riding until after baby is born. Now try not to worry. I have never made a wrong diagnosis in this department yet, and I really don't think you are going to be my first one.'

Elizabeth had started to worry about the twins who finished play school at mid-day but the ever efficient Jane called Lilia who promised to be at the school gates and would look after Felix and Flicka for as long as necessary and would ask Jean-Pierre to pick up Fenella with Eloise.

Rudi had been sitting on Jane's lap and fell asleep as soon as she strapped him into his car seat.

By half past two, Elizabeth was in shock. Inside her womb was a four and a half month baby boy and for once, James' well-ordered life was to be thrown into chaos.

Elizabeth pulled a card out of her handbag and was soon booking a table for two at La Casa sul Verde at eight o'clock that evening.

'Don't tell anyone until I've told James this evening, Jane. He's going to have a bit of a shock to say the very least and I know he will wrap me up in cotton wool until Freddy is born.'

'Freddy?'

'Yes. When we were thinking of names for the twins, we very

nearly chose Frederick. Frederick William Albert Thornley,' and with that she pulled out her mobile again and called Dr. Taylor.

'You were right, doctor. A bouncing boy is on his way in five month's time. I just hope James will be as thrilled as I am.'

'Well, I hate to boast, Elizabeth but as I told you, I have never yet made a wrong diagnosis as far as the womb is concerned but I am so happy for you both.'

That evening, Susan and Bill were giving the twins and Fenella their supper. Fenella had stayed the afternoon at Bramble Cottage with Eloise whilst Trish rode to the Old Manor on Melchior and led Poupèe back to the Centre with a pair of Fenella's jeans and her riding hat in a substantial carrier bag and at five thirty, eight young girls had convened for their dressage lesson with Jean-Pierre.

Elizabeth and James were sitting at a small table in an alcove in La Casa sul Verde. Elizabeth had ordered herself a fruit juice and a glass of the best champagne that was on offer for James, who was puzzled and worried he had forgotten some important anniversary. He thought this unlikely however, as every date of any significance, however trifling the occasion might appear, was written meticulously on the calendar in his surgery.

'What's all this about, shrimpklin? It's not your birthday and I am certain it's not mine?'

'Jamie, I haven't been feeling too well recently. I didn't want to worry you, so I asked Jane to take me to see Dr. Taylor this morning.'

James immediately clutched Elizabeth's hand. 'Little shrimp, you are frightening me. What's wrong? You should have told me straight away.'

'I felt a lump, James.'

' God! A lump?' James had gone as white as a sheet.

'Yes, in my stomach. I was afraid it was a tumour but Jamie – you will never believe this but I promise you it is true – you're going to have another son – Freddy Thornley is already well on his way. He will be here just before Christmas.'

Elizabeth felt a mixture of sticky apple and mango J.2.O. and ice cool bubbling champagne seeping through her fine linen skirt as her ever steady rock trembled and the two glasses flew across the table.

'Please say you're happy, Jamie,' Elizabeth begged as Clarissa and Maria rushed up to the table with warm, damp cloths.

Elizabeth was shaken as she looked at the tears running down her husband's face. 'Pleased, my little sea urchin – it's a bloody miracle. It's beyond my wildest dreams – but how about you – apart from being very sticky and wet?'

'At first I was just relieved and then when the reality set in I felt incredulous. Apparently he's healthy and perfectly formed already.'

Elizabeth was smiling at Clarissa. 'I'm so sorry about the spill but I was just telling my husband he is about to become a father again. We're going to have a little boy, just before Christmas. We shall have a perfect family – two boys and two girls.'

Clarissa was aware of a feeling, which rushed momentarily through her body as she saw the joy on James' face and also the way he was gazing at Elizabeth and she suddenly recalled a memory of Giles, the night she had informed him she was expecting Georgia. She turned quickly away to hide the tears that seemed to threaten so often these days and went slowly to the bar and poured another glass of J.2.O. for Elizabeth and bubbling champagne for James, by which time she had regained her composure and told them. 'Please, have these with the compliments of La Casa sul Verde – I am truly delighted for both of you,' and she handed both James and Elizabeth a menu as the door burst open and Elizabeth recognized her odious cousin, Simon, and his father Rob and Daisy who were making their way to a table for three on the other side of the restaurant where Rob would have an uninterrupted view of Clarissa as she went to and from her kitchen.

'Whatever you do, don't tell Rob why we are here – I don't want anyone else to know before we've told our parents. Maybe we can call at Old Tiles on our way home and we'll tell your Mum and Dad as soon as we get back. I think they might have the surprise of their lives but I'm certain they will be absolutely thrilled.'

James still found it hard to realize Elizabeth was talking about his own parents when she referred to them as *'your mum and dad.'* All his young life, when he and Elspeth had been growing up they had been Mother and Pa and he imagined that was what they always would be. He looked up to see a shadow looming over the table in the guise of Elizabeth's Uncle Rob who was asking them. 'Good Evening, what are you two doing here – is it a special occasion of some sort?'

James was quick with his reply. 'No but we enjoyed our meal here so much on Saturday evening we decided to repeat the experience, and what brings you here?'

'Oh, I'm spending the money Jean-Pierre has just given me for Melchior. This seemed an extremely good place to part with some of it. Excellent food and a lot more to enjoy as well,' and Elizabeth couldn't fail to notice in which way her uncle's eyes were pointing, as Clarissa went to the door to greet her latest diners.

'So you've sold Melchior. Does this herald the end of Simon's riding days?'

'It would seem Simon has already discovered that fillies with two legs are far more entertaining than their four legged counterparts.'

'Well, I'm pleased for Melchior. He will have a really good life. Jean-Pierre treats all his horses with the utmost consideration.'

Rob gave James an unpleasant look. 'Well at least I won't be receiving any of your astronomical veterinary bills for the animal, James.'

James simply ignored his remark, raising his glass saying. 'Here's to us, my shrimpklin,' and as he let the cool bubbles slip down his throat, he sighed in relief as Rob sauntered back to his son and daughter with his eyes still lingering on the unsuspecting Clarissa.

James took hold of Elizabeth's hand, telling her. 'My dearest little shrimp, there is one thing I implore of you. If you ever, ever have a worry of any description, you will share it with me whether it concerns the children, yourself, or anything else, however trivial it may appear at the time You must remember, I am always here for you. I always have been and I most certainly always will be. I am here for you to lean on and I sincerely hope I am your rock that will never crumble.'

Elizabeth squeezed his hand. 'Jamie that's not possible, you are not just a lump of grey stone, you are a solid diamond that can never chip or erode. I may be your shrimp but you are my great white shark, otherwise known as the king of the sea and I love you to bits. Now if we have finished this delicious meal let's go together and face The *General* and my dear old dad.'

As they said goodnight to Clarissa and Luigi, congratulating them on their superb cuisine, Elizabeth noticed her Uncle Rob's eyes were still gazing in the direction of their hostess but Clarissa was totally unaware of the bright blue eyes that were scrutinizing her for as she closed the door behind Elizabeth and James and watched him help his wife into the silver Range Rover, she caught sight of a lonely figure siting on the seat opposite La Casa sul Verde. He appeared to be throwing a small ball to a familiar rotund, little bulldog.

Clarissa went into the kitchen and put a cardigan round her shoulders, at the same time asking Maria. 'Can you serve the sweets for half an hour – I just need a little fresh air?'

'You are feeling alright, Clarissa?' Maria asked her boss anxiously.

'I'm fine. It's such a lovely evening I just feel I must get outside for a few minutes.'

She closed the door and made her way slowly across the green. Giles jumped as he realized he was not the only occupant of the old seat and that Herbie was sniffing at the newcomer's shoes.

He turned and swallowed hard. 'Clarissa. Are you not busy in your bistro?'

'Yes, but I saw you siting on the seat. I could see Herbie chasing his ball.'

Giles gave a semblance of a smile. 'Herbie doesn't chase, Clarissa - he plods – but like his master, he gets there in the end.'

'Would you like to come to La Casa and have a coffee, Giles? I always have one at this time.'

Giles frantically tried to conjure up an excuse. Had she no idea how he felt about her? Did she not realize that it was sheer torture just to be near her? 'Herbie – you can't have a dog in La Casa, surely?'

'Not in the restaurant, Giles, but you can bring him up to my apartment, there are no rules whatsoever there.'

'Your apartment?'

'Yes, at the top of La Casa. I can see your cottage in Back lane and the beautiful old house that Georgia's friends Gus and Abby Wright-Smith have moved into. I can see Georgia's bedroom light and your sitting room lamp still burning after we've finished here. You are sitting at your computer – I imagine with Herbert Holmer.'

'He's all I have once Georgia has gone to bed, Clarissa. He's quite good company actually and a very lucrative friend who has no aversion to prosthetic limbs.'

Clarissa tried to ignore his final words and asked him. 'How about Trish Snowfield? Doesn't she keep you pleasantly entertained?'

For the first time for over ten years, Giles felt he was holding the upper hand. 'Trish, – why yes – she's a really nice girl,' and the new demon now lurking inside him glowed as he noticed the look that crossed his ex-wife's face.

'Now. As for that coffee – it would have been pleasant but Georgia is alone and I always make a point of being back in the cottage by ten o'clock, so I am afraid I shall have to decline your very tempting offer and rescue Herbert Holmer from the seamy brothel in Istanbul that he seems to have got himself incarcerated in.'

Clarissa was fighting with herself. She wanted to tell him she was going to see a counselor next week. 'Giles – I'm.' – but he was already bending over, clipping the smart red lead onto Herbie's collar.

He stood up. 'Goodnight then, Clarissa, perhaps another evening,' and he picked up Herbie's yellow ball. He felt a hand on his arm. 'I'd like that, Giles. I need to talk to you about a brace for Georgia's teeth.'

At last she had his undivided attention. 'A brace? Does Georgia need a brace?'

'I'm not sure but I think the dentist should check. We'll discuss it another time.' And she turned away from him and walked across the green but she could only just make out La Casa sul Verde as the tears poured down her cheeks but as Giles turned in the other direction towards Back Lane, he felt as though his much maligned prosthetic leg was walking on air – he felt different – he felt at last he was the master of his own feelings. He was well aware those feelings involved Clarissa and his ever creative brain was already starting to write his own synopsis. Tomorrow, he would invite Trish Snowfield for a meal for two in one of the secluded alcoves in La Casa sul Verde. His conscience smote him for a brief moment but he told himself he would not give Trish any reason to think this was anything more than a pleasant meal between two neighbours in an ambivalent atmosphere but the look he had noticed on Clarissa's face earlier had been a very familiar one. He took himself back to the year when he had been seventeen years old and had been about to kiss Tansy Mackintosh in response to a dare by his dubious friend Joe Smithson, when Clarissa had clambered up the stairs on the school bus. She had not been amused but the incident had soon been forgotten. Giles smiled again, as he remembered. *'Oh yes, that had been a very familiar look.'* Then he pulled himself together as he kicked his leg in frustration. *'Bloody thing,'*- but he still decided to call Trish first thing the next morning.

Georgia was sitting in the armchair in the sitting room, dressed in her pyjamas, reading a book, waiting to say goodnight to Giles and to give Herbie his bedtime treat. She looked up and smiled at her father. He laughed to himself as he looked at Georgia's perfect set of gleaming, straight white teeth. He felt happier than he had done for many, many years and that night he allowed Herbert Holmer to romp with the beautiful princess he had rediscovered in a nightclub in Istanbul. If he was happy, then naturally, Herbert was too. That was a foregone conclusion!!

CHAPTER 27

Once Elizabeth and James had recovered from the first euphoria of discovering that against all odds they were going to become parents again, they realized their lives would require some changes – not least Elizabeth's four horses.

James had only limited spare time when he could indulge in his favourite hobby and his two horses, Pas de Deux and Top Choice were still reasonably young. Daddy's Girl, Power Point and Amadeus although supremely fit were all nineteen years old. After much deliberation with James, Elizabeth decided Power Point and Daddy's Girl should be retired in one of the paddocks surrounding the Old Manor House and after an initial rest with his long term friends and after Freddy had been safely delivered, Elizabeth would ride Amadeus whenever she escorted her children on their daily hacks and in any of the Riding Club events in which she wished to participate. He had always been her special boy and she hadn't hesitated in deciding which of her three horses she would ride whenever she could. James was trying to persuade her to engage a full time nanny but this was not the life Elizabeth wanted for her children.

'No, Jamie. I want to look after our children. I have managed three perfectly successfully, one more is not going to make me change my mind but I would be happy to have an au pair to help me and maybe someone to help me look after you.'

'Shrimpkin, are you implying I am more trouble than the children?'

'Of course not, Jamie but I want to know you are properly fed and I know you like your meals at the right time. Perhaps we could find someone like Dorcas who would live in one of the cottages and see to the everyday running of the house but I couldn't bear to have a nanny telling me what or what not to do with our children. I think I'm ready to spend more time with the children at the shows now, rather than participating myself. Fenella has become really keen recently and I know Felix and Flicka are soon going to be highly competitive and you must continue with your horses, also I would like to spend more time helping with The Pony Club. My only real concern is for Sweet Dreams. He is only seven and still eligible for the Foxhunter Classes.'—

James broke in. 'I'm too heavy to ride him, I'm not a little shrimp like you.'

'He's got so much talent, as yet unexploited, Jamie. I wonder what your opinion is if I should ask Tom if Joshua would ride him. He will be thirteen after Christmas – the bottom age for him to be eligible to ride a horse is twelve – when he is fourteen in just over a year's time more opportunities would open up and then of course later still they would be able to enter the Young Rider Classes. Josh has exceptional talent and with Tom and Charles helping him I can envisage a super future developing between him and my lovely Dreamer.'

James nodded. 'If that's what would please you, my shrimp, then by all means have a word with Tom. Josh is growing fast. He would look good on Sweet Dreams and the horse would still belong to you.'

'I'll talk to Tom – he and Sam get home late tonight. I'll call him tomorrow morning and see what his reaction is and of course Josh must be enthusiastic too - but somehow I don't really have any doubts about that.'

Having hopefully settled the future of Sweet Dreams, James changed the subject. 'I had a call out to Theobald's Place this afternoon. Anna's rather upset. Her old Topsy Turvy was very lame. I don't like the look of her – I fear it could be the dreaded navicular. I left Anna in tears. I suggested she should ask Pierre about Melchior. He would be a good horse for her – I am sure with Sam's help she would soon get him doing the dressage tests for the club but even if Pierre agreed to sell him, poor old Anna would still have to squeeze the money out of that old Scrooge of a husband of hers. He's still a tight fisted old devil, the only thing he seems willing to lavish his money on is Theobald's Place but he has got a really super home there and somehow or other Anna seems to be able to cope with his reluctance to spend any of his not insignificant fortune. He told me the other day he and Eva have just received a hefty legacy from Miranda's late father now the sale of the haulage business in Lancashire has been finalized.'

Justin was not in the best of moods when he arrived home after a trying afternoon at Lake House. Without Tom's assistance, Eye of The Wind had taken all of three quarters of an hour and six brave people pushing and shoving him from behind before the obstinate horse was finally installed in his compartment in the horsebox. Fortunately, Pickwick was in a considerably more amenable frame of mind and eventually hot and exhausted from his exertion with the reluctant horse, Justin had breathed a sigh of relief as he watched Ricky setting out on her way to Rotterdam where he would join her two days later.

His mood lightened, as it always did, when he walked through the front door of his beautiful home. Anna had placed a vase of freesias in the hall and the fragrance greeted him as he walked past them into the kitchen – opened the fridge, took out a can of lager and after pulling back the metal ring, downed almost half the can in one large gulp, welcoming the refreshing drink before going into the garden where he could hear his youngest son indulging in a particularly vociferous paddy.

His first glimpse of his family was of Anna sitting on the old swing hammock, which had once belonged to his mother, with both Gus and Abby sitting beside her with their arms round her waist. Noah was screaming and stamping his feet as Anna was ignoring his very wet trousers and pants which he was desperately trying to remove. No-one had listened to his plea that he wanted his potty and when nature had taken its course he was more than a little upset, and as the minutes past and nobody was taking any notice his mood deteriorated rapidly and a full blown tantrum had evolved.

Justin picked him up and removed the offending clothes as his young son looked at him. 'Noah asked for his potty but no-one listened to him. Dadda,' he told Justin mournfully. Justin called to Abby. 'Go and find Noah some dry shorts and pants, please. He doesn't appreciate being wet.'

'Can't leave Mummy, Dad. She's really upset.'

'You take Noah to his room and find his clothes, Abby. I will talk to Mummy.'

He noticed Gus was looking worried too. 'What's up, Gussie?' he asked.

'It's Topsy. Mummy was going to take us for a ride but when she led Topsy into her stable she noticed she was very lame. James has been to look at her and he thinks it's called - I can't remember – something to do with the Navy.'

'I think you probably mean navicular, Gus,' and Justin sat down on the hammock beside Anna, who was extremely tearful.

'James is coming back with Mathew this evening – he will give a second opinion – but you know James is very rarely wrong, Justin,' she sobbed. 'Topsy must be at least twenty now, I shall have to resurrect Mary's old bicycle to lead Amelia, your horses are all far too strong for me to manage as well as Amelia and Noah and even Pie can be very lively.'

'Let's not worry until Mathew and James have been this evening, Anna. We will wait for Mathew's verdict. At least there is plenty of grazing for Topsy here even if she does have navicular and has to live the remainder of her days in the paddock here.'

The ponies and Topsy were now installed in the brand new stable block Justin had had erected behind the beautiful old Victorian stables. His own horses were still at Lake House. Justin had put an advertisement for a groom in the Horse and Hound and Anna had been ordered to take details of any replies he might receive whilst he was in Rotterdam.

Fortunately, Noah was happy now Abby had found him dry pants and shorts and he was laughing as he chased the little dog, Santa across the immaculate lawn, which was carefully manicured twice a week by the extremely efficient gardener, Jerry.

Sadly, two hours later, Mathew was confirming James' suspicions and Anna was heartbroken. Topsy was one of the last links with her parents, who had so tragically been killed but she tried to listen as Mathew told her. 'There are various treatments we can try but she isn't a young horse.'

Justin was looking worried. He realized Anna needed a sensible horse from which to lead Amelia and Noah. 'Perhaps Marigold will get something sensible at the sanctuary,' he told Anna.

James looked at him. 'I've known you a very long time you tight fisted miser, Justin – you know damn well you can afford to buy more than a half decent horse for Anna, and I might just know the very one. Jean-Pierre bought Melchior from Rob West only yesterday. He bought him for his school but I reckon you might be able to persuade him to sell the horse to you. He's a good, sensible gelding and with help from Jean-Pierre or Sammy, Anna could soon be back in the Club's dressage team.'

'A horse from the Equitation Centre, James. You must know damn well I would be paying through the nose for it.'

James looked straight at Justin. 'Surely your wife and the mother of your three children deserves a decent, sensible horse, Justin. One she is always in control of. It's not always easy leading an enthusiastic toddler. Excellent little rider that Noah is, you know as well as I do, the unexpected can often happen without any warning.'

'O.K. I'll call Jean-Pierre later and see how much he would want to screw me for and Anna can go and try the horse tomorrow and see how she gets on. God - I always seem to be paying out for something or other and I don't suppose Topsy's treatment is going to be cheap'

'Probably not, Justin, but she is fortunate she has an owner with the wherewithal to help her. Let me know if you want a vet's report if you do decide to buy Melchior. By the way, Lizzie won't be competing in any more Nation's Cup Teams from now on. She's retiring her horses.'

'Lizzie!! Retiring her horses!! What about Sweet Dreams and why on earth is Lizzie retiring?'

'Lizzie is having a baby, Justin.'

Justin's eyes almost popped out of his head. 'A baby!!!' he uttered as if this was the most unusual occurrence imaginable.

'Yes – a boy – just before Christmas.'

'Good God. Well congratulations James, but what about Sweet Dreams – I could buy him for Anna?'

'Justin – Sweet Dreams has a huge future ahead of him – you are baulking at paying three thousand for Melchior, Dreamer is worth ten times that amount and anyway, Lizzie has plans for him. Take my advice and see if you can buy Melchior - he's a really nice horse who deserves a good home after the treatment he has received lately from that obnoxious Simon West.'

When the children had gone to bed that evening, Justin called Jean-Pierre. *'I've been talking to James, Pierre. Unfortunately, Anna's old mare Topsy has developed navicular – it's not looking good – James tells me you've just bought Melchior from Rob West. Any chance of selling him straight on to me for Anna, she needs a quiet, sensible escort when she leads Noah and Amelia, Noah is still only two, it will be a long time before we can let him ride free, even round the lake. My horses are all too strong for Anna when she's got Noah beside her, James thinks Melchior would be perfect and for Anna to ride at the club too. You can help her school him for the dressage competitions she seems to enjoy.'*

Jean-Pierre thought quickly. He was well aware that Melchior would be an asset to the Centre but he already had several good, quiet horses and he agreed with James that most probably the little horse would be ideal for Anna's immediate needs.

'Tell Anna to come to the Centre with Noah and Amelia tomorrow morning at ten o'clock. She can try Melchior in the school and then if she likes 'im, she can take 'im for an 'ack round the paddocks 'ere with Noah and Amelia. I'll ask Trish or Tony to accompany them just to ensure she doesn't encounter any problems.'

'That would be great, but how much do you want for him?'

Jean-Pierre was a friend but above all else he was a dealer who knew full well that the fifteen hundred pounds he had paid Rob West had been an extremely good price. There was undoubtedly a good profit to be made. He was also well aware that Justin Wright-Smith was a wealthy man and a notorious miser.

'Three thousand,' he told Justin.

'Three bloody thousand! For that Australian nag?'

'By the time Sam and I have helped your wife, that 'orse will be worth triple that and well you know it, you old skinflint. Six months lunging with draw reins and regular flat work and Anna will be in the Club's top dressage team. Anna is no mean rider as I certainly don't need to tell you, Justin.'

Justin was still muttering to himself. *'Three thousand for a nondescript nag like Melchior - well I just hope Anna realizes the sacrifice I am making. That's a quarter of the price of the swimming pool I am about to restore'*. Then he recalled Anna sobbing in his arms as she reminded him of the romantic day years ago, when he had taken her to the New Forest and reunited her with Topsy – the mare that had been sold to pay off her late father's debts. That day had been the turning point in their lives and he laughed to himself as he remembered that night in his flat at Lake House. It had heralded the start of what was to become a tempestuous love affair, which after many ups and downs had finally culminated in a rock solid marriage – a beautiful home – and the three children they cherished. He smiled as he told Jean-Pierre. *'O.K. Pierre, but don't worry about Trish or Tony, I'll lead Amelia off Titan and Anna can ride Hamlet. We'll see you at ten o'clock'*. And after putting down the phone he went and sat on the hammock beside Anna.

'Don't worry, Anna. I'll ask James to do everything he possibly can to help Topsy. With the correct treatment she may well recover enough for you to hack her quietly round the orchards again, we shall just have to see what transpires. Meanwhile, see how you get on with Melchior and if you like him, you can have him for your Birthday present but I wish to God I knew what plans Lizzie has for Sweet Dreams. Surely she isn't going to ask Tom to ride him for her. I don't think any of us fellows are light enough, not even Dom, but I'm going to ask Dad to sell me Conchita – she's a really good mare and I want to buy her before Dad sees her jump or he'll sting me for every penny.'

Unfortunately for Justin, his father had no misconceptions about the ability of Conchita - he had already ridden her himself in the school at Lake House and he had already mentally put a large price tag round the neck of the beautiful mare, added to which, Hans Weiss' agent had already been watching – an offer was about to be made.

The next morning, Tom was in the stables at Woodcutters being reunited with his horses who were safely back from Aachen after a more than satisfactory show in more ways than one. Four days and nights alone with Sam had been a rare occurrence. They had eaten in the restaurants around the arena - there had been no tiptoeing around the caravan, endeavouring not to waken any of their five children and above all, the horses had excelled themselves. He was just wondering why Elizabeth had sent him a text. *'Tom, please can you and Joshua come to the Old Manor House this evening? V. important. Huge news to tell you. Lizzie and James.xx'*

Before he could show Sam, another text immediately followed Lizzie's. *'Tom, need your help, Crisis with Anna. Call me at once.*

Justin.' Which Tom obligingly did. Justin always got Tom to call him back – he was well aware a call to a mobile phone cost money!!

'Justin. What's wrong with Anna?'

'Well, nothing actually with Anna except the water works have been running for the past twenty-four hours. It's Topsy. She's got bloody navicular. Going to cost me an arm and a leg I can ill afford. Wondered if you could help?'

'Justin, you have got millions more than I have and I mean that quite literally.'

'I don't want you to give me money, Tom. All I want is for you to get me the best deal from Jean-Pierre for Melchior.'

'Melchior – I don't understand, Justin?'

'Of course. You don't know. Apparently there was a bit of a to do between Pierre and that obnoxious cousin of yours, Simon, culminating with Pierre buying Melchior. Apparently the row blew up a few days ago at the same time as James had been here looking at Topsy. He came back with Mathew who confirmed riding her is out of the question, at least for some time and James has suggested Melchior would be perfect for Anna. Pierre wants three thousand – he's your brother –in-law, can you knock him down to two if Anna gets on well with the horse?'

Tom counted to ten as slowly as he could. *'Justin, I know you are my friend, in spite of being the meanest sod on this earth, as I have so often reminded you. Pierre is my brother-in-law as well as being a really good friend – I am sorry, this one is for you to sort out. I have a policy – never to interfere in other people's money matters. Good luck old chap and tell Anna I'm really sorry about Topsy.'*

'Some bloody friend you are. Tom,' and Justin slammed the phone down.

Tom tried to call Elizabeth but all he got in reply was her voice mail. In the end he decided to leave a message. *'Joshua and I will be at the Old Manor at seven this evening. Can't imagine what it's all about but looking forwards to seeing you anyway. Tom xx.'*

CHAPTER 28

At ten o'clock, Justin was leading little Amelia and Noah from the lofty height of Titan as Anna followed behind on the considerably smaller Hamlet. They put Amelia and Hamlet together into one of Jean-Pierre's stables and Justin led Titan into the indoor school where Ernst was waiting with Melchior – not in his familiar Western gear but in Cassandra's snaffle bridle and deep cut saddle. Jane appeared from the bar with Rudi and took the two little boys to have an ice cream and to play with the building bricks that were kept in a cupboard especially for any young visitors who might be in need of some entertainment.

Anna had soon mounted Melchior and Justin leant against Titan as he watched critically, hoping the horse might give him some reason, however small, to negotiate the price on the grounds of behaviour, but unfortunately for Justin, before Melchior had fallen into Simon West's hands he had been well schooled and although he was slightly green, regular lunging with draw reins would soon improve his rather low head carriage. He responded as soon as Anna asked him to trot and then to canter on each rein, only leading on the wrong leg on two of the corners in the school. He didn't pull and had a very light mouth as Anna discovered when she slowed him to a trot and then to a walk. It was obvious she liked him and Justin couldn't fault his temperament. He stood still whilst Justin felt his legs and picked up his feet and as he opened his mouth and looked at his teeth Melchior's soft brown eyes were gazing steadily at him.

Jean-Pierre appeared with his beautiful Flèche d'Or, leading little Toffee Apple, as Jane arrived in the school with Rudi and Noah. To Anna's surprise, Rudi was attired in jeans and a riding hat. 'I didn't know Rudi had started riding, Pierre.'

'Oh yes, last month 'e get a stool and 'e climb on to Toffee. 'E was sitting in the stable on 'im. That was the beginning, now 'e go every day. Come we all ride together," and with Anna leading Noah from Melchior and Jean-Pierre taking care of Rudi and Toffee Apple, Justin walked behind on Titan and at the end of half an hour, he realized Anna was totally at one with the horse.

'I suppose I should get James to look him over, Pierre, but first, how much do you want for him?'

'Three thousand, Justin. Not a penny more and not a penny less.'

'How does two seventy five strike you. Pierre?'

'It doesn't, Justin. Three or no deal.'

Anna was stroking Melchior who had put his head on her shoulder.

'O.K. but you provide a vet's certificate.'

Jean-Pierre grimaced, but agreed. He realized Justin couldn't bear to pay the full price. There had to be a concession somewhere, however small. He nodded his head in agreement. He would charge the vet's fee to the Centre of which James was a partner, so who in effect would be paying his own fee.

The two men shook hands on the deal and Jean-Pierre told Justin he would call James immediately and in response Justin informed Jean-Pierre he would go straight to the bank and withdraw three thousand pounds from his account which he would leave with Anna.

Jean-Pierre was taken aback, 'God, Justin, all that money in the house?'

'Can't stand cheques, Pierre. I always feel I'm spending more money when I write a cheque, don't worry; Anna can put the cash in the refrigerator until you collect it. Actually, I like the horse. He appears to have a good attitude. Oh, well, that's Anna's birthday present sorted for the next few years – she won't be getting another present for ages. Have to draw the reins in somewhere – money disappears in a flash.'

Jean-Pierre smiled. 'I know, Justin, but it is also there to be enjoyed. Good luck with Melchior, Anna. I'll see if James can come 'ere today and then Trish can ride 'im down to your place on 'er way 'ome. Bonne Chance in Rotterdam this week, Justin.'

'Hue. I shall need every bit of that – Jock's with me which is good but we've got two first timers to contend with – a young lad and an older woman. Philip wants to try them out. We've already qualified for the Nation's Cup finals in Barcelona in September, thanks mainly to Tom and Dad.'

Justin rode home with Anna and Noah and then, leaving them to enjoy the garden for what was left of the morning, cantered through the fields at Old Tiles, then trotted Titan past the lake and after handing the horse to Sheila, went in search of his father who was in his office just putting the phone back on its hook on the wall. He had a wolfish grin on his still handsome face. 'That should put old Hans' hackles up – I've just been speaking with his agent – he's just made me an opening bid for Conchita. I turned it down without even considering it. Thirty thousand pounds indeed – bloody cheek.'

The wind was completely taken out of Justin's sails. He had just been going to offer his father twenty five thousand for the mare.

'So, what is your price for her, then Dad?'

'Well, you've been riding her, Justin, you know what a good mare she is and I found out exactly how talented she is when I rode her myself the other day. Cracking animal. I want at least fifty five thousand for her. She's worth every penny and more.'

For the second time in a few moments, Justin was speechless. 'Y –y –you've ridden her, Dad?'

'Certainly, I have every right to ride my own horses in my own school, Justin.'

'I always understood the horses belonged to the company.'

'Not when we buy them with our personal money, from our own bank accounts, which is what I did with Conchita and Swallow Tail, but don't worry, Justin, you will get your cut of the profit when I sell her and so will Tom. It won't be long before I'm having offers for Swallow Tail I'm certain.'

Justin was silent for a moment.

'Did you want to see me about something specific?' his father eventually asked him.

'Yes I bloody did. How about we become part owners of Conchita. Fifty-fifty. I'll give you fifteen thousand pounds.'

'You can give me give me twenty five thousand, Justin and a third of the mare's winnings goes into my account – a third into Lake House – the other third into yours, added to which for advertising reasons, Conchita keeps the Lake House prefix.'

'So in effect, I would be putting money into Tom West's pocket as well as yours. Dad?'

'Yes, Justin. That's why Lake House Stables is a partnership. We're not a charity – we have Dom and all the grooms to pay let alone the upkeep of all the horses, but maybe you had overlooked that small matter,' he added sarcastically. 'I repeat twenty five thousand pounds and half of her is yours if you agree to my terms. At least you would have the comforting thought that she can never be sold without your consent.'

At that moment, the phone rang again and Justin heard his father talking in German. There was only one thing he could do. 'O.K. Dad. I agree. Fifty-fifty.'

Charles phone call was short as Hans' agent slammed down the phone in his office in Dortmund, and Justin shook hands with his grinning father. However, Charles was pretty certain Justin would have the last laugh – the mare was a cracker.

'That's the second time I've broken the bank this morning, and the second horse I've bought.'

'Good Heavens! Whatever else have you bought?'

'Melchior - Simon West's little horse. I've bought him for Anna's next fifty birthday presents. Topsy has got navicular and Anna is distraught. She needs a good steady horse when she leads

Noah and Amelia. Sam's got all the time in the world now she's not competing at the big shows with Chim anymore. She can help Anna lunge Melchior.'

'Justin, sometimes I really do despair of you. Why do you think Sam has stopped showing Chim or not asked Tom to find her a younger horse? You seem to have totally overlooked the fact she has five extremely lively children – three dogs – a half crazy husband and a business of her own which takes up every spare minute of her time. However, I'm sure if you speak nicely to Dom he would lunge the animal for Anna. Why does it need lunging? What's wrong with it?'

'Nothing, nothing is wrong with it, Dad. It could be a really nice horse – its just rather green and I know Anna would like to try to do the Riding Club dressage competitions. He's got a really kind temperament with the added bonus he is only seven. Jean-Pierre had fallen out with Simon West and that odious boy told his Dad to sell him to Pierre.'

'So you bought him from Jean-Pierre – I bet he stung you.'

'Not so much as my own dad has just done. I paid three thousand for him. If he gives Anna years of pleasure, then that's a small price to pay.'

Before Charles had time to feel guilty about Conchita he told Justin. 'Tell Anna to ride up here with little Noah whilst you are in Rotterdam and I'll lunge him for her – and oh – by the way, let me have that cheque before you leave.'

'Bloody hell, dad, I fly off tomorrow morning.'

'Fine, you can drop it in later this evening,' and as Justin strode out of the office, Charles - the delightful rogue – the best horse dealer in Kent - was gleefully rubbing his hands!!

Justin took the quad bike and rode back to Theobald's Place, then leapt into his Range Rover and shot into Canterbury at breakneck speed to withdraw the three thousand pounds he owed Jean-Pierre, totally ignoring the fact that it would have cost him far less to have written his friend a cheque, as the speed camera flashed on the outskirts of Canterbury and a parking ticket was strategically placed under his windscreen wipers as his silver vehicle straddled the almost newly painted double, yellow lines outside the bank.

Anna was just about to go and fetch the children from school when the Range Rover tore back into the drive, the parking ticket still flapping beneath the wipers.

'Darling, where did you park?' she asked Justin.

'Where do you think, outside the bank of course? I wasn't going to risk walking through Canterbury with three thousand k in my back pocket.'

Anna picked up the ticket. 'Do you recognize this, Justin?'

'Haven't a clue what it is. Stick it in the bin before it litters the drive.'

'It's a parking ticket, Justin.'

'A parking ticket. Bloody hell.'

Anna read it. 'If you pay within fourteen days you only have to pay half the charge otherwise it's sixty pounds.'

'Oh, you deal with it, Anna, you know I can't be bothered with bits of paper.'

Anna sighed, folding the offending ticket and putting it carefully in her pocket. She had long ago accepted the fact that her husband was a total liability – but he was Justin and in her eyes there was no one else quite like him and she loved him to bits.

She was pulling his hand, asking him. 'Come and look, Justin,' and she dragged him towards the paddock where Amelia was cropping the grass beside an extremely contented Melchior. 'Trish brought him on her way home to lunch. James looked at him directly we had left the Centre. No problems at all. I'll take the money to Jean-Pierre after I've picked up the children. I hate owing money.'

'Hmm, I owe my Dad twenty five thousand pounds and he wants the cheque before I go off tomorrow. He's the biggest, old, skinflint on this earth.'

Anna was laughing. 'Darling, talk about the pot calling the kettle black – but what on earth do you owe your father all that money for?'

'Conchita. I've bought half of her. Dad owns the rest, but she's a beautiful girl and I do get to keep a third of any prize money I win with her, which hopefully will be considerable if I can avoid that pain in the neck Thomas West.'

'Goodness, Justin, this has been a massive day of decision making for you – but I love my Melchior already – he's a dear – and I'm sure we shall soon be flying through our dressage tests.'

'Oh, that reminds me, Dad says if you ride up to Lake House with Noah he'll lunge Melchior for you whilst I'm away.'

Anna's face lit up. Charles was brilliant at schooling young horses and only the lucky few were worthy of his attention. Melchior was honoured.

'Smashing, Justin, really smashing – and Justin, Melchior is the best present you will ever give me and I love him to bits already. You're a one in a million husband.'

Justin was surprised. 'Am I? Am I really, Anna?'

'Oh yes,' and she was kissing him until his senses were swimming. 'God, Anna – how long have we got until the kids come out of school and Noah wakes from his nap?' Anna pulled away from him reluctantly, and looked at her watch. 'Minus two minutes, I'm afraid Justin, and actually, Noah is already sitting in his car seat and I think I can hear one of his tantrums brewing.' She kissed him once more and hurried to the car and the now irate Noah – the time of the terrible twos was definitely beginning and she was counting the months until a certain little gentleman would have attained his third birthday.

As Justin was taking the quad bike back to Lake House with his twenty five thousand pound cheque safely in his pocket he passed Tom and Joshua in the woods just outside Woodcutters as they rode

Lily and Kaspar in the direction of the Old Manor House for their liaison with Lizzie and James.

Justin turned off the engine as Lily snorted at the noisy machine. 'Hi, you two. Where are you off to and where is the rest of your brood, Tom?'

'The trips are doing their homework and Rosie is helping Sam get our supper ready. Josh and I are on our way to see Lizzie. Royal summons from the Lady of the Manor!! Don't have a clue what it's all about. What time are you off tomorrow?'

'Ten thirty flight. You lucky sod staying here.'

'Well, Justin, I was in Aachen all last week if you remember, whilst you were most likely doing bugger all here.'

'Actually, I've bought two horses today, at least, one and a half. I've bought Melchior for Anna. He's a really nice little horse.'

'So you bought him.'

'Yea. I'm sure that conniving frog probably made a bloody big profit – he wouldn't even consider my offer. At least I insisted he paid for the vet's examination but he wouldn't budge from three thousand.'

'I believe Melchior is a young horse, Justin – that sounds a really fair price to me. It doesn't look as if you've been too hard done by.'

'Well, at least it's put me well and truly in Anna's good books. Could be in for a steamy night me thinks!! By the way, I told Anna I'm sure Sammy would help her lunge Melchior – she must often be at a loose end.'

Tom didn't bother to answer – sometimes Justin's attitude beggared belief but Sam was perfectly capable of standing up for herself, then Justin's next words took him back as he told him. 'I'm just on my way to see Dad. I persuaded him to sell me half of Conchita. Screwed me for twenty five thousand quid but at least he can never sell her without my consent. Bloody Hans Weiss was after her – I just got to Dad's office in the nick of time. Smashing mare. Did you know Dad had ridden her in the school – underhand old devil.'

'Well, she was his horse after all, Justin. He's surely entitled to ride her. I must go – Lizzie will be waiting. Good luck in Rotterdam later this week. Come on Josh,' and he pressed his heels into Kaspar's sides as they shot off through the woods.

It wasn't until they were way out of sight that Justin remembered about Lizzie and James forthcoming baby. *'Oh well,'* he thought, *'Tom would find out soon enough.'*

Which he certainly did.

Elizabeth and James were sitting in their beautiful sunken rose garden, which Sam was always eulogizing about. There was a fresh pot of tea on the wrought iron table and a variety of biscuits, some of which were beginning to melt in the evening sun. The twins were fighting as usual – each wanting the one and only kit-kat, which was sitting in the middle of the plate. Tom had no time for what he considered Lizzie's spoilt little brats – he picked up the offending kit-kat saying. 'Wow, thanks, Lizzie,' and then licked his fingers as the little boy and girls stared in disbelief, then picked up a chocolate finger and sat on the grass with their arms round each other as Elizabeth sighed. 'Peace at last, thanks goodness. You do seem to have a knack with children, Tom.'

Tom laughed. 'Well, I have had enough practice – more often than not there are at least eight or nine youngsters in our house at one time. Justin has a very crafty way of off loading his kids and Anne-Marie is never far away either, but she's no bother. At the moment Sam is showing her how to knit. She's endeavouring to make a scarf for Oscar! Anyhow why the summons, Lizzie? What's brewing?'

'Something wonderful, Tom.'

'Don't tell me James has discovered another old uncle who has left him a few more millions?'

'No, no. Much better than that. We're going to have Freddy at Christmas.'

'Who the hell is Freddy? Do I know him or is he another equine for you to jump?'

'Of course not, Tom – don't be thick. I'm having a baby.'

'A baby?'

'Yes, Tom. You remember what they are. You and Sam have had enough of them. They sleep in a cot and scream every now and again.'

'A baby – but Lizzie it was so difficult for you to conceive the twins – did you have more I.V.F. treatment?'

'No. I had no idea. I felt a lump and Jane took me to see Dr. Taylor who sent me for a scan and Freddy is due around Christmas, that's why you're here.'

'Why I'm here? Hell, Lizzie, you don't expect me to deliver this baby by any chance, do you?'

'Of course not, stupid – you're here because of Sweet Dreams.'

'Sweet Dreams?'

'Tom, do stop being irritating. Why are you repeating everything I say?'

'I expect I am in shock.'

'Why shouldn't we have four children? After all, you and Sammy have got five.'

'Five and a half, actually. I always add on another half for Ozzie, just for good measure!! Seriously, though, I am thrilled for you and James and it may well knock the stuffing out of those two little monsters,' and he pointed to Felix and Flicka who, having finished their biscuits were now fighting over who was the owner of a large red ball, their furious shrieks breaking the stillness of the balmy evening. James seemed totally oblivious to the screams echoing round the garden as he calmly read a book to Fenella who was sitting on his knee.

‘So what is wrong with Sweet Dreams, then, Lizzie?’ Tom asked his sister.

‘I’ve decided to retire Daddy’s Girl and PowerPoint, after all my horses are nineteen now. Amadeus can have a rest too until after Freddy is born and then I shall use him as an escort when I ride out with the children and Jamie, but I have decided my Nation’s Cup and Grand Prix days are over, at least for a while. Fenella is really keen now. She’s doing well with Poupée, we shall probably look for a second pony for her next year and I am sure the twins are going to be really competitive. I want to spend more time with them at the shows and help Jamie exercise Pas de Deux and Top Choice.’

Tom was laughing. ‘The twins will be fighting each other all the time. Lizzie. You will probably have to find them different shows, but what about Sweet Dreams?’
‘Ah, that’s why you are here.’

‘Why I am here?’

‘Yes, to discuss Sweet Dreams.’

‘To discuss Sweet Dreams.’

‘Tom, you are doing it again.’

‘Doing what again?’

‘Repeating everything I say.’

‘Sweet Dreams is a super little horse with endless scope and ability but he is not for a six foot bloke like me.’

‘There are other good riders in this world as well as you, Tom.’

‘Sure, I am certainly not disputing that, we’ve got one sitting right there,’ and he pointed at Joshua who was now testing Fenella on her theory for her D. Test which she was going to take at the next Pony Club Rally.

‘Of course, Tom, that’s why he’s here.’

‘Why who is here?’

‘Joshua of course.

‘Joshua.’

‘Yes. I want him to ride Sweet Dreams for me.’

‘You want him to ride Sweet Dreams.’

‘Tom, I shall murder you in a minute. Josh would be ideal. He’s light – he’s a strong rider and he has all the ability to take Dreamer a long way. Come on, Maurice is waiting in the sand school with the horse. He’s built a jumping course – I want to see what Josh can do. He will be thirteen after Christmas. You can join him as a Junior Associate.’

‘Does Josh have any say in this, Lizzie?’

‘Of course, but surely he wouldn’t turn down a ride like Sweet Dreams.’

‘He would be competing against adults.’

‘Yes, but Dreamer is still eligible for the Foxhunter and then Josh could easily cope with the Grade C. Classes. He could try for the Junior Championship for fourteen to sixteen year old youngsters in just over a year’s time and then later the Young Riders. He would have the perfect initiation into the more senior classes.’

‘Well, Lizzie, you seem to have got it all worked out.’

Josh was excited. He liked Sweet Dreams and was eager to try him, but Tom was still holding back. ‘Lizzie, nothing is to be decided until Sammy has been consulted. We will go down to the paddock and Josh can have a good school - I will give my honest opinion but Sam definitely has the final say in the matter.’

‘So, Tom, does Sam wear the trousers in your house?’

‘Certainly not, she is Joshua’s mum and therefore I respect her views. We always make mutual decisions, Lizzie. It makes for a harmonious life,’ and then he laughed. ‘But she usually takes my advice anyway, but come on folks, - let’s go to the paddock.’

Sweet Dreams was a beautiful little horse. He had an exquisite head and moved beautifully. Tom couldn’t help imagining Sam in her side saddle habit on this super creature but he had an amazing jump too and that was the way in which his life was destined to travel.

Tom looked with pride at his eldest son, as after a short time on the flat getting acquainted with Sweet Dreams, he, James and Elizabeth who was clutching the twins in either hand, watched Joshua clearing jump after jump.

Fenella was awestruck. She liked both Josh and Orlando – she was slightly afraid of Oliver and kept as far away form Oscar as she possibly could. She clapped as he finally rode back to them. 'Josh, I wish that one day I can ride half as well as you – then I will be really happy.'

Josh was elated. The horse had been superb. 'Please, Dad – let me ride him.'

'Yes, please, Tom.' Elizabeth begged.

'As far as I am concerned Lizzie and James, there is no doubt in my mind, but as I said, I have to talk this over with Sammy. She may want to see this partnership for herself but I think she will most likely trust my judgment. If Josh does ride him, do you want him to come here to ride him or would you want the horse to be at Woodcutters, which would be preferable, especially for Josh – he would have the facilities of the Indoor School close by and his lessons with *the gang* to which he could alternate Sweet Dreams with Ganger and Lily.'

'Oh yes, it would be better if Dreamer was with you, Tom. I'm going to be really busy for the next two or three years, until Freddy goes to Nursery School – Sam has much more free time to help with an extra horse.'

Not for the first time, Tom wondered why everybody seemed to think Sam led a life of luxury whilst everyone else was working.

'Of course Josh can have any money he wins. He can pay it into that account you opened for him last Christmas – one day it could come in very useful. He can keep any trophies he wins too and I am sure there could be a good few of those. I am just happy to know Dreamer still belongs to me with the best rider I can find, who just happens to be my very special nephew.'

'O.K. Lizzie, if that's how you want it, I'll join Josh as a Junior Associate when I renew every one's membership, but I would pay for his keep and his shoes and, oh well, I suppose James would always be on hand if, God forbid any mishap should befall him, and we would obviously pay all the entry fees. O.K. as long as Sam agrees then the answer is yes. I'll talk to her this evening and call you back. Sam could exercise him for Josh sometimes – she would enjoy that.'

'Super. Make sure you persuade her, Tom, but I am quite confident you are perfectly capable of doing that.'

Tom laughed. 'I usually do fairly well in that respect, Lizzie – and seriously I'm thrilled about the baby and Sammy will be too. Make sure she looks after herself, James.'

'Of course he will, Tom and *The General* is being a pain already.'

'Lizzie, you know Mum only fusses because she loves us – she's a super Mum and I do wish you and Jane wouldn't call her *The General.'*

'But Tom, it's only because we think the world of her – but she does love to take control and when she fusses it drives Jane and me mad. Don't forget to call me as soon as Sam has agreed, even if it's after midnight.'

Tom laughed again. 'I doubt it will take that long. Lizzie. I've got a bottle of Chablis – we'll take that into the garden – a few glasses of wine – a nice long snog - and I can pretty well guarantee her answer.'

'Tom, really you are almost impossible but in this case I won't complain. Now get back to Woodcutters and do all that is necessary,' and she waved as he and Joshua trotted back down the drive whilst she would await the destiny of her beautiful, little horse.

Joshua was raving about Sweet Dreams – he had always admired him since the first time he had seen his aunt riding him at the Massenden Show. He had never in his wildest dreams imagined he would be asked to ride him. 'Dad, please, do whatever it takes to make Mum agree.'

'I'll try, Josh. I promise you,' and he didn't tell his son, but he was feeling pretty confident.

'I think it's best if you leave me to tell Mum about Sweet Dreams, you feed and water the horses, whilst I have a glass of wine in the garden with her.'

'O.K. Dad, anything you suggest. I'll give Lily a groom and see to Kaspar for you. Could you ring the bell when supper is ready? I think Rosie and Ollie are on pony duty this evening? I won't say a word to them until you've spoken to Mum.'

'Good boy, Josh.'

Tom poked his head in the kitchen - there was no sign of Sam, but Oscar was whistling as he laid the table and Orlando was spooning strawberries into seven individual bowls.

'Hi, boys, where's Mum?' Tom asked.

'She's just finishing a plan for some old lady's front garden. She's put a cottage pie in the oven and she told us to put the peas on when the clock struck eight. We've just done that and 'Lando's washed the strawberries.'

'Good boys. I'm just going to have a quick drink in the garden with Mum. Ring the bell really loudly when the peas are ready. Rosie and Ollie are with Josh feeding the ponies. Make sure you ring it loudly enough for them to hear it too.'

'Aye – aye, sir,' and Oscar rushed into the playroom as the very distinctive introduction to East Enders could be heard.

Tom shook his head and Orlando smiled. 'It's O.K. Dad. I won't let the peas burn. I can't think why Ozzie persists in watching that rubbish. Anne-Marie gets quite cross with him.'

'Well I have to say I entirely agree with her, Lando. I'll be back with Mum in ten minutes.'

Tom could see Sam sitting on the stone seat under the rose arch, with her head looking up to the sun, capturing its last few rays before it disappeared for the evening. She was clutching her sketchbook, which obviously contained the plans for old Mrs. Blackler's front garden.

He sat down beside her and handed her a glass whilst he deftly opened the bottle of Chianti.

'So how was your evening with the Lady of the Manor, my Thomas?'

'Well, Lady Thornley did indeed have some amazing news. There is going to be another little Hon. Thornley. Namely Freddy. Due around Christmas Day.'

'Tommy!! How wonderful!! Lucky, lucky Lizzie.'

'She had a bit of a fright actually, sweetheart. She felt a lump and was afraid it was something sinister. Jane took her to Dr. Taylor, who immediately told Lizzie she was pretty sure she was four and a half months pregnant. Jane took her to the hospital for a scan and lo and behold, Freddy was confirmed to be well and truly on his way – but darling, don't waste time wishing for the impossible. We've got our wonderful boys and Rosie and above all else, we've got each other. We couldn't possibly wish for anything more. - Actually there is something else I need to talk to you about. Lizzie is giving up competing – she's retiring Power Point and Daddy's Girl but she will ride Amadeus at the Club and when she escorts the children on their hacks but the reason she asked me to take Josh with me this evening was because she would like him to ride Sweet Dreams for her next year when he will be thirteen and can become a Junior Associate which would enable him to ride both horses and ponies. Josh tried him and he rode him like a pro - as far as I am concerned I foresee no problems at all. He's a much easier ride than Oz has to put up with on Hanky Panky. Josh is desperate to ride him but I told him you must have the final say. I can only advise you that it could be good for both Josh and the little horse.'

'Tom, of course I trust your judgment but can Josh compete on a horse at his age?'

'Yes, but sometimes he will be competing against me!! Mainly in the Foxhunters - there are also competitions for children aged between twelve and fourteen who are riding horses, and then there are Junior Classes for fourteen to sixteen year olds followed of course by the Young Riders. Sweet Dreams is a small horse – a lot will depend how fast and how tall Josh becomes but even Rosie could probably ride him eventually. Lizzie doesn't either want, or need to sell him – she loves him - but she is being practical and looking for the best option for her horse. She is desperate for Josh to ride him.'

'Fine then, Tom. I just hope Oscar doesn't have one of his moods.'

'Ozzie has more than enough to cope with at the moment with Humbug and Panky, he couldn't possibly manage any more and he is in for a shock when he gets to the Grammar School next term, his school workload will treble but fortunately he is only eleven, so that will be the end of any discussion as far as that young man is concerned. We'll take the rest of the wine in with us – I think I can hear 'Lando ringing the bell. Oz won't be too pleased, doubtless he's glued to some sordid scene in that wretched soap.'

'Then the sooner we get indoors the better, Tom, and you can give Lizzie a call and put her mind at rest and tell her she's really, really lucky and I will go and be an unpaid nanny whenever she wants me.'

As they reached the kitchen door, Joshua, Ollie and Rosie were running through the gate, which led from the stables. Sam smiled at Josh. 'Congratulations, Josh. I hear you are all set to become Auntie Lizzie's stable jockey.'

Josh's face broke into an enormous grin. 'Mum, so it's O.K.?'

'Of course, Josh. Your Dad says he's happy so of course it's all right. Just one thing, Josh, I would like to exercise Sweet Dreams in the term time for you sometimes. I think he is one of the most gorgeous little horses I've come across. You're a lucky, lucky boy.'

Oscar had appeared in the kitchen. 'Who is a lucky boy. Mum?'

'Josh, he's going to ride Dreamer for Auntie Lizzie next year.'

Fortunately, Oscar was smiling. 'Like I ride for my Countess and can I take my supper into the playroom and watch the rest of my programme it was just getting pretty -pretty – steamed up!!'

'No, you most certainly can't Oscar and your Countess would certainly not approve and I gather Anne-Marie doesn't either.'

Suddenly a little voice asked Tom. 'Who do I ride for, Daddy?'

'You ride for me like Ollie, and 'Lando rides Jet for Charles, so you all ride for someone and you are all extremely lucky young people,' and with that silence reigned as seven plates of cottage pie were quickly devoured.

Tom suddenly remembered and told Sam. 'We met Justin in the woods – he was delivering a cheque to Charles - he's bought half of Conchita. Hans Weiss was after her. I think it could be time I made my move for Swallow Tail. Come to the show with me tomorrow, Sammy and give me your verdict on him. I'll drive the horsebox and Hannah and Jules can take you kids for a ride after school. I'll ask Jane to drop you home when she picks up Eloise, and by the way, Sam, poor old Topsy has developed navicular. Justin has bought Melchior; apparently Simon had a bust up with Pierre and told Rob to sell the horse. Anna is over the moon.'

Sam laughed. 'I know, Justin has already called me. He said I had time on my hands so could I help Anna school him?'

'And what did you tell him?'

'Why, I said yes of course. I'd love to help Anna get into the dressage team with him.'

Somehow Tom wasn't surprised by her answer – Sam was unique – she was an angel – no wonder they were so often in heaven, he thought!!

Whilst Tom had been at The Old Manor, Justin and Anna had hacked across the fields to Ribbenden. Gus and Abby were riding

Hamlet and Guy whilst Anna and Noah trotted side by side and Justin brought up the rear. They waved to Marigold who was exercising her greyhounds in one of the paddocks and then cantered slowly along the bridle path. Noah was bumping up and down, clutching Amelia's not inconsiderable mane. Justin rode alongside Anna. 'Let me take the lead rein – you have a good canter with Gus and Abby – let Melchior have his head.'

'O.K.' and she flew beside Hamlet and Guy. Her cheeks were pink and her eyes were shining when Noah and Justin eventually caught up with them.

'He's super, Justin. I'm going to work really hard with him. I just can't wait to get him hooked on dressage.'

When they arrived back at Theobald's Place there were two messages on the landline phone. The first was from a Mr Peregrine Percival, who stated he was twenty seven years old, both healthy and strong and was more interested in a home for himself, his horse, his twelve year old sister, Columbine and his fourteen year old brother, Cornelius than a large salary. Apparently he had owned a show jumping pony when he was twelve years old and now had a promising novice horse and his brother and sister both had a J.A. pony.

The other message was from a middle-aged couple. Horace Carpenter had worked with horses all his working life and his wife Martha was an excellent cook and housekeeper.

Justin was immediately drawn to the young man. The thought of someone working for him for a small salary immediately appealed to his penny-pinching mentality. He called Peregrine Percival first. He was obviously an educated man with an abrupt but clear voice. By the end of the conversation, Justin had discovered that their father and mother had been drowned in a sailing accident four years ago and he was his young brother and sister's legal guardian. They not only had their horse and ponies but also a large horsebox and Peregrine's Range Rover. He explained to Justin that for personal reasons he wished to move as far away from Yorkshire as possible.

It didn't take a professor to realize Peregrine had recently suffered some personal crisis. 'Have you any daughters?' he asked Justin.

'Well yes, but Abby is only nine – I don't think she would concern you in any way - my older son is eleven and Little Noah is just two. They spend almost all their spare time with their ponies, and Anna, my wife, has her own horse. I am a partner in Lake House Stables with my father and Tom West and our latest recruit Dominic Silvestre. The horses are all pretty top show jumpers – but I want to move my own string here as soon as I have acquired a reliable groom. I go abroad a lot, so I must be certain I am leaving them with a really competent person. Maybe you would like to come and see my set up? I am off to Rotterdam tomorrow but I shall be at home all next week – how about Monday?'

'That should be fine. Where is your nearest airport?'

'Airport. Well, Gatwick.'

'No, no. I mean a small one. My cousin has his own plane, he's a freelance pilot and he happens to be on holiday next week. I'll ask him to fly me down to Kent.'

Justin was wondering who on earth this young man, with whom he was having this weird conversation was. 'Well, Headcorn aerodrome is about ten miles away.'

'Fine, I'll fix it with Ptolemy. I will let you know what time we will be arriving and perhaps you could arrange a taxi to meet us.'

'Us?'

'Yes, I must bring my half brother and sister. – They've had a pretty traumatic life these last few years – especially this last month.'

'That's fine – the kids will be on holiday – they can meet Gus and Abby and young Rosie West. Tell them to bring their hard hats and they can ride round the paddocks whilst we talk and don't worry about getting a taxi, Gus and I will come and pick you up. He would enjoy coming to see the aerodrome.'

As Justin put the phone down he was totally confused. Who the hell was Peregrine Percival who seemed to require a home and help with his horse rather than the sizeable salary, which most grooms would be seeking?

Before Justin had time to call the middle-aged couple, the phone rang again. This time it was Sam offering to come to Theobald's Place in two day's time to see if she could help Anna school Melchior.

'Justin has just had a rather strange young man on the phone, Sam. He's flying down from Yorkshire on Monday with his young brother and sister in his cousin's private plane. He seems more interested in a home and help with his horses than money. Of course Justin thinks that's wonderful – he won't even entertain a middle-aged couple. They sounded much more suitable – apparently the husband has been a groom for the past thirty years and his wife is an excellent cook and housekeeper.'

'Anna, give Lizzie their number. James insists she has more help. Lizzie refuses to have a nanny but I know she would be happy with a housekeeper. I'm sure we could all share the husband around our various stables. Give me the number before Justin throws it away and I will give Lizzie a call.'

Half an hour later, James and Lizzie had arranged to meet Horace and Martha Carpenter the following afternoon.

Elizabeth and James were over the moon and the following morning, Elizabeth took her cleaning lady and her au pair, armed with dusters, mops and buckets to the tiny lodge at the west end of the drive to The Old Manor House. It had stood empty since Bill Cotton's elderly gardener had died and his widow had decided to live with her daughter in Cranbrook. Every now and again, first Susan and then Elizabeth had hired a cleaner from a local agency and twice a year the little lodge had had a thorough spring clean. By the end of the morning the glass in the windows were crystal clear and the whole cottage smelt of lavender polish.

The lodge was simply but comfortably furnished and had its own small garden on three sides including a small vegetable patch. As Elizabeth placed a vase of sweet peas on the small table in the lounge, she crossed her fingers and prayed Martha and Horace Carpenter would fall in love with what she and James hoped would be their new home.

Elizabeth had spoken to Tom at the school gate that morning. He and Sam were on their way to Sussex in the small horsebox and were dropping Rosie and the triplets at the gate before continuing their journey with Kaspar, Clementine and Swallow Tail, who were due to compete later that day.

'If you like, Lizzie, I'll stop on my way back and pick up Sweet Dreams. I've got one empty stall. I can't say exactly what time – Clem and Kaspar are both in the open. If they behave themselves and reach the jump off it could be as late as seven thirty or eight o'clock but if neither of them gets through then it would be nearer six, but I certainly hope one of them does.'

'Super, you can give me a call from the showground when you are leaving and I will have him ready. Good luck.'

Sam opened the widow. 'Lizzie, take care. I am so, so envious.'

As they drove away, Tom took Sam's hand. 'Please, my darling – even if it were possible, do you think I would have put your life at risk again, however hard you had begged. I would never have let it happen – without any doubt it would have been out of the question, because, my Sammy – there is one thing I am quite certain of, I can easily live without another baby but I could never, never survive without you and just think, you will most likely be a granny several times over before you have reached the ripe old age of forty!!'

'Oh, dear, you're so sensible, Tom, but who is going to be first?'

'Well, I suppose it should be Josh, But somehow I think it could be one of the trips.'

'Oh God, darling, not a baby Oscar.'

'Only time will tell, my sweetheart – now could you open those letters I grabbed from the postman just as we were leaving?'

Sam opened the first two. 'Just schedules, Tom, I'll leave them on the shelf under the dashboard.' She opened the third letter and grabbed Tom's arm.

'Hey, Sammy, what the hell are you doing, do you fancy tipping over in that ditch?'

Sam tried not to distract him further but she was reading the letter again. It was from a firm of solicitors in Bromley who she had never heard of.

'Dear Mrs. West. This is to inform you that in accordance to the last will and testament of the late Joseph Smythe you have been bequeathed his entire estate which includes a flat and all its contents in Chislehurst, Kent. Perhaps you could get in touch with me as soon as possible to let me know when you could come to our offices in Bromley. If you are interested in selling the flat, we have received an offer of three hundred and forty thousand pounds from a Mr. Clive Portland who is the owner of the flat above your late uncle's. He wants to seize this opportunity to reinstate the building into one large, family home. The flat is fully furnished and you may wish to keep some of the items, which are very attractive, and some quite valuable antiques, including a collection of silver snuffboxes. I appreciate you may wish to have an independent valuation of the property but I wait to hear from you. May I conclude by saying how very sorry I am for your sad loss? Jeremiah Courtney. Courtney, Courtney and Smithers, Solicitors'.

'Oh, my goodness, Tom,' she gasped and read the letter again, this time reading it aloud so that Tom could hear the contents.

'Great Uncle Joseph was Grandpa Smythe's crusty old bachelor brother. I hadn't seen him since Granny and Grandpa's Golden Wedding Party. You didn't come. You were somewhere abroad jumping at the time. Your Mum had the children and I caught the train to Worthing. Goodness, what a shock, I didn't even know he was ill, let alone the poor old boy had died. I used to get a card at Christmas and when I was little, ten pounds on my birthday but other than that I never heard from him. We'll go and see the flat as soon as you can spare a day but if the valuation is fair I shall accept the offer but we will have to see what the furniture consists of and whether any of it is worth keeping. I am sure there is a good auction house in that area.'

Tom was taken aback. 'Gosh, when is the funeral?'

'It must have gone. Apparently he died a month ago.'

'Oh, dear, I wonder why your Gran and Gramps didn't let you know he was ill.'

'I think they're quite frail now, Tommy. I must tell Mummy. She and I really ought to make the effort and go to Folkestone and see them more often. I don't think Gramp's memory is too good these days.'

'We'll go to Bromley one morning this week, Sam. The kids break up on Friday, it would be good if we could go before then. Give the solicitors a buzz and see which day would be convenient.'

Sam eventually managed to speak to Mr. Jeremiah Courtney, the sender of the letter she was currently holding in her hands. She asked if she and her husband could possibly meet him one morning that week, explaining they had five children and it would be much easier for everyone if they could come before the holidays started, and they could all be left safely at school whilst she and Tom came to Bromley.

Fortunately for Tom and Sam, the solicitor had just had an appointment cancelled for the following morning, and after a quick nod from Tom, Sam agreed to meet the aforesaid Jeremiah Courtney at eleven o'clock the following morning at the flat in Chislehurst, which now apparently already belonged to Mrs. Samantha West.

Sam was still in shock as Tom drew off the main road, which led to Brighton into the show ground, which was bathed in morning sunshine. She held Swallow Tail whilst Tom put on his saddle and bridle and then rode off to join David Mason who was mounted on a Foxhunter horse on which the owner had suffered the misfortune of breaking her leg. The horse looked to Tom to be a real handful and even he didn't envy David the ride.

'She's not my usual type, actually, Tom but Melissa has got a super Grade A. which I'm riding for her later. Poor old Mel is going to be out of action for the rest of the season – so I've got them both for the foreseeable future.' Tom waited to hear no more as the chestnut mare's back leg lashed out towards Swallow Tail's chest. He pulled him away telling David. 'I'll go t'other way me thinks, David. Good luck and I'll see you later.'

Meanwhile Sam was sitting on the grass by the Foxhunter ring with her faithful Boswell lying beside her, his large head as always, placed on her knee – his brown eyes watching everyone that dared to come near his mistress, until suddenly his tail thumped against her knee as he recognized a familiar face. Sam was startled as Charles threw himself down on the grass beside her.

'Charles, I didn't know you were coming here today.'

'Just keeping tabs on your husband, Sam. I want to see how he's doing with that chestnut gelding. Old Hans is furious he's missed out on Conchita. Thought I might be able to mollify him by offering him Swallow Tail. Tom has been unusually reticent about him – that usually denotes he's stumbled onto a good one he doesn't want me to know about.'

Sam was taken aback. 'Charles, Tom never eulogizes about a horse until he is certain it's got something extra, you know that. He has only jumped the horse about three times.'

'Hm – well I want to see for myself and they are having an auction here later today, about twenty horses and a couple of ponies. Could be interested in one or two, one in particular that I know needs sorting out, if he goes cheaply enough. I know just the right person who could do that.'

Sam didn't need to ask, she was certain her poor Tom was going to be presented with a problem and she was well aware Charles was more than a little impressed when Tom and Swallow Tail were receiving the cheque and the blue velvet rosette, at the same time trying to avoid the flailing rear leg of the bad tempered mare David Mason had miraculously steered into second place.

'I knew that two timing husband of yours was hiding something, Sam.'

'But Charles, you do get to have half the prize money.'

'Yes, but he never let on how good that horse is.' But he clapped Tom on the back as he rode round to join Sam.

'Charles, what the hell are you doing here?'

'Keeping an eye on my property, young man and hoping to buy one or two bargains in the mid-day sale.'

'Bargains or trouble, Charles,' Tom asked his boss sardonically.

'They won't be trouble once you have sorted them out, Tom.'

'How about Justin, trying?'

'Justin! He's not got half of your patience, Tom.' *'Or talent,'* Charles thought sadly to himself. 'When is your next class?'

'Not for three hours, there's the Grade C. and the Speed Class first.'

'Good, you and Sam can come to the auction then. I'm sure Sam's brought plenty in her hamper for me to share, then we can see what we can buy.'

'I'm afraid you're out of luck, Charles. I promised Sammy I'd stand her lunch today.'

'Oh well, I'll join you in the bar then, Tom,' and any thought of discussing Sam's latest exciting news would have to be put on hold.

He took Swallow Tail back to the horsebox and having made certain he had a full manger of hay and water at his disposal, walked back to the area where the auction was shortly to take place.

There was a ring around which the horses and ponies would be led and several straw bales had been placed around the edge.

Sam sat down with Boz and contemplated the extraordinary morning which had started with such normality and had suddenly turned into a weirdly exciting day, nonetheless tinged with sadness as she thought about a lonely old man who had no one else to leave his inheritance to other than a great niece he had probably encountered no more than half a dozen times in his life. She wished she had taken more time to visit him and felt almost guilty about the flat and its contents, which she was about to see the following morning. She had as yet no idea what she would do with the money once the sale of the flat had been completed, she knew that interest rates were now at an all time low, but as she pondered the best way to invest her sudden small fortune, her immediate thoughts took a dramatic about turn as she watched her poor husband being persuaded by Charles to try a lethal looking bay stallion from whom two minutes later Tom was flying through the air and then reluctantly clambering back on, as Charles insisted the stallion had only executed a playful buck

A little later, to Sam's relief, Charles seemed to have resigned himself to the fact that even Tom was not going to agree to take on the lethal bay stallion and had already turned his attention to an extremely handsome grey gelding which had been brought over from Ireland by a dealer Charles had heard much about a few years ago after his late godmother, Lady Hermione had apparently visited his yard and been greatly impressed by the quality of his horses. She had spoken highly of the dealer to whom Charles was now engaged in conversation.

'Tell me about this grey gelding, then, Paddy. What's he doing in a sale like this?'

'I've brought him over with a nice young pony. Business is a bit slow at the moment and frankly I'm a bit short of the ready. My daughter is getting married in the autumn – going to cost me a fair packet as far as I can make out.'

Charles looked for Tom but when he couldn't see him anywhere, borrowed a hard hat from a vague acquaintance who was also looking at what was on offer in the sale, squashed it on his head and leapt onto the horse himself.

The reason Charles couldn't see Tom was because he was currently in one of the stables talking quietly to an extremely nervous but beautiful young mare. She was cowering at the back of her stable but with apprehension rather than malice. A young girl was obviously supposed to be in charge of her.

'Is this your mare?' Tom asked her.

'Yes, my dad bought her for me a few months ago but I'm afraid of her.'

'Afraid? Why is that?'

'She doesn't like me going into her stable. She knows I am frightened of her and I can't hold her when she jumps. Dad's not too pleased. He paid an awful lot of money for her in Holland. He saw her advertised on the Internet. She was jumping well then but she had a strong man riding her. Sometimes she just runs round the jump. I just hate her now.'

Tom was talking very quietly to the young horse. She was certainly extremely pretty with a dark liver chestnut coat, slender white blaze down the centre of her face and two short white socks on her hind legs. She had beautiful conformation and when Tom asked the girl if she knew how she was bred, she showed him the mare's papers. He immediately recognized the Dutch stallion that was still jumping very successfully on the international circuit.

'Can I try her?' he asked.

The girl handed Tom the bridle and stood clutching an almost new German saddle. 'Could you put her tack on,' she asked him, 'she won't stand still when I have anything to do with her?'

Tom put his hand in his pocket and gave the mare a couple of pony nuts before attempting to put on the bridle. With just a shake of the head from Alicia, which appeared to be the horse's stable name and then two or three halfhearted swishes of her tail, the saddle was on. Tom mounted as swiftly as he could. The girl seemed too terrified even to take hold of the rein and having got the stirrups to the correct length, Tom walked into the area designated for trying the horses that were destined to be sold.

To his surprise, the first person he saw was his mentor sailing over a large spread on a big grey gelding, with a burly Irish man giving him every encouragement. As he landed, Charles spotted Tom on the smaller liver chestnut mare. They both thought, *'what the hell,'* as Tom watched in admiration as Charles once again soared over the spread, which thanks to the enthusiastic Irishman was now even wider, and Charles watched his one time protégé cantering a beautiful mare round the edge of the ring, stopping to talk to Sam who was still sitting on the straw bale with Boswell, as she contemplated how she would spend her newly acquired legacy.

'What are you doing on that animal, Thomas?'

'I think I've just found another lady, sweetheart.'

'Oh, Tom, what am I going to do with you? Do you want me to spend some of my newfound wealth? You did very well as my servant once before, West.'

Tom laughed –'I'll try her for a quarter of an hour and see how I assess her. She's obviously been allowed to get away with murder but I think it could well be game on,' and he cantered her round the ring.

Fortunately, Charles had finished his trial of the grey gelding and sauntered across to lower the spread for Tom and Alicia. As Tom rode up to the jump, the mare took him completely by surprise, as at the very last stride she ducked sideways, avoiding the jump and almost but not quite depositing Tom on the ground. Tom shortened his reins – tightened his legs on her flanks and rode as strongly as he could, holding her straight with both his hands and his legs and it was in that moment that Alicia became aware she had met her match. She was never to duck out at a jump again, and as Charles raised the jump and widened the spread a couple of times he stood back and watched the World Number One and his magic working again.

Tom walked Alicia round for ten minutes and then took her back to the lethargic girl who he was certain was answerable for this lovely mare's mischievous ways.

'Where's your Dad?' He asked.

'In the bar.'

'Well could you go and fetch him. Tell him a prospective buyer would like to talk to him.'

The girl sauntered off, whilst Tom busied himself looking round the stables at the other horses on offer. There was nothing else to compare with Alicia until he came to the very last stall where a blue roan head and a pair of enormous brown eyes was waiting to greet him, it's ears sharply pricked as it gave a deep whinny. Tom started - although the pony was only just fourteen hands it reminded him of two ponies he knew only too well who were at that moment happily at home in Massenden.

The Irish man who had been talking to Charles was leaning nonchalantly against the stable, thirstily gulping down a can of lager.

'Is this your pony?' Tom asked.

'Sure and it is. I've brought him over from Ireland with the grey gelding.'

'What's he done so far?'

'Four Foxhunters. Won his last two, second before that and a fourth to begin with. He's a good honest little pony. Perfect for a reasonably proficient kid.'

'Who rode him for you, and were these classes in Ireland?'

'Sure and they were. My partner's young son rode him but he's a big lad of fourteen now, this little chap needs a ten or eleven year old. He's not strong at all.'

'Is there anyone here that can ride him?'

'Fraid not. The kids are all still at school in Ireland.'

'Yea, they are here too. But I do know someone who is light enough to ride him – hang on.' Two minutes later, Tom was pulling a slightly less than willing Sam towards the swarthy Irishman. He pushed his hat on her head, grabbed hold of Boswell's lead and watched as Sam trotted round the arena. The pony was willing with a good head carriage and it wasn't long before Sam's confidence had risen and she was cantering on both legs. Tom and the

Irishman, whose name Tom had discovered not at all to his surprise was Paddy, lowered the jump to three feet and with Sam's heart in her mouth she aimed the willing roan pony towards the jump. She barely felt his stride alter as he cantered up to the jump and flew over without any effort.

Tom wished one of his boys was with him – but they weren't and Sam had done her bit. He just had to trust his own instincts, which were telling him this pony from Ireland had to have a close connection with Thunder and Ganger and he knew he had just the little rider for him. Rosie had never done a Junior Foxhunter class before but this would be her chance, she would be ten in the spring. He just hoped Sam would agree with him.

'What sort or reserve have you put on him?' Tom asked Paddy.

'Three thousand. He's worth more than that but I'm desperately in need of money. My daughter is getting married this autumn.'

Tom handed the pony back. 'Thanks, he's a nice pony and I see he is only a six year old.'

'That's right. He's only a young'un to be sure.'

Tom gave the pony a handful of nuts and then went back to find Alicia's owner who had finally managed to drag himself away from the bar. He reminded Tom of the ghastly Jake Strawbridge whom he had encountered at the show in Essex a few weeks ago.

Tom decided to be friendly. 'Hi,' he greeted the man. 'I wondered what you could tell me about your daughter's horse?'

The man had already had more than enough to drink. 'Only that I was stung by some underhanded Dutch dealer a few months ago. Told me that horse had never stopped in her life. First show with my daughter was fine - they came third – then she started ducking out at the jumps and Jodie got more and more afraid, after that the bad manners in the stable began, all I want is to see the back of her and find another nag for Jodie.'

Tom felt desperately sorry for the unsuspecting horse for which this unpleasant fate awaited.

'How old is Alicia and what has she done so far?'

'She's Grade C. and she's eight years old.'

'So what reserve have you put on her?'

'What's that got to do with you?'

'Everything if I'm interested in buying her. I want to know whether or not I am wasting my time, also does she have a vet's certificate?'

'Yes, the vet came yesterday. I have it here with her papers.'

'Fine. Now tell me the reserve.'

'There isn't one. The last thing Jodie wants is to take her home. I just want to get shot of her before she half kills my daughter. I've wasted a small fortune but I suppose that's what happens when you see fit to indulge your children.'

'Well, you can rest assured if I should buy her, Alicia would have an excellent home.'

'I couldn't give a damn where she is, so long as she's no longer in mine,' and the odious man turned and made his way back to the bar.

Sam had tears in her eyes. 'What a horrible, horrible man. Poor, poor Alicia How can people be so unfeeling. Bid for me, Tom, I couldn't bear to let her go back to that creature.'

'How much are you willing to pay, My Lady?'

'Whatever it takes, West.' And Sam gave him her special look, which never failed to make his heart reel.

'I'm going to buy the pony for Rosie, Sam. He's simply got to be related to Thunder and Ganger; he comes from the same part of Ireland they originated from. He's got exactly the same little star and those enormous brown eyes. Rosie will love to do the Junior Foxhunter Classes. I know he's only fourteen hands but he'll hop over those jumps and he already has an excellent track record.'

'Fine, as long as Oscar doesn't kick up a stink.'

'He won't. I'm pretty certain the Countess won't let Ozzie out of her sight. I am certain she has got young horses with Ozzie's future very much in the foreground of her plans. The one who is the least well provided for is Ollie, but he never complains and his time is so much more restricted than the other boys at the moment. Now let's find Charles and grab ourselves something to eat. We've still got three quarters of an hour before the sale is due to start.'

'Have you got room for a possible two more in your box?' Tom asked Charles.

'Two more?'

'Well, yes, I like the liver chestnut mare, she's fallen into the wrong hands and I'm certain I can sort her out in no time, Charles. Compared to Opal and Misty she's a singe.'

'And what's the other one then, Tom?'

'The roan pony – I want him for Rosie. I'm almost certain he has to be related to Thunder and Ganger.'

'You spoil your kids, Tom.'

'Well, I think maybe we are all guilty of that, but they work damn hard and I have never heard one of them say *'I'm bored, Dad, What can I do?'* Not once, and they have all learned to be good sports and Charles, you know we are all mighty proud of them – so why does a bit of spoiling harm them? Not at all as far as I am concerned.'

'You're probably right, Tom, and actually that Irish chap, Paddy is going to send me over a super fourteen two pony which he says Rupert can have on trial for a month, so game on, Tom West - and don't forget we've got the task of choosing the Pony Club and the school jumping teams. The heats are in August and the final the first week in September just before the holidays end. We'll put our heads together next week, Tom.'

'Fine. By the way, I'm taking a day off tomorrow. I think I'm owed a few.'

'Where the hell are you buggering off to?'

'Sam and I are going to look at a flat in Chislehurst.'

'Where the hell is that?'

'Near Bromley.'

'What the dickens are you going there for? You've not suddenly got a whim for a London pad, have you Tom?'

'Well, possibly for a short time. Tell him, Sam.'

'I've been left a flat in Chislehurst by an old uncle. It was totally unexpected. I didn't even know he was ill. Apparently the flat is full of antiques. Tom and I are going to meet the old boy's solicitor tomorrow.'

'So are you mega rich, Sam?'

'In comparison to your millions, Charles it would be a mere drop in the ocean, but to me, three hundred and fifty thousand pounds is a lot of money and we don't know what is in the flat but I gather he had a big collection of silver and lots of snuff boxes too.'

'Invest wisely, Sammy, don't leave it festering away in some bank account for God's sake.'

'I certainly won't do that, Charles, never fear, but I won't rush into anything, I'm not really an impulsive person.'

'Anyway if you do get those two animals, Tom, I've got plenty of room. I can take Swallow Tail home for you too if you don't want him to hang about all day.'

'That would be really super, Charles. Are you driving? Or is Erica lurking around the box?'

'Yea, I am. I didn't bother bringing a groom. I hadn't bargained on having two horses and a pony on board, but rest assured, I've coped with far worse problems than that over the years.'

'Have you by any chance got your cheque book on you. Charles?'

'I suppose you want me to lend you some money?'

'Just until tomorrow. That would be super.'

Charles laughed. 'You haven't bought them yet, Tom. Let the suspense begin.' And they made their way to the straw bales around the edge of the ring.

The first of the lots they were interested in was the roan pony and he was struggling to reach his reserve price. Tom was delighted when he bought him for the maiden bid of three thousand pounds.

Most of the livestock were ageing Grade A. horses that had enjoyed varying degrees of success in their younger days. Several, however, didn't reach their reserve prices and were being trundled back into their disappointed owner's horseboxes to be taken home and then subsequently to another sale in a different part of the country.

After the next six horses had come and gone, the stocky Irishman, Paddy, led the grey gelding Charles had been trying into the ring. Again the bidding was far from brisk and to Charles delight and Paddy's disappointment The Blarney Stone would become the latest bearer of the Lake House prefix for the reserve price of twelve thousand pounds.

They watched as the bucking bronco Tom had sat on earlier failed to sell and then Tom noticed David Mason bidding for a fourteen-year-old Grade A. chestnut mare, which he bought for twenty thousand pounds.

Charles was astounded. 'Hell, what on earth is David buying that old girl for. Once she was brilliant but she's had a hell of a lot of problems in the last two years. She's been lame more often than not.'

'Perhaps he intends breeding from her, Charles. She's a nice type, put her with a top stallion and you never know.'

Jodie was terrified as she led the penultimate horse into the ring. Her nervousness was transmitting itself to the mare who gave a half rear. Jodie screamed and let go of the lead rope with which, as the girl's shrill screams filled the air, Alicia bolted – flying round and round the small sale ring dodging the few stewards who were brave enough to try to stop her. Tom stood up ducking under the rope, which surrounded the ring. He stood perfectly still, calling her gently. 'Come girl, come to Tom, here girl, quietly girl.' She stopped, listening to his voice, looking at him. 'Come girl, come here girl,' and he held out his hand, which contained three pony nuts. She gradually took a step towards him whilst the auctioneer and all the stewards held their breath as Alicia took another nut, all the time listening to Tom's soft voice. One more step and Tom knew he could catch hold of the rope. He stood like a statue, his hand offering her three more nuts. Suddenly she was within his grasp and as she took the nuts from his left hand, his right arm slipped forwards and the next moment he was grasping the rope and walking up to the auctioneer. 'Would you like me to lead her for you?' he asked Jodie who was shaking from head to foot.

'Y yes please,' and Tom trotted Alicia round the ring.

There didn't appear to be anyone bidding. The auctioneer had started by asking for twenty thousand pounds. There had been no response and his voice was now sounding desperate as he asked for five thousand pounds. 'This mare is here to be sold, make no mistake about that – she is here without a reserve – come on now – who will start the bidding?'

Tom suddenly heard Charles' voice. 'Three thousand.'

Tom couldn't believe it. Was Charles really bidding for the mare he himself wanted so much? But he knew he couldn't bid against his boss, and as there was absolutely no one else interested, the mare was almost given to Charles for his first cheeky bid.

Tom was still holding Alicia whose owner was nowhere to be seen – he led her up to Charles. 'Yours I think, boss.'

'Don't be daft, lad. Her new owner is right here,' and Sam was smiling.

'Charles bid for me, Tommy. She's ours. The biggest bargain ever.'

'Sam, darling. You've bought her. You're my mistress.'

'Oh yes, my Thomas, I most certainly am,' and she gave him a wicked smile.

Charles gave them both an odd look. 'What am I missing here, Tom?'

'Maybe you should suggest to Joanna she pays you for that grey gelding you've just acquired. Sammy and I discovered a long time ago, when she first had Black Chintz that it's good to have a mistress, especially when she happens to be your wife!!'

Charles just saw fit to shake his head at Tom in disbelief. 'I always knew you were mad, Tom, but actually, perhaps on reflection I do see your point. I could just suggest to Joanna she might like to be the owner of a grey gelding!!'

Tom still had an hour before his Open Class was due to begin. He called Hannah and Jules on his mobile asking them to get three stables ready, one for Alicia, one for the roan pony who was apparently called Braveheart and the third for Sweet Dreams who he was picking up on his way home.

Charles grey gelding, Blarney Stone, seemed a solid and reliable character and walked calmly into his stall – followed by Braveheart and eventually after more than a little persuasion from Tom, Alicia deigned to follow him up the ramp. Finally, Tom ran back to his own box and fetched Swallow Tail and then loaded him beside Alicia – Charles clambered into the cab and drove slowly out of the showground and up the A.23 towards Massenden. He knew Alicia and Braveheart would most likely be heading towards their forever home but he was already planning Blarney Stone's future and that would involve a few hefty wins with himself C.W.S. on board and then a nice profit finding its way into the Lake House Stables' bank account.

Sam shut Boswell into the cab whilst she helped Tom with Clem and Kaspar and then as he and Kaspar disappeared towards the practice jump she sat down in the cab, took the letter out of its envelope and re-read it carefully, making certain she hadn't been dreaming – but no – there it was in front of her in black and white. She replaced the letter in the envelope and put it back under the dashboard, then taking Boswell's lead, locked the cab securely and walked to the arena. Fifteen minutes later she was watching Tom and Kaspar on their very best form. Clem was not so fortunate when she knocked the middle element of the treble but it was to be

Kaspar's day and the cheque Tom received more than paid for the roan pony, Braveheart, who had probably by now been unloaded and would be standing in his new stable at Woodcutters. Tom hoped the same applied to Alicia, but he knew that however obstinate she might be when she reached her destination, Charles was probably the person he trusted more than anyone else to manipulate her into her new abode.

He wondered not for the first time if Justin was right when he told him he had a screw loose. He had started out that morning with three horses and now somehow he had acquired two more and a mistress!! Even though one was a pony he already had high hopes for it. Braveheart had flown over the practice jump with Sam earlier on and although he would never tell anyone, especially Sam herself, she had been a mere passenger. He would get one of the trips to jump the pony in his own jumping paddock before he even mentioned to Rosie that Braveheart had been purchased with her in mind. He decided he would take Ollie and he would ride Alicia the following evening after he and Sam had been to see her inheritance in Chislehurst. Tomorrow was to be a very interesting day.

CHAPTER 29

Tom had set the sat nav, which should in theory direct them to 5a Madeley Villas, Chislehurst.

They had dropped the children at school after Tom had almost forcibly dragged Rosie away from Braveheart, with whom she appeared to have already formed a strong bond, although Tom had been extremely evasive when questions had been asked as to where he had come from, did he belong to Dad and if so, who was going to ride him.

'Yes, he is mine,' Tom had told them, 'and this evening I want one of you to try him in our jumping paddock.'

'Me- me – me,' – a chorus of voices had echoed round the breakfast table – all except Josh who couldn't wait to ride Sweet Dreams that evening.

'Ollie, you have only one pony to exercise at the moment, Braveheart most probably won't be for you, I am well aware you have two more music exams coming up next term but you can ride him this evening whilst I assess him. By the way, Rosie, those two girls you met at the show in Essex are coming to stay next week. I spoke to their dad last evening and they are going to bring their ponies with them. He will bring them in his horsebox on Sunday. They will be here for the Massenden Show the following Sunday and then their parents will take them home afterwards. Apparently they are really excited and looking forwards to joining *the gang* for a week.'

Oscar was looking interested. 'Cor, Dad. I wish Mike could bring them in his Swallow Tail. I liked Cassie and Clare – they're not as pretty as Annie but they were good fun. I know all *the gang* will like them.'

'I'm afraid they will be arriving in nothing more exciting than a horsebox, Oz, but Mike and Suzie have invited as all for the weekend when the base where the Swallow Tails are kept is open. It's in September and I have promised I'll make sure I can take however many of you want to come. Apparently there's a good horseshow in Lincolnshire on the Sunday, so they suggest we take the ponies. They've got a spare paddock adjoining the house. Just one pony each though, kids.'

'Whacko, Dad. Can Annie come too?'

'I expect we can squeeze you all in. We'll take the big caravan – we may not all fit into Mike and Suzie's house.'

'Whacko,' Ozzie repeated. This was his latest word.

Having left Hannah and Jules with the dogs and instructions not to turn Alicia out until he was back, Tom and Sam were soon joining the slow moving traffic as they approached the perimeter of Greater London.

'I couldn't breathe if I lived in a place like this, Tom – but I suppose if you work in London and it's what you have always been used to maybe you don't even notice all the cars and the noise. Where on earth does everyone put their cars in the evenings, or do you think they all use the tubes or the busses?'

'God knows but whatever you do, Sammy, don't fall in love with this flat, or I am afraid, my darling, much as I love you, you would be living there alone.'

'You can certainly have no fear of that, my Tommy, but this looks a bit better.'

They were approaching the more salubrious area of Chislehurst with well-maintained gardens and many more trees lining the roads. The sat nav suddenly instructed Tom to take the first left and then turn immediately right and No.5 a. Madeley Villas would be found fifty yards down the Avenue on the right hand side of the road.

Sam was surprised. The houses were large, built in Edwardian times and number 5 looked extremely imposing, as she and Tom stood on the pavement completely awe struck by the size of the double fronted house.

Jeremiah Courtney was a small man, with a goatee beard and a shiny pate, surrounded by a few strands of grey hair. However, he was greeting them warmly as Sam stood looking at the beautiful pine doors, which led off a large square hall with the original Edwardian tiles still covering the floors in a mosaic pattern. It was indeed an impressive first impression of her inheritance.

To their surprise, the opulence didn't end there as the solicitor opened one of the pine doors to reveal a large drawing room with a grand marble fireplace with its original art nouveau stylistic tiles surrounding the wrought iron grate. The windows, which looked over the avenue were set in a large bay, which still had their original white painted shutters and beneath the Chinese rugs, Sam could see the beautiful old wooden floorboards. Not only was the room itself beautiful, it was filled with antiques from many periods including a set of Victorian balloon back chairs and a button back chaise-longue sitting under the window. There were numerous cabinets around the walls, housing various porcelain and bronze ornaments and one was filled with literally hundreds of small pieces of silver and bronzes.

Sam's mind was spinning as she entered a similar sized room on the other side of the hall, which had obviously been her late uncle's bedroom. She felt overcome as it was exactly as he had left it the day he had been rushed to hospital but as she looked round, she noticed box upon box stacked on top of the wardrobes and several very attractive silver photograph frames adorning the small bow fronted chest of drawers.

By this time, Sam was clutching Tom's hand but even he was completely dumb struck and for the moment, was incapable of uttering a single word.

The kitchen was at the back of the house behind the drawing room. It had certainly never been modernized and the original dresser stretched along one side of the kitchen wall. An eye catching desert service was displayed on the bottom shelf. Sam picked up a comport, of which there were four - each one and every one of the eighteen plates which made up the set were exquisitely hand painted, each with a garden flower. When Sam carefully turned the comport upside down she was not surprised to see blue crossed swords painted on the base. Without doubt she had inherited eighteen Meissen plates and four wonderful comports.

An art deco tea set adorned the top shelf and even Tom recognized the distinctive style of Clarice Cliff, remembering a salt and pepper pot Mary had cherished and had kept well out of reach when Tom and his sisters had been little children.

The kitchen had casement doors, which opened, onto a long oblong garden – obviously maintained by an experienced gardener. To Sam's surprise there were four Japanese maple trees in various parts of the lawn and she fleetingly wondered whether it was from her late great uncle that she had inherited her love of these beautiful trees.

In one corner, under a rose arch, Sam spotted a heavy, wrought iron table and six matching chairs. She could immediately see they were not twenty first century reproductions and at the same time was wondering whether she could persuade the muscular Erica to drive the horsebox up here and transport this beautiful garden furniture back to Massenden, but by the time they had finished the tour of the house, she had decided they would have to ask the local removal firm to bring several of the beautiful antiques back to Woodcutters.

She decided she would ask Mary, who loved antiques and was very knowledgeable, to spend at least two days going through the flat from top to bottom with her.

Jeremiah Courtney had somehow managed to make a pot of tea in a teapot, which had a spout in the form of an ornate swan's neck. The cups had roses painted all around the outside and a different rose in the bottom of each one. Sam was looking at two pictures she had taken off the wall in the smaller bedroom. One was a scene outside a cottage that had hollyhocks growing around the door and a group of a lady and three small children standing together on the doorstep. It was, as Sam had thought as soon as her eyes had spotted the watercolour, signed by Helen Allingham, one of the most sought after artists of this particular genre.

The other was an oil painting of four small ponies grazing under trees in a moorland setting, typical of the style of George Morland. Sam knew Rosie would love to have this picture in her bedroom and she had immediately recognized the name. Her stepbrother, Andrew had often mentioned it, telling her he was famed for his country scenes, often of small ponies.

'I'm going to take these home with us, Tommy, I simply love them.'

Tom smiled at her. 'Do you think I could indulge myself too, Sammy?'

'Darling, of course you can. Take whatever you want.'

Tom walked across the room and lifted an oil painting of a dark bay racehorse from the wall. The horse's name was written on the mount and the painting was signed by an artist whose name Sam recognized all too well, 'John Frederick Herring.'

She was trying to concentrate on Jeremiah Courtney's rather monotonous voice. 'I told you in my letter, the gentleman upstairs had offered you three hundred and forty thousand pounds for the flat but I have to tell you that in the past two days we have received three more offers, the highest being five hundred and twenty thousand. It appears it is very difficult to acquire a flat in this area that has a good-sized garden. Of course the final decision must be yours but could I advise you that I think it would be prudent to put the flat on the market with a good London auctioneer but certainly the first offer you had appears to be way under the value of the property.

'Goodness. Well I'm in no rush to sell, in fact I would like a little while to sort through all these stunning antiques. I need to go through every cupboard and drawer in the house. I love some of the snuff boxes, I really need time to consider what Tom and I would like to keep for ourselves.'

‘Of course, Mrs. West. I suggest you put the flat in the hands of a really reputable auction house and he mentioned a well-known name. They would also sell all the furniture and small items you don’t wish to keep. Of course you would have to pay them commission but I do believe the advice I am giving you is prudent.’

Before they left, Sam had agreed that Jeremiah Courtney would oversee the sale of the house for her. She knew she was out of her depth and decided that obviously her great uncle had trusted this solicitor to deal with his affairs for many years.

Sam would ask Mary to come up to Chislehurst with her and together they would peruse every corner of the flat, probably once the Lewis girls had finished their stay at Woodcutters the following week.

Tom and Sam drove home in a daze. ‘God, Sammy, I almost need my sat nav to get me home. My brain is all over the place. That flat was like an Aladdin’s cave. I think I must now have a very wealthy wife.’

‘Tom you know very well that everything in that flat is ours, not mine – nothing has changed and it never will – we share everything.’

‘My darling Sam, remember I am only your servant, don’t forget this evening I am going to try my ladyship’s new steed and she can come and watch me.’

‘Idiot, Tom – but we will invest that money wisely – but I think there will be several bits and pieces I will want to keep. Uncle Joseph was obviously a very astute old man and according to Jeremiah Courtney he inherited a lot of those antiques from his father and grandfather. Amazing, quite amazing.’

As Tom drew nearer to Massenden the traffic had eased considerably and just after four o’clock they were turning into the welcoming drive and drawing up in front of Woodcutters.

Sam was clutching the three paintings. Tom had promised he would unearth his electric drill and look for some rawlplugs and after they had exercised the horses and ponies, would hang them wherever she wanted them.

Hannah had made the boys and Rosie a ham sandwich and to Sam's surprise the triplets were all sitting round the table in the playroom engrossed in their homework. With only two more days before the long summer holidays the workload had become a lot lighter and the boys had almost completed their tasks.

'Where's Rosie, boys?'

'She hasn't got any homework. She's taken her library book to read in Braveheart's stable. He seems to be her latest obsession.'

'Oh well, Dad has gone to check all is well with Jules and Hannah, no doubt he will discover her and bring her back here for her tea before we all ride down to the sand school once Joshua is home.'

Tom was walking up to Alicia's stable about to ask Jules how the day had been when he became aware of Rosie's voice talking softly inside Braveheart's stable. He crept up to the door and peeped over the top. Rosie was totally engrossed - lost in her own world. She was sitting on the stool, which was normally kept in the tack room, reading a pony book to her newest friend. The pony's roan head was resting gently on her shoulder, his eyes half closed. He pulled his mobile from his pocket and quickly took a photo – the scene had brought a lump to his throat – it was one of the most touching moments he could recall. He decided to take the photograph to Andrew and ask him to paint a watercolor of the scene he had just witnessed. It would be the perfect present for Sam at Christmas.

'Rosie, sweetheart, what are you doing?'

Rosie sighed. 'Reading to Braveheart, Dads. He loves it – he's listening to every word. He's not like a pony, he's more like a friend. Please will you let me ride him?'

'Ollie will ride him first, Rosie. I agree he seems to have a fantastic temperament but in spite of what you think, he is a pony, but when I've watched Ollie and if I am sure you could manage him, then I won't stand in your way but there is a ham sandwich waiting for you in the kitchen. When you've eaten that and had a drink we are all going to saddle up and make our way to the sand school.'

'O.K. Dads,' and Rosie shut her book and turned to the pony. 'I won't be long, Braveheart – please be a good boy with Ollie and then my dad says I can ride you,' and she kissed his soft, blue roan cheek.

Half an hour later, the horses and ponies were saddled and a small cavalcade was making its way through the woods to the sand school. Josh was more than a little excited as he led the way with Sweet Dreams, Oliver and Orlando were following him with Braveheart and Jet Stream. Sam was riding Madam with Rosie and Sparkler bouncing along beside her and finally Oscar and Tom were bringing up the rear. Alicia was behaving well beside Oscar. Tom had inveigled him into riding the calm, sensible Goldfinger that evening. Oscar had taken more than a small amount of persuasion but had given in when Tom had promised he would ride Clementine round the lake with him and Hanky Panky before school the next morning. Tom had decided Panky's early morning high spirits would not influence Clem. Oscar was delighted and informed Tom he would set his alarm for six o'clock the next morning. Now he was chatting to Tom about the brace the dentist had told Anne-Marie she would have to wear after her thirteenth birthday in two year's time.

'She will look a bit odd, dad. The dentist says she will have to wear them for eighteen months that means she will be nearly fifteen but then she will be more beautiful than ever.'

'Well, Ozzie,' Tom told him with a smile. 'You've certainly got something to look forwards to then.'

'Oh yes, Dad, I shan't kiss her till the brace has gone. It would feel as if she had a bit in her mouth.'

Tom turned the other way to hide the amusement on his face, Ozzie sounded so serious. Tom knew this particular son of his could be difficult but he never hid the truth – Oscar West always said whatever he thought, but he agreed with Ozzie, when she was fifteen, Anne-Marie would most probably be growing into the most beautiful, young woman. He came back to the present as Alicia shied at a pheasant, which suddenly appeared from behind a tree and decided to hold her a shade more tightly until they reached the sand school.

The stables Tom had converted several years ago in the small barn near the jumping paddock were empty and he put Alicia and Madam in them whilst he and Sam organized the youngsters. He could see Josh was consumed with impatience, desperate to try Sweet Dreams over the course he and Sam were about to build.

He didn't put any of the jumps higher than Junior Foxhunter height – Sweet Dreams was still relatively inexperienced and this was a big step up for Joshua. After a quarter of an hour on the flat, whilst Rosie and Sparkler practiced their dressage test in the empty paddock next to the jumping school and Ollie, 'Lando and Oscar were deep in discussion about the ironmongery which would adorn Anne-Marie's teeth in the not too distant future, Joshua had his first jump on Sweet Dreams.

Sam walked over to the paddock and gave Rosie a run through the dressage test which she would be doing at the Pony Club Day the following Saturday with most of the girls from *the gang.* Out of the corner of her eye she could see Josh rising rhythmically over the jumps and she could hear Tom's words of encouragement – making his son feel on top of the world.

She sighed. *'Dear Tom. He was a wonderful dad, no wonder his children looked up to him with so much pride.'* He was praising Josh and telling him to join the others and to send Oliver and Braveheart to him.

Sam came with them and helped Tom lower the jumps to three feet three inches.

Tom and Sam stood together and watched as Oliver schooled Braveheart on the flat. Tom looked at the pony's rounded neck and his even canter; he turned to Sam telling her. 'Super Working Pony, Sam.'

'Absolutely,' she agreed.

'That's your forte, my Sammy.'

'Um. O.K. I'll see if I can persuade Rosie. Somehow I don't think that will be too difficult, she's in love with him already.'

Tom called to Oliver. 'When you're ready, Ollie, see how he goes.' And Oliver turned towards the jumps. Braveheart's ears were pricked as he approached the fences, he didn't pull, nor did he need much encouragement, he just cleared each jump in one smooth movement. Tom raised the poles to four feet and the pony didn't falter.

Rosie was standing by the fence on Sparkler, watching. 'Please, please, Dad let me ride him, I know I can.'

Tom looked at Sam. Her instinct told her Braveheart was a special pony, surely related to Thunder and Ganger with the same little white star on his forehead and the wonderful soft brown eyes. She nodded at Tom and he beckoned Rosie into the school, she handed Sparkler to Ollie and then Tom lifted her onto Braveheart, shortening the stirrups and telling her. 'Just trot steadily round the edge of the school, don't do anything else until I tell you – just get completely used to riding a pony with a larger stride, although actually he's only two inches bigger than The Duc. Tom and Sam finished setting the jumps at 0.80metres

'O.K. Rosie, if you feel quite happy then canter.' Rosie sat still, squeezed with her calves and as Braveheart broke into his steady canter he could hear Rosie singing in time to the rhythm of his feet. After five minutes she rode up to him. 'Can I take him over the jumps now, Dad?'

'Just keep him really steady Rosie, and try the first two.'

They cantered round in a circle before Rosie turned to the first jump and as he had done with Oliver, Braveheart pricked his ears, barely altering his stride and was over the jump and cantering on towards the next one. Rosie turned and rode up to Tom and Sam. 'Please, can I do the course now and then will you put it up higher.'

'If you jump clear, then yes.' Which is just what they did and when Tom raised the jumps to the Junior Foxhunter height he watched his diminutive little daughter with pride. The round had been perfect. Braveheart would be Rosie's pony for the rest of her junior days and he knew without doubt that success was just around the corner.

'Good girl, Rosie, now give Braveheart back to Ollie and take Sparkler, then come and watch Oscar and Goldfinger and 'Lando and Jet Stream whilst I go and get Alicia from the stable.'

Alicia had been bored in the stable and she was delighted to step foot on to the soft grass, she shot forwards but Tom was more than ready for her. Her previous owner might well have found her strong, but she hadn't had years of riding horses like Satin, Invader and Kaspar, to name just a few and she held no fears for Tom, who soon had her in a beautifully controlled canter as Oscar and Josh raised the jumps to 1.30 metres. When he reached the double he felt her faltering but his legs were strong and he was able to keep her straight and with one small tap on the shoulder, she was over with just the slightest hesitation. The second time around she didn't falter at all. Tom patted her and walked her round the edge of the school on a long, loose rein. He wasn't certain how fit she was. He imagined the girl, Jodie, had probably not ridden her for some time. He patted her neck again, and more than satisfied with the evening's work, rode beside Sam and Madam whilst his children followed in his footsteps, which was where they were already most certainly heading.

CHAPTER 30

Sam gathered her group of girls every evening, taking them into the sand school at the Equitation Centre. Life had become much easier since Justin had moved into Theobald's Place and put a gate at the bottom of his paddock, which led into the corner of the cross country course – it avoided the busy main road. It was a little further for Mimi and Anne-Marie but it only took them a short time to canter by the lake to Woodcutters and then cut through the gate at Old Tiles Farm into Back Lane and Theobald's Place.

The dressage test was to be divided into three groups. The first was for riders who had past their D or D +Test or had not as yet taken one at all. The next for those with their C or C+ Test and the last was for the older children who had reached the lofty height of the B or B+ test, like Jacques. Mimi and Josh were due to take theirs in the Christmas holiday when they would join him.

Jacques was the only boy out of all those in the gang who wanted to do the dressage test. Jean-Pierre had coached him tirelessly and there was no doubt that he had inherited much of his father's talent and impeccable style. The girls had all told him they would be staying to watch his test, which was to be the penultimate one of the day, the final one being for the most elite members of all, the mere handful who had passed the prestigious A. test.

Sam was helping the C. test girls, which was the majority of them and Trish was looking after Fenella, Abby, Anne-Marie, Daisy, Virginia Mawgan-Whitely and Eloise who would also be taking her test with Daisy in the forthcoming Christmas holidays. She had started her riding much later than the other girls of her age, but in Sam's opinion, again with much help from Jean-Pierre, she thought she was an extremely strong contender to win the first test.

An hour later, Sam was content with both groups. 'We'll have a rest day tomorrow,' she told them all. 'Now it would be good if you could all manage to plait your ponies. All you C. test girls should certainly be capable of that. Mimi, could you help Anne-Marie and Virginia and Veronica I'm sure either Sheila or Sally would help you. Abby, I will bring Rosie to your house and Daisy you bring Popcorn there early on Saturday morning too and I will help the three of you. Georgia and Charlotte, how about you two?'

'I think we can manage, thank you Sam. We've been practicing and we will help each other.'

'Super, then I will see you all here at the dressage arena on Saturday morning sharp at eleven o'clock.'

'Will Ozzie and Gus be watching us, Sam?' Anne-Marie asked.

'No, the boys are going to a big show the other side of London with Tom and Charles. We will have a nice girlie day on Saturday. Bring a picnic if you want to or you can bring some money and buy some sandwiches here. It's entirely up to you – but perhaps some of your parents are going to come and watch you?'

'I know Mum is,' Mimi told her and both Georgia and Charlotte were certain they would be supported by their families too, the only one who seemed dubious was Tilly. 'I think Mum is probably working,' she told Sam rather wistfully.

'Don't worry, Tilly. I'll pop a few extra sandwiches into my basket. You can share our picnic and you too, Daisy.' Sam couldn't imagine Rob making even a doorstep for her and Tilly and Daisy both smiled with relief.

At Shepherd's Cottage, Amy was fluctuating between the excitement of Adrian coming home after four weeks in a rehabilitation clinic and apprehension as to how she would cope with a husband who had no recollection of marrying her, let alone being the father of their beautiful little daughter. She was only too grateful that Miriam and George would never be far away and whom she knew would give her all the support they possibly could. Fortunately, it was obvious Adrian liked her, maybe she thought, they could start their lives again or one day she prayed he would remember his past and that he had known her since she had been ten years old. So far it was a question no one could answer, not even the top specialist in the hospital he had left a few weeks ago. Tom would be collecting him from the re-hab clinic at eleven o'clock and all being well he would be eating his lunch with her at mid-day on Monday.

The day of the dressage tests had arrived and the boys were off with Tom and Charles to a big show in Bedfordshire. Dom was preparing to pull out of the drive at Woodcutters with Jules beside him and Tom's latest acquisition, Alicia, who was going to make her debut with Tom at the venue they were currently about to head off to. The Wizard was looking at her inquisitively as he stood in the next stall. It would be his first competition after pulling a muscle in his shoulder earlier in the year. It would not be the biggest open and Tom thought it should be ideal for him to begin his comeback. Ganger was standing quietly behind them and looking at Jet Stream and Torchlight who were already pulling at their hay. Oliver's Buck's Fizz was quiet as Humbug and Hanky Panky pulled very odd faces at each other.

Tom followed with the boys in the Range Rover he was currently hiring whilst the enquiry about the accident was still ongoing. He had recently heard a court case would be coming up in six week's time.

At the same time as Dom was leaving Woodcutters, Ricky was loading The March Hare for Rupert, and Pie in the Sky and Hamlet for Gus. Charles himself had decided to try his new horse Blarney Stone in the Foxhunter Class and Stormy Waters in the Open.

As the boys were all safely on their way, back in Massenden, the girls were bathing their ponies and plaiting their manes with varying degrees of success. Trish took pity on Tilly and quickly replaited the tennis balls into a line of neat marbles and Joanna was helping Mimi who seemed to be completely alienated from both needles and thread.

At last the ponies were ready, the picnic baskets packed, the saddles and bridles immaculately clean and everyone appeared to have managed to find their pony club tie, which they hadn't worn since the Easter holidays.

Sam scoured the rose bushes and picked the smallest buds she could find. Wrapped the stems in silver foil and found a small gold safety pin for each one. She had taken one for Rosie and Daisy and two more for emergencies. She very much doubted if Tilly would have thought of a detail like a buttonhole and her mother, Ruth, she was sure most certainly wouldn't.

At ten thirty, all the girls were gathered together. Sam made certain their hair was all carefully folded inside the hair nets and then looked at Mimi, sending her straight to the lady's room, telling her firmly all traces of powder, eye shadow and lipstick were to be completely removed and that when, and if, she should one day happen to attain her Grade A. Test then these cosmetics would be perfectly acceptable but they were not for a young girl with a mere C. Test.

Mimi pulled a face at Sam's back which didn't go unnoticed by her mother who unfortunately for *Charles' little minx* agreed with Sam and personally accompanied her daughter to the extremely upmarket lady's room next to the bar.

As Sam had suspected, Tilly had not brought a button hole and she was smiling at Sam who was pinning a small Samantha rose bud on the blue jacket Mimi had just disposed of and who was now sporting an extremely smart dark grey jacket adorned with black velvet collars, which Rosie was coveting, begging Sam to buy her one for her next birthday.

'Not until you have completely outgrown this one, Rosie and then we will see.'

Rosie sighed, she hated the phrase, *'we will see,'* it didn't usually bode well.

It wasn't long before the candidates having attained their D. Test or had not yet taken a test of any colour were being called to the collecting ring where they were each given a neat square number with black tape to tie round their waists.

Eloise and Pierrot were the first of *the gang* to ride calmly into the arena. With their thick black manes plaited, Pierrot and his sister Poupée were even more difficult to tell apart. Jean-Pierre was standing by Sam who was listening to his criticisms of his daughter, who in her eyes were performing a near perfect test. However, dressage was Jean-Pierre's forté – he strove for perfection in his own tests and perhaps, sadly for Eloise, expected it of her too. As he watched the young children who followed, his opinion of his daughter's test was changing as Anne-Marie, Virginia Mawgan-Whitely and Abby all failed to ride into the corners and Anne-Marie and Tom Thumb were consistently cantering on the wrong leg. However, as she had not the first knowledge of right and wrong legs, Anne-Marie was blissfully unaware of her mistakes.

Jean-Pierre's eyes narrowed as he was suddenly watching Daisy and Popcorn who were immaculately turned out.

Rob had asked Sam to take Daisy to Canterbury and had given her an open cheque, asking her to buy all that was necessary for his daughter to be kitted out to perfection. Sam had bought a blue show jacket and dark brown leather gloves, a cream pair of jodhpurs, short brown leather riding boots and a leather show stick. As Sam filled in the amount on the cheque Rob had already signed, she hoped Tom's uncle had a preconceived idea of how much kitting out a young rider would cost him. She couldn't help giving Tilly a sympathetic look as she glanced at Mimi's discarded jodhpurs and slightly faded blue jacket but Tilly didn't mind, Bits 'n Pieces looked amazing and she was here with *the gang.* She asked for nothing more.

Daisy finished her test with an absolutely square halt and an incline of her head in the direction of the judges and Jean-Pierre knew it was going to be extremely close - just a mark of two would separate his own daughter and Daisy, who he reminded himself was Jane's young cousin. He was, however, being a bit premature as eventually the penultimate rider entered the arena on a replica of his own daughter's pony.

In his Pony Club days, James had been in the event team and had always enjoyed the dressage. He and Maurice had found the flattest paddock at The Old Manor House – the groom had painted the letters in clear, black paint and a very acceptable dressage arena had been created. Every evening at exactly five forty five, James had religiously helped Fenella, and as another of Jane's nieces trotted in a dead straight line, Jean-Pierre acknowledged that without a doubt he was witnessing the winner. James was hanging on to Felix and Flicka who were each sucking a lollipop which James didn't really approve of but had bought in a final effort to bring an end to a fight which had suddenly erupted as the truculent twins both wanted to sit on his shooting stick.

Elizabeth was standing in the collecting ring watching carefully and waiting for Fenella to exit the arena. 'Beautiful, Fen. Good girl Poupée. That was a really nice, steady test.'

Sam was running up to them, 'Well done, Fen,' and Rosie trotted up to Poupée who had been her special pony for nearly two years.

'Darling, darling Poupée - she was brilliant, Fen.'

Mary and John were watching with Jane and Clara who had come to support her sister and much later would be there for Jacques. Susan was with them but as Fenella's test ended she stood up, telling Mary. 'I think I had better relieve James of those twins. I don't know whom they get their quarrelsome nature from. Certainly not from me I hope, and James is so placid it can't possibly be from him. I know we all think Ozzie is the difficult one but the triplets are always looking out for each other – Ozzie perhaps most of all.'

The triplets were enjoying a really good morning. As Tom

parked beside Dom and the horsebox, the first person Oscar saw was Clare Lewis. He put two fingers in his mouth and let out a piercing whistle, terrifying a solid cob, which was being held by an equally solid middle aged lady. The cob reared up – the shocked woman let go – but Oscar was completely unaware of the havoc he had caused as Dom set off in hot pursuit of the cob whilst Tom stammered his apologies to the now irate lady. Fortunately, Charles had just arrived and called out. 'Hi, Tom, how is the West family this morning?' and the owner of the cob which was now being returned to her by Dom, suddenly realized who she had been berating a few moments ago.

Oscar was returning to the family with Cassie and Clare Lewis. 'Come and meet all the boys in *the gang,'* he was shouting. 'Ollie, 'Lando, Josh, these are Cassie and Clare. They're coming to stay tomorrow – here, Gus and Rupert come and say hello.' He turned to Tom. 'You're looking a bit stressed, Dad.'

'Oscar, you need to go and apologise to that lady in the next horsebox.'

'What have I done, Dad?'

'That screeching whistle you emitted terrified her horse – it flew off over the showground, luckily Dom managed to catch it but she definitely was not amused.'

Plump ladies held no fears for Oscar - he tapped on the window, startling Betty Bunting who was pouring herself a cup of coffee from her thermos flask hoping it would help her get over the shock she had just endured as she had watched her beloved cob, Welcome Lad, flying in the direction of the main arena. The coffee splashed on to her jodhpurs making a dark stain in a very embarrassing place. She looked up to see the smiling face of a lad with piercing, blue eyes, gold curls and a scar running down the side of his face. Betty Bunting wound down the window, glowering at Oscar, who was not the least bit perturbed.

'Sorry – Dad says I frightened your horse. When I whistle my pony gallops up to me. You should train your horse. He would soon learn. Oh dear, have you spilt your coffee?'

Betty Bunting was not amused by Oscar's apparent unconcern. 'What does it look like, you cheeky little ragamuffin?'

'Cor – Ragamuffin. I like that. When our next foal arrives I might suggest we call it that if it's a boy. Thanks. I must get back to my pony – he gets a bit worried if I'm not with him. He's only got one eye you see. Sorry about your horse and I hope your jods dry before you go into the ring,' and with one more cheeky grin he helped Tom and Orlando unload Humbug and Jet Stream before riding with Rupert and Gus to join Clare and her bay pony, Flying High. Cassie and Snowman had already won the twelve two class and Josh and Oliver were sitting with her on the grass with the girl's mother and their young brother who was firmly fixed to a pair of reins.

Tom and Charles were busy in the practice area helping the boys and Clare get ready for the next class.

'No Dad today, Clare?' Tom asked.

'No, he's got a display, I think it's over the sea at Bournemouth but he's bringing us to your house tomorrow. Cassie and I are really excited. It's great we've all met up today but where is Rosie?'

'She's at a dressage day at the Pony Club with all the other girls,' Oscar told her. 'Annie is doing it too but she hasn't been riding very long – she is going to take her D. Test in the Christmas holidays.'

Charles answered his mobile, which was buzzing. 'That was Joanna,' he told the boys. 'Fenella and Poupée won the first test. Eloise and Daisy were equal second, Abby was fourth, Veronica Mawgan-Whitely fifth and Anne-Marie got a highly commended.'

Oscar looked pleased. 'Good, Charles, she can pin it up with my rosettes.'

'Your rosettes?'

'Oh, yes. I just keep one or two really special ones, like the first I won with Panky, then I give all the rest to Annie. She says she pins them on her bedroom wall with a little card underneath each one saying which of my ponies won them. I've never seen them cos boys don't go into girl's bedrooms do they, Charles?'

Charles kept a straight face. 'They most certainly don't, Oscar but Anne-Marie is a lucky girl to get all your lovely rosettes.'

'But we shall both look at them one day, Charles. Annie and I know that.'

'I am sure you will, Oz but now could you concentrate on Humbug, please?'

The boys and Clare all reached the jump off which was certainly fast and furious with Oscar and Humbug just prevailing over Gus and Hamlet with Orlando and Jet Stream in third Place. A boy unknown to the triplets was fourth and to her delight Clare and Flying High had scrambled into fifth place after Rupert and The March Hare had tried too hard to catch Humbug's time and run out at the penultimate jump.

Whenever other competitors caught sight of the golden haired triplets, more often than not being aided and abetted by their famous father overseeing their every move, they knew it was not impossible but highly unlikely that they would be able to beat one of the triplets, let alone all three of them.

Whilst Tom was devouring the contents of Sam's hamper, wondering how Rosie was faring with her dressage test, Sam was gathering the second set of girls, making sure to send Rosie to the loo with Mimi.

It was the largest group and Sam knew she was in for a long afternoon. James and Elizabeth had taken the twins and Poupée home as Fenella sat with the rest of the group ready to cheer on Rosie and the rest of *the gang.*

Joanna took a photograph of Mimi as she and Babushka trotted steadily into the arena. Sam had to admit the grey jacket did indeed look extremely elegant against Babushka's lighter grey coat and dark mane and tail. She noticed Tom's Uncle Rob and Simon sitting with Mary and Susan. They had come to watch Daisy but Rob had not seen fit to thank Sam for the hours she had spent helping his daughter or traipsing round Ashford and then Canterbury getting Daisy suitably kitted out. She decided his failed marriage and being forced to be a single parent must have turned him into this egoistical man. There was no sign of Tamara Adams but she noticed an attractive dark haired woman sitting between him and Simon. She looked harder and discovered her eyes weren't deceiving her. It was Clarissa Norton who had obviously come to watch Georgia.

Sam's eyes spanned the rest of the showground, travelling around the edge of the dressage arena. Suddenly she noticed a small, very round dog sitting on his master's knee. Giles was alone - a sad – dejected figure. She was just going to go and talk to him, when to her relief she saw David and Esther joining him, opening a bottle of wine and sharing it with him.

Clarissa didn't want to spend the afternoon with Robert and his obnoxious son. She had met him in the bar when she had been about to buy herself a glass of rosé wine before going in search of Georgia. A voice beside her had said. 'Come and share a bottle with me,' and somehow she had found herself sitting with a man who was almost a stranger, when she couldn't take her eyes of a familiar figure with a rotund dog called Herbie sitting on his knee less than fifty yards away from her.

Simon had grumbled that he didn't want to waste his morning watching his young sister, but he was trying to persuade his father to buy him a new tennis racquet and was well aware he needed to get into Robert's good books, so he capitulated with a bad grace but his mood changed when as soon as he arrived at the Equitation Centre his eyes had fallen on *the chick* who sat behind him every day on the school bus and who appeared to be a good friend of his arch enemy Joshua West of whom there was no sign that morning. His eyes didn't leave the elegant rider on the grey mare. *'Yes',* he decided, *'some chick indeed.'*

Robert was so engrossed trying to hold Clarissa's attention he didn't notice that his son was extremely preoccupied – fascinated by Charles Wright-Smith's *'little minx,'* who was currently halting in front of the judge's box unaware of the scrutiny she was under.

She went and stood with Georgia and Charlotte who were waiting in the shade under a large oak tree. Simon got up and walked casually towards the three girls.

Georgia was the next competitor and as she trotted into the arena, Clarissa stood up saying, 'Excuse me, Robert I just want to have a word with someone,' and to Rob's dismay and annoyance he watched as she walked towards a group which contained a small dog.

Giles had noticed her stand up and leave Rob. He started as he realized she was walking towards him – reaching his side – sitting down beside him saying. 'I'm nervous, Giles. I'm not used to seeing our daughter on her pony.'

Giles took a huge gulp of his Chablis, his mouth suddenly feeling like sawdust but he moved up and patted the grass beside him as David poured her a glass of the wine.

Clarissa already felt a little unsteady after the wine Robert had been plying her with but she accepted the glass David was offering her.

As she sat down and stroked Herbie, Giles felt his heart crashing and feelings flooding his body that had lain dormant for many years. He tried to concentrate on Georgia and her test but all he was conscious of was Clarissa's arm touching his bare skin. *'Christ,'* he thought, *'this is heaven and hell rolled together. God help me. I love her so much.'*

He suddenly realized she was asking him a question. 'I'm sorry Clarissa, I'm afraid I was miles away.' *'God what a lie,'* he thought to himself, *'I couldn't be closer.'*

'I asked if you thought Georgia had done well.'

At least now he could laugh naturally. 'I've no idea, Clarissa, all

I know is that ponies have four legs, a tail, and cost a bloody lot of money to feed, but as long as Georgia is happy then that is all that can possibly matter.'

Georgia had finished her test and had now ridden up to Giles. 'Dad, wasn't Fire Cracker super?' Then she suddenly noticed her mother.

'Mummy, you're here.'

'Of course Georgia, darling. I wanted to watch you but I was nervous, then I saw Dad and I wanted us to watch you together. I don't know anything about dressage but it looks quite complicated.'

'Um. Catherine Wheel is looking good, Esther. I'm going to stand under that tree. It's rather hot for Cracker in the sun. You'll wait until the results are announced and see how I've done, won't you, Mum?'

'Of course. I'll wait here with Dad and funny little Herbie.'

'Oh bliss – oh hell' – Giles was thinking both at the same time.

Mimi was relieved when she saw Georgia making her way to join her under the old tree. Simon was standing extremely close to her, making a play of patting Babushka, who she was sitting on – every so often letting his hand brush her thigh. She pretended to be a sophisticated young woman but in reality was just a young girl about to embark on her teenage years. She was not certain how to cope with this latest phase in her life but she suddenly knew she was missing the company of both Joshua and Jacques, who talked about their ponies, the forthcoming swimming gala at the local leisure Centre and the British Grand Prix at Silverstone, which they had recorded. She didn't want Simon's hands touching her knee and her thigh. She wasn't nearly ready. She looked for her mother and caught sight of her with Mary and Simon's father who was fully aware of what his son was up to. He walked up to Simon, thoroughly fed up that his afternoon appeared to have been wasted as he could see the object of his thoughts looked unlikely to leave her ex-husband and his friends. He addressed Simon – not unaware of the uneasy look in Mimi's eyes.

'Come on, Si. Daize has finished. Let's be on our way. I'm going to the Bear for a pint or two.'

Simon glared at his father. 'I'm fine here, Dad.'

'I think not, Simon. Come on and I think your Mum is looking for you, Mimi.'

It was Mimi's chance to escape. She rode over to Joanna and Mary and watched Charlotte who was the final rider finish her test. With a sense of relief she noticed Simon and Robert West disappearing from view. She picked up her mobile, *'Josh, have you jumped yet?'*

'Yea, Mimi, it was great. Ganger just beat Panky and Pie, now I'm waiting for the Foxhunter to begin. How about you?'

'The test went well. Charlotte's just finishing hers but Georgia's looked really good. And Josh, good luck to your Dad. I'll see you tomorrow.'

'Yea, we've been with Clare and Cassie all day. They're great. Your dad says we can bring the ponies to Lake House in the afternoon and he'll give us a lesson, then we can swim and Sheila and Erica will cook us a Bar –b -que.'

'How nice, Josh?'

'Who?'

'Cassie and Clare.'

'Good fun. Now I must go. There are only two more to jump before me – I must give my mobile to Dad. Cheers,' and he left Mimi wondering just how much fun Josh was going to have with Cassie and Clare who would be staying at Woodcutters.

She sighed. Growing up was not all it was cut out to be. She was learning that very quickly.

An hour later, as she was waiting for Jacques to perform his more intricate test, she heard her mobile. *'HI, Mimi, how did you do?'*

'Actually, Josh, I am holding a small, silver cup and a new head collar for Babs.'

'You mean you won?'

'Yes, and Georgia was second.'

'Wow, we'll celebrate tomorrow. I'll chuck you both in the deep end when we're swimming in Charles' pool.'

'Beast – but Josh – Mum says all the gang are going to Camber on Tuesday before the weather breaks which it is supposed to do at the end of the week. I want to do something special with you.'

'Special, Mimi. Where?'

'At Camber. In the sand dunes."

'Mimi!! We're not ready for a steamy relationship.'

'Don't be an idiot, Josh. I want to take a spade and find your birthday present. The one I buried. I want to give it to you again.'

'O.K. We'll find it, but Mimi you are nearly thirteen, going on seventeen. I'm afraid I am nearly thirteen going on eleven. I don't want to grow up for a very long time but I promise we will find that pen and pencil and I will look after it until one day our ages will have converged and will be running in two straight lines – that's a promise. Now Dad is about to jump Alicia – see you tomorrow.'

Mimi switched off her mobile and went to find Jacques. She was still Charles' *'little minx'* but she was happier than she had been for a very long time.

Anne-Marie had forgotten to take her mobile, but Rosie's was ringing. *'Rosie, it's Oz.'*

'Oz, what do you want?'

'Annie.'

Rosie laughed. *'She's right here, we're just watching Jacques,'* and she handed her mobile to Anne-Marie. She heard her friend's voice, still with its strong French accent.

'Ozzie – where are you?'

'Watching Dad. He's just jumped a clear round with Alicia – his new mare.'

'And how was Panky?'

'Not as good as Buggy who won the thirteen two class. Panky was second – who would want a brother with a cracking pony called Ganger? Still, second was bl--- good.' He quickly managed to bite his tongue before the forbidden word came out. *'But Annie, you were brilliant. Rosie says you got a rosette.'*

'Well, yes, Ozzie but actually everyone got one.'

'That doesn't matter. It's taking part that's important, not winning, Annie.'

Anne-Marie smiled to herself recalling Oscar's determination, desperate to win whoever he was riding – however monumental the task – furious with himself if he should happen to make a mistake.

'Of course it is, Ozzie,' she replied tongue in cheek, *'I'm just following your example and you can have my rosette.'*

Oscar sighed – *'Perfect, Annie. I will hang it next to the first one I got with Panky -- and the last one with Whisky,'* he added poignantly.

Anne-Marie was smiling happily as she handed the phone back to Rosie. 'Oz is just perfect,' she informed his sister - who didn't agree with her friend one little bit.

Georgia was proudly displaying the blue rosette now tied to Fire Cracker's bridle and glancing rather dubiously at the rather technical book entitled *The Rudiments of Dressage,* which had been her prize. She rather envied Mimi the smart head collar she was holding but she was happy, principally because her pony had performed so well and secondly because at least for this afternoon her Mum and her Dad were together.

Giles was telling her. 'I'm going to make a move now your test is over, Georgia but we are so proud of you. I'm going to take Herbie home. I think he's had enough of the sun. It's suddenly getting very warm.'

'Fine, I'll see you later; I'll ride home with Charlotte. We want to see how Jacques gets on in the next test.'

‘Just take care then, sweetheart and I’ll see you later.’

He stood up with Bertie and watched as Clarissa struggled rather unsteadily to her feet, kissing Georgia, telling her to come and have a meal at La Casa whenever she wanted and to bring Charlotte with her.

As Georgia trotted back to the shade of the oak tree to re-join Mimi and Charlotte, Clarissa swayed, clutching Giles shirt. ‘Oops – too much wine, I think. I didn’t realize how many glasses I was consuming. My legs feel rather strange.’

Giles kept hold of her. ‘Herbie and I will walk home via the green. I think you are in need of a strong arm, Clarissa.’

They said goodbye to David and Esther, thanking them for their hospitality and with Herbie rolling on one side of him and Clarissa likewise on the other, Giles set off in the direction of the green.

Clarissa stumbled several times and Giles intensified his hold. He wasn’t certain how he could stem the emotions that were racking his body but somehow he managed to hold a reasonably normal conversation, mainly about Georgia and Fire Cracker.

As they reached the green, Giles sat on the seat opposite La Casa sul Verde. He turned towards Clarissa and for one blissful moment she thought he was going to kiss her until her hopes were dashed as he said. ‘You wanted to discuss Georgia’s teeth the other evening, Clarissa.’

‘G –g – Georgia’s teeth?’ Clarissa whispered in disappointment.

‘Yes, you told me you wanted to take her to the dentist to get his opinion as to whether he thought she would need a brace.’

‘Did – did I?’

“Yes, but personally I don’t think she does. Her teeth are almost as perfect as her mother’s.”

‘Oh – then perhaps I won’t bother – but there’s something else I need to tell you.’

‘About Georgia?”

“No – no. About me.’

‘You’re not about to have an affair with that obnoxious Robert West are you? Or are you about to see somebody else?’

‘Would you mind if I was, Gi?’

‘Please don’t call me that and you know damn well I would.’

‘I am seeing someone actually, Gi,’ she told him, ignoring his request.

‘God. Come on Herbie – home,’ and he went to stand up, holding the little dog under his arm. Clarissa pushed him unceremoniously back onto the seat. ‘I’m seeing a counselor, Gi.’

‘A counselor? Why?’

‘I’m having a course of hypnotherapy, actually.’

‘Hypnotherapy?’

‘To try to overcome my phobia. I want that more than anything else in this world.’

‘Why?’

‘So that I can be with you, near you, love you. It’s all I want in this world. You’ve always been there, even when I was with Paul. I want to beat this ridiculous fear. I have to, Gi.’

‘Is this the wine talking, or is it my Clarissa?’

‘It’s definitely not the wine, Gi.’

‘Please stop calling me that – you don’t know what it’s doing to me.’ But Giles arms had crept round her. He let go of Herbie’s lead as he pulled her towards him, kissing her very gently.

‘I always did say you had a very kissable mouth, Clarry,’ and he kissed her again, pulling her closer. The kiss lasted a long, long time and as they finally pulled apart, Clarissa realized her bare leg had been pressing against his jeans and she hadn’t even given the prosthetic leg underneath the blue denim one single thought.

She heard Giles sigh as he asked her, ‘Clarry, you are doing this for me?’

‘I’m doing it for both of us, Gi.’

'Let's take things very slowly, Clarry. Just dates – fun together. I couldn't be hurt again - I just couldn't take it, but I'll come to La Casa for a meal on Wednesday and maybe afterwards you would make me a very special cup of coffee in your apartment. I'll ask Esther to look out for Georgia. Could that be our first date?'

Clarissa squeezed his hand. 'It most certainly could. A new beginning, but now if I am sober enough I must go and prepare the sweets for our diners this evening.'

'And I must go and retrieve Herbie form old Mrs. Asquith.' and he pointed to a very elderly lady who was being besieged by the rotund little Herbie.

As Jacques was winning the penultimate test with an outstanding score, Rob West was drinking a beer in the garden of The Bear whilst, much to his disgust, Simon was sipping a mango and apple J.2 O. through a straw, enduring a long, stern lecture from his father. This was an extremely unusual occurrence but earlier that afternoon Rob had been watching Simon with Mimi and he did not like what he had seen. He was certain it was no accident that Simon's hands were touching Mimi's thighs and this was not to be tolerated even by the easy going Rob. He had been sitting with Mary and Joanna; he had turned to the latter and asked. 'How old are your two, Joanna?'

'Rupert is eleven and Mimi will be thirteen a week before Christmas,' she had informed him, well aware of the reason for his question. She was not blind and she was going to have a long talk to Mimi that evening.

'Only thirteen,' Rob had replied, looking slightly taken aback. 'I thought she was older than that.'

Joanna looked straight at him. 'She likes to think she is Robert but believe you me, I've got my eyes firmly attuned to what my young daughter is up to.'

Now, in the garden at The Bear, Rob was asking his son. 'Do you know how old Mimi Wright-Smith is?'

Simon laughed. 'Not yet but I shall soon be finding out.'

'Too right you will, Simon. Like this very minute. Mimi has not yet had her thirteenth birthday. I suggest – no – I insist you leave her well alone before there is serious trouble. Charles Wright-Smith's daughter is NOT to be trifled with. You could be in deep trouble. I suggest you either treble your enthusiasm for sport or stick to the girls who hang around the village green, preferably the former of those two options. Mimi Wright-Smith and any of Joshua West's gang are totally off limits and for once you will listen to what I am telling you. Is that totally understood?'

'She's a stupid little cow anyway. She must be if she's a friend of my cousin.' Inwardly Simon was fuming but for almost the first time in his life he was in awe of his father. He stood up, leaving both his drink and Rob – 'I'm off – I'm going to the tennis club and if you buy me that racquet I've got my eyes on I'll forget Mimi Wright-Smith and that stupid gang.'

Rob sighed and as he had done for so many years, in fact ever since his wife had left him with two young children, he pandered to his spoilt son, putting his hand in his pocket, pulling out his wallet and handing him a wad of notes. 'Oh go on then, - buy the bloody thing.'

Simon made his way to the tennis club, happy in the knowledge he still could, as he had always been able, twist his father round his very smallest finger.

At the show the other side of London, Tom was kissing a girl – but as usual it possessed four legs, a mane and a tail. Alicia had just won the Grade C. Class. It was their first competition and he was thrilled. She had soared like a bird - his first intuition had been correct – she had all the scope in the world and he knew their love affair was going to be mutual.

He put her back in the horsebox giving her a handful of pony nuts and wandered over to the smaller arena where Charles was sitting with Suzie Lewis, watching her daughters in the races. He sat next to Charles. 'Congrats on winning the Foxhunter with the Blarney Stone earlier, Charles, he looks to be a super animal. How long is he going to have the Lake House Prefix in front of his name?'

Tom was well aware he and Charles had a totally different frame of mind when it came to parting with their horses. Apart from the long departed little Ninepins, he could only recall one horse that Charles had a true affinity with and that was his beloved mare, Wishful Thinking, now older even than Black Satin but who was still grazing peacefully in the small paddock nearest to Lake House where Charles could see her from the window in his study. Tom's horses meant everything in the world to him they were an extension to his family. Sam had always acknowledged that and they were all a part of her life too, even the notorious Satin and now the devilish Opal. Charles saw his horses as a boost to his ever-increasing bank account – he respected them all and was fastidious about their well-being but he was a philosophical man – every good offer had to be weighed up and considered and that Tom was certain would be the case with this latest grey horse with whom earlier on Charles had cleared jump after jump and had left the arena with a satisfied smile on his handsome, yet still roguish face.

The only offers he never listened to were when they involved his children's ponies – much as he loved his bank balance, there were two things he loved even more and those were his wife, Joanna, and his children.

Tom grinned at Charles. 'Waiting for an offer, Charles?'

'Not just yet, my friend, this one feels good. I'll get him to H.O.Y.S. before I think of off loading him.' And Tom had no valid reason to doubt him. He glanced around the show ground to see what his boys were up to. He thought he could hear the triplets urging Cassie and Clare to success in the races, which were just finishing, and the next moment all the boys were descending on them as they watched the girls collecting their prizes in the arena.

'Bloody good show,' Oscar was shouting, not without receiving a very straight look from the portly lady whose cob he had upset earlier in the day. She had been watching her nephew who had just been beaten by Clare and was not in the highest of spirits. 'Your son's language is disgraceful,' she told Tom.

He laughed. 'I know it is. I'm afraid he takes after his mother!!' To which the lady turned away in disgust saying. 'What hope for her children then,' leaving Tom feeling more than a little ashamed of himself. He would tell Sam, he knew she would forgive him, especially when she discovered her servant had triumphed with his mistresses' horse!!

Tom left Charles and bought six ice creams and an iced lolly for Suzie's little boy and sat round the edge of the arena. He called Sam's mobile only to discover she was in the stables at Theobald's Place undoing a multitude of plaits. *'I haven't jumped The Wizard yet, Sammy.* I *should think it would be about half past eight before we are home.'*

He wasn't altogether surprised when she told him. *'Don't worry, darling, I've made a big chicken salad. You can eat it whenever you get here. Rosie and I are going to have ours as soon as I've finished unplaiting, then we're going to put up the camp beds in Rosie's bedroom for Cassie and Clare.'*

'You're a million dollar girl, my Samantha and I think you are going to appreciate your servant too. Alicia won the Grade C. Class so I think I am due my just reward My Lady,' and he gave a wicked laugh.

"I will consider what it is worth, West. I doubt I shall ever employ such a worthy servant again."

'To right you bloody won't - for the very good reason this servant is never going to give in his notice,' and he switched off his mobile before she could reply. He looked up to see the fat lady staring at him askance.

'Your poor children, both parents using the most appalling language I dread to think what they will be like in ten years time.'

'I can assure you,' Tom told the now red-faced lady. 'If they take after their mother, they will be the luckiest youngsters on this earth.' To which she had no answer.

He made his way back to the horsebox to fetch The Wizard, whistling happily as he thought of his mistress waiting for him at Woodcutters, the girl who had made his heart rock for as long as he could remember – his beloved wife Sam.

The Open Class was small with only fifteen entries. The day was proving to be an excellent one for Charles as Stormy Waters was the easy winner. The Wizard jumped two clear rounds but Tom didn't hurry him. It was many months since the horse's last competition and Tom was more than happy with fourth place and a completely sound horse.

Several hours later, Tom was holding his mistress, telling her. 'You've got a wonderful horse, My Lady.'

'So lot's to look forwards to then, West?'

'Oh, God yes I'm full of hope, but just kiss me again, my Sammy. I think just being your husband is even more satisfactory, but whichever I am, my darling, we are *ad infinitum'* and he kissed her again for good measure.

The Casa sul Verde was finally in darkness. The diners had departed and at last Clarissa was gazing out of her window at the top of the building. She could see Theobald's Place with just a light or two burning on the landing. She looked to the left of the big house at the row of four cottages, letting her eyes dwell on Number Two. She could just make out the back of Giles' head as he bent over his computer. Herbert Holmer was on the brink of solving the trio of murders in Istanbul - the book was nearing its end - soon a new chapter would be starting in the detective's life and maybe, just maybe too, in the life of the man who had created the dapper Herbert Holmer, the author Patsy Sanders, alias Captain Giles Norton V.C.

CHAPTER 31

Tom was already on his way to the rehab clinic in Surrey, whilst Mike and Suzie were driving their Range Rover and trailer over the Queen Elizabeth 2nd Bridge, which spanned the River Thames, dividing the counties of Essex and Kent.

They were soon in the heart of the weald of Kent, admiring the unfamiliar oast houses which were a feature of this part of the South East of England, They were both taken aback when they pulled up in front of Woodcutters and saw the beautiful old cottage with its panoramic view over the lake, stretching as far as Charles and Joanna's Queen Anne House which lay a short way beyond.

Sam and Rosie rushed out to greet them. It was the first time Sam had met the Lewis family but before two minutes had elapsed they were laughing and joking like old friends.

'I'll open the yard gates,' Sam told Mike. 'Tom says leave your trailer here for the week – he presumed you wouldn't be needing it. Our groom, Jules will help you push it back beside the small horse box.'

Mike could barely answer – he was completely taken aback by the size of the immaculate yard and the blocks of stables, which Tom had added over the years and now consisted of eighteen. Mike had already noted the massive cream horsebox with *L.H.S.* written in italics in gold letters on both sides, then he stared askance at the smaller box in the same cream livery and the immaculate automatic two horse box, which now replaced Sam's ill fated trailer.

There were post and rail paddocks reaching as far as the lake and horses and ponies abounding everywhere, including two gorgeous foals grazing with their mothers and two other heavily pregnant mares.

He turned to Sam who he thought was even more stunning than the surroundings he was standing in. Mike was a harmless flirt who appreciated a beautiful woman but he was also a loyal husband and he never went further than very lighthearted flirtations but he laughed as he told her. 'And I thought your husband taught the local kids to ride – but I got my own back – he thought I was going to fly him to Amsterdam or Brussels in a crummy 737 – so we're even Stevens I guess. Where is Tom by the way? Is he out on one of his horses?'

'No, he'll be home for lunch – traffic permitting,' and she told Suzie and Mike the sad tale of Adrian and his little family.

Having unloaded Clare and Cassie's ponies and put them together in one of the smallest paddocks next to Jet Stream and Le Duc – the seven children were tearing round like maniacs – visiting every paddock, whilst Mike manfully held on to Jonty who was struggling to join them.

'Come in and have a freshen up, then we'll take a drink out into the garden.'

'A soft one for me, please, Sam. I'm afraid I never drink when I'm either driving or flying. It's not worth the risk – an accident isn't always your fault as you obviously know only too well after your groom's sad experience.'

Suzie was staring at the beams in the kitchen and the original slate tiles on the floor. She could see through the open door into the sitting room. 'That inglenook is to die for,' she told Sam.

'Well you're welcome to a tour of the cottage – actually Tom and I are pretty proud of it. Tom and Justin Wright-Smith were riding together when they were teenagers when they stumbled on the cottage, neglected and almost hidden by the trees. They could just see the old chimneys. Justin took one look and turned away, he hated the spiders and the cobwebs but Tom went inside – he fell in love with it. A couple of days later he said he had a surprise to show me. We rode here one evening – he took me upstairs and we gazed across to the lake. He promised me one day it would be our home. He jumped the Puissance at The Horse of the Year Show that year – Satin and he won whilst I fainted. He was only seventeen but he wanted the money to buy the cottage from Charles. In the end, Charles had the cottage restored and gave it to Tom on his eighteenth birthday. That was the day we moved in here together.'

'Goodness – so how old were you?'

'Sixteen. Mummy wasn't too pleased but Tom and I had squatted here as often as we could before Charles had it restored. Charles is a fantastic boss but then he has the best rider in the world at his yard. We used the money Satin had won to enlarge the cottage. We always knew we wanted a big family.'

'So you've known Tom since you were a teenager?'

'Longer than that, I fell in love with my prince when I was in a wheelchair –look,' and she showed them the photograph of Tom and Twinkletoes in the garden at Honeysuckle Cottage, smiling at a little girl who was trying to struggle out of her wheelchair.

'I thought I was Snow White,' she laughed, 'and my prince had come to save me, and that's exactly what he did. He spent hours and hours helping me to walk and to ride. There is no one else in this world as kind as Tom, I'm absolutely certain. He would do anything to help any one and I know that is what he is going to do for poor old Adrian, not to mention Amy and dear little Molly. If you are really blown away by old houses, we could walk across the fields to Tom's childhood home, Old Tiles Farmhouse. It goes back hundreds of years. It has king beams and a dragon beam and enormous old inglenook fireplaces and wonderful old stables added in the Victorian era. Tom's Mum and Dad are brilliant people. I'm sure John would be delighted to give you a guided tour, he's terribly proud of his home. His family has lived there for over three hundred years. It used to be a big sheep farm but now John has only got a few Jacobs. He and Mary have turned the farmhouse into a B.and B. mainly for the visitors to the Equestrian Centre who come from all over Europe and they let the lovely old oast house which Tom and John had restored for holiday lets. It's really popular. I'll ask Tom if Jonty can ride Twink. He's rather an old gentleman now but I'm sure he would enjoy a walk to the farm. - We can ask him now; I can hear his car in the drive.'

Tom greeted Suzie and Mike effusively. 'Smashing to see you again, Mike. We had a good day with your girls yesterday in Bedfordshire. The kids all did really well.'

'You are modest, Tom. I gather you and your boss didn't do too badly either.'

'Well, it was what I would term a good day all round. What's cooking, my Sammy? It certainly smells yummy.'

'Roast lamb – one of the Jacobs I'm afraid. Don't tell Rosie for goodness sake, she's verging on being a vegetarian already. How was Adrian? How did he cope with the journey?'

'Yea, he was O.K. with the journey but he seems a bit stressed about living with Amy. He won't acknowledge he has a right to be there – not even after Amy showed him their marriage certificate. The problem is, he can't relate to being Adam Carstairs – he can't relate to having a past at all. Poor, little Amy, Anna was there. Justin is actually giving the kids their lunch then I think all *the gang* is going up to the school. Charles and Justin are going to give them a workout and then a swim afterwards.'

'Tom, I suggested Suzie and Mike walk over to the farm after lunch. The old beams fascinate Suzie – your dad would be in his element!! Could Jonty ride Twink – the little fellow would love that?'

'Sure. Twink is in the paddock with Satin. Actually I might ride Sat over to the farm – he could do with a change of scenery, do you fancy a ride on Clem, Mike? She's a doddle until she see's a jump and even then she is a cool as a cucumber. I can lend you a hat.'

'It's years since I've ridden anything bigger than Clare's pony?' Mike laughed, 'but it does sound a great idea. Is that the big bay you were jumping in Essex the other week?'

'Sure is but she's a real mother hen, I promise you. Sam even let me do a puissance on her a short while ago. That says a lot I can tell you!! The girls can walk with Twink. I'll just give Mum a call to warn her we're coming.'

He came back grinning. 'Dad is already planning his tour of the house and Mum says definitely tea afterwards – and Mum's teas are to die for I can assure you.'

'That's amazing – after that I think we should reluctantly wend our way home. We will say cheerio to the girls before they all go off to Lake House. The traffic in the tunnel may not be too funny at that hour but at least my hawk doesn't need feeding or exercising. That's one advantage it's got over your horses!!'

The gang was finally ready and with Josh and Oscar, who was noisily shouting instructions to the back of the line, they trotted past the lake on their way to the indoor school. Fortunately, Cassie and Clare were used to riding in David Mason's indoor school when they had their lessons with him, and they were also used to being well disciplined, so they took Charles' instructions and criticisms seriously, knowing they were learning an awful lot in a very short time.

Justin took over after the first hour and the afternoon immediately became light-hearted and fun as they did Chase-me-Charlie and seven barrel jumping as well as a speed competition all of which Cassie and Clare were well acquainted with.

They all watched in awe as Oscar and Panky jumped higher and higher in the Chase-me Charlie as his exuberant nature got the better of him and he couldn't resist showing off in front of the absorbed group of girls, until even Justin realized the jump was getting over limits. 'No more, Oz – we all know that pony is a machine. You don't have to remind us.'

They finally turned the ponies out in two paddocks, putting Sailor Boy and Flying High in a stable. Two minutes later they were diving into the pool whilst Erica and Sheila watched over them at the same time as they cooked an enormous pile of beef burgers. It was certainly a day Cassie and Clare would never forget.

Whilst the youngsters were enjoying their day, Mike had fetched his camera and before they left Woodcutters, Suzie was taking a photograph of him perched rather nervously on Clementine beside Tom on his old friend Black Satin who was pulling the ugliest face he could muster at the huge bay mare. Mike was far more nervous of the black monster than of his own enormous mount that was standing like a solid rock.

By the time they were half way to Old Tiles he had completely relaxed and as Satin gave an enormous buck they proceeded at a steady canter to the Victorian stables where they would leave the horses for the afternoon. With the horses settled, they could see Twink in the distance with Sam leading him and Suzie walking on the other side with one hand on little Jonty's leg. They waited until they reached the small paddock where the two donkeys, Cobweb and Moth were standing under their oak tree and let Twinkletoes free to join his old friends.

Mike took his camera into the house and was soon snapping the amazing roof structure inside the attics at the old farmhouse as John showed him the king beams and the old dragon beam that had held the old farmhouse together for hundreds of years.

As everyone who made Mary's acquaintance for the first time did, Suzie felt she had known this beautiful woman all her life, as she looked at the enormous inglenook fireplaces in both the main sitting room and the old dining room which was now the room the many visitors enjoyed. Mary showed her the bread ovens in the corner of the fireplaces and the ratchets from which the huge joints had once hung as they had roasted over the wood fires.

After the tour of the house they walked to the Oast House which Tom and John were so proud of and then showed Suzie the Victorian stables where Satin and Clementine were pulling at a full manger of hay.

Suzie and Mike openly gasped as they sat in the kitchen in front of a table laden with one of Mary's notorious high teas. There was a selection of egg, salad and ham sandwiches, a chocolate Guinness and a lemon drizzle cake and to finish with a bowl of raspberries topped with meringue and fresh cream.

Mike was asking Tom when the next jumping show would be after the one they were going to attend this coming Sunday.

'The weekend before the children go back to school. That's the first one in September.'

'Is the Oast free?' he asked Mary.

'I'm afraid it's booked right until Christmas but you could always rent one of the yurts. They're great. Ask Tom to show you them as you ride back, Mike. They're only a stone's throw from the path you take across the field. If you fancy one, let Tom or Sam know and they will book it through the Equitation Centre. If you should happen to fancy coming to the New Year Show, we've just had a cancellation for the oast. The family who were coming has got a big silver wedding in Germany they feel they ought to attend. They phoned me this morning to let me know.'

Mike and Suzie had no hesitation – 'Done, Swallow Tail will be safely in her stable.'

'Who is Swallow Tail?' John asked. 'Have you a horse, too?'

Mike smiled, 'No, she's is my Hawk.'

'Your Hawk?'

'Yes, I'm a pilot. Swallow Tails. You know.'

John looked impressed. 'Swallow Tails – Goodness it seems a long time ago that I took Tom and Justin Wright-Smith to the seaside to watch the display.'

Tom held Clementine whilst Mike looked inside the yurt as they made their way back to Woodcutters. In no time at all he was instructing Tom to book one of the larger ones for them for the first week in September. We won't tell the girls, we'll keep it as an end of the holiday surprise. Clare is off to the local Grammar School; it will take her mind off the coming ordeal. We will take it for the whole week, Tom. I shall most probably be doing a display on the Saturday, but Suzie will be fine with the kids, especially with your super parents so near. I would feel quite happy to leave her here with the girls and his little nibs.'

His nibs was sitting on Twinkletoes as they re-joined the girls. 'Trot – trot' – He was demanding.

'Twinkletoes is too old. He's almost as old as I am.'

'Are you very old?' the little boy asked Tom.

Tom laughed and gave Sam a special look, which didn't go unnoticed by Suzie or Mike. 'Not too old to enjoy the good things in life,' and Sam blushed as she recalled her servant's behaviour the previous evening.

Having waved au revoir to Suzie and Mike and after a phone call from Josh saying they were still at Lake House consuming beef burgers, Tom grabbed the quad bike and with Sam on his knee, shot through the woods to Shepherd's Cottage. Sam was clutching a plate of cold lamb and salad, which had been left over from lunch and a gooseberry flan.

Adrian was sitting on a seat on the small patio at the rear of the cottage with little Molly peacefully asleep on his knee. Tom joined him whilst Sam discovered Amy in tears in the spare bedroom, hanging Adrian's clothes in the wardrobe.

She put her arms round her asking. 'What is it Amy? I realize it must be an intolerable situation for you.'

'He refuses to sleep in our room, Sam. He says it's not in his nature to sleep with a woman he doesn't know. He just won't acknowledge he is Adrian Carstairs, he says he thinks he once knew someone called Adrian, he says the name seems familiar. Oh, Sam, what am I to do?'

'Amy, all you can do at the moment is be patient. Try not to get upset when he says he doesn't know you. It's bad enough for you and Miriam and George, but imagine what it must be like for him. He is probably terrified. He loves little Molly that is quite apparent. Try to treat him as a really good friend who is staying with you and one day he may want more – or some small thing could jog his memory. You know Tom and I are only yards away and Anna and Justin aren't far either. I know Justin can sometimes be tactless but really he's got a heart of gold. He and Anna will watch over you and little Molly I am certain. Now see if you can at least enjoy a meal together in the sunshine and let him do as much as he is willing for Molly. She may well be a very keen factor in this wretched scenario.'

Whilst Tom and Sam had been entertaining Suzie and Mike, Justin had driven to Headcorn aerodrome. Gus had chosen not to come. He had wanted to be with *the gang,* rather pouring scorn on the small aerodrome, so Noah was sitting in his booster seat singing to himself as Justin turned in through the gates and drove to the car park. A few minutes later, a plane circled over head before landing on the airstrip and soon Justin was aware of a tall, dark haired man, dressed casually in grey denim jeans and a dark blue T. shirt, accompanied by a young lad and a slightly smaller girl similarly clad in jeans and paler blue T. shirts. He decided to drive back via Lake House and trust *the gang* would take pity on them.

After a short time, another young man, obviously the pilot emerged from the plane and Justin took Noah from his booster seat and made his way to the reception area.

Peregrine was certainly no shrinking violet. He held out a large hand and informed Tom, 'I'm Peregrine Percival and this is my cousin Ptomley.' He pushed the two youngsters forwards, 'and these are Cornelius and Columbine.'

Justin smiled and shook hands with the young boy and girl. Cornelius faintly resembled his older half brother.

'My cousin says he will wander round Headcorn for a couple of hours and meet us back here at six o'clock.'

'The village is quite a walk from here. Can I drop him in the centre?'

'That's O.K. he's got his folding bike.' And for the first time,

Justin noticed the folding machine the slightly older of the two men was carrying.

'Fine, let's get going then,' and he led Peregrine, Cornelius and Columbine towards the Range Rover.

The boy and girl climbed into the back with Noah and his booster seat between them, eyeing each one with a large amount of interest and a small amount of suspicion.

Justin endeavored to make small talk but it was obvious Peregrine's main focal point was whether any other grooms worked at the stables and if so how many were of the female gender.

'None at my stables where you will be based. I like my kids to do as much as possible for their ponies. In the winter they will have to be brought in from the paddocks and given hay but in the summer when the evenings are light they are always riding them and I expect Gus and Abby to make certain they have every thing they need. My groom would be expected to drive them to the shows on some occasions but they often go with my Dad's two youngsters, Mimi and Rupert who are my half brother and sister. My Dad has several grooms. How many horses we have between us vary from time to time but there are usually around twenty excluding the kid's ponies. We do bring on young horses and sell them, that's part of our scheme and we also have a number of brood mares, mainly our retired show jumpers. All my Dad's grooms live on the premises. There's Erica and Sheila,'

Peregrine interrupted Justin sharply. 'Two girls?'

Justin laughed – 'Girls!! That word does not quite describe them, especially Erica but she is the salt of the earth and Sheila worked for my dad when I was a young lad. They're both great – actually they are an item – they live in the flat over the garage. Then there is Sally who is married to Dad's gardener and Dom who is our newest partner at Lake House Stables. He's great – a frog - but a super chap and so is his French wife, Genevieve. They have one young daughter of twelve, called Anne-Marie.

Tom West is our third partner. You must have heard of him. He's a pain in my backside as well as being my best pal for the past twenty odd years. He and his wife Sam and their five kids live about a quarter of a mile away in a cottage on the edge of my Dad's estate. They've got four boys. Triplets called Oscar, Orlando and Oliver, Josh who is twelve and little Rosie who is nine, and my son's special friend. She's a brilliant little rider. Dad says she's the best nine year old he has ever come across. Josh could be a really good pal for your brother, Cornelius.

Unfortunately Tom's groom had a terrible accident and at the moment he has a Canadian brother and sister working for him for six months at the end of which, hopefully Adrian will have recovered but he suffered severe head injuries and he still doesn't even remember who he is. Hannah and Jules live in a small oast house that belongs to Tom and Sam. You won't see much of them – just every now and again at the shows. They work exclusively for Tom. I have a gardener and his wife who helps Anna in the house. They live in the lodge with their daughter who is just about to start at the Grammar School in Ashford.'

'What's this Grammar School like?'

Justin laughed. 'Well, I went to the Grammar in Canterbury and so did Lord Thornley, alias James Cotton who lives in the Old Manor House and we haven't turned out too badly.'

'What about Columbine? Where do the girls go to school?'

'All the girls go to the Grammar in Ashford. My own daughter is too young but my sister, Mimi started there last year. Dad seems more than satisfied.'

They had arrived at Theobald's Place having dropped Cornelius and Columbine at Lake House. Mimi was soon weighing up Cornelius – offering him Lord of the Rings for the afternoon, which he had no hesitation in accepting. Charles asked Sheila to fetch Groucho. The Mawgan-Whitelys had gone to London for the day and soon Columbine was suitably mounted and Justin drove off to Theobald's Place with Peregrine.

'So, no scheming women lurking around the place?' he asked

Justin, who recognized from his tone of voice that Peregrine was totally serious, which was a feeling that was endorsed, when the would be groom added. 'They're a species that should never have been put on this earth.'

'*Crikey!!*' Justin, who like his father believed women were one of the main reasons for living, thought, '*this bloke has a serious problem, but there is something I like about him*'.

Anna brought them a cup of tea and a large piece of Mary's chocolate Guinness cake, which she had purchased at the Farmer's Market and he appeared to have no trouble making small talk to her. *'It must just be unmarried women he has a problem with'*, Justin surmised.

'So, what's your story, Peregrine or can I call you Perry?'

'Yes please. I need to get away from Yorkshire a.s.a.p. O.K. you've probably realized I have a problem with women. They're not to be trusted.'

Justin looked straight at him. 'Well, we are all entitled to our opinion of course, but personally I couldn't be without them, especially Anna, but I can promise you there are no women to disturb your peace of mind here and even most of my horses are fellows,' he added a trifle sardonically. 'Just Conchita my latest horse who I part own with my dad. I care deeply about my horses and their welfare and it is important they have the best care possible. What experience have you?'

'I haven't worked with other people's horses before, in fact I have never worked for anyone in my life, but I have always had horses and ponies around me. I have my own Grade C. horse Passe Partout – he's doing the Stairway series at the moment and Will and Binny each have a JA. Pony. Binny's Top Hole is thirteen two and Will's Shining Light is fourteen two.'

'And Wills and Binny are?' Justin asked Perry.

'Cornelius and Columbine, unfortunately, my dad had a passion for exotic names. Cornelius' second name is Wilfred – he likes to be called Wills and Binny is our nick name for Columbine.'

'So are these animals at livery somewhere at the moment. I presume you would want to bring them to Kent with you?'

'No, no, they're not at some livery yard. They live on our estate.'

'Your estate?'

'Yes, Helingbury Castle, in Yorkshire.'

Justin knew it well. It was less than ten miles from his late grandparents old home.

'Helingbury Castle? That's your home. You are Lord Helingbury?'

'Yes. I inherited it and the title from my father when he and my step mother were killed.'

'Why on earth are you applying for a job here, as my groom?'

'Horses are all I know. I've always looked after my own. I would never let dad's grooms touch my ponies or the horse I've got now.'

'But I need to know, why the hell do you need a job? You must be far wealthier than I am.'

'Maybe I am but I told you it's not the money, I'm doing this because I need to get as far away from Helingbury as I possibly can.'

'A woman, I presume?'

'Too true,' and he sneered. 'The scheming blond who I had known for most of my adult life and who had been my fiancée for the past two years – the bitch who ditched me on our wedding day – two hours before the ceremony and one hundred and fifty five minutes before she disappeared with my two timing, young brother.'

'Perry – I need a groom who will stay with me and my horses, not someone who wants to come here on a whim.'

'As long as I can bring Wills and Binny, their ponies and my horse, I don't care about anything else. My cheating, conniving, young brother who is aptly named Romeo and my one time fiancée are welcome to that pile of stones and mortar. I just want to work with horses and if that includes a bit of travel to shows on the continent then so much the better.'

Perry's attitude to life was appealing to Justin more and more. He thought maybe there were some vague similarities to his past outlook on life and he briefly recalled that not so many years ago his opinion of women had not been so far removed from that of the recently jilted Lord Peregrine Percival. He himself had once fled to Hans Weis and Germany, Perry merely wanted to flee to Kent.

'Come and see the Coach House and the Old Stables,' he invited Perry who had by now informed him he was twenty seven years old.

Justin laughed to himself as Perry enthused over the Coach House as though he had been living in a tent for the past few years!

'They're smashing. Where are your horses?'

'They are still at Lake House with my dad's. I will show them to you when we pick up your youngsters.'

'When can I start?'

'Hold on, old man. We haven't even discussed a salary yet.'

'Whatever. I'm quite happy to be more of a working pupil.'

Justin named a rather meager amount but Perry didn't hesitate – money was the least of his worries. He had more than he would ever know what to do with.

'Fine,' he agreed. I'll get in touch with the Grammar Schools for Wills and Binny. Would you have a free stable for Passe Partout? He's a thoroughbred, so he needs to come in at night. My dad bred him.'

'Sure, and for the ponies too. I had more stables than we need built in the modern pony block. One day I expect Noah will have a couple of jumping ponies too. Are the ponies mares or geldings?'

'Wills' Shining Light is a palomino gelding and Binny's little Top Hole is very dark grey and a gelding as well. They're seven and nine years old now.'

Everything seemed to have been conducted in a rather haphazard fashion. Justin was glad his father and Tom hadn't been there to witness this extraordinary interview. He knew it would be no good asking Perry for a reference because he had never before earned a penny in his life but he liked him and that was good enough for the happy go lucky, easy going Justin.

When they got back to Lake House, Wills and Binny were already part of *the gang* it had taken Mimi Wright-Smith less than a quarter of an hour before she was inviting Wills to become the latest member and then as her basic good manners came to the fore she had turned to Binny and included her as well.

Martha and Horace Carpenter were already ensconced in the lodge at The Old Manor House and Lizzie was finding Martha the proverbial treasure. Horace was happily dividing his time between the Old Manor House, Theobald's Place and Woodcutters and Justin felt with the older man's help his stables would hopefully run on oiled wheels.

The next day, the horseboxes were loaded as the entire *gang* made its way to Camber Sands. Sam and Tom followed with Charles and Joanna with the largest picnic they had ever encountered, whilst Justin, Anna and Giles transported the children in their various vehicles.

The sun was already shining as Dom and Erica drove the two biggest horseboxes. Rupert noticed Mimi was carrying a small spade. 'Going to build a sandcastle?' he asked his sister with more than a hint of sarcasm.

'Mind your own business, Rupert.' Mimi retorted and slammed the door of Anna's people carrier in his face but when Joshua got in and sat down beside her, her expression changed when he smiled at her telling her. 'We'll find it Mimi – even if it takes us all day.'

It didn't take all day, Mimi remembered exactly which sand dune she had buried the leather box in and after only five minutes she gave a whoop of joy, *'Eureka,'* and she was handing the box containing the pen and pencil with Joshua's name on the side of both the writing utensils and on the top of the box to it's rightful owner. He withdrew a piece of paper from his pocket and drew a line with the newly found pen. 'Now you draw one, Mimi and on each of our birthdays we will make it a bit longer and a fraction closer – until one day I promise you the two lines will join together.'

Mimi smiled. 'That sounds almost like a proposal, Josh.'

'You never know, Mimi – maybe or maybe not, but that line will move very, very slowly - it won't be fast and furious, I can certainly assure you of that,' and with that vague promise, he pulled Mimi to her feet and put the box with the pen and pencil carefully in the horsebox before taking Sweet Dreams onto the golden sands with Babushka and Charles' *little minx* galloping beside him.

CHAPTER 32

The next morning, Tom was at the stables just before six o'clock – he had already set his alarm and got out of bed at two thirty to check on Black Chintz who had appeared restless when he and Sam had done their late night tour of the stables the previous evening.

Jules and Hannah had just arrived and were on the point of calling Tom and were obviously relieved when they saw him appearing in the yard. An hour later, with Sam and seven excited youngsters watching, Chintz produced her beautiful black, colt foal. He was both extremely strong and undeniably handsome. Chintz was Satin's full brother and to Sam's consternation this cheeky young man bore a huge resemblance to his notorious uncle.

Tom was more delighted than anyone as he looked at the foal's hocks - his sturdy body, his naturally arched neck and his bold eye. The foal appeared to be fearless and within minutes of taking his first steps and whilst Chintz was expelling the afterbirth, he walked up to Tom playfully pulling his shirt. Its mischievous eyes were gazing straight at him and in that moment – at less than one hour old – the cheeky little colt was telling him. 'We're going to have a great time together,' and in the paddock a few yards away, his uncle was nodding his head. Black Satin was totally agreeing and Tom had no reason to doubt either of them.

'Have you thought of a name for him yet, Sammy?'

'Hm – he looks like a load of trouble to me – he reminds me of a wicked pirate. How about The Jolly Roger?'

So a young colt foal that was going to need every ounce of Tom's patience and expertise and whose name was The Jolly Roger would maybe one day be recognized all over the world as his uncle Black Satin had once been. He gave Tom's shirt one more cheeky tug before trotting back to his mother – tossing his head and then pulling viciously at her teats. Trouble had arrived but a bond had already been established. Roger and Tom had already had the first conversation of many they would have in the future. The colt appeared to have inherited all the physic powers of his Uncle Satin, who was now galloping round his paddock, bucking in his customary way.

Tom walked up to him telling him. 'You idiot Satin, you're far too old for these high jinks.' Satin blew softly in Tom's face – Tom understood. Satin was telling him one day his little nephew would conquer the world and Tom knew only too well Black Satin had never yet been proven wrong.

Sam gave the children each a packet of sandwiches and watched as they made their way to Lake House where Dom was going to give them a lesson and then they were all going to have a work out in Charles' gym before swimming, after which, Justin and Dom would take them for a hack to Ribbenden to visit Marigold's Sanctuary.

Sam suddenly felt the house had gone very quiet. Oliver had discovered Clare loved music. Like he did, she learned the piano and had singing lessons after school twice a week. They had been giving their noisy rendition of chopsticks on the piano and Oliver had been playing songs that Clare was familiar with on his guitar. Oliver was unusually happy. He appeared to have discovered a soul mate. Now, with the piano lid closed and the guitar standing in the corner of the playroom, silence reigned.

Sam sat on the seat in the garden thinking about the wicked looking foal her favourite mare had produced. As she closed her eyes, she felt a very familiar arm creeping round her and Tom was kissing her neck. 'You're disappointed, aren't you, my Sammy?'

'I know I shouldn't be Tommy but I'm positive he is going to be a handful – I know you love a challenge but I am all for a quiet, uncomplicated life.'

Tom smiled. 'Here's an offer. I'll take The Jolly Roger and you can take pot luck with whatever Misty produces.'

'Really,' and Sam's face immediately brightened.

'Sure thing. I love that wicked boy, Sam, and darling, we're going to do great things together. Satin has already told me.'

'Tom, how can I bear it? Another Satin in the stables! Truly, I never imagined that could be possible. Yes, please, he's all yours and I shall wait with bated breath to see what your Misty produces.'

She didn't have to wait long. As the children arrived home at seven thirty, Love in a Mist's liver chestnut foal arrived in the largest of Tom's stables.

He was considerably smaller than The Jolly Roger but at least in Sam's eyes, a great deal more beautiful. In fact, she would almost have gone so far as to term him exquisite. He was dark, liver chestnut with two white socks on his front and two longer, white stockings on his back legs. He had a slim white strip, which ran in a straight line down the centre of his face, huge dark brown eyes and an auburn coloured mane and tail. His young body was in perfect proportion to his head with its cheekily pricked ears. He nuzzled his mother before walking up to Tom and Sam who were standing absolutely still, not wanting to do anything to startle the highly-strung Misty.

He ignored Tom, walking straight up to Sam, pushing his soft nose into her cupped hands. She held her breath as she gently moved her right hand and stroked his chestnut neck. He snorted, then stood still, nuzzled Sam once more and then walked slightly unsteadily back to his mother.

Sam had tears in her eyes. 'Tom he's absolutely gorgeous – what's that word you say, Rosie?'

'Supercalifragilisticexpialidocious!!'

Tom laughed. 'Don't tell me that is going to be his name?'

'No, something far simpler. What else could he be called but *Pot Luck* because that's what I took when I gave you The Jolly Roger, Tom? I shall call him Potty, of course.'

'Well it was certainly an excellent gamble you took, Sammy. I doubt whether he will grow to more than 15.2h.h. He would probably not have been big enough for a great six-foot hunk like me. You can do whatever you like with him.'

Sam clutched Tom's arm. 'Tommy, I have just seen Satin in the corner of his paddock holding my side saddle and at the same time I do declare your wicked little Jolly Roger was sticking his tongue out at me. I shall have to be patient; I won't be able to show him in the mare and foal classes. Misty would be impossible but next year – oh Tom – next year maybe the yearling category, but whatever his future I'm so glad I took Pot Luck.'

Tom set his alarm twice that night in spite of Mathew Parker and James both visiting the stables and pronouncing he had two very fit mares and two thriving foals.

Jolly Roger had nipped James' arm. 'God, Tom, who on earth does this little monster remind you of?'

Tom laughed. 'I know, that old black devil who at the moment is giving me furious looks because I am ignoring him. God, James, I am crossing every finger and every toe hoping Chintz had produced a replica of her brother. Roll on five years time, except,' and he pulled a rueful face, 'I shall be thirty seven then but with any luck I should still be fit and able.'

James pulled a grimace. 'Thanks, Tom, you've made my day.' and to Tom's acute embarrassment he realized James thirty-seventh birthday was looming on the very near horizon.

'Sorry, old man – if I am half as fit and handsome as you, I shall be more than happy. How's my young sister, by the way?'

'Blooming – this pregnancy seems to be the most natural thing in the world when I think of Fen and the twins. She went through a lot with that I.V.F. treatment – Freddy was obviously meant to be. She will be watching the School and Pony Club team selections tomorrow. I imagine your boys and Rosie will all be there?'

'Yes, *the gang* is coming in full force. They are all going to try except Anne-Marie but she will be there. She's not letting Ozzie out of her sight whilst Cassie and Clare are staying with us!!! They are great kids – we met them at a show in Essex. Their Dad, Mike is a pilot with the Swallow Tails. Could the two girls jump *hors concours* tomorrow? They've brought their ponies with them. Charles gave them a lesson with *the gang* yesterday – he says they are cracking little riders. Incidentally they are coached by our team-mate, David Mason.'

James immediately agreed. 'Of course, I'll tell Mum. As you know she's District Commissioner again now after a break of a few years. Lizzie is her second in command but I am sure she will be more than delighted to welcome two visitors.'

The following morning, all was well with the two mares and their foals and Tom and Jules led Chintz and Misty into a small paddock and watched as The Jolly Roger bucked high in the air as Pot Luck stayed close to his mother. Roger was already showing signs of joie de vivre as he kicked his back legs in Tom's direction as his master leapt adeptly out of his reach.

'Not so much of that, young man,' but when he went indoors he told all the children that none of them was to venture into the paddock where the mares and foals were grazing.

'Why Dads?' Rosie asked.

'Because Roger appears to have an aspiration to become a footballer."

"What's an aspiration, Dads?"

"He thinks he has the right to kick anything that comes within his sight.'

'Don't worry, Dads. Clare and Cassie and me won't go anywhere near him.'

'That definitely applies to you too, Oz.'

Oscar was well aware Anne-Marie, who had come with Dom to see the new foals was glancing anxiously at him. 'O.K. Dad. Footballers kick balls – could be very painful!!'

'Oscar, please. That is really not funny.'

Oscar merely grinned. 'Oops, sorry, Dad. Forgot there were ladies present!!'

Sam gave her son a stern look. 'Maybe you should go and get Panky ready, Ozzie. How is Anne-Marie getting to the Centre?'

'Her dad is taking her there on his way back to Lake House.' He grinned cheekily at Sam, 'or we could ride tandem on Panky.'

'Oscar, just calm down and go and see to Panky. Anne-Marie is going to take the picnic hamper in the car with Dom.'

Oscar looked horrified. 'Mum, aren't you coming to watch?'

'I need to get on with a garden I am designing, Ozzie. I've been neglecting my work recently.'

'Mum, one more day won't make any difference surely. Dad says he will come. He and Justin are going to help us with the practice jump. It's not the same without you, Mum.'

Sam looked at his pleading face and when Josh and Rosie came up to her saying. 'See you at the Centre, Mum,' obviously expecting her to be there, her mind was made up as her heart ruled her head. 'O.K. Oz. I'll be there, cheering like mad.'

'Mum, you're just great,' and Oscar gave her a hug which squeezed every ounce of breath out of her body and when Tom came up to her emulating his son, saying. 'Ozzie says you've decided to come – fantastic,' – she had already forgotten her plans for the garden at Spring Cottage, The Street, Ribbenden!! Her family needed her, - there was nothing more important.

It seemed to take forever to get seven children and seven ponies ready but at last they had been joined by Rupert and Mimi and had reconvened at Theobald's Place to find Gus and Abby waiting for them with Charlotte, Georgia and also Daisy who was coming with Anna and Noah to cheer on the members of *the gang*.

Every child who wished to try for a place in the team was allowed to do so. The morning would be dedicated to the Primary School hopefuls of which there appeared to be an extremely large number.

Daisy and Anne-Marie had become good friends and they sat on a rug, which Anna had brought, with Noah who was asking Sam to tell him another story about the naughty kitten who chased little birds. Sam duly obliged, making up the tale as she went along – something she had done many times when the triplets had been Noah's age. He was listening intently, sucking his thumb and pulling his hair – a sure sign he was sleepy, until Sam realized he hadn't uttered a sound for some time and Daisy was laughing. 'He's fast asleep, Aunty Sam.'

Sam laid him on the rug, covering his head with her cardigan. It was going to be a really hot day and she was relieved when she saw Justin approaching with Noah's buggy, a large sunhat and an oversize tube of sun cream.

Justin lifted the little boy gently into his buggy and turned it away from the glare of the sun so that it wasn't shining on Noah's face. 'I had better go and find Tom and Anna. The Pony Club hopefuls have ages to wait, they've taken off their saddles and have gathered in the shade under the oak tree. Cassie and Clare are with them. I think they are going to have a whizz round the Pony Club course just for fun. They seem to be enjoying themselves; they appear to be very capable little riders. David Mason has obviously taught them well.'

'They will be jumping here at the show on Sunday before they go home,' Sam told him. 'They are nice girls and they seem to get on really well with Rosie and the boys.'

'There will be two more members of *the gang* soon, Sam. I've acquired my new groom, Lord Peregrine Percival of Helingbury Castle – accompanied by his Grade C. horse, his half brother and sister – their two J.A. ponies and his own horsebox.'

Sam was astonished. 'Goodness, what's he like, Justin?'

'He's a misogynist.'

'A what?'

'A woman hater. He was ditched at the altar – quite literally a couple of months ago, in favour of his younger brother. He's not interested in money – he just wants to get as far away from Yorkshire as possible.'

'Goodness – do you think he has any idea how hard a groom has to work?'

'God knows – but he's dirt cheap, so I'll give him a try. He likes to be called Perry by the way and the kids are Cornelius and Columbine, better known as Wills and Binny.'

'Why Wills?'

'Apparently the lad's second name is Wilfred. Perry is going to see if he can get the kids into the local Grammar Schools. They are arriving next Monday. Binny and Wills met *the gang* when I took them via Lake House on our way from Headcorn aerodrome. They seemed to have enjoyed themselves.'

'Aerodrome, Justin?'

'Yes, Perry's cousin Ptolemy has his own plane. He's known as Tolly by the way.'

'God, what have you taken on, Justin?'

'I don't know but I could be in for a very interesting time. Horace Carpenter is going to help me two days a week. Lizzie, Tom and I have come to an agreement – we are going to share him. Lizzie is thrilled with his wife Martha, so all looks well there.'

At last, the Primary School children had all put their names on the blackboard in the collecting ring. James had asked Tom to judge the children with him but he had declined. 'I really can't, James – with five of my own kids competing for a place it would be too difficult. Someone else must decide whether or not they deserve to be in the team.'

Eventually, Elizabeth, Jean-Pierre and James were elected to be the selection committee with Susan as a final arbitrator should there be any uncertainty.

As the late July sun seemed to be getting hotter and hotter the first young hopeful entered the ring. It was Rosie and Le Duc de Toulouse. After much agonizing and discussion with Tom, she had brought him in preference to Sparkler. She wasn't certain, and neither was her father exactly how big or demanding the course would be and she knew the superior height of Le Duc could be to her advantage.

She was soon leaving the ring with a fast clear round. She rode round to re-join *the gang* who were all assembled under the oak tree, threw her jacket on the grass and sat down beside Cassie and Clare.

'Wow,' they exclaimed. 'What a super pony. You didn't bring him to the show in Essex.'

'No, because Dad wanted to help Oz with Humbug that day, it was Buggy's first show since he had lost his eye.'

The next two youngsters were in the class above Rosie and below the triplets – they both reached the third jump where their ponies decided to dig in their heels and soon the buzzer sounded to tell the unfortunate hopefuls they had been eliminated.

The triplets then followed one after the other and the clear rounds began to mount.

Two sisters called Emily and Iris Fellows jumped their stocky little cobs carefully and cleanly but extremely slowly and then Rupert and The March Hare flew.

By the time Gus, Abby, Eloise, Charlotte and finally Georgia were also basking in the glory of clear rounds, Susan was quickly re-reading the rules of the forthcoming competition.

'James,' she was soon telling her son. 'Thank goodness each school is allowed to enter an A. and a B. team. We'll get all the clear rounds to jump again and see what we can sort out.'

Fenella was the first casualty as Poupée knocked both parts of the double and then the raised jumps proved too much for both Emily and her sister, Iris.

'Right,' James clear voice came over the tannoy. 'Now for a real competition. All those of you who jumped a second clear round will go once more against the clock. This is your last chance to impress the selectors. Your time will count.'

James had the list of names in front of him and a pencil in his hand. First he watched Rosie and put a tick by her name. Then he watched in amazement as Oscar set off on the prancing Hanky Panky who was flying, leaping over the jumps as somehow Oscar mustered the strength to turn him in the air, cutting vital seconds off the time. He was watching Oscar at his very best – he put a double tick by his name.

There were six children who were outstanding. They consisted of Rosie and her triplet brothers, and Rupert and Gus. Not in the same class but giving more than adequate performances were Charlotte and Georgia. That he reckoned would make two teams of the obligatory four riders. He then put a small tick by Abby and Eloise, hoping they wouldn't be required but they had jumped two steady clear rounds and would be the reserve riders.

Susan then appeared with a box of rosettes. The first three, which were Oscar, Gus and Rosie, were each presented with a red, blue and yellow rosette and every other child who had tried for the teams was given a Highly Commended. Susan had found the box in the Pony Club cupboard at the back of the indoor school at the Centre.

James voice came over the tannoy again. 'We have seen all we need – thank you so much for coming. There will now be a break for lunch whilst the selectors decide who will be in the teams. Yes. I did say TEAMS. There will be two teams representing the Massenden Primary School and one representing the Pony Club. There will be Massenden Primary School A. team, and Massenden Primary School B. team. Neither team will be superior to the other. We just have to decide who will be in which team.'

After a hearty picnic and an anxious wait, the tannoy crackled into life once again. This time it was Susan who was announcing the teams. 'Team A. will consist of Oscar and Rosie West, Gus

Wright-Smith and Georgia Norton. The reserve rider will be Eloise Dubois. The B. Team will be made up of Oliver and Orlando West, Rupert Wright-Smith and Charlotte Collins. Their reserve rider will be Abby Wright-Smith. I am sure you will all do your very best and make your school proud of you. For many of you this will be your last chance to be part of the Primary School team but next year, maybe the Grammar Schools will be able to enter a team. I know you have all been very fortunate and have had coaching at Lake House. Dom will make certain you all have at least two sessions a week until we all go to Sussex in three week's time. The top two teams will compete in the National Finals in Warwickshire one week later. Now please could the Pony Club group gather in the collecting ring?'

The Pony Club team was far easier to select when Josh, Jacques, Mimi and Veronica Mawgan-Whitely were the only clear rounds apart from Cassie and Clare Lewis who would be competing with their own Pony Club in Lincolnshire.

The decision was soon made and Susan was informing the group that Joshua West, Mimi Wright-Smith, Jacques Dubois and Veronica Mawgan – Whitely had been the chosen team with Matilda Smith as the reserve.

Susan thanked all the children for coming on such a hot day and told them all to ride home at no more than a walk.

Charles had suggested *the gang* took their ponies home and should then make their way to the swimming pool at Lake House.

Whilst Georgia spent an enjoyable evening with *the gang,* her father was indulging in his excellent meal at La Casa sul Verde. Having satisfied himself Herbie was safely with Betsie as she religiously cleaned every single one of the guinea pig's hutches whilst the little dog eyed the small rodents in his usual laid back manner, and had ensured Esther would keep a watchful eye on Georgia when she arrived home, Giles was sitting on his own in a corner alcove where he had a perfect view of Clarissa as she welcomed her diners – one of whom, and much to his discomfort being Robert West. The two men ignored each other for a very good reason. They were both stalking the same prey and only one of them could be successful. There would be one lucky winner and one disappointed loser.

As the meal drew to a close, to Giles' dismay he watched as Rob ordered two small glasses of crème de menthe, beckoned to Clarissa and soon saw her sitting chatting to him as she sipped the smooth green liquid at his adversary's table.

At last, as he was getting more and more impatient and had mentally written the next chapter in the exploits of Herbert Holmer, Clarissa was standing up, showing an obviously reluctant Robert West through the door. He watched as his heart twisted in pain as Robert took Clarissa's face between his hands as he dealt a lingering kiss on her lips. He wanted to throw up – but he noticed Clarissa's hands pushing Rob away and closing the door firmly behind him. She turned and smiled at him and now his heart was throbbing. He stood up and followed her up the first flight of stairs, which led to Luigi and Maria's apartment and then up a much steeper, narrower stairway to her tiny apartment at the very top of the building.

He walked to the window and saw the lights twinkling in the cottages in Theobald's Row and the brighter lights in Justin and Anna's beautiful old Georgian home.

He pulled Clarissa to the window and they looked together across the green where he could see Robert West at the far end, making his way back to Honeysuckle Cottage.

'I loathe that smart-arse, Clarry.'

'Giles Norton, - do I detect just a smidgeon of jealousy?'

'Let's drink our coffee – it smells inviting.' Giles was determined to keep a cool head. He would not put himself in a vulnerable situation, however tempted he might be. He was not a well drilled ex-army captain without having attained an extremely strong character and however much his body might ache to have Clarissa in his arms or better still in his bed, he was never going to take the risk of being rejected again, and until he was absolutely certain, he would bide his time and if it never happened it wouldn't be for the lack of trying.

Clarissa had classical music playing softly in the background. The apartment was certainly extremely small, comprised of a living room with a tiny kitchen area against one wall, a small square landing with two pine doors leading off it, one to a wet room, the other he guessed correctly into Clarissa's compact bedroom.

They sipped their coffee, sitting together on the small sofa, which was their only option, the room being too small for any other creature comforts except for an oblong coffee table and a cabinet which appeared to house Clarissa's favourite trinkets.

Clarissa was tired – she had worked hard, as she did every day La Casa was open. She let her head drop onto Giles' shoulder. He took a firmer hold of his emotions but he had to ask her one burning question. 'Clarry, you may think I have no right to ask you this but if I don't I shall never sleep peacefully again. Is there anything going on between you and Robert West?'

Clarissa lifted her head from his shoulder and he noticed tears in her eyes. 'Why do you imagine I am putting myself through all this hypnotherapy and counseling, Gi?'

'I hardly dare let myself think.'

'Now I am going to ask you a question. When did you last sleep with a woman, Gi?'

'Not for a very long time.'

'How long?'

'To be precise, the night before I left for Afghanistan.'

'Oh, Gi. I'm sorry.'

'For a start, I never met anyone and even if I had I would never have wanted to have risked being rejected again. So your heart is not crashing every time you catch sight of that womanizer?'

'No, Giles – I can assure you it is most definitely as steady as a rock.'

She put her head back on his shoulder and whispered. 'Steadier than it is now?'

He stroked her neck but five minutes later she was asleep. He kissed her closed eyes very gently and stood up, deciding to visit the loo before making his way home. He opened a door but it didn't lead to the shower room. He was in a small bedroom with a single bed and a table beside it. His eyes were immediately drawn to two photographs.

One was of Georgia jumping Fire Cracker – the other was the same photo that stood by his own bed – the very one that his father had taken the day he and Clarissa had become engaged. He closed the door quickly, found the loo and then whistling happily made his way back to Theobald's Row. Clarissa was going to meet him for lunch at the Equitation Centre on Sunday. They would watch their daughter together.

Two hours later, Herbert Holmer was starting a new adventure. This time an extremely attractive woman accompanied him. They were searching together, trying to discover the whereabouts of her long, lost family. Herbert Holmer felt his heart beating faster as he glanced at the raven-haired beauty that bore a very close resemblance to Patsy Sanders' own Clarissa. At least, Giles hoped that's what she would become before too long. His own Clarissa back where she belonged - with him – Captain Giles Norton, not Patsy Sanders, inventor of a dapper detective with the name of Herbert Holmer.

As far as Cassie and Clare were concerned, the week was absolutely flying by. They loved every second of their time with *the gang* who were organizing a campfire with sausages and baked potatoes on the last night of the girls' stay at Woodcutters. One-time girl guiders in the forms of Erica and Betsy, who were more than a little enthusiastic to show off the skills they had learned many years ago at their Girl Guide camps, would oversee it.

Oliver and Clare had been closeted together in the playroom with the door firmly closed whilst they practiced the songs, which they hoped most people would recognize. Ollie with his guitar and Clare would lead the singing aided and abetted by Oscar and Orlando who, according to their headmistress Mrs. Abrahams had more than average voices that had never been exploited. It would be a large gathering with all the mums and dads and not least the grooms.

Anna had insisted Amy brought Adrian and Molly even if she went and fetched them herself.

The evening was to be held at Theobald's Place. When Justin got wind of the forthcoming event, he immediately saw this as an extremely cheap way to host his long overdue housewarming party. Tom had laughed when his friend had asked him to accompany him to the local supermarket to help him transport the wine.

'The super market, Justin?'

'Why not? £3.50p. a bottle of plonk, that's fine and Tizer for the kids. What more do people want?'

Tom hid round the corner of the aisle whilst Justin chose the cheapest wine he could fine. He quickly dialed Charles' mobile. '*Charles, your son is currently buying the cheapest plonk he can possibly unearth, do you want me to buy us something decent whilst I am here?'*

'Actually Tom, don't worry. I've got a crate of Chateaunoeuf du Pape. I'll bring that for the more discerning but that son of mine will not taste one sip of it. The mean sod. House warming indeed! Poor Anna!'

The day had gone well. *The gang* had been watching the senior competitors at the Massenden Centre. Tom had been delighted – Swallow Tail had triumphed in the Foxhunter Class and Alicia had won the Grade C. Her points were mounting rapidly and soon she would be trying her luck against the top ranked horses. Tom hoped she would succeed and he was almost certain she could. He would find out soon enough but now she had qualified for the Grade C. Championship at H.O.Y.S. in the autumn and after this morning, Swallow Tail would be in the Foxhunter Championship. He decided not to push either of them before then. The Wizard could take his turn after his enforced long rest and Black Opal could join him. Kaspar had won more than his fair share of competitions lately and Tom was determined to give him a well-earned rest with Madame and Clementine. It suited his plans well. He wanted to spend more time with Sam and his children these holidays, especially with Rosie and her new partner Braveheart, who she would be jumping for the first time the following morning.

Justin was delighted when Conchita came second in the Grade C. Class and Pickwick won the Open.

'That's helped pay for the bloody wine we're going to consume this evening,' Justin was telling Tom as he watched the campfire burning later that day. 'God knows what my bank balance is like now. You've no idea what it's like feeding a wife and three greedy children, Tom.'

'Justin, do I detect a lapse of memory? How many mouths do I have to feed and no-one could consume more than Oscar and Ollie?'

'Well, Sam must be much better organized than Anna, that's all I can say.'

'Justin. Anna is like gold dust and you bloody well know it. She's got a lot on her mind at the moment too, trying to help poor Amy.'

'Well, I suppose I would hate to be without her. She's got some very good points, especially in' ----

'I really don't want to know the finer details, Justin – just go and help her hand round your vinegar – oops – sorry Justin, I meant - wine.'

Ten minutes later, Tom walked across to Anna who was sitting with Noah on her lap blowing the steam from a baked potato he was impatiently waiting to eat. Tom removed the drink from between Anna's fingers and handed her a glass of Charles' extremely expensive Chateaneuf du Pape.

'Oh, thanks, Tom, that wine Justin bought tastes a bit odd.' Tom turned his back on Anna for two minutes whilst he searched for Sam and the next time he noticed, the glass he had handed Anna was almost empty. To his annoyance it wasn't Anna who was enjoying the delicious wine – it was in his opinion, the meanest sod on this earth, who also happened to be a millionaire many times over. Tom sighed, as he also had to admit, a chap who had also been one of his best friends for over twenty years. He sighed, stood up and took Anna another glass. Justin looked at him.

'Wow, Tom – this is excellent wine for just £3.50p. a bottle. Good old supermarket!!'

Tom however was well aware of the laughter in his friend's eyes. Justin knew only too well where this particular brand of wine had come from, of that, in Tom's opinion there could be no doubt.

The evening was a roaring success until Giles noticed Rob West making his way towards John and Mary with whom he was sitting, along with David and Esther Collins. John was laughing at his younger brother –'No Tamara Adams or some other beauty queen tonight, Rob?'

'Tamara and I are finito – over. She wanted to move into Honeysuckle Cottage with me. That is definitely *NOT* with capital letters on my agenda.' To John's surprise and to Giles as well he added. 'If I do have another woman it will have to be with Daisy's approval. Do you think I am not aware of the unsettled life my kids have had to endure? There is however, someone I've got my eye on – unfortunately she's a very busy lady. Running a bistro is an arduous task but I am working on her.'

It was the discerning Mary who noticed the look that passed across Giles Norton's face. It was one of fury – amazement – and not least fear. *'Blast Rob and his women,'* she thought. Giles watched Rob as he stood up and wandered over to the large group who were sitting by the glowing embers of the campfire, and then saw him sit down beside a dark haired, young woman who he vaguely recognized. He had seen her in the village store several times and also riding a horse down Back Lane past Honeysuckle Cottage.

'Hi,' Rob greeted her, noticing her glass was empty. 'Can I get you some more wine?'

Oliver was leading the group into a well-known song especially for his dad's sake. It was a rousing rendition of Clementine but when they reached the line '*how could you leave me?*' Rob noticed tears running down the face of the young woman sitting quietly beside him.

'What's wrong?' he asked.

'I'm sorry, it's just that I am missing Glen so much. He would have loved an evening like this.'

'And Glen is?'

'Was – he was my husband. He died last year. It's just those words – they got me. I think I will go home.'

'And where might home be?' Rob asked.

'Back Lane. Theobald's Row. I'm Trish. I live with my brother, Tony and his wife Alicia. I don't want to spoil their evening- I'll be O.K.'

'Stay there, I will go and ask Esther to bring Daisy back with Charlotte and I will see you safely home. Many years ago, I went through hell. My wife left me with two tiny kids. It's been tough. Actually, sometimes it still is, but we manage. Time will help you, even if it does take a long while.'

Having arranged for Esther to bring Daisy home, Rob, who very rarely showed the vulnerable side of his character made certain Trish was safely in the cottage, accepted a cup of coffee and chatted amiably until Tony and Alicia arrived back not too long afterwards but not before Rob had convinced Trish that however hard it might be to lose the husband you loved, you were left with nothing but happy memories – a sadistic divorce on the other hand left nothing but bitterness and hatred.

Rob very rarely spared a thought for his ex-wife. He had long ago decided she was not worth the time, but when he arrived back at Honeysuckle Cottage he lit the fire in the sitting room and by the time Daisy arrived he had burned every photograph he possessed of a women who had not only devastated his own life but those of his young children as well. His mind strayed to Tamara Adams – she was undoubtedly both desirable and glamorous but she had barely acknowledged Daisy, whose happiness Rob valued more than anything else. To many people Rob had the appearance of being a spoiled, egoistical man, but there was one thing these sceptics were completely unaware of – Rob West would put his son and his daughter before anything else in his life.

His mind drifted back to the girl who had told him she had tried to have a baby with her dying husband. She had told Rob it was all she had wanted – a living memory of Glen.

Poor girl, Rob thought. He might take her to The Bear for a meal one night. Not to La Casa – he wouldn't want Clarissa to catch sight of him with another woman, just fish and chips or a steak at The Bear. It was certainly worth considering.

CHAPTER 33

At Woodcutters, everyone was up at the crack of dawn the following morning. The show at the Equestrian Centre was starting with the Junior Foxhunter ponies at ten o'clock. This was always a very popular event and there were usually at least forty entries. Rosie and Braveheart and Jacques and The Flying Fox were the only members of *the gang* who were eligible for this particular class. Jacques and Foxy had already qualified for the Foxhunter Championship later in the year. If they won today they would automatically move up into the next grade.

Tom didn't want to push Rosie and Braveheart. Rosie wouldn't be ten for another six months; she had all the time in the world.

He wouldn't want them competing at H.O.Y.S. this year – next year she would be ten and a half, with longer legs and more experience with the pony. He wanted her to do well but her priorities this year were Sparkler and Le Duc de Toulouse. Her career was moving in the right direction at a fast speed and sometimes he had to stop and remind himself not to let her move at too great a pace. Above all, he wanted her to have fun – not always trying to qualify for some Championship or other. He had to admit, however, Braveheart was probably the easiest of the three ponies Rosie would be riding that day.

Finally, the ponies were all ready and loaded into Tom's two horseboxes. He was driving one himself and Jules would be following with the other.

Sam was taking her car with a pile of raincoats and sou westers. The weather had suddenly changed and it was hard to believe they had been sitting round the campfire on a balmy evening just a few hours ago. It wasn't actually raining, but the sky was overcast and the heavy clouds were hovering over the village. She had Cassie and Clare's holdalls ready to give to Mike and Suzie with their belongings packed ready for their departure to Lincolnshire directly after the show.

Mike and Suzie arrived just before the horseboxes left the yard. Tom helped Mike hitch his Range Rover to the trailer whilst Cassie and Clare were enthusing about the wonderful week they had spent. They couldn't stop talking about *the gang*, the campfire, riding in the sea, lessons with Charles, and swimming in the pool at Lake House almost every day. 'We've missed you, Mummy,' Cassie told Suzie, 'but do we have to go home. Couldn't Swallow Tail come and live at Headcorn aerodrome?'

Mike laughed. 'I am afraid she has to live with her team mates, girls, but don't forget Rosie and her brothers are all coming up to the Open Day at the end of September and we will try to jump here from time to time.'

Suzie smiled when she noticed the friendship that appeared to have been struck between Oliver and Clare. 'Music, Suzie,' Sam explained. 'They've discovered it's something they both really enjoy. It's been really good for Ollie – he has his music school every month but he gets rather swept up by the ponies and sadly none of *the gang* seems to have the slightest interest in music. It's been a fantastic few days for him.'

'Well, luckily we will all meet up again in September, and your boys can have a really close look at Swallow Tail.'

Tom arrived at the showground three quarters of an hour before Rosie and Braveheart's Class was due to start. They walked the course together, joined by Jacques. Jean-Pierre was involved with greeting the judges, making certain a cup of Cappuccino was awaiting them before the long task that lay before them as the forty five entries loomed on the horizon in the first Class of what was undeniably going to be a long, slightly damp day.

Jacques was a tall, slender boy and he towered above the diminutive Rosie, but as she looked at her fellow competitors she realized Jacques was not alone on that count – every single one seemed at least a foot taller than she was. She was, however, not the least bit worried as she laughed with her favourite cousin.

Rosie was jumping early. After coaching her in the Indoor School at Lake House and also Charles' jumping paddock, Tom had full confidence in both Rosie and her pony and Rosie had no fears at all. Unfortunately, Sam did not appear to share their carefree approach and she was not looking forwards to her small daughter's first foray into the Junior Foxhunter Class, which was always full of ambitious, young riders - determined to move their novice pony up the ranks.

Tom was not unaware of his wife's apprehension. She had uncharacteristically snapped at him when he had spilled his coffee at breakfast time. It was totally alien to her usual sunny nature. He had taken a cloth and mopped up the offending beverage and dropped a kiss on her forehead, saying gently. 'She'll be fine, Sammy.'

This morning, however, Sam was not to be easily placated. 'How can you be so complacent, Tom? Don't you care about your children?'

'Sammy, that's not fair,' but before he could say any more, she had run out of the kitchen and he could see her making her way to the stables to join the children.

He had sat at the table sipping the cup of coffee, which he had replenished. He hated it on the rare occasions that he and Sam were not in total accord. He would never risk Rosie or the boys' safety. He was only too aware accidents could happen. He had seen many at first hand but they could be when you least expected them – cycling round the lake – diving in Charles' pool or even something as mundane as crossing the road. He would never let Rosie ride Braveheart if he had one smidgeon of doubt about the pony's capabilities or his temperament.

This was the reason Rosie was going to jump early. Sam's agonizing would be over quickly. Rosie did not question the reason her father had put her in sixth place on the blackboard and was happily attacking the practice jump.

As Rosie was entering the arena, he saw Sam running towards him. She wasn't crying but he knew tears weren't far away. He held out his hand and she took it straight away. 'I'm sorry, Tommy, I was beastly to you. You're the best dad in the world – it's just – it's just – Rosie is our baby.'

'Do you think I'm not aware of that, Sammy? But I promise you her courage and her heart are as big as anyone else's who is jumping this course today. Now hold my hand and we'll watch her together.'

There were twelve jumps to be negotiated and as Braveheart approached the second half of the course, Sam had completely forgotten her lack of faith in both her daughter and her husband and was jumping every fence with Rosie and Braveheart as they sailed faultlessly to the finish and were trotting towards them. Rosie was leaning forwards, kissing the pony's neck. 'Dads, he was brill – you said he would be – he's not nearly as strong as Sparkler or the Duc. He's – he's – super---- oh, you know, - my special word.'

'Pop him back in the horsebox until much nearer the end of the Class. It could last at least another two hours. When is Jacques jumping?'

'Twenty eighth, I think he told me.'

'Mum and I will come and help you with Braveheart and then you can find Gus and *The Gang,* I want a quick word with Mum.'

As Rosie ran off to find Gus, having established Braveheart was happily ensconced in the stall next to Humbug, Tom firmly closed the door of the groom's compartment. He caught hold of Sam, tickling her in all the places he knew after years of experience would have her screaming for mercy. 'Say you're sorry, Samantha West.' He was laughing. 'Say I'm sorry Tom, I'm a horrid girl.' His eyes were wicked and he was tickling her mercilessly – but suddenly he stopped and his eyes gazed into hers as at the same time his mouth put an abrupt end to her squeals. It was turning into a very long kiss and Tom wasn't sure when it would have ended if he hadn't heard a very familiar voice.

'Cor, Dad. Good job I caught you with Mum and not some Dolly Bird,' and Tom found himself looking into the laughing blue eyes of the irrepressible Oscar who was now asking him. 'Why would you ever want a *bit of fluff* - Mum is quite beautiful?'

'Oscar, you are only confirming something I am very well aware of and where do you pick up these dreadful expressions? Now go and find Rosie and help her unload Braveheart for the jump off. I'll be with you in a sec.'

'Yea, Dad, you do look a bit – er – disheveled,' and he was staring at the buttons on his father's shirt before he shrugged nonchalantly and turned away shouting to Rosie at the top of his voice for all the world to hear, "Rosie, come and get Braveheart with me. Dad's cooling off.'

'Cooling off? But it's raining.'

'Yea – but he was just about to boil over.'

'Boil over? You mean the kettle? Why was he making tea in the horsebox? They're serving tea and coffee in the bar.'

Oscar laughed. 'He wasn't making tea, Rosie but here you are,' and he handed her Braveheart.

Tom kissed the tip of Sam's nose. 'Tommy, we're alright aren't we?'

'Darling, Sam, do you ever imagine I will ever let us not be? Come on, hold my hand and we will watch Rosie and Braveheart together.'

Oscar was helping Rosie onto the pony as Tom and Sam joined them. They looked at the jump off course and Tom was telling her. 'No racing, Rosie. Just jump a nice, steady, clear round. It's no good qualifying Braveheart for the Championship this year because I wouldn't let you do it. You need lots of good solid clear rounds first and a real understanding with him. Next year will be a different matter – then I shall not only hope, but also expect to see you at H.O.Y.S. Now, believe it or not there are only ten clear rounds – fourth – fifth – or sixth in the most I am expecting – now go and enjoy yourself, sweetheart.'

Rosie trotted off to join the other competitors who were waiting for the jump off. She walked quietly beside Jacques who was thinking that possibly this could be his last Foxhunter Class with The Flying Fox.

As Rosie had disappeared, Tom had put his arm round Sam. He laughed. 'Maybe Ozzie appeared at a very opportune time – I'm not certain where we were heading.'

'Oh Tom – possibly heaven.'

'Samantha West, you could well be right, but all is not lost. Let's make a date. Ten thirty this evening – bottom of the stairs.'

'Stairs?'

'The golden staircase of course. Where else?'

'Thomas West, you are an incorrigible man.'

'No, just a husband who happens to be a teeny weeny bit in love with his wife.'

'How teeny?'

Tom squeezed her hand. 'That's a leading question, Sammy, but ad infinitum, my darling –but now come back down to earth – Rosie is just entering the arena.'

To Tom's delight, Rosie did exactly what she had been told. She jumped a perfect round, in what he considered was a perfect time. A quarter of an hour later she was receiving a dark green rosette and Tom decided she had finished in a perfect place. Four ponies down the line, Jacques was holding a red velvet rosette and a silver cup. Rosie would not be competing against her favourite cousin next year. - He was bound for higher things. She had decided she would adhere to her father's instructions for the rest of this year but at the New Year Show, at this very venue, she and Braveheart would fly. They had already had a long chat about it. It wasn't only the boys who had inherited Tom's extraordinary ability to talk to their horses. Braveheart and Rosie chatted all the time, they had a unique partnership and she kissed his nose as Jacques closed the lock on his stall and helped Rosie lead Sparkler down the ramp, ready for the 12.2.h.h. Competition. She went to the practice area where she found several members of *the gang,* as well as Cassie who was with her father.

The rain was now coming down in earnest.

'You go and sit in the stand with Suzie,' Charles told Mike. 'There's no sense in us all getting soaked. Tom and I can always nip home for a change of clothes if necessary. Cassie will be fine with us and Justin and James are here too.'

'Well, I won't refuse your offer,' and Mike hurried to the shelter of the stands. When he and Suzie had set off from Lincolnshire much earlier that morning there had not been a single cloud in the sky and he was clad in light jeans and a thin cotton shirt, which was already adhering to his skin.

The riders had taken off their show jackets in exchange for their waterproofs. Fortunately Cassie and Clare's were in the Range Rover with the rest of their luggage.

The ponies were not enjoying the rain as it turned into large hailstones and some little riders were being deposited on the wet grass.

Jean-Pierre quickly opened the doors, which led into the indoor school and hustled the ponies, children and adults into the dry, whilst the class was postponed until this latest downpour was over.

As was so often the case, fifteen minutes later a watery sun had broken through the clouds and there was the obligatory amount of blue-sky to make several sailor's suits.

Jean-Pierre left the school door open in case there should be another sudden downpour, as Tom made certain all Sparkler's studs were fixed securely into his shoes before Rosie cantered into the arena, as the class finally got under way.

Justin was walking round with Abby who was very distressed. Guy Fawkes had been amongst the several ponies that had objected to the hailstones pinging down onto his neck. He had given two huge bucks and before Justin could catch hold of her, Abby had flown through the air.

Justin cursed. Why did these unfortunate things always seem to happen to the most nervous children? Abby had just been beginning to gain confidence on Guy and this was going to be a big setback. Eventually, as she gave no sign of even wanting to enter the arena, he caught hold of Gus and Rupert – sent the latter to the secretary's office to change Guy Fawkes' rider's name and almost threw Gus onto Guy telling his son. 'No way am I going to lose my five pound entry fee, Gus.'

Gus merely sighed as he let down the stirrups and took Guy over the practice jump, whilst Abby's wails reduced to a snivel.

There was no one more delighted than Rosie. 'Gussie, I'm going up in size with Braveheart and you're going the other way with Guy.'

'Yes, Rosie, and Dad needn't think this is going to be a regular occurrence, either. Abby fell off when we had those hailstones and now she wants to ride Fuzz Buzz again but Dad didn't bring him here today and there's not time to go and get him, but Dad won't waste the entry fee. He says if I win more than the five pounds he's paid I can keep the rest. He says now he's got to pay a full time groom he's got to watch every single penny.'

Tom couldn't help overhearing, 'Don't believe a word your Dad says, Gus, take every penny he offers you and make sure he buys you all a really slap up lunch from the bar.'

'Oh, he won't be doing that, Tom. I heard him telling Mum she was being far too extravagant with the butter when she was making the sandwiches this morning.'

'And what did your Mum say?'

'She didn't exactly SAY anything, Tom. She didn't put any butter on his bread at all. Then she put his sandwiches in a foil container, put it in a bag and wrote JUSTIN in huge letters. And Tom, I am going to watch him very carefully. I wouldn't trust him not to try to swap his sandwiches with Noah or Abby's when he discovers what Mum has done.'

'Your poor Mum. It will be hell for her when your Dad finds out.'

'It's strange, Tom. Mum seems to have her own way of dealing with Dad. She just whispers something in his ear and he's in a good mood for the rest of the day.'

Tom grinned to himself – Justin was a mean devil – but obviously Anna had learned where his weakness lay and she had her very own way of dealing with it!!

The twelve two Class had been diminished by more than just Abby – three other young girls had also tumbled to the ground, one being Virginia Mawgan-Whitely, who was the only real casualty. She had fallen awkwardly as the normally placid Pixie Love had shot sideways and with a suspected fractured collarbone, was on the way to Ashford Hospital in Caroline's Range Rover whilst Veronica was trying to load a reluctant Pixie back into their trailer. Fortunately, Jacques had seen her struggling and with his help, at last the pony was safely installed whilst at the hospital Virginia was having her arm put in a sling.

Eventually, including Gus and Guy Fawkes, there were ten entries. Poupée and Pierrot had not been the least upset by the cold hailstones, their calm temperaments prevailing as it always seemed to do. The two small girls followed each other into the arena, as James and Jean-Pierre were both hopping from one foot to another at the edge of the collecting ring, whilst Jane and Elizabeth watched totally unconcerned from the comfort of the director's box in the stand, discussing the forthcoming addition to the Thornley family. Elizabeth shook her older sister's arm. 'Jane, Eloise and Pierrot have just jumped a clear round I think, judging by your husband's reaction.'

Jane sighed. 'Oh, dear, I missed her. Never mind, but don't tell Pierre for goodness sake. He'll be over the moon as usual – watch out, Lizzie we had better not miss Fen's round as well.'

It wasn't long before Fen was joining her cousin in the collecting ring, waiting with their fathers for the jump off. Unfortunately for the two little girls, it wasn't long before Gus, Rosie and Cassie were joining them. Gus and Rosie did a *high five*. 'Game on, Rosie, but Good Luck!'

Unfortunately for both Rosie and Gus the game was definitely not on, as both Sparkler and Guy Fawkes uncharacteristically hit the last fence in their jockey's efforts to beat each other – the proud winner of her first class at this prestigious show was Cassie Lewis with her game little pony, Sailor Boy, and to James' and Jean-Pierre's delight, Eloise and Fenella took second and third places. Tom took success and failure in his stride but Justin was not pleased. 'That boy has just wasted twenty quid – he needs to keep his mind on the jumps – not on your blooming daughter.'

Tom laughed at Justin. 'And who do I remember couldn't keep his eyes off a certain red head when he was jumping in the Pony Club Team a good many years ago, upsetting his dad,' and Justin actually had the grace to blush.

'Touché, Tom, but Gus had better concentrate in the next class. I shall have strong words with him.'

'Well, at least he only looks at Rosie, Justin. That would appear to be the difference between the two of you!!'

It was Justin's turn to laugh. 'I couldn't help it if all the girls fancied me, Tom.' But five minutes later, Tom could hear his friend berating young Gus.

'Concentrate, Gus – keep your eyes off Rosie West and firmly on to the next fence.'

'Sorry, Dad, but I think Rosie must have been looking at me too, Sparkler hardly ever knocks a pole.'

'Well, I'll take the five pounds you won and I am afraid that will leave you with precisely zilch, in other words, nothing.'

'Not to worry Dad. The money doesn't really matter.'

'Not matter!! Money not matter!!' Justin was incredulous that his own son's outlook on life could be so different to his own and then a sense of shame crept over him, as Gus told him. 'Not really, Dad. As long as I am with Rosie and *the gang,* I'm happy and that is good enough for me.' Then he grinned at Justin. 'I will try and win with Pie and Hamlet, but it won't be easy, there's some very hot competition today.'

'Well, put Guy back in the horsebox and then come up to the stand. Mum's got our picnic.'

Gus was wondering how his dad was going to enjoy the sandwiches he was about to sample.

'Why have we all got individual packets with our names on today, Anna?' Justin asked.

'Because Abby doesn't like tomatoes and I've made some banana sandwiches especially for Noah, it seemed easier.'

Justin bit hungrily into his ham sandwich. 'God, Anna – this is as dry as a bone – it tastes like sawdust. You must have forgotten the butter.'

'Oh no, Justin, I didn't forget – you told me I was being too extravagant, so I thought you would be pleased if I didn't give you any.'

Justin said several rude words, which Anna totally ignored before he hurried to the bar. He came back with a bap filled with salad and prawns oozing out of the sides. 'This cost a bloody fortune, Anna.'

She smiled at him and nibbled a prawn that had fallen on his jeans. 'I'm sure it will be worth it later on, Justin.'

He laughed. 'I'll bloody well make sure it is, you conniving little wench,' but Gus was happy as he saw his mother smile and pass one of her sandwiches to his father. It was all Gus had wanted since the day his father had returned into his young life when he had been the same age as Noah was now. He also recognized that his mother knew the perfect way to keep his father in order, he loved them both to bits and so if they were happy, then Gus most certainly was too.

'I'm going with Rosie to get Hamlet and Le Duc, Dad. Tom's coming with us.'

'O.K. I will see you in the collecting ring in ten minutes.' Anna was handing him another of her sandwiches. 'Do you want another, Justin? If not I'll throw them away.'

Justin was horrified. 'Anna, you can't possibly just chuck them away. Take the ham out when we get home and we'll have it with a salad and we can toast the bread for our breakfast tomorrow.'

'Justin, I really do despair of you. Have you looked at your bank statement lately by the way?'

'Oh, yes. It's not too bad.'

'So what in your opinion is not too bad?'

'Well my current account was just over four and a half million - but actually it's quite a bit less now. I wrote two pretty hefty cheques the other day. I gave a quarter of a million to a charity I quite fancied.'

'Justin, that's amazing. You are a really good person. What was the charity?'

'It helps people recover from brain injuries. Sometimes I can't sleep when I think about Adrian and Amy. I paid a cheque for two hundred and fifty thousand pounds into Amy's account too – at least she won't have to worry about money for a while. Oh, well. I had better see what young Gus is up too.'

Anna took hold of his hand. 'Justin – I love you – overtime tonight, darling, and on Amy's behalf, thank you from the bottom of my heart.'

Justin grinned. 'Cheap at the price, my darling,' and he was whistling as he went to find his son.

Anna wasn't altogether surprised when five minutes later the bartender came to find her, carrying a small tray on which a glass of bubbling champagne was standing. 'With the compliments of Mr. Wright- Smith, madam,' he said as he handed her the tray.

Anna smiled – she never completely understood the complex

nature of her husband and she very much doubted if he understood it himself but there was one thing she knew for certain - there was nobody else quite like him and she loved him with all her heart.

The thirteen two class ended with its usual predictability with Humbug and Oscar coming first and Gus and Hamlet close behind. Rosie and the Duc were third with Orlando and Rupert tying for fourth place with Jet and The March Hare. Clare and her pony, Flying High, were fifth and Georgia squeezed into sixth place. It had been an extremely successful hour for *the gang.*

There were two Junior Open Classes that afternoon. The first was a slightly less formidable course than the second, which would count towards qualifying for the Championship the Equestrian Centre was going to hold at the New Year Meeting.

Jacques had decided to jump in both classes. Firstly with Foxy and then with Beau Geste in the larger open. Mimi, Oscar and Josh were going to do the same with their ponies and Gus and Oliver were just going to do the more difficult option.

When Mike suggested they should make their way back to Lincolnshire, it was Clare who begged to stay and watch Oliver and her father good-naturedly pandered to her request, as Jonty demanded his fourth ice cream.

It was definitely to be Oscar's day as he won the fist Open with his Countess' Goldfinger. He carefully picked the pink and green rosette, and then pushed the brown envelope into his pocket patting the ever-reliable palomino pony. He grinned at Josh and Lily who had come second and glanced down the line to Mimi, two girls he didn't know and then lastly to Jacques and Foxy who had just completed his first Junior Open. Jacques had been sensible and was more than happy with his result.

It was the final competition that was the important class of the day. Points were on offer for the first six places to help towards qualifying for the Championship. Tom was looking at the faces of the young boys and girls in the collecting ring – some a trifle nervous – some excited and some determined but it was the expression on one particular boy's face that caught his eye. It was a look that said it all – he was going to win. Sam was standing with Mary. 'Mary, just look at his face,' and she was pointing to Oscar. 'Who does he remind you of?'

Mary laughed. 'His father when he rode The Likely Lad, who else?'

'I know he's a handful, Mary, but his heart is just like Tom's – pure gold. He's already given his first two rosettes he won today to Anne-Marie. Underneath that exterior there is a very vulnerable young man and I just pray Anne-Marie never breaks his heart.'

The sun was now shining and on this beautiful afternoon, Sam's fears seemed highly unlikely – but unlike Satin, she was unable to see into the future and if it had been possible, she would have been extremely disturbed. Life was never as straightforward as it might appear.

Sam shuddered, as someone appeared to walk over her grave, as she briefly recalled the terrible time when she had been sixteen and she and Tom had parted. It had been the worst four months of her life and it hadn't been because of another boy or girl – she had been jealous and afraid of a horse. The horse she had eventually come to love so much – Tom's wonderful Black Satin.

She determinedly pushed all thoughts of the past out of her head and walked to the edge of the arena, watching Tom as he walked the course with Josh, Orlando, Oliver and Oscar. It was certainly large, as the boys could just see over the tops of the jumps.

Gus and Mimi were walking with Justin and Charles who were soon joined by Jean-Pierre and Jacques.

The competition had barely started before the jumps were taking their toll. Mimi and Orlando both had four faults and there was only one clear round by the unknown girl who had come fourth in the previous class, this time riding an extremely strong bay gelding. Josh and Ganger were the first of *the gang* to jump clear and he appeared to start a trend as Jacques and Beau Geste and

Gus and The Pie soon followed. There were eight more hopefuls each who had four faults when to Clare's obvious delight Oliver and Fizz jumped what Tom admitted was the luckiest clear of the afternoon when Fizz clouted the pole in the middle of the treble. It shot at least a foot into the air and then by some miracle, landed back in its cups.

'Bloody lucky, Ollie,' the determined Oscar shouted to his sibling as he passed him in the entrance to the arena.

The lady judge sighed. 'Can't Tom West do anything about that child's language? He's an impossible lad.'

The other judge who was a young man laughed. 'He's also extremely highly talented, just look,' and they watched in silence as Oscar and Hanky Panky pranced their way round the course.

Oscar had been the penultimate competitor and when the last boy in the class had eight faults there were only six clear rounds. There would be points for them all, but by far the most for the eventual winner.

Josh and Ganger were at a disadvantage as they commenced the jump off. Above all, Josh wanted to go clear, which he did, but he knew his time was there to be beaten.

Jacques and Beau Geste were fractionally slower, but Josh was well aware his main adversaries were yet to come and they happened to be Gus and his two younger brothers. Josh thought Gus was faster, but when the time was announced, to his surprise, The Pie had been half a second slower than Ganger and now at the worst he knew he had to come third and that would still give him a good number of points. He stood by his parents and silently watched his brothers. Ollie wanted to show Clare there was more in his life than just music and he set Fizz alight as they shot through the start.

Tom smiled at Josh as Ollie's time was announced. 'Take it on the chin, Josh – there is nothing else you can do. You were unlucky to be the one that had to set the time.'

Oliver came to join them, standing up in his stirrups as he watched the final competitor which, unfortunately for him was Oscar with Panky.

Tom held his breath whilst Sam held his hand. She said nothing except. 'Tough luck, Ollie, but really well done.'

'I'll never beat Oz, Dad. He's special isn't he?'

'You're all special in my eyes, Ollie and by the law of averages one day Panky has to have a fence down, so seize your chance then.'

'I know, Dad, but what about Josh and Lando – Lando was unlucky today – it's bloody hard.'

Oliver very rarely swore but Tom understood exactly how he was feeling.

'I can sympathize Ollie. I had Justin and Lizzie always breathing down my neck – but remember - you and Fizz have picked up a good number of points and so has Josh. I reckon you will all make the Championship and there are two more shows yet with more points on offer. When you have collected your rosettes go and say goodbye to Cassie and Clare all of you. Their dad is anxious to get going. They've got a long drive ahead of them.'

To Tom's surprise he noticed the suspicion of a tear in the usually undemonstrative Ollie. 'I don't want to say goodbye to Clare, Dad. It's been a fantastic week.'

'And you will all have lots more together I am sure, Ollie. Don't forget we are taking the caravan and camping in their field at the end of September.'

'That's a long time away,' Oliver sighed.

'Good things are worth waiting for, Ollie – always remember that. Now off you go and I'll see you back at the horsebox.'

Tom noticed Oscar was on his mobile, texting frantically. 'Oz, you need to get your rosette. Who on earth are you texting?'

'My Countess, of course Dad, I've left her a message, look and Tom read. *'Had a bloody good day. Goldie and Panky both came first. Had to tell you, Oz.*

He immediately received a reply. '*Well done, Oscar. I told you they were both super ponies but they have certainly got a bloody good rider, Lavinia and Totty.*'

Oscar pushed his mobile under Tom's nose. 'Look, Dad.'

Tom read the countess' text. 'I think you have met a kindred spirit, Oscar.'

'She's my Countess, Dad. My bloody own Countess.'

Tom and Sam both shook their heads in despair but when Oscar was out of earshot, Sam whispered, 'and he's a bloody good jockey, Tom.'

'Sam!! – but O.K. it's true, bloody good, but for God's sake don't tell him. He'll find out for himself quite soon enough.'

CHAPTER 34

The following morning Mary and Sam put two sleeping bags and two pillows in Sam's car before setting off to Chislehurst. They also gathered as many card board boxes and newspapers as they could lay their hands on and set off with a feeling of anticipation as they made their way through the traffic in the direction of Chislehurst.

Tom was looking after the children whilst Mary and Sam stayed the night in the flat. They knew they would need a minimum of two days to sort through the mountain of contents inside the rooms and they could carry on with the task well into the evening if they didn't have to make the journey home in the rush hour.

They had packed a hamper of food and they would be more than adequately catered for during the two days.

Tom was going to take the children to Lake House for the afternoon. He wanted to spend time with Rosie and Braveheart and after all *the gang* had had a rare lesson with him, whilst Charles took the rest to the swimming pool, he was going to see if he could restore a little of the confidence Abby had lost the previous afternoon.

'Bring Fuzz Buzz,' he had told Justin who seemed to be in a world of his own. Partly because Peregrine and his entourage were expected at Theobald's Place in time for an evening meal, which Anna was kindly providing at seven o'clock and partly due to the aftermath of a very steamy night.

'Wake up, Justin. What did I just ask you?'

'Sorry, Tom. Anna was on great form, she' ----

Tom broke in abruptly. 'Spare me the details, Justin – just bring Fuzz Buzz and Guy. Daisy can have a jump on Guy – she's well capable.'

'O.K. My new groom is arriving this evening. I must be back by six thirty.'

'Justin – it's now one thirty – if you think I am teaching a gang of kids for five hours, you can think again!!'

The children were excited. They didn't often have the privilege of Tom's expertise. He was not such a hard taskmaster as Charles but his lessons never ended in the raucous chaos that Justin's tended to do. Charles would get the maximum he could from his pupils, whereas Tom always left them with a little more in the tank.

He smiled at Abby. 'You just watch with Fuzz Buzz, Abby, then you and I will go for a ride round the lake. Hannah told me she saw the kingfisher this morning. You never know, if we ride very quietly we might be lucky. I'll ride one of the bigger ponies. You can choose which one whilst you are watching *the gang*.'

Tom was pleased with Rosie, she was absolutely at one with Braveheart and he decided to enter them for the Foxhunter Class in Surrey the following weekend.

After an hour with *the gang*, he smiled at Abby. 'Now, have you decided? Who shall I ride?'

'Babushka,' she told him. 'I think she will be sensible and she's quite a big pony.'

'O.K. Babushka it is. Can I borrow her Mimi?'

Mimi handed her to Tom and held her whilst he lengthened the stirrups.

'Can we come as well?' Eloise and Fenella were asking, 'We would like to see the kingfisher too.'

'Yes, it will be a very steady ride. Certainly no galloping.'

'That's O.K.' and Tom was soon leaving with Abby and Fuzz Buzz close beside him and Fenella and Eloise trotting behind on the almost identical Poupée and Pierrot.

They were in luck. The kingfisher flew from the opposite bank, right down the middle of the lake – a jewel – flashing in the late afternoon sun.

'Uncle Tom, it was so, so beautiful. It was the same colour as one of Mummy's earrings,' Fenella told him. 'I think she said it was an aqua – aqua –aqua' –

'Aquamarine. I think, Fen and you are absolutely right. Look, there it goes back to the bank and watch carefully, it's swallowing a small fish.'

The three little girls didn't move as they watched the beautiful little bird swallow its catch.

'I didn't realize they were so small, Tom,' Abby told him and to his delight she was sitting happily on Fuzz Buzz seemingly without a single care in the world.

Halfway back Tom asked Abby. 'How about a slow canter?'

She nodded and shortened her reins as the four of them made their way back to the end of the lake before walking back to the school.

'Now, ten minutes over some trotting poles, the three of you,' and Abby made no objections, but at the end of the lesson, she whispered to Tom.

'I don't want to ride Guy Fawkes, Uncle Tom – I just want to ride Fuzz Buzz.'

'That's fine, Abby. We'll tell Daddy. He will understand. Daisy can exercise Guy for now. She's several years older than you. Now let's get the ponies in the stables and then join the others in the pool.'

Tom sat down beside Justin who asked him. 'How did it go, Tom?'

'Really good, but she has told me she doesn't want to ride Guy. He's quite a strong pony, Justin – why not let Daisy jump him for a bit? What's Alfie doing these days?'

'Alfie's at Theobald's with Anna's Topsy.'

'Get him in, Justin. He would be perfect for Abby.'

'But Tom, he's twenty four now.'

'That's nothing, Justin. He could get her over this crisis. He's the perfect schoolmaster. Twink was older than that when he taught Rosie to jump.'

Justin thought for a moment then smiled at Tom. 'Thanks, Tom, I'll take your advice. Gus can ride him tomorrow just to make sure he's sound and them I'll get some shoes put on him. Perhaps I did retire him too soon.'

'Well, I am certain you did. He won't let you down I'm sure of that but if you want a small piece of my advice, Justin, I think you should call Lizzie or James and suggest Fen is the reserve rider for the school team. I think it would be a load off your young daughter's mind. She has got plenty more years at the Primary School – there is absolutely no point in pushing her unnecessarily. I'm sure you agree with me.'

'You're right, Tom, as usual. I'll ring James tonight once I've settled my groom into his new surroundings.'

'Lord Peregrine – God – Justin, I'm dying to meet him.'

'Well, I'm certain you won't have to wait long. Now I had better grab Abby and Gus or he will be at Theobald's before I am. I can't leave Anna to deal with a misogynist on her own and thanks a million for helping Abby.' He was laughing as he called his children.

Mary and Sam had made their way safely to Chislehurst. Mary had been taken aback when Sam had opened the door and she had seen the Victorian tiles on the floor in the square hall and the original pine doors, which led to the various rooms. She stared in amazement at the contents that seemed to fill every room. 'Sam, darling, wherever are we going to begin?'

Sam laughed. 'With a cup of coffee, I think, Mary and then how about finding out how far away the nearest recycling skip is, I think more than a few visits will be necessary. Let's start in the most boring room, the kitchen. I noticed a small store at the corner of the road. I'll go and ask them about the rubbish tip and see if they know of any house clearance firms who would take the stuff that's too good for the dump and not good enough for a London auction house.'

'You nip up to the shop, Sam whilst I make us a cup of coffee.'

'O.K. I won't be more than five minutes.' and Sam hurried up the road in the direction of the old-fashioned corner shop. Her mission was successful as having purchased a bottle of wine to fortify Mary and herself that evening, she asked the helpful Indian lady, who was obviously the owner of the shop where she could find the nearest refuse tip. Fortunately, it wasn't too far away and she immediately gave her the name of a reputable firm who undertook house clearances.

They had arranged with the auction house to send a van the following day to remove all the larger pieces of furniture and to pack the smaller, breakable items which Sam had no use for at Woodcutters. She wanted the more valuable pieces to have left the flat before the house clearance firm arrived. She could imagine them eyeing all the silver and bronzes with eagle eyes.

'What about that beautiful Meissen fruit service, Sam?' Mary asked.

'Mary, I don't know. It's a complete set. We have four boys – well four and a half with Oscar – probably six if you include Tom into the equation. It would be dreadful if something got broken. Woodcutters isn't really a Meissen type of cottage. I love the blue and white dinner set Miranda gave us. I think I should be sensible, Mary. It will have to go to London.'

'I agree with you, Sam – it must be worth an awful lot of money.'

Mary soon found marks on the bottom of the teapot with the swan neck. 'Rockingham, Sam, and again it is a complete set.'

Sam sighed. 'Oh dear, it had better go as well.'

In the bottom of the dresser, Sam discovered something she did want to keep. It was an early blue and white Spode dinner set. It almost matched the service Miranda had given them.

'I must keep this, Mary. Look at the gorgeous soup tureens and ladles and this wonderful serving dish and look, four vegetable dishes all complete with their lids. I love it and I know Tom would too. Let's pack it carefully in our strongest boxes and stack it in the corner of the kitchen until we leave tomorrow.'

There were four more complete tea sets. Two were from the Minton factory and one was Worcester. Each piece painted with a bird of some description –the fourth was distinctive – it was Clarice Cliff. Mary knew immediately that it was a rare and sought after pattern. 'Sam, I think it could be worth a lot of money.'

'I don't care, Mary. One day I think Rosie and Gus would love this. Perhaps' ---

'Rosie and Gus?'

'Mary, you know they are just like Tommy and I were. I'm not so sure about the boys, but I am absolutely certain about those two. They are almost like a little old Derby and Joan already!!'

'Well, Sam, at least he will get what his father could never manage.'

'Mary, what do you mean?'

'Sam –we all knew. Justin was in love with you all the time you were growing up. Didn't you realize?'

'I did. He was always a really good friend but you know only too well, Mary, there could never be anyone else for me but Tom. He was my prince – he always has been and he always will be. Thank goodness now Justin has all he could possibly want with Anna, Abby and Gus and my darling little godson Noah. Anyway, this tea set is going nowhere, Mary other than Woodcutters. I'll pack it carefully and put it over in that corner with the dinner set.'

After two more Spode dinner sets were discovered and left to go to the auction house and a mass of silver knives, spoons and forks as well, Mary and Sam stopped for a quick lunch before tackling the sitting room.

This was a massive job. The display cabinets were filled with literally hundreds of mainly small but interesting silver and bronze pieces.

Sam particularly loved the cold painted Austrian bronzes, which mainly depicted a vast variety of animals and birds.

'I love these, Mary. This horse looks rather like Oscar's Panky. I'll give it to him but he'll probably give it to Anne-Marie. He gives her nearly all the rosettes he wins. I still sometimes wonder what it is that attracts him but she is a dear girl – but I worry – I haven't told Tom, but several times Satin has been up to his tricks. He's often showing me Oscar crying in a strange room and Simon and Rob are always there too. That horse is psychic, Mary, it probably means nothing but if he shows me anything else, I shall definitely tell Tom.'

'A problem shared is a problem halved, Sammy. Don't keep anything from Tom. Maybe he can talk to that animal and find out what it is all about.'

'Maybe I will, but everything is fine at the moment,' and Sam changed the subject. 'What shall we sort through next?'

'Lets go through the bureau and get rid of any papers that are of no interest.'

They walked over to a Queen Anne Walnut bureau, which stood in the far corner of the room. It had three large drawers and when they opened the writing flap there was a slide under which they discovered a deep well where Sam found a square parcel, carefully wrapped in several layers of brown paper and tied securely with string. On the top in now faded writing, she could just make out a message. It was poignant and sad – it just said *'Joshua – gone – my heart is broken.'* Great Uncle Joseph had obviously had a very deep affection for his nephew and had been too upset to have the photographs on display after his tragic death.

Sam sat down and undid the knots in the thick string, which secured the precious memories.

There were photographs of her father from the days when he

was sitting smiling in a rather old fashioned perambulator – to the last one which was of her own christening. Joshua was dressed in his army uniform, holding her in her Christening gown whilst her mother was smiling up at him, totally unaware of the impending tragedy that lay ahead.

She looked at pictures of her father doing various activities. Fencing at school, serving an ace at tennis, diving off a high board, standing on his head laughing in the sea and finally in his school uniform with Alice beside him dressed in her navy school skirt and the obligatory checked cotton shirt.

Sam was shaken. She could almost be looking at her own Joshua with his dark, curly hair, beautiful smile and long, slender figure. The only difference was Tom's piercing blue eyes, which Josh had inherited. She felt hot tears running down her cheeks and Mary's comforting arm round her shoulders.

'Sam, these are so special – I am sure you would want to keep them, they are all you have left of your father.'

'No, not all, Mary. Rosie and I are a living legacy. The trips are one hundred per cent West, Josh has Tom's eyes, but Rosie and I have everything my father had to give us and I am proud. I shall take these to Mummy. She must have the first choice. I know Peter wouldn't mind, after all, he has several photos of Rebecca, his first wife. She was an enormous part of his life and that's how it should be. These are all in beautiful silver frames – the children should have one each in their bedrooms. After all he was their grandfather and they must never forget that.'

Sam wrapped them carefully, before returning to the rest of the drawers in the bureau where she discovered share certificates and bank statements, telling her she was inheriting far more than just the flat and its contents.

'Mary, I am totally overwhelmed by all this. I shall ask Elspeth about setting up a trust for each of the children, perhaps to mature when they are twenty-one. They are fortunate young people, the boys already have their cottages in Theobald's Row and Rosie will eventually have The Little Oast, but Tom and I will never cease to forget Charles' generosity when he gave us Woodcutters when we were scrimping and scraping, trying to save the money to buy it. Tom has been lucky with his horses, but it doesn't follow that the boys will enjoy the same good fortune. I'm not certain about Oliver, but I can't imagine Josh and Oscar not following in Tom's footsteps and probably Orlando and Rosie too. If they have a little security behind them, then Tom and I will be happy.'

Mary and Sam worked until ten o'clock that evening, by which time they had discovered many, many treasures. Sam's head was spinning. She had decided to keep all the cold painted bronzes and selected a few of the silver vinaigrettes. Some had intricate pictures worked in enamel on the tops and there was a cigarette box with a famous London retailer's mark underneath which had an enamel picture on the lid of a mare and its foal, which she wrapped extra carefully. That was for Tom. He had never smoked a cigarette in his life but she thought he could put his paper clips and rubber bands in it and have it on top of the desk in his study.

Sam had already arranged for a removal van to come to the flat the following day and she had put a red dot on the pieces of furniture she wanted to keep and a blue one for the items to be taken to London to the auction house.

The bureau and a carved hallstand in the guise of two bears at the bottom of a large tree were destined for Woodcutters. She thought Rosie would love to hang her anorak on the hooks which protruded from the top of the tree under which a large bear and her baby had been intricately carved at least a hundred years ago in the Black Forest in Germany. She wasn't certain what Tom would think about this slightly weird object but if he voiced any doubts about it, she was confident the rest of the family would outnumber him.

The removal van would also transport the beautiful iron garden bench and chairs with their seats interwoven with leaves and flowers, each piece stamped with the mark Coalbrookdale.

She had put a red sticker on the various bow front chests of drawers and some of the small oak tables and chairs which could be stored in one of the barns, She had a feeling that one day they could come in useful. Then, as she looked on the floors, she noticed the old Persian rugs and soon she had earmarked those for Massenden as well.

Mary had discovered another bronze in the bottom of the wardrobe in the spare bedroom. It was an endearing sculpture of two dachshund dogs. 'Look, Sam, Mac and Mabel.'

'Have them. Mary and anything else you fancy. I think John would love those.'

'Do you think I could take this picture of the Jacob sheep for John? I think it's Victorian but I don't recognize the artist. It's very well executed though. It would be so appropriate in his little study.'

Sam was exclaiming after she had opened a box and found it filled with antique jewelry. There was a valuation certificate from a London jeweler written many moons ago and a note, obviously written by Great Uncle Joseph, stating that these items had belonged to his late mother Olive Smythe and his great aunts Ada and Emma Smythe.

Sam was looking at a long gold guard chain and several art deco pendants with peridots, amethysts and aquamarines. In a separate smaller box, she discovered three fifteen carat gold gate bracelets which she slipped into her hand bag with a plain gold chain, long enough to go twice round even the fattest of necks. She would keep them for the boys – maybe one day they would have special girls who they would like to give them to. She picked out one piece for Rosie and one for herself. They were two very simple Victorian pendants; one was a little diamond flower with a ruby in the middle and the other an identical flower but the centre was graced by a beautiful bright blue sapphire. She imagined Great Aunts Emma and Ada when they were young girls, wearing these to hunt balls and coming out parties, dressed in fine dresses and gold sandals.

There was another box with various rings which neither Sam nor Mary wanted to keep. Sam had never once removed the ring she loved so much that Tom had given her at Gervaise Castle, the night he had officially asked her to marry him when she had been seventeen years old and she wanted nothing else, but she insisted Mary took a little gold brooch in the shape of a bee with a diamond for its body and two dark red rubies for its eyes. It was appropriate for Mary who had her own hives of bees and took her bee keeping very seriously.

By three o'clock the following afternoon. Braggs, Braggs and Sons were loading the furniture destined for Woodcutters. The auction house had sent their own van to transport the valuable pieces to London and Jim Brent's house clearance firm had arrived. After much bartering, where Mary came in extremely useful, Sam was holding a cheque for ten thousand pounds. She was certain there must have been some valuable object that Mary and she had overlooked but she was more than satisfied.

Jeremiah Courtney had arranged that the flat would be sold on the 15th October in an auction room in Mayfair and at last she and Mary climbed into the people carrier, which was laden with numerous boxes, pictures and one or two crates of antique toys Mary had discovered in a cupboard in the attic at the very last moment. They hadn't even had time to look through them but they were now squashed on the back seat.

Sam called Tom. *'We're on our way home, darling. Dirty, tired and laden with all sorts of goodies.'*

'Take great care in the suburban traffic, my darling and when you get home, Rosie and I have made you a surprise.'

'A surprise?'

'Yes, for our supper.'

'What's cooking, Tom?'

'Rosie's wait and see pie.'

'Big kiss to Rosie and to you too, Tommy. Love you, oh, and your Mum says a big kiss from her too. See you soon.'

'Ad infinitum, my Sammy.'

'For ever and always my handsome hunk.' And the car sped on to Massenden.

Sam dropped Mary at Old Tiles. She was going to have a quick bath and then enjoy the luxury of a meal at La Casa with John.

'Mary, thank you so much, I could never, never have managed without your help and when I have sorted the boxes tomorrow you must come and collect the bronze figure and the picture of the sheep. I think I shall just lock the car and pray Boswell does his guard job tonight. I'm too exhausted to lift one single box this evening. I must re-charge my batteries before Messrs. Braggs Bros arrive tomorrow morning. Love to John and enjoy your meal, whilst I go and discover what delicacies Rosie and Tom have concocted for our supper.'

As Sam turned off the engine of the car, she wondered whatever could be a more welcoming sight than one handsome man, three identical boys, one slightly older, dark-haired son and a beautiful little daughter all running towards you – there arms outstretched, each one wanting to fling their arm round you.

She had a lump in her throat – it had been an emotional and exhausting two days and after each of her children had almost throttled her - Tom's gentle kiss and the feel of his hand caressing the back of her neck was all she could ever wish for. The money and the wonderful items, which lay unopened in the boxes, were insignificant beside the wealth of love she felt for her precious family.

Rosie was pulling her hand. 'Mummy, Mummy, come in the kitchen. Dads and I have been slaving all day.' Tom and Sam both laughed.

'That's what Mummy does every day, Rosie but I'm sure she is really hungry – let's see if the pud is ready.'

Boiling away on the hob were two enormous steak and kidney

puddings and in the middle of the table, two mouth watering raspberry Pavlovas.

Sam recognized the puddings immediately. Sylvia Charlton was famous for them and there was a long queue at her stall at the farmer's market every Tuesday morning and at the next stall, Anne Grice's Pavlovas were notorious.

'Gosh, Tom, you have been busy. Pavlova, Rosie! Amazing!'

'I did say it was a special meal, my darling and we did have to peel the potatoes and slice the green beans. Oh and fill the saucepans with water.'

Rosie was still hopping from one foot to the other. 'It was fun Mummy, we all rode down to the market. The boys held Madam and Braveheart whilst Dads and I bought our super. It was great. Oscar and Ollie put the puddings in their rucksacks and Dads managed to balance the pavalovas on his knees. We had to walk but we called in to Theobald's and met Justin's new groom and Binny and Wills. They are going to the grammar schools with the boys and Mimi next term. Perry is really nice. He's got ever such a posh voice and a fantastic horsebox. It's silver and blue – it even makes Justin's look scruffy. He was getting the stables ready and this afternoon they were going to move Justin's horses to Theobald's Place. Binny and Wills were going to ride up to Lake House with Abby and Gus but Dads took us to see Marigold.' Sam was slightly disconcerted when Rosie giggled.

She noticed Tom was not looking her straight in her eyes. 'And what delights did Marigold have on offer?' she asked.

'Oh,' Tom replied in an offhand voice. 'Actually, she had a puppy she wanted to show us – a labradoodle the same colour as Bertie. Ten weeks old, called Hector.'

'Oh, yes, and where exactly is this Hector now?'

Tom sheepishly opened the door to his study. Scampering feet, a cold wet nose and a series of very wet licks greeted Sam. The big dog bed was lying in front of Tom's desk in which Holy and

Bertie had just woken up whilst Boswell was growling uncertainly at the newcomer.

Tom was looking pleadingly at Sam – so were four pairs of blue eyes and one pair of soft brown ones – she sighed. 'Welcome to Bedlam, Hector,' and both Tom and the puppy seemed to be kissing her at the same time.

Sam was well aware that Bertie was an old dog, nearly fourteen years old. She recognized that Hector would relieve the agony Tom would undoubtedly have to endure the day his faithful old dog departed this world and sadly she knew this day was approaching more quickly than either she or Tom would acknowledge. She kissed him again, telling him, 'He's lovely, darling – all I hope is that Boswell stops growling before too many days have passed.'

Fortunately for Hector, Boswell was soon to encounter something far more annoying than a playful puppy. Soon, a huge brown bear was going to be sitting in the corner of the utility room. It would take all of Boswell's attention and Hector would be left in peace with little Holly who wouldn't leave his side.

The puddings and pavalovas had completely disappeared and Sam's eyes were almost shutting when Tom asked. 'Should we unload the car? Is there anything valuable in there?'

'Tom, I think there may well be thousands of pounds worth of stuff – but I really can't lift one more box for the foreseeable future.'

Tom looked at the boys who had just finished stacking the dishwasher. 'Come on, chaps, we can't leave the boxes in the car all night, just our luck Boz will decide to sulk and go off duty this evening. Carry the boxes very carefully. We'll put them against the wall in the playroom.'

Oscar was struggling with a particularly heavy box, which contained part of the Spode dinner service. 'Cor, Dad, I need to go to Charles' gym more often. I can't budge it at all.'

Tom laughed. 'God knows what treasures Mum has got hidden inside this one but trips, you take the medium size boxes, Josh and

I will carry these monsters between us and Rosie you bring the odd bits and pieces Mum has obviously chucked in as an after thought.'

Whilst the rest of the family were unloading the car, Sam ran herself a hot bath, poured in a mass of bath salts and foam and laughed, wondering why she was never able to have a good soak without an audience. Usually, it was an appreciative pair of blue eyes that were appraising her shapely body, however, at this moment, the owner of those eyes was currently heaving boxes into the playroom and it was a pair of liquid amber eyes that were staring unflinchingly at her. Boswell was sitting with his head resting on the edge of the bath, jealously guarding his mistress from the new young upstart who had stolen both his bed and his friend Holly. There was no way this mischievous newcomer was going to take his beloved mistress as well and his ever-watchful eyes didn't once stray away from Sam. She smiled. She didn't imagine Boz was appreciating her bath time in quite the same manner as the owner of those piercing blue eyes that were far more accustomed to invading her privacy.

She put on her bath robe and wandered downstairs to find the boxes had all been neatly stacked and her exhausted children and husband indulging in five cans of coke and a large glass of lager.

'God, Sammy, did you and Mum carry all those boxes to the car?'

'Of course, darling. Unfortunately for us, we didn't find an Aladdin's lamp with a Genie to help us amongst Great Uncle Joseph's treasures,' she laughed. 'Boswell doesn't trust your new foundling, Tom. He sat with his head on the side of the bath not taking his eyes of me.'

Tom was about to make a rather saucy repartee until he noticed five pairs of eyes peering at him over the rims of their cans of coke. He gave an exaggerated yawn.

'Come on you lot, drink up, I'm exhausted after moving all those boxes – bed time for everyone – take Hector into the garden, Josh and the other dogs too.'

As the youngsters and the dogs disappeared into the garden with

Boswell still growling at the totally unconcerned Hector, Tom took Sam's hand. 'I think I'll have a bath after heaving all those boxes, you had better come and make sure I don't drown. I could do with a pair of brown eyes watching over me and I am NOT referring to Boswell's!!'

CHAPTER 35

Tom had departed with all the children, in the direction of Lake House. All the youngsters who had been selected for either the Pony Club or the Primary School Teams were going to have a workout with Charles and Dom.

Fortunately for Sam, Tom had decided to walk up to the indoor school with Bertie and Holly following faithfully behind him, whilst Hector tore from side to side of the footpath on his long lead. It was strange to see several empty stables from which Justin's horses had been eyeing all that was going on around them, but yesterday afternoon Perry and Justin had walked up to Lake House and eventually all Justin's horses were now ensconced in the fully restored Victorian stables at Theobald's Place along with Perry's amiable but highly excitable Passe Partout. Binny and Will's ponies had settled in their new surroundings straight away and were grazing happily with The Pie and Hamlet, with Fuzz Buzz and Alfie in the adjoining paddock.

Sam was feeling refreshed after an excellent night's sleep and was now ready to face the excitement of undoing all the boxes with the help of both Alice and Mary.

'I think we will lay everything out on the big table in the playroom,' Sam suggested as she pulled the extending table to its maximum length. Alice gasped when she saw the beautiful Spode dinner service.

'Sam, it's stunning but wherever are you going to put it?'

'I think in the bottom of the dresser until the boys are at least sixteen – the tureens and ladles are to die for and I shall put the Clarice Cliff there too. The small bronzes and little pieces of silver will be fine. I have kept one of the display cabinets that they were in in the flat. I'll find a corner in the sitting room but I really want you to look at these, Mummy,' and Sam handed Alice the pile of photographs she had discovered in the bureau – some but not all in solid silver frames.

'You must take as many as you would like, Mummy. The one I would really like to keep is the one of my dad standing on his head in the sea – it's just the sort of prank our boys would get up to.'

Sam sat her mother on the settee in the sitting room and they spread the photographs out beside her. Mary had stayed in the kitchen hurriedly boiling the kettle. She had the feeling a strong cup of tea might be required.

Sam put her arm round her mother. 'Mummy, this must be so hard for you. I know you adore Peter and you two are blissfully happy, but I know how much you once loved my dad but Peter would understand, he has been through a similar situation.'

'Sam, it's so long ago – when I look at these pictures I find it difficult to believe this young boy was ever my husband. We loved each other and we did crazy things together. He was always doing something bordering on dangerous. Perhaps he was a little like Oscar. I thought he was amazing and I don't think there is ever another love quite like one's first but I don't think I would have had the peaceful life I enjoy with Peter. I would always have been waiting for the next wild adventure to begin.'

'Well I don't know, Mummy. I have only ever had one love and so has Mary, but as long as you are happy now, that can be all that matters.'

Alice was still glancing through the photographs. 'I think I would just like to take this one, Sam,' and she picked out the one of herself and Joshua in their school uniforms. 'That was when my life really and truly started. Magical days.'

'You can take as many as you want, Mummy. I think the children should each have one in their bedrooms – after all he was their grandfather.'

Alice sighed. 'Josh – a grandfather! That is totally unimaginable!

He was like Peter Pan – the little boy who would never grow up, but the dearest person you could ever meet.'

Sam put the rest of the photos back on the table, rather taken aback by her mother's attitude. She had expected tears, but perhaps too much had happened in Alice's life since those halcyon days. There had been the hellish years with Marcus before she had found happiness with Peter. Maybe the past was best left where it was as far as her mother was concerned. She picked up her favourite picture and placed it on the table. She looked at the wide grin on her father's face – so like her own and Rosie's and went back into the playroom and the boxes which were still piled on the floor.

Alice was looking at the Clarice Cliff tea set. 'That's a rare pattern, I think, Sam. I've got a book about Clarice Cliff somewhere. I'll look up the pattern for you.'

'I'm going to make sure I put it somewhere really safe, I think Rosie and Gus might like it one day.'

'Rosie and Gus! What ever do you mean? Sam – you are surely not going to encourage that friendship?'

'Mummy – Gussie is a dear. We have all loved him since the day we prayed for his survival, the day he was born.'

'But Sam – he will be just like Tom was with you. He won't give Rosie a chance to meet other boys.'

Luckily John had just called Mary on her mobile and she was talking to him in the garden, well out of earshot.

'Mummy. I surely don't still have to tell you I never wanted anyone but Tom. If I did miss out on other boys kissing me or maybe wanting even more, then I have not one single regret in this world. My love for Tom has never wavered and I am one hundred percent certain if you asked him how he felt he would tell you exactly the same. Perhaps we are lucky but there is no one on this universe that could have made me happier than Tom has done all these years.' And Sam thought of last night when somehow or other she had ended up in the bath with him!!

'It's hell for both of us when he is away jumping but the heaven when he is home makes up for all that. Rosie is much too young to think of Gussie as anything other than her very special friend but I can assure you, if in a few years time they are still inseparable, then I shall do nothing to try to influence her to broaden her experience. They are a very special duo and frankly I hope and I think it will always be the case.'

'Sam, I only wanted you to enjoy growing up.'

'Mummy, darling, I can assure you it was an experience I shall never forget – it was perfect and it will be for Rosie and possibly Ozzie too. He adores Anne-Marie.'

Alice laughed – 'That funny little French girl – but she has charming manners and her mother is such a lovely person.'

'Anne-Marie is good for Ozzie. She wants to be a doctor. That's a long stint at Uni – their love will have to be really solid to survive that. Only time will tell. Now would you like to choose whatever takes your fancy from this box of jewellery? There's a very pretty bracelet with turquoise and pearls set in fifteen carat gold. According to Mary, that means it is Victorian.'

Alice fell in love with the bracelet and as Sam fastened it round her wrist asked. 'What about putting all these things away, Sam?'

'I want Tommy to see them first. He and the children will help me when they get back from Lake House. He's keeping them out of the way whilst we unpack. They're all having a picnic with the Wright-Smiths by the swimming pool.'

'I must admit, Tom is a very good father.'

'Mummy, I keep telling you – not only is he one hunk of a husband, he's a storming good dad. Ask any of the boys, or Rosie.'

There was a sudden scrunch of wheels on the drive.

'Here's Braggs, Braggs and Sons with the furniture. Some is to come here and the rest Tom said we could put in the big stable at the end of the block until I decide what to do with it. It's empty now all the mares have foaled.'

Mary was soon boiling the kettle again as the three strapping men huffed and puffed down the garden with the solid iron garden bench and chairs, which Sam stood and admired. 'They look fantastic under the weeping willow, Mary. What amazing workmanship but there is no time to admire, ladies. The pièce de resistance is about to be positioned in the utility room,' and the huge carved hallstand with the two bears crouching at the bottom was soon sitting proudly in one corner with Boswell snapping and barking at the mother bear. At last he lay down, still giving deep-throated growls as he tried to protect Sam from the harmless piece of wood.

At last, the bureau was in the sitting room with the display cabinet and all the chests of drawers, small tables and chairs were safely locked in the stable. Sam gave the three men a sizeable tip and as the lorry scrunched out of the drive, opened a bottle of Chablis and sat with Mary and her mother on the beautiful garden chairs, eating the sandwiches Alice had made.

To her surprise, when she looked at her watch she discovered it was almost a quarter to three. 'Goodness, I had no idea that was the time. Tom said he and the children would be home by four o'clock.'

She stepped over Boswell who was still growling at the hallstand and handed Mary the watercolour of the Jacob sheep and the bronze statue of the two dachshunds.

When she was alone, she poured herself another glass of wine and sat on the wonderful bench. At last, Boswell deigned to leave his position by the bears and was now lying by her feet – his ears listening for any intruders. A short while later, his tail thumped and she could hear voices, telling her the children and Tom were returning.

Soon, they were coming through the garden gate and she heard Tom's voice asking, 'Who is skiving then, Sammy?'

'Not skiving, Tommy – planning.'

'Not planning to leave me for six months and go on a world cruise with all your inheritance are you sweetheart?'

‘Nothing so boring, Thomas. I’m planning a new business venture, actually.’

‘Oh, God – not Acorn Antiques, surely?’

‘Not quite – no – Massenden Holiday Cottages.’

‘Come again?’

‘Massenden Holiday Cottages, and you, my darling, will be my sleeping partner.’

‘I don’t really know what you are suggesting – but I fear it’s not the sort of sleeping partner I would like to be. If I become many more sleeping partners I won’t have time for the real thing, my darling.’

‘Don’t be an idiot, Tommy. You are going to be my sleeping partner in more ways than one. You will be a co-director in my holiday cottage business. If you don’t object I am going to buy several old cottages within a ten-mile radius of here, do them up and let them for astronomical prices. The area is perfect. The Channel Tunnel, Canterbury, loads of National Trust Properties and maybe best of all the Equitation Centre. As soon as that flat is sold, I shall start looking for my first project.’

‘Sammy, I think I married a bloody entrepreneur, not just the most beautiful woman for over a hundred miles, but so long as I sleep in your bed, I don’t mind what sort of sleeping partner I am!! I must say these seats look as though they have been here for ever.’

‘Come inside, Tom. Come and look at all the goodies.’

Tom almost fell over Boswell who had gone back to his position in front of the hallstand, lying full length, giving deep-throated growls.

‘My God, Samantha, what the hell is this monstrosity?’ At the same time, Rosie and the boys were shrieking in delight.

‘Mum, it’s fab – can we hang our anoraks on it?’

‘Of course. That’s what it is for.’

Tom shook his head. 'I think I'll just lie down and growl with Boz. I might as well be his sleeping partner too,' he laughed.

Rosie was looking at the collection of Austrian bronze figures. 'Mummy – I love these. What are they made of?'

'Bronze,' Sam told her. ' They are painted when they have been modeled and are cold. You can arrange them all in the cabinet in the sitting room if you like.'

Oscar was glancing at the different animals – he picked up the one that had reminded Sam of Panky. 'Cor – can I have this one, Mum, or is it ever so valuable?'

'Not ever so, Ozzie – quite – but yes, you can have it, but do look after it carefully.'

'Course, Mum, Annie will keep it safe for me. I'll take it to her now before I have a chance to lose it. I'll buzz up by the lake on Buggy. I'll be O.K.' and before Sam could even utter the words *'be careful,'* he was disappearing in the direction of the stables, clutching the little bronze figure.

Sam put all the rest on a large tray, which she placed carefully on the settee in the sitting room. 'There you are, Rosie – that will save you having to run backwards and forwards.' At last everything except the boxes of toys had either been put away in a cupboard or found a place somewhere in the home. Sam was about to undo the first box of toys when Tom took it firmly out of her hands. 'No more boxes today, Sammy, I've booked a table for us all at La Casa. I thought we deserved a treat tonight except that now a certain young man has gone A.W.O.L.'

'Call him on his mobile, Tom. Tell him we're eating Italian this evening – that should get him moving. He loves Italian food.'

Sure enough, no more than fifteen minutes later they saw Humbug and Oscar trotting back into the yard.

'Annie loved the horse, Mum. She's put it on the mantelpiece in the sitting room. She says she will dust it every evening.' And he was humming tunelessly to himself as he stepped over Boswell who had still no intention of coming to terms with a large wooden hallstand.

'Can we be here when you undo the boxes of toys?' he asked Sam.

'Yes, I'll wait until tomorrow evening when everyone is here. Don't be disappointed if it's only a load of old rubbish One of the boxes is extremely heavy. I think it may have quite a lot of books in it."

Oscar didn't look too impressed but Rosie smiled at Sam. 'Oh, good. Braveheart loves it when I read to him.'

'Let's walk to La Casa, Sammy,' Tom suggested. 'It's a super evening.' When they arrived they were surprised to find Giles sitting alone in the alcove opposite the entrance to the kitchen.

'Hi, Giles. Are you dining alone? If so and you can stand five kids, come and join us.'

'Where's Georgia?' Rosie wanted to know.

'She's with Charlotte this evening. Thanks, Tom, that would be nice. I'll tell Clarry I'm moving to your table.'

Clarry, Tom thought and he remembered seeing Giles and his ex having lunch together at the Equitation Centre the previous Sunday. Maybe there were developments in that direction.

'How's Herbert Holmer these days?' Sam was asking him.

'Herbert is on top form. I think there are about to be huge changes in his life. We shall have to see.'

'I'm intrigued, Giles. Has he found a new women?'

Giles laughed. 'If you want to find out, you will have to buy my next book, Sam.'

Giles was watching the bistro as it quickly filled up. It had become extremely popular and customers were coming from the other side of Ashford and Canterbury and a few even from the coast. He would have to be patient – it could be well past eleven o'clock before he could be alone with Clarissa. They were supposed to be having nothing more than a light hearted flirtation and a bit of fun but the kiss Clarissa had given him as he had left her on Sunday had left him reeling and he still felt a tightening in his stomach as he recalled her hands sliding under his shirt. It had only been the sudden appearance of Luigi and Maria that had broken the spell. He knew two things for certain – he loved her and he wanted her but he still couldn't bear the risk of being rejected – it was as simple as that. He had decided to ask her to come to Sussex the following week to watch Georgia jumping in the Primary School Team. He felt safer in the open air, surrounded by people.

At ten o'clock, Tom and Sam stood up. 'Rosie is nearly asleep in her chair. We really must get her home. How about you, Giles?'

'I think I will have another cup of coffee. I'll see you at this school do in Sussex next week.'

'Sure thing,' and Tom was almost certain Giles was waiting for a tryst with his ex-wife once the other diners had departed. *'Good luck, Old Chap,'* he thought to himself – *'but be careful, don't let yourself get hurt,'* - and he took hold of Sam and Rosie's hands as they walked home across the green, passing Rob and Trish coming out of The Bear.

Robert had expected to be bored but to his surprise, over the course of the meal, he and Trish discovered they had several interests in common. One was tennis – the other to his surprise was motor racing about which he soon realized she had in depth knowledge. He discovered the ill-fated Glen had always been keenly interested in the sport, not just as a spectator but also in his teenage years with go-carts, then advancing to formula Ford, enjoying more than a little success with both. She told him they had gone to Silverstone every year to watch the Grand Prix, which had not been too far from their old home.

Trish had played tennis at county level and it wasn't long before Robert was trying to persuade her to join the Massenden tennis club. 'Si is a crack player,' he told her, 'and I'm not too bad either, nor is my brother, John.'

Trish was undecided. 'I'm a bit shy of joining new clubs. Glen and I always went to everything together.'

Robert was not giving up. 'Come as my visitor –Si and I go every weekend.'

Rob could tell she was dithering. 'Two o'clock on Saturday, Si and I will call for you – it's not worth taking the car, it's only a stone's throw away.'

Two minutes later, to her surprise, Trish found herself nervously agreeing to go with him.

Tom looked at Sam. 'What on earth is Uncle Rob doing with a nice girl like Trish? Not his usual type at all, I would say.'

'There's nowt stranger than folk, or so the old saying goes, Thomas, but I agree with you, Tamara Adams must have scared him off loud voiced bimbos.'

Trish couldn't sleep. She was tossing and turning, thinking of Glen. Was she betraying him? Should she have refused Rob's offer to take her to the tennis club? She wasn't even sure she liked Rob and she most certainly didn't trust him, but she missed playing tennis and she didn't want to go to the club on her own. Surely Glen wouldn't mind. She tried to imagine what he would have done if the circumstances had been reversed. She wouldn't have wanted him to be lonely. She hoped he would have tried to make a new life for himself - she thought about the baby they had striven for until he had become too ill to try any more.

She could hear Lilia in the kitchen making a cup of cocoa for Tony whilst he had his shower. She pulled on her dressing gown and went downstairs where she discovered Lilia heating a saucepan of milk. She smiled as Trish appeared in the doorway. 'Do you fancy a cup too, Trish?' she asked.

'No, but have you five minutes to talk to me?'

Lilia was very close to her sister-in – law. 'Of course, Trish – there's nothing wrong, is there?'

'Not wrong, Lilia. I just need some sound advice and who better to ask than you. Lilia, you knew Glen well. Do you think he would mind if I joined the tennis club?' 'The Tennis Club, why would he mind? He would certainly want you to enjoy yourself and you love playing tennis. You would be a huge asset to the club.'

'Actually, it's not only that, Lilia. Rob West has said he will take me as a guest and introduce me. I don't even know whether I even like the man but he was kind to me the other evening when I was a bit overcome by those songs we were singing round the campfire. He took me to The Bear this evening and we discovered we had one or two similar interests – namely motor racing and tennis. That's when he suggested I should go with him and Simon on Saturday afternoon.'

Lilia laughed. 'Well you know my opinion of Simon and the disgraceful way he treated poor Melchior but I really don't know Rob at all – but one afternoon at the Tennis Club hardly constitutes a heady romance. Go and enjoy playing and don't worry about Glen. Sadly he is your past, you must accept that. You will never, never forget him but you are only twenty-nine – you can't live the rest of your life as a recluse. There that's my advice for what it is worth,' and the two girls walked up stairs together. One to a loving husband, the other into a journey to the unknown, which appeared, might include the notorious Rob and Simon West.

Whilst Trish was seeking Lilia's advice, Clarissa was flinging the window open in her tiny sitting room.

'Gosh, this is the one drawback to living in an attic, Gi. It gets unbearably hot. I've bought a fan for my bedroom- I think I will have to get one for this room as well. Do you want coffee or would you prefer a cold drink?'

'Um – have you got something simple like elderflower or lemonade?'

'I've got some elderflower cordial and bags of ice.'

'Smashing, Clarry, that sounds perfect.'

As she went to the fridge she told him. 'Put the telly on whilst I fix the drinks. I've no idea what's on.'

Giles pressed the remote and soon found himself staring in mild fascination at a couple that were obviously indulging in a steamy relationship. It was well past the water shed hour and this had to be an X rated film.

Clarissa was laughing. 'Gi, what on earth are you watching?'

'I don't know but it's quite educational.'

Clarissa laughed and pushed the dark lock of hair away from his eyes. 'Do you miss it, Gi?'

'Miss what?'

'This,' and she pointed at the screen. Giles laughed.

'I don't miss what I never had, Clarry. I don't remember ever executing any of those moves, even in my hey day.'

'Idiot – I meant do you miss making love?'

'Of course, I'm a perfectly normal man. What would you expect, but it could only ever be with the right person. Not just for kicks.'

Clarissa stroked the lock of hair again. 'I love you, Gi.'

Giles swallowed – he wanted her but he didn't want to be hurt. *'Help me please God,'* he begged silently.

'Clarry, we agreed fun. A light hearted romance.'

'But that's impossible, isn't it Gi?'

'Clarry, you know I love you but it's too soon to commit ourselves. Come and live with Georgia and Herbie and me at Theobald's Row. Just as friends to begin with. You can have the spare bedroom it's not palatial, but it's far bigger than your little cubbyhole here. Georgia would be happy, you know that, let's see where life takes us. If we both go in the same direction it could be the best decision we have ever made.'

Clarissa thought, and then took his hand. 'O.K. Gi. Just good friends.'

He laughed. 'As I said, we will see where life takes us but how about sealing our decision with a peck on the cheek?'

It turned out to be a peck that lasted a very long time.

'Gi.'

'Um, hum?'

'I have a feeling the journey has already started. Do you think it's a very long way?'

'It all depends how fast we travel, Clarry but now I had better tear myself away. I will explain to Georgia tomorrow and you bring all your things. No time like the present,' and after another *peck* on the cheek, he finally tore himself away and strolled home across the green, *'Que sera sera,'* he was whistling happily. He and Herbert Holmer were both very happy that night as he wrote the next two chapters of his latest book.

The next morning it seemed as though Giles' good fortune was set to continue as he opened his post and read. *'We are interested in making a film of your book 'A Stranger Riding By' which the American film director, Sinclair Washington is keen to direct with his beautiful wife Lois Carmelo in the leading role. Please get in touch with me as soon as possible so that we can discuss this at length. The location for the film would be in the South East of England.'*

Giles was elated .He had certainly heard of the famous Sinclair Washington but he had no idea that Lois Carmelo was the ex wife of local resident Rob West and the mother of Daisy and Simon. Fortunately for Giles, he had no notion of the storm that he was unwittingly whipping up - one that would break in the very near future.

By the time Jules was driving Tom's horsebox to Surrey on

Saturday morning, Clarissa was ensconced in the spare bedroom at two Theobald's Row, whilst Trish was about to embark on her initiation into the Massenden Tennis Club under the guidance of Rob West, who was totally unaware of the dark, black cloud that was about to descend over himself and his children and of what a huge role the unlikely Trish would play in their lives.

It was still gloriously warm and Sam had taken three large cool bags with sandwiches and a multitude of cold drinks, which they would enjoy at the horse show in Surrey. They had spent the previous evening undoing the boxes, unearthing some strange and interesting toys.

Rosie had grabbed the box of books. They were mostly by Enid Blyton, and she was already reading the first of the Famous Five adventures to Heartbeat. There were several boxes of toy soldiers, which had hardly been played with and several German tinplate toys still with their keys and their various mechanisms in full working order. The most exciting find was a Steiff golliwog and two peg dolls. They were over one hundred years old and after all the boys and Rosie had fought over who should have them, Sam firmly decided they would sit on her bed and there the arguing ended.

The Duc was having a rest prior to The Primary School competition and Sparkler and Braveheart were standing in the horsebox, staring amicably at each other from time to time. Several of the ponies were being rested and just Jet Stream, and Goldfinger were accompanying Rosie's two, along with Tiger Lily. Oliver had decided to stay with Hannah and the dogs, hoping Boswell would soon stop growling at the hallstand.

Tom was taking Swallow Tail and Alicia, but even with the absence of many of the ponies, the horsebox was still full.

Boswell was howling as he watched his beloved mistress firmly shutting the door of the People Carrier and Oliver was beginning to wish he had not elected to stay behind, as he and Hannah hauled the huge dog back indoors where he immediately returned to his position in front of mother bear.

Charles had elected to take the day off too, as Perry arrived at Lake House to pick up Lord of the Rings. Like Oliver, Rupert was staying at home but his day was going to be far more exciting than his friend's. Paddy had kept his promise and the J.A. Pony was due to arrive from his yard in Ireland that afternoon, which was one of the reasons Charles was staying at Lake House. Rupert was to have the pony on trial for two weeks, which Charles had to admit, was a very fair deal.

Perry was driving his own horsebox. It was enormous and capable of transporting ten horses. With Gus only taking Hamlet, and Abby nervously agreeing to ride Alfie, there was room for Binny and Will's ponies as well as Conchita, Pickwick and Perry's own thoroughbred Passe Partout, who was frantically kicking the partition.

Wills and Binny travelled with their brother, as Justin took Mimi, Gus and Abby. Anna had decided it was too hot for Noah and he was screaming as he watched the horsebox pull into Back Lane.

Anna quickly phoned Charles. *'Any chance of your smallest grandson coming for a swim? He's having a tantrum because he wasn't allowed to go to the show with Abby and Gus.'*

'Bring him along, one more screamer won't make much difference. Those monster twins are here with Elizabeth. Apparently there's a problem with the water in their pool at The Old Manor. They're nearly murdering each other already. I've sent Rupert to sort the little blighters out. I think Rudi and Clara are on their way too. The more the merrier. Come as soon as you like.'

The journey to Surrey was uneventful and to everyone's relief, not least the horses and ponies - the horseboxes were able to park side by side in the shade.

As usual, the Junior Foxhunter Class was first in the second ring.

Unfortunately, it clashed with Tom and Swallow Tail and Justin and Conchita's Foxhunter in the main arena, but Perry was soon proving to be worth his weight in gold, which Justin certainly didn't pay him, as he carefully walked the course with Rosie and by the time Tom raced back to find her, having jumped clear on Swallow Tail, Rosie was waiting calmly for her number to be called. 'Gosh,' Tom gasped. 'Thanks a million, Perry.'

'That's O.K. Tom,' he answered in his very ex public school voice. 'I've done this umpteen times with Wills and Binny. It was a doddle.'

He had obviously done his job well as Rosie and Braveheart approached every fence perfectly - finally finishing the class in third place. Rosie knew she could have won but she had remembered the promise she had made her father and she hadn't pushed the willing pony.

In the senior class, Swallow Tail was second, beaten only by Conchita, much to Justin's delight.

The next problem was Abby's reluctance to jump Alfie. Once again, Tom was impressed with Perry who could see Justin was growing impatient. He took the little girl's hand and calmly walked into the arena with Rosie and Tom, telling her about his little twelve two pony who he had fallen off dozens of times. 'And didn't you mind?' Abby had asked him.

'No, You're not a good rider until you have fallen at least seven times.'

'Oh,' and Abby climbed back onto Alfie without another word.

The twelve two class was the smallest as it almost always was, with only eight entries. There was no contest as Rosie and Sparkler flew and to everyone's delight Abby was smiling as she collected the third placed rosette, which she proudly pinned on to Alfie's bridle.

Rosie's day was finished. She tied Sparkler and Braveheart to the rings on the side of the horsebox – made sure the shade was not going to disappear and sat down beside Sam, ready to watch Orlando and Binny.

Orlando and Jet were clear and then Rosie sat upright to watch Binny. She liked the look of Binny's dark grey pony. He jumped smoothly and cleanly and soon she was joining Orlando. 'More competition, Mum, but I like Binny and Wills and Perry is super.'

Sam smiled. 'Good, I hope Justin appreciates him.'

Eventually, Orlando beat Binny by half a second. It had been an excellent contest and everyone was happy. Binny obviously loved her pony and when she sat down beside Rosie to watch her brother, she told her.

'I shall be so sad when I have outgrown Top Hole. I've had him since he was four years old. We went through Foxhunters together, but next year Perry says I should ride Will's Shining Light. He says Wills should have something a bit hotter. Perry likes hot, strong horses himself.'

'Have you always lived with your brother?' Rosie asked.

'Oh, no. Only since Mummy and Daddy were killed. Perry had just finished at Uni – he's actually a lawyer – he had just got a first – then Daddy's yacht capsized off The Needles. Perry came straight back to the castle and saved us from being sent to an aunt who lived on the Isle of Skye. We were really desperate. She was much older than Daddy and had never had any children of her own. Perry never thought twice and thank goodness now he's our legal guardian. He had been going out with a girl called Perdita. He met her at Uni. I think they lived together for a year or two whilst they were in Exeter, then they got engaged. They had a terrible row about Wills and me. She wanted Perry to send us to Skye. He absolutely refused and on the day they were to have got married, she eloped with Perry's brother, Romeo. I think she always had her eye on the castle. Well, she's got it now. Perry made it over in favour of Romeo. He says he hates all women but Wills and I hope and hope that one day he will meet someone that will change his mind. He's such a fantastic person.'

'Is he very rich, Binny?'

'Mega. Romeo only had half the castle, not the title or the money. Perry is still Lord Helingbury.'

James arrived at mid-day with Pas de Deux who he had decided to jump in the Open. He flung himself down on the grass beside Sam, who having noticed the rather fraught expression on his face was soon pouring him a cold drink.

'Lizzie is going to ask Dr. Taylor if she can arrange for the twins to see a child psychologist. We've been up half the night. Now they're even quarrelling about which bed they are going to sleep in. There seems to be barely a moment in the day when they're not screaming or hitting one another. I can remember your trips when they were that age, I know they could be naughty but I can't recall them physically fighting each other.'

Sam laughed. 'Probably because Ozzie was always so dominant. Oliver bowed to him, and Orlando to both of them. You've got a huge house, James. Why don't you give them each a room of their own? When the boys were their age we didn't have the space, the boys accepted they had to share but when Tom and I converted the attic and made our old bedroom into two so that they could each have their own space, they were over the moon. They are very close, but they like having time to themselves, they love the new arrangement. Try that and see if there is any improvement. Maybe Freddy will take the wind out of their sales.'

'In other words, you think Elizabeth and I spoil them.'

Sam smiled as kindly as she could, remembering how many times she had come away from The Old Manor House saying to Tom. *'Those twins need taking in hand a.s.a.p. I know to Lizzie and James they were a miracle after all that I.V.F. treatment she went through but I am really surprised at James. He's so strict with Fenella and yet it seems Flick and Felix can do no wrong.'*

'Well, James, to be honest, perhaps you do but I know how

hard it is not too. Tom and I discovered that after Rosie was born, especially with the knowledge we could never have any more children. Luckily with our rumbustious boys, there wasn't time to indulge her, sometimes I know Tom finds it hard – she can twist him round her little finger – but on the whole he is extremely fair. See whether you can get over the problem without counseling, James - they may calm down when they leave playgroup and join the reception class next term. See how they react when Freddy is born.'

James sighed. 'You're probably right, Sam. At least Elizabeth has a wonderful help in Martha. Fenella follows her like a little shadow; she spends hours in the kitchen with her. Yesterday she showed Fen how to make fairy cakes.'

He finished his drink and changed the subject. 'Fen is really excited about being the reserve rider for the Primary School team – although we've explained to her the chances of her actually competing are minimal, but she doesn't mind – she is just looking forwards to a day with Poupée. I think we shall soon be looking for another pony for her, Sam. Then Flicka can take over Poupée.'

'Why don't you ask Justin about Guy Fawkes? Abby doesn't want to ride him. She was frightened when he shied when those massive hailstones scared him last week, but that was totally out of character. He's usually as solid as a rock. He's a full twelve-two, with masses of scope for his size. I think he is a super pony and of course last year Tom discovered he was sired by a top jumping pony stallion before he got into the hands of those gypsies along with Sparkler and the other ponies Tom discovered at Marigold's sanctuary. At least we know the gypsies hadn't stolen them. It was just a weird quirk of fate that led them to Massenden. Fen is a really good rider, James, not the least bit nervous like Abby. Justin might even consider loaning him to Fen until Noah is older.'

'I'll have a word with Elizabeth first and then I will probably speak to Justin. Have you met his new groom yet?'

Sam grinned. 'Peregrine Percival - yes indeed – in fact he has brought Justin here today and if you glance over there you can see his young brother, Wills just entering the arena and that is Perry standing by the entrance.'

James looked across the showground where he could see a young lad on a shining palomino pony just commencing the course, and a tall, elegant, young man in cream breeches, leather boots and a white shirt watching his every move with Tom and Justin, who were waiting with Mimi and Josh who were about to follow him into the arena.

Josh and Wills appeared to have struck up an immediate friendship, which pleased both Tom and Perry. Tom, because Josh tended to be a loner. Although he was older than the triplets, he often seemed to be overpowered by them, especially Oscar and he relied on his older cousin Jacques for friendship and Mimi, too, when she was in the correct frame of mind. Perry was pleased because he was well aware of the trauma Wills and Binny had suffered losing their parents and more latterly their home and everything they had been familiar with all their young lives. There was obviously going to be friendly rivalry between the two boys and Perry and Tom watched Wills flying, pushing Shining Light to his limit in a vain effort to catch Lilly's extremely fast time. Mimi and Lord of the Rings, who she considered her second string just separating the two boys.

Mimi was in her element as she stood between Lily and Shining Light receiving her blue rosette.

They took the ponies back to the horseboxes and having made certain they were securely tied, made their way back to Sam and the massive picnic she had provided. She was certainly not unaware of the game Charles' *little minx* was playing as she smiled coquettishly at first one boy and then the other but Josh knew Mimi only too well and turned to Binny, asking her about her pony, Top Hole. Wills was asking Rosie where the girl with dark hair who had a pony called Fire Cracker lived. Georgia had not gone unnoticed by the newest member of *the gang*. Mimi was certainly not best pleased and turned her attention to Oscar, who was wondering what his Annie was doing and hoping she would not be too disappointed with the plain green velvet rosette Goldfinger had won that morning.

There was a fun fair at the very far side of the showground. All the junior classes had finished and there was a Young Rider's Class before the Open in which Justin, Tom, James and Perry were all competing. All the youngsters were begging to be allowed to spend their prize money on the various attractions. Tom didn't really want to leave Sam, who was busy clearing up the remnants of the picnic and Justin decided he couldn't be bothered to walk to the far end of the showground. To everyone's surprise, James suddenly stood up.

'I'll take them – I haven't been on a helter skelter for more years than I care to remember. Come on, kids.'

Perry joined him. 'I'll come with you.'

Perry had a very good reason to join James and the large portion of *the gang*. Wills and Binny were extremely wealthy young people. Perry had inherited the castle, the title and most of his late father's vast fortune but his young half brother and sister had inherited even more. Their mother had been the only daughter of a mutli millionaire entrepreneur. The money was in trust until they had both attained their twenty third birthdays but two years ago, on a day Perry would never forget, there had been an attempt to snatch Binny from his horsebox. Fortunately he and his brother, Romeo had returned just in time to foil the attempt. Now, he guarded both the youngsters with his life. That was the reason they would not be on the school bus – he would be driving them to and from Ashford every day, making certain they were safely on the school premises and back at Theobald's Place in the evenings.

When he knew Justin better, he would tell him the reason, but first and foremost he wanted Wills and Binny to have friends and fun with their ponies. He was going to ask Justin if he could have a guard dog. He had overheard Tom and Sam telling James about Boswell guarding Sam from some carved wooden bear and how Tom had surprised her with a labradoodle puppy, which he had got from a nearby sanctuary.

‘Did they have any more puppies or other big dogs?’ he asked Tom.

‘She certainly had at least two other ‘doodles’. Marigold wanted me to have Hector – he’s got slightly bowed legs. She knew I wouldn’t mind and would look after him.’

Sam looked surprised. ‘Has he?’

‘There you see, darling. You hadn’t even noticed. I said only slightly but for some people that would be a huge turn off. For me, as long as he’s not in any pain it doesn’t matter one iota and James has already confirmed he doesn’t feel a thing.’

‘James?’

‘James is not only my brother-in-law, he is also my highly esteemed vet.’

Perry looked at James’

‘But aren’t you Lord Thornley?’

‘So what? There is no law in this land that states that a Lord can’t be a vet. At least not as far as I am aware.’

Perry laughed. ‘Touché, James. Actually I am a lawyer. Not a practicing one but I wanted to achieve something.’

James grinned. ‘Well, Perry, we would appear to have two things in common. We are obviously both industrious Lords with a yen to try those terrifying looking rides waiting for us over there,’ and they set out with their entourage to savour the delights of being thrown upside down and inside out.

Tom looked at Justin. ‘He’s a great chap, Justin, but it’s all a bit surreal.’

‘I agree but he’s damn hard working and the kids love him. I’m going to make the most of my good fortune whilst I have the opportunity. He certainly has a thing about women, though. I introduced him to David Mason’s younger sister. You would have thought I had been offering him a glass of hemlock. He barely acknowledged the poor girl, saying he wanted to check Passe Partout was O.K. in the box. Strange. -- I must say his horse appears quite a handful. Interesting to see what happens in the Open. I hope he remembers to keep an eye on the time.'

Tom laughed. 'Don't worry, Justin, he's got the human version of Big Ben by his side. You know James is never one minute late nor one second early!!'

Justin stretched. 'I'm going to discover the bog, Tom.'

'I'll come with you. How about you, Sammy? You seem engrossed in your book. Is it one of Giles latest editions?'

Sam laughed. 'No, actually, I've pinched it from Rosie. It's called 'Five go to Kirrin Island,' by Enid Blyton!! There are four children and a dog called Timmy.'

'Well, that shouldn't cause you any nightmares, my sweetheart.'

'Tommy, it's much more scary than any of Herbert Holmer's adventures – there's a horrible man called ~Scarface.'

'Oh dear, there could be a few sleepless nights ahead for Rosie then. Justin and I are going to find the loos. Will you be O.K. on your own?'

Sam laughed. 'Darling Tom, I am in the middle of a showground with at least one hundred people surrounding me – I fear it is most unlikely some gallant prince will come and spirit me away.'

'I thought you only knew one prince?'

'Of course I do, Thomas. Now you and Justin go and find those loos whilst I discover whether George and Timmy reach their island before the horrible Scarface,' and she blew him a kiss and then one to Justin, just for good measure.

James and Perry arrived back precisely half an hour before the Open Class was due to begin. The four men walked the course together. Whilst Wills manfully hung on to Passe Partout and Sam held the placid Alicia, Mimi and Josh took care of Pas de Deux and Pickwick.

'I think I will try to go early on,' Perry told Tom. 'Passe Partout gets a bit steamed up if he's waiting around. What about your mare?'

'Oh, Alicia just does what I tell her. We talk to each other you see.'

'You talk to each other?'

'Yea, it's something I discovered I could do when I had my first pony called Twinkletoes. It has come in very useful over the years.'

'Crumbs! Perhaps you could have a word in monsieur's ear. He needs a bit of common sense knocked into him.'

Five minutes later, Tom was totally agreeing as he watched anxiously as Passe Partout plunged and rocked his way around the not inconsiderable sized course as his determined rider stayed seemingly glued to the saddle.

Not only did Tom acknowledge Perry was a very accomplished rider, he was obviously completely fearless as the big thoroughbred completed the course with both rider and horse still in one piece.

It was obvious Perry loved his crazy animal as he stood with his arm round its neck watching his boss jump an immaculately smooth round on his reliable friend, Mr. Pickwick, but it was when he watched Tom and Alicia that he knew he was witnessing a true master at work. He turned to Justin. 'That was truly sensational.'

Justin grimaced. 'Don't rub it in, Perry. Tom has been my best pal for over twenty years now, but at the same time he has also been the sharpest thorn in my side. He deserves to be the world No One even if he is prepared to let it go for the sake of Sammy and his kids. He wants to spend more time with them. It's a hard life, Perry. Especially when you have a big family like Tom does. If you want any help with that maniac then ask Tom. His spare time is almost non-existent, but he has told me he's not going abroad again until the final of the Nation's Cup in Spain at the end of September. He wants to make certain the triplets settle into the Grammar School. They can be a bit of a handful, especially Oscar. Tom is also very protective of Sammy since she was stabbed last year.'

'Stabbed?'

'Yea, by some nutty woman who fancied our Tom. It was quite a horrific scandal, actually. She had just divorced her husband, Lord Michael Foulkes-Williams.'

'Michael!!'

'You know him?'

'Of him. His father and mine were distant cousins.'

'Well, Sophie went berserk when Tom told her to leave him alone. She stabbed Sam in her kitchen and left her for dead. Fortunately, my dad found her just in time.'

'I heard Michael's wife had died.'

'She certainly has, Perry. She committed suicide that same morning.'

'God, poor old Michael. I believe he has two young girls.'

'He has. Michael married again very soon after. Fortunately, his new wife seems a nice woman and has accepted the girls. I'm surprised they're not here today. Florence often jumps against Mimi and Josh.'

Perry noticed Binny and Rosie walking towards them and he changed the subject abruptly. 'So,' he asked Justin – 'is this Tom's number one horse?'

Justin roared with laughter, shaking his head. 'I rate Alicia number five or maybe even number six. Wait until you meet, Clementine, Sea Breeze, Black Opal, Madame Bovary and certainly not least Kaspar. Tom has only had Alicia a few weeks. I reckon by next year she will be up there with the others but good luck to him. He's a bloody workaholic and actually the nicest chap you could ever wish to meet.'

James and Pas de Deux were the last pair to jump and by the end of the competition there were tweve clear rounds.

Perry was the first in the jump off and Tom held his breath, as this time he let Passe Partout have his head. He hurdled the jumps, missing all the poles by a whisker, finishing in a very fast time.

Tom looked him in the eye. 'Perry, You'll break your neck on that monster, for God's sake bring him up to Lake House to the Indoor School and Charles and I will see whether we can persuade him to calm down a bit. There is no point at all in having a good horse once you are dead.'

'Wow, would you really?'

'Yea, but don't ask me to ride him, I've got enough nutters of my own but we will see what we can do with a good deal of basic ground work.'

'Groundwork?'

'Schooling on the flat.'

'I've never done that with him.'

'I'm afraid that's only too obvious, Perry, but Charles and I will convert you between us. Bring him up to the school one evening once my friend here has flogged you to death mucking out his stables!!'

'Oh, I don't mind hard work, it takes my mind off other things.'

'Actually, Justin is O.K. You've got yourself a good boss and now he is desperately trying to beat your time.' However, Pickwick was known for his care rather than his speed and he was several seconds slower than his groom, who Tom had decided was unorthodox in more ways than one. He took Alicia to a far corner of the practice area and Perry watched him canter her in small circles – never letting her alter her stride, until finally he popped her over the two practice fences. Perry then watched in awe as Tom and Alicia jumped as one, cutting every corner, saving valuable seconds. He watched as Sam ran up to him, still clutching the book she had been reading. He noticed the look, which passed between them as she laid her hand on his thigh. He sighed, Tom was obviously lucky, - he had found his perfect woman but as far as he was concerned, those were very few and far between. He had once thought he had found his but she had betrayed him and in his prejudiced mind the entire female species were devious – underhand - scheming and certainly never to be trusted.

James was riding out of the arena patting Pas de Deux. She was a sweet natured, honest mare and they had finished in sixth place. He was more than satisfied.

As they rode out of the arena, Tom was chatting to Perry and Justin when a large, red faced man who he vaguely recognized, grabbed hold of Alicia's bridle, making her give a half rear, almost unseating him.

'What the hell?' and then Tom realized who he was. It was the father of Alicia's previous owner. He recalled a young girl being eliminated early in the class – of course, now he realized that had been young Jodie.

He looked at the man who had obviously had far too much to drink. 'I'm off to see the stewards. That mare must be drugged.'

Tom stared back but stayed completely calm. 'Fine. I've no objection to the vet looking at her. Let's go and find him.' And he rode Alicia to the marquee, which was clearly marked vet.

James had accompanied him and as he saw the duty vet, he immediately recognized a former university pal. 'Hi, Mark.'

'James, what's up? Is there a problem?'

By this time, Jodie's father had puffed his way to the marquee. 'I'll say there is. This mare has been drugged. This fellow bought her from me at the sale in Sussex last month. Lethal creature – my daughter was terrified of her. Lost a small fortune. She ducked out at every jump. She's doped, I tell you.'

By now, a small crowd was gathering round the marquee including Sam and all the children. Oscar was well aware of the accusations that were being made against his father. He marched up to the irate man. 'My dad doesn't have to dope his horses, you ignorant fool – he's the best rider in the world.'

Tom looked at Sam. 'Get the kids in the car, sweetheart – it's probably best if James and I deal with this matter. They can take all the blood they want from Alicia - they won't find a thing – she's as clear as a bell.'

By this time, the head judge had appeared. 'Tom,' he asked. 'What on earth is going on?'

Jodie's father almost pushed Tom over. 'This horse has been doped, I tell you,' he yelled at the judge. 'My daughter couldn't manage her. She was lethal.'

The judge gave him a withering look. 'I'm afraid your daughter can't manage any of the horses you buy her, Mr. Wainwright. I judged this mare several times in Holland – she was extremely promising. I presume you are aware of who Tom is?'

'No idea. All I know is he got her for a paltry three thousand pounds.'

'Tom is Thomas West. Currently number one rider in the world and as I understand, your mare was sold at auction and you had not seen fit to put a reserve price on her.'

The man had suddenly become subdued. 'Tom West. Well I --- Well I ---. Perhaps I have made a mistake.'

James had decided it was time this contretemps came to an end. 'I am Tom's vet. There is no way he would ever contemplate drugging any of his horses. He spends hours and hours schooling them on the flat – over cavaletti – out hacking. That's why he is so successful – not bloody drugs. I am sure Tom would be happy for your vet to test her.'

The man was looking away.

'O.K. O.K. I was obviously mistaken,' and with a final glare at Tom and Alicia, turned and made his way back to the beer tent.

'You're really welcome to test her, George,' Tom told the judge.

'No way, Tom, we wouldn't insult you. She's a lovely mare – good luck with her,' and with that, the unfortunate episode was over.

CHAPTER 36

Later that evening as Mimi unloaded Lordy she saw a strange head looking out of the stable Conchita had recently vacated and her brother standing in front of the door stroking a dark grey head with a small star and a large, dark brown eye. To her surprise, when the pony turned his head to look at her, she noticed his right eye was brilliant blue – not unlike Josh and the triplet's.

Mimi put Lordy in his stable - checked he had fresh water and plenty of hay and then joined her brother. 'Hi, Rue. So this is Hawkeye – quite an appropriate name I must say,' she said, pointing to the flashing blue eye. 'Gosh, he's definitely more than two-toned, Rupert, he's like '*Fifty Shades of Grey!!*' Is he friendly?'

'Very, considering by all accounts he had a horrendous time crossing the Irish Sea. He's been travelling over twenty-four hours. We're going to let him out in the small paddock with Groucho tomorrow and then Dad is going to give me a school with him on Monday before all *the gang* get here for our last practice before our School and Pony Club trials on Wednesday. His full name is Captain Hawkeye of Killarney. I hope I don't let him down - he has come here with quite a reputation. He was the top pony in Ireland last year but his rider was a boy of sixteen.' Rupert flexed his biceps and laughed. 'A few extra hours in Dad's gym I think, Mimi. How was your day?'

'Good. Lordy came second between Josh and Peregrine's half brother Wills.'

'What are Will's and Binny's ponies like?'

'I can't lie to you Rue. Top class,' she laughed, 'and so is Wills.'

Rupert was well aware of his father's nickname for his older sister. 'For God's sake, Mimi – surely Josh and Jacques are enough for you.'

Mimi tossed her head. 'Safety in numbers, that's my policy Rupert.'

She gave Hawkeye a final pat before she went indoors to text both Jacques and Joshua to see if they would ride out with her the next day.

Perry was whistling as he gave Passe Partout a small feed. Charles had agreed to have a look at his beloved thoroughbred the following afternoon. 'Dad's always happy to help if he knows there is potential,' Justin had told Perry, ' and I have persuaded him you and Passe Partout have certainly got bucket loads of that.'

Perry had taken the opportunity to ask Justin whether he would object to a dog living at the stables.

Justin was delighted. The only reason he hadn't got a guard dog himself was because he knew large dogs ate their way through bags of dog food. Santa was perfect, he fed mostly off the food Abby and Noah almost invariably left on their plates with some dog biscuits soaked in the gravy Anna served with their meals.

He smiled – nodding his head. 'Of course, Perry, so long as you take full responsibility for it.'

'Smashing. I would just like to be certain Binny is safe.'

'Binny?'

'Yes. This is strictly between you and me, Justin, but Binny has already been the victim of one kidnap attempt.'

'Kidnap?'

'She will become extremely wealthy on her twenty-third birthday, Justin. She and Wills will both inherit a fortune from their late mother. They have no idea. I want them to have a normal life – growing up with good friends – learning to be good sports. Please, Justin, not a word about this to anyone, not even Anna. Luckily I have no wish to lead a social life. Passe Partout is all I require and a dog would be fantastic. I left my two labs with Romeo at Helingbury. After all, it was the only home they had ever known.

Tom was telling me about a sanctuary in the next village. Apparently the old lady has got some labradoodle puppies. Probably not the best guard dogs under the sun but I have always had a weakness for them and I do want a dog Binny can love.'

'Have as many as you want, Perry. Are you quite happy here?'

'Oh, yes. Your horses are really easy to look after – super natured. If you like I'll hack Conchita out with Binny and Wills this afternoon. We may go and discover this sanctuary.'

'Smashing. Do you think Binny could ride Guy? Abby won't go near him – I shall have to get someone else to take him over for a bit. I want to keep him for Noah eventually. Alfie really will be too old in four year's time.'

'Four years? How old will little Noah be then?'

'Six and a half. He can start with Fuzz Buzz when he is four and a half, the same as my young half brother, Rupert did.'

Perry was surprised but he was sure Charles Wright-Smith knew what he was doing. Who was he to question his methods?

When he had finished the stables, he looked up the phone number for the sanctuary and five minutes later was talking to Marigold.

Marigold was taken aback when the distinctive Old Etonian voice explained he was speaking from Theobald's Place Coach House and was Justin Wright-Smith's newly appointed groom who was seeking one or two guard dogs. He understood she had some labradoodle puppies.

Marigold was always honest. 'I have just one left. A big boy but I can't guarantee he will be a guard dog. I've also got a two-year-old Heinz 57 and a Jack Russell who was found tied to a gatepost just outside Ashford. Now that little girl really is a feisty madam.'

Perry was interested. 'I know it's Sunday but it's my afternoon off. Could I ride over to the sanctuary with my brother and sister?'

Marigold never turned a prospective customer away. 'Of course,' she told Perry. 'Anytime before five o'clock, I always go to evensong on the last Sunday of the month.'

'Super. We'll be with you around three o'clock. I'm not certain exactly where the sanctuary is but I'm sure Justin will be able to tell me.'

'Just follow the bridle path opposite the Equestrian Centre and you will eventually be passing the back of the sanctuary. You will see my old black and white house across the fields and you can't miss the new barn. Just open any of the field gates and take a short cut through. It's a lovely day, you will find me in the vegetable garden.'

Perry went to find Binny and Wills who were preparing a salad for their lunch – or rather – undoing the plastic around the ready-made prawn and chicken concoctions he had bought in the super market.

'How do you fancy riding over to the animal sanctuary in the next village? I've just spoken to Marigold, the lady who runs it, and arranged to look at some rescue dogs she has. I thought a couple of dogs wouldn't go amiss to keep us company and Justin has agreed to us having them.'

Binny was jumping up and down clapping her hands whilst Wills was asking if he could call Georgia and see if she could come with them on Fire Cracker.

Perry agreed. 'Well, yes, but do you have her number?'

Wills laughed. 'I pinched it off Josh's mobile. He asked me to hold it for him whilst he was jumping Lily yesterday.'

Perry wasn't certain he approved of his young brother's devious move but at the same time admired him for his enterprise.

Georgia happened to be at a loose end. Apparently, Josh was going to help his dad with Bamboozle's first lunging session in the indoor school, then having a jumping lesson with Sweet Dreams. She was losing heart with her pursuit of Josh's attention and she was pretty certain Mimi wouldn't be too far away from the school that afternoon. 'O.K. Wills – that would be super – I've been to Marigold's sanctuary several times. I can show you where it is. I'll wait for you at the end of Theobald's drive at two thirty.'

‘That’s excellent news,’ Wills told Perry. ‘Georgia has been to the sanctuary before – she can show us the way.’

‘Fine, Wills, but don’t go losing your head over a silly young girl. They’re not worth the agro.’

Wills held his counsel. He had already formed his own opinion of the fairer sex and they certainly didn’t concur with those of his brother.

At half past two they were setting out in an orderly file, trotting along the bridle path which passed through the woods and then beside the fields, until they could see Marigold’s beautiful but neglected old Elizabethan house at the end of the paddocks. They opened the gate and cantered steadily across the grass with Binny holding the fiery little Guy Fawkes beside her brother and Georgia. She could understand why little Abby didn’t want to ride him. He was certainly stronger than her own Top Hole, in spite of being a whole hand smaller.

Perry jumped off Conchita who he had found biddable and steady in comparison to Passe Partout. He handed the reins to Wills whilst he went into the garden in search of the vegetables and Marigold.

He gazed at the beautiful old house, which according to a plaque on the wall informed him dated back to fifteen thirty-five. He noticed the decaying wood around the windows, the wattle and daub with cracks everywhere and a multitude of tiles now lying on the ground in broken pieces, having slipped from the roof over several winters. He decided the elderly lady, who in spite of the warm afternoon was making her way towards him in a heavy tweed skirt and jacket, bending over two sticks, was either too frail or too poor to do the urgent repairs this lovely old house was in need of.

Perry was used to moving amongst the highest society and he immediately recognised the aristocratic aura that surrounded this frail lady. Likewise Marigold was immediately recognizing the voice of a young man who had obviously received an education at a highly esteemed public school.

‘Good afternoon.’ Perry was greeting her. ‘What a beautiful

house you live in. I come from Yorkshire where most of our houses are built of rather dark stone – they don't have quite the same charm as your wonderful wattle and daub – and what a fabulous walled garden.'

Marigold sighed. 'Ribbenden Manor has been my home for all of my life but sadly I have no one to inherit it. Luckily I have a wonderful band of volunteers who help me with the sanctuary but one day I fear I shall have to sell the old house and move into one of the lodges. I am putting that day off for as long as I can but as you can see, the house needs a fortune spending on it and unfortunately that is something I just don't possess. However, that's enough of my problems. Let's put your horse and ponies in the stables and I will show you the dogs.'

She led them into a large new barn, which was divided into three sections. At the far end there was a row of cages right around the perimeter, housing guinea pigs, rabbits and some smaller rodents. The middle section was a cattery with accommodation for at least a dozen felines and the front of the barn was divided into ten kennels, each with it's own small run. Some were larger than others and Perry's eyes had flown straight to the honey coloured labradoodle.

Marigold carefully closed the main door of the barn and let Digby out of his kennel. He immediately leapt at the youngsters and Perry, and then lay on his back waiting for his tummy to be tickled.

'So what is his history?' Perry asked Marigold.

'The usual, I am afraid,' she told him. 'People who buy a puppy not realising how big it will grow. In this case a young couple decided to try breeding. By the time the pups were only two weeks old they had had enough. Digby has been here eight weeks. One of my volunteers fell in love with his mother and then Tom West took the puppy which had slightly deformed legs – but that's typical of Tom – it's a very slight condition and Hector will have the best home imaginable with Tom and Sam and their five children. They got Boswell from me and little Holly. I am so happy for Hector. The other boy went to another really nice family who also live in

Massenden. A Mrs. Mawgan-Whitely. Her two girls were thrilled but no sooner had he gone when a gentleman rang me in great distress. He had found this little lady tied up to a stake by the old water mill, along with this gigantic softie. James came to look them over a day or two ago. He thinks the little Jack Russell is no more than two. Someone must have cared about her at one time because she has been spayed and thank goodness this monster has been neutered."

The little Jack Russell bitch wouldn't leave Binny and Georgia's sides and Wills had obviously fallen for the mongrel, which was almost as large as Sam's Boswell. According to James he was no more than eight months old and both he and the little bitch had been pronounced to be in perfect health.

Perry was soon passing a large wad of notes to Marigold who was delighted, telling her they would ride home and return in the Range Rover to collect the three dogs.

They gathered three stirrup leathers to put round the dog's necks and were back within the hour. A very short time later, the labradoodle was following Perry everywhere and Georgia and Wills were sitting on the grass in front of the Coach House with Bollocks – which was what Wills had decided to name his Heinz 57. Binny had found an old deckchair, which Justin had left in the tack room and Belinda the little Jack Russell was sleeping peacefully on her lap. Marigold had given Perry a bag of the dog food they had been accustomed to eating at the sanctuary and with Perry's old anorak making a temporary bed, later that evening all three dogs obviously thought they were in heaven.

Whilst Perry had been increasing his livestock, Tom and Josh had been introducing Bamboozle to the routine that lay in store for him for the foreseeable future. He was five years old and unlike Whisky and Humbug instead of being piebald, was dark grey like his mother, Tom's little speed horse, Shooting Star. He was fourteen hands one inch high and with just a few more months in which he might grow, Tom reckoned he would remain safely inside the requisite fourteen two hands. He was a strongly built pony and Tom could already feel his strength and eagerness and with Josh running beside him, he was already learning the rudiments of being on the end of a lunging rein. He was obviously highly intelligent and Tom was determined to try and school him three or four times a week and hopefully back him before Christmas. He was already having second thoughts about letting Rosie ride him. He was immediately aware Bamboozle was going to have a mind of his own as well as an extremely strong body.

Charles had been hinting that he thought it was time for Jet Stream to move on. Apparently, Jean-Pierre had made him an extremely good offer with Eloise in mind. In spite of Rudi's perfect feet, which Jane had high hopes of he also had perfect hands and his father's beautiful seat. Jane had already decided she was never going to fall out with Pierre over their children's futures again and if Rudi chose to ride, then so be it. Even at the tender age of two he was always trying to clamber onto the long suffering little Toffee Apple and next year Jean-Pierre knew there would no better pony for him other than the admirable little Pierrot.

'What are your plans for the triplets?' Charles had asked Tom.

'Well, nothing different at the moment. Oz certainly has his hands full with the Countess' two and Buggy as well for another year. I don't think I shall let Rosie take over Buggy – he's so strong. I couldn't put Sam through that worry every time she went to a show. She and I wondered whether you would lend us the governess cart, Sam would quite like to see how he would go in harness. He's a cute little fellow and with blinkers, no one would know he only had one eye.'

Charles was immediately intrigued. 'We could hire Buggy and the trap out for weddings,' he laughed.

'Actually, Charles. I think Sam's idea was to show him. Anyhow, we shall certainly never sell him. I shall probably think of getting a Foxhunter pony for Oz at some time but I think the Countess already has a pony in mind for him. Some young relation of Panky's I believe. If you do decide to sell Jet, I think I will let 'Lando ride Bamboozle. He was originally intended for Rosie, but my first impressions are no – leave her with The Duc and Braveheart. She will never part with Sparkler. We might see if Noah can ride him in a few year's time but I hope when Josh is out of Juniors she will have two or three years with Ganger. As long as you give 'Lando some warning he will understand if you sell Jet. I think he could do really well with Bambi. Hopefully Rosie will have that lovely High and Mighty who was born the other day. When he is four and ready to back, she will still only be thirteen. We shall have to wait and see, but the future could be exciting.'

The following morning, Erica was giving Rupert a leg up onto Hawkeye, and then waking beside him into the indoor school where Charles was waiting.

Rupert was well aware that not only was his father still one of the best riders in the world, he was also one of the most patient but demanding tutors.

He listened intently to every word he was told. At first he found Hawkeye's stride much longer than The March Hare's. Charles told him to sit up, shorten his reins and sit deep in the saddle and after half an hour on the flat he could see his young son relaxing and beginning to enjoy the experience of riding the bigger pony.

He built a spread and an upright fence, which Rupert successfully manipulated and then with the help of Tom and Josh who had brought Bamboozle for another lunging session, built a small but inviting course, which Rupert proceeded to jump to his father's satisfaction.

Charles looked at Tom. 'Now can we see what he is really capable of?'

'Sure, do you want Josh to ride him?'

'No, Tom, I want you to. You're light enough. He's as strong as an ox. I want to see how much scope he really has got.'

Tom sighed but could see no valid reason to object. He sighed again when he saw the size of the jumps he and Hawkeye were expected to clear. Five minutes later he was certain if Rupert was capable of holding this strong pony, even Oscar and Panky would have a real challenge on their hands but bring it on, for in his heart he was pretty certain his gutsy young son and the effervescent Panky would still reign supreme.

CHAPTER 37

On Wednesday morning the excitement in several of the homes in Massenden was at fever pitch, as the ponies were being brushed and groomed ready to be loaded into the horseboxes before setting out for the Schools and Pony Club Trials.

Erica would be taking eight of the ponies in Charles' horsebox and Jules was driving Tom's largest box with the remaining seven ponies. The Primary School was taking a coachload of supporters who would be in the capable hands of Messrs. Abrahams, Clarkson and Clive Sanderson. It was the first time the school had entered anything other than the music festival Oliver had once taken part in at Hastings, which until now had been the highlight of the school year.

Clarissa had worked extra long hours the previous day and the sweets on the Casa sul Verde's menu were safely in the fridge and the freezer under the surveillance of Luigi and Maria. She was smiling at Georgia who was sitting in the back of Giles' Range Rover with Binny and Wills who had already joined the Pony Club and were keen to support their newfound friends. Belinda was asleep on Binny's lap and Herbie was sitting on his special cushion beside Georgia, growling occasionally when Belinda deigned to so much as glance in his direction.

Josh was travelling with Jules, and Tom and Sam's People Carrier was filled with not only the triplets and Rosie but Daisy and Tilly as well. With all the Wright-Smiths, the Dubois family and Charlotte's parents, Massenden Village was going to be very well supported.

Sam had brought three large tartan rugs and soon everyone was settled at a point where they had an excellent view across the whole arena.

Tom and Charles had agreed to be joint chef d'equipes for the school teams and later Jean-Pierre and Justin would look after the Pony Club team.

Tom soon realized his first task was to try to calm all the excited children, which was certainly no mean feat.

The Pony Club teams were jumping after the schools – so Mimi, Josh, Jacques, Veronica and Tilly settled on one of the rugs to give encouragement to the Primary School. The teams that finished in the top eight places would jump again in a larger arena after a break for lunch. The victorious team and the runner up would go on to the National Championships in Warwickshire two weeks later. If by any chance the teams both happened to come from the same School or Pony Club, the team in third place would then qualify as well.

Whilst the Junior School competition was taking place in one ring, the Senior Schools were jumping simultaneously in an adjacent arena.

Tom was in charge of Massenden A. Team and Charles the B. Team and soon they were very busy getting their first riders, which were Oscar and Oliver ready. There were twenty-five schools competing and Oscar would be fifth to jump and Oliver twelfth.

The course wasn't big but to some children who only jumped at very small, local shows, they appeared enormous.

Massenden were at a huge advantage having the offspring of three International riders at their disposal – five of which belonged to the World famous Tom West and three to the almost equally notorious Wright-Smith dynasty. By the time all four members of each team had jumped there were only four teams on zero faults. All four of the teams and four that had incurred eight faults had all automatically qualified to jump in the main arena after lunch and all eight teams would start again on zero faults.

The course was being altered for the Pony Club teams and Charles couldn't help wondering whether the course builder wasn't being a little over ambitious.

Giles was happy for Georgia who had jumped an excellent round.

He knew she wasn't in the same class as the Wright-Smith and the West children but for this reason success was all the sweeter and he was happier than he had been for years with his daughter sitting on one side of him, Clarissa on the other and Herbie asleep between his knees. He kissed Georgia and smiled at Clarissa who was tickling his cheek with a long piece of grass. At the moment he was living in both torture and paradise at the same time. Paradise when Clarissa was making him tea, pouring him a drink, sitting on the settee sometimes stroking his neck – torture when he could hear her singing in the shower, closing her bedroom door – the squeak of her bed – he wanted her so much and he couldn't help wondering whether she wanted him too.

Charles and Tom were almost as exhilarated as their offspring. The large group of supporters and the three teachers from the Primary School had watched in awe as their pupils and classmates had excelled themselves. Mrs. Adamson reflected that maybe it had been a sad day when Oscar West had solemnly shaken hands with her saying, 'Goodbye, Mrs. Adamson, I shall miss you,' and she had thought, *'Yes you little scoundrel and I shall miss you too.'* She had watched in fear as he had twisted and turned on the prancing Panky and then had felt a lump in her throat when his young sister had flown round on The Duc. She noticed the special smile Gus Wright-Smith was giving Rosie West and shook her head. *'Just like Tom and Sam – in ten year's time we shall all be on the village green throwing confetti again.'*

Justin and James stood up. 'Come on, Pony Club Team, to horse – to horse.'

Mimi, Josh, Jacques and Veronica jumped to their feet and walked the course with their mentors.

'Take care at the double but it's no different to any others you have jumped. Neither is it as high but a spread and an upright of fairly flimsy planks afterwards is always a challenge and needs extra precision.'

Jacques was to be the trailblazer for the Massenden Pony Club, followed by Veronica and Groucho, then Mimi. Josh was to be the anchorman.

They had been drawn to jump in tenth place out of twenty-two different Pony Club teams from all over the south east of England.

Jean-Pierre was holding his breath and lifting his right leg every time Jacques approached a jump but they made their way steadily and safely round the course. One down – three to go!

Veronica was the most nervous of the four members of the Pony Club team but fortunately Justin's laid back manner appeared to rub off on to her and with the help of the evergreen Groucho the team accomplished their second clear round. Unfortunately it was destined to end in drama. Having passed through the finish, for no apparent reason Groucho tripped almost tipping Veronica out of the saddle. She gallantly clutched the pony's mane and left the arena unscathed but sadly Groucho was limping. It was all too obvious he would be taking no further part in the competition if they should qualify for the main arena that afternoon.

The team's reserve rider, Tilly was in shock. She had not for one moment imagined she would be jumping in a huge competition at a large venue in Essex, but before this could happen Josh and Mimi needed to jump clear rounds, which they did with no problem at all.

Three other Pony Clubs were on zero faults too, automatically qualifying along with the Massenden team. Eight other teams, each with four faults selected one unfortunate member to jump against the clock. Only the four fastest would join the other teams that afternoon.

Justin had taken Tilly to the horsebox and was soon schooling her in the warm up area. Bits n Pieces was now twenty years old but he was as healthy and fit as a ten year old and he and Tilly were sailing over the practice jump in perfect harmony.

The team put all the ponies back in the horseboxes whilst their parents opened the various picnic baskets and hampers and some of the Primary School pupils came to join them.

‘I wish Mum was here,’ Tilly was saying. ‘I’ve no family to watch me.’

Virginia Mawgan-Whitely smiled. ‘Yes you have, Tilly. You’ve got Veronica and me. You know we’re your half sisters – we’ve got the same rotten dad.’

There was a socked silence until Sam put her arm round Tilly – ‘You’ve got all of us. Tilly. Every one of us will be routing for you. We’re all so proud of you,’ and apart from Veronica Mawgan-Whitely who was crying in the horsebox, everyone wholeheartedly agreed.

By the end of the afternoon, Massenden village was a place that would not be forgotten by any of the Junior Schools or the Pony Clubs. The Primary A. Team had beaten the Primary School B. Team by four faults. The A. Team had all jumped superb clear rounds and only Charlotte had incurred four faults for the B. Team. They would both be going to Warwickshire in two week’s time along with the Pony Club who had qualified in second place with just two time faults from Tilly and Bits n Pieces.

Mrs. Abrahams was almost in tears as she shepherded the supporters onto the mini bus promising she would try to organize a larger coach which they would share with the Pony Club to take them all to Warwickshire. It would mean making a very early start but Massenden Village was determined to be at the showground giving the teams their full support.

The only downside to the day was the unfortunate Groucho. James had broken the news to Veronica as gently as he could that it was highly unlikely that Groucho’s leg would have recovered in time for the finals in two week’s time. Fortunately for the Pony Club, one of their newest members had an excellent pony and before the afternoon was over, Wills had learned that he and Shining Light would be the fourth member of the team. The jumps would be considerably larger for the Championships and Tilly was more than happy to revert to her previous role as reserve with the ageing Bits n Pieces. She had played her part today helping her team to reach their goal of competing in the Championships. Now she had a superb red rosette and a sash, which had been placed round Bits n Pieces neck as a memento of an amazing day.

As Georgia returned to her father's Volvo, she stopped abruptly when she noticed her mother's head resting on his shoulder. She wasn't certain, but she thought he had been kissing her neck. She crossed her fingers tightly – was it possible? Could it be? Was her dream really going to come true? All Georgia wanted in this world was for her dad to be happy. She was an intelligent girl. She was well aware of the reason he had bought Herbie – why he had walked round the village green so often, sitting on the seat opposite La Casa hoping against hope for a glimpse of her mother. She had noticed him kicking his prosthetic leg and when she had seen the reaction her mother had shown when she had introduced her to Oscar she was almost certain she had discovered the reason for her father's tormented mind and why she had left him eleven years ago.

Her dad had explained that her mother would be sharing their home. Her apartment at La Casa was tiny and hot, he had told her, and he had persuaded her to use the spare bedroom at 2. Theobald's Row. They were after all, he had continued, still good friends.

Recently, Georgia had noticed the way her mother's hand often rested on his knee and she had seen a softening on her father's face as he smiled in response.

'Um – just good friends,' she thought to herself and clambered into the back of the Volvo with Binny and Wills. This time, Herbie had placed himself firmly on Clarissa's smart trouser suit. Like her father, the little dog seemed to be winning her affection as well.

Georgia smiled at Wills as Giles started the engine, he stroked Herbie, letting his hand rest for a moment on Clarissa's knee before putting the gear into drive and gliding out of the showground towards Kent. He was realizing that for the first time since he had moved to Massenden, 2. Theobald's Row was indeed home.

The next morning, Tom and Josh worked Bamboozle for an hour

and then Tom rode the quad bike to Shepherd's Cottage. He was going to use all his persuasive powers to encourage Adrian to come back to work at Woodcutters. He would suggest he started with just the mornings from nine until mid-day. Adrian's eyesight was now almost normal, however, his memory did not seem to be showing any sign of improvement at all.

Amy was trying her best to cope with the situation but it was almost impossible for her. Adrian and she were without doubt the best of friends and there was no question that he loved little Molly.

When Tom pulled the quad bike to a halt in front of the cottage, he could see Amy hanging a large basket of washing on the line, whilst Adrian was picking blackberries from the hedge which ran along the back of the garden for Amy to make a blackberry and apple pie for their lunch.

Tom walked over and joined him, nonchalantly popping some juicy berries into his mouth. He looked straight at Adrian. 'Time you came back to work and earned some money, Adrian.'

'Back to work?'

'Yes, Adrian – at Woodcutters with my horses, with whom you worked for the past fourteen years.'

' I don't remember working with horses – I don't remember working at all.'

'Well you most certainly did and I need you back at the stables and you need to earn some money. Jules, who you have already met, will call for you at eight thirty tomorrow morning and this week you can work until twelve thirty. Amy can push Molly up to the stables and you can walk home together until you are certain of the way. Hannah and Jules will tell you what to do and tomorrow morning I will make sure I am close at hand. You can ride Madame round the lake whilst I give Kaspar some exercise. Once you get back to working again you will find having a routine will give you a reason for waking up in the morning and when I hand you your wages on Friday you will be happy when you are able to give Amy some money to help pay for the food you are consuming.'

'Amy, yes, Amy. She looks after me and she is an excellent Mum. I like Amy – a lot. I think she expected me to share her room but I can't, Tom. I might have a wife somewhere. I just don't know. You keep telling me I'm married to Amy and I wish I could believe you. Sometimes I want to kiss her – love her - but how can I, Tom? Some girl might turn up out of the blue – my wife or my fiancée. I can't take the risk, but I seem to be spending my life fighting my feelings. Maybe you are right – working at your stables may well help me. I certainly hope so.'

'It will, Adrian, I'm sure. One day everything will work out for you. Satin has told me it will.'

'Satin?'

'Yes, we talk to each other. Satin very rarely makes a mistake. So tomorrow morning Jules will be here at eight thirty and I will see you at the stables. Now I will just say au revoir to Amy.'

He went into the kitchen where Amy was giving Molly her lunch. The baby had just started enjoying little jars of baby food; he smiled at them both, running his finger down Molly's cheek, which was as soft as a peach. 'Adrian is coming to work at the stables tomorrow morning,' he told Amy. 'I am going to throw him in the deep end and get him mucking out with Jules and Hannah. There is nothing physically wrong with him now. The sooner he gets back in the groove the better.'

Tom didn't tell Amy the message Satin had sent him a few days ago. It had been extremely bizarre. One of the triplets had been riding a huge bicycle – it had been flying through the air above Adrian, who appeared to be pushing one of Tom's metal wheelbarrows. Tom really began to wonder whether Satin was beginning to lose the plot in his old age.

By the end of the week Adrian was asking Tom if he could work full time. He got on well with Jules and Hannah, whose time at Woodcutters was passing all too quickly.

'Do you want us to move on now Adrian seems to be coping?' Jules asked Tom at the end of that week.

'No way. The longer you both stay with me, the better. Luckily the horses are all jumping well. I really need all three of you. With the ponies as well as the horses there is a lot to do, not to mention the young stock. Four foals will be a lot of work once the colder days come and they need to be brought in every evening.'

'Actually, if you would like us to, Hannah and I would love to stay with you permanently. We've just received our dual passports. Our grandmother was British so there was no problem. We are both really happy here and actually, Hannah and I have made lots of friends in and around the village, especially at the tennis club.'

Tom was already well aware of this. His father had told him. 'Your young Canadian lad is really popular. He and his sister are excellent players and he seems to have found a pretty girlfriend. Nice little thing. Her parents have the butcher's shop in Ribbenden. She's a nurse at the vets. James speaks very highly off her.'

Now Tom was smiling at Jules. 'Are you sure it's my horses you want to stay with, Jules?' he teased. "Or is it young Cindy Carter?"

'You know Cindy, Tom?'

'We know her dad well. He used to buy lamb from Old Tiles for his shop and my sister was at the Primary School with her older brother. Cindy was just a pretty little girl in those days.'

Jules smiled. 'Well she certainly hasn't changed then – I think she's downright gorgeous, but to be honest, Tom, so are your horses and your kids are terrific. Hannah loves having them around and she enjoys looking after their ponies.'

'Fine, you and Adrian can be in charge of the horses, and Hannah can be responsible for the ponies. It won't be too arduous for her – the boys and Rosie love looking after them in the holidays. It's really all they want to do.'

Tom was smiling as he made his way back to the cottage, where a delicious aroma was wafting through the kitchen window. It smelt very like his favourite toad in the hole. He liked Hannah and Jules – Adrian seemed really happy working with them and all his equine friends were really well looked after. There was only one person who was not going to welcome a pretty Canadian girl living in Massenden, especially when he discovered she was working for his own boss's partner. As far as Peregrine Percival was concerned there was no place for young women, especially attractive ones like Hannah in any corner of this earth and it wasn't long before he would be making his feeling lucidly clear.

After seven days of fun with Cassie and Clare who had thoroughly enjoyed a week of sunshine in the yurt, school was looming and with clothes to be marked for not one, nor two, but three boys, Sam and Miriam had spent every spare moment sewing what seemed like a myriad name tapes onto various pieces of clothing, but at last everything was ready for the boys foray into the Grammar School in just over a week's time.

First, there was the question of a trip to Warwickshire for the Primary School and Pony Club Championships.

Much to *the gang's* delight, Cassie and Clare's Pony Club had also qualified and they would all be meeting up once again.

The horseboxes were loaded for the final time these summer holidays. The ponies had all been carefully bandaged, protecting their legs and each had a full net of hay before leaving Woodcutters with Dom in the driving seat. Anne-Marie and Oscar were sitting beside him in the cab whilst Tom and the rest of the family followed in Tom's new Range Rover with Boswell sitting proudly in the back. Hannah and Jules were looking after the other three dogs but Boswell had seized an opportunity when no one was looking and jumped into the boot and nobody had the heart to drag him back to the cottage. He refused to take his eyes off Sam for one second and since his arrival at Woodcutters now over a year ago, Sam had never once had to endure the recurring nightmare that had plagued her, or seen Sophie Stevens in her dreams again.

She was busy tying a small bunch of heather onto the mirror. 'What's that flower for, Mum?' Rosie wanted to know.

‘It’s from the garden – it’s heather. The gypsies maintain it brings good luck. So let’s see if it is true.’

‘I shall put a tiny piece in the side of the Duc’s brow band then, cos Massenden Primary has got to do well. Mrs. Abrahams is coming in the coach. They’ve hired a really big one. The Pony Club is going to share it. They’re going to leave the village at five o’clock tomorrow morning. Mr. Sanderson is coming too. Gus says he’s really nice but I wish I was going to the Grammar with Gus and the trips. I won’t have any friends at the Primary.’

Sam sighed. It was at least the twentieth time she and Rosie had had this particular conversation. ‘Darling,’ she told her for the umpteenth time. ‘You’ve got Abby and Fenella – and’-

‘But it’s not the same. Gussie won’t be there. I won’t have anyone to look after me.’

‘You’ll be fine, Rosie. The Grammar school is especially for boys. When you leave the Primary in two year’s time, you will be going to Ashford with Mimi and Eloise and all the other girls.’

‘I won’t see Gussie every day.’

‘ *The gang* will be meeting two evenings a week. You’ll see him then and all the girls.’

Fortunately, Boswell caused a commotion as he clambered over the back seat, trying to get in the front with Sam and Rosie’s attention was diverted as Tom stopped – put Boswell firmly in the boot and tied him securely to a hook. Sam fervently hoped she wasn’t going to have to endure histrionics when term commenced the following week and breathed a sigh of relief as Oliver opened his iPod and engaged his sister in a game of naughts and crosses.

They arrived at mid-day and once the ponies had been stabled, Sam opened the packets of sandwiches and bottles of lemonade whilst Tom laid the tartan rugs under the nearest oak tree and beckoned to the Lewis family to come and join them.

Soon the rest of *the gang* was running towards them. Joanna laid out another rug and for the moment as Gus sat beside Rosie, school was not given another thought.

The ponies had half an hour hacking quietly round the showground and then Justin produced his cricket stumps and bats. Having persuaded Tom, James and his father to participate, he looked hopefully at Dom and Jean-Pierre.

'I think the ponies need grooming,' Dom said with a sly smile at Jean-Pierre. 'We will make certain they are beautiful for tomorrow – you enjoy yourselves with your strange English game. We might have a beer afterwards. Enjoy yourself, Anne-Marie and I will see you later.'

'Mais, Papa, Oscar loves cricket. He says it's the best game he plays.'

'He's English, Cherie. I told you they have some very strange ideas,' with which he and Jean-Pierre ambled towards the stables whilst Justin's mouth was gaping at the insult to his favourite sport.

'Ignorant frogs,' he muttered good naturedly to James before pushing the stumps into the ground.

Strict rules were adhered to that evening. Every one with the exception of Jacques and Wills were in bed by nine thirty and the other two boys followed shortly after, as the clock on the church opposite the showground struck ten o'clock.

At nine o'clock the next morning, Tom and Charles were walking the course with the Primary School children. Out of the corner of her eye, Rosie could see a huge group of boys and girls hurrying towards the arena, followed by Messrs. Abrahams, Clarkson and Sanderson who had escorted the Primary School supporters and Susan and Bill who had gamely kept an eye on the rather more vociferous Pony Club, who had shared the coach. Bill Cotton had not been exactly enthusiastic but Susan had been adamant.

'You must support the children, Bill. After all you are a governor of the school and I am the District Commissioner of the Pony

Club.' To her relief he had finally agreed to accompany her. Since his retirement he appeared to have receded into a shell, pottering in the garden or immersing himself in The Times crossword. Susan had spoken to Dr. Taylor who she had known since James had been in the Prince Philip team with her son Adam, now longer ago than either of the two ladies wished to admit.

'It sounds as if he is suffering from a mild form of depression, Susan. Can you persuade him to come and see me; otherwise I will call at the oast and see if I can catch him unawares. I know how difficult it can be to get an obstinate man to seek advice!!'

Susan laughed. 'You don't have to tell me that, but come and have a coffee next week. I'll get Bill to show you his rose bed – that's all he seems to be interested in at the moment.'

This conversation had taken place over a week ago and now, thanks to Bill's roses and a very understanding doctor, he had been subscribed a mild antidepressant and Susan could already detect a slight improvement in his general demeanour.

As usual, Rosie was one of the youngest competitors but she was smiling happily as she walked between Gus and her father, whilst Oscar and Georgia listened carefully to everything Tom was telling them.

Charles was walking a little way behind with Orlando, Oliver, Charlotte and Rupert who was the only one of *the gang* who was feeling the slightest bit nervous. After a highly successful Junior Open at the Massenden Show the previous Saturday where he and his new pony Hawkeye had caught everyone's eye, finishing just behind Oscar and Goldfinger, he had begged his father to let him bring the big grey pony to the Championships. Tom agreed with Charles that he could see no reason why he should not, the result being Hawkeye was about to show more than just the Massenden Equitation Centre that Rupert Wright-Smith had arrived. However, Oscar had other thoughts. As far as he was concerned, his friend Rupert would have to fight for every single trophy – in his eyes,

Panky was *the best* and he was pretty sure Joshua had no fears for Ganger either.

Today, however, he and Rupert were both jumping for the honour of their school and they were clapping each other on the back saying 'good luck and bonne chance' as Annie would say, as having completed their scrutiny of the course, they had re-joined the rest of *the gang* before going to the stables to fetch their ponies.

Oscar was pleased his dad had agreed to him bringing Panky instead of Humbug. He knew if there should happen to be a jump off and he was involved, as long as he could control him on the turns, there was no pony faster than Panky. Orlando had brought Torchlight and with Gus and Rupert, the two teams from Massenden Primary were extremely well balanced – it could be anyone's game and there were twenty other teams equally determined to get through to the final Championship in the afternoon. Only eight teams would progress and the ponies had arrived from schools from far and wide across the British Isles. All the parents sitting around the arena were on edge knowing there would inevitably be tears of joy but also some of woe.

At nine-thirty, the first young rider was entering the arena. 'Let battle commence,' a steely eyed Oscar was saying to Rupert who was now half wishing he was sitting on the familiar back of The March Hare, as Hawkeye tossed his arrogant head high in the air almost catching Rupert's nose as he watched Oscar and Panky prance round the arena, exiting with a broad grin on his face.

Tom had one arm round Sam as they sat on the rug, surrounded by what seemed to Tom, a whole classroom of extremely noisy children. His other hand was hanging on to Boswell who was good naturedly enduring a series of snarls from the little Jack Russell who was guarding Binny as Boz was watching over Sam, whilst the lazy little Herbie was fast asleep on Giles' knee. Giles, however, was clutching Clarissa as Georgia and Firecracker were finishing their round with just one time fault.

‘I’m sorry,’ she was saying to Tom. ‘I’ve let the team down. I should have pushed harder.’

‘Then you could easily have had faults, Georgia. You did well and by the way the first two riders from each team have gone and we’re in a really good place, second to our B. team. Rupert has just jumped a really super round for them.’

Eventually, by the time all four members of every team had jumped, thanks mainly to Rosie and Gus’ clear rounds and the one Oscar had jumped earlier, the Massenden A, team were in fourth place with Georgia’s one time fault and Massenden B. were in equal first place with two other schools who had all jumped clear rounds. Both teams would be in the big Championship in the afternoon.

Justin had already got Jacques and Mimi warmed up and they were walking round the practice area together making certain Babushka and Beau Geste stayed warm and supple but not hot. There were twenty Pony Clubs competing, including Lincolnshire South for whom Clare Lewis was riding. Their team’s selectors had deemed Cassie’s pony too small and to her disappointment she was merely a spectator. She felt like a traitor as she left her parents and went and sat by Rupert Wright-Smith who was beginning to show signs of having inherited a good many of his father’s genes, not only in the art of show jumping. His eyes were already appraising the extremely pretty, young Cassie Lewis. They had spent many hours with *the gang* the previous week and Rupert had singled her out for attention on several occasions, on the final morning pulling her behind the yurt and kissing her goodbye, as at the same time, Oliver was promising to text Clare.

The kiss hadn’t gone unnoticed by Clare who had teased her sister as they had passed through the Dartford Tunnel on their way home. Cassie was more than a little annoyed. ‘It’s not funny, Clare. Rupert and I are in love.’

‘Don’t be daft, Cassie – you’re only ten – you don’t know what love is.’

'Well, what about you and Ollie?'

'That's different – I'm almost twelve.'

Later that evening Suzie had asked Mike. 'Do you think the girls should see less of *the gang*, Mike?'

Mike laughed. Like Charles, by the time he was fourteen he had kissed so many girls he couldn't even remember some of their names. His parents had despaired, as his father once told a friend. 'As soon as one girl goes out of the front door of the house another seems to come in through the back!!' He had been twenty-four when he had met Suzie and his life changed dramatically. Fortunately for Suzie, he had sewn his wild oats and although his eyes still appreciated an attractive woman, he knew where to draw the line and their marriage was as steady as a rock. Now he got all the kicks he wanted from the dare devil feats he performed in his Swallow Tail.

'Darling Suzie, how many boys did you fancy when you were Cassie and Clare's ages?'

Suzie looked shocked. 'Certainly none, Mike, I was still playing with my dolls.'

'Suzie, how old were you when you finally grew up?'

'When I met you.'

'Suzie, you were twenty two.'

'Maybe I was. I was fussy. It had to be someone special.'

'And that was me?'

'You were a dashing young pilot. Everyone knew of your reputation. You were nicknamed *Maid a minute Mike*. I was afraid.'

'Afraid?'

'I didn't want to be 'just a minute, Mike. I wanted to be 'forever Mike.'

'But you took the risk.'

'I couldn't help it – you were the person I had been waiting for.'

'And has it been worth it, Suzie?'

‘What do you think? But did you really deserve that terrible reputation, Mike?’

‘Probably, but I can promise you one thing – I found what I wanted in the end.’

‘And that was?’

‘The perfect girl. I recognized her as soon as I set eyes on her and she always will be but don’t worry about our girls, with a Mum like you they won’t go far astray.’

Suzie and Mike pulled their attention back to the competition. Cassie was smiling at Rupert as he handed her half his Kit Kat whilst they watched Jacques and Beau Geste. The course was fairly testing and so far there had been only one clear round from a team from South Yorkshire but soon, to the delight of Susan and all the Massenden supporters, Jacques was making it two.

Mimi however, was a shade too cautious and she and Babushka finished with two time penalties but half an hour later, Wills and Shining Light were fast and clear. Georgia and Binny were standing applauding him and he was wishing Perry had been there to see his round.

‘A smashing addition to the Pony Club,’ Susan was saying to Elizabeth, ‘and what a charming boy. I had a phone call from Peregrine yesterday asking me to keep an eye on young Columbine – he seemed rather anxious. I can’t think why – she seems a very well behaved girl.’

‘According to Justin, Peregrine is a super groom. He’s a smashing rider and can manage all Justin’s horses. He’s really Lord Helingbury but Justin says he’s had a bad experience with a woman and now he hates every female of a certain age on this earth.’

‘Oh dear but perhaps that’s Justin’s good fortune. Knowing Justin Wright-Smith I expect he is paying the fellow the most basic wage imaginable. The old scrooge!’

‘Yet he has spent a fortune on that old house. Fortunately Anna loves it as well.’

'And she loves him too, Elizabeth. I shared a lesson with her and Melchior. Jean-Pierre helped us with the next dressage test we're going to do with the riding club in the New Year. We are hosting it this time. Melchior is coming on in leaps and bounds. His head carriage has improved no end. I'm so pleased for the horse, he's a dear.'

At last it was Joshua's turn and by this time there were five Pony Clubs on four faults with five more ponies and riders to jump. Josh needed a clear round. If he should have four faults, with Mimi's two time faults it would become a nail-biting scenario.

Sam said nothing. She didn't think Tom was aware of how tightly she was clutching his hand. Mimi was holding Jacques' arm cursing her two time faults. She knew she had been over cautious. It was not in her nature to be slow but she had been desperate to jump a clear round. She watched as Ganger covered the ground between the jumps. The concentration was on Josh's face for all to see.

Charles could scarcely breathe as he recalled the many times Tom had saved the day for the Nation's Cup Teams. Josh definitely had inherited his father's temperament and the understanding between the pony and rider was obvious and soon the whole of Massenden cheered as he flew through the finish. There was now no doubt that with only two faults, The Massenden Pony Cub would be jumping again.

The Senior School's competition was still in progress and Charles and Tom walked to the second arena and took note of the course, the size of the jumps and the standard of riding. They both nodded their heads happily. Next year both the girl's and the boy's Grammar Schools would field a team, of that they were more than certain. With Gus, Rupert, Wills, Jacques and Tom's four boys they already had their two teams. They were sure the girls could find one; they just hoped the heads of the schools would agree to enter.

They smiled at each other, as the top six teams were all from extremely well known public schools, the final two slightly less so. *'Next year,'* Charles thought to himself, *'we will show what an ambitious Grammar can do.'*

The schedule for the afternoon was that the Junior School Championship would be held first with the Senior Schools next and then finally the Pony Clubs.

Oscar was to jump first for his team. Tom had decided if there should be a jump off and their team were involved, no one would be better than Panky and his irrepressible son and if he jumped first the pony would be rested.

Some of the younger children had never had the experience of jumping in a really large arena before and the one that was confronting them was most certainly that – it was huge and *the gang* was at an enormous advantage. All with the exception of Charlotte and Georgia had represented their country in the Junior European Championships the previous year and that had certainly given them a wealth of experience.

The fences were falling and there had already been two eliminations when Oscar and Panky entered the arena. Completely unbeknown to him, a middle-aged countess was watching beside her friend Lionel. They had been asked to present the awards. Lionel turned and smiled; 'I thought that lad was going to ride Goldfinger for you, Lavinia?'

'He does but when he came to try him he noticed Panky turned out in a field and fell in love with him. He begged me to let him try him and now here he is back on the circuit big time.'

'Well I never, when your grandson came out of juniors I never expected to see that pony in the arena again. That boy of Tom's is – well – there is really no word to describe him, Lavinia.'

'Unusual, I think you would call him, Lionel. He's got everything. Courage – ambition – charisma – and a funny little French girl friend who he gives all his rosettes to.'

'You mean Dom Silvestre's girl. Dom's a good fellow. Never quite hit the top spot but just exactly what they need at Lake House to bring on their youngsters. Now, watch out, here comes the next future star. Goodness, he's got that fantastic, strangely marked grey pony that won practically everything in Ireland last year. They will give young Oscar something to think about.'

'Rupert Wright-Smith is an excellent rider, but what else could he be with a father like Charles but I have made up my mind, it's Oscar who is going to ride for me when he leaves school? I shall make certain of that. They can't all ride for the Lake House Stables. I've even got a tiny cottage on the estate. He can bring his little French girlfriend with him.'

Lionel smiled. With Lady Lavinia and Totty's money, added to their love and excellent eye for a horse, Oscar's future certainly would appear to be assured.

By the end of the competition there were just three schools with four faults. Georgia and Charlotte had both knocked the upright, which had been the second part of the double. They were both despondent but Tom and Charles brushed aside their apologies. 'It was a huge track, girls – your ponies are both only just over thirteen hands – they did brilliantly.'

'But Rosie and The Duc went clear.'

'Yes, but The Duc has been in these arenas many times and so has Rosie. There are three teams in the jump off and only one of you from each team has to jump. I have elected Oscar and Panky for the A. team and I think Charles has chosen Orlando and Torchlight for the B. team. I don't know the third team but they had four very good contestants, –so – bring it on – and may the best team win.'

The schools drew lots for the order in which they would jump. Massenden B. would go first with Orlando - Saint William's Prep School from Derbyshire would be second and Massenden A. with Oscar had the benefit of going last.

Tom was doing his best to keep Oscar and Panky calm as they watched Orlando. His time was fast but both Tom and Oscar were well aware it could be beaten, which it was by a young lad from Saint William's.

As Sam was watching her son, all she could see was Tom – he had been eleven and her own special prince, jumping Twinkletoes. Oscar's expression, the way he drove with his legs and had the ability to turn in the air was identical. As Panky approached the final double, if he could clear it, the contest was over.

Messrs. Abrahams, Clarkson and Sanderson were leaping up and down along with all the supporters from Massenden Primary and as Oscar sailed through the finish three seconds ahead of Saint William's, the cheers became deafening.

Eloise was thrilled – she hadn't even sat on her pony but as reserve rider she too rode into the arena to receive her award.

Oscar suddenly saw a very familiar figure walking towards him carrying a blue velvet sash with Winner Junior Schools Championship written on it in gold letters and a huge blue velvet rosette. There was a large Challenge Cup with a smaller replica for each child, which Lionel was carrying.

'Lady Countess, madam – I didn't know you were watching. I told you Panky said he was special and that's Rosie, my little sister.' He pointed to his young sister as he looked at the rosette, 'Oh, blue. I think I will keep the sash in the tack room but I think Annie likes blue velvet. Thanks ever so much. Will you be at H.O.Y.S next month?'

'I most certainly will, Oscar.'

'I'll try my best to win for you with Panky, but Goldfinger is bloody good too.'

The countess gave her pony one more pat and then moved on to Rosie. 'You've got a super pony,' she told Rosie. 'He can't be much more than thirteen hands?'

'He's thirteen hands and one inch and he's called The Duc.' She then pointed to Gus. 'That's my special friend, Gus Wright-Smith. He was great too,' and her lovely brown eyes smiled at both the countess and the young man who was grinning from ear to ear, looking the absolute image of his still extremely attractive grand father.

After the Countess had reached the end of the line and the last rosette had been given, which was to Fenella, who like her cousin Eloise hadn't, until that moment even sat on her pony, Oscar and Panky rode round the arena in the Middle of the Massenden A. team clutching both the trophy and Panky's reins, somehow quite miraculously staying in the saddle.

Oscar leapt off Panky, solemnly handing the blue velvet rosette to Anne-Marie who was waiting with her father at the exit to the arena. 'Look after it, Annie and I'll take care of the sash, then one day they can hang together in our cottage.'

Anne-Marie's eyes were glistening with tears 'tu es merveilleux, Ozzie. Vraiment merveilleux,' and she reached up and gave him the briefest kiss on his cheek. He blushed, *'Cor,'* he thought, *'and I thought this day couldn't get any better.'* It was a very first innocent kiss but Oscar was sure it would be the first of very many and even at his tender age he was quite certain they wouldn't all be so innocent, as images from EastEnders flashed in front of his eyes. As he walked back to join *the gang* having handed Panky to Dom, he met Mrs. Adamson who was rushing towards him – arms outstretched waiting to clasp him to her generous bosom, at the same time planting an extremely wet kiss on his forehead. He tried not to shudder and then found himself held tightly by his nemesis, Mrs. Clarkson who was giving him a peck on his cheek, not quite able to forget the morning Oscar had pushed her bra down the swimming pool toilet. Last of all, Clive Sanderson was slapping him on the back saying, 'Well done, Oscar – the school is really proud of you.' Oscar West, for so long the bad boy of Massenden Primary was leaving in a blaze of glory.

He sat down beside Anne-Marie, telling her. 'Yours was the best, Annie.'

'The best?'

‘Kiss, Annie. Mrs. Abrahams almost gave me a bath and Mrs. Clarkson’s was almost as bad but yours was perfect.’

Anne-Marie blushed but took hold of his hand, not letting it go all the way through the Senior School Championship. Sam and Tom were well aware of the situation. ‘Don’t worry, Sammy. When I was twelve even if I didn’t kiss you, I certainly wanted to!!’

‘Maybe, darling, but that was you – this is Oscar we are talking about. I don’t think you were quite as hot headed as he is and I’m sure you didn’t watch East Enders.’

Tom laughed, ‘I couldn’t Sammy. I never had a television at my disposal. I’ll have a little word with Oz. I’ll get the boys together when we get home and just make sure they’re all aware of the facts of life. We’ll have a dad’s hour. They are growing up fast and they have a lot to contend with in front of them but they are great kids, Sammy. We are lucky.’

The standard of the Senior Schools was not as high as in the previous Championship. The majority of the boys and girls were at boarding school. Their ponies were turned out to grass during the term time ridden very occasionally at the weekends and when Tom and Charles glanced at the score sheet there was only one team on four faults, the next was on six and the third team on eight. There was no need for a jump off and soon the course was being set for the Pony Club Championship.

James and Justin walked the team carefully round the course. It would be a real test and certainly require careful jumping. There was a jump with a water tray underneath it, which with the sun shining directly on it was not for the faint hearted.

‘Don’t go mad there whatever you do,’ Justin told the team. ‘If you fly at it you will more than likely take the top pole with you – keep on a bouncing stride – hold your pony’s head and push two strides out – definitely not before. The rest of the course is pretty straightforward apart from the double of gates right at the end. Again, don’t rush at those. It’s far better to get one time fault than crash straight through them. You go and get ready Jacques. Yours is the fifth team to jump.'

Susan could barely bring herself to watch and Eloise had her eyes shut as her older brother cantered into the arena. Jacques' lessons with Charles and *the gang* had taught him much and with his naturally good seat and hands, his ponies always seemed to do their best for him. He remembered Justin's advice about the water tray, which had already caused two eliminations. He held Beau Geste's head not letting him go until he saw a perfect stride – he did exactly the same as he approached the double of gates. His time had been steady and he had two seconds to spare – he had set the team off to the very best start.

By the time the next rider, which was Mimi, was waiting by the entrance, the second rider from Clare Lewis' team was eliminated at the ominous water tray. Sadly for Clare she and the fourth member of her team would not be jumping. It was a bitter blow. Clare tried to take it well but it was the end of all the hope and practice of many weeks. She sat beside Oliver – now her own team were out of the competition and was willing her new friends to win.

Babushka was on song and Mimi was acutely aware of the time. She was determined not to have time faults again and she finished half a second inside the time limit.

Justin breathed again. 'Well done, little sis.' He called to a delighted Mimi, and then crossed his fingers for the next team rider who would be Wills.

Wills was desperate not to let his teammates down. They barely knew him and they had accepted him into the team without question. He had ridden Shining Light for the last three and a half years and the course held no fear for him. He felt the pony hesitate as he caught sight of the light shining on the water tray – he used his legs hard and tapped Shining Light's shoulder with his stick. The pole rattled but fortunately settled back into its cup and two minutes later they were flying through the finish.

The water tray was really taking its toll and only five teams were left in the competition with only one rider left to jump for each team. Only Massenden and a team from South Yorkshire had remained on zero faults.

When the final boy from Yorkshire jumped clear, all Justin said to Josh was. 'Good luck. Josh,' he knew Josh was only too aware that he and Ganger could not afford to make a single mistake.

For once it was Rosie who couldn't watch. She hid her head in Gus' chest. Sam couldn't look either as she hid behind Tom's back with her hands over her ears trying to blot out the sound of any pole, which might fall.

Oliver, Orlando and Oscar were leaning against the wooden fence, which surrounded the arena with Anne-Marie, Charlotte and Clare. They jumped each fence on their own feet as Joshua and Ganger cleared jump after jump. The pony was seemingly being extra careful, clearing each obstacle with several inches to spare.

The triplets were screaming so loudly Sam could even hear them through her hands, which were blocking her ears. She gazed at Tom who kissed her gently. 'Brilliant, Sam.'

'Oh dear, I missed it.'

Tom kissed her again. 'Well, you will just have to watch the jump off then, Sam and I warn you it is going to be very tight, that kid from South Yorkshire is bloody good. I am sure their chef d'equipe will choose him for the jump off and I am pretty certain Justin and James will opt for Josh and Ganger,' and his prediction proved right.

The boy from Yorkshire, who had been announced as Paul Petherington and his pony Dick Turpin were flying but Tom knew long before he had reached the water tray that baring a miracle it would be impossible for him to clear it and he knew from personal experience miracles didn't often happen if you were approaching a difficult fence on a completely wrong stride and sure enough, there was an ominous plop as the pole fell into the water tray. Now all Josh and Ganger had to do was go clear.

Josh had been talking to Ganger – whispering in his ear. 'Do it for the team, not just for us, Ganger.' The pony blew gently back at Josh – they could afford to have time penalties but that wasn't in Josh's nature and they set off at a fast canter. Tom watched his son carefully as they approached the water tray. He saw him steady Ganger – bounce – bounce – bounce – let go and over and the same at the gates – then gallop through the finish.

'That was bloody good, Sam but don't tell Josh I said so. I don't want any of our boys to get big headed.'

The entire Pony Club and all the supporters from Massenden Primary School had erupted. Only last year Mimi and Josh had been head girl and head boy before they had left for their Grammar Schools and two years before that, Jacques had also had that honour.

Once again the Countess and Lionel were presenting the rosettes and the sashes and Josh was holding the large trophy.

As the Countess handed it to him she asked, 'You must be Oscar's older brother. Your father must be very proud of his family and of all the team. Do you all live in Massenden?'

'Yes, we're lucky. We have our own gang. Charles and Justin Wright-Smith give us loads of lessons. Sometimes it's Anne-Marie's father, Dom Silvestre and when Dad's not abroad he helps us too. We train in the gym and swim every morning before we get the bus to school.'

The Countess was impressed. 'Goodness, what hard work.'

'Yes it is, but it's fun. Dad works out every day too – we know if we want to get to the top like him that's what we must do. Even Rosie understands that.'

The Countess smiled as she turned to Mimi, thinking what a startling contrast Joshua's character was to Oscar's. He was calm, polite and charming but she smiled as she thought of Oscar, his exuberance – his rather indelicate use of the English language and his affection for a little French girl. They were undeniably both lovely boys but she was glad it was Oscar who was riding her equally unconventional Hanky Panky. She moved away from Mimi and found herself confronting Wills. She stopped when she found herself staring into the face of the son of her deceased second cousin. 'Cornelius,' she asked him, 'what on earth are you doing here and where are Columbine and Peregrine?'

'Binny is here with *the gang,* and Perry is at Theobald's Place looking after Justin Wright-Smith's horses. He's working there as a groom.'

'Peregrine! A groom! What about Helingbury Castle?'

'Perry has made that over to Romeo and his new wife. He doesn't want to be anywhere near Romeo or Perdita. He just wants to live an ordinary life with no attractive women within a hundred miles of him.'

'I heard that scheming young woman had left Peregrine at the altar and married Romeo. Well good luck to Romeo is all I can say. It looks as though he might definitely need it. But Peregrine – a groom! What would his father have said?'

'I hope he would have admired him, Aunt Lavinia, as Binny and I do.'

For once the Countess was silenced and moved on to give Jacques his spoils.

Binny was calling Perry. *'Perry, we've had an amazing day. The Primary School teams came first and third and the Pony Club team have just won. Cousin Lavinia is just giving out the rosettes and sashes. Wills and she seem to be having an awfully long chat.'*

Perry groaned. *'I bet they are, Binny. I wonder what the hell Wills is telling her. She's a nice old trout but a snob of the first order.'*

'I believe she owns both of Oscar's ponies, Perry – so you might well meet her sooner than you think.'

'Well, luckily for me and for you and Wills, I am old enough to run my own life and both yours and Will's too. As far as I am concerned, Theobald's Place and Massenden are perfect and that is

exactly where we will stay. Now I must go and feed Justin's horses. Say well done to Wills and I'll see you both later.'

Perry was thoughtful as he turned off his mobile but of one thing he was certain – no Countess or Duke - no one in this world would get him to go within a hundred miles of his younger brother or Perdita. He didn't care if he never set foot inside Helingbury Castle again.

Two days later a reporter from a leading pony magazine and two from the local paper visited Massenden. The triumphant teams and their ponies were called to Lake House where they stood first this way and then that way whilst at least a dozen photographs were taken.

When the local paper fell through the doors a few days later, there was a picture of the school teams with a huge caption *Success for Massenden Young Riders as their Primary School and Pony Club Triumph. 'IT WAS BLOODY GOOD FUN,' SAID 11 YEAR OLD OSCAR WEST, having beaten two other riders including his triplet brother to secure the Championship for the Massenden School A. Team which included the youngest rider in the competition, his nine year old sister, Rosie who truly sparkled. Massenden B. Team led by Orlando West was third. Later on in the afternoon, Joshua West secured victory for the Massenden Pony Club in a fiercely fought jump off with a young competitor from South Yorkshire. It was a thrilling climax to the afternoon in Warwickshire.*

There were photographs of all the teams and one of Rosie and Le Duc jumping Charles' red brick wall.

The report in the 'Just My Pony Magazine' was far more circumspect. *Success For Talented Young Riders. The future looks bright for the British National Team. Tom West and Charles and Justin Wright-Smith's children help other talented young riders from the small Primary School in Massenden, a village in the picturesque Weald of Kent to victory in the Junior Schools Championship in Warwickshire last week. Later, after an enthralling jump off,*

Joshua West, Tom's oldest son snatched victory for his Pony Club team. The dedicated youngsters are coached regularly by Charles, Justin, Tom and the talented French riders, Dominic Silvestre and Jean-Pierre Dubois, whose son Jacques was in the Pony Club team.

There was just one photograph of all the children sitting on Charles' red brick wall.

Sam was staring aghast when she read the local paper. She folded it and ran to the study where she found Tom laughing on the phone. *'Here's Sam with a face like thunder, clutching the local rag. See you later, Charles.'*

He turned to confront his wife. 'You've read it then, darling?'

'Of course I have, Tom. Now every home in the county will know we have a son of eleven who swears like a trooper.'

Tom opened a drawer and pulled out an old newspaper – now yellow with age and dated exactly twenty years ago. There was a photograph of a young boy with gold curls, riding a small black pony, holding aloft the Prince Philip Cup with the caption, *Massenden Pony Club Triumph – It Was Bloody Fantastic* were the words of local sheep farmer John West's twelve year old son Thomas' etc.etc.

Tom was laughing and pulling Sam onto his lap as she held out the current edition of the very same paper. 'You're always telling me Oscar takes after his dad, Sammy, and I'm not too bad, am I?'

'Thomas West, you know you are incredible but whatever will Anne-Marie think when she reads this?'

'Anne-Marie has to learn to accept Ozzie for who he is, just as his Countess has done. I bumped into her as I was walking back to the horsebox the other day. *'Your son is quite enchanting,'* she told me. *'Straight talking – straight thinking – and the salt of the earth.'*

'Are you certain she didn't mean Joshua, Tom?''

'Quite sure, she also told me her naughty Panky has definitely found his soul mate.'

'Oh well. If he's good enough for a Countess, why should I

worry? You will have a word with the boys about you know what though, won't you, Tommy?'

'You know what? Now what exactly do you mean by that?' he grinned at Sam. 'Perhaps you had better show me.'

'Thomas West you are quite incorrigible. You certainly don't need reminding of what I am referring to. Now you and I both have work to do. I will see you at lunch time.'

Tom grinned again. This time even more wickedly. 'You certainly will and if I haven't remembered, maybe then you will have time to remind me.'

'Thomas,' but Sam blew him a kiss before hurrying to her office and the plans she was designing for a garden surrounding a block of retirement flats in Folkestone.

CHAPTER 38

Sam was waving good-bye to four handsome, young men; three of who were sauntering slightly unwillingly passed the lake to the bus stop at the end of the drive to Lake House.

She had persuaded – no - she told herself – insisted Tom had taken them to Timm's Trims in Ashford, which still had its old fashioned red and white striped pole protruding skywards above the door and which had a board advertising gentlemen's hair styling.

Mr. Timms had groaned inwardly when he had seen Tom West and his four boys striding up to the door of the small shop. Tom was the worst fidget of all of his many customers and as usual, twenty minutes later, Tom was staring at a short back and sides. Albeit still with tight, gold curls clinging to his scalp. As always after a rare visit to Timm's Trims, Tom would be searching for a smaller riding helmet. His own ordeal over, he watched the triplets squirm one after the other as they suffered a similar fate and then finally, Josh who sat as if he were made of stone.

Oscar had pulled his baseball cap low over his eyes, even more conscious of the scar, which ran down the side of his face.

'Now everyone will notice and tease me,' he moaned.

Josh put his hand on his younger brother's shoulder.

'Well, Oz, they won't do it more than once because my left hook will swing. If anyone bullies you, come straight to me.'

Tom was beginning to wish the trips were still at the Primary School with Rosie, who had still been complaining to Sam that she was going to be lonely and miserable.

At last, Tom and Sam were heaving a sigh of relief. The boys would meet a number of *the gang* once the bus was under way. Jacques, Mimi and Rupert would be waiting at the top of the drive and an even larger number would have assembled at the bottom of Back lane, including Gus Wright-Smith who had just sent a text to Rosie. *'I'll meet u after school. Will call u when I am on my way. Will bring Hamlet. Let's ride tandem round the lake.'*

Rosie, who was about to refuse to get into Sam's People Carrier was immediately uplifted. *'Great,'* she text back and without further ado, sat down on the passenger seat next to her mother.

When she arrived in her new classroom, Mr. Sanderson, her new form master, was looking out for her well aware she was going to miss her brothers and many of her friends. He smiled at her and told her.

'I've got a little task for you this week, Rosie,' and she noticed a young girl her own age standing beside him. 'This is Katie Greenside. She has just moved to a house in Back Lane. She has got a pony, so I thought you would be the perfect person to keep an eye on her until she gets to know all her classmates.'

Rosie found herself looking into the face of a young girl who was clutching a satchel and a bag, which contained sandwiches and an apple. She took her hand and pulled her towards the desk Mr. Sanderson was indicating and within two minutes was gazing at a plethora of photographs of a black cob with feet the size of dinner plates and a coat resembling a hearthrug. She was biting back her laughter as she asked Katie. 'What's his name?'

'Actually, Rosie, Dainty is a she. She was my dad's horse. He rescued her from some gypsies when he was a teenager. Now she's twenty five.'

'Where do you keep her?' Rosie wanted to know.

'There's a paddock behind our cottage. Dad asked James Thornley who it belonged to and it was his. He agreed we could rent it for Dainty. She's lucky – it's got an old shelter in one corner and a stream running down one side. Dad says Tom West lives in Massenden. I watch him on television whenever I can. I would love to learn to show jump more than anything in this world but Dad can't afford to pay for lessons. Have you ever met Tom West?'

Rosie was laughing. 'I haven't only met him, Katie, I live with him. I'm Rosie West – he's my dad - and we live in Woodcutters near Lake House. You can come back after school one day and meet our ponies. There are a lot of them – I've got four brothers and we all ride and so does Mum. I'll ask her which day you can come. Where does your dad work?'

'At the veterinary practice, he's a vet. He trained with James Thornley at Cambridge.'

'Well, he's bound to come to Woodcutters before long then. James and Lizzie Thornley are my aunt and uncle by the way. Fenella and the twins, Felix and Flicka are at school here, too. The twins are in reception and Fen is two years behind us.'

In less than half an hour, Rosie had forgotten all about being lonely and she had already invited Katie to join *the gang.* By the end of the first week, to Sam and Tom's relief, everyone appeared happy. Wills had formed a good friendship with Josh and Jacques and all the girls liked Binny, although they couldn't quite understand why Perry took her to and from school in his Range Rover. On the first morning Oliver had met Katie's brother, Jonathan. They had sat together on the bus and had discovered they had a mutual love of music. By the end of the week, the two boys had joined the extremely talented jazz group, which the school was so proud of.

'Did you have that chat with the boys, Tom?' Sam asked as they sat down to a rather lonely lunch, the silence broken only by Boswell's deep growl as he glared at the wooden bear and the occasional yelp as Hector became a little too over exuberant with Holly. Bertie was sleeping, which seemed to be all he did these days. Tom was worried and had arranged to take him to see James at half past two that afternoon. He smiled at Sam, his soupspoon held midway between his chest and his mouth.

'I did exactly as you asked me, Sammy. However, I wouldn't have rated the conversation a resounding success. Josh laughed and said they had received instruction in these matters at school since they were seven years old and Oscar told me not to embarrass myself – he and Annie had discussed the matter and were intending re-considering the situation when they had left their grammar schools. I felt I was being very gently put in my place.'

'But did you tell them how growing up isn't always easy?'

'Sammy, I promise you I didn't have to. Fortunately whoever visited the school to instruct them appears to have been very explicit. I was let off the hook. Now stop worrying, my sweetheart, think how you are always telling the boys how much they take after me!!'

Sam kissed him. 'Tom, that is just what I am worried about.'

At twenty-five minutes past two, Tom was confronting a stranger who was shaking hands saying. 'Hi, I'm Steve Greenside. I've just joined the practice. Apparently our young daughters have palled up at the Primary school. James and I were at Cambridge together. We kept in touch - they wanted another vet and I needed a new life – so here I am. I'm afraid James has been called to Ribbenden to attend a horse that has fallen into a ditch but how can I help you?'

'I'm Tom as you have probably gathered. I'm worried about Bertie. He's fourteen – I – Sam gave him to me for my eighteenth birthday – he's – he's – special. He's still eating well, but he doesn't appear to have any energy. He sleeps most of the time.'

The vet was extremely thorough. He realised the dog was very special to Tom.

'He is a good age for a big dog, Tom. It's not good news but I think there are definitely some tablets, which will help him. Unfortunately his heart is very noisy – that's not unusual for a dog of his age. Let's see what a course of these tablets will do. I'll give you enough for a month and then I would like to see him again. If there is no improvement, we'll ask James or Mathew for a second opinion but I am sure you realize he is an old dog.'

'I know. I've still got my first ponies and my wonderful old horse, Black Satin. It's the downside to working and owning animals. At the moment they all appear fine but I am well aware there will be some dark days in the not too distant future but on the upside I've recently acquired four super foals from my older jumping mares. Life goes on – it goes round in circles.'

Steve smiled. 'I've, or rather little Katie has got my old cob Dainty. I rescued her when I was twelve from a dreadful gypsy camp where she was being ill-treated. That was the day I knew I wanted to follow in my dad's footsteps and become a vet. Katie keeps begging me to let her have riding lessons. I'm afraid Dainty just plods from pillar to post but there have been other priorities in our family for the last few years. My wife suffered from M.S. She was confined to a wheelchair when Katie was two. I had to employ private nurses to look after her – I wanted her to be at home with her family round her. She died four months ago. That's when I decided to make a new life and when I met James at a University chum's wedding and he told me they were wanting another vet here it seemed as if fate was taking a hand.'

Tom tried to smile. 'I know Rosie has asked Katie to join *the gang*. They are a group of like-minded boys and girls who meet at Lake House as often as they can. One of us is always there to instruct them. It won't cost you a penny. The children are of many different standards. Katie could probably borrow a pony if your cob isn't up to participating. In fact, Justin Wright-Smith has got a super little chestnut wiling away his days in one of his paddocks. The kids are all meeting after school on Friday in the indoor school. Get Katie there. I'm taking the session with Justin – let me see if I can help her.'

'Katie would be over the moon. I can't begin to tell you how grateful I am. It's not been easy for her or Jonathan, they can barely remember a time when their mother was well.'

'Nor for you either, I imagine, Steve?'

'Sadly, it's life, Tom. When I married Jessie she was a dancer. She had her own ballroom studios in Hertfordshire and she also played the trombone in an amateur jazz group. She was the sparkling light wherever she was – no-one would ever have imagined her life would end as it did.'

Tom noticed there were tears in Steve's eyes as he turned to the computer to ask the receptionist to have the pills ready for Tom to collect. He felt ashamed. He had been whinging about his horses and ponies getting old when this poor man was obviously still trying to come to terms with his wife's untimely death. He vowed he would help young Katie achieve her ambition to jump.

He helped Bertie into the Range Rover and drove straight to the Primary school to pick up Rosie who was walking down the drive with a girl he didn't recognise. He assumed this was most probably Katie. He saw Steve draw up at the gate, the girl jumped into the car beside him, then turned and waved to Rosie. When he got home, he took his mobile out of his pocket and called Justin.

'Justin, what is Guy doing at the moment?'

'Bloody nothing, Tom. He's out in the paddock with Topsy, eating his head off and doing bugger all.'

'Could Perry get him to Woodcutters this afternoon?' and Tom explained about Katie and the tragic life she had led.

'Sure thing. Perry is out with Conchita and leading Pickwick at the moment, but I will ask him to get Guy in and lead him over to your place as soon he gets back. He can tack him up so that you have got his saddle and bridle.'

'Thanks a million Justin, It may not work out, apparently the girl has been riding an old cob – we shall just have to see.'

At two o'clock that afternoon, Hannah was pulling Kaspar's mane and tail in the yard at Woodcutters. Fortunately for Hannah, he was enjoying the attention he was getting and his eyes were half shut as he dozed in the bright sunlight.

Suddenly, there was a loud bang as the gate blew shut behind Passe Partout and Perry, who was valiantly hanging on to Guy

Fawkes who was not enjoying being in such close proximity to the exuberant thoroughbred.

Unfortunately for Hannah, she hadn't notice Kaspar's rope had come untied. He awoke from his reverie with a start when he heard the gate clatter and the sound of cavorting footsteps in his stable yard. He knocked over the bucket, which contained his grooming kit and charged towards Passe Partout. Perry had let go of Guy as he struggled to control his horse and avoid being kicked by Kaspar who was not best pleased to see a stranger in his yard. Fortunately, Guy had noticed his life long friend Sparkler and had galloped over to the small paddock and was talking to him over the fence.

Hannah screamed as she tried to get hold of Kaspar's head collar but Passe Partout shot sideways, depositing his rider on the ground.

Perry cursed as he picked himself up, hanging grimly on to Passe Partout with one hand and grabbing Kaspar's head collar with the other. His eyes were flashing contemptuously at Hannah. 'Get hold of this horse, for God's sake, you incompetent girl – you shouldn't even be in charge of a kitten. Look at my bloody leg.'

Perry wasn't swearing – he was pointing at his ripped jeans, now saturated with blood from the deep graze on his right knee.

Hannah was shaking even though she now had a firm hold of Kaspar's head collar. 'I'm sorry - I'm sorry,' she was almost whispering – not frightened of Kaspar but of this tall man with flashing eyes and fury and contempt sparking from every part of his being.

'I didn't realize his rope had come undone. He was almost asleep until he heard your horse.'

'That's right – that's right - blame my innocent horse. Typical woman. Typical. Always think their stupid fair sex can never do any wrong,' with that Perry leapt back on to Passe Partout and shot through the gate, almost knocking Sam over as she came to talk to Jolly Roger and Pot Luck. She leapt out of the way, just missing Passe Partout's rump.

'Excuse me, Sam. I do beg your pardon. I think however maybe you should sort out that empty headed girl. I can only feel sorry for Tom if he has to put up with her stupid antics every day,' and with that he raised his hand to Sam and disappeared from sight, the blood still running down his jeans.

Hannah was crying. 'What a truly hateful man. He came bursting through the gate on that maniac of a horse. I didn't realise Kaspar's rope had come undone. I was pulling his tail. I think he must have been chewing it whilst I wasn't looking. He had been unusually quiet – I thought he was asleep. The next thing I knew, that horrible man was calling me names – slighting all women. He's the vilest person I've ever met in my life.'

'Oh dear, Hannah, I know Justin thinks he's marvelous. Apparently he's wonderful with the horses and Gus and Abby too.'

'If I were Justin I wouldn't let Abby within a hundred miles of him. I hope I never have to speak one word to him again.'

'I think that could be rather a big wish, Hannah. Massenden is quite a small village, but don't worry, no harm was done, except I couldn't help noticing the blood that was pouring down the gentleman's leg. Come on. Worse things have happened at sea. Let's tie Kaspar up again and I'll go and fetch Guy and take his tack off before he gets caught up in his reins.'

As Perry took off his jeans and soaked his knee in iodine, the harder the wound stung, the more he muttered to himself that God should never have even contemplated putting a single woman on this earth, especially ones with huge brown eyes that filled with tears when you shouted at them and he reminded himself firmly he hated all women, today and as far into the future as he could see. Once bitten – absolutely definitely twice shy. 'Stupid little cow,' he muttered to himself.

When Jules arrived back at Woodcutters from a hack with Adrian, he realized his sister was unusually quiet. Eventually he heard of her encounter with Perry. He leapt back on to Madame

Bovary and five minutes later was confronting Perry. 'I have just found my sister in an extremely emotional state for which I have every reason to believe you are wholly responsible,' he told Perry

'I think not. I imagine you are Jules. Your sister was totally at fault. She had omitted to notice the rope of the horse she was grooming had come undone and detached from the ring by his stable door. He knocked me off my horse – bloody ripped my jeans and gashed my leg.'

'Anyone can make a mistake.'

'They most certainly can. Especially when a woman is concerned. I learned that to my cost not many moons ago. Now if you will excuse me I have to go and fetch my brother and sister from Ashford.'

Somehow, Jules felt he had been well and truly put in his place. There would certainly be no love lost between the two young men.

On Friday evening, after Sam had given Katie some tea with Rosie and the boys, she walked beside her on the lively little Guy Fawkes. She didn't have to be a professor to realise that for Katie and Jonathan childhood had been far from the happy one their own children and their friends had enjoyed and although it seemed very hard, maybe life would now be a little easier for all the family once the initial shock of their mother's death had passed.

Katie seemed quite relaxed on Guy as they made their way to the indoor school. 'He's quite, quite different to Dainty,' she told Sam. 'He's a lot smaller, but much, much more lively. He's super.'

Hannah had been helping Tom with Bamboozle. He was improving every week; already trotting over poles and jumping the cavaletti as Tom lunged him round and round the school. She accosted Justin as he walked into the school with Gus and Abby. 'You've got the most uncouth man I've ever met working for you,' she told him.

Justin shook his head. 'I would never call Perry uncouth – maybe a trifle unconventional.'

'Well, he was absolutely vile to me.'

'Don't take it personally, Hannah. Perry hates all girls since his fiancée ditched him.'

'Well, Justin, I certainly don't blame her. He's the rudest man I've ever set eyes on. No woman in her right mind would want him.'

Unfortunately Binny overheard this interchange and grabbed hold of Hannah. 'Perry is the best brother on this earth. You don't know what he's like. If it weren't for Perry, Wills and I would be living with a bad tempered aunt on the Isle of Skye. He's the best person in this world.'

Hannah shook herself free of the angry young girl. 'Well, I am sorry, Binny. We obviously see your brother from a totally different perspective. As far as I am concerned, I hope I never have the misfortune to set eyes on him again,' and she walked off to stand beside Katie and Guy.

There was no doubt that Katie was completely self taught but her enthusiasm and her willingness to learn were obvious from the start of the evening. She had no fear and handled Guy with confidence. She could certainly rise to the trot and was not the least bit concerned when Guy cantered round the school behind Rosie and Braveheart even though she was bumping up and down in the saddle. Tom immediately knew the best person to help her and knowing that person as well as he did he was sure she would agree to help Rosie's new friend. He walked up to Sam.

'Could you take Katie and Anne-Marie down to the far end of the school, Sammy and see what you can do to help them both with their canter? We'll keep the rest of *the gang* at this end of the school. Hannah is going to walk Bamboozle back to Woodcutters.'

Sam did not hesitate. 'Of course, come on girls, let's see what we can do.'

Justin was pleased when he saw Katie was obviously enjoying

herself on Guy Fawkes. Sam had told him of Katie's situation at home and the charismatic side of Justin, which was actually never too far away, wanted to help the girl and the mercenary side, which never left him, realized if he loaned Guy to Katie he would have one less pony to feed and he knew only too well winter was approaching. He liked Guy Fawkes and wanted to keep him for Noah when he was older. He would be perfect after his little son had learned the rudiments of jumping from the elderly but totally reliable Fuzz Buzz.

'We'll take Guy to Woodcutters for the moment, Justin and see how Katie gets on with him over the next week or two. I'll ask Sam if she can help her – she really needs lunging and going right back to basics. After that, if all goes well she can have him at their cottage. Apparently Steve has got the old cob he had as a teenager so Guy would have company.'

'That's fine with me, Tom. I'll leave you to sort that one out as you have already met Katie's father.'

'Before you depart, Justin, Sam says Hannah was really upset this afternoon. Your new groom was really out of order. Apparently he was really rude to her.'

'Tom, I am not getting involved with petty squabbles between our grooms. I saw the state of Perry's knee. Kaspar got loose whilst Hannah was grooming him and rushed up to Passe Partout who exploded causing Perry to fall in the middle of the two horses. They are both adults. They must fight their own battles,' he laughed. 'They will probably end up in bed together one day. Stranger things have happened.'

'Well, according to Sam, that could be difficult. Hannah told her she hopes she never has to set eyes on your precious groom again. Anyway we will look after Guy at Woodcutters temporarily – he would have a good home with Katie. Her Dad saw Bertie the other day. He seemed a really nice chap and just think Justin, you won't have to pay any vet's fees if anything should befall Guy.'

'Better and better – let's hope the girl gets on with him.'

‘To Sam’s relief, Rosie had taken the task of looking after Katie seriously not only at school but with Guy as well and two evenings each week Sam took both girls and Anne-Marie for a hack round the lake or to Tom’s sand school where she worked hard with Katie and Anne-Marie’s sitting trot and canter. They were both intelligent girls and keen to catch up at least with Abby and Daisy and Sam was pretty certain it wouldn’t be too long before they had achieved their goal and by the end of two weeks, Guy Fawkes was on loan to Katie. He was to stay at Woodcutters until the spring. It was easier for Sam to collect the girls from school and they would be tacked up alongside either Goldfinger or Sweet Dreams ready for Sam to accompany the girls to Tom’s sand school, which, much to Katie’s astonishment was floodlit.

Steve was indebted to Sam. Every sentence Katie uttered started with *‘Sam says* or *Sam showed me.’* He realized at last Katie had the stability that had been lacking in her young life and it was the same for Jonathan. He went to Woodcutters twice a week too, and whilst Katie enjoyed her outdoor pursuit, he and Oliver practiced their trombones and clarinets whilst sometimes the other boys sang lustily if they happened to know the songs.

Steve realized it had been the best move he could possibly have made, especially when he met Mary and John who had taken Mac and Mabel for their boosters. ‘Stock up at the Farmer’s Market.’ Mary had told him. ‘Have you got a big freezer?’

Steve laughed. ‘Actually, I seem to have acquired an extra one. I brought my own from Hertfordshire only to find the couple I bought Penny-Farthing Cottage from had left theirs behind for me in the garage.’

‘If you can’t get to the market, John and I will get anything you want and we will pop it into our freezer. You can collect it from the farm after surgery. I am there every week. I have a stall. I make bread and cakes and I sell our eggs and my honey too. I shall never get rich, but I love chatting to all the other stall holders and the village people who support us.’

Steve smiled, thinking what a beautiful mother Tom was blessed with. 'I'm on holiday the week after next,' he told her. 'I thought I should be at home for half term. The children and I will have a shop up, and then I might well take advantage of your really kind offer. I'm afraid my cooking skills stop at a drive to the supermarket and ready-made meals or a Pizza from the van every Thursday.'

At the end of September, Tom and Sam took their five children plus Gus, Rupert and Anne-Marie to Lincolnshire for their long awaited visit to the home of the Swallow Tails. Sam and Suzie took the girls into Lincoln for some retail therapy whilst Tom accompanied the boys to a rather bleak air base in what appeared to be the middle of nowhere, where large grey hangers housed the squadron of Swallow Tails. Under the supervision of Mike, the boys climbed one by one into the cockpit of Swallow Tail Two, which was Mike's particular hawk, exclaiming at the many dials surrounding the controls.

'Wow,' Oscar grinned as he fingered the controls. 'Which one fires it up?'

Tom poked his head anxiously into the cockpit. 'Oscar, don't you dare touch a thing. It could well be the last you would ever see of your beloved Hawk, Mike.'

'He won't figure out how to start Swallow Tail, Tom, don't you worry. Sometimes even I have to think twice before I have remembered. There's a simulator inside the building, Oscar. You can have a go on that if you like, boys.'

The boys were enthralled for the rest of the afternoon. 'Cor, it's just like jumping Panky upside down,' Oscar was shouting. 'If I wasn't going to be a show jumper I'd be a pilot, Mike. Cor!!'

At last, Tom managed to get the boys back into the Range Rover. 'That was the best afternoon EVER, Mike. EVER, EVER!!' The boys were telling him in chorus. They had all bought a small framed print of Mike's Swallow Tail, and Rupert, who loved making things, bought a model which he was going to hang on a wire from his bedroom ceiling.

That evening, all the girls slept in sleeping bags on the floor in Cassie and Clare's bedrooms whilst the boys shared the large caravan Jules had towed behind the horsebox.

The show the following morning was only five miles away from the Lewis' house. Tom was resting all his horses except The Wizard who would not be going to H.O.Y.S. Rosie and Braveheart and Rupert and his new mount Hawkeye were the only two ponies participating, as all the rest would be jumping at the big show in the middle of the following week but Cassie and Clare were both entering Snowball and Flying High.

Sam zipped up her anorak, noticing how bracing the air was in Lincolnshire. The wind seemed to be blowing straight off the east coast. She rummaged in the caravan and found a rather elderly thick woolen jacket for Rosie. She had complained of a sore throat at breakfast time that morning and the last thing Sam wanted was an ailing Rosie in a caravan at H.O.Y.S.

Whilst Tom and Rosie walked the course, Josh fetched Braveheart and rode him to the practice area where he helped his young sister in to the saddle.

It was one of the last outdoor shows of the autumn and unusually for the Junior Foxhunter Class, which was generally large, there were only twelve entries. It was to be Braveheart's first win without even trying, as he and Rosie jumped the only clear round.

Tom quickly pulled a small handful of pony nuts from his pocket and stroked Braveheart's nose. 'Good pony. Good boy - that was excellent – good girl, Rosie.'

Rosie was smiling. 'He's my best friend, dads, - he told me he would be really careful.'

'Well he most certainly was just that, sweetheart. Josh, can you help Rosie put him back in the horsebox and then we'll all watch Cassie's twelve two and Clare's thirteen two classes. Rosie suddenly gave three enormous sneezes. 'Here's a five pound note. Gus. Take Rosie into the refreshment tent and have a hot chocolate. The wind is really biting. Does any one else want one too?'

Rupert obviously wanted to watch Clare but Oscar pulled Anne-Marie to her feet. 'Annie is shivering, Dad. Can we go with Gus and Rosie?'

Tom produced another five-pound note. 'Anyone else before I put my wallet away?'

'Cassie and I might like one after her class, Tom, but I am going to sit here and watch her first,' Rupert told him.

By the time Rupert had won the Junior Open with his new, supercharged Hawkeye and Tom and The Wizard had won a very poorly supported open, Rosie was sneezing every five minutes and everyone scrambled back into the Range Rover. Jules started the journey back to Kent with Josh beside him in the horsebox – goodbyes had been said until the New Year Show at the Massenden Centre when the Lewis family would be staying in Old Tiles Oast House.

There was an unusual silence in the car. Rupert and Oliver were both thinking New Year's Day was a long way away, Rosie was asleep, Gus was upset because she wasn't well and Anne-Marie and Oscar were playing a game on Oscar's iPod. Only Tom and Sam were chatting compatibly, laughing as Tom related Oscar's enthusiasm in the simulator the previous afternoon and then discussing the forthcoming H.O.Y.S., crossing their fingers that the entire family wouldn't succumb to Rosie's virus.

Unfortunately some of Sam's fears became a reality. As they were preparing to leave Massenden on Wednesday morning, the triplets were all complaining of sore throats, each one sneezing at five-minute intervals. Rosie now sounded as though she needed her adenoids removing and Sam's throat felt as though a piece of sandpaper was wedged from one tonsil to the other and she felt a sharp pain in her side every time she drew breath. Only Joshua and Tom appeared to have escaped the virus.

Gus was asleep in the back of Justin's Range Rover beside Abby, who was holding a handkerchief doused in eucalyptus, trying to stem all the germs, which were flying round her father's car.

Tom and Joshua were shaking their heads. All this coughing and sneezing did not augur a good start to H.O.Y.S. When at the last minute, Dom had to be called to replace Jules who had woken up with a blistering headache, the men felt even more despondent. Even Oscar felt too wretched to show more than a mild reaction when he heard the news that Anne-Marie would be accompanying her father and she too was speaking in a tiny whisper.

Tom opened the window of the Range Rover hoping to blow the germs away, only to be remonstrated with by Sam, who enquired whether he wished to be visiting all his family in hospital. They would doubtless all develop pneumonia.

The atmosphere in the car was definitely not good. The triplets were unusually quiet for the simple reason they were all three asleep and Rosie was now complaining of feeling sick. Even one of the dogs was emitting obnoxious smells from the boot of the car.

Tom went back into the cottage, rushed to the bathroom and unearthed a rather elderly bottle of *Rescue.* He snorted several drops up each nostril, praying it would work all the miracles it was purported to do on the label, pushed the bottle into his pocket for future use and rushed back to the car. He gasped at the mixed aroma of eucalyptus, Fisherman's Friend, Vick Vapor Rub and not least, doggie farts and looked at Sam. 'I have to open this window for two minutes, Sam or my vomit will very soon be adding to the terrible stench in the vehicle.'

There was no reply for the simple reason Sam was asleep. Tom put his hand gently on her forehead – it was burning hot. He rushed back indoors again and found an unused packet of Paracetamol, ran back to the car, closed the window and finally set off towards the M 25.

In the horsebox, Josh was chatting to Dom as they ground to a halt behind a long queue of traffic near the Sevenoaks junction. It was going to be a slow, tedious journey – not one to be relished.

By the time the showground came into sight, the triplets had all three been sick and Sam's teeth were chattering. Tom sniffed more drops of *Rescue* before he unhitched the trailer, helped Sam and the triplets to bed and made everyone a drink of lemon and honey. Finally with the help of Rosie, who was now feeling better, and chattering non-stop, making up for the last two days, he helped Josh and Dom unload the horses and ponies. He took Rosie and Josh to the refreshment bar and bought the three of them steak and chips, before hurrying back to the caravan where all four invalids were still fast asleep.

The next morning, the triplets all had very deep, husky voices and extremely runny noses but no sign of a fever and were a quarter of the way back to their usual exuberant selves. Sam was not so fortunate. Tom felt her burning forehead and called the secretary. 'This is Tom West – can you give me the local medics phone number, Sam seems to have quite a high temperature.'

It was a new secretary. 'Are you certain it's not a vet you are requiring, Is Sam your horse?'

'No, Sam is my wife and she definitely needs a doctor. She's burning hot.'

An hour later, Sam was being admitted to the local hospital with viral pneumonia.

'It's precautionary,' a frantic Tom was told. 'We need to get this fever down and a caravan is not the best place for your wife at the moment. You did the right thing – she might even be back with you tomorrow.'

Sam was crying. She wanted to be strong but she felt too weak. 'The children, Tom. What about the children?'

'Don't worry about that, darling. I'll go back to them and buy them all lunch and then I will ask Dom to keep an eye on them and come straight back here.'

'You can't, Tom. You've got a class this afternoon.'

'Damn the ruddy class this afternoon, do you think I am going to leave you in hospital in the middle of Birmingham on your own?'

'Tom, please jump.'

'No – emphatically no, you are all I care about at the moment. That's how it always has been and how it always will be.'

'Tom – you are one in a million.'

'Yes, and you are one in two million, my Sammy. Now you have a good sleep whilst I go and see to the children. I'll be back A.S.A.P. Love you.' He blew her a kiss and rushed back to the showground.

Rosie burst into tears. 'Where's Mummy?'

'She's had to stay in hospital until her fever has quite gone. I am going back when you have all eaten. Dom will look after you.'

Rosie refused to eat anything – the triplets merely toyed with their food - Tom ate only because he knew it was the sensible thing to do and only Joshua seemed to enjoy his beef burger and chips.

Rupert and Gus were still in bed but Anne-Marie was recovering and she and Oscar spent the afternoon watching a speed class, which Charles and Stormy Waters won.

To Tom's relief by the time he left that evening, Sam's fever had almost gone and she was told if it was the same in the morning she could leave the hospital.

The next morning, after a call to Sam's ward, Tom was told his wife's temperature was completely normal and he could collect her as soon as he liked.

Gus and Rupert were also recovering and at last everything seemed much brighter for the Lake House Stables.

Whilst Tom rushed to the hospital, Dom got Swallow Tail ready for the Foxhunter Championship.

Tom asked Josh to stay with Sam to make her tea or a lemon

drink whenever she wanted one and raced into the arena just in time to walk the course. He waved to Justin and they walked together.

'How's poor old Sam?' he asked Tom.

'Weak but miles better, thank goodness. I know I tend to panic about Sammy but she does give me good cause to do so sometimes. Josh is with her – he's a good boy, he will make sure she has everything she needs. Thank goodness the kids are all improving so rapidly.'

'Yes, and thankfully Noah seems to have escaped this horrible virus. He's in good voice, shouting at everyone. He loves it here. Can't wait until he's jumping Sparkler.'

'Sparkler?'

'Oh yes, Tom. Rosie told Gus Noah could ride Sparkler for her. Smashing! It means I won't have to splash out a small fortune on a good twelve two pony for him.'

Tom was left speechless but he loved little Noah and obviously Rosie and Gus had discussed this between them. Much water would flow under the bridge before a final decision would be made. Rosie had three more years when she would still be eligible to ride Sparkler if she hadn't grown too big – which, looking at her diminutive stature would appear highly unlikely.

He pulled himself back to the present and leapt onto Swallow Tail. He was a lovely young horse and Tom was almost certain he wouldn't be riding him for much longer, especially if they should do well within the next hour. Which is exactly what they did, coming second to Justin and Conchita.

Charles grimaced as he turned down a huge offer for the mare as Justin and Conchita exited the arena holding the trophy.

'I'll have a talk to my son,' he told the Canadian who was the agent for one of the well-known riders from the U.S.A.

'How about Lake House Swallow Tail?' the man then asked Charles.

'Oh! That's an entirely different matter. He belongs solely to me.' The Canadian made a more than generous offer and before Tom even had time to dismount, Swallow Tail belonged to Buzz Brightling – the former number one rider in the world.

Tom was philosophical. He had once thought he would like to buy Swallow Tail from Charles but that was before Alicia had appeared on the scene. He patted the gelding and two hours later he was saying goodbye to yet another excellent horse, but Justin refused to sell Conchita. He knew she was a future International mare and Charles was left to rue the day he had shaken hands with his son.

When Tom got back to the caravan he found Sam dressed, sitting in a chair sipping a bowl of chicken soup, which Joanna had made for her. There was also a small bowl of trifle. She smiled as he walked through the door and held out her hand. He grasped it and put his head gently in her lap.

'Please, please, Sammy, don't frighten us like that again. Thank God you look one hundred times better this afternoon.'

Sam smiled as she squeezed his hand. 'Perhaps not one hundred yet, Tom but certainly seventy five times. I will take it really quietly today, then I should be fine to watch the children jumping tomorrow.'

Tom kissed her forehead. 'I'll just make myself a sandwich and then I've got to get Alicia ready for the Grade C. Championship. We'll be one horse lighter on the way back on Sunday, Charles has just sold Swallow Tail to Buzz Brightling. At least I shall get ten percent of the money. That's a good lump of cash for the old savings account.'

'Don't forget I'm going to London for the sale of the flat next week. Exciting times ahead, methinks.'

Tom left to get Alicia from her stable, relieved to see Sam's empty soup bowl. She was tackling the trifle enthusiastically and his heart was considerably lighter as he gathered his mare.

Dom held Alicia whilst Tom walked the course with Josh. He felt it was a good education for the future as Josh carefully counted the strides alongside him. Next year, Josh would be jumping Sweet Dreams for Elizabeth but Tom knew that for the moment, his eldest son's heart was set on winning the Leading Junior Championship with Ganger the following afternoon. He also knew all too well that Oscar was fired with the same ambition and he was certain the other twenty or so boys and girls who had qualified for the competition would all be filled with the same desire.

Tom had been certain Alicia was a special mare from the moment he had first set eyes on her with the terrified Jodie and he was hoping he wouldn't let her down.

Joanna visited Sam to see whether her tasty offerings had been appreciated and she was delighted when she was confronted with two empty bowls.

'Rosie and the boys are watching Tom and Alicia in the Grade C. Championship, Joanna I think I shall take advantage of their absence and have a short snooze. Do you think you could make sure I get to the loos without toppling over – I hate using the one in the caravan?'

'Put on a warm jacket then, Sam and we'll be as quick as we can. There's a bitterly cold wind today.'

Sam was more than a little surprised to discover how wobbly her legs felt and she was glad when she got back to the warmth of the caravan. She took her antibiotics and snuggled under the duvet, wishing it were the old feather bed at Woodcutters.

Two hours later she was woken by the boys excited voices and soon they were bursting through the caravan door.

'Look, Mum,' and Josh was holding a huge trophy. 'Dad's like a dog with two tails. Alicia was brilliant – she beat twelve other horses in the jump off including Charles and The Blarney Stone. Dad has just turned down a huge offer on your behalf for Alicia. Buzz Brightling's agent wanted her to go off to America with

Swallow Tail. Dad told him *'No Way.'* The man increased his offer but Dad told him he was merely wasting his time.'

Rosie broke in. 'He's the best dad in the world. He loves his horses much more than he loves money. Not like Charles. Gus told me his grandpa wanted to sell Conchita but his dad wouldn't let him. Horses make you much happier than money, don't they Mum?'

Charles had been about to knock on the caravan door to enquire after Sam. He stopped when he heard Rosie's still slightly husky voice. For a moment he felt guilty – he readily acknowledged nothing gave him a greater kick than watching his bank balance grow. He heard Sam telling Rosie. 'There is an old saying, Rosie, *'Money is the root of all evil.'* It's not always true but I am afraid it very often is.'

Charles turned and walked pensively back to his caravan. He called Justin. 'Meet me in the bar in five minutes, Justin.'

'Now what does the old devil want?' Justin thought, but ten minutes later he thought his ears were playing tricks on him.

'I've been thinking, Justin,' his father was telling him. 'Give me ten thousand pounds and Conchita is yours.'

'But, Dad, you turned down ninety thousand for her only this morning, that would have been forty five k each.'

'Maybe I did – but I am offering you my half for a fraction of that. She's entirely your responsibility then.'

Justin had never shaken hands so quickly. He banged on the door of Tom's caravan asking his friend. 'Have you got your cheque book here, Tom? I left mine at home.'

'No, Justin, but Sammy has hers.'

'Can you lend me ten k. Sammy? Just until we get home. I need to buy a horse a.s.a.p.'

Tom looked amazed. 'Justin, where on earth have you found a horse for ten grand in the middle of Birmingham?'

'Here. Right here. Please, Sammy, I'll repay you the minute we get back to Massenden.'

Sam sighed. 'I don't keep ten thousand pounds in my current account, Justin.'

Justin handed Sam his mobile. 'Ring your bank, Sam and get some money transferred.'

Sam's head was beginning to spin. She dutifully looked in her diary, found the number of her bank, managed to remember her password and the deed was done. She handed Justin a cheque.

'Thanks a million, Sammy.'

'Well, I hope whatever you have bought brings you success, Justin.'

'Oh, she will. Dad has just sold me his half of Conchita for ten grand.'

Sam looked surprised. 'Why didn't you just tell your dad you would pay him when you got home, Justin?'

Justin laughed. 'Do you think I trust that old wheeler-dealer – he would probably say he had forgotten all about selling her to me. I trust you though, Sammy. I'm sure your cheque won't bounce,' and with this final remark, he hurried back to give his father the cheque.

Tom and Sam both shook their heads. 'That father and son are both as nutty as a fruit cake – I really don't know which one is worse,' and Tom hid his latest trophy in the fridge.

The next morning the only people up bright and early were Jacques, Tom and Jean-Pierre. Jacques was the only member of *the gang* involved in the Junior Foxhunter Championship. He had got up really early and plaited Foxy's mane. Now he was walking the course with his Uncle Tom, whilst his father held the Flying Fox. Foxy was a beautifully built pony with near perfect conformation. He was strong and agile but not a difficult pony to ride, always attacking every jump with both enthusiasm and an enormous amount of scope.

It was a large class and by the end of the first round eleven competitors had jumped clear including Jacques and Foxy.

Jock, who had sold the pony to Jacques, was watching almost as anxiously as Tom and Jean-Pierre, as Jacques entered the arena for the jump off. Four competitors had already jumped and as so often happened as soon as time reared its ugly head, panic set in and poles flew all over the place and the odd run out occurred. There was not yet a clear round. Tom had told Jacques not to go mad but he had pointed out two time saving maneuvers where Foxy could cut across the jumps saving valuable seconds. They were clear in a quick but beatable time; all they could do now was watch and wait. When the penultimate rider came into the arena, Tom recognized her with a start, for looking exactly like her late mother, Florence Faulkes-Williams was attacking the jumps with determination and style. She was certainly an extremely accomplished rider but to Tom and Jean-Pierre's relief, finished her round just half a second slower than Jacques.

Jacques couldn't watch the large screen in the practice area as the final pony and rider cantered towards the first jump. He was so near and yet so far from the biggest achievement of his short career. He buried his head in Foxy's neck and listened. Suddenly, he heard a loud plop and a big *Ahhh* from the spectators. He opened his eyes and saw the five bar gate lying prostrate on the ground. He felt his father and Tom both slapping him on his back and heard Jock saying. 'A bonnie round – well done laddie.' Mimi and Josh were running towards him shouting. 'Brilliant, brilliant, Jacques.'

Jean-Pierre was calling Jane who had stayed at home with Clara and Rudi as Eloise was running a few yards behind Mimi, and then hugging her brother. It was the perfect start to the day for *the gang.*

Tom made his way back to the caravan to find Rosie and get her ready for the next Championship which was for the little twelve two ponies. It followed the sidesaddle class which Sam and Chim had previously won so many times.

Rosie still sounded extremely adenoidal and had the occasional bout of coughing but nothing in this world was going to stop her doing her very best with Sparkler.

To Tom's relief, Sam was already making a remarkable recovery. He had met Lionel with Oscar's Countess who had insisted she should sit with them in their box well away from the biting wind.

Oscar and Anne-Marie each held one of her arms as she made sure her still rather shaky legs got her safely to the box.

It was one of the largest boxes and Totty wrapped a rug round her as she sank rather thankfully into one of the comfortable chairs. He patted Sam's arm. 'You must watch all your children and Tom from here, Sam – pneumonia is definitely not to be trifled with.' He heard Anne-Marie and Oscar coughing. 'You two had better stay here as well. There's plenty of room. Can't have Panky's rider having to pull out.'

Oscar smiled at him. 'Wow, thank you –smashing,' and he glued his eyes on the course Rosie was about to jump. He then endeared himself even further to his Countess as he watched Tom walking the course with his small sister.

'We're really lucky,' he told her. 'We wouldn't win any of these big classes if Dad didn't spend so much of his time helping us. He shows us where to save time without going crazy – where to take off and when to hold back – he's a brilliant dad, but he doesn't just help us, he helps all *the gang*, even my Annie who is really nervous.'

Anne-Marie smiled at the Countess. 'He's just like Ozzie, Lady Lavinia, really special.'

The little twelve two ponies were having varying degrees of success, the best result so far being a young boy on a skewbald pony with just four faults.

'Here's my cousin,' Oscar told the Countess as Eloise and Pierrot cantered into the arena. 'My other cousin Fenella has got Pierrot's sister Poupée, she qualified too, but Auntie Lizzie's having a baby in December and Uncle James decided not to come to the show this year. I don't think Fenella realized she had qualified, which was lucky.'

He watched as Pierrot trotted through the start before breaking into his steady canter and Eloise was on her way. He had a similar temperament to Fuzz Buzz. Nothing fazed him and nothing really hurried him as he was now demonstrating as he and Eloise jumped the first clear round. Jean-Pierre was so delighted he increased his offer for Jet Stream to Charles, who was watching beside him. Charles couldn't refuse. It was more than he had paid for the consistent little mare almost four years ago. Unbeknown to Orlando, he would be riding Jet Stream for the last time that afternoon. Tom had no idea the transaction had taken place – he was standing by the entrance holding Sparkler whilst Rosie blew her nose for the last time before entering the arena.

Tom watched with pride. He was well aware Rosie was probably only sixty per cent fit. She had a streaming head cold, but she gathered Sparkler, placing him perfectly at every fence, sailing over the final double and through the finish.

She was smiling as she trotted out of the arena straight up to Gus who had been peeping through his fingers.

'Brilliant Rosie, just brill.' Tom watched as he saw Gus catch her as she jumped off Sparkler. He smiled nostalgically as he remembered catching Sam after she had won the working pony class on Twinkletoes. Rosie was smiling at Gus. It could have been Sam, smiling at him over twenty years ago. At that moment he was almost certain it would always be like this for Rosie and Gus. He was sure that like Sam and himself, they too would be *ad infinitum.* Their's was a very special friendship. He walked up to Rosie, breaking the spell. 'Well done, Sweetheart, perhaps Gus would hold Sparkler whilst we study the jump off course.'

Three boys and three girls who had managed to jump clear rounds were eyeing each other up as they waited for the jump off to begin. As always, Tom had told Rosie. 'Don't and I emphasize, don't go mad – keep steady and cut the corners.'

She listened carefully, and obeyed his instructions and soon Sparkler and she were the worthy winners. Eloise, who had also listened to Tom's sound advice, was in second pace. The other children had flown, scattering poles all over the arena.

In the box, Sam, who was still feeling rather fragile was wiping her eyes. 'I don't usually get emotional but that was such a classically *Tom West* round. He has spent the whole morning in the practice area with first his nephew and then Rosie and his niece, Eloise. He never thinks of himself. He's got a huge class with Kaspar this evening. He will crash out for an hour after the boy's fourteen two Championship, have a shower and then be off on Kaspar. I'm going to insist he has a break for at least two weeks. No one can keep on pushing their body at the pace he does.'

Totty had disappeared, only to be seen in the arena presenting Rosie with the trophy and the very special rosette.

Gus was asking Tom. 'Can I take Rosie for a beef burger, Tom?'

'Yes, but promise you will look after her.'

'Off course I will, Tom. You need never worry when she's with me. She's special.'

'She is Gus, very special, just like her Mum.'

Lake House Stables triumphed again in both the thirteen two and the fourteen two Championships. Oscar was in tears when Humbug beat Gus and Hamlet into second place and Orlando into third. Orlando was receiving his rosette in total ignorance of the huge shock about to confront him. As he exited the arena, Eloise grabbed hold of Jet's reins. 'Give her to me, 'Lando,' she demanded with the over exuberance of a young girl who has just acquired one of the best thirteen two ponies in the country.

'Why do you want her, Eloise?' Orlando asked his cousin, confused by her attitude.

'Because she's mine. Papa has just bought her from Charles. She is coming home with us to the Equitation Centre.'

Orlando looked for his dad and to his relief saw him making his way towards him with Oscar and Humbug.

Tom looked at his son's ashen face. 'Lando, is it the bug? Do you feel poorly again? Where is Jet?'

Orlando was struggling not to cry. 'No, Dad I don't feel ill, but I shan't be riding Jet again. She's with Eloise. Charles has sold her to Uncle Pierre.'

'Sold her!' Tom was incredulous. He was aware Charles had been thinking of selling her but not without letting him know so that he could talk to Orlando first. In his opinion, Charles had acted cruelly and callously. He marched up to his boss who was in the middle of telling Rupert he had thrown away his chances on The March Hare, turning far too wide into the penultimate oxer.

Rupert, who was wracked by a coughing fit couldn't be bothered to explain to his dad that his whole body felt like a ball of cotton wool. The bug had hit him hard and he was glad he wasn't jumping Hawkeye in the next Championship. Fortunately, he was for the future.

Charles was not at ease when he saw the expression on Tom's face.

'Charles, I have always been well aware your main priority is making pot loads of money – I know we beg to differ where horses are concerned but I am shocked that you saw fit to let Orlando find out he would never ride Jet again by his exuberant new owner. I don't care if my horses disappear like Swallow Tail, this morning. God, after riding for you and Lady Hermione for over twenty years it's something I had to come to terms with many years ago. Fortunately, Orlando has Torchlight for whom I have turned down an offer of ten thousand pounds from some over ambitious parent. Orlando knows I will never sell him and as soon as possible I shall be backing Bamboozle. Jet is your pony and of course Orlando has been lucky to ride her and win so much money for you,' Tom couldn't resist adding. 'But you could at least have let him get the fourteen two class out of the way and let me break it to him gently.'

Charles knew he was in the wrong but he was the last person to admit to his wrong doings. 'Your son wants to be a show jumper I believe, Tom – then it is best he learns the hard way. It won't be the first or the last time I accept a good offer and the sooner he and all the kids learn that, as far as I am concerned, the better.'

'So, if I offered you twelve thousand pounds for Babushka, you would accept?'

'Good God, no, Mimi would never forgive me.'

Tom turned away. He felt sad that the man he had looked up to since he had been twelve years old and whom he knew would help any child who was having a problem, could have this mercenary side to his character. To some people, six thousand pounds was their life savings and he thought of Tilly's mother, Ruth, who most likely didn't even have a bank account, but to Charles Wright-Smith it was a drop in an enormous ocean. No wonder even Justin didn't trust his own dad. He had obviously had to fight to keep Conchita a few hours ago.

He looked for his boys and saw Orlando and Oscar trudging back to the stables leading Humbug, their arms round each other, as Rosie and Gus followed them with Hamlet and The Duc. Rosie had captured the last rosette with sixth place and Gus was well satisfied with coming second. No one could possible deny Oscar the joy of winning with his brave little Humbug.

Tom strode past Rosie and Gus, not failing to notice she was still sneezing and coughing. 'Rosie,' he told her, 'when you have settled the Duc go straight to the caravan and put on your warmest jacket then go to Box H. and find Mummy. It's Lady Lavinia's box – Oscar's Countess. Anne-Marie is there. Go and find her and sit in the warm.'

Rosie was pleased, she knew she hadn't been at her best with Le Duc but her throat was still sore and her nose felt like a red beacon. She was surprised she had even been placed at all.

Tom collected Torchlight's tack from the horsebox and made his way to the stables to find Orlando. As he approached Torchlight's stall he could hear the triplets who had gathered inside.

'It's bloody rotten 'Lando,' Oscar was telling his brother. 'We'll jolly well beat Miss stuck up Mimi in the next class. I bet Charles would never dare sell Babushka. --- Gosh, I hope my Countess won't have a huge offer for Panky.'

Tom's head appeared over the stable door. 'You can have no fear of that Oz. I doubt if anyone else could ride him and the Countess is not obsessed with money. She would have sold Panky and Goldfinger years ago is she was. Now come on boys – let's get you ready.'

Charles was feeling unusually at odds with himself. 'Why are you so quiet, darling?' Joanna asked him as she brushed the collar of Mimi's jacket. 'I hope you're not coming down with this nasty bug all the Wests seem to have had.'

Charles shook his head. 'No, it's definitely not the bug. I've upset Tom I am afraid.'

'Tom. You've upset Tom?'

'I sold Jet to Jean-Pierre for Eloise this morning. Unfortunately she was waiting to claim her after Orlando had collected his rosette. I hadn't had a chance to tell Tom or Orlando. I think he was a trifle upset.'

Before Joanna could put her thoughts together, Mimi had leapt onto Babushka.

'You stink, Dad. Don't bother to walk the course with me – I'll find Justin or Tom. Poor Orlando. You're foul.'

Charles leant against Lord of The Rings who he was holding. 'Well, talk about straight from the horse's mouth. Did I deserve that?'

For the first time since he had met Joanna he didn't like the look in her eyes as she answered shortly. 'Yes, Charles, you most certainly did,' and for the second time in five minutes he had noticed scorn on the faces of the two most important women in his life.

He made a lonely figure as he trudged back to the caravan. He pulled his cheque book out of the small safe, opened it and wrote, *'Orlando West. One thousand pounds'* – and signed it Charles

Wright-Smith. To Charles, money sorted out everything – but in his heart he knew it wasn't always the case and he feared he had lost the respect of the person he admired most in this world.

He saw Tom talking to his boys and walked up to Orlando. 'Here's your commission for Jet. I always give some money to the rider.'

Orlando just stared nonplussed at Charles, but Tom put out his hand.

'Thanks, Charles. That will be very useful when we buy Bamboozle's tack. I'll put it straight into Orlando's bank account. We'll be pushing Bambi harder now. We'll aim to enter him in the Junior Foxhunters a.s.a.p.' He put the cheque in his pocket and turned to his boys.

'Come on you lot, let's see what you can do.'

Which turned out to be a lot as Oscar and Josh tied for first place with an identical time and to Tom's delight, Torchlight and Orlando were just behind them. Mimi and Lord of the Rings were fourth and Oliver and Oscar fifth and sixth with Buck's Fizz and Goldfinger. It had turned out to be a massive triumph for the Lake House Stables.

Oscar's Countess was smiling as she tried her best to hand the cup to both Oscar and Joshua. It was no easy feat as Panky whirled round and round in circles, whilst Ganger stood like a solid rock – his soft brown eyes gazing at Lady Lavinia. 'He's a beautiful pony,' she told Joshua.

Josh smiled. 'He's the best, Lady Lavinia. My dad had his brother when he was my age and now my young sister is jumping his half brother.'

Panky was finally standing still. Oscar was looking worried. 'Lady Countess – if you ever decide to sell Panky, please will you tell my dad or me before he goes to America or some other far away country.'

'Oscar – I promise you Panky is yours all the time you wish to ride him and I am going to ask your father to bring you to my stables in the Christmas holidays. My groom has just started jumping Panky's half brother and I would like to see what you can do with him. He is the same colour as Panky and full of spring and promise. I think you will love him but get rid of that horrible cold before you come. You will need all your strength.'

'Wow. Has he got a name?'

'Of course, he's called Hoity Toity. I will speak with your father. I have already mentioned the pony to him. I am sure he will agree to you riding him, but it's up to you. Only if you want to.'

'Wow – yes please. Hoity Toity – bloody good name.'

Having won the big class with Kaspar that evening, the following morning the show came to an abrupt end for the West family when Tom and Josh both woke with rasping sore throats and splitting headaches. Tom sent Dom to cancel all his entries, then asked Justin to help Dom load all the horses and ponies into the horsebox and with Oscar sitting with Anne-Marie beside Dom, and Sam driving the Range Rover with Tom asleep in the passengers seat and Joshua likewise in a corner of the back of the car, they made their way back across the country until thankfully Sam came upon the first sign post that mentioned Massingham. In twenty minutes she was drawing up in front of Woodcutters.

She gave Tom the rest of her antibiotics and he and Josh fell thankfully into their beds.

On the Sunday afternoon all the West family were watching the Grand Prix. Tom felt a tinge of guilt at the pleasure he felt as he watched the final plank fall behind his boss and mentor – with the plank went the first prize of twenty thousand pounds. It was finally won by the Dutchman Mikel and the now ageing Grey Knight, once the mount of Charles – sold without warning by the imperious late Lady Hermione MacDonald, one time sponsor of the majority of Charles' horses.

'Sods law,' Tom thought to himself but he noticed Joanna putting

her hand sympathetically on Charles' knee. He grinned. 'He's obviously wheedled his way back into her good books,' he laughed.

To which Sam replied. 'Jo adores him. She is well aware he's a crafty old devil but that's part of his charm. I've realized that since I was eleven years old!!'

CHAPTER 39

By the middle of the following week both Josh and Tom had almost completely recovered, and on Wednesday morning Joshua was once more making his way by the lake with the triplets, to the main road and the school bus.

Tom suddenly decided he would forgo his horses for a couple of days and accompany Sam and his mother to the auction house in Mayfair where 5a, Madeley Villas, Chislehurst was to be sold the following afternoon. Unbeknown to Sam he arranged for Hannah to come and stay the night at Woodcutters before booking a hotel in London for the night and seats for Agatha Christie's, The Mousetrap. It was the longest running production in the world, but in spite of that, none of them had seen it and he knew Sam would love trying to workout whodunit. She had just been through a rough time and he thought she deserved a treat.

The children were all happy to be left with Hannah, although he had a sneaking suspicion that Oscar might well have company when he watched East Enders. He had overheard him at the stables discussing the latest scandal with Hannah, but after his talk with the boys it would appear Oscar had his personal life in good order. Perhaps, he thought, he worried too much about his young son's propensity to watch rather explicit programmes.

The next morning, Sam barely recognized her own husband in his dark grey suit, white shirt and sporting his one and only tie with little galloping horses printed on it, which Rosie had given him one Christmas. And to her astonishment not a sign of his customary trainers but to finish the outfit, a pair of highly polished, black shoes.

'Darling,' she told him. 'You look very dashing – you would have made an extremely sexy city worker.'

'Sammy, you may rest assured, two days in London in a grey suit and a tie is stretching my powers of endurance. I couldn't be away from my jeans and favourite sweatshirt one moment longer I can assure you, however alluring I might appear to you and however sexy you may look in that extremely fetching creation you are attired in.'

Sam was wearing a suit she had discovered when she had visited Eva in Rye two weeks ago. She had felt guilty. She had merely gone to Rye to meet Eva and Tabitha for lunch and had ended up purchasing the extremely elegant, chic but expensive powder blue fine woolen suit with a lawn blouse with tiny forget –me – nots printed in sprays in exactly the same shade of blue. Eva had taken thirty pounds off the price but in Sam's mind she had still been vastly extravagant. However, she put this thought completely out of her mind when she saw the way Tom was gazing at her with something more heady than mild appreciation blazing in his cornflower blue eyes.

'Sam, come on darling, we'd better go and fetch Mum,' and Sam was sure it wasn't the recent cold that was making her husband's voice so husky and she gave a thought to the scanty nightdress in her overnight bag with a shiver of excitement. She took his hand tightly and hurried with him to the car.

Sam was perched on a gold chair with a padded, blue, velvet seat, looking round the exclusive and ornate room in obviously what had once been an elegant, Georgian family home but was now an auction house specializing in selling extremely upmarket properties.

The only auction Sam had previously been to had been in Canterbury when she had watched Tom's despised Louis Wain pictures of weird looking cats go under the hammer. That had been exciting enough, but now the suspense was almost unbearable. She glanced through the catalogue where there was a photograph of every property, of which a mere handful was under a million pounds.

As she turned the page, her eyes fell upon a massive property in Maida Vale with an estimated price of six to eight million pounds. Sam felt she had entered an entirely different world.

5a. Maideley Villas, Chislehurst was lot No. 25. Sam realized each lot took much longer to sell than the tables and chairs had done in Canterbury, as most achieved far more than their estimated prices. She glanced round the room trying to see who was bidding but it all seemed very discreet and many of the bids were either on the internet or the telephone.

Finally at fifteen minutes to four a photograph of 5A. Madeley Villas appeared on the large screen above the auctioneer's head. Sam clutched Tom's hand and Mary's with the other as the bidding began. The reserve price was six hundred and fifty thousand pounds, which was the opening bid on the telephone. Very quickly the price had risen to nine hundred and fifty thousand – obviously two people really wanted the property as finally at one million, two hundred and fifty thousand pounds, the hammer finally fell.

Tom was holding both Sam and Mary as they crept out of the room and took a taxi to their hotel in Knightsbridge, where instead of the cup of tea they had intended partaking of, they ordered three large brandies.

'Goodness,' was all Sam kept repeating.

'How are you going to invest all that money, Sam? Have you given it any thought?' Mary asked her daughter-in-law.

'Yes, I've already discussed it with Tom and he's agreed to be a sleeping partner – I'm going to keep my eyes open for two or three old cottages within a few miles of Massenden and start my own holiday let business. Massenden is so well situated for the channel tunnel, Canterbury and so many beautiful National Trust Properties, including my favourite Sissinghurst Castle. I hope I can discover some cottages that need renovating and enlist the services of wonderful Jim Griggs again. He's excellent and really reliable. I'll wait and see how much the furniture and all the pictures and the sliver and porcelain sell for and there are quite a lot of investments the old man had – Mr. Grainger, the solicitor thought about eight hundred thousand but I want to put some money in Rosie and the boy's accounts. I will see what it all amounts to before I make up my mind but I love old property – it fascinates me. I won't do anything without Tommy's approval, Mary. You know we always share everything but I have decided I shall cut down on my garden designs. Now Martin is a partner in his firm and Sarah is expecting another baby. I think she wants to be a *stay at home Mum.* I think I will make sure I only have one design on the go at any one time. I would like to spend some time working on my little colt, Pot Luck and in another year the plan is to put Humbug to work pulling Charles lovely governess cart.

Actually, if I had been forced to live in London, I think I could have lived in that flat in Chislehurst – it had a really calm atmosphere. I think most probably that lovely garden was quite a rare feature being so close to London. That probably made the flat really desirable, but Mary, I would forgo all that money to have my dad alive and inheriting it instead of myself. Mummy seem to have put him almost out of her life but I can't, even though I have just one tiny, vague recollection of him playing with me on the sands at Camber. That's why I want to invest the money and make some of my inheritance over to his grandchildren. I'm sure that's what my dad would have done."

Tom hailed a taxi, which would take them to theatre land where the Mouse Trap was playing. They ate beforehand in a small Italian Bistro. Tom had to laugh. The food was not a patch on La Casa Sul Verde and each dish was at least more than three times the price.

He wasn't a great theatregoer but he had to admit he thoroughly enjoyed the suspense of the long running play, along with the pleasure of Sam's hand clutching his.

They kissed Mary goodnight having seen her safely to her room on the floor below their own and then walked together up the wide, curving staircase to the second floor and their room which looked over what appeared to be a million roof tops.

Tom gasped as Sam appeared through the bathroom door. She was still his perfect Sammy, as beautiful as she had been in the scanty nightdress he had given her one Christmas - he thought he had been eighteen at the time.

He held out his arms smiling and telling her jokingly. 'My darling, you know I have just been a very sick man.'

Sam laughed, flashing her huge brown eyes at him. 'Then let's hope I am the perfect tonic for you, my Thomas,' with which she fell into his open arms.

The next day before they caught the train home they discovered a very exclusive shop, which sold all the latest riding gear. Sam found exactly what she was looking for. Rosie would be thrilled – her Christmas present was wrapped in tissue paper inside a very upmarket carrier bag. On Christmas Day, Rosie would be unwrapping a grey riding jacket with black velvet collars.

Tom closed his eyes as he sat in the corner of the train seat. 'You're very quiet, Tom,' his mother remarked. 'Do you feel run down after that horrible virus?'

Tom smiled at her. 'I'm fine, Mum – maybe just a bit whacked. It was quite a day yesterday, one way or another.'

Mary had turned to look out of the window – Tom reached for Sam's hand, gently rubbing her palm as his eyes glinted at her wickedly. He sighed – 'quite a day wasn't it my Sammy?'

She squeezed his hand tightly as a pair of soft brown eyes gazed into two bright blue ones and as the train plunged into darkness as it flew through the tunnel near Sevenoaks, Tom pulled Sam to him and kissing her very gently, whispered so that only she could hear, 'and quite a night too!!'

CHAPTER 40

The evenings were soon drawing in. The gang had all gone to the big bonfire night, which was a yearly ritual, held on the large playing field and organized by the cubs and scouts.

The ponies were turned out except for Bamboozle with whom Tom was working. Schooling him almost every day. He had asked Hannah, who was not much heavier than Mimi, to back him and now he was trotting and cantering round the indoor school, making light work of the cavaletti at the end of the grid of poles.

At the end of November on a misty Saturday morning, Orlando was riding him for the first time, making his way to the indoor school with Clementine and Tom walking calmly beside them as the mist swirled eerily over the lake.

With the help of Hannah, Tom had worked his usual magic and Bamboozle, or Bambi as he was affectionately known, was compliant and sensible and Tom could immediately sense that he and Orlando were at one with each other. He appeared to have inherited Shooting Star's sweet nature and by the end of the term, Orlando was already jumping three-foot courses with him.

Tom registered him as Lake House Bamboozle and in January at the Massenden Equitation Show, not only would Orlando be jumping Torchlight in the new Pony Championship to be held at the Centre for the first time, but also Bamboozle would be initiated into the world of show jumping in the Junior Foxhunter Class.

The foals were now coming in every evening. They had all grown considerably and were each developing their own characteristics.

It was Rosie's task to put a halter on to High and Mighty, lead him into the stable and give him a small feed. He waited by the paddock gate every evening, whinnying as soon as he saw Rosie and Sam who went with her to feed and water Pot Luck. Sam was really excited. Pot Luck already walked beside her and would now trot as soon as she asked him. He moved beautifully and she couldn't wait to show him in the yearling classes.

Finally Jules and Hannah would bring Spellbound and The Jolly Roger into the last two stables.

Roger was strong and playful, invariably giving two large bucks as Jules led him across the yard. When Jules had shut him securely in his stable, he would go to the paddock nearest the house and fetch Satin. Satin would always whinny to Roger and Jules was certain he was telling the colt. 'Yes, my nephew, keep those bucks coming!' Jules was almost sure Black Satin was winking at the mischievous colt.

To Tom's delight, Adrian had slotted back into his old job like a duck takes to water.

'I'm really enjoying myself – I love working for you,' he told Tom as they were enjoying an early morning ride around the lake. He and Tom were riding Chintz and Sea Breeze, getting them fit to resume their jumping careers again in the New Year, whilst all Tom's other horses who had jumped so well for him over the past months were enjoying a sabbatical.

In the middle of November, Sam received a letter from the London auctioneers who were selling the furniture and the multitude of smaller lots, including the beautiful Meissen dessert service and several pictures, some of which Sam and Mary had thought were beautifully executed, especially one of a woman and two children on a rocky beach and another of a seascape. Sam had dithered, half tempted to keep them, but after much thought had placed them back with the other paintings, which were destined for the auction house.

When the catalogue had arrived at Woodcutters, Sam had lit the fire in the inglenook in the sitting room, made herself a cup of coffee, pulled her favourite chair close to the merrily burning logs and enjoyed the next hour looking at the photographs of many of her lots including a half page photo of her Meissen desert service. On the cover of the catalogue she was surprised to find she was looking at her picture of the woman and children by the seaside. She didn't recognize the name of the artist but obviously the auctioneers were holding it in high esteem, and it was valued at several thousand pounds.

Sam put more wood on the crackling log fire, fetched her laptop – found the calculator and took the lower end of each estimate. Half an hour later she was rechecking her figures. If each lot sold for these prices she would be richer by over three hundred thousand pounds.

She had already received the cheque for the flat and it was now sitting in her already healthy bank account. Interest rates were at an all time low, earning her very little and she had already contacted Messrs. Swain Long and Swain in Canterbury and two other leading estate agents asking them to let her know immediately any likely period properties should come on the market.

She had shown Tom the catalogue and he had just said. 'Fantastic, darling.' He had just got back from a visit to the vets with Bertie and the news was not good. His heart had not improved and Steve had called the most senior vet, Mathew, who happened to be in his own surgery that morning, to come and give his opinion.

Mathew had known Tom a long time. 'Not good, Tom, I'm afraid he is slipping away all too quickly.' Tom's eyes immediately filled with tears but he asked Mathew bravely.

'If he was your own dog, what would you do?'

Mathew put his hand on the top of Bertie's head. 'As a vet, Tom, I would have no choice – his quality of life is getting poorer by the week.'

Tom stood up holding Bertie's lead. 'I'll take him home for one more night with the family. Can you come to Woodcutters tomorrow morning, there is no way my wonderful old friend is going to suffer.'

Mathew nodded wordlessly.

‘Maybe James would come. He knows Bertie well.’

Sam was worried. She had cooked Tom’s favourite toad in the hole and he wasn’t touching it.

‘Darling, what’s wrong?’ she asked. To her horror Tom put his head on the table as sobs wracked his body.

Sam leapt to her feet. ‘Tom – Tom, what is it?’ She threw her own knife and fork on to the table and rushed to his side.

‘It’s Bertie,’ he managed to gasp between his sobs. ‘One of the vets is coming tomorrow morning.’ With which he sobbed his heart out in Sam’s arms as the tears poured down her face as well.

Sam recovered first. Bertie had always been Tom’s dog. Sam adored him, but Boswell came first in her affections – always guarding her, never leaving her side if he could help it. She removed the uneaten meal from the table and scraped it into the dog’s bowls. Boswell, Holly and Hector rushed up to sniff what was on offer but Bertie merely raised his head, looked at Tom with sad eyes and then laid back in his basket with a huge sigh.

Sam left to fetch Rosie from school. She waited until the little girl had settled in the car and then told her as gently as she could. ‘Rosie, Daddy is very upset today. You know when you are really unhappy you can’t help crying – well, that is how Daddy is at the moment.’

Rosie looked unbelievingly at Sam. ‘Daddy crying! Daddy’s never cry.’

‘They do when they are very, very sad, Rosie.’

‘Is Daddy terribly sad then?’

‘Yes, I am afraid he is.’

‘Why?’

‘You know Bertie has been sleeping an awful lot recently.’

‘Yeees.’

‘It’s because his heart is very old and tired. Daddy took him to see Katie’s father this morning – he was very worried and asked another vet to look at him too. He told Daddy Bertie is very weak. Tomorrow morning Uncle James or Katie’s daddy will come here and give Bertie something that will make him sleep for ever and never feel tired again.’

Rosie was quiet for a moment then asked Sam. ‘Like the Sleeping Beauty, you mean?’

‘Well, sort of like that I suppose, Rosie.’

‘Then he won’t be able to snap at Holly when she wants to play with him?’

‘No – he certainly won’t be able to do that.’

‘That’s alright then, Holly can play with Hector,’ and Rosie smiled at her mother. As far as she was concerned, as long as her little Holly was happy everything was all right in the world.

Sam took Rosie straight to the yard to get the foals in for the night. There was not a sign of Tom and as she correctly surmised he was sitting on the kitchen floor with his arms still around Bertie.

She saw Adrian, Hannah and Jules who were bringing in the horses and ponies before darkness fell.

‘Is Tom O.K.?’ Adrian asked. ‘Only we haven’t set eyes on him since early this morning.’

‘He’s very upset,’ Sam told the three grooms. ‘Bertie has to be put to sleep in the morning. Tom is devastated. I doubt whether you will see him before tomorrow afternoon. You all know the routine for the morning, but I will come and see you once the vet has gone.’

The mood in the yard was sombre as they proceeded to fetch the rest of the ponies and Sam took Rosie into the house.

She seemed far more upset by her father’s swollen, red eyes than by the fact that Bertie’s life was about to end. She climbed onto Tom’s lap and gently stroked his face before asking him. ‘Daddy, your heart isn’t getting old and noisy is it?’

‘No Rosie – fortunately as Dads go, mine is still relatively young. It's is very sad at the moment but I'm pretty certain it's still in excellent working order.'

Rosie sighed. 'That's alright then, Daddy, and if Bertie goes to heaven, you and Mummy can see him, cos that's where you and she sometimes go, isn't it?'

It was the first time Tom had shown the slightest hint of a smile that day.

Sam watched for the boys coming down the path by the lake. She knew they would go straight to the yard and say good night to their ponies. It was a daily ritual they never failed to do.

'Come here a minute, boys,' she called to them. 'When you go into the kitchen you will notice Dad is very sad.'

They glanced at Black Satin's stable and relaxed when they saw his head appear over the door with a large piece of hay dangling from the corner of his mouth.

Orlando looked anxiously at Sam. 'Not Twinkletoes, Mum?'

'No, 'Lando. It's Bertie. I told you last week his heart was very noisy, well I'm sorry to say it has got much worse. The vet is coming tomorrow morning to give him an injection so that he doesn't suffer any more.'

The boys were all very quiet but they appeared to be accepting the situation. Later that evening as bed time was approaching and having finished their homework, Oscar was sitting on the floor with his arm round his father, who still had Rosie, who had fallen asleep, on his lap. 'I'm, going to stay here all night with you, Dad.' Oscar informed Tom. 'I know exactly how you are feeling – just like I did when you told me Whisky was dead.'

'Oz. you've got school tomorrow,' Sam reminded him.

'I don't care. I am staying here with Dad and Bertie,' and Sam knew from the expression on his face, nothing was going to change Oscar's mind.

Oliver, Orlando and Josh were still in their rooms doing their homework when Sam gently lifted Rosie off Tom's knee and carefully carried her up the stairs to her room. She barely opened her eyes as Sam pulled her nightdress over her head and then tucked her under the duvet. She left the small light on by Rosie's bed and opened Orlando's bedroom door. To her surprise, Oliver and he were sitting together on the bed with Oliver's ear pressed hard against Orlando's chest.

'Ollie, whatever are you doing?'

'Lando and I were worried in case our hearts were getting noisy, Mum.'

'Darling boys – you have absolutely no need to worry whatsoever. Bertie is a very old dog. If he was a human being he would be almost a hundred years old.'

'Are you sure, Mum?'

'I'm quite, quite certain. Now finish your homework and then hop into bed.'

Finally Sam peeped into Joshua's room. He was lying in bed staring up at the ceiling. 'Josh,' Sam asked him. 'Are you O.K.?'

'Just thinking, Mum. It's sad animals don't live longer isn't it? It's as if we are just lent them for a little while.'

'It is Josh – you are absolutely right. One day we shall have to be really brave and say goodbye to Twinkletoes and the donkeys and maybe even Satin and Thunder. Not just yet – but we have to know that day will inevitably come.'

'Poor Dad.'

'I know, Josh – but your dad is strong – he'll be better once tomorrow morning is over, I promise you.'

It was James who came to Woodcutters, after Hannah and Jules had taken the other three dogs for a walk round the lake. Sam held Tom's hand as they sat on the floor together with Tom holding Bertie until he was deeply asleep. James was used to dealing with heartbroken owners several times every week but it was difficult when it was your brother-in-law and your best friend.

'Sam,' James told her. 'Ring through to the stables and ask Adrian to tack up Sweet Dreams and Breeze. Go off for a long hack with Tom. Get right away from here for the next two hours. I will deal with Bertie's body. I know Tom wants it cremated, and then he can be with Honey under the Acer tree. Please go with Sam, Tom. I promise you it is the best thing to do.'

Tom agreed with James – kissed Bertie one final time and followed Sam out to the stables.

James was perfectly right – by the time they were back at Woodcutters, Sam had persuaded him life must go on and he was eating his lunch with Hector's gold head on his knee.

'Thank God for Hector', Sam thought.

Whilst Tom was gradually coming to terms with the loss of Bertie, Giles was still struggling to get used to living in such close proximity to Clarissa, who was now happily settled in 2. Theobald's Row.

Georgia was totally happy. She loved having both her parents under the same roof, even though she saw very little of her mother who spent all day at La Casa sul Verde, hosting her lunchtime customers and preparing the sweets before getting ready for her evening diners.

Giles didn't like the idea of Clarissa walking across the village green at eleven o'clock at night and he made a point of taking Herbie for a late evening walk and sauntering back with her to Theobald's Row. They would often have a cup of hot chocolate, sitting compatibly by the wood-burning stove in the cosy sitting room.

Once they had drunk their chocolate they would kiss each other goodnight at the top of the stairs, opening the doors of their rooms on opposite sides of the square landing, unbeknown to each other both longing to turn in the same direction.

Giles was currently in correspondence with Sinclair Washington.

It was looking very likely the filming of To a Woman Scorned would start in early spring. Giles was going to be a very wealthy man. Sinclair Washington would be in London during the first week of December and would like to meet Giles for dinner at the Savoy Hotel.

Giles and Clarissa were enjoying a glass of wine after she had endured an exhausting evening at La Casa after a group of young men had enjoyed a few two many bottles of wine and had become extremely raucous and rather too boisterous. Clarissa had breathed a sigh of relief when their cabs had arrived and they had made their noisy exit.

She was happy to see Giles and Herbie sitting on the seat opposite La Casa.

'God, I'm exhausted, Gi. I hope I never see that lot from the other side of Maidstone again. I gather they were some rugby club or other. I've brought a bottle of Pinot Griggio from the cellar. I need something to calm me down when I get home.'

The logs were still smoldering in the wood burner as they enjoyed their wine together.

'I won't be home tomorrow evening, I'm living it up. I'm having dinner and staying the night at the Savoy,' Giles informed Clarissa.

She was more than a little surprised. 'The Savoy?'

'Yes, I'm meeting a rather important person who will have a huge impact on my future.'

'A woman,' Clarissa whispered.

'Would it matter if it was, Clarry?'

She looked into his eyes. 'Yes.' She was direct with her answer. 'It would, Gi, very much.'

The look in her eyes was making his heart thump - he felt the love he had for her cursing through his body.

'Clarry, would I be such a fool to tell you if I was meeting a special woman? Of course I'm not. I'm having dinner with the film director Sinclair Washington and his leading lady Lois Carmelo who also happens to be his wife.'

'Sinclair Washington! What is he doing in London?'

'Clarry – it's not public knowledge yet, but he wants to make a film of my book '*A Stranger Riding By,*' with Lois starring in it.'

'Gi –darling, congratulations, that's totally amazing.' And she flung her arms round him kissing his lips.

It was the *darling* that tipped the control he was holding on to so tenuously overboard, as the kiss that had started out so innocently became more and more sensuous.

'Please, Gi,' Clarissa was imploring him, 'don't say goodnight to me on the landing.'

Giles groaned. 'Clarry, I haven't wanted to do that since the day you moved into the cottage.'

'Neither have I. Gi, please let me be with you.'

'Clarry, there is something you need to know. I love you - I have never stopped loving you for the last twelve years. I have wanted you every night – I hated Paul for taking you from me – I could have killed him.'

'I'm sorry. Oh Giles, I'm sorry. Please, please give me another chance. Why do you think I never married Paul or wanted his child? You were always there, in the background, always.'

As they clung together, Giles picked Clarissa up in his arms and with Herbie panting behind them, carried her up the stairs and kicked his bedroom door open.

'I need my nightdress, Gi.'

He laughed. 'Not necessary, sweetheart, I'm certainly not letting go of you for something as unimportant as a nightdress.'

This was to be the night when Clarissa knew she had beaten her phobia forever. She hadn't given one single thought to Giles prosthetic leg – there had been far more pleasurable things to think about.

'Don't ever stop loving me. Gilie.'

'Darling, I never have and I never will. You are in no fear of that.'

She snuggled closer to him as her eyes were closing. Giles was happy and tomorrow before he caught his train to London, he would make certain that Herbert Holmer would capture his woman too. He kissed Clarissa's neck very gently as sleep was slowly overcoming him too.

The next morning, Giles kissed Georgia as she left to catch the school bus.

'I'm staying in London this evening, sweetheart. Go to the Casa straight after school. I've spoken to Esther - she has agreed Charlotte can go with you and have a meal there as long as you both do your homework. You can walk home with Mum after she has finished work.'

'I must give Cracker his hay, Dad,'

'Joyce has offered to do that and Esther will feed Catherine Wheel and Bouncer. So you have nothing to worry about.'

'O.K but why are you staying in London?'

'I have to meet a business colleague but I shall be home early the next morning. Herbie is staying with Betsy and Joyce until then. Now, off you go or you will miss your bus – work hard and have a really good day.' He kissed Georgia and watched her run up the road with Charlotte. Tomorrow evening he would tell her that he and her mother would be changing their life-style. He was pretty certain she would be happy.

That evening, in the bar at the Savoy Hotel, Sinclair Washington introduced Giles to his wife Lois. Giles was sure she would make an excellent leading lady, but had given him the impression she was a hard, calculating woman. During the course of the evening she had told him her ex-husband, who she hadn't set eyes on for years lived in Massenden.

Giles didn't enquire who he was or where exactly he lived – he wasn't particularly interested but the offer he received for his book to become a film was significant and he arrived back at Theobald's Row the next morning an extremely happy man.

He went to his computer – there was an important wedding for Herbert Holmer to attend. It would be the dapper little detective's own big day. As he sat down at his computer to write the final chapter of his latest book, he picked up an envelope, which was lying on the keyboard. He opened it with shaking hands as he recognized Clarissa's handwriting. Was she already regretting their wonderful night – he ripped open the envelope and extracted a card. *'Giles, darling – will you marry me? If the answer is yes, then come to La Casa sul Verde with Georgia this evening at seven thirty. We will dine together – whatever you decide – I love you Gilie – I promise I will never let you down again.'*

Giles got back into his car, forgetting all about Herbert Holmer's forthcoming nuptials and drove to the nearest florists. He found a large bouquet of deep red roses, and a card with one red rose – inside he wrote just three words. *'Yes please, Giles.'*

When Georgia came home from school, he made a cup of tea and cut two slices of Mary's lemon drizzle cake. 'Georgia, I have some news I hope you will be happy about.'

'Daddy, please tell me we're not moving. That's not why you went to London is it?'

'We won't be leaving Massenden I promise you, Georgia. Mummy and I have decided to get married again. We know we can't live apart any longer, we love each other too much.'

Georgia was beaming. 'Daddy, is it possible I can have a little brother or sister?'

Giles laughed. 'We're getting a bit long in the tooth for that now, I think, Georgia.' He suddenly stopped laughing as a thought flashed through his mind. *Last night – my God – was Clarissa on the pill?* – He had not the slightest idea. In the heat of the moment he had never thought to ask her.

'We're going to have dinner at La Casa this evening,' he told Georgia.

'Gosh, two evenings in a row.'

'I hope it will be a very special one, so put on your favourite dress.'

Georgia laughed. 'I don't really do skirts, Dad, but I'll find the one Mum gave me last Christmas even if I can't still do up the zip!!'

Giles, clutching the bouquet of red roses and Georgia with the zip pinned at the side of her dress arrived at La Casa sul Verde at precisely seven thirty. Clarissa greeted them at the door, dressed in a black skirt and a midnight blue blouse, which she had bought on a trip to Brussels.

She glanced nervously at Giles' face, and then took the bouquet and the card he was offering her. She led them to the table that was laid for three in the most secluded alcove and opened the card with shaking hands. She gazed at Giles – her eyes bright with tears – Giles was already opening the champagne, which was in an ice bucket beside their table. He poured three glasses. 'To us, Clarry, and to our lovely daughter,' and they all three clinked their glasses.

Georgia was already sending a text. 'Who are you on to, Georgia?'

'Wills and Binny, this is the best evening of my life.'

'Mine too,' her father told her not letting go of Clarissa's hand, whilst Maria put the beautiful, red roses in a vase and placed them in the middle of the table.

Perry was eating his evening meal with Wills and Binny. It was a steak and kidney pudding he had purchased at the Farmer's Market the previous day. He had been about to buy a chicken flan when the person in front of him had picked it up. He looked at the slim figure; there was no mistaking the slim waist and the elfin hair cut.

'Bloody girl,' he thought as he glared at the back of Hannah and picked up the steak and kidney pudding before she could get her hands on that as well.

The pudding was delicious and Perry was just helping himself to another plateful when Wills' mobile bleeped.'

After a moment Wills was smiling at him. 'Wow, wonderful news. That was Georgia. She's dining at La Casa with her mum and dad. They're getting married again.'

Perry gave his young brother a withering look. 'Crazy idiot – what on earth is the stupid fellow doing that for – he'll be in for a muck load of trouble. That's all women are – nothing but a load of bloody trouble.'

CHAPTER 41

In no time at all the triplet's first term at the Grammar School had come to an end. It had passed remarkably smoothly and to Sam's relief even Oscar appeared to have settled into the new regime, most likely she thought because he had Anne-Marie beside him on the bus each morning and evening. After she had dropped Rosie at the Primary School on the final morning, she got back to Woodcutters to find her friendly postman about to deliver a large pile of letters. She took them from his hand and glanced through them quickly. There were three schedules for Tom - a host of Christmas cards, an invitation from Eva and Andrew for lunch on Boxing Day and a long thick, brown envelope. She turned it over and saw it was from the London Auction House.

She went indoors where she found Tom who had just had a phone call from Oscar's Countess, Lady Lavinia.

'She wants me to take Oscar tomorrow, Sam, so that he has all the holidays to get used to the pony. I know Dom and Trish intend to have a session with the gang tomorrow morning and Ollie and 'Lando can stay and help with Charles' horses in the afternoon. Josh and Jacques are going to get the bus to Ashford with Mimi and do some Christmas shopping, so that only leaves Rosie. Come with us Sammy, I know Lady Lavinia doesn't mind how many of the kids come. She's asked us for lunch and she is half expecting Anne-Marie anyway.'

Sam had enjoyed her previous trip to Lady Lavinia 's Oxfordshire home and she smiled at Tom. 'Lovely. I'm really fond of the Duchess and dear old Totty.'

Tom wasn't so certain about Totty. The elderly gentleman still had a wicked glint in his eye and reminded Tom very much of Charles' late father.

Tom soon disappeared in the direction of the stables. Sam refreshed her cup of coffee and then slowly slit open the thick, long, brown envelope.

She gasped – she couldn't believe it. There was a long list of every item sold - they had nearly all either reached or surpassed the top estimates. Several had exceeded these by a vast amount of money, including the Meissen dessert service and the Spode dinner sets, but the most exciting of all was the painting of the woman and children on the beach. The name Dorothea Sharp meant absolutely nothing to Sam but she must have been extremely well known to several of the bidders and they must have wanted the painting very much. Sam's hand was shaking as she looked at the cheque. After the commission had been deducted, she had another one million, two hundred and seventy nine pounds to put in her bank account.

She decided she would send a sizeable donation to the local children's hospice and another to Marigold's Sanctuary. Life felt surreal. Not too many years ago Tom and she had been saving every twenty pounds they had won, scrimping and scraping trying to buy the then derelict Woodcutters Cottage. Now, partly thanks to Tom's dedicated hard work with his horses and an elderly old Uncle who through a sad twist of fate had left her his entire estate, she was about to embark on buying a portfolio of period cottages. She was almost in a trance as she wandered to the stables to find Tom. Her holiday-let business was becoming more and more of a reality, not just some wild fantasy.

The following morning, Tom borrowed Jean-Pierre's trailer and hitched it behind his own new Range Rover. The insurance had finally been settled and this time Tom had elected to have an automatic gearbox so that Sam could drive if necessary, but this morning, he was behind the wheel and Sam was beside him with Oscar, Anne-Marie and Rosie chatting non-stop in the back. Oscar was more than a little excited. If this pony were to be anything like Panky then he would be on top of the world.

The journey was uneventful and just before twelve thirty Tom was cruising down the long drive towards the old house, which stood proudly amongst the trees.

Lady Lavinia greeted them warmly and Anne-Marie was remarking at the amount the little dachshunds had grown, although the Countess had only kept the two bitches.

Oscar could barely contain his impatience as he waited for his first glimpse of Hoity Toity. He sighed as his father accepted another cup of coffee at the end of the meal, thus prolonging the agony.

At last they had all piled into Lady Lavinia's very elderly and none to clean Land Rover. Oscar thought he was hallucinating - he knew it couldn't possibly be Panky because he had kissed his cheeky nose just before he had climbed into the Range Rover at Woodcutters - but all the same, he seemed to be here in Oxfordshire – looking out of one of the stables.

Lady Lavinia was saying. 'There he is, Oscar. That's Hoity Toity,' and she was pointing to the bay pony looking out of the stable.

Anne-Marie and Rosie had stayed in the house playing with the young dachshunds. There was a bitingly cold wind and Sam was certain snow was not too far away. She wondered if they were going to have the first white Christmas for a very long time.

Oscar had rushed up to the stable, Tom was giving him a leg up and Oscar was very soon realizing that not only did Hoity Toity look like his half brother, he obviously had exactly the same exuberant temperament.

Lady Lavinia's groom had schooled him over the rather ramshackle jumps. The pony obviously had no fear and neither had his young rider, as they were soon cantering round and round the sand school, completely at one with each other.

The little group watched as Oscar turned towards the jumping course, which was set at a reasonable height of three feet. The pair was flying and the Duchess and Totty, who had just arrived in his golf buggy, were clapping.

Lady Lavinia was looking appealingly at Tom. 'If we put the jumps up to four feet, Tom, would you see how he re-acts?'

As Oscar slid to the ground, Tom jumped onto the strong pony and let down the stirrups. Soon the Countess and Totty were holding their breath as they watched a maestro at work and the pony was reacting. His scope was tremendous – Hoity Toity had as much if not more to offer than his brilliant half brother.

Four hours later, two identical heads were stabled next to each other, staring at a young boy who would surely one day be conquering the world like his dad.

Hannah went into the kitchen, which was next door to the tack room. It was small but it housed a microwave, a toaster and an electric kettle. A door at the back led into a washroom and toilet and a large washer drier, where the rugs and blankets were laundered. It was bitterly cold again and everyone's fingers were feeling stiff and frozen and no one turned down her offer of a hot cup of tea. She opened the tin, which should have contained the teabags, but to her dismay someone had obviously used the last one and not thought to replace them. Hannah was pretty certain she knew who the culprit was and she looked no further than her brother, who would avoid shopping of any description at all costs.

She picked up the keys of the very elderly camper van and called to Adrian and her brother, 'Just going to pop to the village shop. I won't be more than ten minutes.' And she shot out of the yard.

Hannah parked on the hill behind a pristine Range Rover and her heart sank as she noticed the man emerging from the driver's door and marching into the store. It was an all too familiar figure. Unfortunately for Hannah, in her consternation, she omitted to leave the van in gear added to which, the elderly vehicle was not endowed with the most efficient of hand brakes.

She was trying to avoid her nemesis, which was not easy in a shop the size of the average living room but eventually she had found what she was looking for and was standing on tiptoes trying to reach a box of P.G. Tips tea bags. She had just achieved her objective when she was aware of an ominous bang, which sounded extremely like metal coming in to contact with metal.

She and Perry both ran. Hannah screamed and Perry swore. The front of the camper van was completely entangled with the tow bar on the rear of Perry's immaculate Range Rover. He turned on Hannah.

'You bloody stupid, incompetent girl. I've half a mind to call the police. You shouldn't be anywhere near a car. My God! You can't control a horse and you are obviously totally incapable of even parking a car.'

Hannah was shaking, partly from shock but mostly from her fear of this furious man, whose dark eyes were blazing.

'I'm sorry,' she whispered, 'but I had a shock when I saw you get out of your Range Rover, I must have forgotten to leave the van in gear.'

'Well, if that doesn't take the bloody biscuit!! How can it possibly be my fault?'

To Hannah's relief, she noticed John West walking across the green with his two little dachshunds, Mac and Mabel. John noticed there had been a slight coming together of the two vehicles.

'Hi, Hannah, what's happened, love?'

'John. Oh thank goodness. Please can you help me? My brake didn't hold and the van ran down the hill into this person's Range Rover.'

John was his usual calm self.

'Don't worry, Hannah. We'll soon get this sorted.' He turned to Perry. 'Come on young man, I'll try and lift the front of Hannah's van whilst you drive your Range Rover forwards.'

Perry was glaring at Hannah who was still shaking and still clutching the box of P.G. Tips. John called to two young lads who were walking towards the store.

'Hey, lads can you come and help? Hannah can you hold Mac and Mabel whilst I lift the van?'

Perry looked at John. 'You're surely not going to trust her with your dogs, she couldn't even take care of a guinea pig in a cage, she's a walking disaster.'

John chose to ignore this outburst and with the help of the two young lads, with one almighty effort, they all three lifted the van and Perry drove slowly forwards. He got out, thanked John and the boys and having made sure there was no damage to his Range Rover, with one final withering look at Hannah, strode back into the store to pay for the groceries he had left by the till.

John was surveying Hannah's van with some concern – he ran into the store and came out with a ball of strong twine. He pulled a penknife out of his pocket and proceeded to tie the bumper and the number plate back to the main body of the van.

'That should get you back to Woodcutters, Hannah. You will have to get it welded at Jim Smith's in Ribbenden, I doubt he will be able to do it before Christmas though.'

At that moment, Hannah felt she never wanted to sit behind a steering wheel again. She hated Peregrine Percival – he was the most bad tempered, terrifying person she had ever had the misfortune to meet and it wasn't until she got back to the stables that she realized she hadn't paid for the tea bags.

She borrowed her brother's bicycle and made her way back to the village store.

'Oh no dear,' she was told, ' that nice gentleman told me to put them on his bill, he realized you had forgotten to pay for them. Such a gentleman. No, dear. You certainly don't owe me anything.'

'How much were they,' she asked.

'One pound thirty five pence, dear.'

Hannah went back to the stables, took out her purse and carefully counted one pound thirty five pence. She placed it in an envelope on which she wrote, '*Money for tea bag's*' and asked Oscar and

Joshua to ride round to Theobald's Coach House and make certain Peregrine Percival received the envelope.

Perry opened the envelope and tipped the money into the palm of his hand, then dropped it casually into his pocket.

'Stupid little half witted bitch. Typical incompetent woman,' and he pushed the thought of tearful brown eyes firmly out of his obstinate head.

CHAPTER 42

It was a cold but bright Christmas Eve and Oscar had just had a really successful school on Hoity Toity. Tom had taken him to the indoor school with Orlando and Rosie, giving them all a good work out prior to the Junior Foxhunter Class, which would be held on New Year's Day.

It was obvious Oscar and his latest acquisition were going to be a force to be reckoned with and he was extremely satisfied with the progress Bamboozle and Orlando were making. As usual, Rosie and her beloved Braveheart had been their usual reliable selves.

Tom had hacked Breeze up to the school with them and they rode back round the lake before putting the ponies back in their stables.

Oscar ran up to his bedroom and carefully wrapped up Anne-Marie's Christmas present. She had recently had her ears pierced and he had bought her a tiny pair of gold earrings in the form of horseshoes. He had also bought her a thick wooly hat with a bobble on it to keep her warm when she watched him in the chilly indoor schools.

He was singing happily to himself as he walked by the water and could see Lake House in the distance and he knew South Lodge was only about two hundred metres past the big house, when he suddenly realized he had left the woolen hat in the tack room. He cursed and then remembered he had noticed Rupert outside the front door at Lake House tinkering with his now functional bicycle. He turned and walked back towards the house. Rupert was still in the front garden.

'Hi, Rupert,' he called to his friend. 'I've left one of Annie's Christmas presents in the tack room at Woodcutters, can I borrow your bike for ten minutes?'

'Sure thing Oz,' Rupert was happy to oblige his friend and handed him the bike.

Oscar was soon peddling at full pace past the lake, and then swooping into the stable yard at Woodcutters. He pulled on the brakes but to his horror there was absolutely no response. He yelled to his father. 'Watch out, Dad.'

Tom leapt to the side just in time, pulling Hannah with him, watching the quick thinking Oscar steer the bike towards the soft but unpleasant muckheap. Unfortunately, Adrian appeared around the corner, wheeling a large metal wheelbarrow also on his way to the same destination. Oscar was going so fast it was impossible for him to avoid anything or anybody. Soon Adrian was lying on the floor with an upturned wheelbarrow on top of him and a crack on the head, whilst Oscar flew over the handlebars straight into the middle of the dung, with Rupert's bicycle following him.

Tom swore. He saw his young son was already scrambling, dirty but seemingly unscathed from the muck heap and rushed to Adrian who had fallen against Panky's stable, currently still lying stunned on the concrete. As Tom reached him, he struggled to sit up. He was shaking his head.

'Tom, Tom. Whisky isn't here because he's dead. That crazy lorry crashed into us. I remember it flying out of that turning a few miles away. Oscar and Annie were in the back of your Range Rover. I was towing Sam's new trailer. Tom, please can you get this blasted wheelbarrow of me. – I remember everything. Kissing Amy goodbye before I left that morning – Amy and me getting married in the registry office near the river. Little Mollie being born. God, Tom I feel odd, but my brain is as clear as a bell.'

'Sit still, Adrian for God's sake. Hannah get him a really hot, sweet cup of tea and Oscar for goodness sake go indoors and have a shower.'

'Dad. I can't. I've lost Annie's present – her earrings are somewhere in the dung.'

'God, Oscar. Jules, can you get a pitchfork and look for a small parcel in Christmas wrapping paper. Oscar's lost it in the muck heap.'

After five minutes Oscar was shouting. 'Eureka,' as he spied a now extremely dirty parcel.

By this time, Tom had helped Adrian to the tack room where he was drinking his tea and recalling almost his entire past life.

Tom had called Amy, and within ten minutes Adrian's father, George turned into the yard with Amy and Molly in the back seat of his car.

Amy flung herself at Adrian, handing him Molly.

'Amy. Oh Amy. Whatever have I put you through? I'm so, so sorry. Now I remember our wedding day. You looked so beautiful and the day little Molly was born. I remember taking you to shows a long time ago with Bits n Pieces and riding Fling and winning at H.O.Y.S. with Thunderbird. I can remember every single thing, Amy, even that dreadful morning.'

For Amy, it was the end of a nightmare. She had her husband back and it was going to be the best Christmas present anyone could give her.

Sam screamed when she saw Oscar, looking like a chimney sweep and smelling like a human sewer, clutching a filthy Christmas present.

'Oscar, whatever has happened to you?'

'It was Rupert Wright-Smith's bloody bike, Mum. The brakes didn't work. I borrowed it because I remembered I had left Annie's wooly hat in the tack room. I knocked Adrian and his wheel barrow over and then shot through the air into the muck heap.'

'Adrian?'

'Yea, he banged his head on Panky's stable door and now he can remember everything. Anna, Molly, Whisky, everything.'

Tom burst into the kitchen. 'Wonderful news, Sammy. We've got our old Adrian back, thanks to Oscar and Rupert's lethal bike. Oz, for God's sake get into the shower and make sure you get every bit of that dung out of your hair. When you are thoroughly clean I will run you up to Anne-Marie's.'

'Her present is all dirty.'

'It's only the paper, Ozzie,' Sam told him. 'Give it to me, I've got a whole roll of Christmas paper – I'll wrap it up again for you.'

It was a wonderful Christmas Eve, the only person who was not too happy was Rupert, but unbeknown to him on Christmas morning he would find a brand new red bike under the Christmas tree. Charles had always had his doubts about the efficiency of the brakes, but they had served a purpose, they had brought back the Adrian everyone was so fond of. Amy had her husband, Molly her father and above all Miriam and George had their son.

Sam was putting Oscar's clothes in the washing machine. 'Oh, Tommy, I never dreamed this would happen. I thought poor Adrian might never remember.'

'Oh,' Tom told her, 'I always knew he would one day, Sammy. Satin showed me one of the triplets flying over Adrian and a large wheelbarrow on a bicycle. You know Satin is always right.'

'Tom, I do hope he will make a mistake one day He's been worrying me lately, the wretched old fellow.'

'What is he up to, my Sammy?'

'He keeps showing me Anne-Marie. Oscar is crying in a room, which looks like a surgery or a hospital and for some weird reason, Simon and Rob are always there too. Has he shown this to you, Tom?'

'Never, Don't worry darling, he would definitely have told me if he knew anything sinister.'

'I hope so, Tom. Oh God, I hope he would.'

The year, which had seen more than its fair share of ups and downs, was suddenly drawing to its close on a bright note. Adrian's clothes were now back in their rightful place in the main bedroom and Miriam was singing as the turkey spluttered in the oven at Crofter's Cottage where all the Carstairs family were going to spend Molly's first Christmas.

Sam was loading the back seat of Tom's Range Rover with a multitude of goodies, which would be enjoyed at Old Tiles, which had been the family tradition for as long as Tom could remember. With twelve grandchildren, which included the quarrelsome twins, it had taken almost the whole morning to get the table set but as always the atmosphere was carefree and happy as Tom and Jean-Pierre uncorked the first bottles of champagne, which James had brought from the cellar at The Old Manor House.

Elizabeth's baby was due in two day's time and she was half heartedly trying to stop Felix pulling the head of Flicka's Steiff teddy bear that Father Christmas had brought her that morning, when she leapt up with a scream. 'Where's Jamie?'

James was in the kitchen with Tom and Jean-Pierre, just about to take his first sip of the bubbling, gold champagne when John's head appeared round the door. He took the glass from James.

'Stop right there, old man and get your wife into the car. Her waters have just broken.'

Mr. Cool became Mr. Flustered for the briefest of moments before he picked up the bag Elizabeth had been carrying around for the past month, extricated the screaming Flicka from the clutches of her brother and handed her to John – then helped Elizabeth into his Range Rover.

Precisely one hour later as Sam was ladling bread sauce onto her plate, the phone in the kitchen rang. It was James.

'Freddy has arrived,' he told Tom who had been nearest to the phone. 'He was born at exactly forty two minutes past two after only four strong contractions which came at precisely two minute intervals."

Tom was laughing. He was really fond of James but everything, even the birth of his son had to be monitored by James' watch. Woe betides his sister if she had suffered one more contraction with only one minute between the previous one. But according to James, Freddy was perfect and Elizabeth was already walking round her room. He had been informed he would be taking her home first thing on Boxing Day morning.

Jean-Pierre produced another bottle of champagne.

'Let us drink to the Honorable Frederick James Thornley and of course to Sam and her new venture. Raise your glasses everybody.'

The whole family raised their glasses and for once Felix and Flicka, who had lemonade, were in accord as the glasses clinked and Tom's eyes glinted wickedly into Sam's as he reiterated.

'To little Freddy and to my perfect sleeping partner and I shall most certainly make certain I am that,' he grinned at Sam and then added seriously. 'To success in our venture into property together and to a brilliant year with our horses and ponies.'

'A Happy New Year, especially to Adrian and his family and we mustn't forget Giles and Clarissa. There is a lot to look forwards to, and now a toast to Mum and Dad – another perfect Christmas,' at which everyone pulled their crackers together.

A metal ring with a bright glass stone in the middle fell out of Oscar's cracker and rolled on the floor. He scrambled under the table, quickly retrieving it and putting it in his pocket. He knew exactly whom he was going to give it to and his smile grew even brighter. He quickly found his mobile and text *'A Happy Christmas, Annie',* as he patted his pocket.

That night Sam and Tom looked out of their bedroom window across to the stables and beyond, past the lake to Charles' beautiful old house. Tom had brought two glasses and a bottle of Chablis with him. He filled the glasses and handed one to Sam. He raised his own.

'To next year, Sammy and to old period cottages, but however many you may find, there will never be one quite like Woodcutters. It just isn't possible,' and he glanced across to the stables where Black Satin was nodding his head and Tom could have sworn Jolly Roger was mischievously sticking out his tongue in his direction.

He pulled the curtains and took Sam's hand. 'Are you ready to step into next year with your sleeping partner, my Sam?'

'Oh, yes,' and she kissed him gently on the lips. 'It's going to be great, but with you by my side how could it possibly be anything else?'

Other books in the *Massenden Chronicles* by Emma Berry

Ribbons and Rings

The Interlopers

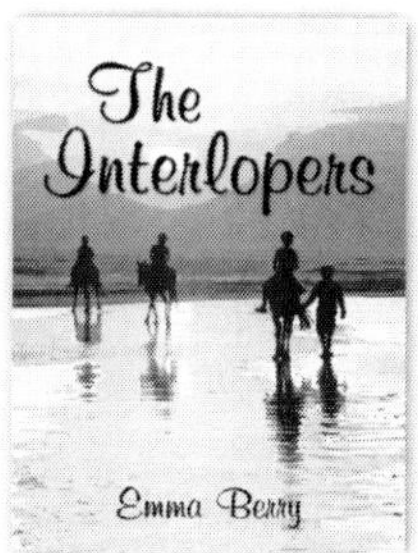

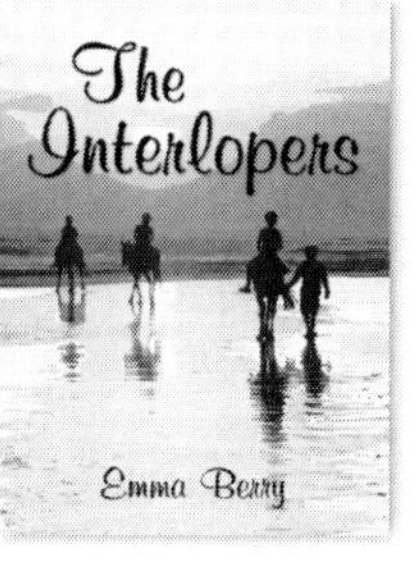

Riding High

Perfect Partners

Time Will Tell

Twists and Turns

Full Circle

A Family Affair